I0779205

Cover Art by Eyes of a Crow

First Printing: 2018

ISBN 978-1-988301-45-7

Kings Toe Publishing
kingstoepublishing@gmail.com
Burlington, Ontario. Canada

Chapter One

We should tell her now! I can't stand the way in which the child lives.

No, not yet. She isn't ready. When the time is right, we will. For now, she must wake and live the day as she always does and we must be there to help and protect her as we promised.

But the prophecies, she will need time...

There are some things she must learn for herself. Too much too soon, and she could be lost to us forever. Remember, she is different from the others. Now, pull yourself together and bid her good morning.

*****

It's time to get up, sleepy head, a soft voice sang out gently in the dark. Willow opened her eyes and scanned the room slowly, instantly adjusting to the dim lighting that came part and parcel with early mornings. Darkness of any sort simply didn't affect her. Having night vision wasn't something she ever considered questioning. It was merely a normal part of her everyday life.

Tilting her head from side to side, she glanced over the room. Nothing had changed. She lived with the bare minimum: a table, cupboards, and a few storage chests. A bucket in one corner overflowed - rain water seeping into the cracks in the floor at its base. Fixing the leak in the roof was on a list of one-day-to-do chores that she hadn't yet gotten to.

All her furniture was on that list, each piece requiring one repair or another to be done. Being made out of the same aged wood as the exterior of her shack, it stood to reason it needed almost the same amount of attention. That included the bed she was lying on. It creaked its agreement as she moved, tossing aside her bedding. Martha, the seamstress, had made it for her - it being exactly one blanket and one pillow, both of which were tattered and torn from use.

With no lights or windows and only the one door, being inside was dingy at best, not to mention a tad bit stuffy. The shack was nothing more than a place to lay her head every night and definitely not worth calling a home. Scanning the room one more time, she sighed. As always, she was most certainly alone.

Come or you will be late, and you know how the Council dislikes tardiness, a new voice, this one deeper, harsher and unmistakably male, sounded loudly in her thoughts. She didn't bother to look around. There was no point. She already knew no one was there.

For as long as she remembered, she had fantasized the voices were those of her mother and father. But how could they have been? She had been told her parents died long ago. At the time, she was barely six cycles old. Her limited memories from that age didn't include what had happened to them. Nobody in town talked about how their deaths occurred, just that they were gone - if they talked about it at all.

Willow sighed. Of course, the voices were right; they always were. She had work to do, and if she wasn't on time, trouble was sure to follow. The Council wanted things done a certain way - their way. She could already hear their voices lecturing her, the same as they had each and every time they claimed she stepped out of line. "Our lives are like a puzzle. We all have to find the place where we fit in to make the bigger picture whole."

Her duty to the common good had been assigned to her. She grew fruits and vegetables. That was her place in the puzzle. Accepting that fate and doing her very best in her assigned role was the key to keeping her world functioning properly. If any one person slacked off, the whole system failed. But still, she couldn't help but feel there was something more; something she was missing; something else she was destined to do.

Her feet slid to the floor. Grabbing a pile of clothes from a cupboard, Willow pulled a shirt over her head. The female voice returned. *Make sure you are completely covered. Remember what we discussed.*

How could she forget? They only reminded her every waking day, and multiple times at that. On her back was a beautiful portrait of two stunning midnight-black cats with crystal blue eyes and their kittens. The voices warned her to never show the pictures or tell anyone about their conversations. If the Council found out, they would have been less than lenient with her. Her companions never told her why, but deep inside she knew there was a connection with the past - to what happened to her parents. History was ruled a taboo subject and no one, not even the voices, would give her any information.

Willow opened a wooden chest and picked up a hand mirror. The small crack forming in one corner didn't faze her. Why would it? She hated her reflection. All it showed was each and every one of her imperfections from an up close and personal vantage point.

Her eyes were her only redeeming grace, being an unusual green and blue mixture with hints of red speckled throughout. Everything else, she considered completely unremarkable. Her skin consistently remained the same lightly tanned, bronze colour, even though most of it never saw the sun. Those few places that did ended up with an assortment of freckles. Work kept her in a physically fit state, which made her somewhat less feminine than all the other girls. Her above-average height didn't help in that department, either. Shorter girls tended to be daintier. Willow was sure there was a direct correlation between the amount of awkwardness a person had and their size. She was living proof.

Her long, curly hair hung down around her shoulders. Today, it was blonde with a few blue and black strands. As with all girls, her hair colour changed on its own, as if it were matching her moods, abilities, or personality. In any given day there were an infinite number of combinations of hair colours that could have formed. In fact, the prior evening she had gone to bed with pure white hair. That trend continued for girls until their sixteenth cycle. Then her hair would choose the permanent colour it wanted to be. At one time, it was common belief that the final colour of a girl's hair was directly influenced by the strength of her abilities. The Council, however, recently renounced that idea, declaring only their members and families were endowed with the most powerful gifts. That at least partially explained the abundance of hair colours that could be seen while visiting the castle grounds.

Like most of the under-aged, Willow had no clue what her abilities were yet. When she was younger, and out with her friends, they would often sit, dreaming about different abilities and which ones they wanted. They were all told the signs were there somewhere - subtle indications of the future, and if they looked hard enough, the answer would surface. Once, she sat in a corner concentrating for an entire evening, trying to make something, anything happen. Falling asleep out of boredom was the only result.

Having the right abilities wasn't a matter to be taken lightly. It was important, maybe even the most important thing in their lives. It meant the difference between acceptance or a long, hard life of work, and at times, ridicule. Being able to do something dazzling or entertaining enough, made all the difference. There was even a chance, albeit a slim one, of being invited to stay on the castle grounds. The accommodations there were far more comfortable than anything the town could offer. Of course, on the flip side of the equation, some abilities were considered utterly useless.

Her mind wandered to Victoria, who was only in her tenth cycle and already showing signs that she could heal bruises and cuts. Her parents tried as hard as they could to hide it, but to no avail. Rumours got out, as they tended to do in a small town, and the teasing began. The ability to heal, although a good quality to have, was useless in a world where there was no sickness or war. Oddly enough, Willow couldn't even remember the last time someone died outside of what the Council declared. She wasn't about to strain trying, either.

At least Victoria had a chance. There was still time to develop other abilities. Willow wasn't as fortunate. She was nearing the end of her fifteenth cycle and the clock was ticking. She could hear it as clearly as her own heart beating.

One final glance in the mirror and she tossed it back into the chest from whence it came, not concerned in the least about adding to the cracks already there. A frustrated groan passed through her lips as she haphazardly tied back her hair, not bothering to use a brush to help. It was already changing to a golden colour as it disappeared under the fabric of her hood.

"Just get through the day," she chanted. A deep breath and a tug on the door handle finished the morning routine. The last few remaining drops of the daily rainfall hit her outstretched hand, rolling between her fingers before disappearing to the ground.

Rain fell at the same time every day. It started two hours before sunrise and its final drops dribbled down an hour later. It was always the perfect amount of water needed for the trees, plants, animals, drinking, and for other daily uses. In fact, the weather in general was always perfect: not too hot, not too cold, not too dry, not too wet and always the same.

Taking her first step outside, she was greeted by a warm breeze. Closing her eyes, she deeply inhaled the fresh air, enjoying every vibrant scent it carried with it. Long ago identifying each had become her own personal game, one she shared with only the voices, although they never joined in. Today the fragrances included: the wild of the forest, a variety of herbs and plants, the flowers blooming in the castle gardens and a touch of the lingering smell of the recent rain, fading ever so slightly away. This was what made living worthwhile.

She loved nature, but most of all the fullness of the forest, with trees reaching high into the skylines - often spending her free time climbing to the highest limbs of the tallest trees just to peek over the stone walls at the castle gardens with its beautiful flowers in all colours, sizes and shapes. Then there was the great hill that sat like a giant, overseeing everything that happened. Its lush green slopes were covered with grass and four leaf clovers soft enough to cushion a bare foot's every step - like walking on a cloud. Sadly, no one was allowed to visit the top. The Council had forbidden it, but it was beautiful to look at. In some strange way, it gave her world an unusual sense of calmness.

Walking around to the back of the hut, she came to a large plot of land, filled with vegetables and fruit trees, their numbers in abundance. In a daily ritual, she gestured with her hands from side to side, thanking all the plants, trees and bushes for growing the finest produce. Her friends often expressed how unusual they thought she looked talking to vegetation, but in Willow's mind, she knew that they provided enough food for everyone. For that they deserved a thank you. Besides, she was pretty sure almost everyone in town already thought she was crazy anyways.

Her mind wandered back to the voices and how quiet they were at the moment. Imagine what people would have thought if she ever told them about that tiny secret. A little chuckle escaped from her throat.

So don't tell them, echoed through her head. *We have told you before not to tell anyone.*

Sometimes, she forgot as much as she could hear them, they also heard her. In reality, it probably was much better that she didn't have to verbally communicate out loud with them. The glares and stares that talking to herself brought with it was too much for any one girl to handle. It was better to stay unnoticed in the shadows rather than risk drawing the attention of the Council.

She didn't, however, resent hearing the voices. In fact, deep down, she was thankful for them. Over the years, she'd learnt their advice was usually sound and always had her best interests at heart. They basically had raised her since her parents left. It was also nice to not always have to be alone. Having someone to listen to her most serious problems made the hard times that came with life that much easier.

She placed empty baskets and bushels around the trees and plants. It was time to begin harvesting the produce for market. After filling several bushels with a variety of tomatoes, squash, and peas, she pushed her overloaded wheelbarrow around front to the stands. By the time she returned, all the rest of the baskets were waiting, already full of various fruits and vegetables. She never questioned where the help came from, but thanked whoever was responsible and went about finishing her work.

The sun began its ascent over the great hill, but for the moment, everything remained quiet. The town was made up of a series of buildings that all looked identical from the outside. Each one was built using the same greyish coloured, ageing wood. Patches, made out of whatever materials happened to be available, covered spots where rot could no longer be ignored. Appearance wasn't the main concern: covering any holes as best as possible was. There were no fancy designs or gardens. These houses were built strictly for need - the bigger the family, the bigger the house. Some people added a couple of steps or a porch out front, in an attempt to make a more inviting sense of home, or perhaps it was merely to facilitate the front rooms where they worked and showed off their products.

The town's one main, dirt and rock road ran from the castle gates to the north, down through the town, before ending at the orphanage. The forest bordered the buildings to the south, where it connected to the base of the great hill to the east. To the west the forest bordered the town all the way to the stone walls of the castle. No one had ever been curious enough to venture to find where, or if, the forest ended, although a few joked about it from time to time.

Directly across from Willow's hut was Mrs. Waddington's place. She was the finest, albeit only, book writer in town, not to mention a most talented storyteller. Unfortunately, there was less and less need for books since the Council declared learning to read... actually learning at all, unnecessary. Still, the under-aged found a way to sneak out after dark whenever possible to listen to one of her wondrous tales of great beasts, love, deceit, war, and peace.

Off her tongue and lips words flew through the room, circling those listening below and bringing life to visions of the very stories being told, as if it was happening before their own eyes. The highs and lows of her voice captured the very emotions of each of the characters she spoke of. There wasn't a lot of entertainment for youth in the town, and story time was a favourite on all of their lists.

Beside Mrs. Waddington's place was the seamstress, Martha, who made everything sewn, from blankets to clothing. Her husband, Olie, handcrafted shoes. Beside them was the Posh place, specializing in dishes and candles. At the end of the street sat the Shinning house. They made anything one might need out of gemstones, which amounted to mainly jewelry and flashy items for members of the Council. Across from them was the Miller bakery. Its ovens baked the most wonderful fresh bread, a taste of which melted in mouths and danced on the taste buds.

There were, of course, other homes not located on the main market street, housing the masters of various different professions such as woodworking, metalworking, as well as tool making and sharpening. They were the ones responsible for making the larger items the town needed - things ordered for a specific need, as well as various forms of crafters and animal farmers.

By the time Willow finished setting up her market stands, the last of the night had silently whisked away to make room for the light of day. Still, it was at least an hour later when the town started to show signs of life. Not that they needed to; most of the store fronts wouldn't open for hours yet. She preferred to finish up early. That left her nothing to do but to sit and watch the others as they slowly began moving about, starting their chores and gathering water from old barrels for their daily needs.

Jessie, Dezi, and Pete, the gem worker's boys, plopped down on their own front porch, joining in the sightseeing. From there, they weren't under foot while their mother and father began preparations for the day ahead. Willow didn't envy them, knowing their only customers were the Council members and their families, who were always hard to please. Each one always wanted something bigger, brighter and more outstanding than the next. That was a tall order to have to fill.

Across from the produce stand, Mrs. Waddington swept clouds of dust from her porch. After her husband, son and daughter-in-law were all declared dead by the Council, she was left raising her grandson, Nathan, alone. All of a sudden, she motioned a fast wave and darted inside.

A silence crept over the marketplace, leaving a chill where the rays of the sun had previously warmed. That could only have meant one thing: the Council had arrived in town to pick up their fresh produce for the day. Its members enjoyed a fresh fruit breakfast every morning and it came with the unspoken rule that they were always to be served before anyone else. They had the pick of the crop, literally.

Willow looked down the lane and held her breath. Today wasn't starting off well at all. The Council had sent their children into town this morning to fetch their needs. Rumours had been flying around town that Council family members, the ones closest to their sixteenth cycle, were being given more duties. It was time for them to prepare for the future.

They would, one day, run things. Unfortunately, it looked like those weren't just rumours anymore.

Malarchy and Nebulah's daughter, Jade, led the teen group as usual. She was slim, with a white complexion, perfectly rosy cheeks and plump red lips. Her deep green eyes flickered with specks of emerald in the light in such a way that their colour matched her name. That wasn't her only claim to fame: she was also the only girl in town whose hair hadn't changed in three cycles. Its light blonde colour shimmered in the sun and she always seemed to effortlessly control the style, which changed more often than her clothes did. Today it was curly - not a natural curl, but more a manufactured one.

It was hard to tell if it was just the different hairstyles or if her facial features were different daily as well. Everyone knew appearance, especially her hair, was one of her talents and she was quite proud to show off all the different glamours in her fashion arsenal. To complete today's look, a frilly white dress hugged the curves of her body, which were far more developed than any of the other girls her age. Sabrina and Camile followed closely behind, both trying their best to copy the same look as their leader, right down to the curls.

Willow winced as she imagined the two girls having to roll pine cones in their wet hair and then even worse, remove them when their hair was dry. For the moment, she didn't feel quite as cursed about having her own natural curls.

Behind them walked two boys, Justin and Neil, who weren't paying much attention to anything going on, except the rock they were kicking back and forth between them. They were as good looking as boys got. Both were tall, with sandy coloured hair and hazel eyes - their medium builds were masked by fine clothes.

Willow didn't understand the other girls' fussing over boys. They were okay. Some were fun to hang out with and play games, but she hadn't ever felt love-struck, like the other girls her age did, especially at the mere sight of any one or another.

"Too bad she has to open her mouth," Clairity joked, referring to Jade.

Willow was so distracted by the morning's events, she completely missed her best friend coming over to sit beside her. "What would get you up so early?"

Clairity laughed and replied, "I couldn't leave you to deal with that lot alone, now could I?"

Clairity was short with an average build. She wasn't a stunning beauty, but she had style. Her hair was cut in an uneven bob, which hugged her face in all the right places - highlighting her high cheek bones. Today her hair was black. Of all the colours, it was the one that suited her the best. That was probably because it also matched her eyes. As dark brown as they were, they easily could have been mistaken for the midnight colour, from near or afar. The pale white complexion of her skin perfectly matched the porcelain dishes and figures her mother made. Seeing Clairity's mother desperately trying to add a little colour to her daughter's face by pinching her cheeks as hard as she could, always brought a smile to Willow's face. Although Clairity hated it.

"Can we get some service here? Or do you think wasting our time is in your best interest?" the girl in front of her snarled.

Willow looked up, her gaze caught by a pair of icy green eyes staring back at her, freezing her body and soul. They were as cold as they were beautiful. She shivered as if a chilled wind had suddenly blasted against her bare skin, leaving goosebumps as a calling card. In those few moments of hesitation, she briefly lost herself to intimidation. Luckily, Clairity was there, already starting to put baskets together for the impatiently waiting group. It was odd, but lately it seemed her friend knew exactly where and when she needed to be.

"Staring into space as we wait, pathetic. Wait till Father finds out about this!" Jade complained in a voice loud enough to be heard by most of the town. "And what is she wearing?" The three girls burst into high-pitched laughter before heading down the road, not back the way they came, but further down the lane.

Willow knew the three girls were strolling toward the Shinning boys still sitting on their front step. Sure enough, they offered a flirtatious wave and a giggle. That was all it took to gain the boys' attention and soon the group of them were all talking and laughing together. All the while, the two boys from the Council remained oblivious to what their female counterparts were doing. The pair were far too preoccupied with the delightful aroma of fresh-baked bread coming from the stone oven out-back of the bakery.

Clairity gave her a nudge. "Anyone home?" she asked.

Willow shook her head, breaking free from the trance that completely engulfed her. She looked up at her friend, who motioned to the rest of town waiting in line for their baskets for the day. They both knew everyone, and after the line ceased, baskets were made for those few who hadn't yet been by. Together, they delivered them, Clairity taking the last one home for her own family.

All that was left to do was pack the remaining fruits and vegetables into boxes for the orphanage. The children living there had it the hardest out of all the townsfolk. They shared everything with one another and had very little to start with. Compared to the way these kids lived, Willow was in a dreamland. Any time she thought of them, her heart cried. The only hope they had was to develop an ability the Council found entertaining or extremely useful.

Willow took it upon herself to try to brighten their days, making sure there was always something especially yummy in the boxes - a sort of treat the kids could look forward to. After all, if circumstances had been a little bit different, she might have been stuck living there as well. In fact, she didn't actually know why she wasn't, but figured the orphanage had been already overfilled when her parents died.

She felt a tap on her shoulder. "Need some help with those?" Jessie asked. Usually, one of the three boys would offer to carry some of the boxes and she was always eager to accept. Help meant making one trip instead of two, not to mention having company along for the walk. As much as she wanted to help the orphanage, she hated going there. There was an aura that surrounded the building as if it was the place from whence shadows were born. The last few times she visited had left her with an uneasy feeling - one she couldn't shake. She was sure someone was listening and recording her every move.

Jessie was the tallest of the triplet brothers. Usually, children born together looked identical - not in the case of these brothers. They were each different in appearance and personality. It was almost as if they were three parts to one whole person, each getting different qualities from the other. The only thing they shared in common at all was their similar light brown shade of hair and matching eye colours.

Jessie was muscular and very strong looking, but quiet. Dezi was just shorter than his brother, although not overly muscular, but there was a definition to the shape of his arms and chest, which suited him. He was loud, fun and exciting - always the life of the party. The final brother, Pete, was the shortest of the three, albeit still taller than most boys their age and was quickest to offer his opinion when he had one. He was neither boring nor remarkable, but could captivate an audience when he chose to. Most of the time, however, he was lost somewhere in the shadows of his brothers.

The orphanage was located on the far side of town and was the largest building... other than the castle. The outside showed signs of its age and the life it had managed to weather through. Now, major repairs had passed the point of simply being needed - much more than was seen in the rest of the town.

Inside were four rooms. The first was a small sitting room for visitors, not that they had many. In a way, it made Penelope and Micca, the couple that ran the orphanage, feel prepared in case someone did happen to drop in.

Peeking in the door, the living area appeared exactly as she imagined - lack of use and all. A thick layer of dust had made its home on every surface possible. In the centre of the room was a table with a tiny porcelain vase filled with what appeared to be dead wild-flowers. The seating, composed primarily of high-backed benches, was decorated with faded cushions that were sentenced to a lifetime of remaining in the exact same spot. Directly across the hall was the second room - Penelope and Micca's bedroom.

There was an unsettling silence, especially for a house that so many children called home. Following the front hallway led to a tall wooden door, which opened into a food preparation room. The makeshift kitchen wasn't by any means large. Cupboards lined all of the walls. In the centre of the room was a single wooden table - the sort one stood at, rather than sat.

Willow and Jessie lifted the boxes onto it. Usually, someone would have greeted them earlier. Neither had been past that point before or seen the large room that the orphans spent the majority of their lives in. Out of concern and a little curiosity, the two agreed to explore further. Willow stepped aside, motioning for Jessie to take the lead. There was no hope of her budging the door that stood between them and satisfying their curiosity. It had been well constructed using a heavier wood than the rest of the building.

"Explains why the front is so quiet," Jessie said, almost stealing Willow's exact thoughts. She nodded in agreement.

The room that had been previously hidden from them was by far the largest either of them had ever seen, with over double the space of the rest of the house combined. Long tables and benches were set up, clearly meant for dining. Later, the children would have to move them to one side of the room in order to find a spot on the floor for their pillows and blankets to sleep for the night. There were seventeen children who lived in the orphanage, all between the ages of ten and fifteen. Most had been under four cycles when their parents were declared dead. This was the only life they knew, and there was a good chance, it would be the only one they ever would know.

All of the house's inhabitants were there, going over what looked like a long list of rules. Lately, the Council had been coming down hard on children for playing unsupervised outside. They even went so far as to threaten to put the whole lot to work, keeping the castle clean if they had nothing better to do than pester citizens. That translated into reduced outdoor time and stricter rules for behaviour in the presence of others. The majority of the children sat on the floor in a semi-circle around the adults, attentive as if it were story time.

Off to one side, Willow noticed a lone boy leaning against the wall, staring at her. There was no sign of emotion whatsoever in his dark eyes. He was short with brown hair and a few freckles or dirt spots - it was hard to tell which. His clothes weren't in any better shape, layered with patches and stains that would never wash out. A long blade of grass hung out of his mouth to one side, bobbing up and down as he chewed on the opposite end.

"His name is Arnold," Jessie said, breaking the silence between them.

"I know, but shouldn't he be with the others?" Willow asked, her gaze never straying from the sight of the boy.

"The new arrangements probably have him going stir crazy. It has to be rough hardly ever leaving this room," Jessie whispered.

Looking around the room, she agreed. Being locked up would have driven her over the edge too. Still, she couldn't help but feel there was something else behind that chilling stare.

Micca was the only other one to notice them standing just inside the doorway. He lifted a finger in the air, signalling for the children to remain seated before hurrying over to offer his thanks for bringing the food and an apology for not meeting them sooner. The conversation was over in seconds, Micca excusing himself to head back to his discussion and leaving them to show themselves out. It was, after all, almost dinner time.

The pair retraced their steps out of the building. Simply stepping outside felt like a heaviness had been removed from the air. Willow inhaled, enjoying the sensation of being able to breathe freely.

Jessie took several glances at her from the side. "Diana is having story time tonight. She asked me to tell you there is going to be something special you need to hear. I think you should go."

Willow smiled all the way back to the marketplace. The return trip went faster than usual, with a part skip to her step. That was the best news of the day. After the two parted, she headed home to clean up the mess and prepare for the evening's excitement.

Chapter Two

In the distance, sitting on a slightly higher elevation and to the north of the town, was the great castle constructed completely out of different types of hand-carved stones and metals complimented with brightly coloured glass windows. High peaks, boasting elaborate statues of great majestic birds in flight, enhanced the grandeur of the building. The large doors of the front entrance were big enough to allow a giant to enter, each elaborately decorated with a carving of a magnificent tree embellished with beautiful sweeping limbs. On either side of the doors stood two massive statues: the first of a feline lunging forward; and the other an unusual cross between a wolf and bear, standing on two feet with arms outstretched and growling fiercely.

Inside, carvings told tales - a picture book of sorts, its pages dancing their way across the walls. Ask a question and the answer sought could be revealed or, in the event of disaster, prophecies uncovered. The floors resembled polished marble, enhanced with fine golden accents. Overhead, lights twinkled against a dark background, forming stars in the ceiling. A grand stairway, in the middle of the room, twisted magnificently in a circular motion to the upper levels, where the sleeping quarters were located.

There was enough space in these living quarters to house more than ten times the town's population, but only Council members, their families, the guards, and some entertainers were permitted to stay anywhere on the grounds.

To the right from the stairs, two golden doors permanently remained open wide, lending a view to a magnificent ballroom complete with a shimmering ceiling made entirely from rare gems and crystals. Past that was a hallway that led to the main dining room filled with tables decorated with crisp white linen and set using only the finest of porcelain dishes. Further down were food preparation rooms, including a door which led outside to the brick ovens for cooking.

To the left of the stairs was a hallway, which led to the common rooms - mainly used for sitting and furnished with all the comforts one could hope for. Soft, golden coloured cushions lined every chair and grand vases filled with delicate flowers from the gardens sat on top of brown, polished marble tables.

At the end of the hallway were two blue glass doors, which opened to a walkway leading all who passed through on an adventure of winding paths edged by gardens that tantalized the mind and offered utopia to the senses. Floral aromas filled the air; a beautiful array of colours caught the sight; and a sweet taste danced on the tip of the taste buds of anyone who was lucky enough to venture for a stroll. Stone benches and smaller versions of the same statues as found out front added additional beauty.

The path ended at a large iron gate, the highest point of which was shaped in a semi-circle. Within, the words *E Pepvo Eco Glay Callum* were displayed - an ancient language that no one, even those currently living in the castle, could read or write. Malarchy, however, insisted the meaning was, *The Council above all others.*

In the hours before sunset, a humming, musical in nature, whimsically rose from the garden as beautifully coloured flowers transformed into bright, glowing blossoms, capable of lighting up the pathways at night. The sun always set in the same place, slowly disappearing behind the great hill, but not before setting it ablaze in a brilliant, glowing green radiance.

Security for the castle was of the utmost importance. A stone wall surrounded the grounds with only one set of iron gates leading into the property from the town. Once through, it merged with a path heading to the elaborate front entrance. Four guards were always posted at the opening, two on each side, to ensure only those invited were allowed to enter. There were twenty-six guards who took turns in rotating shifts. Directly behind their post were the barracks used to house security and staff. That building was made of a similar rock as the rest of the structures on the property, adorned with its own set of carved pictures. These, however, were of guards protecting open doorways, not any of the doorways that could be found in the castle or the iron gates, but smaller ones with their own carved stones in each corner. Some of the pictures even depicted the guards defending the opening from something coming through, although there were no clear images of any enemies.

The staff were permitted to send two people to town daily for food and other needs. Other than that, they remained in the building unless called for by the Council or on duty. At special events they were instructed to have extra guards posted inside the grounds, ensuring control was kept at all times.

Entertainers were only allowed to practice on certain days, at certain times and performed something different on a daily basis for the Council's amusement. They were not permitted to leave the castle grounds at any time. Any entertainer who disobeyed risked not being allowed back in and would have to return to their former life - which, of course, none of them wanted to do.

The grounds themselves were vast and included a practice area for all the different types of abilities, a courtyard for dances and events, and a games area for entertainment. The practice area provided targets for shooting at, an obstacle course, an arts and crafts section, an invention studio, a stone patio, a grass area, and a fenced in area. It was mainly used by guards intent on keeping their combat skills sharp and any entertainers preparing for a show.

The games area consisted of an outdoor arena where two or more people could test their abilities against each other. It also had been closed for as long as anyone could remember. No one bothered to question why.

The courtyard was the most used area outside, with a beautiful stone patio surrounded by benches. At the front was a stage-type platform where all instruments and entertainment props were kept. Although the castle contained a beautiful ballroom inside, the courtyard was the popular place to hold dances and other forms of nightly entertainment.

During the daytime, children who lived in the castle were periodically allowed to play outside. These young heirs and heiresses to Council positions were rarely heard of or seen by the townspeople, mainly because they were never allowed to step foot outside the castle gates. The majority of times, the youngsters were restricted to common-use rooms hidden well away from everyday activities even from their own kin. It was only at larger events that they were paraded around for their cuteness factor, giving moms and dads a chance to beam with pride over their little bundles of perfection.

This didn't always have a good effect on the older sons and daughters who would occasionally become jealous over the toddler spotlight. Jade was one of those. Over the last year, she had wished countless times her younger brother, Jordan, would go away or disappear completely. She craved the limelight. It didn't matter if she never saw Jordan again as long she could have the full attention of her parents, especially her mother.

Just outside the garden gates sat a large stone table and chairs where, almost every evening after dinner, the Council would meet to discuss current events, business, if any, and laws. There were six chairs on each side and one at the end. A giant glass bowl of water sat directly in the middle.

The Council itself was made up of thirteen people and although they were all deemed to be equal, Malarchy and his wife, Nebulah, led the meetings and decisions.

"Old business?" Malarchy's voice rang out over all of the small talk going on at the table.

The rest of the Council scrambled about, hurrying to take their assigned places for the meeting. Malarchy claimed the single spot at the end of the table. Behind him, the glow of the sun setting beneath the great hill illuminated his head and face in an eerie green aura, adding to his illusion of power over the rest of the Council.

Malarchy was one of the oldest on the Council, although he looked no older than thirty. He wasn't remarkable in appearance, standing at average height with a build that could be considered on the slim side. Male pattern baldness was something he'd never admit to, claiming instead to shave his head bald on purpose. When he spoke or smiled, uneven teeth created the unnerving impression of fangs. He dressed flamboyantly in fine linens of bright colours with golden trim and gemstones adorning every place possible. Most of the town weren't sure exactly what his abilities were, but they were too frightened to find out.

"None," replied his wife, Nebulah, to the left of him. As one of the smallest adults, her golden blonde hair was almost equivalent to her height in length. Even so, her most noticeable feature was still the size of her chest, doubling the size of any other woman in town and matched with a small waistline and hips. It was a wonder she didn't lose her balance when she walked simply from being top-heavy. Whenever she spoke, a noticeably fake smile crossed her face directed at whomever her audience might have been at the time.

"New business, then?" Malarchy's voice sounded again, loud and confident.

"The children have asked us to consider having a dance to celebrate their sixteenth cycles," his wife answered immediately.

"We haven't for others before, why now?" argued Aurora. She was one of the newer members of the Council - appointed only four cycles ago as a cousin of another Council member, Zebulon. Seated directly to the right of Malarchy, she was medium height, but the thinnest lady at the table. As usual, she wore a crisp white suit - illuminated by the natural glow that radiated from her body. The rest of her ensemble enhanced her overall appearance. She kept her hair short and spiked at the top, adorned with gold, silver and copper tones that highlighted the electric hues of blues and purples shimmering in her eyes. Unlike other Council members, Aurora never felt the need to wear jewelry or to add anything flashy to her appearance.

Aurora was known as a *light* - a person able to read energies who, in an advanced form, could also lend energy to another person, enabling them in turn to enhance their own natural abilities. Unfortunately, the lack of training for her talents meant she couldn't control them properly, often misreading auras. Larger groups of people, more often than not, proved painful, driving her to the point of almost becoming a recluse. In her room there were no headaches, so that was where she stayed with the exception of some meals and daily Council meetings. Events and trips to town were avoided at all costs. Her lack of knowledge of her craft also meant she was a target for exploitation of her energy-enhancing abilities and was rarely aware when someone was tapping into them, afterwards left wondering why she had become very tired.

"There are an unusual amount of children this cycle who will be coming into their powers. Jade suggested it might be a nice gesture and the girls are happy to see to all the details. I don't see any reason not to allow them a small celebration for their generation. Of course, all of the castle will be invited to join in the fun," Nebulah rebutted.

"And the children from the town?"

Nebulah's face seemed to have to work a little harder to keep its smile while she answered. "Of course, the boys from town will receive invitations and can bring a date of their choice. There are a few young ladies who don't own a dress or know how to dance. We don't want to pressure them into something they may find uncomfortable - to say the least."

Malarchy interrupted before anyone else could reply. "To vote then - in favour?" He counted the raised hands then added, "Against?"

Nine of the thirteen voted in favour, three against, being Aurora, Zebulon and Lynnea and one, Ozias, was asleep.

"A dance it is, but before the new cycle begins, so no unusual abilities arise at the event. I think that is best." After a slight pause, Malarchy added, "Is there anything else to discuss this evening?"

Zebulon stood and asked to speak from the other side of the table. He was a short round man who never denied enjoying bread from the bakery a lot more than vegetables. His brown curly hair matched a full beard, well-trimmed and tidy. His clothing wasn't exceptional, but he did adorn his fingers with rings of various gems, which he claimed aided him in his interpretation of the skies and the meanings of symbols and signs.

"I think we should revisit the prophecies," Zebulon announced.

The faces of all the others became stern and uneasy as each one turned and stared at the man who remained standing. After an uncomfortable pause, Zebulon took his seat to wait for the answer, which didn't take long.

"We have dealt with the prophecies already," Malarchy snapped.

"I agree, we took steps to try to change the course of the future, but there are no longer any prophets left in our world to ask if we succeeded. What if we set in progress the fate we so desperately tried to avoid? Should we not take some action to prepare in case we have failed? Perhaps make a Plan B, since we are talking about the complete destruction of our homeland."

Sheer annoyance began inching over Malarchy's face, moving faster by the second, a red flush creeping into his cheeks as he answered, "Are you not the symbol interpreter? What do the skies say? The pictures on the wall?"

Zebulon's face turned solemn. "The wall has gone quiet. The pictures are gone and the skies offer no answers. The stars do not rise at night to form any signs, nor do clouds hold visions. I can no longer see anything pointing to any future."

Malarchy motioned to his wife to check the carved pictures on the walls inside the castle while the rest of the table sat quietly, anticipating the returning news. There was no smile when Nebulah resurfaced. She simply nodded confirmation to her husband, who turned his attention back to the small, plump man.

"And what do you suggest we do? We have no prophets anymore and now no symbols to interpret."

Staring down at his interlocked hands, Zebulon replied, "We revisit the prophecies - look at them again... see if we can find any clues we may have missed and then decide on a plan of action should any of it still come true. Perhaps there is something we can change."

"And are you willing to answer the questions which will arise as to the decisions the Council made?" After looking at several Council members, each nodding, Malarchy added, "Very well then. Lynnea, would you mind?"

Lynnea, Zebulon's wife, sat beside him at the table. Her hair was a dull grey, which she unsuccessfully attempted to spice up with silver and crystal hair pins. Everything about the woman was awkward to the point of her being mousy. It was a safe bet that, on any given day, her sweater would have at least half of its buttons in the wrong holes. Choosing clothes which were always a bland colour: a shade of beige or tan and usually untidy, also wasn't helping the situation. She was shy and quiet, often not speaking a word to anyone except her husband and even then in nothing more than whispers. She did, however, possess an unusual ability which allowed her to take the minutes of all the meetings. She could save pictures of everything she saw and later replay them by projecting the images onto the face of water, allowing others to see it.

Lynnea nodded, standing directly in front of the large bowl, its contents clear and calm. Looking directly into it, she raised her arms, hands wide open and palms facing upwards to the sky, ushering her commands. The water obeyed, forming a large cube over the table. After a few seconds, an image came into view on each of four screens of flowing liquid - a woman with long midnight-blue hair.

The picture focused on her upper body and head. From what could be seen, she was wearing what appeared to be a black uniform, the type made specifically for combat. The top was a sleeveless vest and on each of her arms, just below the shoulder, were pictures on her skin - a single wolf on each side. A distressed look covered her face, one which could have rivalled the purest form of fear. The entire Council was transfixed on her.

The woman began to speak, a shakiness expressed in her voice. "I have had a vision of the future our world is heading towards and we must take action. There is no time to waste. We have less than nine cycles before we are invaded by an army dressed in black and red. They carry weapons, the likes of which I have never seen before - glowing swords, bows and guns with an unknown power source. There are hundreds of them, if not thousands.

"They are by far the most cruel and strongest enemies we have yet faced. There will be people murdered in the streets and others taken away as prisoners. Stone statues will crumble as a storm fills the skies and the weather turns deadly, with booms of thunder and lightning strikes more severe than I have ever experienced before. The gardens will be destroyed and the forest set ablaze with fire. In the end nothing remains except for destroyed and deserted ruins. No life survives.

"We must fight this evil at its root before it destroys our very home and spreads its vicious will to all other worlds. Please consult the other seers and interpreters. Ask them to look into our future. I am scheduled to leave to aid Petra's expedition to the main world at sunrise. I have consulted with the guardians and am transferring some of my abilities to the walls of the castle to offer guidance and aid in making decisions. The changing pictures shall show what course the future is taking. Be strong, friends, and train as many as possible in my absence. The more of us who are fully able to use their abilities, the better the chances for survival if the portal teams fail to destroy this threat before it reaches our homeland."

The picture faded and the water fell back into the bowl. Lynnea returned to her seat, satisfied her role in the evening was complete.

Aurora spoke first. "Who was that? Was she a Council member? Where is she now? Should we be worried?"

Malarchy glanced at the Council members again, rubbed his face and replied, "Her name is Iris and she was a Council member in the guardian days of our world. After this prophecy, she did as she said - transferred some of her abilities to the castle walls before leaving the next morning to help in another world. Over the next cycle many teams were formed and deployed, to not only combat regular threats to the portals, but also to locate and stop this invasion from ever happening. After news of a battle gone wrong, all remaining guardians and trained teams left to offer aid in the war. A cycle passed... none returned and no news had been received.

"The remaining Council members decided to take action to protect the citizens left in our world. The portals to other realms were disassembled and the parts destroyed so that no one could enter or leave. We then appointed new Council members to replace those who were gone. In order to keep the population safe and calm, and considering many family members who left to aid in the battle hadn't returned, we made up news of their deaths. We implemented plans so people would forget and not discuss the past. I stand by the decision of closing the portals so that no malevolent force could ever use them against us by entering our world and invading our sanctuary. The time of the guardians was finished. They would offer us no salvation. We were, and still are, left to our own devices."

"If it was that easy, don't you think the others would have thought of that plan instead of putting their lives on the line?" Aurora argued, signs of exhaustion taking hold in the form of dark bags under her eyes. Her glow dimmed, her face turning three shades whiter.

"I think we made the best possible decision we could. Leaving the portals open would have meant an unnecessary access point to our world for an invasion. Unless anyone else knows how an army could enter to attack us, I don't see the problem."

Zebulon interrupted. "The problem is there are no signs for our future. We need to do something. Reinstate the training program and advance abilities so people can defend themselves if it does happen."

"Do you enjoy your life as it is now?" The tone in Malarchy's voice raised an octave. "Do you think the good townspeople will not ask questions? Perhaps you believe they will understand the choices we made condemning their loved ones who may have still been alive?"

It was Aurora who rebutted. "Some of us were not involved in any of those decisions."

"Do you believe this life you have is because you deserve it? You are who you are because we made you that way. We gave you your seat on the Council and your comfortable room in the castle. If you think for one minute people won't turn on you if the truth comes out, if the Council loses control, or if people find out how strong some of their abilities really are, you are mistaken."

A confused look came over Aurora's face. "You mean our abilities aren't the strongest?"

Malarchy rubbed his temples before replying with a sigh, "You can't really believe glowing makes you powerful. You can hardly even read the energies you see and remembering pictures that you can play back in water is a nice trick, but hardly threatening. Then there are Rowan's balls of light, which I admit are great to use to see by at night, but would hardly help in a fight."

Rowan darted a look of dislike at the speaker but remained quiet. He did, after all, only illuminate Council meetings that ran late and nightly entertainment or events, with circular orbs of light.

"Each of you, think about what you can do and what we know the townsfolk can do. They have displayed great strength, speed, control of fire and ice, control of metals - and that only names a few. We don't even know what some of the kids can do yet! Even with my powers of illusion and Nebulah's gift of persuasion, we wouldn't be able to hold on to control. We would be overthrown, our families removed from the castle. The life we have would be over. Are you willing to give all this up for something which may never come true?" Malarchy asked, turning the charm back on.

In an unusual turn of events, Lynnea offered, "There is a child who we know can heal. If her power was trained, if she was given direction, she could save lives if there was a war."

"Do you believe that child will bother to save any of us after the way she has been ridiculed? Are you willing to take that chance? Or perhaps the young lad we have juggling at night for your entertainment, learning how much more he can do with his mind. Do you think he will thank you for the ridiculous outfits and exploitation of his abilities for your amusement?" Malarchy snapped back.

"No, my friends, if we teach them more, enhance what they can do, they will turn on us. We will lose control. Perhaps we should vote. Now, I don't want to be too hasty. Let's give everyone a chance to think about the lifestyle we have and what could happen, what we could lose... for no reason. So the vote will be in the evening after the fourteenth sunrise, unless disaster strikes before then or more pressing business takes precedent.

"Until then, look around, see how life could change not just for you, but for your families... your children. There is to be no talk of this meeting outside the Council and we are each to go on, as if none of this was ever discussed - everything as normal. We will announce the sixteenth cycle dance to take place on the eve after the thirteenth sunrise, which should give the girls plenty of time to arrange everything and still be soon enough that we can implement any decisions after. Think hard, there will be no meetings until the vote unless an emergency arises. For now, the meeting is adjourned."

The Council members went their separate ways. The majority of them headed to the courtyard for the evening's entertainment. Aurora, however, returned to her quarters, exhausted. Nebulah, Nyssa, and Ashley went to find their daughters to discuss the plans for the dance and make invitations. Even with all the sobering talk tonight, they were still energetic and excited about the upcoming gala their girls would be attending. It meant new dresses, new jewelry, new head pieces to adorn their hair - it meant shopping. Malarchy remained at the stone table for a few minutes collecting his thoughts. Even borrowing Aurora's energy boost, he was far more tired than he had ever felt before from merely controlling a meeting.

Malarchy's head had been resting in his hands, elbows on the table, for some time, when he heard, "Sir." He looked up to see a guard in front of him. *How awkward*, he mused. The guard's name, if he even had a name, had escaped his memory.

"What is it?"

The guard replied, "A boy, sir, at the gate. He says you told him to come speak to you if he heard anything."

"Bring him, then."

Castle guards shared a telepathic link, gifted to them by the ancients to make it easier for emergencies to be handled. Now, however, the ability was nothing more than a parlour trick used primarily to save time. He closed his eyes and sent a message to his partner to bring forth the child. A few minutes passed before a second guard appeared with a boy walking beside him. As they drew near, the boy's appearance became apparent. It was none other than Arnold from the orphanage.

When Malarchy first discovered Arnold possessed a gift he could exploit, he pounced on the opportunity. Enhanced hearing was the perfect tool for spying on the town. All the Council leader had to do was offer the boy all of his desires for any useful information he might over hear by *accident*. Curiosity took over rational thought. In light of the evening's meeting, whatever the boy had overheard could have been important. Malarchy dismissed the guards.

"You have something to report?"

"Yes, I overheard someone tell the girl, Willow, that Diana Waddington was telling a story tonight - one that is very important for her to hear," the boy offered.

"What is the story about?"

"I don't know, sir. The story isn't to be heard till some of the children gather secretly at her house tonight after dark. I have never been to one, but I hear the stories run for a couple of hours. Can I move in now?"

Malarchy laughed. "No child, not yet. First, I need to know if this information is actually important. It will be dark soon. I want you to go and listen to the story and any other talk you might hear. Watch how Willow reacts. I need to know if there is a message for her and, if there is, if she understands it. Go now and report back here tomorrow. Then, and only then, we can discuss your reward."

Chapter Three

Willow was so excited about the evening's scheduled activities that she arrived early. Mrs. Waddington's house was always open. She never wanted anyone to knock, since she never heard the knocking anyways. Willow opened the door and headed into the visitor's room where books lined shelves that completely covered the walls. There was one large chair, firmly planted as close to centre as possible. It looked comfortable, albeit well worn. That was where Diana sat to tell her stories. Numerous old pillows and blankets were neatly stacked beside it. Later, the children would take them from the piles and settle into positions on the floor. In the corners of the room were four tall tables where people could stand and read. Each was just big enough to hold a couple of books. Nathan stood alone at one of the tables.

Mrs. Waddington's grandson was twelve cycles and unusually short for his age, although tall enough to read from books at the standing tables. His dark-bronzed skin and golden brown coloured eyes were identical to how his mother's had been. His hair was black with tightly woven curls, each one forming its own perfect little spring.

The books on the table lay closed. Nathan hovered over top, studying the cover of one with some interest. His left hand moved over the book in front of him, caressing it without actually touching it. Suddenly, a beam of energy in the form of a white light exploded from the book to his hand. He closed his eyes and smiled as if he was seeing utopia.

Willow moved forward, watching his every move. Aware of her presence as she neared, Nathan glanced up at her. The beam of light vanished. His lips opened, letting out only a squeak, followed by a gasp. His eyes pleaded with her before his words did. "Please. Please don't tell anyone. They can't know."

Confused, she answered, "Know what? What are you doing? What was that light?"

"I," he stuttered, "I was reading."

"But..."

Nathan motioned for her to stop by shaking his head back and forth while waving his hands in front of him in a similar pattern. With a gulp, he continued, "About a week ago, I was looking at the cover of a book and noticing the worn spots... where it had been held by people in exactly the same place for many cycles. Then it happened. This light appeared and within seconds, I knew everything the book said, word for word, fully understanding it."

Willow smiled and moved closer, alternating her glance between him and the book. She picked it up, examined it, and commented, "That's amazing! I wish I could do that. These stories are brilliant."

"No - no, you don't. I don't, either. Gran, she would be heartbroken if she knew. She has such hopes for me to develop a useful ability. This... well, if the Council found out, they would be less than impressed, especially since they don't want us reading books. They don't want us learning. I can't break her heart. She can't ever know."

"I still think it's great and saying that they don't want us learning is exaggerating a bit, don't you think? They just don't want us using all our time reading stories instead of handling our daily duties is all."

She was cut off by him. "You really don't get it," he said, grabbing her arm. "I wish I could show you what I see."

Both the arm he was holding and his own began to radiate a white glow. Willow's eyes opened wider than ever before, taking in a wondrous amount of sights. Then the glow faded. She picked up the book Nathan had been looking at and opened it. She knew the story, word for word, picture for picture... every detail. She could see images playing in her head the same as if Mrs. Waddington were telling it. She looked at him in amazement, jaw hanging open.

"I know this story. I can see it. You shared it with me."

His eyes starred back at her. He blinked a couple times. "Something new I will have to be careful of."

"But this is a gift you can share with everyone, you need to..."

She was cut off again. "No, I don't want anyone to know. Now promise. Willow - please promise me you won't tell."

"I won't tell. But promise me, when no one is around, you will show me more stories," she said, looking at the second book. A perplexed scowl came over her face. "Nathan, this book isn't written in any language I have ever seen before."

He took it from her, placed it in front of him and repeated the same process. Again the white light connecting hand to book appeared and a few moments later, he smiled and said, "I understand it! Zoz ta'qu rogram! I understand it!"

Her eyes widened in disbelief. "Did you just speak a different language?"

"I did," he replied with a smile so big it took up most of his face. "Here," he offered.

She extended her arm. The light bound the two again and when it was finished, her eyes darted back and forth as if they were trying to help process information.

"Amazing!" she blurted out. "Zzz'hq!" She spun around in a circle, grabbing Nathan at the end in a bear hug. "I can speak another language." Looking as if searching for information, she added, "An ancient language used by only those who were present at the beginning of our time. Do you know how incredible this is? And the story - the meeting between the guardians and the ancient snakes - the arguments over territory, over power, leadership - the needed to be recognized as more important, stronger and better than subjects below them. It's riveting, compelling... treacherous yet beautiful. Do you think it's real, a history of sorts?"

"More likely it's a story, to teach a lesson about corruption - the good and bad in everyone, and choose the right path kinda deal. It's a big theme in many of Gran's books. But it's the oldest book here and it's not written in Gran's handwriting. I think it probably is a very old forgotten language. Anyways, it means we now have our own secret language, which is brilliant."

"Brilliant! This is the ultimate! Are you sure you don't want to share with others? I think they would be impressed." Her excitement spun out of control, leaving her giddy and a bit dizzy at the same time.

"Yeah... well, you are a geek."

She steadied herself with the help of the table. "I am not." It was impossible to avoid the look of disagreement on Nathan's face, sending her into a full burst of laughter. "Okay, I guess I am... a little," she added. "But you have to admit, having our own secret language is exciting."

The two moved away from the table just in time for the doors to open.

Diana Waddington always carried herself with an air of royalty. Not because of fancy clothes or gemstones, but because of the true regal appearance of her face. Her hair was dark and always tied up in a bun, without a single strand out of place. Her naturally stunning features were like no other in town.

Her cheek bones were high, but with soft lines which traced upwards to a pair of cool baby blue eyes, spaced perfectly and graced with long eyelashes. Her nose was small with a curved point at the end, and sat directly above full and naturally red lips. When she smiled, she showed off her pearl white teeth, all correctly spaced and sized. She was posture perfect with a straight back wherever she went, accentuating her beautiful figure with curves in all the right places... none too big and none too small.

Diana always wore full-length dresses, in one solid pastel colour, that were clean and crisp. There was no doubt she spent time attending to her appearance daily in some ritualistic form or another. When she spoke, she pronounced every word clearly as if they formed off her tongue and lips perfectly. Her voice lifted and fell with emotion in all the right places, creating an almost musical form to speech.

"You two look like you are having fun. Continue. I am just getting ready for tonight," Diana said.

In all the excitement, Willow completely forgot about her conversation with Jessie. "What is so special about tonight's story? I was told you wanted me to hear it."

"Patience, my child. You will hear it with the others. Private readings might be construed as treacherous in some way by the Council. I don't think either of us need to be considered as a threat by them, now do we?"

Diana had a point that couldn't be denied. Willow and Nathan each grabbed a pillow and blanket from the piles and chose a place to sit before the others arrived. Over the course of the next hour, the room began to fill. Jessie, Dezi, Pete, Victoria, Clairity, and Ashlyn arrived in time to take the seats directly around them. Other children filled the remaining spots, including the metalsmith's son and daughter and two of the woodworker's daughters.

A boy in the corner caught Willow's eye. She nudged Jessie beside her and motioned towards him. It was Arnold, the boy from the orphanage. With the way he had his eyes locked on her again, she felt like a target.

"He must have heard us earlier when we were talking. I hope it's worth it because I wouldn't want to be him later when someone notices he isn't at the orphanage," Jessie said.

Diana Waddington took her place in the chair. On the table beside her were candles with glass covers that illuminated the area perfectly for reading and a single book with a brownish red cover.

"Everyone, settle down and find a comfortable spot now. We are about to begin," Diana said, blowing the dust off the book away from all the children and opening it to the first page. Silence fell across the room in anticipation.

"Once long, long ago, there was one world, which contained all of the different realms and every type of being or creature one could possibly imagine. There were small pixies whose wings would light up at night, no bigger than the size of your pinky finger and pointy-eared elves dwelling in the trees of the largest forests - faeries who dusted the skies with playful magic and large ugly trolls who hid in the darkest caves of mountains - witches who could practice the best and the worst magic had to offer - half-beast half-man creatures with enhanced senses of sight and sound - mighty giants with one eye - goblins and gnomes - beings who lived underwater - wizards and winks - dwarfs and men of all natures.

"Sitting in the middle, on top of a hill, watching over all, was an ancient tree named Acacia - taller by far than any tree that could be found. Its beautiful green leaves on large drooping branches gently swept the ground beneath them in the wind. She was one of the first ancients ever in existence. Together with guardians, she protected the right of each and every culture to exist and grow in its own way, in its own time and, most importantly, on its own path. Their purpose was not to judge what direction a realm chose to take, nor to involve themselves in regulating right and wrong for these realms, but rather to ensure that every type of creature in the realms had a chance to evolve on its own.

"You would not see the light if there was never any dark. Likewise, you could not distinguish what was right and just if there wasn't any wrong. All things are balanced.

"It wasn't long until another group of ancients with ill intent emerged, comprised of beings once considered guardians, who had chosen to act on impulse and desire rather than reason. They believed their powers made them better than the rest of the realms and that they should be treated as such - bowed down to, served and worshipped. A great battle began between the remaining guardians and those who left the order to pursue personal gain and power.

"Realizing the battle was not advancing and that both sides would be bound in a stalemate forever, the Xiuhcoatle, a race of large serpents, began a search that would change history forever. The snakes hunted high and low for a weak man who could easily be manipulated and charmed with promises of wealth and power to wage a war between the realms, so that the guardians would be forced to intervene. Apopp, one of the largest of the serpents, at long last found what they were looking for, a man named Adom and his wife Evila. They were mortal, with no extraordinary talents, living a modest life. The couple were offered a drink of the blood of faeries, which Apopp promised would enhance their strength and speed and allow their family to claim other lands as their own, taking riches for themselves. The two drank and a great war followed.

"They conquered many lands with the aid of the great serpent's potion. Within the realms, news of the benefits of drinking blood of the magical spread like wildfire and so did a new obsession with obtaining the power granted by such blood. Men began to try to conquer those who showed signs of magic in any form. Creatures were captured and persecuted. Wars broke out. Forests were burned. Lives were lost. Great kings obsessed with gold and riches were born, with one wish, to extend their kingdoms and enslave those who opposed them. The blood wars were in full swing and such would be the theme throughout much of the world for some time.

"The remaining guardian races and Acacia decided they could not both fight the other ancients and protect the realms from each other. A decision needed to be made and, after much discussion and thought, the one world was split into many realms - with only portals left connecting them to each other. For added protection, all portals required a guardian to activate them.

"The magical folk were safe again. The men were left to bicker and fight amongst themselves in their own lands. The power of the potions wore off and the ancient races were each given their own worlds to be bound to. The final decision was less than popular with many, especially a few of the kingdoms of men and the ancients.

"Before creating a land for themselves, the guardians chose a group of gifted and honourable beings to join them. There were many possible choices, but only so many could be chosen based on their disposition to act upon temptation and the emotions that can be found within each of us. As a gift for their service, Acacia granted them and their families to come extended life. They weren't immortal, but without sickness or war, they would live to the end of time. Their age would not show, nor would their bones ache or bodies fail.

"A beautiful world was created with vast forests and gardens. A great house sat overlooking the rest of the world. It was a home for everyone. All were equal and all would train to ensure the safety of every being and to ensure that only the guardians and their new friends had use of the portals. There could be no doorways into or out of the main world which could allow corruption to enter or leave.

"It was soon discovered that by creating the portals, the guardians syphoned off some of their powers and, as a result, they could not travel through the very gateways they created to the other worlds. They searched for a solution for many cycles. It wasn't until a young prophet suggested that the guardians might merge with another being, that an answer presented itself. Shortly after, the prophecy rang true and certain men and women were able to act as a host for them. Two guardians were the maximum any one person could handle. In this combined form, the guardians could pass through the portals and once safely on the other side, the two could separate again.

"The arrangement proved to be advantageous in other ways as well. The host person could take on some of the guardian's traits: agility, balance, advanced perception, rear sight, tracking abilities and they could communicate in a telepathic form, with each other, while merged. There became three distinct groups in this new home world, the guardians, the keepers and the guardian friends - all still treated equal, but each with their own unique purpose in regulating the safety of all life.

"Teams were trained for their future adventures in the main world and different realms. There were many adventures over the cycles, but those are other stories..."

Diana Waddington used a piece of paper to mark her place in the book and placed it back on the table beside her. She looked up at the children already stretching and starting to move off the floor. From the looks on their faces, she knew they were happy with the tale she told.

Jessie bumped Willow's arm as they were leaving. "So? What was so special you needed to hear that story?"

"I don't know," she replied. "Maybe the whole good and bad in all of us thing, you know, the *You are growing up - don't murder anyone, it's just hormones* kinda deal."

Jessie laughed. "I could see that."

"I did read a book earlier that mentioned the same races, though. Do you think they could be real? I mean a race of evil snakes is disturbing to say the least, and all that drinking of blood. Yuck. Who could do such a thing?"

"That's what makes the story so great." Dezi stuck his head between them and laughed. "You aren't scared of a little sensationalism, are you? You sure you can handle being all alone tonight? Who knows what might find a doorway into our world and attack you? Now, if you need some company to keep you safe."

"Don't ask, Dez, cause you definitely wouldn't be safe!" Clairity laughed. The laughter grew louder as everyone else joined in. The trio were dressed similar to each other tonight and held the attention of several of the girls over the story for most of the evening. In a way it made sense. They were, after all, the three most eligible prospects for young girls looking for a future husband. That included several from the castle as well.

"I think if there was anything, including doorways to other worlds hidden in the forest, someone would have found it by now. Think of all the times we have played hide and seek and never came across anything," Willow answered.

"No one has ever found where the forest ends though, so... who knows what could be out there." Pete smiled as he teased the girls.

"Okay, enough, I am going to have night scares in my dreams." A real sense of worry crossed Clairity's face. Willow understood the feeling, all the talk of monsters and blood was frightening, even if she wouldn't let the others see how she felt.

It was late and she needed to be up earlier than the others, so she turned to say goodbye, catching sight of something out of the corner of her eye that stopped her dead in her tracks. It was Arnold and he was standing in the space beside the Waddington house. It was almost as if he were hiding in the shadows. She motioned again to Jessie, who turned and looked. The boy backed up and started walking away as if nothing unusual happened.

"He was watching us. It's a little creepy," Willow whispered to Jessie.

"That story really got to you, didn't it?" He laughed. "Arnold isn't creepy. He is just another kid. He probably wanted to join in the conversation but was too scared of rejection. I think you should call it a night."

Willow agreed and muttered, "See you tomorrow," as she headed back to her one bedroom shack to turn in. Once inside, she changed into her bed wear, laid down and pulled the cover over her head.

Closing her eyes, images of the story haunted her imagination. Sleep wasn't going to come easy, if she kept thinking about frightening things. She put the thoughts out of her mind and concentrated on the forest and its trees. The thoughts soothed her, righting all that was wrong and easing her emotions.

Sleep child, you are safe tonight, the female voice whispered gently. The world swirled around as Willow drifted off into a deep sleep.

Chapter Four

The motion of Willow's breath rhythmically moved in and out of her chest. A cool breeze brushed against her face. She opened her eyes to find herself standing in the middle of the town road wearing nothing but a full-length, white, silk nightgown. Her long, red hair hung loose, flowing behind her gently as if harmonized with every breath she took.

A fog crept low to the ground, rolling in from the forest. The eerie mist swirled around her bare ankles. In thinner patches, she noticed the ground was littered with faceless bodies - none moving. She wandered down the street towards the tree line, finding what she had believed to be fog was actually smoke. The forest was set ablaze in giant, blue flames. Clouds began to rumble with thunder; lightning illuminating the sky. Rain began to pour down. She tried to scream for help, but couldn't make a noise. Her mouth fell open, gasping for words.

Her feet began moving, running aimlessly up the road. There was no other life - no sign of people. She approached the castle gates, but they were destroyed. Broken stone was scattered throughout the grounds and only parts of the castle still stood amidst the rubble. The coloured glass windows were shattered - the stone table cracked in half. Disaster and destruction were everywhere.

There was nowhere to go. Then, out of the blue, she found herself running as fast as she could - climbing to the top of the great hill to a tree that was dying. She tried to help it, to heal it, to comfort it. A branch broke off, hitting her in the head. She fell to the ground and watched as the rest of the tree burst into blue flames.

Willow tried to scream again. This time she burst out, "Help! Please someone help me!"

"Come towards my voice," she heard from the distance. Looking around, she could see the face of her friend, Ashlyn, in what appeared to be a hole in the sky. A hand extended through the opening. Willow reached as hard as she could, finally grasping the hand. She felt herself being pulled up... escaping.

Like a jolt of electricity hit her, she sat up straight in bed - sweat dripping down her face and her heart racing. *It was a dream, just a dream*, she told herself.

What was it about, child? The male voice asked with concern.

You don't know? I thought you were always with me, she said.

We cannot enter your dreams. Only a dreamwalker can do that. Dreams are for you and you alone. You can choose to share what happened with us and we can try to help you decipher the meaning, if you would like.

Willow went over the dream in her mind and decided, with the help of the voices, that the visions were just the result of her imagination playing on the story from the night before. There was little time to linger over it. She needed to prepare for the day. Everything around her seemed normal. She jumped - no one ever knocked on her door.

Ashlyn stood in front of her, still in her night clothes and holding on to a little rag doll as tightly as possible. She lunged forward, throwing her arms around Willow in a hug, bursting out, "Are you okay?"

"You mean that was real? You were there? How?" Willow placed a hand over her mouth, her mind racing with questions.

Ashlyn shook her head. "I can't explain it. I have never gone into another person's dream before, just called my mom into a few of my night scares. It started about a month ago. The dreams are similar to the one you had. Mom thinks they are a warning of some sort... of something that is coming, but we don't know what." She looked down at the ground. "They scare me - the bodies with no faces. Who do you think they are?"

"I don't know. People, I guess - maybe from here, maybe from somewhere else," Willow replied.

"Can I stay with you today? I can help if you want."

Willow smiled. "Sure, but you will need to change into regular clothes first. We can meet back at the stands and sit together."

Ashlyn headed off across the street to change. Already behind, Willow began her daily ritual. She finished bringing the produce round front when her friend returned. After filling the stands, the two girls sat down.

"So you are a dreamwalker," Willow said, breaking the silence.

"I don't know what that is."

"You can move through the dreams of others and pull people into your own. It's a rare ability, I bet." Willow added more apples to the fruit display in front of her.

"Yeah, I guess," she answered with little enthusiasm. "Not what I would have chosen. I can't think of a situation where it would ever be helpful."

"You pulled me out of that night scare. Do you think you can die in your dreams? Could something have actually happened to me? You said the dreams were the same. Do you know what happens next?" Willow sat down again, her legs fidgeting.

"No," Ashlyn answered with a mouth full of berries. "I get to the same point, on the great hill when a branch falls and the dying tree catches fire, then I call out. Mom pulls me out - the same way I did to you."

"Should we try to see the rest? You know, see what happens?" Willow asked.

"No, I don't think that's a good idea. Something bad could happen. I just wish it would go away."

The town's daily activities commenced while the girls were chatting and, coming towards them, Willow could see Jade and her entourage as well as their mothers. The three girls had almost a skip to their walk and smiles that reflected the sun in such an intense manner that they forced squints from onlookers from the sheer brightness. The castle boys also seemed happier, but for a different reason: the group was moving faster than normal. Nebulah, Nyssa, and Ashley strolled behind them, a look of pride plastered on their faces like a thick layer of makeup.

When Jade reached the produce stands, she barked, "Just put together baskets. You should know what we like by now. We will be back in a bit." Without even stopping, she continued on.

"They are going to order new jewelry, I bet." Ashlyn didn't take her eyes off of the girls until they reached the Shinning house and entered. "Aha, I knew it!"

Willow looked up from the baskets she was preparing just in time to see the group disappear into the gem maker's house. Shortly after, Victoria emerged from the house and ran over to where they were sitting. The young girl was still dressed in her sleep wear and looked as if she left home in a rush. Normally, her long wavy hair would be neatly tied back in a ponytail or braids, but today it was loose and hadn't even been brushed.

"Can I join you? It's getting crowded at home," the young girl asked.

Ashlyn was quick to answer, "Of course you can. So what's going on over there, anyways? Why the rush for new shiny stuff?"

"Something about a dance at the castle." Victoria was more interested in choosing something to eat from the fresh fruit in front of her than discussing details of some dance.

"A dance?" Ashlyn smiled. "Do you think we will be invited?"

Willow glanced at her, perplexed. "No!" she snorted. The two broke out into a round of laughter at the thought of Jade extending an invitation to either of them to join in anything.

A few moments later, the Council group emerged, swiftly moving on to Ashlyn's house.

"I bet that's a lot of clothes they are ordering. Looks like I am going to be busy helping out for a while." The tone in her voice reflected her lack of enthusiasm in making beautiful outfits for a dance she probably wouldn't ever see.

Two guards sent to town for supplies stopped at the stands and were looking over what was available. Faramund pointed at corn. From the corner of her eye, Willow noticed a rather crude picture on his lower arm, unlike her own, which were more detailed and realistic. Iskander, the other guard, made a similar motion towards the grapes and peaches. The same image appeared on his arm. A scowl crossed her face. How was it she never noticed before?

"What does that symbol mean... the one on your arms?" she asked.

The two guards looked at each other and then at the girls - bursting with curiosity. Both guards were tall and muscular. Iskander's complexion, however, was so strikingly different from his friend Faramund's golden skin tone that it made him look distinctly paler than he might have appeared if he had been alone. That, combined with his fair hair, and one might have thought something frightened the colour completely from his body.

Faramund pulled his sleeve back, revealing the entire picture to the girls. It was an oval shape with four swords, one representing each direction: north, south, east and west. The tips of each sword met in the middle. The entire picture was coloured in an unusual shade of blue.

"The oval represents a door, or..." he paused for a moment, looking at the other man as if they were somehow discussing what to say. "A gate, with the four intersecting swords representing two guards on each side. The swords meet in the middle allowing no one to pass. Put simply, it is a sign of our birthright to protect."

"So every guard has that picture?" Willow continued her interrogation.

"Yes," Iskander answered. "When chosen for service as a guard, the symbol appears. It is a great honour to be given the responsibility."

"If I wake up one day and have the same symbol, I would just be a guard?"

Both men laughed. "Something like that, but guards are appointed based on need, and there hasn't been a need for new guards in a very long time," Faramund replied.

"Does that mean something would have to happen to one of you for another to be needed?" Ashlyn asked with a mouth full of berries, a red ring forming around her lips from the ripe juices.

"I hope that doesn't happen, but, it is a way in which a new guard could be needed. The most common way still is an increase in the number of... gateways that need protecting," Faramund replied.

"In other words, a new guard won't be appointed unless there are not enough guards alive or available in relation to the number of gateways needing guarding," the other man offered.

As interested as Willow was to continue the conversation with the two men, Jade and the others were emerging from ordering their new clothes. There was no desire start out the day on the Council's bad side or get anyone else in trouble. She thanked them for the conversation, handing them their baskets. The two men were on their way to the baker's when the Council group picked up their orders. As they suspected, no invitation to the dance was extended.

The rest of the day was dreary. Victoria returned home. The whispers in the line of who was invited and who wasn't was too much for Ashlyn, so she headed home to help her parents. Since very little happened on a daily basis, the dance was going to be the hot topic for the next couple weeks - until the event was over. Willow herself was glad when it was time to drop off food at the orphanage.

Dezi came over to help with the delivery. He was fun to be with, quick with the jokes and always made Willow smile. All the way there, she managed to avoid the dance topic. She already knew the brothers were invited and in her opinion there was nothing to discuss.

Today, Micca was already waiting for them out front. There was no need to go inside. The thought crossed Willow's mind that it had something to do with Arnold sneaking out the night before. There was no sign of the boy.

The way back was unusually quiet, almost to the point of being awkward. A couple times, it seemed Dezi was going to start to say something, but changed his mind. He would sigh, rub his hand through his hair, then shove both hands in his pockets before continuing the walk. They were about halfway back when he came to a complete stop.

"So, I guess you heard about the dance?" he said, his voice cracking. He swallowed and coughed.

Just the topic she hoped to avoid. Holding her breath, she answered, "Yes, I wasn't invited though." There was a pause for a moment before she added, "I am sure you will have a great time. Everyone is talking about it. It is going to be the biggest event in... forever."

"Yeah, it sounds great. Thing is, no girls were invited," he replied, kicking the dirt beneath his feet.

"How can you have a dance with no girls? Sounds rather awkward," Willow said, starting their walk again.

He laughed. "Well, the guys were given an invite for two. We are supposed to bring a... date," he said, matching her pace.

"Oh, I get it. Have you decided who you want to take?"

Dezi stopped walking abruptly. "I am trying to ask you," he blurted out.

"Me?" she squealed out in shock. "I thought you would go with Jade or one of the other Council daughters." She looked down at a few pebbles on the ground. "Are you sure?"

"Jade is pretty to look at, but I would have a much better time with you. You know when to laugh and don't ruin my jokes," he said, winking at her with a twinkle in his eye.

She let out the air she seemed to have been holding through the whole conversation. "I can't dance. I might hurt your feet, but if you still want me to go with you, I will."

"Excellent!" The two returned to walking. "See you later," he added as they approached his house.

Willow felt as if she was going to burst if she didn't tell someone the news soon. She was going to the dance! As soon as Dezi disappeared inside, she changed her direction to find Clairity and Ashlyn.

Her friends had managed to sneak off to a quiet spot under a tree in the forest. The girls beamed with enthusiasm as they listened with excitement to the story. When she finished, they all simultaneously let out a little yelp, which someone walking by might have considered to be the cries of a hurt animal.

"Can you believe it? Me going to the dance! I have never been invited to anything in my life. It's the most amazing feeling," she said, grabbing Ashlyn's hands and spinning round in circles.

Clairity smiled at the two. "I can't wait to see the look on Jade's face when she finds out. That is going to be priceless."

Willow stopped in her tracks, wobbling - her head dizzy from spinning. She fell backwards, landing in a sitting position. "I forgot about that." The smile faded from her face. "What was I thinking? Oh... why did I say yes? I can't dance - I have no dress - and Jade is going to cut me into pieces. I have to tell him I can't." Panic set in.

"No," Ashlyn complained. "Why should she ruin your fun?"

Clairity agreed, smiling. "She is right. You need to do this for all of us wretched folk who won't be invited."

"You don't know that. There are lots of boys that got invites for two." After a pause, she added, "What am I going to do? It's a disaster."

Ashlyn smiled. "A little dramatic, don't you think? Come on." She motioned for her friends to join her. "Let's go."

"Where are we going?" Willow asked.

"To my house. You will see."

The three headed back to Ashlyn's. Her whole house was more comfortable than a typical family would have. Different fabrics, cushions, and finished clothes filled the front room, as well as standing figures with dresses in the process of being made. Her sleeping quarters were down the hallway to the right. A body cushion rested on a patchwork quilt that covered her bed and cupboards remained open, filled with clothes.

"Let's try some of these on," she said, motioning to Willow while removing a handful of dresses from her closet.

After trying on one after the other, it became apparent that their figures simply weren't compatible. There was no way any of the dresses would fit her.

"Thanks for trying."

"What are you girls doing in here?" Ashlyn's mother asked, peeking in the doorway. "Oh, my. Dress up time?"

The girls took turns explaining the story to her. The whole time her face seemed to hang on every word with excitement.

"One of our own going to a dance at the castle. It's about time, I say. Oh, this is good news. These dresses won't do! No - not at all... Ashlyn, fetch me my bag. We'll make you a new dress. You will be the belle of the ball after I am finished."

Seconds later, Ashlyn returned with a tapestry bag, filled with: tapes to take measurements, pins, needles, thread and a sketchbook with notes and designs. Martha immediately started to measure, standing on the bed to reach Willow's chest, shoulders and arm span. After each measurement, she recorded information in her book and added an "Ahuh" or "Aha." The whole process only took a few moments. The seamstress looked deep in thought. "Hmm." A slight pause. "If only we knew what colour your hair would be that night. I could pick something that wouldn't clash."

Without thinking, Willow added, "Red." She wasn't sure why she was thinking back to the dream at that moment. Her hair was a dark brown at that moment.

"Don't be silly, child," Martha said, smiling. "No one has had red hair in ages and I doubt that is going to change any time soon. I think black might be the best choice for the dress. It goes with everything. Don't you worry about a thing. You will have the finest dress I have ever made. Now, off you girls go and stay out of my hair while I work."

Martha was the closest thing to a real mother Willow knew. She was short, a little plump, with curly black hair and always wore floral print dresses with a white frilly apron over top. She never felt like she was assigned a job. She loved to sew. No one knew how, exactly, she made the material she used, only that the process involved leaves, flowers, broken branches and weeds. *Trade secrets* was the answer she would give if anyone asked. On numerous occasions the girls scrounged through the forest to collect various *materials* for her.

"Maybe gather some wildflowers for me over the next few days if you have nothing better to do," Martha added.

The girls agreed and headed outside, still bubbling in excitement over the dress - so much so, that they almost bumped into Mrs. Shinning trying to go in.

"Oh, Willow darling, are you getting a dress and shoes? Dezi told us you two are going together. It's so exciting, isn't it? Don't you worry about a thing. We will take care of all the details. Mr. Shinning just wanted to know what colour you would be wearing."

"Black, I think, but I really don't need anything too fancy. I am not sure I would feel comfortable," Willow answered.

"Don't be silly. We have already started designing a couple pieces for you. You two will be the couple to admire," she said, closing the door to the seamstress's house behind her.

"What have I gotten myself into?" Willow asked her two best friends. Over their shoulders, she caught sight of a boy strolling towards the castle gates. "Is that Arnold? What's he up to?"

The two girls spun around and watched the boy, steadily increasing his pace, until he was out of sight.

"He is probably going to try to ask someone at the castle to the dance," Ashlyn offered, trying not to snicker at the thought of Arnold on a date with Jade.

"Yeah, maybe," Clairity responded, still staring down the road. The half-scowl on her face let on that she not only didn't quite believe that answer, but also wasn't going to offer an alternate explanation. After a few moments, she added, "We should get some rest. I have a strange feeling something big is going to happen tomorrow." She looked at her friends faces and continued, "It's just a feeling. I don't know why exactly, but my intuition has been bang-on lately."

The three hugged.

"Goodnight and happy dreams," Clairity said with a half-smile. "And guys, stay away from Arnold. I feel all kinds of bad vibes coming from his direction. I know it's weird, but please, just tell me you will."

The two girls agreed.

Chapter Five

It was already getting dark when Arnold arrived at the castle. Approaching the gates, he addressed the guards. "Take me to Malarchy and make it fast. He won't want you messing around with me standing here waiting."

The four guards exchanged glances and a smirk before Eudard took the assignment. He headed off to see if the boy could enter or should be turned around and sent home as a nuisance. To his surprise, upon finding Malarchy, he actually agreed to see the boy. Using the guards' natural telepathic connection, he sent a message to the others to escort the child into the garden area.

Arnold wasn't even in front of the self-declared Council leader when he blurted out, "I have the information."

Malarchy glared at him and motioned to the two guards. "Wait outside the garden gates. This won't take long." After they left, he turned his attention to the boy. "Do not address me in public unless I have indicated I want you to speak. Are we clear?"

Arnold held his gaze - not backing down, then the edges of his lips curled upward just a touch. "Fine, as long as you remember our deal. I have information and I want what's coming to me."

"And you will get it and so much more, as long as the information is something I can use and you remember your place. So spit it out. What is so important that you are out after dark?"

"This is the only time I could escape after the other day. Those people don't know who they are dealing with... yet," the boy snarled.

"Yes, yes boy, time is precious. Let's get to it," Malarchy demanded.

"The writer, Diana Waddington's story - I went and listened like you asked. It was about ancient races, guardians and Acacia, a giant tree. Sounded to me like she was hinting the tree used to stand on the great hill. It was quite the story, with portals to different worlds and wars - even included the drinking of blood. Pretty sure the girl didn't understand any message from it, though. Not sure that group is bright enough to understand much."

The colour drained from Malarchy's face. "Very well, we will look into it. Now away with you."

"No! We have a deal. I am not going back to that place anymore. I want a room here, tonight, and to be treated as one of you," Arnold barked back.

"Who do you think you are talking to?" Malarchy snapped, grabbing the boy's arm and dragging him towards the garden gates. "You will do what I say, when I say and right now, I say you will go back to town as if nothing has happened. After I check out your tale, I will decide what it's worth to me and not a second before. Do you understand me?" Without waiting for an answer, he added, "Good." Then he turned the boy over to the guards with instructions to remove him from the grounds and send Zsiga to the gardens.

It took less than a minute for Zsiga, the head guard, to reach the stone table where Malarchy sat. His skin, hair and eyes were darker than night, allowing him to move in the shadows with ease. That was one of the skills which helped him secure the position of leader over the other guards. His impressive muscular build was another. "Sir, you sent for me?" he asked.

Malarchy snapped out of deep thought. "Yes – yes, I did. Gather a team of men. There is something that must be done to protect the greater good of our citizens. I will meet you at the main gates with instructions in two hours. Make sure your men are prepared with weapons ready and torches lit." He dismissed the guard and moved inside the castle, where he stared at the blank wall silently until it was time to give his instructions.

Chapter Six

Willow bolted straight up, taking in a deep breath, filling her lungs to capacity. She must have been dreaming again. That was the only logical explanation. It was hours still before she needed to be up. She lay back down and closed her eyes again. A scream sounded outside. This time, she knew she wasn't dreaming. She jumped out of bed.

What are you doing? Where are you going? The female voice shrieked. *Stay inside. You don't know what is happening out there. You could get hurt!*

"Sounds like someone else is hurt. I need to try to help," she said out loud. Truth be told, she was scared and wasn't sure who exactly she was trying to convince, the voices or herself. Things were changing so fast lately. Her life was a mystery that she needed to solve. She opened the door and stepped into the street.

Go back inside! The voices cried louder now, as if upset. *You aren't even dressed. Someone could see.*

Willow didn't hear the voices; in fact, she didn't hear anything for a moment. She stood swaying - stunned at the sight of guards piling books from Diana's house on a big bonfire in the middle of the street. There was one guard on each side of the house stopping people from getting too close. Diana was screaming and crying, held by her arms by two men. On one side of the porch, Nathan curled up in a ball. Without thinking, she ran towards him. Seeing her moving toward him, Nathan rushed to meet her at the edge of the porch. A hand grabbed her shoulder from behind.

Faramund, the guard she had spoken with earlier that day, pulled her back into the shadow between the two houses. "You shouldn't be out here, girl." He turned his gaze to the boy holding on to Willow's waist. "He doesn't need to see this. Take him to your home. You can't help the woman now." He removed his jacket and placed it over her shoulders. "Quickly now, before anyone else notices. The Council will be far harder on you than they will be on the storyteller if they find out." He moved out of the shadow, returning to his post.

Willow looked down and realized she was wearing her night dress. It was white and sometimes hung off one shoulder. Suddenly, she understood. Faramund had seen the pictures on her back. He was helping her. As the guard suggested, the two ran across the street, back to her shack. Once inside, Nathan turned around, allowing Willow to change into clothes - ones that covered everything.

She didn't understand what was happening around her, but had a strong feeling she knew who did. After Nathan lay down to rest, she took a position as if meditating and called out inside her head, *I know you can hear me. I think it's time you told me what is going on.*

When it's time, we will. You have to understand, there are things you must discover on your own. Unless you are in direct danger...

Willow cut the voice off. *Danger, you don't think what is happening to Diana is danger?*

A dangerous situation perhaps, but it doesn't impose direct danger to you and that is our concern. What is happening here is wrong, but you can't fight it alone and definitely not before you mature to your full potential. Until that time, you must be patient and trust us.

She stood and moved to the door. Opening it a crack, she saw the guards escorting Mrs. Waddington towards the castle - her hands bound in rope behind her back. Willow glanced back at Nathan on the bed. *People are getting hurt. How can I do nothing when I know they would do everything for me?*

You are more special than you know. Others see that, the male voice responded to her alone.

She left the door slightly open and backed up to the wall, sliding down to a sitting position. Her vision locked on the fire burning the books she loved so much. Tears pooled in the corners of her eyes until she could no longer handle the burning. She cried.

At the same time, rain started to pour down, harder than she remembered it ever raining before. Within minutes, the bucket in the corner was overflowing again. She made no effort to move to empty it - water puddled on the floor. Tears raced down her cheeks, soaking her collar. She watched the downpour turn fire to smoke, oblivious to everything else.

Clairity ran across the street and knelt down beside her. "What are you doing? It's late. The Council will be in town any time now and the stands are empty."

Willow looked at her and replied, "It's still raining. I never start work till the rain stops."

"It's been raining for hours. No one knows why. It's never happened before. Come on. I will help you," Clairity offered.

The two girls left Nathan in bed, agreeing he needed the sleep and headed out back. Willow felt better with a friend to lean on. The rain started to let up. She was too absorbed in getting the stands filled to notice when it stopped completely - allowing herself to be distracted by voices telling her people counted on her and she couldn't let them down.

Four guards came to her stand, two picking up the Council's needs, because of the unusually wet weather, and the other two attended to the needs of the guardhouse. After they left, people darted from their homes, picking up essentials before hurrying back again. Even when the sun was shining again, no one lingered outside. Talk was kept short and without eye contact. People were scared.

Ashlyn joined her friends behind the produce stands. "Where do you think they took her? I hope she is okay," she said, sitting down, a blank stare on her face.

The other two girls glared at her, both placing one finger in front of their lips. "Nathan is still sleeping inside," Clairity whispered.

"Sorry," Ashlyn whispered back.

"It's okay, I am up," Nathan said from the door. He moved over and sat down, staring across the road at his grandmother's house and the remains of charred books in the middle of the street. Time passed in complete silence. It was quiet, almost too quiet.

Ashlyn motioned for the others to look up. Jade, Camile and Sabrina skipped by, like nothing happened. They headed straight to Ashlyn's house, most likely to check on their orders.

It was only a few minutes later that the girls emerged, Jade slamming the front door. Even from a distance, it was obvious from their faces that they weren't happy about something. Jade practically stomped holes in the ground on her way over to the Shinning house with the other two trying to console her. Martha appeared in her doorway and motioned for her daughter to stay where she was. Seconds later, everyone in town heard a blood-curdling scream. People peeked out their windows and doors at the jewelry maker's place, trying to catch sight of anything they could.

Jade emerged from the house, yelling, "I'll be back with others! Don't think you'll get away with this!" She stormed down the street back to the castle, her two friends running behind her.

"What was that about?" Nathan asked.

"Not sure," Clairity replied. "But I have a feeling we need to stay here. This isn't over yet."

The four of them continued making baskets for people as they sporadically appeared. It was about an hour later when they were packing up the remaining food that Jade returned with her mother and headed straight to the Shinning place. The raised voices meant there was no doubt someone was in the middle of a heated argument, but none of the girls could make out any words. It lasted for about ten minutes, then Nebulah and Jade emerged and walked to the dress maker's house.

This time, Nebulah motioned for her daughter to remain outside. Jade stood, glaring in Willow's direction while waiting. Another argument erupted. When Nebulah returned to her daughter, they exchanged a few words.

Jade voice raised. "I don't care! I want them and I will have them. They are making fools of us, Mother, and you are letting them." She stormed off back to the castle - her mother walking slowly behind her.

Willow started to head over to the jewelry maker's house when Martha ran out and sent her back. "Not now. Let this settle. We can handle it. You four just deliver those boxes and call it a night. Get some extra sleep." She handed Willow an extra blanket and pillow for Nathan and turned to go back inside.

Willow was glad the group did as Martha suggested. After the night before, she was exhausted and fell right to sleep.

Sometime during the night, the pile of charred books disappeared from the road. All that remained the next morning was a black spot on the grey and brown path where the fire once burned.

Willow attended to her normal duties, trying to start the day as if nothing happened. It was impossible to not see something was going on. Her beliefs were all but confirmed when the Council sent guards for their daily needs again.

Nathan, trying to lighten the mood, suggested perhaps the Council realized they could do less if they made the guards do daily errands for them. Having a giggle together was the highlight of the morning.

The day stretched on with people hurrying to get their food and trying to avoid talking. She wondered how long they would live like this, scared to interact with each other. Suddenly, to her surprise, Jade appeared in front of her.

"Do you really think you can be anywhere near better than me? This is a warning to you. I will get what I want, no matter what it takes. I'd move aside if I were you before you or your friends get hurt." Jade flipped her hair as she turned and headed towards her home.

It took a moment for Willow to fully process what had just happened. Had Jade really threatened her? Why? With no one jumping out at her with an answer, It was time to go for a visit and find out for herself.

The Shinning house was always open during the day. Inside, Augusto Shinning was working on what, from where she stood, looked like a necklace. He was a funny-looking little man with pure white messy hair that was well overdue for a cut and a big white moustache, which curled up at the ends into circles. The door closing forced his gaze in her direction.

"Opaque, we have company." Stopping his work, he smiled. "How are you today, Miss Willow?"

She wasn't sure how to answer. Under the circumstances, it almost felt like a trick question. Luckily, she was saved by Mrs. Shinning.

"What a lovely surprise. Does Dezi know you are here? I can call him."

"No, thank you," Willow said, her voice shaking a little. "I came to see you."

"Oh," Opaque replied. "What can we do for you, my dear?"

"Well," she said, thinking about her words for a moment before deciding to just tell them out right. "I had a visit from Jade today. She was angry at me for something. I am not sure I understand why. Earlier, I heard parts of your argument. I wondered if they were in some way connected."

Augusto took in a deep breath and let it out slowly. "I am afraid it is the things some people in town are making for you for the dance. Jade decided she wanted them for herself and when we refused to give them to her, she became enraged."

An expression of horror overtook Willow's face. "I don't want to be the cause of any problems. Please, make the items for her so she will be happy."

"No, my dear, it doesn't matter if we give the things we are working on to her. The second we make you something else, she would want that too. Greed has overtaken that girl. The town all agreed we would not give in. The items we make for you will be for you. Don't worry about Jade. She will have to get over it. Now, head on home and put it out of your mind."

Willow did as they requested, not wanting to cause further problems within the town, but a part of her feared that which was still to come.

"Guess they told you, huh?" Ashlyn asked, meeting her part of the way back.

Willow bit her bottom lip, nodding. Normally talking things through eased her mind. This time, however, she only felt a slight twinge of relief after retelling the story of Jade from earlier to her friend.

"That's terrible. She actually threatened you and your friends?" Ashlyn asked, her eyes bulging. "I wouldn't worry. What can she do? Her parents aren't about to take on the whole town."

It was the next day when Jade and her mother returned again. This time she was carrying something in a handbasket and her two girlfriends, Camile and Sabrina were on either side of them. They headed straight to the Shinning house again. Jade and Nebulah entered while the other two stood outside, more rigid than statues. When mother and daughter appeared again, whatever Jade carried in was gone. They entered the seamstress's house. This time, all four went in and emerged a few minutes later.

They moved across the street in Willow's direction. Behind them, she could see Ashlyn in her doorway - shrugging her shoulders. Martha closed the door.

Jade stepped forward, smiling. "I am sorry for the way I acted. I hope you will forgive me. I am sure we can be friends. We can't wait to have you come to the dance."

Willow almost fell off her seat. "Thank you," was all she could manage to say after catching her balance.

The group strolled up the street, heading back to the castle.

What was that? she asked with her inside voice.

Trust your instincts, was the only answer she received back.

Martha and Opaque both ran across the street to see her, smiles beaming.

"See! We knew no parent would allow their daughter to act like that." Mrs. Shinning smiled.

"Everything is fine now and you will have a wonderful time at the dance," Martha added, placing her arm around Willow's shoulders and squeezing.

"I suppose." Willow said, still unsure. "If you don't mind me asking, what did Jade bring you?" she asked Mrs. Shinning.

"Not me, dear. She felt bad about the way this affected Dezi and his brothers. She wanted to make sure they still attend the dance, so she made them a small cake. The four of them enjoyed it together while we adults talked about designs for the Council girls."

Willow couldn't imagine Jade cooking anything. But over the days leading up to dance, she came every day with a baked cake made especially for the three boys and only them.

The following days and nights remained relatively uneventful - each one seeming to pass by more quickly that its predecessor had. Before she knew it, the day of the dance was upon her. Everyone in town busied themselves, preparing last-minute details. Ashlyn, Nathan and Clairity agreed to run the produce stands for the day so Willow could get ready for her big night.

It was probably a good thing her stomach had been too queasy for her to eat anything. She couldn't imagine anything she swallowed being able to pass by the lump that had formed in her throat. At least she had Mrs. Shinning and Mrs. Needle to help her. They both had jumped at the chance to use her as a living dress-up doll. When they arrived, the two ladies carried with them the most stunning dress and jewelry Willow had ever seen. Seeing their offerings in-person put Jade's jealousy into a new perspective.

The two women stepped outside while Willow slipped into the dress. It was pure black and started with a collar around her neck. Two straps extended down the front, attaching to a sleeveless, backless top. The upper half connected at the waist to a skirt that gently kissed the floor as she moved. A gold chain ran from the collar at the back to the top of the skirt at her waist. She gasped, suddenly remembering the pictures. She stretched her neck, trying to see her own back. There was nothing there. Puzzled, she continued searching until she heard a giggle.

Alright you two, where did the cats go?

She received her reply right away. *To your stomach.*

They can move? Why didn't you tell me? She asked.

Relax, it's new, the other voice said calmly. *The further you go into your sixteenth cycle, the more changes will happen.*

Martha peeked her head back in the door. "Can we come back in? Oh, you look beautiful." The two ladies walked in without waiting for an invitation.

"Stunning," Opaque added. "Your hair, it's… red," she added, looking at the seamstress. "I haven't seen that colour in... a very long time."

The two ladies helped Willow fix her hair up off her neck, allowing a few wispy strands to flow down around her face, then put on the earrings, necklace and hair pin that had been meticulously designed just for her.

It was time to try the shoes. The two women insisted she walk back and forth until she could manage the full width of the room without toppling over. In the end, it wasn't perfect, but on the arm of a strong young man, she'd make it through the night. Confident they had done their best, the two mothers left, heading home with Willow's friends. Nathan was staying at Ashlyn's for the night, leaving nothing to interrupt the evening.

Clairity came over a few minutes later. "Wow, you look amazing."

"What are you doing here?" she asked.

"I had a feeling you might need some company," Clairity replied.

"Right again," Willow said. "I am so nervous. What if I make a fool of myself? Or fall down? Or…"

"Don't be silly," her friend interrupted. "You will be brilliant."

The two girls sat and waited. The sun went down, and from where they were, the girls could hear the music from the dance.

"He isn't coming - is he?" Willow said, more as a statement than a question. Her gaze focused down at the ground.

"Maybe something happened. You don't know for sure. He wouldn't just not show up. You two are good friends." Clairity turned around, seeing that her friend wanted to change out of the pretty dress. "You could wait a bit longer."

Once back in her own clothes, she handed the dress, shoes and jewelry to Clairity. "Would you return these for me? I am sure someone will be able to put them to good use." She said, her hands shaking.

Clairity agreed, not knowing what to say or do. She could see the pain in her friend's face - the way she was straining not to cry. Reaching out, she touched her friend's shoulder. That was enough to make Willow bolt, running faster than she ever had before, disappearing deep into the forest.

Clairity for once didn't want to listen to her intuition. It was telling her to leave Willow alone for now - that she would be fine and this was how things needed to be. She hadn't been wrong since developing the ability, and until this moment, hadn't questioned it once. In the end, she decided to let her friend have space for the rest of the night. She headed across the street to return the items and share the sad story of the evening's events.

Chapter Seven

Willow slowed her run to a walk and then stopped, bending over to catch her breath. There was only running, not thinking, not listening - just running. Without a planned direction to her path, she found herself near the castle wall. Climbing one of the largest trees gave her a bird's eye view of the courtyard.

Music drifted up to her ears. Her vision blurred at the sight of couples dancing, twirling in time to the beat. Floating balls of light lit up the sky, sending a gentle glow down on the festivities. To one side, a man in a bright red and orange suit juggled three spheres of fire with his bare hands. At evenly timed intervals, a lady dressed in shimmering silver and gold, would motion upwards to the sky, following which, sparks of glitter would rain down from high above in pretty patterns. Those lucky enough to be in attendance were all dressed in fancy clothes - beautiful flowing dresses and crisp suits. It was more glamorous than she had imagined. Her eyes stung with unshed tears.

First love is always the hardest, time will heal. It was the female voice she had become so accustomed to over the years, trying to console her - worried about her.

Willow sighed. *It isn't love. Dezi is a great guy and a good friend, but I don't think I even know what love is yet. I hear other girls talk about a single touch sending shivers down their spines, their thoughts filled with one person, one face. Truth is, I haven't felt anything even remotely close to what they describe. No, it's my pride that is hurt. I wanted to be there... to be good enough to be there. I wasn't and Jade was right. She won and it leaves me feeling defective in every way possible.*

We are proud of you. Few of your age could see the difference.

That doesn't help how I feel right now, Willow responded. As a single tear trickled down her face, grey filled the skies. As if feeling her sadness, the clouds wept with her. Rain began to fall over the castle grounds. "Did I do that?" she asked out loud.

"Yes," whispered on the wind. This time, it wasn't a voice she remembered hearing before, yet it was somehow familiar. She looked around, expecting to find someone who followed her from town, but there was no one.

"Who said that?" she demanded.

"We did," came the answer.

She slid partway down the tree with ease, without losing her footing. She never did. For as long as she could remember, she had climbed the highest trees, swinging from branches without ever falling once. She placed one hand on the trunk of the tree she was in and realized that was who had spoken to her. Leaves rustled words of pleasure that she could finally hear them. As they swayed in the breeze, they sang to her as a mother sings to her child.

"Trees? Am I talking to trees?" She slid further down towards the ground.

"Yes, you always have. You just didn't realize it until now. Since the first time you climbed up on our limbs as a young child and almost fell. You called out for help and a branch steadied your feet beneath you. Through the years, we have shared your most intimate feelings. When you were sad, you came to us and we cradled you. When you were mad, we listened to you. When you were happy, we danced with you."

Willow thought back and remembered. It was true. Whenever anything happened in her life, she would go to the forest, climb the trees, run across the branches, sit secure on the tallest limbs. There she felt safe, protected, loved.

She slid the rest of the way down to the ground and realized she hadn't been climbing at all. A branch beneath had lowered her slowly to the base of its trunk. She muttered a *thank you* and began walking without direction. There was so much to think about - to let soak in. So this was her ability - this was what she could do.

Partly, there is still so much more if you choose to learn, the familiar female voice returned.

Are you a tree too? she asked.

She heard laughter all around. *No, we are not,* the male voice answered.

She was about to ask another question, but up ahead she saw something unfamiliar. She quickened her pace through to a clearing that surrounded a building made of white stone with intricately designed columns and a flat top. There were no doors, but rather steps on both sides leading up to an open platform with a table in the middle. On either side of the platform were round semi-circular shaped rooms with carved shelves, lined with books.

Stepping inside, the structure seemed far bigger. There were thousands of books, more than she could ever imagine reading.

What is this place? she asked.

Home to the keepers, the male voice answered.

"Keepers? As in guardian keepers? Like in the stories?" she asked out loud. A shiver in her voice let on she was almost afraid of the answer.

The stories are true, every bit, every part. Diana has an unusual talent of recording history in writing and teaching it to others. She was the official historian of our world and used to teach past events in school at the castle. The books here are references keepers felt necessary to keep protected. Some contain the different abilities of every living person in this world, others with maps and languages of all the different realms. Every question you want to ask, the answer is here.

"Why haven't I seen this place before? Or anyone else I know, for that matter?" she asked, astounded by her find.

Only a keeper or someone led by a keeper can find it. The forest protects the way, blocking others and changing their course to go around or head back towards where they came from. It's like a magical barrier.

So why am I here? A sensation came over her that she already knew the answer.

Because you are the last keeper of this world.

She slid to a sitting position on the ground against one of the bookshelves and brought her knees to her chest. Hugging them, she rocked back and forth. This information was so much to process. Only a few moments ago, she was crying like an infant because she wasn't at the dance. That all seemed so insignificant now compared to what she was being told. "So you, who are you?" It was easier for her to speak her thoughts out loud as if she were having an actual conversation with someone.

We are the last guardians of this world. My name is Aslo and my wife is Kiera.

"You have names. All this time you had names and didn't tell me. I thought I was crazy." A look of disbelief crossed over her face, draining it of colour.

Perhaps this is too much for you to take in all at once, offered Kiera.

"No, I want to know everything. I want to know what happened to my parents," she barked.

Alright, Aslo responded. *The other night, you heard the basic story from Diana. Any extra details you need are contained in the books here, which you can read any time. The world was divided by portals after the blood wars and guardians, keepers, portal guards and friends are the defence system meant to keep all realms safe. Another ancient race found a way to contact men, ones who could be weakened and easily led. Another war broke out. Teams from here were sent to combat the threat. Your father was on one of the first teams deployed.*

The threat was far more extensive than anyone first believed. Weapons which could open up rifts in the space between worlds were being designed. An army had been growing behind our backs. More and more teams were sent to aid those already locked in battle. Soon our vulnerability was exposed. Although we guardians are immortal, we cannot travel the portals without a keeper and keepers are not immortal. Added on top of that was the fact that only certain beings could become keepers. It was a recipe for disaster. The enemy figured out guardians could be trapped in worlds or specially-made cages. They tricked keepers into worlds where guardians would be useless and either killed or captured the keepers, leaving guardians stranded. Some were captured and confined in worlds which we do not know the location of.

"Couldn't another keeper just go through and bring back the guardians?" Willow asked.

Yes, in theory, but each keeper could only carry two guardians. Keepers were low in numbers and it would have meant taking a big chance. At the time, losing more keepers wasn't in the plan, especially since word had been sent that all keepers were needed to join the fight.

"How did they send word?" she interrupted the story again.

Portal guards are telepathic. Each portal was to have two guards on each side. When a portal is open or active, telepathic messages can flow through to the other side. Aslo paused for a moment, then continued. When a message was received here that help was needed, the remaining keepers had no choice but to answer. Your mother was one of them. She stayed with you as long as she could and then asked Kiera and myself to take care of you while she was gone. Less than a half a cycle after they left, communication between the worlds stopped. Only silence remained.

Kiera picked up the story. *Before the wars, a prophecy was made foretelling the destruction of this world and everything in it. The remaining Council members took that to heart and decided the best thing they could do would be to close the portals so no enemies could use them to travel here. All known portals were destroyed. We don't know who survived on the other side, if anyone. The Council later declared they were all dead. On that day, things changed in this world.*

No one knew that Aslo and I existed. We didn't choose a keeper because I was pregnant - a rare occurrence for our kind. The Council removed all information they could find on guardians. We needed to take care of you, and yet if someone saw us, it could put you in danger. Your parents were our friends. We decided to join with you, something that had never happened with a child under sixteen cycles. It worked, but we could only speak at first. Slowly, we began to be able to move around and when the time came, I gave birth to eleven. Not only are you the only keeper underage, but you carry thirteen guardians, when no one else could carry more than two. The downfall is, we cannot separate from you until the exact day your sixteenth cycle begins.

"My parents, they could be alive? They were just left? Abandoned?" she asked, tears pooling in her eyes again.

Aslo answered. At the time, the Council was trying to protect those who were left here and, in all fairness, there are thousands of different worlds, making the chances of finding anyone slim if a rescue was attempted. The Council changed after that from carrying out the role of teacher and mentor to that of a ruler. They replaced the keeper spots with family members and removed everyone else outside the gates in hopes that memories would fade quickly, and they did. At the same time, the Council forgot as well. They tasted power and, similar to other stories you have heard, their appetite grew. The same struggle we were fighting outside this world was taking over here as well. Their own self-importance will be the downfall of this world if not from a battle within, then as the prophecy foretold. If they trained people how to use their powers to their fullest potential, perhaps you could have fought back. Most of you haven't even begun to discover the tip of what you can do.

"My dream … the attack … it will come from a hole in the sky, not the portals. That is what the dream meant - isn't it?" Willow asked.

We believe so, Aslo added. We just don't know when. Only the Council heard the original prophecy. We lived here and never mingled outside. That is why no one ever knew we existed. Only keepers had seen us before. The pregnancy was the first in thousands of cycles. We chose to stay put at the time.

"You risked their lives, your children, to join with me," Willow mumbled.

We loved you as our own. It was the only way. It was the right choice. All of us are fine and we were able to all be together. Pick a few books then walk to the left.

Willow chose a book about the main world and an encyclopedia of creatures the keepers met in the different realms, then moved to the left. There was a space between two book shelves. As she got closer, a staircase appeared winding downwards. She followed the stairs to a hallway.

"What is this place?" she asked.

The keepers' living quarters. There are sitting rooms, weapons rooms, rooms to eat in and separate rooms to sleep in. Yours is five doors down on the right, Aslo answered.

"Mine? But I'm not even old enough to be a keeper yet."

You were always special. We always knew you would be a keeper, prophecies confirmed it as well, and we always knew your abilities would be extraordinary, Kiera explained.

"I talk to trees and make it rain when I cry," she snorted.

In time you will see, child, it is so much more than that. We can help you develop those abilities you know you have but, you and only you, must discover what your abilities are for yourself. No one can tell you what you can or cannot do.

Her room was bigger than the shack she lived in. A large bed sat in the centre, with a body cushion to lie on and warm blankets. On one side of the room there were cupboards and drawers filled with clothes, mainly black and all in her size. They were similar to the uniforms the guards wore and made of a material that could stretch, but still protect.

They were made for you - try them on, Kiera said.

Willow was already changing. She pulled on black pants that were tight to her skin, but still offered incredible mobility and a sleeveless, black vest which left areas of her back exposed. She chuckled at the number of pockets the outfit had.

Out of the blue, she asked, "Can I bring someone here who isn't a keeper?"

If the need arises, yes, Aslo answered. *The boy, Nathan?*

"Yes, he could help me with all of the reading."

On the other side of the room was a desk with hair brushes and accessories in front of a large mirror. She tied her hair back, jumped on the bed and began to read a book on the main world. Her mind swirled with images of tall buildings and metal objects that could move called cars.

The day was so exciting, time flew by. Willow drifted off to sleep with visions of the strange new world she was reading about.

She opened her eyes and glanced around. There was nothing - plain white was everywhere she looked. It took her a few minutes to figure out why she was there.

"Of course, I am dreaming," she said, smiling. "Ashlyn, can you hear me? Ashlyn?"

"I am here. Everyone is worried about you. Are you okay?"

Willow spun around to greet her friend with a hug and a smile. "Yes, I am fine, but I need you to do something for me. It's very important," she said. "I need you to ask Nathan to go to the forest and follow the path. Can you do that?"

"What path? To where?" Ashlyn's frowned, worry lines forming, her face reflecting the confusion she felt from the request.

"Just ask him to trust me. When he gets to the forest, he will find the path I am talking about. He has to come alone. I will find him."

"Aren't you coming back?" her friend asked.

"Yes, soon. Please don't tell anyone else about this either, just Nathan. We should go now," Willow said.

The room faded into the darkness of deep sleep.

Chapter Eight

The sun was already shining when Willow walked back up the winding staircase and replaced the books she had borrowed. As she walked around the semi-circular shelves, her fingers ran gently across the spines of the volumes of literature that lined them as if taking in every title.

Her attention turned to the stone table. Walking over, she rounded it three times, looking at all of its features. In each of the four corners was carved the same symbol that was on the guards' arms. The corner pieces appeared to be separate from the table, yet no matter how hard she pushed or pulled, she couldn't move them. Each was a smooth rock with a flat top and a carving in the centre. Scanning the table again, it seemed it had been built to match the rocks and not the other way around. She wondered if there might be a book that might explain it, but her thoughts were cut off.

"Willow, where are you?" Nathan's voice echoed on the wind.

She ran down the steps into the forest. The trees made way for a path which led right to the boy. Taking his hand, she led him back to the building where she had spent the night.

"What is this place?" he asked.

"Your Gran - her stories - they were all true. These books contain information on everything... all the different worlds the guardians visited, maps, in-depth knowledge of creatures and beings, locations of portals, encyclopedias and even languages. There is also some material on us - records of abilities and instructions on how to train to maximize them."

His eyes widened in disbelief. "How do you know these books aren't just stories themselves?" he asked.

She decided right then to trust him completely. She couldn't do this by herself and, if the end of their world was coming, she at least wanted to try to survive.

"A guardian told me," she answered. "I need your help. These books - I have to know what each one says. It's important. Things are changing and I think they are about to get a lot worse. People could get hurt."

Nathan began scanning books. At about the third, he looked at her curiously. "Red hair, huh?"

"Sorry?"

"Red hair... according to this book, it means you have extreme abilities. It's very rare. In fact, it refers to the person as having powers which could make them a saviour of worlds. You must have pretty amazing talents. Do you know what they are yet?"

"I can talk to trees," she replied.

"Not sure how that can save a world, but it's definitely interesting." He laughed. "Sorry," he added. This time they both broke out into laughter.

"I don't know, either, but I can make it rain when I cry too," she said after the two settled down.

"That explains all the wet weather we have been having." He tried to not laugh, but instead ended up letting out a snort - starting the two giggling again.

"Let me see what you have read so far."

Nathan shared two books with her and over the next few hours, he continued to read and then share what he learned. In between, the two discussed some interesting points in one book or another. They talked about what the different shades of a pixie's wings meant, what a plane was and how big a world needed to be to use one and how to find a dark elf that was cloaked in invisibility. Occasionally, they spoke in different languages they learnt from the books. They finished over seventy without making a dent in the first shelf.

Willow went into the forest for a few minutes. "Kiera, Aslo, are you there?" she asked.

We are always here, Kiera answered.

"Is there a room downstairs that isn't being used? One that Nathan could rest in if he gets tired?" she asked, whispering.

Yes, the one past yours is empty. He could use that, Aslo responded. *Oh, and you don't have to speak out loud. We can still hear your thoughts.*

"Right," she said, still whispering. "I forgot for a moment."

She returned with a basket of fruit, which she set on the stone table.

Nathan's eyes bulged, glistening at the sight of the fresh produce. "Thank goodness! I was starting to wonder if I was ever going to see food again," he complained, taking a bit out of an apple.

"A little dramatic, don't you think?"

After eating, she showed him how to find the staircase and his room if he was tired. Nathan's comments about being hungry made her think about the other townsfolk. It was time for her to go back and make sure they had food as well. After assuring him he would be safe and that she would be back as soon as possible, she headed to town.

Stepping into the forest, she heard a playful whisper, "Ready to see what you can do?"

Willow smiled. Her eyes opened wide to take in what lay before her, a world she only partially noticed before. The tree in front of her swayed as if bowing - its branches forming a staircase for her to climb. She reached the top and peeked her head up above the tree line.

From beneath, she could hear a whisper. "Go ahead, we won't let you fall."

With that, she stepped on the branches and leaves, taking her first steps across the top of the forest. It was beautiful - the sun's warmth shining on her while the wind tickled her face. She lay down and rolled around, taking in the different scents of each of the trees beneath her. Then she lay motionless on her back, her arms and legs outstretched, enjoying the feeling of the branches beneath her, moving slowly in the wind, massaging her body gently. She closed her eyes - visions of her friends entered her mind. Suddenly, she realized time was passing and she hadn't accomplished anything she had hoped to. Standing up, she ran towards where the forest bordered the town.

Chapter Nine

Jade decided to go into town earlier than the rest of her friends. She was still ecstatic about how well the dance had gone the night before. Even the short downpour couldn't ruin her victory. There was only one last conquest to make. She would have what she wanted and show that town of ingrates their place.

She added a skip to her walk as she came down the lane, carrying a closed basket on her arm - completely oblivious to anything going on around her. Most of the town's population was standing in the middle of the road. She smiled as she passed them, stopping at Mr. and Mrs. Shinning with Victoria wedged tightly between them.

"Good morning. Are your boys up?" she asked, not even noticing the solemn looks on their faces.

"They are inside," Opaque answered without looking at her.

She thanked them and continued on to their house. Opening the door, her eyes fixed on a glass case, elegantly displaying the jewelry that had been made for Willow to wear to the dance. A devious smile crossed her face as she walked by and called out for the brothers. Pete answered her, extending his hand to offer her a seat in the visiting room behind the shop area.

"Where are your brothers?" she asked. "I brought you some more cake."

Pete's eyes widened at the thought of the treat she was offering. He had never been overly fond of sweets, but this was like nothing he tasted before. Just the thought of it made his mouth water and his heart race. His adrenaline pumping; he needed to have it and needed it now more than anything else in the world. He yelled for his brothers in a booming voice, letting them know Jade brought more of the cake. His mouth filled with saliva as he watched her bring the baked delicacy out from the basket that adorned her arm. The other two boys were there in a flash, both experiencing the same reaction as their brother.

Jade served them each a piece, watching carefully as they quickly devoured it. As she filled their plates again, finishing the rest of the cake, she mentioned there were some things that would make her happy - very happy. The boys, their attention still consumed by the food before them, didn't answer her. A frown crossed her face, aggravation momentarily taking hold. Even frustration broke to her will as she quickly changed back to displaying a pleasant smile, pulling out a second cake from her basket.

"I thought you boys might be extra hungry today, we were out so late and all," she said, watching the boy's eyes following the second cake as she set it on the table.

When almost all of it had been consumed, Jade spoke again. "You fellas happy?" she asked.

The three brothers' attention switched to the girl in front of them. They nodded, longing for more words to be sung to them. Jade wasn't about to deprive them of it.

"I wish I could be happy. Until this sadness is banished from my mind, I cannot give an answer as to who I will chose to live out the rest of my life with. I want to, but I just can't think of feeling such joy," she said, her face wet from fake tears.

"What can I do to make you feel the same joy your presence gives me?" Jessie asked, kneeling before her. "Name the task. There is nothing I wouldn't do to see your beautiful face smile again."

Turning her head to fake more tears, she replied, speaking to them all, "Perhaps." She paused for a moment, letting the brothers hang on her word. "The dress and jewelry that were made for Willow for the dance, I cried for days when I found out such beauty would be worn by someone else. If I could just wear them once and feel worthy of such items." She sighed.

That was enough for the boys, who rushed out to the front shop. Jessie and Dezi began fighting each other, tugging the jewelry case back and forth, while Pete slipped out the door and headed to the seamstress's shop. He found the black dress lying on the counter. Without a word to anyone, it was in his arms. On the way back, he didn't even stop to notice the state of his parents' shop, filled with broken glass and destroyed furniture, or his brothers still battling. He slipped past it all to present Jade with her prize.

Jade held up the dress and smiled. Folding it neatly, she packed it safely away in her basket. The two other boys emerged, bruised and cut, each carrying items she longed for. Dezi presented her with the necklace and earrings, while Jessie bestowed upon her the hair piece.

"For me?" She squealed with delight, putting the pieces into her basket and closing the lid. "This is so much to process. You all have made me so happy. I have to think about my choices, but I will have an answer for you tomorrow. Until then, dream of our time together."

The boys sat back - silly lovestruck smiles plastered over their faces as they watched the object of their affections take her leave.

Jade added a quick skip to her step, smiling ear to ear. Stopping to pick up food for the day, she realized the stands were empty. Turning around, she saw the whole town standing behind her. She walked closer and asked, "Where is the vegetable girl?"

"We don't know," Clairity answered. "She has been gone since last night."

"I see," Jade replied with a shrug, continuing her walk to the castle without a thought or a care.

Most of the Council members were gathered at a table in the dining room deciding who would go into town today for supplies when Jade walked in.

"Where have you been so early today?" her mother asked.

"I went to town to thank the boys for such a wonderful evening," she said, still beaming from the prizes hidden within her basket.

"You should have brought back some fruit," her father said without looking at her. "That would have saved us sending someone else."

"I tried, but couldn't. The useless girl ran away or something," she responded with a dismissive tone.

"What have you done?" Nebulah demanded.

"What have I done?" Anger spiked in Jade's voice. "What have I done? I can't help it if I am more beautiful than her. How is that my fault? I am sure she just went off to pout because her date decided he wanted to be with me more than her."

"Didn't you have enough dates last night without one more? Couldn't you let that girl have a little bit of happiness? Did I bring you up to feel nothing?" Her mother waved one hand in front of her face as if it were a fan, her mouth slightly open. She looked upwards, in a poor attempt at stopping tears from falling.

"You brought me up to see that we are far better than those losers. That we deserve to be treated better and have everything we want. None of them deserve to make me or anyone else from the castle feel inferior and in no way should those people show us up or make fools of us and, let's face it, lately that's all they have been doing while the lot of you sit here and do nothing. They need to be put in their place. All I did is what this Council hasn't had the nerve to do," Jade said, a green fire burning in her eyes.

"How dare you pretend you know the business of this Council and try to hide your deeds behind its name?" Malarchy stood, fury written on his face. "You will go to your room and remain there until a proper punishment has been agreed upon. Do not test me further, child."

Jade let out a little scream before stomping off to her room.

Malarchy stood silent for a few moments, staring at the still blank wall before speaking. "Nyssa, Zebulon, Nebulah, would you please take a few guards into town? See if you can find out what happened. Assess the damage and see if the guards can harvest any food from Willow's gardens. Albeit, I fear they will not."

"Why wouldn't they be able to pick our food for us?" Aurora asked.

Malarchy chuckled. "Do you really think that much food grows naturally every day? That fruit trees have new fruit every day? No, I am afraid it was the girl who made it happen. That is why I let her remain on her own and not join the orphanage years ago. Without her, we could all starve."

"There is still the bakery, Malarchy," Aurora added.

This time, he laughed. "The bakery - yes well, behind the bakery is a plot of land where the grains grow that the bakery uses to make its food. Who do you think makes them grow every day? And then there is the matter of the weather."

"The weather?" Nyssa asked as if surprised.

"Yes, the weather," he answered. "Since the day that child was born, we have enjoyed bright skies, warm temperatures, only adequate rainfall and at the same time every day, while we sleep so it disturbs nothing. The sun sets and rises at the same time."

"Are you saying she controls the weather as well - and did so as a baby?" Nyssa asked.

"That is exactly what I am saying. She is a terraformer. It's a rare ability, not to mention it has been with her since her birth. No, I am afraid if we can't somehow fix this mess, things will get worse. The sooner you get going, the faster we can try to resolve this. The rest of us will work on alternate plans taking the worst possible scenario into account."

When Nebulah, Zebulon, Nyssa and the four guards reached the city, they found the town still congregated in the street. They approached the gathering, sending everyone back to their homes, while the guards examined at the gardens. Some of the townsfolk moved to their porches, but were still watching as the guards returned with bad news. There was nothing growing - nothing at all - not even a single fruit tree. All they found was plain open space.

A chilling scream came from the Shinning house. The Council members hurried to the door and let themselves in. At first glance, one might have thought the mere sight of their front shop was enough to let out the screech of terror they had just heard. Glass lined the floor - all of the display cases destroyed. There was damage to the walls and windows. After carefully stepping through the mess, they saw the Shinnings kneeling over their sons on the floor. The boys were all having some sort of seizure. All three lay unconscious, froth spilling out of their mouths as bodies twitched in unnatural ways.

"Send for Micca!" Nebulah yelled to the guards behind her. "And quickly, there is no time to waste. Your fastest must go!"

"Help is on its way," Nyssa said to Augusto. "Can you tell us what happened?"

"I don't know. We were outside with the others. The only one who came by was Jade," he answered.

Opaque stood. She picked up the broken case which once held Willow's jewelry and glanced over at the bits of cake left on the table, before turning her wrath to Nebulah. "Your daughter did this!" she exclaimed.

"I don't think now is the time for accusations."

"The things we made for Willow for the dance are gone - stolen. She threatened she would have them no matter what the cost." Opaque picked up a plate and took it to Jade's mother. Shoving it in Nebulah's face, she continued, "This cake... your daughter brought it here this morning."

No one noticed Martha standing in the background until she added, "The dress I made Willow is gone as well."

"Stay here," Nebulah said to Nyssa and Zebulon. "I will take a guard and return to the castle. If my daughter is involved, I will find out."

Leaving, she almost bumped into Willow coming over to see what all the commotion was about.

It only took one look inside for her to see the three boys convulsing on the floor. "What's wrong with them?!" she shrieked. "Victoria - she could help. She can heal."

She felt a hand fall on her shoulder and turned to see Micca behind her. He pushed past her, and knelt beside the boys.

"She can't help," Micca said. "It's not anything a healer can cure. They have consumed a potion of some sort. The only way to save them now is to find out what the ingredients were and make an antidote."

"Who would do this? Why?" Willow asked.

Augusto answered. "We think it was Jade."

"Is this over me? Did she do this because of me?" Her eyes stung. The pain of the realization that she was the reason her friends were hurt was too much for her.

Zebulon put his arm around her. "Come now, child, you need some air. Let's not have tears and flood the town. We will figure this out. How about you tend to some food for the rest of the townsfolk? There are hungry, scared people."

Willow looked at him with a blank stare and stepped outside. He knew what she could do. What she didn't understand was, why the people didn't just go harvest their own food? She stumbled across the road, still in shock from the sight of the boys and went to her garden. It was empty. She stood dumbfounded. There was nothing there.

Clairity and Ashlyn came to her side, both just as shocked by the sight of the empty fields as Willow was. What came next was an even more unusual sight.

Willow stood tall, raising her arms above her head. What looked like a golden dust rained down on the field. Within seconds, there were bountiful fruit trees, bushes of berries, vines with grapes and vegetables of all types, all fully grown and ready to pick. She turned, taking only one step towards her friends. The weight of the day's events became too much for her. Her legs buckled, sending her tumbling to the ground.

Chapter Ten

Nebulah walked right by the other Council members, into the castle - her pace never faltering. She climbed the staircase, heading straight to her daughter's room. Flinging Jade's door open, she moved to the bed.

"What are these?" she demanded, pointing to the missing items from town.

"Can't knock?" Jade snarled back at her.

"What is going on here?" Malarchy, having seen the state in which his wife had returned, followed her. He stood at the door, peering in.

Nebulah turned to him. "These items were stolen from town today," she said, choking back tears.

"They were gifts, Daddy, from the Shinning brothers. Go ask them," she said, giving her mother a look of disgust.

"He can't ask them. They are unconscious - all three left on the ground having seizures. And the only one who saw them today was you, Jade," Nebulah replied. "What did you do?"

"Don't be so dramatic, Mother. I am sure they will be fine tomorrow," Jade snapped without concern.

"If something happens to those boys and you have information that can save them..." Nebulah's words cut off. She grabbed the dress and gems off her daughter's bed.

"Hey, those are mine! What do you think you are doing?" Jade yelled.

"Returning them to their owners," Nebulah replied. She was about to leave when Nyssa appeared behind Malarchy.

"I am afraid there is bad news. The boys ingested some form of a potion. Without an ingredients list, they won't make it," Nyssa said, passing Malarchy in the doorway - glaring at the items Nebulah was holding. All three turned their attention to the girl.

"Why are you looking at me?" Jade demanded. "Fine, it wasn't poison. It was just a little love potion and I didn't make it." She looked straight at Nyssa and added, "If you want to know what was in it, why don't you ask Camile? Their fate is her fault... not mine."

"You have broken so many rules..."

Jade interrupted her father with a cold voice. "So change them. That's what the Council does, isn't it? Makes things fit the way they want them to?"

"You have no idea what you have done. I am not sure we can help you out of this mess." A sadness lingered in his voice, something Jade hadn't heard before.

"I can't believe you are my daughter," her mother sobbed.

"I wish you were dead!" Jade yelled back at her.

The three Council members left the room and locked the door behind them. They found Camile in the front sitting room. News of the situation in town was already spreading throughout the castle, reaching every ear it could find.

"I'm sorry," the girl blurted out in tears. "I didn't mean to. I told Jade not to use so much. She went crazy over that girl getting invited to the dance - said she needed to teach her a lesson or all our futures would be ruined. She said our parents would be proud. I don't know why I believed her. I didn't think she would hurt anyone, honest."

"Later," her mother said, placing a hand on each of her daughter's shoulders. "Right now, we need to go to town and tell Micca everything you did to make that potion."

Nebulah told her husband she would join the two heading into town and return the missing items. Before leaving, she faced her husband. "Are we being punished for what we have done?" she asked.

Malarchy answered, "I think so. This is my fault. I have been so blind. Do what you can in town. Jade is locked in her room. There will have to be a hearing and she will have to answer for her actions."

*****

Jade looked around, less than impressed she was locked in her room and furious her mother had taken the items she worked so hard to get. Why didn't they see what she did was for everyone? The Council was getting soft: losing control: letting inferiors have their way and running to their aid. Her anger spiked at the thought of her own parents taking the sides of those nobodies over her.

With nothing to do, she lay down on her bed and hugged her favourite doll. Somewhere between the state of sleep and wakefulness, she heard a voice call her name. Opening her eyes, she found herself in an unfamiliar in a white room - a beautiful man standing in front of her.

"Where am I?" she asked.

"In a dream," he replied. "My family can all dreamwalk. We unlocked the secrets of that ability long ago. But that is not important now, what is important is you. I heard your cries, my dear. What has happened to you is unjust. A beautiful talented woman like yourself should be bowed down to, treated as a queen - not locked up like a common criminal. The people around you don't understand your brilliance the way I do."

"You do?" she asked, licking her lips to gloss them.

He moved next to her and brushed the side of her face gently. "Yes, I have been watching you in your dreams for some time. I have seen your thoughts and desires… your plans and aspirations. You are exactly what I have looked for to stand beside me, to be adored by all as I adore you."

"Who are you?" she asked.

"Forgive me. I am Prince Joseph, son of King Cornelius, saviour of worlds, at your service," he answered with a bow. He now stood directly in front of her, yet she hadn't seen him move.

He was beautiful, with short platinum blonde hair, cold blue eyes and stunning features. His body looked chiselled to perfection like a statue, with just enough muscles in all the right places. She couldn't help but feel they would make the perfect couple and produce the most beautiful children.

Knowing her thoughts, he smiled. "Yes, together we could rule worlds. I would give you only the finest jewels and clothes. Others will dream of being you. Everything your heart desires, I could hand you on a golden platter with the snap of my fingers. I will make anything you have ever wished for come true."

"Please, I want to go with you," she answered without thought.

"And I want nothing more than to take you, my darling, but I need your help to enter your world so we can leave together and live the life you deserve," he answered.

"What can I do? Tell me," she pleaded.

"Is there someone in your world who can mutate or bend objects like metal?" he asked.

"Yes of course, Neil can."

"Good, I need you to convince him to stretch the sky," he said.

"I don't understand," she answered.

"Yes, of course. When he bends metal, he is actually changing the molecular density of the item for a short period of time. If he concentrates hard enough on the sky, he can weaken the boundaries between our worlds in a similar manner, allowing me to open a way in and out. It would only need to be long enough for me come for you," he explained.

"How do I convince him to do this?" she asked.

"You are a beautiful woman. Convince him you know a way to run away with him. Tell him you two will be together forever if he helps you escape the wrath of the Council. We both know their punishment will be severe."

"Okay, how will you know when it is done?" she asked.

"I will watch the skies, my queen. Do not doubt, when it is done, I will come and you will have everything you have ever wished for. Oh and one last thing, should the Council wish to impose a punishment on you, they don't have the right. Tell them that only Acacia can decide your fate." His lips gently grazed her cheek before he faded away into the distance.

*****

By the time Nebulah, Nyssa and Camile arrived back at the Shinning house, the guards had cleaned up all the broken glass and debris in the shop and removed all furniture from the sitting area. The room was now bare, with only the three boys lying on the floor and Micca hovering over them, trying to do whatever he could.

The way his long black hair was neatly tied back in a ponytail, so it wouldn't get in the way, showed off the other features of his face. His high eyebrows and intense brown eyes, together with the stubble of a beard made him look almost attractive in a rough, manly sort of way. He noticed the new visitors and moved towards them.

"Do we have any information?" he asked, anxiously.

"Camile can tell you what was used," Nyssa offered.

Nebulah motioned that she would be back and headed over to Martha's to return the stolen items - hoping to avoid the boys' parents for the moment. At least until their sons were cured of the condition her daughter had caused.

Camile stepped forward. "It was a love potion. Jade wanted the boys to ask her to the dance instead of any of them taking Willow." She took a piece of paper out of her pocket and handed it to Micca. "I told her not to give them too much. I warned her things could go wrong. I would never hurt anyone."

Micca read over this list and let out a breath of air loudly. "This is an advanced potion - the items in it are hard to obtain. I don't even know how you came about this recipe. We could search the forest for days and never find the plants and roots we need to create an antidote, and to be honest, we don't have that much time."

"Willow!" Nyssa exclaimed. "Is she still in town?"

"Yes, she is resting at her friend Clairity 's house. But how will that help us?" he asked.

"She can grow anything. It's part of her abilities. She could grow the plants you need right here in seconds," Nyssa said.

"If she can do that, we could save these boys. Could someone bring her here? Time is running out."

Two guards woke Willow from her sleep, summoning her to Micca. They filled her in on the details of what transpired on the way.

"What do you need?" she asked upon arriving, skipping all pleasantries.

The next hour the two spent outside. Micca would describe a plant and Willow would grow any that resembled its description. He could then pick the one he needed and harvest the flower, leaf, or root required for the potion. After that came the juicing, cutting, blending of ingredients and a touch of magic. Once finished, the antidote was administered to all three boys and all there was left to do was wait.

Nebulah hovered in the background, not wanting to disturb the process, but anxious for information as to the outcome. "Will they be okay?" she finally asked, drawing the attention of everyone else waiting.

"We won't know for a bit yet. The antidote needs a chance to run through their bodies. It should work, if the list I was given was complete. Timewise, it is close, though. The poison has been in them for a while," Micca answered.

"And Jade?" Willow asked without looking at Nebulah.

"She will be treated as anyone would who committed such an act. Punishment will be severe, I am sure, and the town will be invited to the hearing, should they wish to attend," Nebulah answered without emotion. "The afternoon of the second sunrise from now should give sufficient time for the fate of the boys to be known and a trial before the Council to be readied." She turned and left the house, heading back to the castle to give the news to her husband. Camile and Nyssa followed behind her, not knowing what to say, but understanding that Camile too would have to answer for her part in the deception.

Willow joined Clairity on the front steps. There were still a few hours of daylight left. The town was quiet and empty.

"It isn't over yet," Clairity said, breaking the silence. "Something is coming. I can feel it. I'm afraid."

"No, it isn't over," Willow replied to her friend. "Everything is happening so fast, I don't know if I can keep up. I don't know if I want to. Three weeks ago, my life was so much easier. Ignorance is bliss."

"What do you think they will do to her?" Clairity asked.

"Not sure, I guess it depends on whether or not..." Her words stopped. It was the first time she realized her friends could actually die. A lump grew in her throat and tears began to pool in her eyes. At the same time, clouds appeared in the sky and bits of rain began to fall. She took a deep breath and said, "stop," out loud. The clouds swirled and vanished from sight.

Her friend's jaw dropped. "You did that!" she exclaimed, not as a question but rather a statement. "I totally saw you make those clouds come and go."

Willow would have normally been happy to share every detail she had learnt about her abilities in the last day, but now wasn't the time. She couldn't be enthusiastic about anything with Jessie, Dezi and Pete fighting for their lives. She nodded to her friend, affirming that the weather change was her doing.

The girls heard the door close behind them and spun their heads around to see Micca. He sat down beside Willow.

"They seem to be responding well so far. The seizures have stopped and colour is returning to their bodies. It was lucky you were here. That's some talent you have," he said.

"How long before they wake up? I'd like to be here, but I have to be back to the forest before dark. I have some research I am doing with a friend. It's important."

"Research? That sounds interesting. What exactly are you researching?" he questioned.

Willow thought quickly. She wasn't ready to let everyone know about Kiera and Aslo - not until they could officially separate from her. She also couldn't mention the prophecies about the end of the world, and knew that it was probably not a good idea to say she was trying to figure out if her parents were still alive. "How to talk to trees," she blurted out. Seeing the strange looks she was getting from both sides of her, she added, "I think we have discovered that they react differently to common words. It's fascinating, really."

Micca chuckled. "I bet it is. If all goes as planned, the boys should be moving about soon, so you should get back to your tree conversations on time." He fired off a wink before standing up and heading back inside the house.

After the door closed, Clairity turned to her and said, "How to talk to trees? Really? You are so bad at lying."

"Come with me tonight and I can show you." She hoped her friend would catch on to her reluctance to discuss things in front of listening ears.

"Not much else to do around here at the moment. I'll ask Mom." Clairity replied, shrugging her shoulders.

Only a few moments after Clairity left, the door behind Willow opened and Jessie stumbled out, still shaky on his legs. He plopped down on the steps beside her, rubbing the back of his neck.

"How are you feeling?" Willow asked.

"Like I almost died. Stiff and aching everywhere, every muscle and joint," he answered.

"Your brothers?" Willow enquired.

"Fine, just taking a bit longer to walk about. It would be nice if someone would tell us what happened." Jessie answered, grimacing.

"You don't know?"

"No, last thing I remember I was talking with Dezi and Pete about the dance. I was thinking I would ask Ashlyn and Pete would ask Clairity so we could all go together." Jessie replied.

"Would have been nice," Willow said, looking down.

"Did something happen to one of the girls?" he asked with a look of concern.

"No - no, but the dance was last night. You went with Jade - all three of you." Willow explained, her gaze directed at the ground.

Micca stepped outside right at the end of the conversation. "Perhaps Jessie should take some time before getting into the details of what happened. I don't want him to receive too much information too fast. It could cause shock."

"Sorry. I didn't know," Willow replied.

"I want to know," Jessie complained, holding his head.

"Later, your parents can fill you in with the details. For now, you need rest. Back inside," Micca ordered. "It will take much longer to fully recover if you don't rest now."

After saying their goodbyes, Willow walked up the street to the Posh house. Clairity and her mother were already standing outside, waiting for her arrival. Willow wasted no time filling them in on the condition of the brothers. After which, it was time to go. Clairity's bag was ready, packed with some clothes and personal items.

"Where will you girls stay?" Mrs. Posh asked in a motherly tone.

"A fort," Willow answered. "In the forest. You don't have to worry. It's well-hidden and safe."

"Sounds exciting. You girls be safe and if anything happens, anything at all, come right back. You understand? Both of you?" Mrs Posh, pulled a tissue from inside her shirt. Lifting it to her face, she daubed under her eyes. "They grow up so fast!" She waved one hand over her head, holding the other tightly to her chest.

The girls nodded, waving back as they headed off together into the forest. Once out of sight, Willow asked her friend, "Do you trust me?" Without waiting for an answer, she grabbed her friend's hand, pulling her up a staircase of branches to the top of the trees.

Clairity was both speechless and excited. What that translated to was a few incoherent noises instead of words. Rather than trying to talk, the girls simply walked on top of the forest all the way back to where Nathan was waiting. Following a staircase down, Clairity was just as stunned by the sight of the stone building standing before her. Before she attempted to speak, Willow tugged her inside and explained the entire story with Nathan's help.

The three spent the evening learning from Nathan about the books he had read and talking about far-off exotic lands. Later, when the two girls were alone for the night in Willow's room, they shared the secrets that only best friends could before falling asleep side by side. Nathan took the bedroom beside them, having no problem falling soundly asleep, after whispering words of love in the hopes that his gran, wherever she was, could hear them.

Nathan, after waking early, took the opportunity to begin his research again. Neither of the two girls noticed him sitting in a corner reading as they set out a variety of fruit for their breakfast. Tossing a book on the table beside the food, he grinned. His smile widened as he glanced from one girl to the other.

"I found a book specifically outlining how to train a seer to develop visions more clearly," he explained. "I thought we could spend the day trying to expand Clairity's psychic abilities. It seems rather straightforward, but then I've never tried to train anyone before."

"Perfect," Willow replied. "I need to head to town. Everyone will be getting hungry. I also wouldn't mind checking on the condition of Jessie, Dezi and Pete."

Keeping her visit short, she managed to return to the library in the afternoon without anything of consequence to report. The boys were stronger, but still lacked memories of what happened, and the hearing for Jade was still scheduled for the next day. That was one event Willow wasn't about to miss.

Chapter Eleven

Sabrina and Justin walked into the castle's sitting room and sat down, joining Neil. The scandalous events of the last few weeks were glued to the tips of their tongues. The news of Jade's and Camile's confinement to their quarters, pending the outcome of the following day's hearing, spread quickly.

"If you came to discuss Jade, I don't want to hear it. She is still my friend and she isn't around to tell us exactly what happened," Neil said, not wasting time.

"Poor Camile is locked up because of her, or did you forget she is our friend too?" Sabrina snapped back.

"How do you know it wasn't Camile's idea?" he asked.

Everyone was sure Sabrina had known about the love potion and perhaps had even been in on the plans, but she wasn't about to confess to anything and end up in the middle of her own hearing.

"I just believe Camile. That's all," she responded. "If you want Jade's version, why don't you go talk to her? Let's face it, we all know the reason you are taking her side is because you have a crush on her. The way I see it, you simply don't want to believe she gave a love potion to three other guys."

"Even if she did give a love potion to that lot, it wasn't because she was interested in any of them... I guarantee that."

Continuing the argument any further than it had already gone was pointless. Neil wasn't about to take any chances since it was still possible his name might come up at the hearing tomorrow as a supporter if he wasn't careful - guilty by association. But after giving thought to what Sabrina said, he couldn't argue with the logic. She was right. He needed to go talk to Jade and to hear her side of the story for himself.

Each step felt like a mountain as he climbed the winding staircase that led to the door to Jade's room. There was a magic lock on the door which could not be opened by anyone other than Ozias. His fist stopped mid-air, falling back down to his side. He'd never been to her room before. The palm of his hand slid across the smooth wood, looking for courage. After finding the smallest bit hiding, he knocked.

"Jade, are you there?" Neil called out.

Jade moved to the door on the other side and put her ear against it. "Neil? Is that you?" She bit her bottom lip waiting for a reply.

"Yes," he said with a smile. "I wanted to check on you... make sure you were okay. Well, as best as you could be."

Both of their backs slid to the floor where they sat in front of opposite sides of the door - connected without touching.

"Yeah, I guess... It isn't how people are making it out. It didn't happen that way. You believe me, don't you?" she asked, spinning her trademarked pout into her words.

"I figured that. Camile is having her hearing after yours, so hopefully she will admit to what she did." Neil said.

"Camile is having a hearing? I figured it was just me." The touch of remorse residing in her voice threatened to escape. "I don't want her life ruined too. The Council is going to come down hard on me - make an example of me. I know that."

"There must be something we can do."

"Well… there is one chance, but it's risky and I would need your help." Jade carefully listened for the tone of Neil's voice. That alone would tell her if she had a chance or not.

After a few minutes, he responded, "What would I have to do?"

Jade smiled. "You know how you do those tricks: changing the way a rock looks and bending metal without touching it?"

"Sure." Neil replied. He loved making things look strange and getting a reaction when people saw it.

"If you could do that … with the sky." Jade suggested.

"What?"

"Hear me out," she pleaded. "If you concentrated on doing that to the sky, it would weaken the boundaries between worlds and create an opening, for a short period of time, just long enough for us to escape to another world and start a brand new life together."

"How do you know this?" Neil asked.

"I… found a book in one of the restricted rooms that Dad forgot to lock. It outlined the whole procedure. Seems easy enough, and it's not permanent, so no one would get hurt and I would be free. If I don't, I won't see you or anyone else again for many cycles."

"You don't know that, Jade. Your parents…"

"My parents," she snickered, "are the ones looking for the most severe sentence. They are going to use me to show the town they have the people's interests in mind - to stop any possible fallout, uprising or riots. They don't need me. They have my brother. He has been their favourite since he was born. No, my parents aren't going to lift a finger to help me. They already sealed my fate."

"I don't know, Jade. We don't even know what's out there. We could walk right into something horrible," Neil argued.

"How horrible could it be? Think about it. We would be together, forever," Jade replied.

"Someone is coming. I have to go. I will see you tomorrow. Don't worry, I will figure something out," Neil promised before standing up and walking towards the stairs. Two guards passed him, turning the corner. He motioned a hello to them before heading down to find solitude. He definitely had a lot to think about.

Chapter Twelve

Clairity and Nathan chose to remain in the forest reading books for the day, so Willow met Ashlyn. Together, they headed to the castle, arriving shortly before the hearing was to take place. All of the adults from town were already assembled to hear the Council's sentence for the crimes that had been committed.

Jade sat perched on display on one side of the Council's table and Camile was seated on the other. Presumably, the distance between them was to keep the two from talking, or worse, fabricating lies about the events that happened during the past few weeks. Jessie, Dezi, and Pete hand been politely asked not to attend the hearing. They wouldn't have been much use anyways. None of them were able to recollect exactly what transpired. Instead, they remained at home with Victoria.

The Council, donned in their best outfits, took their positions. A handful of the younger children of the castle were also in attendance. Jade's brother, Jordan, who had only just reached his sixth cycle, ran up to his sister. He threw his arms around her neck, hugging her tightly. Tears threatened to fall from the corners of his eyes. A chorus of *awe* rang out from the crowd. Jordan was precious. He was the sort of kid people couldn't help but pay attention to. His personality demanded no less than total adoration. From his short mushroom top haircut, to the dimples that activated with every smile, he reeked of cuteness and, no matter what he did, someone always found it entertaining and delightful.

Nebulah left her spot at the Council table, leading her son away from his sister, choosing to have him sit with her so as not to interrupt anything important once the examinations were under way.

Zebulon had been chosen to head up the hearing. He called for silence before explaining how the proceeding would be held. The first part was fact-taking from witnesses. That was to be followed by questioning the two girls; deliberation of the Council; and finally a summary of the results and punishments, if any.

Most of the morning was spent calling witnesses. There was Augusto and Opaque, Martha and Olie, Micca, all of the guards who went to town over the past few days, and various others who saw the basket or heard the threats made against Willow and her friends. After having to wake Ozias one too many times, Zebulon called for a short break for lunch, before the questioning of Jade began.

*****

"Order," Zebulon demanded, waiting for silence before proceeding. "Jade, did you use an unauthorized love potion on Jessie, Dezi, and Pete Shinning?" he asked.

"Yes," Jade answered without hesitation.

"When did you decide to do this?"

"When I saw the things people were making for vegetable... Willow. There was something special about them. They were better than the items that were made for me. I felt inferior and angry, so I made a plan." She twiddled her thumbs, waiting for the next question.

"Who did you tell your plan to?" Zebulon asked.

Jade decided right then, she was going down, but Camile didn't have to. She felt sorry for involving her friend and being less than honest with her. Perhaps, telling the truth might get her some leniency. "No one," she answered.

The crowd buzzed with talk after hearing that answer and Zebulon called for silence. "Who made the potion?" he questioned.

"Camile, but she didn't know my plan," Jade replied, her voice shaky.

"But she did make the potion?"

"Yes, but please, let me tell you what happened," she pleaded.

"Very well," Zebulon replied. "I will allow this. Please continue."

"I was upset after returning home for the second time and still being told I couldn't have the beautiful things that had been made for someone else. I was outraged they said no to my mother as well. There is a place I go to when I am upset... downstairs in an old sitting room, but this time a door had been left open to one of the restricted rooms. I went inside. It looked as if it used to be a library. I peeked through some of the books and found one on potions.

"I was hoping to give Willow a few warts or something on the day of the dance, but instead I found the love potion. I ripped it out of the book, thinking I could steal her date and end up with the things I wanted that way. No one would ever know. The recipe said that the recipient wouldn't remember once it wore off. I asked Camile to make it for me. I told her it was a prank I was playing on Willow. I offered no other details. I made it impossible for her to say no. I also asked her to make extra, just in case it wore off earlier than expected. She warned me not to give anyone too much or something bad could happen. I didn't listen. I gave the boys the cake. I alone deserve the punishment."

"That is very honest of you. Why would you offer up such honesty now, when we have already heard you incriminated Camile as responsible?" Zebulon queried.

"I had time to think while sitting alone. I don't want to ruin Camile's life when she did nothing wrong," Jade answered.

"But she did do something wrong. She made the love potion for you," Zebulon argued.

"Because I made her do it and I convinced her our parents would be proud," Jade cried out.

"Very well. The Council shall review this information and be back with our decision." Zebulon said, leaving the makeshift court.

Jade looked through the crowd, her eyes coming to rest on Neil. She wondered what he was thinking right now - if he knew how she tried to trick him into making a passage for her to be with her new found love.

Jordan returned with another round of hugs. He didn't care how much she disliked him and the attention he stole from her. He still loved his sister. She looked into his eyes and hugged him back for the first time.

The Council returned quickly. Nebulah took Jordan's hand again, but this time with tears in her eyes. They remained close by. Malarchy stood on the other side of his daughter. The crowd was loud with anticipation of what was about to be revealed. Zebulon stood and again called for silence.

"Jade, it has been decided that you did cause harm to another, wilfully or not, by use of an illegal substance, for personal gain. The Council has decided that you shall be kept under lock in the guard house, without visitation rights, for five cycles, and during such time you shall be delegated work to be done to aid the orphanage."

Jade's knees went weak. This was far worse than she anticipated. She remembered the words she had been told in her dream and blurted out, "You have no authority to cast such a sentence. Only Acacia can pass judgement by law."

The colour drained from Malarchy's face. He screamed, "No!" It was too late. The earth rumbled and quaked as a great tree rose up on the hill. "Foolish girl, now your life is forfeit."

Ashlyn turned to Willow. "It's now - it's happening now," she cried, before running off in the direction of the hill.

Everything was moving so fast. People were scared. Neil took a few steps backwards, almost tripping over Willow. His gaze was fixated on Jade while mumbling *No* over and over. All of a sudden, he glanced upwards and raised his hands. For a moment, it looked as if the sky was a rubber ball, bouncing up and down. People were running. Malarchy was holding Jade with Nebulah holding Jordan beside them.

In one swift motion, the sky ripped open. An army of men instantly appeared, dressed in red and black. Willow noticed Neil frozen on the spot. She grabbed his arm, pulling him behind her increasing the pace from a jog to a full run. Camile caught up to them when they stopped at the gates. Willow grabbed Faramund's arm, pleading him to tell her where Diana was being kept.

"In the guard house," he answered. "You all go. I will make sure she gets out safely. I promise."

Willow nodded. "Head with Diana into the forest. It's the only place with cover from the army. I will find you and lead you to shelter." She disappeared with Neil and Camile into the trees, heading to the only place she knew they couldn't be found.

Chapter Thirteen

"Well boys, looks like we hit the jackpot!" Joseph said to his brothers as they walked through the newly-formed hole in the fabric between worlds, an army of men following behind. "Our sisters will be buying dinner tonight."

"How do you want to split it up?" Lance asked.

"You and Simon head to town, empty it, then move into that forest area. Split it up how you want. My team will take the castle and the grounds. How much time do we have?"

"Just over two hours," Simon replied.

"Men, we have about two hours. No fooling around. Let's get to work!" Joseph yelled. "There is pillaging to be done!"

It took only moments for Joseph and his men to reach the stone table. "Secure that lot," he ordered, motioning to Jade and her family. He stepped up on the table. "And the rest at the table here. Put them in one group beside the beautiful princess Jade. Leave a few men to help keep them here." He turned his attention to the others in the grounds. "Ladies and gentlemen," he yelled. "If I could have your attention. If you run or give my men any issues, they will kill you. I suggest you stay put and wait to be processed as a prisoner of war."

He jumped down with a smile. "This is fun, isn't it?" he said, brushing Jade's hair with his hand. "And I want to thank you for your role, darling."

"This wasn't what we agreed to," Jade said, shaking.

"Ah, now - now. We never actually discussed what would happen to your world. Did you think you could have all those things you want without people to serve? Worlds to rule are conquered worlds, my dear. Maybe you should have asked more questions before you were willing to sell your soul? Ah, but don't worry. I am a man of my word and you shall have everything you have ever wished for."

He turned to one of his men. "Take the brother."

"No! Jordan. No. You can't! What are you doing?" she cried.

"You wished he would go away, leaving you as an only child. I am making that happen for you," he smirked as he watched his men drag the crying child away.

"That's not what I wanted!" she shrieked.

"Perhaps not, but it is what you wished." Joseph rounded up the group gathered before him, tapping on their shoulders. He enjoyed the pain he was causing her. It was his game; his amusement for the day.

He stopped behind her mother, looked straight into Jade's eyes and snapped her neck. Nebulah's lifeless body fell to the ground.

"NO!" Jade cried hysterically.

"You wished many times she was dead."

"I didn't mean it. I was angry. I would never. I take it back. I take it back. Please!" she pleaded.

"It doesn't work that way, I am afraid. Death even I can't undo. Lesson learned - careful what you wish for, it just might come true," he said, still walking.

"I wish you would leave us alone!" Jade cried out. Her father was hugging her now, trying to keep his own eyes off the lifeless body of his wife at the same time.

"Interesting," he said, treating her statement as a twist to his game. The blade of a dagger tapped on his puckered lips. "I was going to enjoy your company this evening. I suppose another one of these young girls will make a suitable companion for me. Very well, as you wish."

He motioned to a man who came running, awaiting orders. "Take these two to the town and leave them there. They are not to be harmed." He turned to Jade. "You and your father will be alone, as you wish... the only people left in this world when the necrid flames engulf all you know and burn the flesh of your body. I hear it is excruciatingly painful, and I promise you will feel every second of it." He sat cross-legged on the stone table, laughing, as he indicated to the other men to bring the remainder of the group for processing. His lips puckered together, whistling a tune in celebration of his unfolding victory.

Chapter Fourteen

It didn't take long for Willow to move Camile and Neil through the forest. They were almost at the hidden quarters when they stumbled upon Jessie, Dezi and Pete, with Arnold tagging along behind them.

"Follow me," she said. "I know the only safe place we can go." There was no time to explain. She needed to keep moving. The invaders were close behind. Words of caution whispered on the leaves of the trees, providing her with news of others hiding in the forest. All she could do was find as many people as she could before the invaders did.

The group arrived at the library and were greeted by Clairity and Nathan. Both were worried, sensing something was wrong and seeing the state of those who were arriving. Willow had forgotten they knew nothing of what had transpired in the past hour.

"They can fill you in later," Willow said, catching her breath. "I need to get back out there and look for others who may have survived."

"Survived?" Clairity shrieked.

"Yes. Listen to me, everyone, this is the safest place you can be. No one can find you here, but you have to stay inside. If you stray to the forest, you will not find your way back. Clairity, Nathan, explain to them when I am gone, please."

The two nodded their response, words forsaking them. Willow prepared to leave, turning back to once again add, "No matter what you hear or think you see, no one can find you. You must trust me." She disappeared into the trees.

The next moments were complete chaos as the group went about trying to fill each other in as best they could, each trying to add details the others had left out. Fear thickened the air, choking them of their sensibility. The situation became dire when the voices of strangers, discussing plans to track people, were heard loud and clear. Their enemies were close.

"This is crazy," Arnold said. "We are waiting to be picked off one by one. This is not even a proper building. When they find us, they have an open shot. I'm not waiting to die in this death trap. We found this place, they will too." He ran for the forest before anyone could stop him.

After only a few steps, he turned around to see if any of the others followed. He stopped dead in his tracks. The building, the others... everything was gone. He tried to backtrack but ended up running directly into a group of the invaders armed with bows.

"Stop there!" a man yelled.

Arnold disobeyed a direct order for the second time, running. Once he realized the mistake he had made, it was too late.

"Bring him down," another voice ordered. Almost instantly, an arrow flew through the air and with exact precision pierced the boy's kneecap. He tumbled to the ground, screeching in pain.

Simon walked up to where Arnold lay. "You should have listened. We don't take the injured. They slow us down."

A deathly scream carried on the branches of the trees, reaching Willow's ears and forcing a shiver. There was no time to think about who it was. She had only just found Diana, Faramund, Iskander, and Zsiga. "Quickly this way," she ordered, as they raced for the white stone building.

"Prince Simon, over there," a man called out.

An arrow whizzed by her head, barely missing her face. Another hit a branch which had moved to protect her. *Almost there,* she thought, as an arrow pierced Faramund in the shoulder. He stumbled, barely catching his footing. Willow grabbed his arm, pulling him along. She motioned behind them, sending tree branches flying at any enemies that followed. New trees began growing, block the path behind them and anyone in pursuit. Her heart raced. She could feel it pounding in her throat. Her mouth was dry. At last, the building came into view. As they set foot in the clearing, she knew they were safe for the moment. She flopped on the ground, breathing heavily.

"Gran!" Nathan exclaimed with joy, as he ran into her arms.

Willow motioned to Jessie to help Faramund with his injury. He looked at her, his eyes longing to hear news of his sister. She shook her head. There was no time to rest. Instead, she inhaled deeply and headed back out to search for Victoria.

It wasn't long before she heard another scream, one she recognized. Willow rushed in the direction it came from, arriving in time to see a man firmly holding onto Victoria's arm.

"I don't want to hurt you, girl, just come along quietly," he demanded.

A branch from the tree behind him swung straight at his legs. The man tumbled to the ground, releasing his hold on the girl. Willow lunged forward, picking her up. Looking down at her enemy, she was stunned for just a moment. She felt something move in her stomach and a new lump formed in her throat. His two bright blue eyes locked on hers. His jet black hair with blue highlights blew in the wind majestically. Willow couldn't remember anyone looking as beautiful as he did at that moment.

Now? Kiera's voice sounded, knowing what Willow was feeling. *Now you decide to get interested in boys, and did it have to be the enemy? Really?*

"Lance," a voice yelled out, too close for comfort. That was enough daydreaming for one apocalypse. In a flash, she was running again. From somewhere behind she heard, "What happened to you?" and a reply, "I didn't see a branch," before the voices faded out of her earshot.

Up ahead, two figures stood over a body on the ground. She approached with caution, but saw it was Malarchy and Jade and the boy on the ground, Arnold. There was nothing anyone could do for him. It was already too late.

Could this day get any worse? she thought to herself.

Shielding Victoria's face, she passed by them, pausing for a moment before motioning to them to follow. They were only steps away from the building.

When Willow set her down, Victoria ran straight into her brothers' open arms. After she finished thoroughly smothering all three, she greeted the others, using her talents to heal anyone who was hurt as best she could. The rest of the group stood and stared in disbelief at the sight of Jade and her father. The tension grew - stress reaching alarming levels. The two were at the very heart of the reason they were all there, huddled together and frightened of what the future might hold.

"I couldn't leave them out there," Willow said, knowing what everyone was thinking. Seeing the others weren't in agreement with her, she added, "They made wrong choices, I agree, but like any of us, they can learn and change. They will have to carry the burden of what they did with them for the rest of their lives. If we leave them out there, we will be making a wrong choice, too - one that we would have to live with."

"She is traumatized," Malarchy blurted out, referring to his daughter. "She watched them kill her mother and take away her brother."

"A lot of people are dead or taken!" Neil shouted back. It was the first time he had spoken since the invasion first began.

"We have to do something to stop them," Malarchy pleaded.

It was Willow who responded with a touch of anger in her voice. "Look at us. We are all that are left. What do you suggest we do? They would wipe us out in a second. No, we are waiting until they go and then we can regroup and decide what can be done."

"I don't think that is an option," Malarchy stated, looking at the ground.

"What do you mean?" Willow asked.

114

He took in a large breath of air. "Joseph, one of the leaders, told us he was leaving us behind to burn in some kind of fire... necrid flames is what he called it."

"That's bad," Nathan said, pressing his lips together. He stepped away from his grandmother. "It's a blue flame that burns anything living. It makes ghost worlds. The direct opposite of terraforming. The flames keep burning until there is no more life - nothing else can extinguish it."

"We don't have much time left if they are heading back!" Malarchy exclaimed. "When they leave, they will set the flames."

Clairity almost fell to her knees. "Ashlyn, she is hurt on the hill. She needs help."

"I will go," Willow started, turning her attention to her friend.

"No, I will. I have increased speed. I can make it faster. Just lead us back here once we get to the treeline," Jessie said.

"The trees will show you a path, I will meet you for the last part," Willow said. "Thank you."

Jessie ran to the hill, racing against time.

"We need to find some way." Willow's thoughts exploded through all of the information that bombarded her mind. *Portals,* she thought. *All known portals closed... known portals... there must be a hidden portal... but how do we find it? Prophecies, there are prophecies about...* "Diana, would there be a book containing prophecies? I know some were only heard by the Council, but other ones the keepers would have kept?"

"Yes, *The Portal Prophecies*. It's quite large," the historian replied.

"Nathan, have you seen it?" Willow said, hoping the boy already read it.

"No, I haven't," he replied.

"Where haven't you read books yet?" Willow asked.

He pointed to a section on the opposite semi-circle to where he was standing.

"Quickly, I need to find this book. Only look for the very largest books," Willow ordered.

Clairity found it before she even finished speaking. "I had a feeling," she said.

Placing it on the stone table, Willow turned to Diana again. "This is your writing. You recorded all of these as historian. Is there a prophecy about the blue flame?"

Mrs. Waddington looked as if a light turned on inside her head. "Yes, yes there is!" She turned the pages of the book. When she stopped, she read out loud:

When the blue flames engulf the land, only one whose will is steadied,

By that discovered can break that which is set in stone to escape.

Jessie called. Willow ran out to meet him carrying Ashlyn over his shoulder. They joined the others, watching as she returned to her steady pacing, back and forth, while repeating the prophecy, over and over.

Her mind raced. "Some things only you can discover... an ability - it has to be... break that which is set in stone... in stone." She looked at the book lying on the table. She handed it to Clairity to hold before running her fingers over the four corners of the table.

"Shouldn't we try to do something?" Malarchy yelled. "We are out of time."

"She is trying to do something," Clairity replied. "Let her concentrate."

Willow looked up and, for the first time, noticed above the stone table there was an opening in the ceiling. A small square that let light shine down on the stone.

She turned to Ashlyn. "The dreams... in our dreams, there was a giant storm. It was in the other prophecy as well about today. Everything else has happened, but the great storm... the thunder and..." her words cut off. She understood.

"Stand back! Everyone inside one of the two side rooms, against the walls. Don't lose that book, Clairity!" Willow yelled.

Raising her hands to the sky and looking upward, a gold dust appeared, flowing from her hands. The clouds swirled above as rain began to fall heavier than it ever had before. The winds howled and, within seconds, thunder boomed through the air. A single bolt of lightning struck the table, breaking it into pieces. The four corner stones broke loose, flying into position as if drawn by a magnet. A portal opened before them with a rainbow of lights in the middle.

"Go!" Willow screamed. The necrid flames were almost upon them. She watched as each of the survivors ran through, then jumped through herself with only seconds to spare, not knowing where they would end up on the other side.

King Cornelius

The three princes returned to their homeland. Here, whether day or night, the skies remained the same: orange with red highlights and purple clouds. Red sands covered much of the world, bordering on seas of black liquid - a place where some of the most vicious sea creatures ever to exist called home. Towns scattered along the shorelines of the seas, housing the population not enlisted in aiding the war efforts. Fishermen would risk their lives to capture any one of the deadly water creatures, which, when cooked properly, were considered a delicacy by their King, and in turn, worth more riches than could be earned in any other trade.

In the centre of the land was a great mountain of black rock - the royal palace carved directly into its base. One lone path rounded up the sides, with several large platforms of flat sheet rock along the way, leading to a gate at the top. This area was the living quarters and King's Court. Under the main levels, buried deep in the mountain were the servants' quarters - below that the dungeons, filled with all sorts of beings - all having been captured from different worlds. Some would be forced to join the army. Others were merely there to be studied and exploited for whatever happened to be of use or need by the king or his children. They were nothing more than glorified lab rats.

A black forest bordered the foot of the mountain, filled with large dark trees, which in any other world might appear to be dead or dying. Their wooden limbs always remained bare. They stood silent. Several large branches protruded from their tops, growing downwards - each dividing into five separate vine-like branches, resembling large hands with long fingers. These appendage-shaped vines sensed even the tiniest movement, instantly wrapping around any living thing. Once snared, they pulled poor creatures to their bases. The bark of a tree would then open to surround its prey, absorbing the very essence of its life. There was one road through the forest which was used by tradesmen, hunters and fisherman, at their own risk. There was little choice but to use it weekly to bring items to a marketplace located on the first stone platform heading up the mountain. The other levels all contained vast amounts of housing for the king's growing armies.

Today the halls of the castle echoed with laughter and celebration for the victories the princes and princesses were to bestow upon their father.

"A toast to Prince Joseph, Prince Simon and Prince Lance, for the conquest of yet another world. Come, my sons. Tell me tales of today's adventures," the king's voice trumpeted as he raised a glass of wine in the air, its precious liquid overflowing in every direction he turned.

"A perfectly flawless attack, no injuries except for Lance. He picked a fight with a tree and lost, ending up on his backside," Joseph answered, laughing.

"To be fair, the tree was twice my size," Lance added with a smile. "And nothing was hurt but my pride."

"Do we know the name of the world you so boldly conquered?" Cornelius asked.

"No, Father, but one of our new guests will be willing to share, I am sure." Joseph prided himself on being the most ruthless of the three princes. He executed his father's requests without question and was quick to claim the glory as well.

"Casualties?" One of the King's royal eyebrows raised as he gulped back his wine.

"Limited, a few struggled and were executed or left behind," Joseph answered.

"Without knowing what world this is? I explicitly instructed you that I am looking for someone. How do you know she wasn't one of your casualties?" the king yelled, a red colour creeping up his cheeks.

"I highly doubt this was that world, Father," Joseph argued. "There was nothing there, except a small town of wooden huts and one castle. Even the prisoner count is minimal."

"Find out quickly. Ask the captives the names of who is missing so I can be sure." Cornelius turned to Lance. "The necrid flames? They have been lit?"

"Yes, the world should be consumed by now and barren of all life, useless to anyone," Lance replied.

"Your gift is a blessing, my son. Soon we shall have destroyed all of those who imprisoned us and the walls they built, not just around us, but around thousands of other realms as well. They imposed their will on us unjustly, took our friends and relatives, turned them against us and made them betray us. They told us we were not good enough for their utopia and denied us the right to make our own."

"Have my sisters returned?" Prince Joseph asked.

"Not yet," the King answered. "When they do, we shall celebrate till the morning. Until then perhaps you can work on a few of our new guests... find some information."

"As you wish, my King," Joseph answered, turning to the steps leading to the dungeons.

The stone staircase was dark and cold. The three princes headed down, passing the servants' quarters as well as the next two levels, which housed beings who were being reformed or chosen to join the king's army and were in training, to the very lower-level dungeons. Here, there were several different rooms which spread across a few levels, including interrogation rooms and holding cells all carved from rock and virtually escape free.

"Bets? I think I can crack one first," Simon said with a smile.

Joseph smiled. "Brotherly competition, my favourite."

"I will sit this one out, you two enjoy yourselves," Lance replied. "I may visit some old… friends." The prince disappeared into the deepest darkest part of the castle's lower levels.

The first two holding cells were full of the castle's new guests. Simon chose a young girl to interrogate, motioning a guard to have her brought to a private room.

"Hello," Simon said, smiling. He was able to turn on the charm when he wanted to on the same level as Joseph. In fact, women found all three of the princes to be irresistible. They were all handsome, tall, well-built, and eloquent speakers. "I am Prince Simon, and you are?"

"Sabrina," the girl answered in a shaky voice.

"Sabrina, very nice to make your acquaintance. I believe there has been a misunderstanding. I want to fix things, but to do so, I need your help. The sooner I sort through the answers, the sooner we can improve your situation here. Okay?"

"I am not sure what help I can be. I don't know anything," she answered.

Simon laughed. "I haven't asked anything yet, so how could you know whether or not you know? These questions aren't difficult. They are about your home. For instance, what was the name of your town and world?"

"Name? It didn't have a name, at least not one I have ever heard. It was just our home. We didn't speak of other places." Her voice shook in fear that her answer might anger the man before her.

"No name at all? There was only the one town and it had no name?" Simon asked.

"Just the one town. I don't think we ever needed it to have a name, or maybe *the town* was its name," she answered.

"Okay," he said, smiling. "It makes sense, there was no need. There are some people missing - correct? Do you think you could name them?"

"Yes, there are some. Why do you want to know who they are?"

"Like I said, I just need to rule out that the person we are looking for wasn't hiding in your town," he answered convincingly.

"Hiding? Like a criminal? Odd things were happening lately. Do you think that is why? Was this person scared you were coming for them?" Sabrina squeaked.

"Yes - yes, it most likely is. Why don't you tell me the names so we can try to bring this evil person to justice?" Simon listened and wrote down all the names the girl listed. "That's all, you are sure?"

"Yes. Wait, I almost forgot... Diana. And, thinking back, she was taken away bound with ropes by the castle guards for something," Sabrina answered.

The young prince's face went white. "What did she look like?"

"Tall, thin, very pristine, hair always very neat, tied back in a bun, clothes always clean and proper. Nice features, some of the girls wished they had her cheekbones. She was pleasant to look at and well-spoken. Is it her?" Sabrina asked without hesitation.

"I don't know," he answered, leaving the room to find his brother.

Joseph chose a woman from the town named Martha, but hadn't gotten very far. He was about to slap the woman for the fourth time for not answering his questions when the door flung open. Simon demanded to speak to him. After leaving the room, he listened to the story and read the names on the list, which was a little more extensive than he had expected.

"There are many worlds, brother. I am sure there are many women by the same name as our long-lost aunt. The whole thing seems unlikely, don't you think?" Joseph asked.

"How so?" Simon asked.

"Guardians were creatures of great power. When they separated the worlds to their own taste and created their utopia, do you think they would have designed beaten-up old wooden shacks for their keepers to live in? Our dungeons are better accommodations. Also, wouldn't there have been a guardian or two left to protect their homeland? No, I think this was a trial colony of some sort - an experiment. The size of the world itself was so small; one town, no bodies of water. Surely a powerful ancient race would have made a better home for itself." Joseph motioned to one of his men to return the captives to the holding cells with the others.

"Wait!" Simon smiled. "The girl in the other room, have the maids bathe her and find her something appealing to wear, then bring her to my room to wait for me. I do enjoy celebrations."

Joseph laughed. "Let's find Lance."

Lance was on the lowest level of the dungeon when his two brothers found him. He stood in front of a special rock enclosure which was clear to see through and naturally blocked many special abilities. Inside was a woman with light strawberry coloured curly hair, shades paler than the girl from the forest earlier. They shared similar facial features, *perhaps related,* he thought. The vision of the girl in his mind was proving stubborn, unwilling to leave his thought of its own accord. There was something different about her somehow. Whatever it was, it intrigued him like no other girl had before. His thoughts were interrupted.

"Something wrong?" Joseph asked, handing him the list of names that were collected.

"No, just wondering how to get her to give up the other creature," Lance lied while looking over the list.

"Why? The other one is immortal. We have eternity to torture it for its crimes," Simon offered.

"It no longer responds. Look for yourself. I think it is broken beyond repair, as good as dead, but trapped in life. It has given up and is useless to us now," Lance responded.

Joseph entered the cell beside the woman his brother had been watching and returned with the motionless body of a black bird. One wing had been removed and all of its bones repeatedly broken. It had endured the worst forms of torture until it could endure no more.

"Immortality isn't always a blessing," Joseph mused.

A loud noise came from down the hallway. Three girls, all dressed in black, their skin a pale olive green, headed their way.

"Do we have victory, sisters?" Joseph asked.

"Victory - there was nothing to be victorious over. This was the first world we have seen with no intelligent life forms. At first, we thought there were some humanoids, but it ended up being just a bunch of beasts with sharp teeth and claws... vicious, yes... but usable, no. The land, however, was perfect to assimilate into the new world once the barriers between space come down. We made sure any plant life would die off quickly and water sources would dry up fast. It won't be long before it is barren land that we can later transform into whatever we want," Zoe responded. She was the impulsive one of the three princesses, quick to make decisions. "I thought those things couldn't die," she added, referring to the bird her brother was holding.

"They can't, but it is broken beyond help now. I don't know what to do with it. Seems such a waste to use valuable space on it," Joseph answered.

Without a word, Zoe grabbed the bird and rushed back up the staircase. Several minutes later she returned, smiling.

"What did you do?" Lance asked.

"The doorway was still open to the world we were just in. I threw it in. Let the beasts play with it some before they expire and it's out of our hair. We can use that room for other things now," she answered.

"I may be starting to understand why you are Father's favourite, Zoe," Joseph said.

"Why don't you share the good news with the lady, Lance? I am sure it will jolt her some, maybe even anger her enough to let the other one out to play," Simon suggested.

"Actually, I think I will have a chat with her and catch up to you later at the celebration." Lance entered the stone room and closed the door behind him.

"Hello," Lance said. He had never actually paid any attention to the women before. "Raven, isn't it?"

"I have no desire to speak with you," she snapped.

"I have information for you, about your friend and... daughter," Lance said.

Raven's eyes widened. "What has happened to the guardian? Return her to me and we can speak."

"I am afraid I can't. The guardian gave up hope. The torture you let it endure on your behalf was too much for it to bear. The broken body was discarded moments ago."

"You are a vile race, without any signs of morals or decency!" she yelled, spitting in the prince's face.

Lance took a cloth from his pocket and wiped it away. "It was your precious guardians who imposed their will on us. They took our lands, our property, our family and our right to grow. They imprisoned us with walls created between worlds, designed to hold us back from our true potential. We are not the villains here. We are the victims. If you are as civilized as you pretend, then why weren't we consulted as to our future?"

"Your father was angry, furious, his sister was chosen by guardians to help in the restructuring and he was not. That is what you fight for, a man's jealousy," she cried, turning away.

"And you? What do you fight for? Your daughter? No, you left her - didn't you?" Lance fished for information, anything he could find out about the girl from the forest. Could she have escaped? Would he meet her again? His blood rushed through his body at the thought, blue flames blazing in his eyes.

"What are you looking for, Prince?" Raven asked as if reading his thoughts. Perhaps the clear rock wasn't as good an ability blocker as previously thought.

"Her name," he answered honestly.

"I must disappoint you, then. I have no daughter... If I did, her name would never cross your lips. I can assure you of that," Raven replied.

"Your world was destroyed by necrid flames a few hours ago. Tell me, did she have the talent to escape?"

"Nothing can escape necrid flames. Is that not true?"

Lance smiled, she had given him all the information he wanted. The look in her eyes told him the girl was her daughter, and her lack of concern meant she was alive somewhere. Their paths would cross again one day, and he looked forward to the confrontation it would bring.

Chapter Sixteen

Willow landed with a thud, banging her head on something on the ground. Years of being joined with several Leanders, the cat-like race of ancient beings, meant she picked up a few of their traits including night vision, stealth, agility and she always landed on her feet, at least before that moment.

There had been no choice but to leap headfirst through the portal as the necrid flames engulfed the forest around them and even less time to worry about how she would land on the other side or what she would find. Rubbing her head, she realized she hit it on the book she asked Clairity not to lose, *The Portal Prophecies*. Without that book, she never would have figured out how to escape in the first place. She looked up to see if the others were okay, but it wasn't a friendly face that greeted her.

A weapon, some form of a gun that she and Nathan read about in one of the encyclopedias they found, was pointed in her face. *This day just isn't going to end,* she thought to herself.

"Get up!" a male voice ordered.

Willow got to her feet. She staggered a bit, the bump on her head making her dizzy. Looking at her captor, she couldn't tell much, other than he was a tall man. A baseball cap hid the features of his face from sight.

"Turn around," the man ordered.

Willow turned her back to the stranger, trying to search for signs of her friends who travelled through the portal before her.

"Hi, I'm..."

The stranger cut her off. "Don't speak. We know about your kind and what you are looking for."

"My kind? What kind?" she asked.

"I said no speaking," he repeated. "Walk over there and join the others you came with until we can figure out what you are doing here."

"Might be easier to figure that out if I could talk." she said under her breath, but loud enough that her captor could hear.

"Just shut up, okay? Don't get me mad," he barked back.

"Okay, okay. Just saying, you can't know what we are doing here if we are the only ones who know and you won't let us tell you."

"Enough, I am not listening to your tricks!" he yelled.

Real winner this one is, Kiera said telepathically.

Can you see him, what he looks like? Willow asked in her mind.

No, we can do a lot of things but seeing through a jacket isn't one of them, Aslo answered.

Right, forgot I was still wearing it, she answered silently.

Ahead of her, she could see the others now. They all seemed fine, at least for the moment. There were several men with guns keeping them in a line. She took the place beside her best friend, Clairity.

"Well, this is much better," Malarchy whispered.

"You could have stayed and fried in the flames, pretty sure I didn't twist your arm," Willow whispered back. Malarchy and his daughter had little right to complain. They were right at the heart of the actions that led up to what happened.

"Can you ever be quiet?" the stranger's voice asked.

A few of her friends in the group let out a little giggle, forcing Willow to tilt her head down the line and ask, "Really?"

"Just shut up," the stranger said, a strong sense of authority resonated in his voice.

"Yes, yes, scary man with a weapon. I am just a little confused. You want us to stand here until what? You magically figure out how and why we are here?" Willow asked.

"You left out without speaking," he added. "It's been a bad day. Don't test me."

Willow chuckled. "Wanna compare notes?"

"Someone get some duct tape for her mouth, please," the stranger yelled to the other men.

One of the men ran to a truck. She recognized it from the pictures drawn in one of the books Nathan shared with her. This world used them for transportation, an idea she found fascinating. The thought of a place having so much space that they needed to use something to move people from one spot to another was mind-blowing. This world must have been huge or people would just walk. When the man returned, he was carrying something round and silver. He pulled part of it and it seemed to stretch, then rip. He placed it over her mouth. It stuck. Her mouth was stuck shut. She tried to move her lips, but no matter how hard she tried, only muffled sounds came out. *How rude,* she thought.

Time seemed to pass by unusually slowly. Willow attempted complaining a few times but her suppressed voice just made the stranger laugh. When she looked at the others to say something, she ended up just sighing. It was clear none of them wanted to have the stuff put over their mouths. Of course, she couldn't blame them for that. It was uncomfortable and irritating. She wasn't sure how long she was standing there before another truck pulled up and a man stepped out. Her captors seemed to have their own little meeting. Then the new man moved in front of her group.

"Who is in charge?" he asked.

No one moved or talked. The stranger moved to Willow's side, pushed her away from the others, then pulled the sticky stuff off her face in one swift motion.

"Ow!" Willow screamed. "That hurt! You really have some nerve. You can't just go around gluing people's mouths shut like that!"

"This one should have no problem answering questions," he said. "We should talk here, where the others can't hear."

"Perhaps I don't want to answer your questions now!" Willow exclaimed, crossing her arms across her chest.

"Oh, I think your need to speak will take over without problem," he said with a chuckle.

"Enough!" The man who had just arrived raised his hand. On his arm was a picture Willow knew.

"You are a portal guard?" she asked.

"My name is William and I am the one asking questions. Who might you be?"

"Willow," she answered. "Are you all portal guards?"

"No, and I am asking questions, remember?" he complained.

"Yes, but it seems strange that you are a portal guard and they aren't. Why were they at the portal and you weren't?" she asked.

"It's a long story, but I need to know who you are and why you are here," he replied.

"Why should we trust you?" she snapped. "You capture us, point weapons at us, refuse to listen to our story, put stuff over my mouth, then want to know everything."

Signs of frustrated filled William's expression. "You recognized the symbol on my arm, and you seem to know what it means. That tells you what I am..."

She cut off his words. "And three of us have that same mark. Did anyone trust them? Or extend hospitality? I can answer that - No!"

William looked at the stranger, "Is that true, Mike?"

"I didn't look," Mike replied. "They were all just sneaking around, so we rounded them up and waited for you."

"The book might have been a giveaway." She held up the large book she was still carrying, titled *The Portal Prophecies*.

Mike shrugged. "I thought it was one of those conspiracy books that keep popping up. This group looks like a bunch of groupie wannabes looking for a supernatural thrill."

William walked over to the others and asked to see a portal guard symbol on any of their arms. The three guards stepped forward and put their arms together so all the pictures were beside each other, matching perfectly. William dismissed his other men before leading the group to a house, about a five-minute walk away.

Outside a cabin, more men and women were stationed, each carrying weapons similar to the ones the men in the forest toted and positioned at fairly even intervals from one another.

Inside the main room was a couch, some chairs and floor pillows, all situated around a lit fireplace, which heated the room to a balmy warm temperature. To the back was a separate space with just enough room for a wooden table and chairs.

William and Mike motioned to most of the group to sit down in front of the fireplace. The guards followed them to the table. Willow took it upon herself to join them.

"Why don't you sit with the others?" Mike motioned to Willow.

She looked at him, then William, then the guards. Faramund muffled a laugh. She turned around and faced Mike. "I think I am more qualified to be at this table than you are."

William laughed. "There will be time for argument, but for now if we could sit down, maybe we could figure out what is going on."

"I only know parts of the backstory about the ongoing war with the Serpent Ancients, the Xiuhcoatle and the prophecies." Willow paused.

"What happened tonight? What brought you here is what we are most curious about," William said, smiling.

Zsiga responded. "Our world was invaded and destroyed. We are all that escaped death or capture. We are the last of our kind."

"Forgive me if I don't look surprised, but we wrote off our home world long ago when no further reinforcements were sent." William's facial expression embodied all the qualities of a boy who had recently lost his best friend.

"Communication was non-existent and the Council feared the worst," the head guard explained.

"That we can explain, the serpents and their allies found a way to weaken the space between the worlds, in short punching holes in them," William said, leaning back in his chair so that the two front legs lifted off the ground.

Mike picked up the story. "Some of your portals, when active, created a strain on the weakened space, so the forces you left here at the time disabled them and hid the stones needed to activate them again. That way no further damage could be done."

"So, we lost contact because you disabled some of the portals, disrupting the telepathic connection?" Willow asked.

"You catch on fast. A guardian could still open a portal from the other side to move through, but they closed after use. No one did," Mike replied.

"They separated our forces. I am the last guard left in this world. These men and women working with me, are individuals whose lives have in some way been touched by the war. They have all lost family and friends and joined the cause to help protect this world. They are good people, but we are still losing the battle. Perhaps with your help we can hold on a bit longer," William said.

"With the portals closed, what are you fighting?" Willow asked.

"Not all the portals are inactive. There are a few we monitor. There are also a few rogue holes in space that have been created that we don't know how to repair. All manner of beings have come through. From what we know, they open and close on their own and only for a certain amount of time."

"We are lucky this world has an imagination and loves conspiracy theories. They make their own stories up about everything that happens. A few rumours in the right ear and they cover it up for us. That's what we thought your group was, thrill seekers looking for proof of something or anything." Mike added, "Sorry about that."

Willow didn't believe at all that he was sorry. There was something about his sheepish grin that said he had overly enjoyed annoying her.

"It's late and most of us have had too much excitement for today. Would you mind if we slept here?" she asked.

"Of course, we have extra buildings with beds that are all empty at the moment. Mike can get you all settled and tomorrow we will show you around," William answered. "Then, perhaps you can explain how you opened a sealed portal."

"Easy," Willow said. "I read the book." She pushed the book of prophecies across the table.

Mike showed them round back of the house where there were a series of additional buildings. They were directed to the third building. Inside were beds with full-body cushions, evenly spaced throughout the main room. Each bed had a storage chest and a small closet for personal items. Mike informed them this was their own place, since no one else was staying there, and showed them the bathrooms and showers.

"Someone will be by in the morning to show you the rest of the facility," Mike said. "You should be safe here. The patrols are out."

Before Willow and the others could thank him, a gunshot sounded in the distance, followed by some shouting.

"Stay here and lock the door. Don't open it for anyone!" Mike yelled as he ran out towards the sound of another gun firing.

Malarchy bolted forward and locked the door, then moved away from it and began checking the windows to make sure they were all also locked.

"What are you doing? We should try to help." Willow wasn't sure what the noises outside were about, but she was certain someone could be hurt and need their assistance.

"We don't even know what we would be up against and we don't know anything about this world. We need to wait till morning," he replied sternly.

"As much as I hate to say it, Malarchy is right. We can take shifts sleeping until daylight and hopefully someone sends for us." Zsiga was already setting up with the other two guards to have at least one of them awake at all times till morning.

Willow sat down on a bed and Clairity joined her. "They are right, you know. We will be more help in the morning. I have that feeling."

"Thanks." Willow smiled at her friend's words. Clairity's intuition had been extremely accurate these past few days.

"One thing I wanted to ask you, though. Back at the stone table, why didn't Kiera and Aslo just tell you how to escape? We almost died."

Willow took a big breath and let it out while trying to find the words to explain. "Because there are some things I needed to find out for myself. When I read the prophecy, I knew I could do it. I had never used anywhere near that amount of power before, but I knew I could. If someone simply told me I could, there would have been doubt. I wouldn't have believed in myself enough to create the force that was needed."

"I get it." Her friend smiled. "Best we get some sleep. Tomorrow I think may be a full day."

Willow laid down. Sleep wasn't going to be easy. What was out there? Would there be anyone left to come for them in the morning?

Chapter Seventeen

A loud knock on the door jolted Willow awake. She wasn't sure how long she slept for, but it wasn't long. The yelling outside continued through the night. Iskander opened the door, letting Mike in. With daylight shining in the windows, she was able to see more of his features. His hair was cut very short and, if it were longer, she imagined it would be a similar colour to her own. His eyes were a dull green, which matched the clothes he wore. From the dark circles under his eyes, she could tell he had little sleep last night as well.

"We have arranged an escort for you back to the main building. Bring anything you need. You won't be back here again till later tonight," Mike said to the guard, his voice loud enough for everyone to hear.

There wasn't any time to think. The escort was waiting and they were on their way within minutes to hopefully a few answers about what had happened during the night.

When they arrived at the room they were in the previous night, it looked completely different, having been transformed into a command centre. There were large boards with maps and coloured flags inserted at different points. Men and women were buzzing around with handheld devices they were talking into.

One woman with her hair tied back in a neat bun wearing all green, in the same colour as Mike's shirt, was pinning more flags in several of the maps. William was going over additional papers at the table. He looked up and brushed the hair from his eyes. With a smile, he extended an invitation to join him at the table.

"Sorry things are a bit crazy around here today. We had a... problem arise last night," He said.

"What happened?" Willow asked. "Maybe we could help. It doesn't look like you have solved the problem yet."

"Best you stay here where you won't get hurt and let the experts handle this," Mike answered.

William shook his head, still smiling. "The opening of the portal you came through created one of those holes we told you about and a dozen or so creatures managed to come through, maybe more. We haven't seen anything like them before. We don't even know what world they came from."

"What did they look like?" she asked.

"Humanoid, pale greyish skin, razor sharp teeth, hands and feet that looked more paw-like than human and the females appeared to have wings of some sort. Rather ugly really, but super fast and deadly," Mike answered.

"Hannulate!" Nathan blurted out.

"Sounds like it," Willow agreed. "They were once one of the most beautiful races to exist. They were peaceful and fun-loving creatures who lived in magical realms. A direct cousin to faeries and pixies."

"That doesn't sound much like the creatures I described," Mike snorted.

"Because they changed. During the blood wars, an evil king captured them, all of them... the entire race. Kept in chains in a dismal dungeon, they were tortured but kept alive to harvest their blood to fuel the kingdom's war. Their species has a unique ability to adapt, and they did just that: developing sharp teeth and razor-like claws that could extend at will and were strong enough to cut the chains that bound them. Then one night, while the armies were away waging war to acquire more possessions, they escaped and murdered any person they met. They considered all of mankind a threat, and probably still do. It took less than an hour for them to wipe out the entire kingdom."

"Great… any good news?" William asked.

"Yes and no. They are, at the moment, nocturnal and during the day they will want to hide and rest. You have a window of opportunity to find them in daylight," Willow offered.

"And the bad news?"

"I told you they adapt. It won't be long before the daylight won't bother them anymore. When that happens, they will be harder to track," she answered.

"Except by following the body count. We need to double up the search now. Call everyone back and double shifts till dusk. Let's destroy them before nightfall," Mike said, speaking to the men and women waiting for instructions around them.

"Destroy them?" Willow shrieked. "No, you can't! It isn't their fault."

"They are killing people. We should just let them?" Mike argued.

"Did anyone try talking to them? Did you even listen to what they have been put through? People made them this way. They adapted to being abused in order to survive. With a little compassion, they could change back into the beautiful creatures they were meant to be." Willow squared her shoulders to Mike. The two were standing only inches apart from each other, as if having their own argument and no one else existed.

William cut in. "This isn't a capture operation, Willow. Even if we could, what would we do with them? They pose a threat to everyone around. We aren't going to take that chance. They will be destroyed and the people of this world will be safe."

Willow heard a gasp from Kiera. She didn't even have to think what it meant. She already knew. "When did you change our purpose?" Willow asked with tears welling in her eyes.

"Hope this place is rain-proof," Malarchy said to Diana.

Willow didn't notice the comment, being too directly involved in what was happening. Malarchy was right, of course; the clouds were forming outside - rain ready to pour down on them.

"What do you mean?" William asked, moving closer to her. An anger brewed inside him at being accused of wrongdoing.

Faramund rushed to Willow's side, poised to protect her at all costs, but remained silent. His job was to ensure the safety of the last keeper, and to him, nothing else mattered.

"Guardians are meant to protect all worlds and all creatures, not just this one and these people. As portal guards, you defend against threats, yes, but these beings didn't choose to come here. They didn't come through the portal to attack. They are victims. Yet you feel you have the right to condemn them, judge them and sentence them. That isn't and never was our birthright or purpose," Willow said, not backing down.

"Look around, little girl, this isn't a game. I am all that is left. These people are here helping me hold on and protect this world. They didn't sign up for Guardian Philosophy 101. Without them, I would have been gone long ago and then there wouldn't have been any of us left in this world." William's anger raged, blood rushing to his face.

"You aren't one of us," Willow said, wishing she hadn't. But she was right. He had forsaken the duty he was bound to for the well-being of one world and had been doing so for some time.

"What do you know about it? What makes you the expert on what the guardians would approve of?" William snapped.

"I know the mark on your arm is fading as we speak. I know you could be removed from your duty if you do this," Willow said, echoing Aslo's words as they formed in her mind.

William looked at his arm. What once was a dark shade had already faded to a light baby blue. "I have followed this policy for some time now. Why all of a sudden?" His words faded off, confusion taking a hold of his thoughts.

"I guess you didn't notice until now. It was probably a subtle change taking place over time." Willow heard Aslo's voice again and relayed his message. "I believe you will find it will darken again should you chose the path you were meant to follow."

The pain in William's eyes was undeniable. He moved to the table, collapsing into a chair, burying his head in his arms on the table. "We have done our best here. It hasn't been easy."

"I am sure it hasn't, but our best isn't always what is right. These creatures deserve a chance and I plan to try." She turned her attention to the others. "Nathan, can you take a yellow flag and mark on the map where the portal to their homeland is, please?" Turning back to William, she asked, "Is the portal at that location active?"

Mike looked at the placement of the flag pin on the map. "Yes, the pink flags are known closed portals. That one, if it is there, hasn't been discovered yet."

"Okay, so all we need to do is round them up and send them home," she said.

"You forget they are savage," Mike argued.

"You forget they are beings who have great intelligence. They learnt to be savage from men in order to survive. Part of them can still be reasoned with," Willow said. "We can divide into three teams, two search parties and one to remain here. Nathan and Diana, can you two complete that map with each of the portals that are missing?"

Nathan and Diana agreed. Willow was about to split up the teams, when Mike interrupted, "I do hate to butt in and all... actually, no I don't. You arrive here after how many thousands of years, waltz in, insult the man who has dedicated his life to protecting a portal and preserving life here and try to take over? This man watched everyone he knows disappear or die. This isn't your show, so back off!"

Silence overcame the room as everyone stopped what they were doing, staring and waiting for new instructions from someone. Willow glanced at William sitting at the table alone with his hands on his face, elbows on the table. As much as she hated to admit it, Mike was right. This was William's place, his army, his supplies; it was his show. They needed to agree. She asked everyone to clear the room for a few minutes so she could talk to the guard alone. William looked up and nodded to his people to step outside.

"I am sorry. I was wrong to take over like that. I will prepare to leave immediately. Most of my people will join me; however, a few may prefer to remain in your hospitality. They won't interfere with your operations."

"How do you know all this? That what I am doing isn't what I was meant to do? That the mark will reappear?" William asked, his head hung low, still facing the table.

"I..." Willow felt a tug in her left shoulder. Seconds later a black cat jumped on the table and sat staring at the guard.

"I am Aslo, Leander and guardian. I spoke the words to the girl. She is my keeper. She only repeated what I asked her to."

Both William and Willow gasped out loud, as if they were seeing a ghost. Silence followed for several minutes before Aslo spoke again.

"We don't have time for this, daylight hours are passing and there is work to be done. You are a good guard, William, but your path has been lost over the years. Not just one world has the right to survive; they all do. We do not have the right to judge how they live. Our job is simply to ensure they have the right to live as they choose."

"It isn't always that simple," William said without emotion. "To protect one means to destroy another in some cases."

"Yes, there is no exact science, but we must try rather than just condemn. There are cases where the innocent must be defended and others destroyed, but in this case both parties are innocent. They are both fighting to exist and neither one has more right than the other to survive."

"I understand and will step aside," William offered.

"No!" Willow exclaimed. "These people look to you for direction. You need to lead them. We will do as you request. Ask us to leave or stay and help. I must follow the way of the guardians, but I will respect your choice."

"What do I... we do? How do we save both?"

"We try," Willow answered. "First, of course, we have to find them."

That comment earned a half-smile. "Yeah, that should be easy enough," William said.

"We do have some skill sets that may help a little," Willow said, sensing the sarcasm in his voice.

"I completely forgot about that. I have unique radar to locate portal stones within walking distance of me. I expect you each have something different."

"You could say that, but for the moment, we are out of time. We need to find the missing Hannulate and get them home before more damage is done," Aslo said as he jumped to Willow's shoulder and disappeared onto the surface of her skin again.

Chapter Eighteen

William got up from the table and summoned the others back into the room, giving a short speech that everything had been worked out and a common goal found. The details of which would be made known later after the urgency of the day had been settled.

Tactical teams were formed. William headed the first, picking several of his own men as well as Iskander, Jessie, Dezi and Pete to cover ground to the north. Willow was to lead the second group to the south, consisting of Mike, Faramund, Zsiga, and Neil.

The remainder of the people stayed at the base of operations. Some were left to protect the camp. All others waited in the command centre.

Nathan, Diana, Ashlyn and Clairity were assigned to helping the young girl who maintained the maps, Sarah. Over the course of the morning, they heard her story about how she lost her parents and younger siblings to the vamprite, a race she knew as vampires. Back in the time of the blood wars, when humanoids were looking to drink the blood of the magic folk, a young prince, Drake, decided turnabout was fair play. He captured young women and drank their blood. It soon came to light that drinking human blood could keep his race of shapeshifters young, strong, and beautiful. Given the chance, the vamprite would gladly invade and live in this world. They had once before found a foothold here.

It was believed a few hundred came through one of the holes in space between realms and took up residence. It was easy to understand the folklore people built up about vampires and why cover-ups weren't a problem in this world. The people here made up stories to explain the unknown themselves.

The jobs in the command centre were basically all about filling in information. Nathan had read in books about portal locations and which worlds they connected to. He marked those on the maps. Sarah was also marking whether individual portals were disabled or not and any known information about where portal stones were hidden.

Everyone else had been given communication devices to stay in contact with the two mobile groups. The guards themselves could stay updated since they could communicate telepathically with each other.

Within moments, the groups were prepped and on their way. The command centre was busy locating possibilities for dark places where the creatures could hide for the groups to search.

Willow's group took the truck south, agreeing chances were high the Hannulate would have travelled at least to dense forestland, as there weren't as many mountains or caves in their location as there were to the north.

The trees were tall and reminded her a little of home, although packed much tighter together. Willow fought the urge to take off her shoes and climb. She placed her hand on the trunk of the tree in front of her and felt the warm whisper of welcome vibrate through her body. A feeling of complete relaxation came over her. She was safe, protected, loved. Taking rhythmic breaths in and letting them out, she closed her eyes and saw exactly as the trees did. She thanked them and turned to the others in her search party.

"They aren't far. There is a dark spot in the forest where they stopped for rest. We can be there in less than ten minutes," Willow said to her team.

"Great, lead the way," Mike answered.

"I don't have to. We can just follow the path."

Mike's eyes widened with surprise as the trees parted in front of him, creating a dirt trail through the dense forest. He looked at Willow as if he was going to speak, but ended up shaking his head as he stepped forward to take the lead.

The trail ended at the darkest part of the forest. Mike stopped and turned to Willow, questioning where to go, but not wanting to speak out loud and disturb the creatures he was sure were resting nearby.

Moving forward, Willow placed her hand on a tree. Within moments, the branches of all the surrounding trees swayed and parted, revealing camouflaged bodies scattered on the ground like fallen leaves. The creature closest to her opened an eye and seeing the strangers, titled its head upward with a growl, showing off its sharp teeth. Seconds later it was on two feet and threatening to attack. The wild war noises spitting from its jaws quickly awoke the others from their slumber and Willow's team found themselves face-to-face with danger.

"We mean you no harm. We want to help you return to your world," Willow said, showing both hands in front of her with palms forward.

"Why should we trust you? We have been tricked by the humans before," it hissed.

A black cat appeared by Willow's feet, rubbing against her legs. The creature turned its attention to the animal.

"So, there is hope left then. We understood you were all… disposed of," it said with more of a hissing noise than normal speech.

Kiera looked up and jumped forward, transforming into the largest animal Willow had ever seen. She assumed the guardian's normal form was that of a cat. Now Kiera stood before her, towering well over her height with a face similar to a black panther but a larger body, more like a black lion, if a lion came in an extra large size.

Kiera spoke. "As you can see, we are not, and our keeper isn't either. We will help you return to your home. The humans in this place are not the same ones who hurt you in the past. They are helping us return order. We ask for your friendship and trust, offering ours in return."

"Where were all of you when we were being tortured for generations? We had no friends then!" it exclaimed angrily.

"We did not know what happened to your people. But now we wish to make sure that no atrocities like that happen to other races. There are fewer of us now, but our duty remains to protect the innocent," Kiera answered calmly, flicking her long tail back and forth.

"Then you are too late. Our world was invaded today. It has been left barren of all water and plant life. There is nothing for us there. You cannot help us."

"We can still help you, more than you know. There is a terraformer in our company who can rebuild what was destroyed, perhaps make it even better than before." Kiera stated.

"That is an unusual ability, very powerful, it is. Show us if you wish us to believe." Another creature from the back moved forward to join in the conversation. "Perhaps an apple tree? We have not eaten for some time."

Willow stepped forward and looked at the ground space available. "We will need a clear area. There is no room here for a full-grown tree."

"I can transport us to a location close to the portal if I am allowed," Faramund offered.

"The others of your kind, will you help us to convince them as well? They separated from you in the other direction, correct?" Kiera asked.

"And you know where they are? We will permit you to transport us and show us the power, then we will talk about other details. If you lie, we... take action," a third creature spoke.

Kiera nodded. Faramund asked everyone to gather together in a group before him. He raised his arms and a green fog released from his palms. The coloured gas swirled around them, creating a wall, above, below, beside, until there was nothing but green. The guard said the approximate coordinates of the portal to the creatures' homeland and seconds later the gas was retreating, back into Faramund's hands and new scenery unfolded before their eyes.

They were within walking distance to the portal now, about five minutes away and in an open area, with no signs of human life nearby.

Willow stepped forward, away from the group, and asked an apple tree to grow for her. A small green sprout appeared, slowly getting larger. The group watched as the seedling transformed into a fully grown apple tree, then with blossoms and finally with red apples, sparkling in the sunlight.

Sunlight, Willow thought. She looked at the creatures who were already trying to find a place under the tree for shade. Looking up at the sky, the clouds swirled and a darkness fell over the area, but no rain fell. She quickly apologized for not shading them earlier, when they had first arrived.

The Hannulate were impressed by the girl's actions. She showed respect and great strength. They agreed to return to their homeland, if she would come through and help rebuild a place where they could live. Faramund once again summoned his transportation powers to move himself and a creature who identified itself as Shakine to the location of the other team, where they approached Aslo before confronting the other Hannulate with news of the agreement that had been made. In the end, the whole process took less than thirty minutes before they returned to the portal location. They found Willow and the others at the stone base where the doorway between worlds would open.

Several more apple trees were already grown by the time they arrived, to feed their starving new friends. The creatures ate as if they had never seen food before.

"Those teeth and claws are for… eating fruit?" Mike mused.

"More of a defensive tool they developed to escape captivity. They are naturally a peaceful race," Willow answered. She moved forward to the portal base and looked at the stones which were still embedded in the corners, the same as the one in her homeland. She knew exactly what to do.

"Stand back, this is going to take some electricity," she yelled so that everyone could hear. Holding her palms face-up, she looked directly into the sky above. A gold dust appeared from her hands and swirled up as if caught in a mini tornado high in the clouds. A darkness fell over the area and a rumble turned into a loud boom of thunder. Rain fell over the stone base and a bright flash lit up the sky as a single bolt of lightning hit its mark, releasing the corner stones which sprung into the air forming four corners of a door with a glowing light show of colours in between them.

Willow smiled and turned to Shakine. "Your doorway home." She bowed.

"We would ask for you to go through the portal first, as we agreed," it hissed back.

Willow took a step towards the open portal. Mike grabbed her arm and pulled her back. "You can't actually be serious about going through. There is a good chance something horrible is waiting for you. Keepers are a hot target."

"I gave my word, I would help them rebuild their home. You can't expect them to return there to await certain death with no water sources or food," she answered, pulling her arm away. She barely began moving towards the portal again when she was almost knocked over.

"I will go first," Mike said, pushing in front of her through the doorway.

Willow sighed, following his lead and disappearing into the lights.

Stepping off the stone base a wave of heat hit Willow's face. She took a moment to look around at her surroundings. The land was as described - barren. The earth appeared as golden sand, stripped of all nutrients that could sustain plant life. There were what was left of trees, now dead, similar to that which might be found in the darkest nightmare. The ground around them was scattered with tall, yellow, dead grasses. The Hannulate who remained, huddled under make shift roofs constructed from dead leaves, wood and grass. They looked weak, most likely from lack of food and water. Mike stood beside her taking in the same sights, Shakine and the others behind them.

"You better be a real magic worker to fix all this," Mike said.

"Best get to work."

Willow took a deep breath and let it out slowly, then knelt down, picking up handfuls of dirt. She let the soil pour between her fingers like sand in an hourglass. Moving to a second spot she did the same again, except instead of letting it fall, she took a deep breath and blew the dirt from her hands. Grains of soil flew through the air with only a few granules falling at a time. As they touched the ground, the colour of the earth changed to a deep brown colour, rich and moist. She stood, looking at the ground. Sprouts of life began appearing at equal intervals. Within minutes, an orchard of fully grown apple trees with ripe fruit stood before her. Looking to the skies, she asked the clouds to form, providing cover from the sun.

The returning creatures helped their friends and family over to the living trees so that they could eat and regain their energy. Shakine moved to Willow's side.

"Can you show me where the water pools were before?" she asked.

"There to the north and one larger to the east. There were rivers that flowed between, with dense forestland around," it answered, pointing.

"And what other types of fruit or vegetables would you like for your food source? Are there any plants that are dangerous to your kind that I should not create?" Willow questioned.

The Hannulate listed off preferred foods, as well as those which were not to be included. Willow began her work. Their world was about twice the size of what her own had been. It would take her a while to complete the necessary changes to allow it to sustain life on its own again.

Her first task was to create large storms over the place that the two main bodies of water used to be located. The water would take several hours to pool back up to levels that were previously available. This was an unusual task for her, as her homeland had no such water reserves, but as promised, she complied with the Hannulate requests.

Taking more handfuls of sand she turned her attention to rebuilding the nutrients in the dirt allowing it to sustain life as it had before. She blew the soil granules once again, but this time a gust of wind picked them up and moved them over larger areas. She continued replenishing the earth until all of the world's ground had been transformed.

Willow touched the dirt and like a wave, a lush green grass grew covering all open areas of ground. Fruit trees grew in orchards of peaches, plums, cherries, pears and oranges. Vines grew with grapes and assorted berries. Wild patches of pumpkins, squash and melons appeared as well as patches of tomatoes and legumes. Moving towards the smaller lake of water she turned her attention to the river creating a line of rain clouds connecting through to the larger sea. Along the river beds lush green forests grew with beautiful flowers of all colours and sizes, that would bloom continuously and glowed at night, reminding her of the castle gardens of her own homeland.

The tasks Willow had been asked to perform all required an enormous amount of energy. Expending such power as quickly as she had left her felling a bit weak. She took a moment to relax under a tree beside Mike. Together they shared an apple.

"I have to say, you didn't do too bad, squirt," he admitted, smiling.

She was about to reply when several Hannulate approached them.

"You have created a beautiful world for us. We give you our thanks," Shakine said. "There is something we must show you that we believe you may have interest in. It was left here by the ones who brought the destruction."

One of the creatures moved forward, holding something very small, black and motionless in the palms of its hands.

"Is that... a bird?" Mike asked.

"It is an Allaren, one of the avian guardians," Willow said, moving closer to see the mutilated body. "What did they do to the poor thing?"

"Torture comes in many forms. For those who can beg for death there is escape, but for the immortal, it can continue until the mind breaks as badly as the body. This Allaren is broken. We fear it may never recover, but perhaps you can bring it to a more comfortable place for it to spend eternity," Shakine said with sincerity.

Willow reached her hands out and took the motionless body. Silently she stroked the bird as gently as possible, not wanting to cause any additional pain. She could see from a basic glance over the creature that a wing was missing, bones were broken, including its neck and its eyes were gone, along with a good portion of its feathers.

"What are you doing?" Mike asked.

"I need to bring her back with us," Willow said as she looked up at him, her eyes watering. Placing her hand on the bird's head, she barely heard Aslo and Kiera's voices pleading with her to be careful. There was no going back; she had already asked the motionless guardian to join with her so she could transport it to the main world. The bird began to transform into a sparkling dust that looked like thousands of tiny diamond specks floating in the air, flowing towards her left forearm where a picture began to form. It was an exact picture of the black bird as it had appeared, including all of the injuries.

Willow turned to Mike. "I have to get back now." Her arms clenched tightly around her stomach, the colour quickly fading from her face.

Mike wasted no time. He picked her up and ran through the portal. Appearing on the other side, he yelled for help. Willow was fading in and out of reality, drifting into an unconscious state.

Chapter Nineteen

The world was swirling around... images... colours... lights... voices. Peering left and right, there was nothing familiar. Her reality was distorted... then there was blackness. When Willow opened her eyes, she was somewhere else - somewhere she hadn't been before. Visions surrounded her in all directions, dancing pictures on a circular screen, like a broken movie, flashing an immortal lifetime of experiences, jumping from one to another. The images began speeding up. She spun around trying to keep up, but it was moving too fast. The pictures appeared and disappeared before she knew what they were, as if whoever was playing the movie was looking for a particular scene.

Of course, she thought. *It's you. Your mind must be injured and this is the only way you can communicate with me. Aslo, Kiera, the others - they aren't with us. They must have escaped, good. Well, I am not awake and I know you can't communicate with me in dreams, so I am not asleep. Guess that means I am somewhere in between. So, what is it you are trying to show me, my new friend?*

There was no indication of how long she had been in this state, watching random pictures moving so fast that she didn't have time to make sense of the shapes or voices. Then to her surprise, the pictures began to slow. It was some sort of a fight. There was a woman she recognized, but wasn't exactly sure from where. The woman's hair was strawberry coloured, much lighter than Willow's, but with the same curls. A loud bang sounded. Willow covered her ears as she watched the woman's body tumble to the ground, where she lay without movement. A group of men surrounded her. Willow recognized the uniforms they were wearing as the same as the men wore who attacked her home world just days ago. They took the woman through a hole in the fabric of space into another world. Everything went dark.

Willow could hear voices. At first they were mumbled, but then they became clearer. It was a familiar voice, one from the day when the attack on her home world happened. It was the first man who had come through the rip between realms and caused the destruction.

"Your keeper is injured and we will kill her - unless you surrender yourself to us. We know your partner is still joined with the woman. It would be terrible if he was also lost. Of course you could remain here, but we both know, with no keeper, you would be locked here alone. There would be no way for you to leave and nothing to do but think about how you let your family die. Choose well. You have ten minutes."

Willow could feel exactly what her guest guardian had felt: the indecision, the guilt, the pain and the final surrender. She realized she was seeing, hearing and feeling everything the injured guardian had. The way it had. She was witnessing history.

The vision shifted to another world. They were moving quickly now. It was no longer a picture, but rather Willow was the bird, as if she was there in its place. She was restrained in some way. It felt like heavy chains, although she couldn't see them. The skies and the ground looked as if they were on fire and the seas were shiny and black. They passed several small towns before coming to a forest. The plants and trees all looked dead, but were moving, as if sensing their presence. She shivered, the hairs on the back of her neck standing at attention.

The men transporting her walked in single formation on the road as if scared to come too close to the forest's edge, until they ran into a man going in the other direction. From his appearance, Willow deducted he was some sort of worker. His clothes were dirty and ripped. Signs of age showed on his face and fear was painted as a picture, his eyes the canvas. He lowered his line of sight, bowing his head down, so not to make eye contact with the officers in front of the procession. They, however, were not willing to share the road. The men stopped, knocking the worker to the side. A large vine grabbed the old man and pulled him in, wrapping around him as if tying him to the trunk of the tree. Willow clenched her eyes closed tightly at the horrific sight. The bark started to engulf him, bit by bit. The tree was eating him alive. The man screamed for help, pain resonating in his voice, as the soldiers just stood by and laughed. Then a silence fell over them. The old man was gone. The group started walking again as if nothing had happened.

At the end of the forest was a mountain of black rock with a single smooth road carved in a circular motion. Along the way to the top, they passed several plateaus. One resembled a marketplace with items for everyday use, probably where the old man had been coming from. The others looked more like the barracks in William's camp. At the top was a grand entrance way to what looked like a castle, built out of the same rock as the mountain.

The stone doors were open and people inside were cheering, celebrating, welcoming them. She could hear echoes of *good job, well done sir* and *caught another one, brilliant isn't he?* The group stopped before a man and woman who dressed as if they felt themselves important, in fine silk clothes of bright colours, adorned with animal furs - both wore excessive amounts of jewels. The man stepped forward.

"Well done, my son! Well done indeed! Another filthy creature." He turned to the others standing around in admiration. "A toast to my son!" He lifted his cup. "We protect the worlds from oppression and confinement. This beast took away our freedom and now we take away the same from it, so it can no longer impose its will on innocent people." The man drank.

The room broke out in a chorus of "Hail, King Cornelius! Long live the king." Then Willow was moving again. This time to a set of winding stone stairs. She lost count of how many levels they went down, leading her to conclude that they must be inside the mountain. At the very bottom were what appeared to be rooms, but made out of some sort of glass on one side and rock on the other. She could see inside the rooms, each housing guardians and keepers, all injured, worn, tired and sad. In one room she saw the strawberry-haired lady.

"You said you would let them go if I surrendered, honour the agreement, prince." Willow found she was the one saying the words - as if scripted.

"No, you are mistaken." The prince laughed. "I said I wouldn't kill them and I won't. Anything else is fair game."

"We have done you no harm. Let them go," she pleaded.

"No harm? No harm? You destroyed our world, our people. You tried to oppress us. You deviated from the true path of a guardian. You chose to impose your will on others by forcing them into worlds of your choice. If it weren't for Apopp and his kind, you might have gotten away with it. They will help us regain our dignity and rights," he said then turned to an empty cell. "Put it in there and if it gives you any trouble, hurt it and its keeper."

He disappeared back up the steps. Willow was cold, sad, afraid - so many emotions were running through her at once. Every so often, a few guards would enter and accuse her of plotting something, then hit her with sticks which gave off bolts of energy. Welts formed on her skin from the abuse. Gasping for air, her eyes stung until tears flowed freely down the sides of her face. Hours faded to days and time passed. The guards continued their attacks daily, leaving enough time between beatings for her to heal herself. Then something changed.

The prince returned. "We need some information. My Father, Cornelius, would like his sister returned. She was taken from us when the division occurred. If you can tell us where she is... well, we can be lenient on you and the woman."

Willow found herself speaking the bird's words again. "Even if I knew who you were speaking of, I would not tell you. No creature deserves the daily torture you inflict."

"She is my aunt. Why would I hurt her?" Joseph asked, pacing.

"Jealousy, prejudice... I am not sure why you torture any of us or how any person could be so cold as to gain pleasure by inflicting pain on others."

The prince stormed out of the room, slamming the door behind him. There was no question, she had enraged him. A shiver ran down her spine, knowing she would pay a price for refusing to answer his questions. He returned a few minutes later with several men and a case of tools.

"Wrong answer. Perhaps your keeper will speak to save you," he said, smiling. "Since you don't want to talk, maybe you shouldn't be able to."

The men secured her with chains to a rock wall as Joseph removed knives and pliers from the case. Within seconds, she felt pain - its effects were so severe that even some of her senses hid from it, leaving her blind and deaf. It was everywhere, swallowing her whole until nothing else existed. She begged for relief, not knowing how long she could continue to live with the torture. It felt like cycles passed, each filled with nothing except continuous agony. Her mind began shutting down, unable to handle any more.

Chapter Twenty

"Quickly, move her to the infirmary." William motioned to Mike to bring Willow's limp body to a bed where they could give her medical attention. Searching the camp, they needed to find both Victoria and conventional medical help. Returning with their on-site doctor and nurse, they were greeted by thirteen black cats.

"What has happened? Why have you separated from her?" William asked, his eyes bulging.

"We can help more from here. She is weak. We don't know what is going to happen. Right now, she is neither awake nor asleep, and comfortable, but soon she could feel all the guardian bird experienced, and share in it. Such torture is too much for anyone to endure," Aslo answered. "If her body shows signs of pain or stress, she needs to be sedated. We must ensure she is asleep. It is the only way to break the telepathic connection between them."

The door flung open and Victoria ran in, followed by her three brothers. Without speaking the young girl ran to the bedside and placed her hands on Willow's arm. Silence fell over the room, no one wanting to disturb the healer's concentration. After several minutes, Victoria turned around looked at her brothers and shook her head. Tears formed in the young girl's eyes. Jessie stepped forward, putting his arms around his sister just in time. She burst into sobs. Everyone knew there was nothing she could do. Willow's health now rested in the hands of the human medical team, which consisted of a young husband and wife, Richard and Mary.

The doctor and nurse proceeded to hook up machines and wires to monitor the patient, took scans and ran tests. It would be hours before any news would be available. Aslo and his family insisted on staying to watch over their keeper, while the others returned to the main house to tell the rest of the camp what had happened.

It would take the next hour for William to try to explain to the others in the command centre the events that occurred as best as he could. The mood was solemn and the air went stale. Everyone tried to come up with ideas on how to heal the young girl lying in the medical building. Not knowing what could be done was ominous. So many questions needed answers.

"How did she manage to bond with an avian guardian when she is a feline guardian keeper?" Diana asked. "That has never been done before. I thought cross-guardian race bonding was impossible."

"There are a lot of things we don't yet understand," William answered. "How could she carry not just more than two guardians, but fourteen? No keeper has ever been able to heal their counterpart before. How will she do that?" He rubbed the back of his neck. "There are harder questions to ask as well. How could she escape from a broken mind? What will her mind be like if she does wake? Will she carry the same scars as the guardian she is trying to heal?" He paused for a moment. "We just don't know the answers."

Mike noticed a boy sitting alone at the table in the corner. He was looking at various books, but never seemed to open any and didn't appear to be concerned at all. He nudged William, motioning in that direction. Everyone turned to look at the boy.

"Nathan," Diana said. "Are you alright? I know you and Willow are close."

"Yes, Gran, I am fine, and she will be too," he answered. "It's in the book."

"Which book? What do you mean?" Mike asked.

"*The Portal Prophecies*," Nathan answered. "Prophecy number twenty-three, although I don't think they are in any particular order."

Diana walked over and picked up the book. She rubbed the cover as if for luck and then opened it, flipping the pages to the exact prediction her grandson spoke of and read it out loud:

A race forgotten shall appear again, in need of intervention

One soul so pure shall see the cause and alter what could be,

Devastation averted, a world now saved,

One life shall be the reward, within its mind a soul has been lost

And another shall fall to slumber, the signs on doors to show the way,

With rest and time life shall renew and mind shall mend

All shall emerge with questions answered

Life preserved and new hope granted.

"Once you figure out what the wording means, you can see it applies to what happened today. The problem is figuring out what they all mean before they come true. That might be difficult. It is something we should work on, though. Some of the stuff in there sounds pretty bad, so if we could avoid them happening it would be beneficial," Nathan said.

"The problem with prophecies is that the future isn't set in stone. They guide you as to what could happen, but we don't know if something we do causes them to happen or stops it. Not an exact science," Clairity said, chewing on her fingernail.

"The ones who wrote this book felt these particular predictions would be something needed in the future. They were insistent that I record them. No explanations were given. I was just told that one day it would be important. They are the only prophecies our world ever recorded on paper," Diana added.

"You didn't ask what they meant?" Mike asked.

"No, it was before the war. I was just a bookmaker. It was my job. There was no reason for me to ask." Diana rubbed her arms as if she were cold, although there was no chill and a fire was raging in the fireplace.

William flipped through the book. "There are a lot of prophecies in here. Do we know if any of them have happened already? Ones that we can cross off the list?"

"We know the one about leaving our home world happened. It's how we got here. Willow deciphered it." Diana took the book and flipped the pages again then read the passage out loud:

When the blue flames engulf the land,

Only one whose will is steadied by that discovered

Can break that which is set in stone to escape.

She handed the large book back to the guard, who examined the page. "From that she figured out how to open a portal?" he asked.

"No, there were other things too, like our dreams. They were about the last minutes on our world. Everything was the same except, in the dreams, there was a massive storm over the forest... and I think she mentioned another prophecy. I don't know where she heard about it, but it was about her. Something about being different from birth and needing to figure things out for herself." Ashlyn had been withdrawn through the whole meeting, as if thinking. "Maybe I could contact her. If she is asleep I mean, in her dreams... make sure she is okay."

"We aren't sure she is asleep at the moment. If we sedate her... it's an option we would be willing to discuss." William looked around the room for any reaction from the others.

"Is that dangerous?" Diana asked.

"We don't know, but we do know that if she seems to be in pain, we will have to induce sleep to calm her."

"You should make her sleep, the prophecy says so. It is the only way!" Nathan exclaimed, not believing they were discussing this. He headed for the door.

"Slow down, dude," Mike said, grabbing the boy. "The doctor is running some tests first. We will have the results soon. Aslo and Kiera are watching her. If she looks stressed they will make sure she is sedated. Okay?"

Nathan nodded and sat down again.

"So Nathan, Diana - you two should head up a team to try and figure out some of the prophecies. Look for patterns or indications of something that could be happening at the moment or in the near future first. There are too many to do every single one at once. Eventually we will need to know them all, though. Pick a team to help you... and call a meeting when you have anything to brief us on. Sarah, you continue working on the maps and location of missing stones for portals. I would sleep a lot better if we had them in our possession. Work in shifts so everyone gets some rest and we have fresh eyes. Anyone not on a team please head to bed, tomorrow we start training for your abilities and self-defence."

William rubbed the stubble growing on his face. A couple of days passed since he had time to shave. Looking around the room, he could see several of the other men were in the same position. *It's definitely going to be a long haul this time,* he thought to himself.

He motioned to Ashlyn and Mike to join him and the three headed back over to the medical centre. There was no change in Willow's condition and the test results weren't back yet. Suddenly, her body began to shake and twitch. Aslo jumped up, eyes widened and focused on the redhead.

"She is in pain!" the guardian exclaimed. "She needs sedation now. There is no time to wait for test results. You have to trust me. She must sleep."

The medical team had seen enough strange things happen in their time at the camp, that they knew better than to argue with a talking cat. A cat, who might one day be the only thing standing between their world as it was and complete destruction. They prepared a sedative to make Willow sleep.

Ashlyn lay down in the bed beside her friend. "Could I have a light sedative so I can try to reach Willow in her dreams?" she asked.

Ashlyn only discovered the gift of dreamwalking in the past few weeks and was still experimenting with what that meant. She knew she could call someone close to her into her dreams if she was emotional, especially scared, although so far she only contacted her mother. Willow was able to call her for help once as well. They shared the same dream - a foretelling of the devastation of their home world. She wasn't exactly sure if she could enter her friend's dreams or not yet. This would be a completely new experience, but she was determined to try.

Mary handed a tiny white pill to Ashlyn. "This will only help you fall asleep. You will be able to wake up if necessary within a couple of hours."

Richard gave some form of medication to Willow through what he called a needle. Ashlyn heard them say her heart rate and blood pressure were already returning to normal levels and she showed no more signs of pain or stress. *Time to go in,* Ashlyn thought to herself as she swallowed the pill. Her body flopped back on the bed. She was worried her nervousness might hinder her ability to sleep and was considering other ways to help herself relax enough to drift off. She sighed, blinking her sight into focus. Everything was white for as far as she could see.

She was asleep. Now all she needed to do was find Willow. She called to her a few times, concentrating as hard as she could on her friend. How she looked. How she talked. Glancing around, the room was white, the walls were white, her dress was white. She mused at how her hair had chosen its final colour in the last two weeks and it too was white, although with pastel pink streaks. It was perfectly straight and hung down just above her shoulders, except for bangs which covered her forehead. She was happy that it no longer changed with her moods. Her hair colour now highlighted her facial features perfectly. She was petite with grey eyes, so light they were almost silver colour, a tiny nose, perfectly pink cheeks and small red lips.

Walking forward, she noticed up ahead closed doors were forming before her eyes, hundreds of them. She began turning knobs, but every one she tried was locked. Frustration set in. She ran frantically from door to door, trying to find one she could open, but none would. After about thirty doors, she stopped. Bending over at the waist, she gasped for air. Slowly her red flushed face returned to normal and her heart rate slowed.

Now what? she asked herself, knowing there would be no answer. She was at a loss. How was she supposed to know which door led to her friend? Her small-framed body slid to the ground and she pulled her knees to her chest. She sighed. Tilting her head upwards, something caught her attention. Getting up, she moved close to the door in front of her. There on the knob was a green gem, a jade. The prophecy had told her what to do.

Of course, she thought. On each door there was a sign indicating who was behind it. A symbol: something that spoke to her; something she could understand. There would be a door for everyone she knew who was currently sleeping. Unfortunately, that was most of the camp, so she would have a lot of doors to examine in order to find the one that led to Willow.

After examining several doors, she came across one with a black bird on the handle. *I wonder,* she thought, *maybe*… She turned the door knob and it opened. Stepping through, Ashlyn found herself in another white room with a single door in it. On the floor was a black bird.

"Are you trying to go through there?" Ashlyn asked.

"I can't. Someone has to open the door and let me through," the bird answered. "It's the door you are looking for. You can help her. Don't leave her alone. She needs someone to protect her."

Ashlyn moved closer to the door and examined the symbols on the handle. They were changing so fast, she couldn't make out what any of them were.

"What does this mean?" she asked, pointing to the signs.

"The girl is someone to whom everything and nothing applies. She chooses her own path and then can create it. A strength which, until now, had never been seen. It is unclear how far she can stretch the reality the rest of us are bound to."

Ashlyn reached for the handle and was shocked when it turned easily. She opened it slowly and turned back to the bird still standing behind her as if she wanted to ask a question.

"She isn't ready to see me yet. I am here if you need anything. She will need to talk to you about things she has seen... felt. She needs a friend she already knows," The bird explained.

Ashlyn walked through, closing the door behind her. The room she entered was still white without any furniture, but sitting in the middle was Willow. She was wearing a white dress, which made her deep red curly hair stand out and her skin tone look much darker than normal.

"Willow!"

The girl in the middle of the room looked up at her with relief written all over her face. "How did you find me?"

"Getting better at this, I guess." Ashlyn smiled. "Are you okay?"

"I saw them... the ones who destroyed our home. They were the same ones who hurt the guardian bird." The colour quickly disappeared from Willow's face as she thought back to the images. "I saw their home world, where the others are being held. They have our people and guardians locked up in rooms. They hurt them; torture them. We have to save them." Her mind wandered to the boy named Lance. She hadn't seen him there, but she knew he was a part of that world.

"How? They have an army, Willow. We aren't strong enough."

"I don't know yet, but there has to be a way. We can't leave them and that will be where they took the survivors from the attack on our homeland as well."

"Did you see them?" Ashlyn asked.

"No, what I saw happened before that. It was what the bird saw and felt. The torture that was inflicted on the poor thing. I thought I was going to die from the pain," Willow explained.

"I think you almost did. Richard, the doctor, gave you a sedative so you would sleep. Aslo said that would help you."

"Oh." A smile came over Willow's face. "Of course, they can't enter my dreams. But I can't stay asleep forever."

"I know. We are working on it." Ashlyn thought about telling her friend about what was outside the door she came through, but decided it was better to wait.

"Did you feel that?" Willow asked, standing up to look around.

"Feel what?" Ashlyn began to answer when the room shook like they were in an earthquake. "Whoa!" she said, putting her arms out to catch her balance.

The room shook again, this time harder than before, then it started to change. A fireplace appeared, complimented by comfortable chairs and a soft rug on the floor. The changes were coming closer and the white room was disappearing. Then a boy dressed all in black appeared. He had blue and black hair with bangs that hung down over his piercing blue eyes. He smiled at Ashlyn and said, "Sorry, private party," while waving.

Ashlyn felt her body propelling backwards. The door opened, throwing her out before slamming behind her. She could hear Willow scream. Looking up, she saw she was on the floor and the bird was looking over her.

"Are you okay? The girl?" it asked her.

"I don't know," Ashlyn described what happened during the visit.

"Lance, the boy you described, is one of the princes in the world that we are fighting. This is dangerous. You need to open the door again and help her."

"I can't, he knew I was there. He won't let me back in." Salty tears cascaded down her pale face, kissing her lips.

"Then let me in!" the bird yelled.

Ashlyn looked at it. "I can do that? How?"

"You can do more than you know, child, you just haven't tried. This world belongs to you, with practice you can do anything," the bird explained.

"So the boy, Lance… he is a dreamwalker too? That is how he made the room?"

"Yes, their whole family has the gift and they have had many years to practice," the bird said. "Just open the door and tell it you are allowing me to enter."

Chapter Twenty-One

Everything happened so quickly. One minute Willow was talking to her friend, Ashlyn, and now here she was standing in a lavish room face-to-face with the boy from the forest. His piercing blue eyes stared straight into hers, as if seeing her soul.

"Hello," he said with a smile. "I was wondering if we would ever meet again. Tell me, how did you escape the necrid fire?"

"How... how did you get into my dream? What happened to my friend?" Willow barked.

"How?" he laughed. "You called me here. Actually, seems a little unfair that you know my name and I don't know yours."

Willow realized earlier she thought of him for a brief moment. "Lance... your name. I was thinking of the forest and what happened. That was enough to call you here?"

"Yes, but how exactly do you know my name?" Lance moved to the back of a chair and rested against it waiting for a reply.

"I heard someone call you in the forest when I was running away," she said.

"So, back to the beginning. You know my name, but what is yours?" Lance pressed for some answers.

"Why did you do it? Why did you destroy my home?" Willow asked, ignoring the prince's question.

"That is a long story. Why don't you tell me how you escaped?" he asked, getting a bit aggravated.

That seemed to be an ongoing theme for her with boys; she aggravated them. Willow's mind turned to a similar conversation she had with Mike. After remembering the duct tape, she decided that she needed to come up with an answer for the prince.

"I… don't know," she answered with a sigh. "I know I was in an accident and a doctor sedated me so I could rest. If you had let my friend stay longer, she might have told me more." She wasn't really lying about that, so even if he had the ability to sense an untruth, he wouldn't question what she said. She wasn't about to give him more information than she needed to. He might have been cute, but she wasn't stupid.

"So where are you?" he asked.

"I... don't know." Again, she wasn't lying; she never asked where exactly she was. Thinking back she realized how odd that was, and she also didn't know where her body was either; maybe a medical facility of some sort, maybe a room, or maybe lying in a field.

"You don't know anything?" he mused.

"My friend… she was trying to see if I was okay. That's why she was here to contact me." This all not only sounded true, it was all true.

"That sucks." He moved around and sat in a chair by the fire.

"Your turn," Willow said, moving closer. "Why did you do it?"

"I told you, it's a long story."

"I have nowhere to go," she answered.

"Okay, well a long time ago, there were six ancient races: the serpents, the spiders, the sea creatures, the cats, the birds and a dog-type animal. They monitored the world and called themselves guardians. The guardians possessed... powers - abilities stronger than any other creature alive. They watched over things, but their policy was not to get involved in the world - to let other beings live out their lives without influence.

"Three of the races felt things weren't being handled correctly. They split off and decided that to keep things the way they wanted, they would have to confine all worlds - separate them from each other, especially locking in serpents, spiders and sea creatures in different places... to ensure their way would not be challenged. They kidnapped people from the stronger realms, thinking that would stop any uprisings.

"The serpents were the original dreamwalkers and contacted different leaders among men to find one who could help them stop the oppression which was being forced on us all. They chose my father. Together they began working on a way to make the walls between worlds disappear. At first just a small hole was all that could be managed. Knowing how much time it was going to take to complete the task, the serpent leader, Apopp, sent through a chalice of his venom for the King and Queen, my parents, to drink. It granted them and their family line new abilities and extended life.

"Now we can create an opening for long enough to enter and search worlds for the rogue guardians and make sure they have nowhere to hide. Our goal is to eradicate them, break down the walls that were put up and ultimately protect all beings from them."

Willow couldn't believe what she was hearing. "You actually believe that?" she shrieked without thinking. Ignoring the anger building in his eyes, she continued. "It doesn't make any sense."

"Really," he answered. "What doesn't make sense?"

"You say your goal is to save people from oppression and destruction. Yet you enter worlds uninvited, kill or imprison the people, force them to join your army and do what you want. Then you destroy everything in their homeland."

"It's the only way to find them, to imprison the ancients that are still hiding. We need to ensure they don't stand in our way or destroy any other families," he yelled loud enough to make her stumble backwards.

She caught her balance. "How many families are you destroying by doing this? How many in my world did you kill or take away? How do you even know these serpents are telling you the truth? How do you know what you are doing is right? What gives you the right to decide?"

"We are setting right an injustice that was done to us and all other creatures. We were the victims, imprisoned in a small world to ensure we could not progress further and challenge them for power."

"You're the victims?" Willow yelled. "You kill parents and children and take away free will from others for what? To ensure your world advances in power? To help a bunch of snakes take over all existence? Just because you feel you were wronged, doesn't give you the right to wrong others or take life away from anyone or anything."

"My father was there. He saw what they did. Lives were lost. My Aunt Diana was taken by them as their prisoner. If it were you, wouldn't you want your family back? My father longs for the day he will see his beloved sister again," Lance argued.

Willow snorted. "Yeah, it is me. I want my family back. I guess I need a hero world to go get them back for me and kill my oppressors. Oh, sorry, that would be you."

"You don't understand." Lance said, his hands forming fists.

Willow interrupted. "Yes, I do. You are doing exactly what you say was done to you, except to other worlds and then justifying your actions by saying you are stopping it from happening again." Anger took over. Clear thought was no longer an option. "And when I get out of here, I am going to find my friends and family and set them free. I will spend my lifetime making sure you and your sick family never hurt anyone ever again."

"You stupid girl," he said, grabbing her arm hard. "Do you think you can challenge an empire? What is to stop me from killing you right now? Do you know what happens when you die in your sleep? You die in real life, too. Our minds can't distinguish between that sort of trauma."

She broke free from his grasp and slapped him, but he was more amused than hurt by it. His eyes laughed at her - mocked her. Still, through all of this, there was something about the boy that excited her. He was dangerous and made her feel free... alive.

The room shook and both of them stumbled backwards. The scenery was changing again. Within moments, they were standing on a field surrounded by forests. Looking up, there was what looked like a large bird flying over them.

"That's... impossible," Lance muttered.

"What is it?" Willow asked. It was unlike anything she had ever seen. Its wingspan alone must have been three or four times the size of the largest man she knew. It was gliding majestically above them, circling as if searching for prey, yet she didn't feel afraid, but she could tell Lance was. The young prince took a few steps backwards and the bird landed between the two of them.

"I recognize that scar. How did you get here? Your mind was broken."

"It has been healed," the bird answered. "And I was let in by someone who cares for this girl. Now it is time for you to go." The bird opened its wings and flapped them, creating a wind that blew the boy back through the doorway he entered through. The door slammed behind him and he was gone.

"Are you alright?" the bird asked.

Willow was still unsure. "Yes," she answered, "but who are you... are you the guardian I helped?"

"Yes, my name is Shelby. I owe you a great debt. It is an honour to meet the one the prophecies spoke of."

"You know of the prophecies?" Willow asked.

"Yes, sight is an ability of all avian guardians, which we can extend to the person we are joined with. For the clairvoyant, it enhances their powers. That is how many prophecies came to be, which meant at least one of us was present and experienced predictions as they happened. There was also one visionary named Iris. She shared her predictions -

what she saw, with my keeper. They were the ones who decided to record the book, *The Portal Prophecies*."

"So you could tell us what some of them mean?"

"No." Shelby seemed to laugh. "The interpretation of the words of a prophecy are important. They can mean one thing to you and apply, but they can mean another to someone else and also apply. While you are the one spoken of in some prophecies, they do not all have a message for you. It is important you understand that. There are others who must contribute to your goals as well. You are not alone, nor are you meant to be alone."

"What about what happened to you? Will there be a time when I can safely wake up? Is there something I can do to help you?" Willow asked.

"You have already done all that you can. I am healing, it won't be long now. You are a brave girl with a real talent for bending rules. Thank you for saving me. Now we must rest. Think of no one, my friend, just sleep."

Chapter Twenty-Two

Ashlyn sat up instantly, as if she had never been asleep or sedated. She had no idea how long she was in the dream world. Time there was much different from real life. Minutes asleep could be hours awake and vice versa. It wasn't morning yet and, to her surprise, Mike was asleep on an extra bed beside her. Probably some macho protection thing he came up with, to keep the sleeping beauties safe. The thought made her chuckle a little. Then she looked over at her friend and wondered what was happening. Had the bird been able to help, or was Willow trapped with that boy?

Walking over, she looked at the picture on the sleeping girl's arm. The bird looked different. It wasn't as mangled anymore. It was healthier - healing. But would Willow be safe until it healed completely? Could people be hurt and die in a dream? She didn't know the answers, but figured she needed to wake Mike up to gather the others together to discuss what she discovered.

Ashlyn learnt quickly that waking Mike from a sound sleep could be dangerous. He grabbed her and almost hit her before he realized there wasn't a threat. For the first time, she wondered what had happened to him. She heard the stories from the others about their experiences with unusual creatures and how it affected them. Something horrible must have been in Mike's past, she thought, something that made him so subconsciously aware of his surroundings that he could perceive a threat.

Mike released his grip and apologized. Ashlyn was quick to tell him her news.

"It can't wait till morning, a couple more hours? Everyone will be tired," Mike said, yawning.

"No," she insisted. "It can't wait. Willow may still be in danger, as well as others."

"Others?" Mike seemed a bit confused. "Okay, I will wake the troops. We can meet in the command centre." He walked out, brushing his short hair with his hand while heading towards the building William was sleeping in.

Ashlyn sat for a moment on the edge of Willow's bed and whispered, "Hang in there," to her, then added, "both of you," looking at the picture of the black bird on her arm. For a moment, she thought she saw it wink, maybe because it had eyes again, or the light was playing tricks on her. Thinking about it, a smile formed in the corners of her lips. She winked back, before heading over to the command centre.

To her surprise, the main room of the house was already bustling with activity. The prophecy team was busy at work, two people would sleep in the back bedroom or on the couch, while the others read and tried to decipher meanings from the ancient text. It wasn't going well from what Ashlyn could tell, but at least there was good news. Nathan was right. The prophecy they discussed yesterday was about Willow sleeping, but there was also a message for her as well. It told her to follow the signs on the doors. That was what led her to Willow.

Behind her, the door opened. The others began filing in, some yawning, some still in night clothes. She was particularly amused by the fuzzy pink bunny slippers Sarah was wearing. It was such a contrast from the usual orderly appearance she had grown accustomed to over the past few days. Ashlyn wasn't the only one who noticed. Mike was already teasing her. Sarah's face turned numerous shades of red.

In the corner, Zsiga was standing at the coffee maker. It had fascinated him since he first was shown what it was used for. Since then, he insisted on making fresh pots of coffee every time he was in the command centre. The first few pots were less than desirable and the others, to be nice, pretended to drink them, then suggested he use a little less coffee next time, throwing it out when he left. Now, he wasn't too bad at it. Maybe practice did make perfect. The smell of fresh coffee was already filling the air, luring several people who were half-asleep. They followed the aroma with mugs in hand waiting for a cup of instant wake-up.

The three portal guards were all interested in the technology of this world. They hadn't been exposed to anything even remotely similar to the devices and machines they were finding here and spent most of their free time learning about how different things functioned.

William stood in front of the large map board by the fireplace. He called for the attention of everyone. Once the last few found seats, the guardians, Aslo, Kiera and their family, were lying comfortably by the fire in their house cat forms and everyone looked ready, he motioned for Ashlyn to come to the front of the room and tell them what she learnt.

She began to explain the story of her night with the prophecy and its hidden meaning for her. The deciphering team was very interested in the information. This meant that every prophecy could mean several things to different people and perhaps needed multiple interpretations. Then Ashlyn told them about Willow. How she was: what she experienced: and the images of the world where their friends and family were being held.

A slight grumble erupted at the thought that the young keeper might want to attack a world with an army that could defeat large forces when they were so few.

"We should wait to disagree until she is here to tell us how and when," Ashlyn said. "But our friends, our family, if they are imprisoned and need us, I will stand by Willow and try to help them."

"I have a feeling there is more information somewhere, a prophecy or something we are missing that will tie everything together about who we are fighting and why. I think that will help us decide where we are heading," Clairity added.

She had been Willow's best friend since birth and there was no question of where she would stand in a fight. Not that she knew exactly how much help she would be. Her gift was sight, but it wasn't fully developed yet. In fact, she still just had *feelings* about things that always rang true. The last few days, she often thought that since heading into her sixteenth cycle the only thing she developed was a permanent hair colour. It settled on midnight black - the colour Willow always insisted she liked the best.

"I did learn something else from the guardian bird," Ashlyn said. "Each of us still has a long way to go to discover what we can do. Our abilities can extend as far as we choose to expand them, literally limitless. We all need practice."

"Agreed. We can begin training as soon as possible - today even. Unfortunately, we are limited to lessons we know or have been taught and, from what I understand, there wasn't much mentoring going on back home," William said.

"I can help with that," Malarchy offered, causing an uproar of whispers. "I know I made mistakes, but long ago I was an original Council member and I helped set up classes to train people. I want to make up for my mistakes. I want to help. I want to see my son again."

He began to weep. Everyone else was at a loss for words. Malarchy had never displayed any emotion to them before and now this, such sadness and regret. They almost felt sorry for him. Many of them were not sure if they should feel contempt or pity for the man who was partly responsible for their world's destruction.

"Fine," William said. "You can work with Mike and pick some people to help you set up training later today. We need to advance everyone's abilities, as well as learn hand-to-hand combat and weapon use. Now, what about our Willow? Where did you leave things with her?"

Ashlyn's face drained of colour as she retold the story of how she was kicked out of the dream by the boy and what the bird told her about him. She explained that she let the guardian into her dream to protect her.

"That is what happened to me." Jade spoke for the first time since leaving their homeland. "Except it was Prince Joseph. He was supposed to take me away, just me. We were going to start a new life together. He seemed so caring. I believed him. I know that doesn't change what I did and I don't expect anyone to ever forgive me, nor will I ever forgive myself. I close my eyes and I see him killing my mother over and over." Her words faded off into sobs.

Neil snorted a *Figures* in the background, which everyone chose to ignore.

"Isn't that defeating the purpose? We sedated her to get away from the guardian," Mike asked, directing attention away from the obviously emotionally unstable girl and her disgruntled wannabe boyfriend.

It was Aslo that answered. "From what she has told us, I believe the avian guardian has healed to the point where it can put the torment experienced behind it. A most unusual occurrence. Until now, it was thought a guardian needed to self-heal, if it was to heal at all. Did anyone happen to look at the picture on her arm to see if the image changed at all?"

"Yes," Ashlyn answered. "The bird is much better looking. It has eyes and the wing has regrown."

"Then we need only worry about the boy. Bad things can still happen in dreams and, if the mind believes them, some can be as real as if they were happening while awake," Aslo added.

"How do we help her, then?" William asked.

"We trust that she is strong enough to get through it and that she has some help. Hopefully, it won't be too long before she is awake again. I suggest we discontinue the sedatives," Kiera, the other feline guardian, answered this time. "Until then, train as hard as you can. We will also help with development classes as needed."

"Okay, trainers, pick your helpers and everyone, I suggest we change, have something to eat and meet in the training field to discuss your abilities in a couple of hours," William said, ending the meeting.

Chapter Twenty-Three

It was a few hours before the training field was set up and ready to use. Much of the training would be based on physical skills and exploring uses of different physical talents. For those like Ashlyn, whose abilities could not be practised on a field, Mike provided different forms of combat lessons.

Mike chose Sarah, Iskander, Faramund and Zsiga to help him, as well as a couple of other men from his world, to replace the portal guards while they trained their other skills on the field, if necessary. Malarchy was with Aslo and Kiera, as well as William and Diana on his team, trying to help advance magical skills.

The first step was to explore what exactly everyone could do and figure out possible uses and advancement of their different talents.

Malarchy began with Ashlyn, since she already saw firsthand how her abilities could advance and the things she could do in the future with training and hard work.

Ashlyn started by explaining what she could do up until that point and that her next steps were to locate people faster, change scenery, bring other people in and out of dreams and learn how to control the dream itself. This gave each of the others an idea of what they were trying to figure out about their own gifts.

Clairity offered to be next. "I have feelings, sometimes as to a place I should be or whether things are true or not. I think I should be working towards full prophecies and lie detection. Ironically enough, I have a feeling there is also a physical aspect to my abilities I have not yet experienced, although I do not know what it is."

"Very good," Malarchy said. "The two of you would be good exercise partners. During the day, work on simple mind reading in your extra time and at night, work on dreamwalking and exploration. For now though, I think you both should join up with Mike and work on self-defence basics. We have already seen the physical aspect of the attacks of our enemy and should be prepared for it."

Aslo and Kiera agreed and the two girls headed off to join Mike. Nathan was the next to step forward.

"Pretty much everyone knows I can read books without opening them and very quickly. I can also transfer the entire book to another person - word for word with full comprehension. Since I am only twelve, I have four cycles to develop my gift. Your time would probably be spent better on other people. I can continue working on the book of prophecies."

Diana smiled at how grown up her grandson had become over the past few weeks. She saw so much of his father in him and was proud. There was no doubt in anyone's mind that the boy needed to continue his work inside the command centre. With their approval, he headed back to his table and books.

Jessie stepped forward. "I have extraordinary strength and speed. I would expect I need to develop how to use both at the same time. I may be able to move a large object, but if someone is attacking me I need to be able to evade them at the same time. I am not sure there will be anything other than brute force that I can develop, but I also think I will be naturally proficient in most forms of combat."

"Excellent, why don't you test that idea with Mike's team and see what happens?" Aslo commented and the others agreed.

Pete stepped forward. "Things can't hit me," he said. "I mean like weapons. It's like I have an invisible shell around me. Not very exciting, I am afraid."

Aslo moved close to the boy and examined him. "This is the best news we have heard. Your next step is to extend a shield to protect others and, if I am correct, one day you may be able to create containment fields and even enforce the barriers between the worlds which have grown thin. I will walk over with you to talk to Mike. I would like to see you trying to protect people against physical attacks."

Pete looked quite proud of himself as the two walked off to join the other team. He had always been the understudy to his two other brothers being the shortest of the three, albeit still taller than most men. He was, for lack of a better description, the one in between, not really spectacular in any way, but now he was finally getting some recognition and stepping out from behind his brothers' shadows.

Malarchy motioned for Dezi to go next, thinking the triplet brothers would stick together, but was surprised by his response.

"I don't know yet," Dezi said, looking at the ground. It was unusual for him to shy away from anything and, it was even more curious that he was the only brother of the three that hadn't figured out what his ability was. "I think I should just work on combat for now." Without waiting for an answer, he headed over to the other team, leaving them wondering what happened.

The next to step forward brought with him an unnerving silence. It was Neil, the one who everyone now knew as *the boy who ripped open the space between worlds and let the invaders in*. It wasn't his fault, of course. He was bewitched by Jade into believing they were running away together to start a new life. He wasn't sure which was worse: being known as a weapon of destruction or Jade's love-struck pawn.

"I can bend the reality of items," he mumbled quietly. "I can rearrange the way they appear, their texture. I can change space. After stretching the barrier between worlds thin enough to break, I am not sure if there is anything else I will advance to. It was terrible, but still sort of epic."

"That it was!" Malarchy answered. "That it was! But, there is always room for advancement. For instance, you can change the way this rock looks and whether it is rough or smooth, but could you make it appear as a rock, but feel like a sponge? On a side note, let's stay away from bending space and making holes for now and concentrate on something a little smaller. Perhaps Diana could work with you on that?"

Diana nodded and headed off away from the crowd to work individually on Neil's talents, and keep an eye on what he was directing his attention to so no further *accidents* happened.

Malarchy turned his attention to his daughter, the only remaining family member he had. "Jade, darling, can you tell us what your talents are?"

"Nothing worth anything," she said without looking up. She hadn't looked anyone in the face since the last day on their home world. "I... can make myself look good. I can convince people to do what I want sometimes. That's it."

"Illusion can be a strong gift if you work on it. In one form or another, your mother and I have the same gift," Malarchy said.

"Had."

"Sorry, dear?" he answered. The tone of his voice told everyone he had forgiven the girl for what happened, or perhaps blamed himself. Either way, she was his daughter and he loved her unconditionally. It didn't matter to him what she had done.

"Mother had that gift. She is dead now... and it's my fault. There is no illusion in that." Jade ran off back to the building in which she had been sleeping for the past few days.

Victoria moved forward and tugged on Malarchy's sleeve. "I can practice healing anyone who gets hurt in practice combat if you like. I am still learning, though, and have a long way to go before I am sixteen."

"A wonderful idea. You head right over there and tell Uncle Mike you will be assisting with the wounded." He flashed a devious smile at Mike.

Victoria skipped away happy as could be to her new job. After a few looks from Mike for sending him the young girl to deal with for the day, Malarchy continued on. Looking over his list, Faramund was excused to help with combat. They already discussed his teleportation powers and practising with accuracy.

"Camile?" he said loudly.

"Potions," she replied. "I can make potions for just about anything. Right now, I use known potion recipes. The next step for me is to work on making my own new recipes using ingredients readily available."

"Good, perhaps we should stay away from consumption ones for the time being and stick to ones that you pour on objects," Malarchy said, thinking back to the love potion she created that almost killed Jessie, Dezi, and Pete. "And work on identifying the different ingredients and their purposes."

Zsiga spoke next. "Stealth," he said. "I can hide in plain sight, blend into shadows, escape detection. I would imagine the next step for me would be invisibility, if I advance any further."

"There is no reason why you shouldn't be able to advance further. Our teachers were always geared towards continual advancement of skills during our lifetimes. You may be surprised at what you could be able to do," Aslo said, returning from the combat team with Iskander beside him to switch places with Zsiga.

"Your talent?" Malarchy asked.

"Seems a little strange for a big guy like me, but..." Iskander closed his fist and opened it again. There sitting inside it was a small ball of light. "I call it *my little star*. I can send it places and it shows me what it sees. It can give off a pretty good spark too, for a little thing. Not too sure how I could expand it, though."

"How far can you send it? How many can you make at once? Can you make it larger, more powerful? Can it go underwater? In any weather? If you answer *I don't know* to any of those, that is what you should be working on," Malarchy said.

"Never thought of all that. I guess there are ways to make her better," the guard said, smiling.

Malarchy signalled to Mike, William, and Diana to come over. When they arrived, he looked at his chart, and back at them a few times then let out a sigh. "Good news... we have an enormous amount of defence. Bad news... we have hardly any offensive skills. Those who are portal guards have a certain affinity for combat, which may help, but we are a long way from being able to mount an attack to bring our people back."

"We do have thirteen and, assuming Willow pulls through, fourteen guardians. Not to mention, the redhead has some unique skills too," William added.

"Undeniably she does, but it's a far cry from growing fruit trees to fighting an army. I hate to have to say it, but, if she doesn't wake, without her skills we may be stuck. Guardians can't go through any portals without a keeper and she is the only one we have," Malarchy replied.

"If that is the case, then a defence is what we will need in the end. For now, though, I suggest we train in as many combat techniques as possible. Prepare them to fight as a regular army and use their defensive skills to stay alive," Mike said and the others agreed.

While the new mentors were talking among themselves, Clairity approached Dezi. "You okay? I heard what you said, about not knowing what your gift was. It's not true. You do know. So why not tell them?"

"You should mind your own business," he snapped, instantly feeling guilty. "Sorry, I have known what I can do for a long time, but I never wanted to end up being a freak show for a bunch of people to make fun of."

"You won't. It's different here," she answered. "They honestly want to develop our abilities so we can help in combat. It's elemental, isn't it?"

"Yeah, fire and water, I can create both," he said, looking at the ground and kicking the grass.

"You need to tell them, you know."

"I will in my own time... maybe. I won't perform tricks, though," Dezi said.

The group leaders returned to their stations to begin setting up training routines everyone could practice daily. Malarchy headed towards the sleeping quarters to find his daughter in the hopes of training her how to use a few illusion abilities that might one day help her escape if the need arose.

At the end of the day, Dezi asked William and Mike for a minute of time alone and explained his situation and how the Council made people with his abilities dress up and entertain. They were sympathetic as to why the boy wasn't willing to share his skill set with others, especially William, but also happy to hear they now had a little more offence to work with. They assured him they would train him how to use his skills in combat, not for the circus and, after trying to explain what a circus was for a while without success, they gave up and let him know they were a team working together towards one goal.

Mike and William were the last two remaining in the practice field that evening, practising their combat skills against one another as they often did to relieve stress.

"Do you think any of this is going to help? They aren't exactly militia material," William said, lunging forward with a sword at his friend's chest.

"They need a lot of work," Mike answered as he blocked the attack. "And you sound out of breath, old man," he laughed.

"I am old compared to you. Ten thousand of your years pass my people by for just one of our cycles. I age much more slowly than you," he replied, attacking again.

"Willow too, huh?"

William stopped the fight and looked at his friend. The two had become close since they met years ago. "What's this about? You got a thing for the girl?" He smiled.

Mike laughed as he returned the weapon he was using to a rack. "It's more of a red hair thing. There are so few of us around that we have to stick together."

Chapter Twenty-Four

Willow opened and closed her eyes a few times, trying to focus on her surroundings. Everything was blurry. *I must actually be waking up*, she thought to herself.

Yes, we are.

She recognized the voice, not one of the voices she grew up with, but one from her dream. It was Shelby.

Things were becoming clearer now. There was a woman walking back and forth, checking numbers on some machines, which were making odd noises, and writing them down. Attached to one arm was a band of material which started getting bigger. Willow winced as it squeezed the upper part of her arm so tightly that she thought it was going to explode.

"You're awake!" the lady said, rushing over.

Willow was preoccupied with the wires and tubes that were attached to her. "What is all this? Ow! I want it off. Get it off of me," she tried to scream, but the words came out coarse and her throat ached. Panic set in; everything was confusing her. She wanted to get up, but the woman was holding her down and yelling for someone named Richard. Who were these people? Where was she? Where were Aslo and Kiera, or the kittens? She hadn't even had time to learn their names yet. What if she never did? What if she had been captured and this was all for torture? Why couldn't she speak properly?

She was fighting as hard as she could, kicking and scratching, when the man arrived and held her down tightly.

"Relax, don't try to speak. Willow, you need to relax now or you will hurt yourself," he said to her in a calm voice.

She wasn't about to relax when these people had her hooked up to who knows what. "Let me go!" She tried to scream. Again, it was nothing more than a squeak and pain shot through her throat.

Richard looked at the woman and asked for something that Willow hadn't heard of before. She left for a moment and came back with a strange looking tube filled with liquid and what looked like one of Martha's sewing needles on top. She pushed on the bottom and some liquid sprayed out the top. The sight of it made her more nervous.

"Calm down now. You are going to hurt yourself. It's okay. We are trying to help you," he said.

Help me? she thought, putting wires into her body didn't seem much like help. The woman moved up to a tube which had a sack of clear liquid on one end and was attached to her arm on the other. She inserted the needle and within seconds everything was flashing before her eyes. She couldn't struggle anymore. Her eyelids closed.

"I think we need to have someone she knows here before she wakes up again. We will need William, as well," Richard said, sending his wife to find the others.

Mike was the first to notice Mary, the nurse, running across the field towards the area where they were practising combat moves. He left the training group and ran over to meet her halfway, curious as to what news could be so important she would track them down.

"Mary, is everything okay?"

"The girl, she woke up," she said while trying to catch her breath. "She completely freaked out. We needed to sedate her before she hurt herself. Richard wants someone she knows and trusts in the room with her at all times till she wakes up again and he wants to see William too, as soon as possible. Maybe you could take a break here, just for a few hours. The sedative should wear off fairly quickly."

"Sure, I will fill in William and the others and we will be right over. I am sure Aslo and Kiera will want to be there as well," he said, turning to head back to the others, many of whom were already staring and wondering what was going on.

Mike approached William and the two guardians first, taking them aside to fill them in. He didn't think everyone needed to know Willow had awoken afraid of the technology around her. He could see now why she would and couldn't believe that none of them had the foresight to anticipate her reaction. Her world never had any doctors, medical rooms, or hospitals. This would all be foreign to her and then adding on top of it all she didn't recognize anyone. The scenario was a recipe for disaster.

After telling them what happened, Aslo and Kiera decided to go straight over so as not to take any chance that their keeper would wake up alone again. William sent everyone back to the command centre to wait, except for Clairity and Ashlyn. Since they were Willow's best friends, he wanted one of them to always be by her side. They could take shifts three or four hours at a time for the rest of the day. Both girls agreed, Clairity offering take the first shift. She headed over with William, while Mike and Ashlyn discussed what to tell everyone else back in the main cabin.

When they opened the door to the medical building, they saw that the guardians had changed back into their house-cat forms and were on the bed beside Willow, while Richard and Mary were standing on either side. Richard was talking to them when he noticed there was someone else in the room.

"Oh good, William, I want you to help make the choice. The IV and equipment really spooked the girl. We could unhook her from everything now, which might make things easier the next time she wakes. The downside is we won't be able to monitor her vitals anymore and, if she doesn't wake as we expect, we would have to put it all back," the doctor said.

"Aslo, you know her better than me. What do you think?" William asked.

"I believe we should remove everything. She is doing well. The avian guardian looks well too. I see no reason to keep her hooked up to your machines and scare her further."

"Do you think there is a prophecy for this?" William asked, rubbing the back of his neck and pacing. "Okay, let's take her off of it all. We will give her twelve hours to wake. That should be long enough and still not dehydrate her body too much. Any longer and we will need to put the IV back in."

"Agreed," Richard said.

William pulled Clairity aside before leaving and asked her to keep him informed if anything happened. When she turned back, the nurse pulled a curtain around the bed her friend was lying in, to detach all the wires in private. She was glad. The machines always made her nervous when she visited the room. She couldn't imagine all the things that were attached to Willow could feel very comfortable. Oddly enough, she thought, with everything in this world being so advanced in comparison to their home, their medical department was definitely lacking.

When the curtain opened again, Clairity pulled a chair over by the bed. Time seemed to drag, passing by slowly for her. There was nothing she could do but practice summoning visions, in between bouts of awkward conversation with Aslo and Kiera. They were doing their best to be cordial to her, but she had never actually spoken to them before. She told herself she would feel the same if she was left alone in a room with people she didn't know, but deep down she knew she felt nervous alone in the presence of the guardians because they were ancient beings of great power, the true protectors of everything. After what seemed like ten cycles had passed, Willow began to move.

"She is waking," Clairity said.

"It could just be muscle reflexes. Let's not get too excited yet," Aslo responded.

"No, I can feel it. She is waking up," the young prophet said.

Kiera was curled up in a circle. Upon hearing the news, she lifted her head to look at Willow's face, her eyes widening with anticipation. Within moments, the young girl opened her eyes a little, then again a little more, trying to focus.

When she regained normal eyesight, she bolted into a sitting position, wishing she hadn't immediately after. Everything started spinning. She could hear voices she recognized, but couldn't make out what they were saying. It was all muffled. She fell backwards onto the bed again. She tried to speak, but her mouth was dry and the words wouldn't form. Her throat was too sore from earlier. She had never felt so terrible before, so out of control of her senses, so weak. Lying down with her eyes closed, she realized that she could focus better on what was being said.

"Relax child, please, it will take some time for you to feel better. You have been asleep for several weeks. Your muscles and eyes will need to adjust to being active again," said a voice she was very accustomed to: a voice she trusted. It was Aslo and he would never do anything that would harm her.

"Willow. It's me, Clairity. The healer here said you could have some frozen water if you woke up, to wet your mouth. He said it would help you until you could sit and drink water. If you open your mouth, I can put a little piece in."

That was good news for Willow. She parted her dry, cracked lips, allowing her friend to slip a little piece of ice in. It felt wonderful; cold and wet. She played with it with her tongue, letting it dance across her teeth and gums. When the first piece was gone, she opened her mouth again and within moments she was rewarded with another small piece of ice.

"Good, she is taking some ice chips," said a voice Willow recognized. Panic set in again. It was the man who restrained her earlier. They did something that made her go back to sleep. She wanted to run as fast as she could, escape to a forest and climb to where she knew no one could follow, but she couldn't. If she opened her eyes she would feel sick again and she definitely couldn't walk yet. If she was in a forest she wouldn't have to. The trees would send their branches to cradle her and lift her away from all her problems. They would protect her.

"Don't be afraid, Willow," Clairity said, sensing the emotions of her friend. "It's just the healer. He means you no harm."

Was this a trick? Willow could hear Clairity's voice and she trusted her best friend, but deep down she was unsure. Everything seemed so foreign to her, especially the way she felt. She had never been sick before... never needed a healer. She was scared.

A new voice appeared. "She is frightened. This experience is overwhelming for her. She is not yet able to communicate verbally. Earlier, her screams were pure adrenaline. Now she is calmer. It could take a while. I suggest only voices she knows well talk in her hearing range until she has regained the use of the rest of her senses."

"Shelby?" Kiera said. "Is that you?"

"Kiera, my friend, yes, your keeper saved my life. Without her, I would still be broken beyond repair."

"Lasel? And your keeper?"

"Prisoners, deep beneath a castle at the heart of a stone mountain, in a world ruled by madmen convinced they deserve to bring retribution. I am afraid they are lost to us, with many more," Shelby said.

"I am sorry. Is there nothing we can do?" Kiera replied.

"Perhaps, but now is not the time. Willow must recover fully before we discuss the possibilities. Unfortunately, I believe that may take weeks, if not longer. She was subjected to a taste of the torture I endured. The torture that broke me. We must tread carefully, make sure she is back to normal before she takes on any more."

Willow wanted to shout out to them she was fine, but the dryness of her mouth and throat still only let her make a few squeaks. In truth, she wasn't fine. She was dizzy, felt sick to her stomach, very tired, and weak.

"Perhaps I can help steady her senses," Aslo said as he joined with her, becoming a picture on her arm in the same spot where Shelby had previously been.

"How does that help?" the doctor asked.

"When the Leander - feline guardians become one with another being, we give some of our traits to that being. In Willow's case, when she is joined with Aslo or myself... or one of our children, she receives the benefit of agility, stability, additional balance and night vision, to name a few," Kiera explained.

Willow felt more like herself almost instantly and her mind began to race through information of what happened over the past weeks to share with Aslo.

Shh, child, now is the time to relax. We can discuss everything when you are better. I don't want you to strain yourself, Aslo's familiar voice sounded in her head.

Okay, but I feel better with you here. Do you think I could open my eyes without spinning in circles now? I should very much like to go to the restroom and then wash up, she replied back so that only her guardian could hear.

Yes, slowly open your eyes and adjust, then try to sit up first. No sudden movements. Everything you do must be slow. Also, keep in mind you haven't used your muscles for a bit and they are considerably weaker now than you remember.

She followed Aslo's advice, opening her eyes and adjusting to what she saw directly in front of her first, then looking around to see everyone. She made sure she was in control of her eyesight before attempting to slowly move to a sitting position. Once she sat up, Clairity offered her a cup with some water, which she gladly accepted. After a few sips she found she could speak, just a word or two. The feeling wasn't pleasant, but it was progress.

"Thank you," she mumbled to her friend. Shortly after, she asked if she could try to get up with one word: *restroom.* Clairity agreed to help her if Richard would allow it. She let out a little sigh of relief when the healer agreed to let her try walking.

As soon as she set her feet down on the floor, she realized what Aslo meant. Her knees instantly began to buckle, no longer accustomed to supporting her weight. Clairity steadied her so she didn't fall flat on her face. After a couple steps, she felt a little more in control, but couldn't imagine she would be running across tree tops any time soon.

Clairity helped her wash up and dry off. It wasn't until she looked in a mirror that she realized what she was wearing. It was an off-white colour and similar to an apron of some sort. To her shock, she had nothing on underneath and the back was open, except for the part that tied together at the neck. Anyone would be able to see her backside while she walked.

"Where are my clothes?!" she screamed as loud as her voice would let her.

"It's okay, just relax," her friend answered. "They needed to take them off you to keep you clean and washed while you were out."

Okay? she thought no part of this was okay by any means. What part of people seeing her without clothing would ever be okay? She spent her whole life making sure she was covered as much as possible.

"I am not leaving this room without clothes," Willow said in tears.

The sound of rain outside was clue enough for Kiera that something was wrong with her girl and she headed into the restroom to see what it was.

"She wants her clothes," Clairity explained.

"Of course, I will find someone to bring her some. There was an extra set of her keeper clothes in the backpack you brought through the portal," Kiera answered and headed off to find someone to bring the outfit over to the medical centre.

The guardian returned quickly with Mike carrying the backpack containing clothes. Clairity came out to retrieve the bag. Willow was still weak. Leaving her alone for any amount of time, even resting in a chair, wasn't an option. After dressing, she tied her hair back off her face. It was limp and dull and seemed somehow thinner than she remembered. She made a comment about how horribly thin she looked in the mirror. Her face was pale, her bone structure peeking through as if her skin was transparent.

"I look sick," she said.

"You have lost weight and muscle. There is a medical program in this world they call physical therapy. People use it to rebuild strength after being immobile for long periods of time as you were. It could help you. Aslo and I have discussed it with the medical healers and think it is the fastest way for you to recover, although it will still take a long time," Kiera suggested.

"Time is something we don't have a lot of. There is an invasion coming and it will come here. We just don't know how long we have to prepare for it or try to stop it," Willow said, leaning hard on her friend.

"Don't worry," Clairity said. "Nathan found a prophecy about the bird guardian. It says when you wake up, things will be better."

"What prophecy? What did it say?" The last time she saw Nathan, he hadn't read the book yet. She was happy to hear that someone was working on figuring out what they all meant.

"Nathan shared the book with me," Clairity said, just before reciting the prophecy exactly as it appeared in the book:

A race forgotten shall appear again, in need of intervention

One soul so pure shall see the cause and alter what could be,

Devastation averted, a world now saved,

One life shall be the reward, within its mind a soul has been lost

And another shall fall to slumber, the signs on doors to show the way,

With rest and time life shall renew and mind shall mend

All shall emerge with questions answered

Life preserved and new hope granted.

"See, it fits perfectly," her friend said in an excited voice.

"I am afraid I am too tired to think right now, but keep in mind prophecies can have messages for more than one person. There is usually more to them than just the obvious, or else they would be... well... useless," Willow replied.

"I see what you mean," Clairity replied with a puzzled look on her face. "So, how do we learn what they mean?"

"I think the best we can do is know them, study them and figure out a rough timeline. Then when the time comes, hopefully we will see the answer and be able to use it to our advantage." Signs of stress from all the activity were beginning to surface.

"We best get you back into bed now," Kiera said. Willow agreed. From the short trip, she was tired and sore.

Back in the main room of the medical centre there were a few more people now. She was definitely glad she had clothes on so no one was staring at her bare bottom. Mike and William spoke in whispers to the healer, while looking at her walk slowly across the room with concern. Shelby was sitting on a chair. Ashlyn was doing something at the table beside where her bed was. As she came closer to the bed she saw there was a vase of water with something in it. A flower she thought, straining her eyes to see that far. No, not a flower, but a branch.

"Ashlyn, is that..." Willow's knees buckled and she collapsed, luckily on the bed so she didn't hurt anything else.

"Willow!" her dreamwalker friend screamed.

Everyone rushed over to her side, multiple hands helped her into the bed again. She closed her eyes for a few moments before finishing her question "Is that what I think it is?"

"I thought it meant something in the dream when it fell, so I brought part with us through the portal. I was hoping it would make you feel better."

Willow interrupted her. "Ashlyn, you are brilliant, you know that? I need to get outside," she said, trying to stand.

"You are too weak to go anywhere, little girl," Mike said.

"If this means what I think it means, it is the most important thing that could happen to any of us. Carry me if you have to, but I need to get to the middle of the field by the sleeping quarters."

"The training fields? What for?" William asked.

"Just please, trust me. I am getting tired very fast, so I need to do this now," Willow answered, grabbing the branch from the vase. Aslo appeared back in his cat form beside her on the bed.

"Do you really think this will work?" the guardian asked.

"I think so, as long as I have enough energy..."

Aslo nodded to Mike to go ahead and move her as requested.

"Okay, squirt, hang on tight," Mike said, picking her up and heading out the door to the training yard.

There were still groups practising combat skills outside. Word spread quickly that something strange was happening. Soon, every building emptied. Everyone was watching Mike carrying her. At first, she couldn't help but feel self-conscious. She looked like a fragment of the strong girl everyone had known - thin and sickly, not even able to walk across a field, but then she realized her task was far more important. If she was right, this could turn the tides for them. It was all there in the prophecy Clairity recited. It was so obvious. This had to be what it meant.

Chapter Twenty-Five

Without the guardians connected to her, Willow was much more wobbly on her feet. She noticed the difference as soon as Mike put her down.

"I will have to sit to do this," she said to him.

"Sit to do what? Are you going to tell me what you are going to try to do?" Mike asked.

"Just help me get down on the ground, please. I would prefer to do it with some dignity rather than a face-plant."

The faint laughter that escaped her lips made Mike smile. "Alright," he said, helping her down on the ground.

"Thank you. Now back up and keep everyone a good distance away. It is important no one gets too close," she said. All in all, she figured for a normal man he was a great addition to their team, even if he could be a bit of a jerk sometimes. In fact, there were several men and women who made her feel fortunate that they were on their side.

After everyone was a safe distance away, she mustered up her strength and drove the branch into the ground. She took a deep breath and lifted her arms up. A gold sparkle appeared around the branch like a small twister surrounding it, getting larger and larger until it looked like it touched the sky.

"She is failing, I can feel it!" Clairity yelled out.

Mike and William went to move towards her, but Aslo changed to his full form and blocked their way.

"She has to do this. I will not let you interfere. This is the most important thing she will ever do. This is what she was destined for. If she fails, all will be for nothing," Aslo said, snarling, his large teeth exposed.

Moments later, Willow fell over. Her body was lying motionless on the ground. The twister dissipated, revealing a large tree with sweeping branches. No one moved. Was Willow okay? Was it safe to move closer to see? William ran his hands through his hair and let out the large breath of air he had been holding through the whole display.

"Can we help her now?" he asked.

"Wait just a few more moments," Aslo answered.

"She could be dying. We could help her!" Mike yelled.

Sobs came from the crowd as they watched Willow's body lying limp and lifeless in a pile at the base of a tree.

Although there was no breeze in the air, the long sweeping branches of the tree began to move. They picked up Willow's motionless body and lifted her high, surrounding her with a glowing aura. Physically, her body began transforming back to the girl she had been before she helped the avian guardian.

Her hair broke free from the tie that bound it and swayed gently around her face, brilliant red, thick and radiant, perfectly complimenting the return of the light bronze colour of her skin. The transformation mesmerized everyone watching. Willow sat up and opened her eyes - their colour spectacular. The sprinkling of red against a sea of green and blue portrayed an image of dancing flames on water. She looked around, reaching out to touch one of the wispy branches of Acacia, the ancient tree of justice. It astounded her. She believed at one time, Acacia to be a story made up to entertain children. Now, she realized everything she knew before was a lie. Eventually, she would have to relearn the truths of her world and uncover all the secrets that had been hidden from her and everyone else.

"You have saved me from an eternity of torture, always burning in necrid flames but never able to extinguish my life. That part of me has now withered since you called me here through that branch. I owe you my gratitude," Acacia said, breaking her train of thoughts.

"I had some help with that. They are a good team. We could use your help," Willow said.

"I am bound by the same rules as the guardians. Sworn only to pass judgement on the worst crimes, committed by those who choose to act on that part of themselves capable of committing the most terrible acts possible and enforce punishment if needed. I cannot intervene directly in your search or in physical battles. These things you must do for yourselves. I can help you in another way, provide tools to help you help yourselves and when the time comes, you will know and call me."

Everyone was so preoccupied with the grandeur of the great tree that no one noticed another girl approach its base. Willow looked down, her eyes connecting with Jade; well, what looked like it could be Jade. She was somehow different, her hair was without style, lacking brilliant colour. Her face and eyes had lost their luster. She was almost homely, compared to her former self.

"I am here for your decision, my punishment for the atrocities that I caused," Jade said, bowing.

"Hmm, yes, it is true you did make some poor choices. Are you sorry?" Acacia asked.

"Yes, of course, but that doesn't make things better," Jade cried.

"No, it doesn't, but you can make things better than they are now. What has happened, has happened. Hopefully you learnt from it."

"I did," she sobbed.

"Then return to your father. He needs you now. When you go forward from today, help others to see and change. Your part in our future is not yet over," Acacia said and paused for a moment before adding, "Whether within an individual or an entire kingdom, there is the ability to do good, bad, or nothing at all. The choice is ours to make, and to choose one way does not mean we will always choose the same again. Remember what you feel now and make the most of your choices in the future."

Jade did as Acacia suggested, returning to her father who had been nervously watching from a distance. A look of instant relief came over Malarchy's face at the sight of his daughter walking back. A display of any form of affection had never been his style, but he too was somehow different. He hugged her tightly as if he never wanted to let go.

A bright glow filled the sky with shimmering lights of purple, red, green, and gold. A dusting of sparkles of gold and silver rained down on William's property and the people outside watching the events of the evening unfold, disappearing upon contact. The branches of the great tree set Willow down on the ground safely. She noticed immediately that she felt strong and healthy again. She was herself.

"Thank you," she said.

"It is you that I thank. You will find now and over time you have what you need to continue. I am anywhere you need me if you ask," Acacia replied.

Willow started walking towards her friends. She noticed a glow was circling around them. Shelby was flying above and found a branch to land on. Aslo and his family nodded at her, joining the avian guardian at the tree.

When she came closer to her friends, she saw something unusual. They had all changed. Even without them moving, she could see they were stronger, faster, more powerful and there was something else. Willow stopped and smiled. She looked down at the inside of her arm and there it was, the symbol. She was a portal guard now and so were many of the others. She walked over to each and turned their arms to see, Clairity, Ashlyn, Jessie, Dezi, Pete, Neil, Camile, the younger Victoria, and Nathan, even Jade and Malarchy all had the portal guard symbol. To her surprise, others had it as well, new additions to her family, Mike,

Sarah, Richard, Mary and others who aided William over the years were given the honour, with it extended life and perhaps other gifts. Only time would tell.

Shelby left her perch and circled around in the air. *It must feel good to be free again,* Willow thought, watching her soar high above, then dive down and land on Ashlyn's shoulder, disappearing. Could it be? She ran over to her friend and asked to see the shoulder. There was a picture of a black bird, looking happy and content with her new home.

"You're a keeper!" Willow said.

"Me?" Ashlyn said in disbelief. "Why me? How?"

I knew in the dream we were compatible, that you would be the one to carry me forward until I find my keeper and my mate again. There will be other guardians who have lost their keepers and will need you. I can help you develop your gifts in dreams if you let me, Shelby's voice said to Ashlyn alone.

She looked at Willow with excitement. "I can hear her in my head. Is that what it's like for you too? All this time you never told us."

"Voices in my head wasn't something I wanted to share, especially since I didn't know where they were coming from until recently," Willow replied.

Looking down, she noticed two of Aslo and Kiera's children were rubbing against her legs and purring. There was a pattern to it, a rhythm. She could hear a message in it, almost like a song. They were telling her they loved her. They needed to help another, but they could reunite again later. They would always be a part of her. She smiled, knowing there was another new keeper to be born tonight and she thought she knew who.

The two cats left Willow and walked over to her friend Clairity, rubbing against her bare ankles a few times before appearing as pictures on her lower legs.

The three girls hugged. There was something new in their lives they could share. Willow realized how much she missed their time together in the forest. Now, there was a reason to go off on their own and discuss keeper matters.

Looking up, she caught a glance of Diana walking away. She wasn't chosen to join the ranks of guards. *It wasn't because she wasn't worthy,* Willow thought. Diana Waddington had always been an outstanding person. Like a light bulb clicking on inside her head, she understood. It was because Diana was Lance's aunt. She was the one King Cornelius was looking for - the one their enemies considered imprisoned somewhere, stolen from them.

Chapter Twenty-Six

Willow was already joined with Aslo and Kiera when she caught up with Diana entering the main cabin. The command centre was empty. All of its usual inhabitants were still outside buzzing with excitement. Mike and William walked in behind her before she had a chance to say a word. The look on the storyteller's face was solemn. It was clear she didn't understand why she wasn't chosen to join the ranks of portal guards and felt it was because of some shortcoming of her own doing. Nothing could be farther from the truth. The guardians agreed with her.

"Don't be upset," Willow said, unsure how to start the conversation. How do you tell someone their brother is an evil maniac bent on the destruction of everything?

"What's wrong?" William asked.

"I wasn't chosen," Diana said. "I am not as worthy as all of you. Perhaps I do not belong here."

"There must be some mistake," Mike said.

"No, I don't think so," Willow replied, turning her attention to Diana. "But it isn't what you think."

"Then why?"

"To protect you," she answered. "Your brother, his name is Cornelius, a king?"

Diana nodded with a look of curiosity in her eyes. "How did you know that?"

"In my dreams I met his son, your nephew… they are the ones who attacked us and they are searching for you."

"What?" the storyteller gasped. "Why?"

"I was hoping you could provide some details to fill in the blanks of what I know," Willow said.

Mike and William looked at each other then back.

"I have a feeling there is a story here we need to hear," William said.

"It begins somewhere in the time of the blood wars," Willow started. "That part of the story I know few details about, but something happened and according to them, it was the three races, snakes, spiders and sea creatures, that remained guardians, and the cats, wolves and birds that split from them. In other words, they believe we are the bad guys. Skip forward to the time of the portals and the splitting of worlds and it becomes an evil plot to control all creatures and enforce a vision of what the world should be. It's all very backwards, but very real to them. In this version of reality, you were stolen from them, against your will. In fact, they believe all those chosen were taken as hostages to stop possible uprisings."

"That's insane!" William said.

"Insane or not, they truly believe they are righting a wrong... that they are justified in their actions and saving worlds from us. They mean to destroy every guard and keeper."

"I chose this life," Diana said, tears falling down her face.

"I know, but when the time comes, when you meet your brother face-to-face, I believe it is important you do not show the mark of the portal guard. Can you tell us what you remember?"

Diana sighed. "I was young - a teen your age. It was the end of the blood wars. Our kingdom managed to stay clear of the conflict, but it came close to our lands and one day my parents, the King and Queen, were out visiting a border town. They were killed. No one invaded us. It was a spill off of a fight from the neighbouring kingdom... not planned. They were simply in the wrong place at the wrong time. It is possible we would have been a target next.

"My brother took his rightful spot as King the next day. He was full of grief and anger. I begged him not to act on emotion, but he ordered that his guards obtain magical blood and drink it in case an invasion occurred... only as a precaution. He never intended to use it as a weapon. I tried so hard to change his mind. We were so close to each other. He wasn't a bad person." She paused for a moment and wept.

"Against my advice, he and others drank the blood. It was never necessary. The portals were created almost immediately after, but the damage was done. When the guardians came and asked me to go with them, I agreed. My brother offered to help as well, but he was denied. I believe it was because he slayed those creatures and drank their blood. It tainted him. He was no longer pure and innocent. He was angry, so very angry. They didn't want him - a king. I left, but I was given extended life. This was a very, very long time ago. How is he still alive?"

"The serpents must have felt his anger. They gave him venom to drink. It runs through the veins of all his family, giving them gifts, including extended life. In exchange, he raises armies, seeks out other worlds, destroys or imprisons our kind and if he finds them he will release the other ancients from the worlds they are now contained in. They plan to remove the barriers between worlds and rule all in the end. Nowhere is safe," Willow said.

"Well, now we know who the enemy is and why they are attacking us, just the where left to figure out," William said, breaking a few minutes of silence. "Anything either of you two remember and want to add would be helpful. The prophecy deciphering team will need to know these details. Maybe something in that book will lead us in the right direction."

He placed his hand on Diana's shoulder. "There is nothing you could have done. Many men went mad after drinking the blood, power hungry, believing they were better than others. Once he tasted it, his fate was sealed. Willow is right. There may come a time when you will be face-to-face with him again and you have a better chance of survival without the mark."

"I do not wish to survive and live a lie. I am one of you!" she yelled.

"It's not just you. There may be others whose fate rests in your hands. There is a reason for everything. You must trust Acacia has one," Willow said.

Diana looked at her, surprised. She never considered there could me more at stake than her own life. It made more sense now. There were possibilities for what her role in the future might be. She nodded, indicating she understood, and took a seat quietly reflecting on everything.

"Nathan," she said after a few minutes. "Can we tell him first before the others? It is his family we are talking about, after all."

"Of course," William said. "I am asking him to come here now." Having a telepathic link to almost everyone would definitely have its advantages. It would also mean a lot more people talking about things he didn't necessarily need or want to hear and at all hours. He would have to have a lesson or two on when it was appropriate to use the link.

"Gran!" Nathan said moments later, running in. "Isn't it great! Did you see? They called me without saying anything. Not even leaving the room. Just think, I can call them when I find something or when I need help or if I want a cookie."

"No!" Mike said sternly, causing the boy to turn and look at him.

"I think there are some things you need to do for yourself still. Imagine if you were working hard and heard twenty people all ask for soap in the shower or a drink outside. It would ruin your line of thought," Diana said.

"Soooo... no cookie?" he asked, scrunching up his nose.

"No cookie," Mike said, smiling this time.

"We will have a class or two to go over what is appropriate to ask and what is not, as well as to teach you all how to communicate with just one person at a time rather than all of us at once," William added.

"Phew," the boy said, motioning as if he was wiping sweat from his brow. "I was worried there I might always be in trouble."

Diana laughed.

William had already turned his attention to Willow. She wasn't moving and was staring at the picture on her arm. The picture was fading in and out.

"Surely that doesn't mean that you are being reconsidered as a guard," he said. The others turned their attention to her as well.

Willow looked up. The two black cats appeared. She wasn't sure what it meant, but Aslo would answer for her.

"No… Willow has a unique talent. She must have developed it during all those years we were together. She was a child and, no matter how much we drilled into her that no one was to see the pictures on her skin, a slip-up most certainly should have occurred. We always thought it was dumb luck, but now it appears she can hide marks on her skin on command. We never noticed because we were the pictures. No one else did because they never knew we were there."

"The picture hiding doesn't mean it's gone?" Mike asked.

"No, it is still there and still has the same effect as it does on anyone else, it's just invisible and she can choose to show it again when she wants to. A talent that may come in handy for her one day," Aslo responded.

"I don't suppose you are tired?" Mike said, smiling at Willow.

"No, definitely not. I think I have had more than enough sleep for today," Willow answered, returning the smile.

"How about I show you some sights of this world? I promise you'll love it," he offered.

The invitation caught Willow off-guard. She didn't ever expect Mike to be nice to her. Things really had changed while she was sleeping. "Sure, I would like that," she answered. It was the truth. She was excited to finally see some of what she read in books and it still bothered her she didn't know exactly where she was.

"Make sure you two are back for the meeting tomorrow morning," William said, smiling. "Oh, and Mike, you might want to remember you still don't know how to keep all your thoughts private yet."

Chapter Twenty-Seven

Mike went to get a vehicle and, a few minutes later, pulled round in what he called a Jeep. It had no top or doors, but other than that, it looked pretty much like a small truck. She hopped in. Mike leaned over, pulling a belt from beside her around her waist.

"It's for safety," he said, connecting it to a metal piece by the edge of her seat. A click sounded.

For the first time, she noticed he had a musky smell to him, manly and strong. She liked it. When he sat back in his seat, she had an urge to lean towards him, close her eyes and let the aroma fill her senses.

Probably not a good idea, she thought, blushing, then hoping no one else heard her thoughts, causing her to blush a little more. She also realized she was grateful Aslo and Kiera decided to stay behind and help Clairity and Ashlyn adjust. The last thing she wanted was for anyone to think she had gone boy crazy.

"Everything alright?" he asked, noticing the flushed colour on her skin.

"Yeah great, I was just thinking how odd it is having to worry about what everyone else hears. I mean, am I safe having thoughts to myself? I am used to guardians hearing everything, but not everyone."

"I know what you mean, but I don't think they can hear everything. It has a trigger, emotions I think control it. William can request the mental connection with other guards on and off. May take us some time to get used to it all," he answered with a big smile on his face.

The drive itself was fairly uneventful. No top on the Jeep meant a lot of wind and noise. She tried to yell, hoping he might hear her, but the results were inconclusive. He would nod and agree mostly... probably trying to be nice. She quickly decided not to speak until they stopped, settling on taking in the surroundings instead.

They passed fields and farms, animals and forests. Occasionally, they drove through a town, with lights and storefronts. Signs captured her attention and imagination. This was all so much more than she was used to and nothing she had read even began to describe what she was seeing.

When they finally stopped, they were on top of a hill of some sort. Looking down, she could see a city below that was all lit up. It was spectacular. Her eyes widened, taking in as much detail as possible. There must have been thousands of lights. She imagined herself down there. There was no chance it could look like night at all. In the distance, she could see a lake. She hadn't yet gotten used to big areas of water, especially ones that were deeper than her height. The thought terrified her. Nathan had read a few books on boats and swimming, but it wasn't something she felt the need to experience any time soon. Past the water, there were more lights, another town perhaps. She couldn't help but wonder how many this world held.

"How many towns are there?" she asked.

Mike laughed. "Too many to count," he replied.

"Really? I mean, I had an idea it was big from the maps, but this goes way past anything I could ever imagine. How do you keep track?"

"We don't, really," he answered. "Generally, people live in one area. They get to know their area of the world pretty well. If they go outside that area, they use a map, or if they go long distances they hire someone to show them around."

"Can we go down there? I'd like to see what a town that big looks like up close." Willow begged.

"Sure, hop back in. If you are hungry, we could stop for some food somewhere. I am sure we could find something open," he answered.

"I thought we passed all the farms on the way here. You mean there is land to grow things down there too?" she asked.

"No, it's complicated to explain in full, but food is sent to places where they prepare it and serve it to other people for money," he said.

"Money?" That word was something she hadn't learnt about in any book yet.

Mike let out a big breath of air. "I can see this isn't going to be easy." He couldn't help but smile at her. She was staring at him with such interest. "In your world everyone had a job, correct?"

"Yes," she answered.

"Here it's the same. Because there are so many people, we assign values to jobs they do and a system to exchange services. You do a job, you get money for it, then you use the money to get things from other people."

"I don't have any money," she said with a frown.

"I do. I will get you something," he promised.

By the time he started driving again, she was thoroughly confused by it all. Everything was so big here. There were so many people, so many things. As they approached the town, more and more vehicles appeared on the road. People were out walking about, even at night. Some had strings attached to animals. She made a mental note to ask someone about that later. The lights made everything bright, just as she thought they would. They stopped at a building.

"This is a fast food restaurant," he said. "They can make your food in a few minutes. What do you like to eat?"

"Apples, berries, tomatoes, oh and I very much like peaches," she answered.

"They have burgers and fries that are pretty good," he said.

"What are burgers and fries?"

"Hamburgers, ground beef cooked and served on a bun?" he said, trying to explain.

"Ground beef?" she asked

"Meat, from a cow," Mike answered.

"How do you get it from the cow?" she asked with a look of worry on her face.

Mike must have missed her concern. "Well, it is dead first."

"Dead?" she screeched. "You eat dead creatures?"

"Yes..." he said, unsure if that was the right answer.

"Oh, I would like to go back now, I think. I am sorry. I was taught the only thing worse than eating something that has died is killing it to eat." Thinking of all the discussions about wars they had been having lately, she added, "Or drinking its blood."

"Okay. Well, I didn't realize you were a vegetarian. They do have salads, fries are fried potatoes. There are other options."

"Vegetarian? Maybe I should have read a few more books before experiencing your world in-person," she answered.

"A vegetarian is someone who doesn't eat meat, just vegetables, fruits, some eat cheeses and drink milk - as well as breads and grains," he explained.

"Yes, I guess that is what I am. I can grow what I need anywhere," she said, looking around. "You go ahead and have whatever it is you like to eat."

"How about we go somewhere else? There is something I want to show you. This I think you will like."

Willow agreed and before long they were walking across a field of cars towards bright lights and loud sounds. There were people everywhere, all ages, some holding hands, some using weapons that squirted water, some with gigantic stuffed creatures. People were laughing, screaming and a few vomiting. There was loud music and all different things that spun around in circles. In the middle was a gigantic wheel that caught her attention.

"It's a ferris wheel... a ride. People go on it for entertainment," Mike said. "Do you want to try it?"

"Yes please," she answered, smiling.

They waited in a line for quite a bit of time; however, Willow hardly noticed. She was too busy watching the big wheel turn around, carrying so many people. She was fascinated by their faces going on and off the ride. Then it was their turn. She could hardly control her excitement. The attendant showed them to their seats and listed off some rules about not standing or leaning over while the ride was operational. Then he moved on to the next couple. The wheel turned to let another group off and on. She sat watching all the people and attractions on the ground. She could see everything. Mike pointed out a few interesting places they could go to while they were there. The wheel went round a few times. The feeling was indescribable. Willow couldn't imagine there was anything much better to experience anywhere in this world than that ride. All too soon it was stopping, letting people off and the two of them were back on the ground again.

Mike took her hand, leading her over to a stand selling all different kinds of foods. He bought her something he called cotton candy. It was pink, sweet and melted in her mouth. Then they were on to another ride, which spun round in circles and made her scream, not so much a frightened scream, but an excited one. Everything happened so fast there. They played games. He won her a fake creature, which was soft and huggable and after a few more rides, they tried apples with a candy coating on them. The taste was sweet and tart at the same time.

The two spent time looking around, just walking through the crowds of people and seeing everything. This was by far the best night of her life. She had never done anything more exciting and free. Willow felt a tug on her arm and turned to see a short older lady dressed in bright colours with scarves and jewelry. She wore dark makeup around her eyes and a bright red lipstick covered wrinkled lips.

"Be forewarned, on Hallows Eve those who are not of this world shall take to the streets, blood shall flow and death shall follow. Your presence attracts what we cannot explain. Your destiny is written. You best make sure you listen," she said in a voice with an unusual accent.

"Hey!" Mike said, turning around and realizing someone had a grip on Willow. The woman turned, disappearing into the crowd.

Willow felt her world spinning. This feeling had become far too familiar since coming to this realm. Her knees buckled and everything went black. Mike reached her just in time to stop her head from hitting the ground.

Chapter Twenty-Eight

When Willow woke in the Jeep, they were already turning the corner to enter William's property. Looking at Mike, she could see the concern on his face. A wave of guilt came over her for ruining the evening. She had been nothing but a pain all night, especially with the eating meat thing, which in her own defence, caught her off-guard. Admittedly, she probably could have handled that better. Then she passed out in the middle of what Mike called a park. Why had the woman's words affected her so much? Maybe everything all together overwhelmed her, a combination of the excitement of all the different sights she experienced during the evening. She did know one thing. She was having the best time of her life and she doubted Mike would want to take her anywhere new again.

Mike parked and came round the Jeep to her side. He hadn't realized she was awake, but even after seeing her eyes open, he lifted her out of the seat and carried her towards the main building. She didn't mind, not that she was tired or light-headed, but she enjoyed resting her head against his shoulder and inhaling his aroma again. It made her feel safe and warm, something she couldn't remember feeling, at least this strong, in all her memories.

William, Aslo and Kiera were still in the command centre. They sent everyone else to get a good night's sleep, except for a few men who were doing perimeter watches. Mike put Willow down on the couch. He retold the story as far as he knew it, leaving out the part where she freaked out over eating meat, which Willow was quite happy about. Then it was her turn to fill them in about the woman. She described the old lady, her clothes, jewelry, makeup and voice. Then she recited the eerie words:

Be forewarned on Hallows Eve

Those who are not of this world shall take to the streets,

Blood shall flow and death shall follow.

Your presence attracts what we cannot explain.

Your destiny is written. You best make sure you listen.

"A prophecy?" Mike asked, looking at William.

"I don't know, but I think we should treat it as one. Tomorrow, everyone is back to work on the prophecies. If something is coming, we need as much information as we can find," he answered. "As for you, young lady, perhaps some time in bed just to make sure you are really okay is called for."

"No - no, I am fine. I think it was just too much to process at once, the lights, the people, the noise. It caught me off-guard. I can help," she pleaded. "You need me. I have a way with the prophecies."

"She is correct. We do need her insight, since it seems so many of the prophecies are about her in some way," Aslo said. "It makes sense she can decipher them. I also think we need a training session on this world before anyone else ventures into populated areas."

"Agreed," Mike said.

That one word played on her emotions, bringing back out the guilt she was trying to swallow. She wanted to tell him she had fun. She hadn't even thanked him for taking her yet. But she couldn't, not in front of others. It would be too weird.

"Okay, off to bed with you," Kiera said. "They are shorthanded tonight, everyone is resting for a big day tomorrow so Aslo and I are helping patrol. We will see you in the morning."

"Are you okay to walk?" Mike asked.

She wanted to say no. She wanted him to lift her up, carry her to her bed, and place her down gently, but answered *yes* with a meek smile instead. The whole walk to her sleeping quarters, she beat herself up inside for giving up her opportunity to thank him for showing her so many things; to let him know this was the best night of her life; to apologize for being rude about the food. She figured he would probably never talk to her again.

She hopped back in bed and the kittens immediately joined her. She made a mental note that she still didn't know their names yet and needed to learn them. She could hear little giggles in her mind, which made her smile. Even with all the sleep she had lately, it didn't take long until she drifted off into a deep slumber. There would be no fear of night scares tonight. She would dream of one thing, being back at the park having fun with Mike.

For tonight, she was content. The promise of tomorrow brought with it a new day. Worrying about tackling everything else could wait until then.

Chapter Twenty-Nine

A place has always existed between sound sleep and wakefulness - the only place where one could experience all that happened on either side of the fence. While there, dreams were controlled without the need for a dreamwalker: destiny held by the hand and shaped by desires, leaving reality begging in the background to be heard.

*****

"Willow... Willow!"

She opened her eyes and stretched before realizing Clairity was standing directly over her.

"Hey," she said, still trying to wake up. Her mouth opened, allowing a yawn to escape.

"We have a meeting, remember?"

"Is it late?" Willow asked, worried she was sleeping way too much.

"No, but we will be late if you don't get up and get ready," Clairity replied, handing her friend some clothes to change into.

Willow did as requested. She got up and did her morning routine of washing, brushing and changing. Stopping to look in the mirror, she realized for the first time, she didn't hate what she saw anymore. Perhaps Acacia took pity on her and changed her just a smidge.

"Do I look different to you?" she asked Clairity without taking her eyes away from the mirror.

"No, why should you? Did something happen?"

"No, maybe it's the light. It's nothing," she answered.

The kittens remained in bed for the day. All the voices could be confusing for them as well. After seeing them settled, all curled up together in little balls of fur, the two girls headed out to the training field to meet the others.

They were the last to arrive. Mike was working with Jessie, Dezi, and Pete already, and didn't even look up to acknowledge her, but William did.

"Nice of you to join us, ladies," he said. "I guess we can begin then. Right, everyone gather round. In this first exercise I want each of you to close your eyes and imagine a line connecting yourself to a person who is here, someone close. When you have that, concentrate on saying *hi*."

Willow chose Clairity and said her *hi*. For a moment, she thought everyone chose to say *hi* to her. Voices were coming at her from every direction, all mixed together. It hurt.

"Let's try one at a time," William said, still shaking his head from the noise.

It didn't seem to matter who he chose. The *hi* rang out to everyone. It was Willow's turn. She said *hi* to Clairity again and looked back to William.

"Are you done?" he asked. "Who did you speak to?"

"Clairity," she answered.

"I heard it. Did anyone else?" her friend asked. No one else did. *Score one for the good guys,* she thought.

Clairity and Ashlyn also mastered the technique with ease. They chalked their success up to being a by-product of a keeper's natural telepathic link. Whatever the reason, it meant the three of them were excused to practice among themselves using bigger messages. Training continued for several hours before breaking for lunch.

There was ample time for Willow's latest plan to form and hatch. It was all but decided. As soon as everyone returned, she would take Mike aside and thank him for the previous night. She even returned to the training site early, hoping to find him alone, but Mike didn't come back. Everyone else, however, did.

William went over a list of rules for when to use the telepathic link and when not to. Nathan's cookie story became the example, which made Nathan happy and almost everyone else giggle.

He concluded the meeting by asking everyone to practice and report any unusual abilities that might have showed up uninvited. At the end, he emphasized a warning that for some, advanced fighting skills meant the ability to call weapons to appear. That particular skill had only been seen in proficient fighters before. Although he didn't think any of them needed to worry about it yet, he also didn't want a limb to be lost during practice fights, or worse.

Concentration wasn't Willow's friend; her mind wandered off in places all on its own. It was hard to pay attention when she was preoccupied with wondering where Mike had disappeared to. Why hadn't he returned with the others from lunch? She had the urge to run up and ask William right there in front of everyone, but thought that might seem a little strange. Mike had been nice to her, once, but they certainly weren't a couple. It was more likely she was reading something into the situation that wasn't there. He made her feel warm and safe. That was something she wasn't used to coming from another person.

Her thoughts betrayed her, throwing Lance into the picture. He was the complete opposite, offering her feelings of excitement and danger. The mere mention of his name made her feel wild and alive. She hadn't thought about the prince at all since just after the dream, but now she could see his piercing blue eyes locked on hers - feeling the intense way he watched her. It was a different connection and yet somehow the same.

"Willow!" William yelled, breaking her trance.

"Sorry," she replied. Looking around, everyone was gone. She was standing there looking silly. "I was thinking about... the prophecies," she added, figuring it was the most believable thing she could say.

"How about thinking about them with everyone else inside the command centre and maybe... I don't know... sharing your thoughts?" he asked.

"Yeah, sure," she answered. The tone of his voice told her this wasn't the time to ask about Mike.

Nathan was sitting at the table with Diana when she walked in. The first order of business was for Nathan to share the book with her, so she would remember every prophecy. The group had already implemented a policy of sharing *The Portal Prophecies* every week to ensure it remained fresh in their minds. They also worked directly out of the book itself.

"So, where should we begin?" William asked as Sarah took a seat beside him. Kiera and Aslo joined them, sitting on the table while waiting for everyone to settle.

This was her chance, she thought. "Aren't we going to wait for Mike?" she asked. She couldn't seem to think of anything else.

"No, he had something personal to take care of," William replied without looking up from his notes.

"When will he be back?" Nathan asked.

Willow covered her mouth, disguising a sigh of relief as a yawn. Luck was on her side. Someone else was the one pursuing the conversation. As much as she wanted the answers, she also didn't want anyone knowing she might have developed a crush on Mike.

"Not sure. We should concentrate on the prophecies," William answered, arching his eyebrows as his gaze returned to the faces around him.

On the outside flesh rots, but under is fine

The captors look dead, the prisoner fine,

No one notices, no one hears, a scream for help disappears

Hidden in darkness, unable to move

The ones with power have something to prove

Look for the signs that something is near

Unusual and strange, that people fear

Under a store which sells that which can be made

You will know the place by the woman with the blade

Some powers real, some not

Rope, fire and water punished the lot

Willow wasn't sure why she chose to read that particular prophecy out loud, but she felt the need. Even worse, she had no idea what it meant. Maybe her mind wasn't clear enough to do this today. No matter what she tried, all her thoughts kept returning to boys, over and over.

"Okay, so any ideas? Willow?" William asked.

"I don't know. It popped into my head. I just had a feeling it was relevant. It mentions signs. I think since Ashlyn's interpretation helped her find me, she took signs to mean symbols of something. We should use that as a start," Willow answered. "We are looking for something unusual and strange that people fear. Didn't you say people of this world make things up for whatever they can't explain?"

"Yes," William said, deep in thought. "It could be the signs we are looking for are a creation of the human world meant to signify something they fear. I guess we should start some research into myths and legends." He walked into a back room, returning with a pile of books. "Start with these, Nathan, and share them. I will start on the computer."

Weeks of study went by and the group found out very little about the actual prophecy. They studied various different stories about monsters and strange happenings. A few of which Willow tagged as requiring further attention at a later date, including: The Black Mountain in

Australia; The Bermuda Triangle; The Lost City of Atlantis; and creature sightings such as Yeti, Bigfoot, Loch Ness Monster and mermaids. But somehow none of them seemed to fit their situation.

Nathan was able to find a reference to one type of creature thought to have rotting flesh called a zombie, but after reading hundreds of books and watching hours of shows on the creatures, no one could find any signs as to where they could actually be located. It seemed zombies might have been the one being that did not originate in another world and was merely born from someone's imagination. Not knowing for sure, they continued to research.

Anxiety levels were on the rise. They were going nowhere with this prophecy. William finally suggested they move on to another and Willow reluctantly agreed. Even with a strong feeling this particular one was important, she conceded the other prophecies were probably just as significant as well.

The group decided to look at the strange message from the amusement park for the rest of the afternoon. They started with Halloween, delving only slightly into its history. The in-depth analysis of the celebration was something William needed to gather books and information on for them to look at another day.

What they did learn about Halloween night came from Sarah. It was a strange holiday during which people dressed up as monsters, celebrating with candy and feasts. The most common costumes were the scary ones: vampires, ghosts, mummies and witches. She explained in detail what each was supposed to look like as she went along.

Diana remembered another story. The one that led to Sarah's involvement at the camp and the loss of her family. "Perhaps each of these creatures, like the vampires, could be from another world and are just named differently," she suggested.

It made sense and tied in with the prophecy. That was enough to win William's approval. He agreed to find as many books as possible on each of the creatures so they could be studied separately. Feeling like they had at least accomplished something, he dismissed the group until morning.

There was still no word from Mike. Although William didn't seem concerned, there was talk around camp that Mike had left them, or run off with some girl. Rumours aside, Willow knew something was amiss. She also knew a way to find out what that something was. All she needed to figure out was how to suggest her plan without looking as if she was some stupid girl with a crush, or worse, a stalker.

Ashlyn and Clairity found her attempting to think things through at the edge of the tree line and insisted they take a well-deserved afternoon alone to catch up and gossip, all guardians left behind. When they were safely hidden away in a tree fort Willow had created, Clairity spoke.

"I actually had another reason for wanting us to talk alone. I have a feeling... something is wrong. I know William and the others don't trust my intuition much, but you two... you know I am accurate," she said. "It's about Mike."

"About Mike?" Ashlyn spun around, her eyes sparkling with interest. "Everyone is wondering what happened. Do you know?"

Willow was in awe: leave it to her best friends to say everything she wanted to and ask the same questions she wanted to ask.

"No, I don't know exactly, but it isn't good. I think he is hurt," Clairity responded. "My visions are getting stronger, but none of it makes any sense. People dressed in black robes so you can't see their faces and big black pots over a fire. There is a bunch of chanting of some sort, but I don't understand the words."

"You wouldn't happen to know where, would you?" Willow asked.

"No, I don't know enough about this world to recognize anything," Clairity answered, frowning.

"We should tell William," Ashlyn suggested.

"No, I don't think he would believe us," Willow said, leaning back on a branch so her head hung upside down. "No, if we are going to help him, we need to figure this out ourselves." She paused for a moment to sit up, before adding, "What if you bring us into your dream and we search for him? If we can find him and talk to him or see more about where he is, at least then we would have something to go to the others with."

The two other girls agreed to try that evening.

Chapter Thirty

The three girls met up after everyone else was sleep. It wasn't hard to convince the guardians to take a patrol overnight again. Years of being constantly joined with another being meant Aslo, Kiera and their family enjoyed having some freedom and Shelby was glad to stretch her wings and soar like she never thought she would again.

They each took their place, ready to fall asleep and hunt for clues. With the beds pushed close enough to each other, they were able join hands while falling asleep, hoping that bond would help them meet up in the dream world. At the very least, it wasn't going to hurt. Convincing Richard the noises from their new telepathic connection were keeping them up at night and they needed help to fall asleep had been the easiest part of their plan. All three swallowed the sleeping pill the doctor had been good enough to provide at the same time.

Ashlyn was the first to open her eyes. She was in a familiar white room, which she decided to call a staging room. It was where she started every dream now. There were doorways that led to other people or dreams she could enter. She began looking for the symbols and calling to her two friends.

A knocking noise grabbed her attention. She followed it to a door to find Willow standing behind it. The two then continued searching doors together until they came across one that was a mirror. The girls glanced at each other, silently agreeing to try the handle. Finding Clairity waiting on the other side was worthy of a high-five. They had already beat the odds by merely finding each other.

It felt as if they were walking in circles for a very long time, calling out to Mike without an answer. A different door appeared. This one was all black with gold carvings on it - symbols none of the girls had ever seen before.

"I think that's it," Willow said.

"Feels like," Clairity agreed.

"How did I know you were going to say that? We couldn't pick a door with daisies or sweets? Noooo. We have to pick the door of darkness and the unknown." Ashlyn shivered. "Go on, then. You two open it."

After the three exchanged glances, Willow grabbed the handle, planning on pulling the door open just enough to take a peek inside. Unfortunately, that strategy worked better in theory than it did in practice. As it turned out, the three girls didn't even have to step through. As soon as a crack appeared, they were sucked smack dab into the middle of the dream.

There was no warning; the three simply found themselves in a town of some sort at night. Although there were street lamps, they were flickering on and off so they actually gave off very little light. Willow imagined how the Leander's night vision might have come in handy about now, but shrugged it off as a lesson learned. Pride got in the way of practicality. That led to further questions of whether Ashlyn could bring all of the guardians into a dream as well. She shook her head. These were discussions best left for another day.

The girls slowly strolled down the street, trying to take in as much of their surroundings as possible, all the while looking for clues as to why they were there or where exactly they were. The road itself was paved: smooth and even. Storefronts and businesses, all appeared to be closed. Signs in their windows caught their attention - one boasting a sale on magic wands, while another had ingredients for *All Your Potion Needs* written in the window. There were also people, all dressed the same, wearing dark brown or black cloaks. Hoods covered their faces, although they all turned towards the three girls as they passed by. Being dressed in bright white made them stick out worse than a sore thumb, even if it was only a dream.

The next block was made up of six stores, three on each side. At least, they assumed them to be stores. There were no windows to see in this time. Each one had a sign that hung above its door engraved with a different picture. One side of the road featured a black cat, a raven and a wolf - the other side had a spider, a sea creature, which Willow identified as a kraken, having seen pictures of it in a book earlier that morning, and a snake.

"Where did all the people go?" Clairity asked, knowing neither of her two friends had an answer.

Continuing on to the next block, they found exactly the same stores, with the same signs. The pattern continued to loop, over and over again. Willow grew a small flower in her hand and placed it on the ground in the middle of the road. The three continued walking straight until they came to the same flower. It was sitting in exactly the same place Willow had left it behind them.

"Guess that means we need to pick a door," Willow said.

"Why do I have a feeling you aren't picking the fluffy kitty door?" Ashlyn questioned, shivering.

"Serpent?" Clairity asked.

"Serpent," Willow agreed, heading over to the wooden door. Without waiting, she pulled it open and stepped through.

The girls were greeted with a blast of musty, sickly-sweet smelling air. The store itself was dimly lit using only candles. Willow could make out some dead flowers and plants hanging from the ceiling, recognizing a few as ingredients Micca had needed to make a potion to help the Shinning boys. There were some dead animals that had been stuffed to make them appear still alive, not that any of them knew why someone would want to do such a thing.

Everything around them was dusty and appeared old. Books lined the walls, some for making spells and potions and others which described the meanings of herbs and scents. For a moment, Willow thought she had seen a copy of *The Portal Prophecies*, but how could that be? She took a step closer, stopping when she heard a voice.

"I'd be careful not to touch anything, my dears," a woman said from behind them. Willow swung around, recognizing the voice. There, in front of her, was the woman from the park, still dressed the same and holding a large knife. The woman returned to cutting up something black and slimy that looked like it might have been still alive.

"Where are we?" Ashlyn asked.

"Did you not find what you were looking for? There is a button there for help." The old woman pointed to Ashlyn's side.

"That wasn't there before," Ashlyn said.

Before Clairity and Willow could scream "NO!" the young dreamwalker reached forward and pressed the big red button marked *help*. A trap door in the floor gave way, sending all three crashing to a lower level.

"Brilliant!" Willow exclaimed.

"How was I supposed to know that would happen?" Ashlyn cried.

"I don't know... maybe when she said don't touch anything, it might have been a hint," Clairity barked. "I know it was for me."

"Oh," she answered. "I thought she meant anything else."

"Could you two get off me now?" Clairity wasn't willing to wait patiently for much longer, being squished beneath the weight of both of the other girls.

The three stood up and dusted off. For a dream, it felt real, complete with all the aches that normally would accompany a fall. There were other things to worry about too. If they had thought it was dark upstairs, it was a hundred times worse where they were now. None of them could see a thing.

"Ashlyn, you can control the dream world. Try to create some light," Willow suggested, nudging her friend with an elbow.

"I'll try, but I haven't been very successful in the past," she replied, concentrating as hard as she could on light.

Willow felt something in her hand. She looked down and then said, "Matches? Really? Couldn't be a lantern, ball of light, torch, one of those flashlight things Mike uses?"

"I told you I wasn't very good at it yet," Ashlyn complained.

"Never mind, maybe we can find something to make a torch out of. Feel around." Willow crouched down to the ground, feeling the dirt covered floor for anything that might help.

It was Clairity who ended up finding a piece of wood. After trying a few matches to light it, the girls agreed that wasn't going to work. They needed something to light to get the wood burning, but there wasn't anything.

"Wait!" Clairity exclaimed. "I have an idea!" She ripped her white dress and wrapped some of the material tightly around one end of the wood.

"Brilliant!" Ashlyn yelled.

Willow used a match to light the cloth. If nothing else, it gave them a chance to look for something better or move on to another, hopefully better lit, room. Once their torch was ablaze, everything around them came into view. Unfortunately, there really wasn't much to see. The hallway they were in was made from grey bricks. The whole area was damp, and strangely enough, now they could see the moisture, a musty smell that was far from pleasant appeared as well.

"I am glad we didn't pick spiders right now," Ashlyn said, imagining the cobwebs and creepy crawlers all over the basement that waited to jump out at strangers behind that door.

The hallway continued for a lengthy stretch before ending at a choice. They could go left or right. Both ways were equally dark. There were no signs to tell them which way was best.

"So now what?" Ashlyn asked.

Willow continued examining the walls, looking for any indication of where they were heading, but couldn't find a single mark or clue. "Guess it's up to you, Clairity. Choose."

"Me? Why me?" Clairity asked, stunned.

"I figured you were the psychic. Go with your gut," Willow answered.

"Gut… gut… okay. We go left because nothing we choose can ever be right in this place," she replied, frowning.

"Okay, left it is. I like that reasoning."

"I don't," Ashlyn mumbled, following behind the other two.

Before long, they came across several empty rooms with what sounded like mad dogs barking in the background. A few seconds later, they found themselves in a room filled with smaller rooms with bars on them, like cages. Strangers reached their hands through the bars, grabbing at them. Some were moaning for help. Others were screaming in pain. Throughout the whole ordeal, not a single face could be seen.

"Do you think Mike is one of them?" Ashlyn hopped on her tiptoes trying to see to the back of the cells.

"No, everything tells me he isn't in there," Clairity answered.

Willow had the exact same feeling. He was down there somewhere, but not with these people - somewhere else. Up ahead, on the other side of the room was an old fashioned wood doorway. She headed towards it and swung it open.

Sitting upright in bed, Willow opened her eyes. The prophecy they had been working on so hard was about Mike. He needed help.

Chapter Thirty-One

Willow's jaw clamped down on the jagged edge of one of her fingernails - a click and it was shorter, albeit no less uneven. She examined the others on both hands for any signs of growth long enough to gnaw at, but found none. One lone hangnail was all that remained to keep her focus while waiting for the others to wake up and shuffle in.

The past few weeks had been such a roller coaster of events, it was the first time she had a few spare moments to toss feelings around in her mind and put everything into perspective, or at least try to. Her thoughts kept wandering back to Mike and the horrible image of him from the previous night's dream.

Willow shifted positions in her seat. Sitting still without doing anything was driving her crazy. She twirled a strand of red curly hair around one finger in an attempt to cope with the anxiety bubbling to a boil and threatening to spill over from inside her.

Dreamwalking with her friend Ashlyn was a fairly new experience for all of them. It was the only way they knew how to contact someone who was missing if all other forms of communication failed. When they first decided to look for Mike, she hadn't known what to expect and, as far as she was concerned, their experience in the dream world confirmed the worst. There was no doubt in her mind now that Mike was hurt and needed help. All that was left to do was convince William and the other guards of that.

The camp command centre seemed different today. Map boards were neatly pushed up against one wall in such a way that, if one didn't know they were used for finding portals and rogue holes in space, one would probably believe they were decorations, placed there on purpose. They made this ordinary cabin feel more like a hunting lodge. Flames raged in the stone fireplace built strategically in the centre of the main room, casting a warm glow onto the sitting area. Blankets, normally seen wrapped around tired researchers trying to power nap, were now covering furniture as decorative throws. Character, etched in wood from years of use, lay exposed - the table usually covered in papers and notes now notably empty - except for one large book in the middle, *The Portal Prophecies*.

The book saved Willow and her friends from being destroyed with their home world; gave them direction; and showed them there was hope. It was a compilation of predictions from before she was born, made by visionaries who once resided in her homeland. The only problem was, it was like reading a book of riddles, making it difficult to decipher. Diana and her grandson Nathan now spent countless hours at that very table, trying to make sense of the meanings of the words written within the book's pages.

Of course, the two of them had certain abilities that gave them an advantage when working with books. Diana was a historian in their home world. Her abilities to keep a record of things allowed her to put anything into book form quickly and easily. *The Portal Prophecies* itself was in her handwriting. Nathan's talent was a smidgen more unusual. Not only could he read a book without opening it, he could also transfer its contents to another person.

The aroma of fresh-brewed coffee snapped her out of her trance. Looking around, Willow realized how many people had already arrived. Zsiga busied himself in the corner, making the coffee. While most people were addicted to drinking the mellow blend, the guard was different. Brewing it quickly became his addiction shortly after arriving in this world. Now, he couldn't walk by a coffee maker without fixing a fresh pot. Most of the camp was glad his skills at making the hot beverage had greatly improved over the past month.

Willow wasn't surprised she hadn't noticed him enter the room. Everything about him seemed to blend into shadows. She imagined he could disappear in front of her eyes without ever moving. The lines on her face made a half-smile. How ironic would it be if the robust aroma of coffee one day was what gave away his whereabouts?

William was the last to walk in. Looking at him, Willow figured he didn't ever have time for much sleep. His sandy coloured hair was a mess and hung over his eyes, causing him to brush it back with his hand every so often. When his chocolate brown eyes could be seen, it was the bags underneath them she noticed, rather than their rich, dark colour. He definitely didn't look impressed with being summoned to another meeting in the early hours of the morning. She almost regretted calling him.

The group assembling had been chosen carefully so as not to disturb anyone who didn't need to be involved this early. It consisted of Willow, Clairity, Ashlyn, William, Zsiga, Sarah, Faramund and Iskander. It was easier to wake someone up later, if they were needed, rather than tell them *Sorry, go back to sleep*.

William made himself a coffee, then settled in the seat at the table which was reserved for him. "Okay, so what's the new emergency?" he asked, emphasizing the word *new*.

The three girls exchanged glances, wondering who should speak first. None of them wanted to be the one to narrate what they saw. The others, who clearly would rather be sleeping than deal with anything at this time of day, found the pause irritating.

"We know what the prophecy means," Willow blurted out. She opened the book in front of her and began flipping through the pages without actually reading what any of them said.

"Can we be a little more specific?" William replied, sipping his coffee with an audible slurp.

Willow could feel the weight of the stares that were locked on her. She closed her eyes and recited the prophecy, carefully articulating every word.

On the outside flesh rots, but under is fine

The captors look dead, the prisoner fine,

No one notices, no one hears, a scream for help disappears

Hidden in darkness, unable to move

The ones with power have something to prove

Look for the signs that something is near

Unusual and strange, that people fear

Under a store which sells that which can be made

You will know the place by the woman with the blade

Some powers real, some not

Rope, fire and water punished the lot

William sighed. "Enlighten us… and this better be good."

After spending weeks trying to decipher that prophecy, he, only just the day before, decided it was too frustrating to continue. A plan to start working on the meaning of a new one was made. They all agreed to move on to figuring out a meaning behind what the old woman in the amusement park had said to Willow and leave the other prediction alone.

Her mind wandered back to the woman's voice - the sound etched in her mind.

Be forewarned on Hallows Eve

Those who are not of this world shall take to the streets,

Blood shall flow and death shall follow.

Your presence attracts what we cannot explain.

Your destiny is written. You best make sure you listen.

"It's about Mike," Clairity burst out.

Willow felt the weight of the world lifted from her shoulders as her friend offered that information. Letting the others think she had a crush on Mike was the last thing she wanted - mainly because she did, or at least she thought she did.

Oddly enough, she didn't find him all that attractive. He had short hair, which was a shade of red similar to her own and a nice build, as did most of the men at the camp. But there was nothing that made her say *WOW* when she thought of Mike's appearance.

William rubbed his weary eyes and let out a puff of air, causing the hair hanging down in his face to shoot straight up and flop back again. "I know you girls are trying to help, but Mike is fine. I am sure he is perfectly safe. He is following up on some information for me and had some... personal business to take care of."

Since Willow and her friends had arrived in the camp, sleep had been hard to come by for everyone. It seemed far too often they were all being dragged from bed for one emergency or another, most of which couldn't actually be dealt with until later in the morning. That caused a certain level of frustration, which was reflected in William's voice and agreed upon in everyone else's.

"Personal business?" Willow immediately regretted asking - all eyes turned their attention to her. She felt a warm flush racing to her face. Seeing that the others were preparing to head back to bed, she pushed aside her pride, scrambling to recover. "Give us a chance," she pleaded, quickly adding, "We went into a dream last night. It was the same as the prophecy. All three of us were there with Mike. He was hurt badly. We need to help him."

William took his seat again, the others following suit. "You did what?" he asked. "We are a team here. I thought we agreed we would work together. Do you girls have any idea how dangerous this is?"

Three guardians entered just in time to hear the guard's last question. Aslo and Kiera were both Leander, feline guardians, and Shelby was Allaren, a bird guardian. It was only a few days ago that Clairity and Ashlyn discovered they possessed the ability to bond with guardians, which meant Willow was no longer alone in that department. Being a keeper meant that two guardians could travel with them anywhere, appearing as pictures on their skin. It also meant that, when in that form, none of their thoughts were private. The girls were still getting used to having ancient beings knowing everything and trying to control their lives.

"What happened?" Aslo asked.

"Seems our three young keepers have been doing some investigating on their own," Zsiga answered, pouring water into the coffee machine to make a second pot.

"No one would have listened to us - just like right now. All of you are dismissing us as three silly girls." Willow's forehead wrinkled, matching the pout forming on her lips. Her voice teetered on the side of anger. "It's done now. We went into a dream and found answers. If we had suggested it, none of you would have agreed to let us try." Crossing her arms tightly, she turned her face away from the others, pretending to focus on the window.

Shelby flew over, landing on the table. "The dream world can be treacherous. One or all of you could have been hurt, or worse."

"We know," Ashlyn answered. "That's why the three of us went together... safety in numbers. We had each other's backs."

"And what would you have done if the three princes appeared and attacked you?" the bird asked.

"So, am I not in danger whenever I dream? Or is it only dangerous when I am trying to help?" The dreamwalker's eyes locked on the bird's, as if the two were having their own private conversation.

Tension in the air grew as thick as a poisonous gas starving its victims of oxygen. Ashlyn was right, of course. Any time she dreamt could have ended in a dangerous situation. Being with friends at least made a bit of sense.

After a brief moment of silence, Clairity spoke up, requesting they simply take the time to listen to the story. Regardless of how they got the information, it was important. She threw in that they could punish them for their actions later, which seemed to make William a bit happier and Willow a bit grumpier.

"I was the one who got the three of us together. I had a feeling something was wrong... really wrong... with Mike." Although Clairity's skin was normally porcelain white, it somehow managed to go a shade lighter. The colour drained from the only place that had held even a touch of pink - her cheeks.

"I did, too," Ashlyn tossed in the conversation.

"Together, we came up with the idea of going into the dream to look for him - just to see if he was okay. We didn't think anyone would listen to us without something substantial to tell." What was left of Willow's fingernails clicked on the table. "You have to admit, you haven't even considered checking on Mike. He could be in trouble and we would never know."

"He can contact us telepathically, or have you forgotten about that?" Zsiga sat down at the table, satisfied the coffee would last for at least a little while. He reached over, his large hands steadying Willow's in an effort to stop the tapping noise that was aggravating almost everyone.

"Tell us what happened," Kiera said.

"We found each other and began calling for Mike. For some time, there was no answer," Willow said. She closed her eyes - her mind drifting quickly, fading between the veils of time, back to the events of the dream.

Willow shook her head, snapping back to reality. She'd completely missed her friends filling in much of the details. Clairity was already describing the inside of the store, the sickly sweet smells and the old woman from the amusement park chopping up some slimy creature - then the warning she gave them about not touching anything and the red button.

"Really, I had no idea she meant not to touch the button," Ashlyn added, trying not to look silly. It didn't help.

Clairity rolled her eyes. "As soon as the button was pressed, a trap door gave way under our feet. We fell to the lower level. It was dark. We couldn't see anything."

She continued on, describing how Ashlyn tried to use a form of dream control to make light for them and ended up with only a pack of matches. A low rumbling of laughter indicated at least some of the group found that amusing.

Ashlyn's face turned completely red, her mouth bone dry from the attention. Being in the spotlight frightened her. Alone with her friends, she didn't mind being teased, but here, in front of everyone, was different.

"We found a stick and made a torch. It was good enough to help us through the path. In the background, we could hear dogs howling. It sounded like they were being tortured in the worst possible way. It was eerie." Clairity's eyes fixated on nothing - lost somewhere between the cabin she was sitting in and the haunting memory of the sound.

"I guess I need a lot more practice calling for items in dreams. At least we could light the torch." Ashlyn hadn't wanted too many people to know about the red help button or her poor excuse for a light. Her words shook to the point of stuttering as she continued to tell the others of their experience. "Then we came to a room. There were people in cages. We couldn't see their faces, but their hands were reaching out to grab us. Some were calling for help, others screaming in pain and some crying. It was horrible." The look on her face went blank as if all expressions were erased from existence, as she too remembered the events in the dream. "The whole place was horrible."

"The air held a damp smell, mixed with an earthy rot. Not a normal rotting smell. It wasn't wood or food. It was something worse. On the far side of the room was a wooden door. There was nowhere else to go, so I opened it." The colour of Willow's eyes dulled. "Inside were what appeared to be men, but they looked like they were damaged. It was still dark and exact details of their faces weren't clear, but I could make out cuts with dried blood. Their peeling greyish coloured skin revealed gaping holes in their flesh in spots. They were hitting someone chained to a chair and asking questions. At first, I couldn't make out any words, everything was muffled. I moved in closer to see if I could find out more and it was

Mike. He was hurt badly, with a lot of bruises and cuts. They were torturing him for information about… me."

She felt her face burning and the sting of swelling tears. Outside, the weather turned for the worse. Willow still hadn't learnt how to stop her emotions from changing the forecast. When she cried, the clouds did too. That was one of the areas of her magic she needed to work on. "We have to help him. You can't deny the dream is what the prophecy describes."

"Yes, it is," William said as if he were thinking. He paused, tapping his fingers on the table. "I am going to try to contact Mike. We will figure out where the place is that you saw in your dream and put together a team to go investigate as well. There is little we can do this second. I suggest everyone head back to bed… until we see if Mike answers. Then we will know the urgency of the situation."

"There must be something we can do now!" Clairity exclaimed, standing up. Her hands slammed palm-down on the table. She slunk back down into a sitting position again.

William's eyes locked on the young psychic's with disapproval. "No, it's late. We don't have a location yet. We don't have confirmation Mike is missing and we are all useless without sleep."

From the tone of his voice, the girls could tell arguing wasn't a good idea. They could hear his authority in every word. Reluctantly, they agreed to his terms and returned to bed, albeit none of them believed they would be able to sleep.

Chapter Thirty-Two

The three young keepers were up early, dressed, and waiting in the command centre for the others to join them. They chose to remain up the rest of the night, partly not wanting to waste a minute of the day and partly because none of them wanted to drift back into the dream again - at least not this soon.

It didn't take long for everyone else to arrive. There was little chatter this morning, even though more of the camp was at this meeting than the earlier one. Zsiga's coffee was brewing again. It dawned on Willow for the first time that she actually enjoyed the familiar smell. It was compelling enough that she might even try some one day. Her eyes browsed over the others as they lined up, still half-asleep, each wanting a taste of the magic liquid. Every one of them would swear that drinking a cup would give them energy and make them more alert. In a sense, it was a different type of magic than she was accustomed to.

A thud came from the front of the room. William's feet dragged, causing him to almost trip on the carpet as he entered. He gazed around, peeking out from beneath half-closed eyes and messy hair. The strain of always being the first up and the last asleep showed in his sluggish movements.

Thinking about it, Willow realized how much work he actually did. He was their link to this world. He found all the books and materials they needed for research, monitored events around the world, put together the camp, provided food and other necessities of life, investigated disturbances and coordinated their forces. When there was a decision to make, everyone turned to him to make the right choice. Nothing would happen without him.

"Did you hear from Mike?" Clairity blurted out before he had a chance to settle in, oblivious to the lethargic mannerisms he was displaying.

Willow turned to look at her, finding her friend's concern for Mike a little odd. Did she have a crush on him as well? Pushing the thoughts from her mind, she convinced herself that Clairity was entirely motivated by psychic feelings. Her friend was simply worried for his well-being. She allowed the rhythm of her breathing to calm her. Without proof otherwise, it was silly to start acting like a jealous girlfriend.

"No," William said, taking a seat. He thanked Diana for handing him a fresh cup of coffee. After one sip, he straightened from his slouched position. He turned his head from side to side, forcing a loud crack. "And I couldn't contact his sister, either."

Sister, she thought. She hadn't known Mike had a sister. Thinking about it, she didn't really know much about him at all - none of them did.

"We are going to need to hear everything," Willow demanded. "I know you respect his privacy, but if we are right, he needs help. He has been gone for a while."

"Yeah." William yawned. "Okay, we have to go back a few years and there are some things I need to explain to you along the way. Mike's sister, Annabelle, is a witch." Letting out another yawn, he moved to the coffee pot to fix another cup.

"A monster!" Willow screamed.

"No, give me a chance to explain," William said. "Here in this world, there are people who practice witchcraft - Wicca. Keep in mind, this is how it was explained to me. I don't study Wicca myself, so it may be a bit of a crude description. Witches, warlocks, wizards, whatever name they go by, do have rituals, spells and potions, but their beliefs are based on nature and balance. Of course, as our wise tree said, there is always the potential in every living thing to choose to do something good or bad. People who practice witchcraft are no different. Believing in balance, however, means they know whatever they do is coming back to them, or has consequence. If you cause something bad to happen to someone, there has to be an adjustment of sorts to make up for what you did - to even things out, so to speak. It's a way of life and you couldn't tell someone who practices the craft from anyone else by looking at them. You all need to do research and learn what is fiction and fact on this topic. I don't want anyone insulting someone because they don't have all the facts. That includes me."

Willow thought for a moment about the ancient tree he was referring to. Most of the camp were now portal guards because of Acacia's gracious gift. For Willow's people, that meant their natural abilities were stronger and combat skills came naturally. For the others, who lived in this world, it meant extended life as well. She shook her head, forcing it back into the topic at hand. "So why do people dress up in costumes?"

Willow's question was almost cut short. "I was coming to that." William put an aggravated tone in his words hoping to avoid being interrupted too much. "Throughout history, witches have been depicted in legends and stories as some horrible evil. They usually have extreme powers, controlling nature, casting curses, calling devastating storms, sacrificing babies or young women to further their abilities. In stories, myths and legends, their kind are mostly described as ugly, wearing all black, big hats with points, warts, flying around on broomsticks and even sometimes with green skin. You get the idea. Obviously, that isn't true."

"I wouldn't necessarily say that," Shelby said.

"What? Which part?" William asked, staring at the bird.

"If we consider that these stories are based on this world interacting with other worlds, which is what I believe we are thinking, the princesses, King Cornelius' daughters... well, the venom their parents drank had a slightly different effect on the women of their family line. They do in fact have green skin and they are known to be powerful witches, the likes of which have been depicted in many of these stories. There is no doubting their abilities when it comes to casting spells. They also happen to wear all black. It is possible that it is people's interaction with these three that has been documented at various times throughout this world's history. Other strange occurrences that have been recorded from time to time could be attributed to witchcraft as well," the bird answered. "The men of the family are necromancers. They practice death magic. I would imagine as we delve deeper into legends there will also be mention of sorcerers with the ability to control or manipulate the undead."

"Eerie how this all sort of ties together, isn't it?" Ashlyn shivered, her hands trembling. Sometimes her statements made people wonder if there really was a light clicking on and off inside her head.

"But if the three of them have been to our world, why didn't they destroy it? Is that not what they do?" Faramund asked.

"Because," Willow answered, pausing for a moment. "Of course." An expression came over her face as if she solved all the secrets of the universe. "They don't want to destroy this world. They want to rule it. That's the master plan. That's what they are building the army for. This world is too big for them to invade just yet. They are still building forces."

"So we need to figure out where they are able to enter and exit this world and take that access away from them," Faramund said.

"I think we need to figure out where Mike is first. My gut tells me there is a connection." A pencil on the table in front of Clairity spun without being touched. Her gaze locked on it, hypnotizing her into some deep vision.

"I think you are right. Let me finish the rest of the story," William said, ignoring the pencil. "Annabelle was young and new to the craft. She had just joined a coven of her peers. There were thirteen in the coven, including her. One evening, during a gathering, a strange occurrence happened. One family member of each of the witches in the coven died in a freak accident - all thirteen, at the same approximate time and on the same evening. Mike's older brother, Joseph, died that night. In another strange coincidence, the wakes, where people can view the bodies of their loved ones to say goodbye, for each of the deceased were all held at the same funeral parlour. Again, it all happened on the same day."

He took a sip of coffee from the cup sitting on the table in front of him before continuing. "After all of the services and visitations were completed and the families had left for the night, the coven gathered again. They decided they would attempt to contact the departed to find out what happened and if it was an attack on them directly. When I interviewed them later, they claimed there was no response."

"Is it possible to contact the dead?" Ashlyn asked. Their extended life meant there had been no recorded death in her world for as long as she could remember. At least until the day she was forced to flee through the portal. The concept of passing on and what came after was a new idea for her and the others from her world to ponder. None of them ever considered the possibilities of what happened after life, or if there was something more to go on to. Even after the devastation of their home world, not one of them wondered if their friends and family went somewhere else.

Willow looked down, her bottom lip quivering with a deep remorse for never taking the time to contemplate if there was some other place where her parents might have moved on to. In all the years she had thought they were dead, she had simply accepted they were gone. Now, although there was a chance they were still alive somewhere, there was also the possibility that if they were dead, they moved on to a new existence. She jolted back to reality at the sound of William's voice.

"There is no definitive answer. It depends on who you ask," he said with a look of contemplation on his face. He blinked twice before continuing. "The topic is too large for us to cover at the moment. It requires a lot of self-reflection. I think we should just continue the story for now. After Halloween, if there is time, you can research the different possibilities on your own… draw your own conclusions."

The others agreed and he resumed: "When Annabelle returned home, she found Mike on the floor holding their father's gun. All of their family was dead, having been brutally murdered in bed. Mike claimed it was their brother Joe, but the police ruled it a botched robbery. The strangest part is that the same thing happened to every member of the coven. Mike was the only family member to survive out of all thirteen families. He claimed to have shot his dead brother in the shoulder."

"Well, whoever it was couldn't have gone far then, right? They must have needed medical attention. Were they found?" Clairity asked, her attention locked on every word. It was like being huddled around in

Diana's sitting room back home, where storytelling had been the best and only entertainment available.

William raised an eyebrow and looked at her. "No... and another break-in occurred that evening as well. All of the bodies from the funeral parlour disappeared, all thirteen. They were found two weeks later - all exactly the same as when they went missing. There were no signs of decomposition at all. The only thing the medical examiner could find that had changed was that one of the bodies had a bullet hole in his shoulder... Mike's brother."

"For real?" Willow's eyes fixated on the guard as if they were sitting round a camp fire, listening to ghost stories. Goosebumps formed on her arms.

"The story caught my attention and I went to check out what happened to see if there was some other world connection. I found Mike. He blamed his sister, had nowhere to go and was going to be lost in foster care. So I took him in. He hadn't spoken to Annabelle since. That is, until the other day. She mysteriously called saying it was urgent they talk and left out why. I told Mike to take some time and work things out with her. You all know the rest."

"In the dream, they wanted information about... me." Willow looked down at the table, her fingers entwined in a nervous fidget. "Could this all be about me?"

"We don't know what this is about. Let's figure that out. Dreams can be difficult to decipher - as hard as the prophecies. There can be some things that are exactly the same and others that are vague, or even signs and symbols. Don't jump ahead of yourself. It may not be about you at all," he answered, getting up and moving to the maps. "Okay, so there are several locations that are well known for, or have a long history of witchcraft. They are..."

"Wait!" Willow screamed, looking up. "I know this is going to sound weird, but I don't want to know where."

"What?" His face contorted in the strangest manner as if forming a question mark from expression. "This was your idea... to find Mike."

"Not what I meant, exactly. When I was asleep in the medical facility, in the dream with the prince, he wanted to know where I was - as in where he could find me."

She paused for a moment. The memory of being in bed for weeks, healing Shelby's wounds, raced through her thoughts. Richard, the doctor, called it a coma. All eyes locked on her, questioning her silence and waiting for her to continue.

"I didn't know, so I couldn't tell him," she explained. "Knowing now that they could potentially have found us if I had that information, I realize it was a good thing I wasn't aware of the location. If I don't know where I am, where I am going, or where I have been, anyone reading my mind would just get random images of places. It wouldn't make any sense. They wouldn't be able to use it against us."

"That makes sense in a strange, off-the-wall, kind of way." Sarah stopped where she was, waiting to pull out the maps for the group to look at. "The less of us that know how to find us, the better off we are, wherever we are."

Her face and nose crinkled up, knowing how awkward her statement when articulated, actually sounded. She slid back into her seat at the table without making eye contact with any of her peers, hoping none of them noticed.

"Okay, but that makes our job even harder. There are hundreds, if not thousands, of places around the world where witchcraft has a history. Unless Clairity can use her third eye, we will have a problem narrowing it down." Sitting again, William scrunched up the piece of paper he had been writing on and tossed it at a small garbage pail in the corner of the room. The ball teetered on the rim for a moment before falling in. William clenched his fist and pulled his arm towards his chest, satisfaction dripping from his smile.

Malarchy raised an eyebrow. "Third eye?"

For a moment, Willow imagined an eye right in the middle of Malarchy's bald head. A little giggle escaped her lips. William cleared his throat in disapproval before anyone else noticed. Changing the noise to a cough, she moved her arm to cover her mouth.

"Yeah, her ability to see things others can't. Our world calls it that. It's considered a sixth sense. You have sight, sound, smell, taste and touch already. Some people develop an extra sense. Since it involves sight into the unknown, it became known as a third eye." William's stare remained locked on Willow.

"Maybe she could," Sarah said, getting up. "I was reading an article a few weeks ago. It studied the senses. In all cases where a person didn't have use of one of their senses, the others compensated and became stronger. It didn't exactly deal with the sixth sense, just the normal ones, but the idea behind it should still apply."

"So, if we blindfold her and give her a pin, she may be able to show us on a map where to go." He left the room and came back a moment later with a piece of cloth. "This should do as a blindfold."

"Wait!" Clairity stood, inching backwards towards the door while waiving her hands in front of her. "I have no idea what you are talking about. I don't know if I have another eye, nor do I want to grow one!"

A few chuckles exploded around the room at the thought of Clairity magically growing an additional eye. William, having heard the joke once from Willow already, quickly cleared things up. "No, it isn't actually an *eye*. It just refers to you being able to see the unknown - things that others can't."

"What do I have to do?" the young seer asked, leery of whether this plan was a good idea or not.

"I am going to blindfold you - put something over your eyes so you can't see using your normal sight. Then we will pull out maps. We'll start with a world map and narrow it down from there. You just put a pin in the map where you feel it is that we should go."

"I... I don't know if it will be right. I haven't done anything like this before." She shivered.

"Just give it a try." Willow put her hand on her friend's shoulder. "Your feelings have been spot-on every time. Let them tell you what to do. Don't overthink it."

Clairity nodded. She swallowed the saliva pooling in her mouth with a loud gulp as William tied the cloth around her face, leaving her blind. William asked everyone else to step outside for a moment to eliminate unnecessary noises. Only Clairity and Sarah remained in the room with him.

Sarah pulled out a world map attached to a standing board and placed it in front of the blindfolded girl. "Okay, this is a world map. We want to narrow down which part of the world we need to be looking in. Just place the pin in the general area."

Clairity stood still for a moment and then moved forward. Unlike most people with their vision impaired, she walked directly to where she wanted to go. There was no bumping into anything or stumbling. She placed the pin in the map with confidence. The other two glanced at each other, a look of disbelief on their faces, both wondering if perhaps she could see through the cloth. Even when playing childhood games of pinning tails on animals, neither could remember anyone, who could find a place to pin the tail to, with such ease. Part of the fun of the game was watching kids stumble around and miss the picture altogether.

"Are you sure you can't see?" Sarah asked.

"Positive. Did I miss the map?" the girl reached up to her face trying to move the blindfold.

"No! No, not at all." William moved her hand away from the cloth. "Okay, let's try a more detailed map of that area."

The new map concentrated on the area in which Clairity had placed the first pin, showing towns and cities. Both Sarah and William were shocked when the girl asked for two pins this time, saying she *had a feeling* she needed the two to properly answer the question. After receiving another, she proceeded to place both on the map in two distinctly different places, once again having no problem finding her way without being able to see.

William smiled, shaking his head. "Perfect!" He removed the pins and motioned for Sarah to remove the blindfold while he called the others back in.

Everyone settled back into seats eagerly awaiting information as to whether their little experiment worked or not. Even Clairity wasn't sure yet.

"So?" Willow asked, her eyes bugged out.

William looked at all the faces directed at him with anticipation. "Well, it's interesting. She picked two witchcraft hotspots. Even more interesting is that one is where Mike was heading."

"So let's form a group and go check it out." Willow jumped up from her seat, heading for the door, eager to get started.

"Hold on there. We need to take a look at that dream a bit first. There may be some important clues we need to know. The symbols on the door, can any of you draw them? The signs... you said you picked the snake picture. What were the other pictures? Was there anything else unusual that any of you noticed?"

"The symbols were lines and letters." Clairity took some paper and a pen and drew *XIII*, *MCCCXIII* and *XXVI*. "It doesn't mean anything, if you ask me."

"Those are Roman numerals." Seeing a look of confusion of the face of the others he added, "A form of numbers. The first one represents thirteen, the second one; one thousand three hundred and thirteen, and the last; twenty-six. It seems thirteen is becoming a common theme."

"The signs. On one side of the road was a picture of a cat, a bird and a wolf and on the other side of the road, a spider and sea creature and a snake." Ashlyn sighed, thinking back to how she had wanted to choose the kitty sign and not the snake.

"Well, I don't think there is any coincidence that those are the original six forms of guardians. Interestingly enough, however, they are also all considered a type of witch's familiar, a helper of sorts... a supernatural being thought to have powers of their own and that could take on the shape of an animal. In lore or sensationalism, a cat, bird or wolf tended to belong to a white witch, the 'good' side. Whereas the others were more common for those who practice darker magic." William paused for a moment. "Was there anything else?"

"Well, yes," Willow answered. "On one of the book shelves, I thought I saw a copy of *The Portal Prophecies*. I know it isn't possible because there is only one copy."

"What if someone wrote a book by the same name? If it has to do with witchcraft, maybe we should track a copy down, find out what it is about and who wrote it." Sarah didn't even pause long enough to look up from making notes on her laptop.

"Agreed," William said.

"Then there was the old woman. Why was she there and what was the slimy thing she was cutting up?" Part of Willow's top lip raised. She made a sour face, sticking out her tongue at the memory of the black worm-like creature being chopped to pieces before her eyes. "Maybe we should figure out if her prophecy is connected to all this?"

"If it is a prophecy," William answered. "Her description and her clothes suggest that she might be a gypsy. There are some swamp areas that have black leeches like the creature you saw her cutting up, bloodsuckers. These areas are known for gypsy witchcraft. The second location chosen by Clairity on the map is one of them. If she is a friend, it is a prophecy. But if she is an enemy, it could be a curse... a Halloween's curse. We need to figure out which she is and how she is connected to all this."

"Something tells me we need to look for Mike first. Answers will come whether we look for them or not." Clairity gazed off into the distance. "I am not in a hurry to face bloodsucking worms, either. That is worse than any creature we read about in books back home."

William chuckled, considering how leeches could appear to be worse than some of the most hideous creatures recorded in keeper books. Their description was rather frightening now that he thought about it. He glanced quickly at his notes and moved his thoughts back on topic.

"Interestingly enough, there are some hidden portal stones somewhere at that location as well." He shifted his eyes from one person to another, studying his options. "We will need to infiltrate the witch community and appear to fit in. Any suggestions?" His attention turned to Willow, knowing she would be the one to reply.

"Well," she started, "I would suggest that the team to go to the first location be made out of some or all of the following possibilities: myself, Clairity, Camile, Jade and Sarah."

"Me?" Sarah screeched, although it sounded more like a high-pitched noise. "Why me? I have no abilities or knowledge of the occult that could help. I am definitely not the one for the job. I am sure I would be much more help here."

"We will need someone who knows certain things about this world, like money. Where to get it. How to use it. Not to mention how to drive. I don't think a crash course can get any of us ready to interact in your world fast enough for this job."

William grunted. "She has a point. I never thought of all that. Guess the other night did you some good after all."

Willow couldn't help but wonder what he meant by that. Had Mike said something to him? She couldn't ask in front of everyone. Actually, she couldn't see asking William at all, at least not yet.

"And the others? Why did you pick them?" he asked. "They are... unusual choices."

"Since we are trying to blend into a community rich with witchcraft, I figure it should be people who can appear magical who go. My abilities, I think, are self-explanatory. Someone disbelieves I am gifted and I can make a large branch unexpectedly fall or clouds swirl followed by an unexpected downpour. Clairity, her sight gives her a pass into the witchcraft world and could help us out of a bad situation. Camile has potion knowledge. Need I say more?" She turned her attention to the girl sitting as far away from the group as possible. "And Jade, your illusion powers will come in handy."

"For what?" Jade said without looking up.

Willow grabbed her arm and turned it so the portal guard mark was facing up. "Make it disappear," she said. "Use your abilities to hide it."

Jade looked at her arm and the mark vanished like it had never existed. William stood up and looked at where the symbol used to be.

"How?" he asked.

"Easy, it's an illusion. Jade is very talented with it, even if she doesn't believe in herself. She has been using her gifts for as long as I can remember. Hopefully she will find her confidence on the way," Willow said. "Faramund will have to teleport us to a remote area fairly close to where we are going. Sarah can navigate. If you wish to send a second group in for added protection, you can. We will need to keep contact to a telepathic form, unless there is an emergency and even then as little as possible."

"And the second group?" William asked, looking at her out of the corner of his eye.

"I thought you would want to figure that out. The less we know, the better. We will keep contact with only you and Faramund. Then you two can share whatever is necessary with whoever else needs to know."

"We will need a place to stay," Sarah said. "I will make arrangements and let you guys know when we have rooms. I am still not sure I am the one to go, though." She hadn't left the camp since arriving, her family having been brutally murdered by vamprite, a race this world referred to as vampires.

"It'll be great!" Clairity squealed. An electricity flowed from her words encasing anyone near her in excitement. "Just us girls. I can't wait." Her attitude was contagious.

"Alright, you girls start packing. As soon as we have accommodations in place, you will be on your way," William said. "Oh, and Willow, be careful. If someone is trying to find you, we could be offering you to them on a silver platter."

Willow looked down at the ground and back up at William. "Why would I stand on a silver platter? I promise, I won't take one with us." She darted a perplexed gaze at him before heading out to start packing bags.

William mumbled to himself in a low voice, "What are we getting into?" He shook his head before going back to work, choosing his team to offer the girls the backup he knew they would need.

Chapter Thirty-Three

Each of the girls were beginning to put a few items in plastic bags when Sarah came into their sleeping quarters and broke out into hysterical laughter. The thought of travelling using plastic bags instead of luggage somehow hit her directly in the funny bone. "I figured we would need a wardrobe trip," she said, motioning for them to follow her to one of the last buildings on the property.

Opening the doors, the girls looked in and each one, even Jade, smiled. It was filled with clothes, accessories, shoes and makeup. A teenage girl's dream room, waiting for them to explore.

Sarah's grin spanned from one ear to other. "Well… get in there and try stuff on!"

She didn't have to tell them again. The girls ran in and began trying on different outfits, giggling at silly ones and *oohing* and *awing* at the fanciest. They tried on belts and jewelry; matched outfits with purses; and modelled hats of all different sizes and shapes. After having fun for a while, the girls settled into choosing outfits for their mission.

"I think we should wear all black." Willow held a revealing black outfit up to her frame while turning from side to side, admiring the possibilities in a mirror.

"You don't have to tell me twice." Clairity always wore dark colours - somehow, they suited her looks. Her hair had settled on midnight black, and when in the sun, one could see deep blue hues glistening in it. It was cut in a short bob style which framed her face, accentuating her porcelain white skin and dainty features. Like a china doll she was lucky enough to have a perfectly molded bone structure, from her high-cut cheekbones, to her cute nose and tiny feet and hands. Each of her petite, thin fingers were topped with a perfectly shaped, long fingernail. Painting them different colours was a recently discovered passion. Nail polish was new and exciting, something their previous world never offered. She looked through the different colours available, displaying an expression of intense satisfaction when she found a jet black one.

Jade picked out some outfits in bright flashy colours and pastels. The others flashed her a strange look. "It doesn't matter what I wear." She held an outfit under her chin in a mirror. "I can make everyone see something black." Turning around, she stood in front of them dressed in a black one-piece sundress with a large southern style black hat. The girls giggled.

"That would be fun." Clairity smiled at her. "Changing into anything, just by thinking it. I can see why you changed clothes so much back home." Seeing the gloomy look on Jade's face was enough to tell her she struck a nerve. Trying to recover from her faux pas, she returned to looking at the clothes.

This was the most civil Jade had been with them in... forever. Willow couldn't help but think this new Jade might one day become a good friend. If Acacia could give her a second chance, surely she could. The girl had experienced as much suffering as anyone else, if not more, having to watch her mother die in front of her eyes and knowing it was a result of her actions. Her brother, Jordan, had been taken away as well, now a prisoner of King Cornelius somewhere. Jade lived every day realizing she might never see him again on top of everything else. A thought crossed her mind, erasing evidence of joy from her face. How many people from her town actually survived?

Sarah pulled out some large material bags she called luggage and the girls quickly packed all the things they would need from frilly black dresses to jeans and sleepwear. The smaller bags they loaded up with accessories and makeup.

"That's it," Sarah exclaimed. "The reservations are all made. So, whenever you girls are ready, we can head out. You may all want to pick out something to wear now, for when we arrive. Maybe something with a little mystery." She picked up a hand fan. Flipping it open to cover all of her face except her eyes, she blinked numerous times. The building echoed with silliness.

"Someone's getting a little adventurous." Clairity smiled, nudging Sarah slightly, knocking her over into a pile of soft feather boas.

"Might as well enjoy it. I don't get out of the camp much." She buried herself in the feathers then jumped out, startling everyone into another round of laughter.

Returning to the task at hand, Sarah chose a full suit, black dress pants with flared legs, black short boots underneath with half-heel, a silver blouse and black tailored jacket. Her hair was tightly wound in a bun on her head and she wore square black rimmed glasses. The others couldn't help but agree the look suited her much better than the camouflage green baggy pants and shirts she usually wore.

Clairity wore a form-fitting short black dress with full sleeves to cover her arms and a black leather half-jacket. Dark sunglasses and red lipstick finished her look. Jade stuck with her belle of the ball southern dress and hat illusion. Camille picked out dress shorts, a tank top and a blouse over top tied at the waist, all in black as well.

Willow went for a black one-piece pant set with bell bottoms and a top that tied around the neck with an open back. She wore a jacket which resembled a cape, a wide brimmed hat and long black gloves. The look was definitely mystifying.

The girls filed out and joined the rest of the camp who were waiting for them to depart. After a chorus of whistles and wows, William motioned for everyone to settle down. He pulled a feather boa off of Sarah and handed Faramund the coordinates for where to take the group. The girls said their goodbyes, with especially big hugs to Ashlyn.

Shortly after, the green teleportation fog was disappearing and they were somewhere new. After watching their personal transportation leave, Sarah pulled out a map and directed everyone which way to go. The walk wasn't as far as Willow expected. It was only about fifteen minutes before they were entering a tall building called a hotel.

Everyone was surprised to see how nice the lobby was. The rotating glass doors continued to turn for a moment after they stepped out of their spins and into elegance. The grandeur within took their breath and words away. A large crystal chandelier hung in the middle of the ceiling, illuminating the whole area in a soft white glow. A large wooden desk stood in front of one wall, giving off a blinding glimmer as if it had been polished until it shone brightly just for their arrival. A sitting area was arranged around a double sided gas fireplace, which was lit, providing the perfect setting for a meaningful conversation. A beautiful tapestry carpet made with vibrant shades of red lined the floors. There was brass and glass everywhere. All of it shone to perfection, reflecting the images of anyone who looked at any surface. Even Sarah was shocked at the sophistication offered for such a low price. She asked the others to stay together and not speak to anyone, before heading to the desk to sign in.

Camille and Jade quickly became mesmerized by the tall backed, oversized chairs in the sitting area. They were so soft and comfortable - much nicer and bigger than anything they had seen before. The two girls were quite happy to take a seat and wait. Willow and Clairity moved to a stand of pamphlets offering different events to attend in the area. One in particular caught their attention: an evening walking tour of thirteen witchcraft 'must-see' stores, museums and places of interest.

"Are you interested in that tour?" a voice asked from behind them.

The two girls turned to see a woman dressed in jeans and a black t-shirt with white words that read *Witches gone wild*. She was older, maybe thirty, with messy brown hair. A pink hair clip had been thrown in on one side, presumably to keep her hair out of her face. It definitely couldn't have been for style. Her fingers fiddled with a necklace. Its charm engraved with a strange symbol on it that looked similar to a warped, sideways number eight.

"Do you like it? I just got it today. I thought I would wear it for luck." She extended her hand, holding the charm around her neck out for them to see while offering her other hand to shake hello. "I am Denny. I came for the tour too. It starts tonight, so if you want to join in you should get your tickets from the desk."

"Thank you," Willow said, looking back over her shoulder while pulling Clairity over to the front desk to ask Sarah to book the tour.

When the girls tapped on her back, there were still two women in front of her, who had already been at the front desk for some time. They were being helped by a woman wearing a burgundy suit with a crisp white blouse. Sarah turned around with a look of surprise on her face. After taking the pamphlet from them, she nodded that she understood. Surprisingly, the two people in front of her had just booked the same tour. The women turned around, leering arrogantly at the girls before walking away. Sarah began the check in process, requesting tickets for the tour right away. There were only four spots left.

"We'll take them," Willow demanded from behind Sarah, who added in a "please."

The girls agreed taking the stairs up to their floor was a better idea than using an elevator for the first time. Most of their senses were on overload already from the seemingly never-ending array of new experiences. On the way up the stairs, Sarah explained, there were two rooms that connected through a door on the inside, with two double beds in each room, suggesting each of them take turns sharing a bed. There were no arguments.

Entering the first room, the girls stood with their jaws hanging down for a few minutes as if waiting for something to fly in. It wasn't until after Sarah finished putting away her clothes that she noticed the others were standing perfectly still just inside the door.

"Are you guys okay?"

"This is where we get to sleep?" Willow asked, still not moving.

"Yeah, why? What's wrong?"

"Wrong? Nothing. It's... so nice." Willow walked to a bed and sat, then bounced up and down. "It's comfortable too, like a gigantic pillow." She took a deep breath in through her nose and closed her eyes. "It smells so fresh and clean. I love light floral scents."

The others mimicked her actions. Camile did a full-body dive onto one bed and the others gleefully bounced, excited by the sensation.

"I forget sometimes all the things you have never seen that I take for granted. Most people in this world grow up with all of this in their homes. We don't think twice about having comfortable beds and furniture." Sarah opened the inside door between the rooms, suggesting a bed rotation schedule. After everyone was settled, she opened her laptop and began typing. "I am going to look up some extra information on witchcraft while we wait until it's time for your tour. There must be a lot of information floating around out there that could be helpful."

The girls listened to stories of rituals and spells, as well as witch trials and executions. In between articles, Camile unpacked a case and proceeded to give the group certain items.

"Okay, so I brought one for everybody," she said, handing out umbrellas. When Sarah explained what they were back at that camp, Camile had been ecstatic. A device that could keep you dry if it rained meant never again having to worry about being outside after spending hours making curls. "They are all black. I thought we could take them with us... you know, just in case." She winked at Willow and quickly threw in, "You never know, it can't hurt to carry them."

The girls all giggled, but agreed to take them 'just in case' a 'freak' storm 'might' happen. Camile jumped up and down clapping her hands, giggling in a high-pitched tone.

"Wait, I have one more thing," she said, handing out timepieces to everyone. Camile was having trouble in this world being on time for anything. To solve that problem, William gave her a watch.

"They are brilliant!" she exclaimed, handing a pocket watch to Willow. "The short line tells you the hour and the big one the minutes. I made sure they were all set the same, so we will all be in sync."

Most of the girls received regular wind-up watches, not fancy but dainty for women, except Willow who was given the pocket watch, because she was wearing gloves and happened to have pockets. Camile was still wearing the big, bright, light-up digital watch William gifted her: an eyesore that appeared out of place on her wrist. She had set it to play a recording of "*You are late! Move it! Move it! Move it!*" in William's voice, over and over again on the hour until she pressed a button on the top to make it stop. She thought it was grand. Everyone else thought it was annoying.

"Listen to this," Sarah said, interrupting the girls' accessory party. "There is a Wicca celebration on October thirty-first, which is Hallows Eve or Halloween. It is a celebration of the dead, on a day when the space that separates the realm that contains the spirits of those who have passed on and the realm of the living world is thinnest, making contact possible. It's called Samhain. That sounds a lot like a split in the boundary between worlds. Maybe we can find out more information about it while we are here. Try doing some snooping while you are out tonight about the best places to be this year." She continued reading the article. "If we can figure out where to be, we might just be able to stop whatever the prophecy is about, from happening."

The girls agreed. Snooping was something they could do and would probably be good at.

Camile checked her watch in a way in which everyone couldn't help but notice and said, "Time to head down. We don't want to be late. Mission or not, I think tonight is going to prove most interesting."

All four decided to change into jeans with black tops, making walking shoes a priority. They also took a couple of backpacks, which they could take turns carrying. It was a walking tour and none of them knew if there would be anything in the stores they were going to visit, that they would end up buying. There was no sense carrying a bunch of shopping bags around for the night when they could put their treasures safely away in a bigger, easier to carry bag. Sarah handed them each some money for whatever they would need and gave them all the best lesson she could on the use of the currency.

It was time. After saying goodbye to her, they headed out the door to the staircase and started their descent to the lobby.

Chapter Thirty-Four

The lobby was deserted except for a small group of people lined up by the front door. Willow recognized the first person in line as Denny, the woman who had spoken to them about the tour earlier. After her were the two women who bought tickets right before Sarah and then turned their noses up, walking by them as if they were somehow more important. Following them was a couple, a small balding man with a bow tie carrying a black bag, and a large woman, who was obviously in control and barked orders every so often.

The couple were followed by a young group, who looked out of place. Willow imagined they were slightly older than her friends, but definitely under twenty. The two dark-haired women wore black tank tops and long skirts with slits at the side. Both tied their hair up in a messy bun, showing off curls, hanging out here and there. Their necks were adorned with black bead necklaces and a series of round rings of different sizes went up both arms, making clanging noises when they moved. Large earrings dangled from their lobes and each had a single black diamond pierced through the side of one nostril. If it weren't for the fact that one of the girls' skin tone was chocolate and the other was more a dark bronze, they could have passed for twins. The other two were male, wearing black muscle shirts and jeans, both with shaved heads and matching tattoos of some symbol on their arms. The four were busy making jokes about the people who were in front of them and hadn't even noticed there were people behind them now as well.

The girls made thirteen in the group, the number coincidentally appearing once again. By the look on her friend's faces, they noticed it as well. Why was that number coming up so often? What did it mean? Her thoughts were interrupted by a strikingly beautiful woman who glided out of the revolving doors at the entrance of the hotel.

"Good evening. I take it you are here for the witch tour?" she said with a smile, while she counted everyone in a whisper.

"Oh yes." Denny clasped her hands together. Her shoulders lifted up slightly as she smiled, then fell back to their usual place. "I have been waiting my whole life for this. It took me a while to save enough money to get here, but I know it will be worth every penny. I have a special gift too. I can tell if you possess the power by touching your skin."

The woman stopped dead in her tracks and turned around. Her face held about as much emotion as a painting of a bowl of fruit. "How interesting. Perhaps later you can tell us about our other guests."

"You can start with me," the lady behind her offered politely. "I am Delilah, a seventh-generation witch. My birthright allows me certain… advantages, as I am sure everyone knows. And this is my apprentice and assistant, Jessica."

"I don't know anything about birthrights, but I got the gift," the heavy-set woman behind the self-proclaimed witch said. "I can make things happen and, well, I made sure we won these tickets to be here tonight. I'm Mildred and this is my husband, Lester. He fetches me my supplies and carries things for me."

"Naomi, Delphine, Russ, and I am Gavin, just here to see what haps." Gavin was the bigger of the two men. He pointed to each of his group while naming them. Then the group engaged in a ritualistic little chuckle as if they all suddenly understood the punch line of a joke told days ago.

Attention turned to the girls. The tour leader glared directly at them. At first, none of them answered. Willow, realizing that no one else was moving, stepped forward and smiled. Her hand fidgeted with the watch in her pocket.

"I am Willow, this is Clairity, Jade and Camile. We came here to visit and look for a book or two we wanted for a collection of sorts and... well, we saw this," she said, holding up one of the brochures from earlier. "It spoke to us."

"It was a feeling. We needed to be here tonight... on this tour," Clairity added, knowing her best friend was faltering in front of the crowd.

"How interesting," the tour guide replied. "A coincidence. You just happened to be at the right place at the right time. Those are usually the most interesting. We aren't expecting rain." She smiled, pointing at the umbrellas before returning to the front of the line. "I am Lilabeth, your guide for the evening. I am going to show you the best stores, open especially for this tour and the best historical draws, a church, graveyard and ritual site. There are thirteen stops on the tour in all. If you make it through them all."

There were a few rumbles about who wouldn't get to the end and why. It didn't make any sense at all to the girls, a perplexed look forming on each of their faces.

Lilabeth was tall with black hair. Perfectly curled ringlets were left free to hang well past the midsection of her back. When she walked, each bounced up and down like a metal spring. She wore all black, except the inside of her jacket was lined in a shiny satin red that matched the colour of her lips. It was impossible to figure out what colour the guide's eyes were; they seemed a different shade every time she blinked. All four girls glanced up at the chandelier, wondering if perhaps the lighting was causing the effect.

I have a feeling we are missing something. There must be more to this tour than they advertise. We should stick together, Clairity spoke in a purely telepathic manner, ensuring no one else in the tour heard.

The line started shuffling out the door and down the street. The moon appeared full and bright, with clouds passing over every so often - the sky noticeably void of stars.

As if reading minds, Lilabeth spoke to the group, "Although the sky appears as if there are no stars, I assure you they are there. It is just an illusion they have vanished. Why, you ask? Perhaps to show the beautiful full moon more clearly. Possibly magic? Illusion or glamour is a strong gift many witches would love to possess. Or possibly clouds or smog and the illusion is caused by human parasites destroying nature. Imagine if you were locked in a world where there were never any stars. Would you miss them?"

"The common have no respect," Delilah scoffed.

"They can serve... a purpose," Naomi said, licking her lips, drawing attention to their unnatural bright red colour that stood out as if coated with a thick layer of lipstick. Her friends cackled loudly at the comment.

"I hope no one here is... non-magical. That would be awkward," Gavin added, still laughing.

What is going on here? Do all these people believe they are witches? Do they all have powers? Are we in trouble? Jade asked, communicating through her thoughts.

No, remember we all have power and relax, but let's cut the telepathic chit chat, girls. I think someone here can read our thoughts. Keep it under grips and think about finding that book, nothing more. Understand?

Willow hoped the other girls would receive her message and focus their thoughts on the book. She wasn't sure what abilities the rest of the tour group possessed, but she did know they weren't all witches. They all had powers, albeit different somehow and not anything she could pinpoint, for the moment.

"Probably not everyone here practices the craft," Lilabeth said without turning around. Willow knew if she did, she would be smiling.

"Do you read futures as well or just minds?" Willow asked, fishing for information and taking a chance their guide was more than she appeared.

Lilabeth laughed. "The future is not mine to see. Perhaps someone else in the group has an active third eye. As for reading minds, I have done this tour enough times to anticipate what is being thought by the participants. It's nothing more than that, I assure you. We are coming to our first stop. It is the first place on the itinerary I gave you earlier."

"You didn't give us anything. I would know if we got something." Mildred planted her feet solidly in one spot.

"Check your bags or pockets. I gave them to you." The guide twirled one hand in a spiral above her head. "Remember to keep them."

Everyone stopped for a moment and checked bags, purses or pockets, whichever they brought, each finding a piece of paper outlining the first place they would be stopping at. Camille glanced at the other girls with a *how* look on her face, receiving back three *I don't know* shoulder shrugs.

The first stop was actually a trio of stores. Willow spun in a circle, clasping her hands together at the sight of a sign in one window about magic wands on sale and a second boasting *All Your Potion Needs*. Grabbing Clairity's hand, she directed her attention to the signs. They were on the right track. Those were the same signs the girls had seen in the dream.

"We should look in each," Clairity declared loudly. "We don't know where we might find the book." It wasn't really a lie. They were looking for a book called *The Portal Prophecies* but references to *the book* also become a way of talking about finding Mike without anyone knowing what they were up to. The girls agreed with a nod and a few awkward winks.

Lilabeth explained the three stores would be open for shopping exclusively for the tour. When they were done, they were all to meet outside in the small circular park between the shops. There were picnic benches to rest on, if there was a wait.

Gavin and his groupies claimed a table for themselves, showing no interest in looking in any of the stores. Everyone else headed towards the shops, eagerly looking for magic.

The four girls entered the first store, chosen out of proximity rather than interest. It was exactly as advertised. All it sold was wands and staffs. They looked at a few different types and pointed, whispering between themselves about what they might be used for.

"For channelling power, my dears." An older woman moved out from behind a curtain. She was completely bald and wearing an unusual blue and yellow tribal dress.

"Channelling power?" Jade questioned. "I am not sure we understand what you mean."

"Ah, new to the world of wands, are we? No problem... no problem. I can tell you all you need to know. As I am sure by now you know, the magic in each of us is different. We are not the ones to decide if any type of magic is stronger than another. I rather prefer to think of it as falling snowflakes. Each one is a snowflake, but no two are the same. The craft in us may manifest itself in any number of different ways. Some are outwardly more obvious than others... the things other people can see happen." She moved towards a wand and picked it up, caressing it gently as if it were her pet rather than a hunk of wood.

"So you mean you can see someone create fire, but not necessarily see someone reading minds or making a potion?" One of Camile's eyes twitched in anticipation of the answer. Practising potions proved to be a difficult task with the limited resources the camp offered.

"Yes, precisely. That is where wands come in. You see, you can channel any form of magic through a wand and turn it into any form of physical magic you like. For instance," she said, turning to a spoon on the counter behind her, "you can channel a single beam of power to cut through metal." A stream of light escaped from the tip of the wand the woman was holding and cut the spoon in two.

"Any power can do this? Clairvoyants, sleep walkers, illusionists, any?" Jade squinted, puckering her lips as if she was sucking on a lemon.

"Yes, any. All of us have some form of the craft within us... just not everyone admits it. You simply have to direct your power to the wand - will it, so to speak. It takes a bit of practice and a lot of concentration," the woman answered.

"Does it matter which we choose?" Clairity picked up a dainty wand no bigger than her pinky finger. She raised her eyebrows in curiosity as she spun the wand around in her hand, examining every detail before returning it to its case on a shelf.

"Oh heavens, yes. You must choose a wand that suits you. It is an extension of your personality - a part of you. It must fit. Look around carefully. There is one that will feel right when you see it. There is one for everyone, but you must decide it is the one for you. If the style of the wand isn't in tune with your essence, it won't work for you."

"So I couldn't borrow one that a friend of mine uses?" Camile's lips angled downward, not quite frowning.

"Definitely not. You are two different people."

"What if I lose my wand? Can I never use one again?" A genuine concern could be heard in Camile's words.

"You could get another one that suited you. There are those who have wands for every different type of magic they wish to practice. There is nothing to say you can't own more than one, if that is what you desire." The woman's eyes locked on Willow for a moment, watching her browse the different wands, but not picking up any.

Clairity lifted up a wand that was a little smaller than the others, all black with a dark blue stone on the tip. It wasn't fancy, but wasn't plain either. Funny enough, Willow hadn't even noticed that wand when she was looking around. She did however find a wand she and the others agreed would be perfect for Ashlyn. It was white, long and thin with a pink stone perched on the tip. Clairity added it to the one she was buying.

Camile found one which was made from a blonde wood with golden accents and a crystal diamond on top, while Jade chose one with all different hues of green and a large green gem on the top. The girls brought their choices to the counter and paid for them.

"None for you, my dear?" the woman asked, motioning to Willow.

"I am not sure any of these could help me," she replied.

"Well, seeing as you bought so many, the next one is free. Pick any that interests you. Look closer. I have a feeling perhaps one of these might captivate your attention." She pointed to shelves of wands behind her.

Willow took a moment to look around again. She was about to say she hadn't felt anything positive and perhaps the girls should pick out one for someone back home, when she noticed what looked like a plain stick behind the counter. "Can I see that one?" she asked.

"This one? How unusual," the woman said, handing the wand to Willow.

"Unusual how?" The smooth plain texture of the wood in her hands enticed her, drawing her in. A frown found its way to her face when nothing happened. She expected something more… maybe an aura to explode from it illuminating her face and making the choice obvious.

"Only the most trained witch would consider such a wand. For this wand to be your choice, you must be quite powerful. It is made from a branch provided by one of the oldest willow trees alive. The tree, when asked, gave its permission for only one branch to be used. A willow tree in some circles is considered a magical being in its own rights."

How couldn't that be perfect, she thought. *A willow tree, just like my name.* She paused for a moment, realizing she hadn't known before then that she was named after a tree.

The wand was no more than a glorified stick, straightened and smoothed, with a small tip on one end and handle on the other. There was no paint or gems or designs. Its plain new wood scent made her feel at home.

"Can I take this one?" Willow asked.

"Of course. I am a woman of my word. You can have your choice. May it serve you well," the shopkeeper said, handing it to her.

Willow put the wand in her back pocket and covered it with her shirt. She thanked the woman. Within a few moments, the girls were outside once again, heading across to the next shop - the potions store.

"You're up, Camile," Willow said, opening the front door. Inside, the room had a mixture of scents. Trying to separate them would be close to impossible.

"Mm, peppermint, rose petals, ginger, lilac, orange, lemon, sandalwood and jasmine. I love those scents." Camile stood still with her eyes closed, letting the smells fill her senses. Her face glowed as if a bucket of liquid sunshine had tipped ever so slightly, causing its contents to gently flow down on her, illuminating every line of contentment it could find. She took in a deep breath and let it out again before opening her eyes to a man standing directly in front of her.

"You know your ingredients, I see," the shopkeeper said. He was tall with white hair and glasses, wearing black pants and a white shirt. A plain white apron over top of his clothing showed off a variety of different coloured stains. "It is the more unusual ones that you need to know though, right?" He nudged her gently with his elbow, grinning, his smile showing off a golden tooth.

"Unusual?" Camile repeated in a question form.

"Yes, dead ladybug's wings, volcanic ash, whiskers, the juices from a poison ivy plant, dirt from an empowered graveyard, blossoms from a Christmas cactus, or lightning-struck wood - all powerful additives," he answered, tending to watering a plant. "Of course, you need to figure out what each is for. That takes time and dedication. But there are no shortcuts in magic. They lead to unnatural things."

"Is there a book?" Camile asked.

"A book? A book? There are no books for these ingredients. No. I am afraid I mistook you for a potion master. Anyone can memorize everyday ingredients from books. A real expert can see possibilities in everything around them. Using a book of someone else's work is as dangerous as are certain items used in potion making. You, my dear, are a weak link. Taking such shortcuts in your magic will doom you. Perhaps another store is for you girls. Good day."

The girls walked out silently exchanging looks of *what just happened?* They hadn't even had a chance to look around before they were thrown out in the street.

"I... I am sorry," Camile said. "I guess I need more work." Tears crept out of the corners of her eyes and trickled down her face, dripping off where her lips curled downwards to form a full frown - a direct contrast to the way she looked only a moment ago.

"It isn't your fault. That man was odd. Don't worry about it," Clairity said, hoping to make the girl feel better. "Okay, so one shop left then. Cheer up. I am sure we will find something marvellous in there." She entwined their arms and tried to put a skip in their step. It failed miserably, the two almost tumbling to the ground.

The girls walked across the park, passing Gavin and company still sitting on their picnic bench, to what looked like the smallest store from the outside. It was described in the pamphlet as a *Curiosity Shop, filled with every sort of treasure that wouldn't disappoint.* The store inside definitely didn't disappoint them. It was at least a hundred times bigger than the other stores they visited and filled to the brim with unique items, antiques and hard-to-find needs. Lilabeth and the rest of the tour group were already inside, busy searching every nook and cranny for exactly what they wanted.

A smash rumbled through the store followed by a high-pitched scream. "Lester, you idiot! See what you have done! Go wait outside for me before you destroy anything else I will have to pay for!" Mildred yelled.

"Yes, dear," her husband answered, pushing abruptly by the girls to reach the exit, having no desire to anger the woman more than he already had.

The four girls smiled at each other at the commotion before continuing on to look for something unusual that would in some way help them in their quest. They split up, heading in different directions. It didn't take long for Willow to find a bookshelf filled with the most unique and unusual books. Her fingers ran across the spines of each on the shelf, highlighting the titles.

She sulked after going through them all. *Drat, I was hoping The Portal Prophecies book would be here,* she thought to herself. Before she had a chance to turn and walk away, the exact book she was looking for fell on the ground, almost hitting her toes.

But that wasn't there before, she thought. *How can the exact thing I want appear?* She scanned the area to see if anyone was watching her or maybe reading her thoughts, but found no one.

She wasn't going to argue, but instead picked up the book. On the way to the front to pay for it, she passed Camile talking to Denny - both admiring something in a small black case. She couldn't quite see what it was from her vantage point, but thought it might be a piece of jewelry of some sort.

"Did you find everything you were looking for?" a little woman asked, breaking Willow's fixation on the conversation going on between her friend and the strange woman from the hotel. She faced forward to the woman speaking to her. The store owner stood on a stool. Willow had never seen a little person before and the look of shock must have been obvious on her face. "Something wrong dear?"

"No, no. It's just... I looked through the bookshelf and the book I wanted wasn't there. When I said the title in my mind, it was. Threw me off-guard is all," Willow answered, trying to hold her face in a manner in which to hide her obvious lie. She wasn't trying to be rude. With all the new experiences this world had to offer, surprises were always jumping out at her from left and right. In time, hopefully she would learn how to control her reactions.

"Well, I don't have a lot of room, so you have to ask for what you need for it to appear sometimes," she said, taking the money. "There are free samples in the bags on the way out. Make sure you take one."

"Thank you," Willow replied, smiling as she turned to where her friends were waiting.

Camile had in fact picked out jewelry - a charm of some sort. The symbol on it was familiar, but she couldn't remember from where. Neatly tucked under her friend's other arm was a book of potions that guaranteed success.

"Are you sure that's safe?" Willow asked.

"Yeah, it'll help me get up to par. No worries. There is no way sitting in that camp I am going to learn anything new. This is the best answer," Camile replied.

There was no time to argue as soon as they walked outside, they could see there was something else going on. The rest of the tour was already gathered and it looked like they were having a disagreement of some sort.

"He just came outside to wait. It was so crowded in the store," Mildred said, muffling words through her sobs. "You must have seen him. There is nowhere else to go. Why don't you tell us where he is?"

"We told you, lady. We didn't see your husband," Gavin answered, leaning on the side of the picnic bench. Naomi squatted on the table, with Delphine sitting cross-legged beside her. Ross stood at the other end.

Willow noticed they were all wearing leather jackets now. Had they had jackets before? She couldn't remember them carrying any.

"Well, he couldn't have just disappeared." Lilabeth flung her hand in the air again. "Spread out and everyone look. We can't have Lester missing. How long has he been gone?"

"About fifteen minutes," Mildred said, blubbering frantically. "Something broke and I sent him outside. I shouldn't have gotten so upset with him."

"Maybe he ran off with another woman," Russ laughed, his friends joining in.

Willow flashed a disapproving look. Her gaze caught Gavin's. His eyes mocked her, trying to provoke a response. She had no intention of backing down. Clarity tried to break the connection between the two, but failed.

"Watch yourself... witch," Gavin said, before turning back to his friends.

"What was that?" Camille asked. "Are you crazy? They are powerful; you shouldn't mess with them. Let's stay out of their way. Let them have their fun. They aren't hurting anyone by making jokes." Her sentences seemed disconnected and abrupt.

"Are you okay, Camile?" Clairity asked. "I feel something different."

"I am fine," she huffed. "Maybe you should try feeling where the lost guy is so we can move on," she barked back, walking away.

"I have a bad feeling right now and I don't know if it's about Lester or Camile," Clairity whispered to Willow.

An hour passed with no sign of the missing man. It was as if Lester never existed. There were no clues or leads. He simply vanished.

"We can't stay here all night. We have to finish the tour. We can contact the authorities as soon as someone has a working cell phone.

The land lines in the stores aren't working, either. All we can do is move on." Lilabeth tilted her hand, gesturing towards a dark empty road.

"I am not leaving without my husband!" Mildred yelled. "You… well, I am too much of a lady to tell you what I think of you and your tour right now. This is your event and I demand you help find my husband."

"Okay," Gavin said. "We feel bad we didn't see the old guy come out of the store, or where he went, so we will stay with Mildred and keep searching. We can catch up to you when we find him."

"How nice of you!" Lilabeth exclaimed, relieved she didn't have to spend the whole evening standing in a park. "But how will you find us? There is no map of the tour."

"No worries, we will follow your direction. I have a strong tracking ability. It's… in my blood," he answered, a coy smile creeping up on his face.

"You can follow the pamphlet, albeit there is no exact map showing roads between the places. It outlines the order in which we go to each. The next stop is the court house, which was turned into a museum, followed by a church and graveyard. You need to catch up to us by then to finish the tour as we continue on a pathway through dense forest land to ritual sites. It's far too easy to get lost in the woods if you don't stay with the group," Lilabeth answered.

She then turned to everyone else and said, "Okay, on to the courthouse for the rest of us. Many were accused of witchcraft and tried there. You will see the judge's quarters first, then where the victims of the witch trials were held, hanging poles and more. After that we continue on to the church and graveyard where bodies of the accused who had been sentenced to death were buried." Her eerie tone left visions of the murders in the minds of those who heard her.

The smaller group continuing on consisted of just Lilabeth, Denny, Delilah and her assistant, Willow, Camile, Clarity and Jade.

Chapter Thirty-Five

Sarah was sitting in the room alone, wondering what she should do while the girls were on the tour. She tried reading, managing two pages of a book: then resting, but her eyes were glued wide open: then doodling, but the images were frightening. She threw her sketchbook across the room and resorted to pacing.

Thinking back, she realized she hadn't been alone since the vampire attack claimed the lives of her family. Since then she stayed at the camp, where there were always people about - rarely even contemplating leaving. She looked down at the goosebumps growing larger amongst the tiny hairs standing straight up on her arms. She shivered, deciding it was time to check in with William and the others to let them know what happened so far.

William? Can you hear me?

Yes, Sarah, is something wrong? Do you need us?

No, I… just wanted to fill you in while the girls were busy was all.

Busy? Aren't they with you?

No, they found a pamphlet in the things-to-do rack in the lobby for a midnight witches walk, but there were only four tickets left, so I stayed behind.

What was it called, the tour?

It just says thirteen must-see witchcraft sites, a walking tour.

I just sent Zsiga to the lobby to find a copy. We need to know where they are. Have you heard from them since they left?

No, they left just before eleven.

I think we better meet. Is there a coffee shop near you anywhere?

Yes, just down the street. Why? Do you think something is wrong?

I don't know, Sarah, but seems odd there were only four tickets left for a walking tour. If there was a car ride or something to limit space, I could understand. Walking? I would have thought the more, the merrier.

I see what you mean. I never thought of that.

Sarah gave William the location of the coffee shop, then got dressed and walked the three blocks to meet up with them. She was the last to arrive.

"Hi. You guys got here quick," Sarah said.

William motioned for her to have a seat. "I think we have a problem. We couldn't find any pamphlet like you described and no one at our hotel has ever heard of it. I also did an online search and it brought up nothing. Did you bring a copy of the pamphlet? I tried to contact you telepathically, but the connection seems to be broken. We don't know why. We can't contact the girls, either."

"No, I just got dressed and walked over. The hotel is just three blocks away. My copy is in the room. We can go fetch it and talk to the lady behind the desk who booked the tour at the same time. No telepathic connection means the girls can't ask for help. They could be in trouble." A hair-raising sound of gnashing and grinding came from her teeth. She clenched her hands in tight fists, as if ready to do battle.

"Good idea. Let's go. Try to remember this is not your fault. You couldn't have known this tour might not be what it seemed." He took her arm and moved swiftly out the door to a car where Iskander, Faramund and Zsiga were waiting.

Sarah gave directions to William. When they pulled into the hotel, she let out a small shriek. Her mouth dropped open as if her jaw had been dislocated.

"You must have the wrong address, Sarah," William said.

"No," she answered, holding up the keys to the two rooms - the exact name of the hotel imprinted on a wooden key chain attached to them. "I don't understand. How can this be? It didn't look like that before."

The hotel was abandoned, and from the looks of it, it had been for some time. The windows were boarded up. A condemned sign swung loosely on what was left of the glass revolving door. William pushed through, with the others following behind him, except Zsiga, who stayed outside to keep watch for the missing girls.

Inside, the lobby was dusty and smelled as if it was used as a toilet for all manner of creatures. What little furniture was left was ripped and broken. There was no electricity. The giant chandelier had been removed or stolen, its dangling wires now the only indication of its existence.

William motioned to the overturned stand, which once housed the pamphlets of things to do in the area. Iskander checked all that were left, but shook his head. Nowhere in the pile was the particular one they were looking for.

They moved towards the front desk, which was covered in a thick layer of dust. Its wooden sides were smashed in by what appeared to be several footprints. Obviously, vagrants used the hotel as a place to stay for free - a fight breaking out between them resulting in the damage. There was a guestbook sitting on top of the counter. Although it too was covered in the same dust, it looked out of place. William blew the dirt off before opening it to the last entry. He read out loud the fourteen names appearing inside.

"Fourteen, so with you staying behind, thirteen went on the trip. That number is showing up a lot, isn't it?"

Looking down at the book again, a name vanished before his eyes. He blinked a couple of times, thinking his eyes were playing tricks on him and counted again. There was definitely one less name on the list. But where had it gone?

"Not anymore," Sarah said, looking from beside him. He was glad she confirmed his findings. "Lester just disappeared. That can't be good. I am so stupid. How could I let them go off like that? We need to find them. In the room I have the pamphlet. Maybe you can track them down by following the same route."

They walked carefully across the broken glass and furniture that was now the lobby, passing the door-less elevators. "How did you get around using them?" William pointed to the long fall down that would await anyone who tried to use one.

"Clairity thought they were all on information overload and it would be safer to take the stairs. She said it was just a feeling. Guess it was bang-on." Goosebumps ran up and down Sarah's entire body at the sight of the gaping hole. She rubbed her arms and shoulders, trying to shake off the feeling of utter fear.

They climbed the stairs using Iskander's little star for light and found the two rooms. She used the key to open the first door. Their luggage and clothes were all there, as well as her laptop, open as if she was using it, but the room was disgusting. It was dirty - the mattresses ripped with no sheets and springs popping through - bugs and rats crawling all over. The bathroom looked like a scene from a horror movie. Sarah screamed, grabbing the brochure from under a mouse.

"Here," she said, handing it to William, using two fingers so as to touch as little as possible. She shivered again, this time in disgust. Her skin began to turn a particularly odd shade of grey. At least adding vomit to the room couldn't make it any worse.

William looked at it, but the words were already fading and within moments, the pamphlet crumbled to dust in his hands as if it never existed. A perplexed look crossed his face. "Why don't you go outside with Zsiga and wait? We will pack up your things and get another room where we are staying." He wandered around looking for any clues that might have been overlooked.

Iskander escorted Sarah downstairs to wait. It didn't take long before all their luggage was outside and loaded in the car. William left instructions with Zsiga to stay out front in case the girls returned, but to stay in the shadows so no one knew what he was doing. He asked Faramund to return to camp for reinforcements. They basically needed all hands on deck. He continued trying to contact Willow's group telepathically with no answer. They were going to have to form search parties and find them the old-fashioned way, by looking.

The group returned to the strip motel where the men were staying and rented an extra room for Sarah. The signs of stress were undeniably written all over her face. Rest was the best thing for her.

By the time she was settled, Faramund had returned with Dezi, Jessie, Pete, Malarchy, Diana, and Nathan. William threw the guest book from the hotel down on the table as their only clue, explaining how there were fourteen names, including Sarah and the girls, and that it had changed to thirteen before their eyes.

Malarchy picked it up and opened it. "There are only twelve names now. Are you sure you didn't miscount?"

William took the book from him and looked at the names. He couldn't remember who was on the list before, but one was missing. Luckily it wasn't one of the girls. He did notice that Sarah's name was now fading. He figured that was probably because she was out of the hotel and away from any magic used on the building. Just to be safe, he sent Jessie over to her room to watch her for the night. Diana agreed to check in on her as well, in case she needed someone to talk to about what was happening.

"We need to form search parties. Keep in mind something is disrupting telepathic communication and we don't know how far that reaches. We may not be able to contact each other, so keep a look out for signs. There should be one person who can create a sign in each group. That means Dezi, your fire and Iskander, your little star. Diana and Nathan, you stay here. Track down whatever you can and find a prophecy to help if you can."

Dezi, Pete, and Malarchy formed one group and Iskander, Faramund, and William the second. They started from the abandoned hotel, each taking one direction. With all the traffic and people walking about in the evenings, someone had to see something. A walking tour of that many people would be hard to miss.

By the time it reached about two in the morning, most of the stores had closed. Only a few bars and restaurants were left open. Both groups quickly realized that stopping people randomly to ask if they saw the tour group was useless. Most patrons trying to walk home were drunk, barely knowing where home was. People working inside establishments had just as much information. Almost everyone they spoke to answered using the exact same language, "Do you know how many people come through here every day?"

The two groups took different routes, following the information Diana and Nathan provided them before they left. Nathan used his abilities to quickly read every pamphlet in the motel lobby about things to do and places to go in the area. They were looking at anything that might be significant to the witchcrafting world and be accessible in the wee hours of the morning. There were a few graveyards, churches, parks, memorials and known hanging sites to explore. In the end, each one came up empty. They were running out of places to check. How could the whole tour group just vanish?

A somber mood filled the air they breathed, suffocating any happiness that was left in them, leaving only misery. Where were the girls? What was happening to them? They continued to search down streets and alleys - anywhere they could find to look. Time was running out. It was an hour later that Camile's name began to disappear from the hotel registration book.

The search parties' paths crossed. They were both checking out the graveyard of an old church, thought to have the bodies of witches buried in it. With the six of them together, William opened the guestbook again. This time, Camile's name was gone. He stood still for a moment. His face told the story of a man who had given up hope. Wherever the girls were, they were alone. He couldn't help them and he knew they needed help.

"Come on, Willow, give us a sign, something..." He stood motionless, staring into space. It was unusual for William not to know what to do. Everyone always looked to him for answers.

"Are you okay?" Iskander asked.

A smile formed on William's face. "I don't believe it. Look! Above the forest over there." He took Iskander's shoulders and physically turned him around. The others followed suit. He pointed to clouds swirling, as if a storm was about to hit over top of a wooded area. "It has to be! No storm forms like that on its own."

The group of six headed towards the forest. They had a place to look now. There was hope again, at least for three of the girls. Only time would tell what Camile's fate was.

"We need to move quickly, in case it dissipates." William motioned to the others to follow him. "No one enters alone. We stick together. Last thing we need is to have to look for someone else."

Chapter Thirty-Six

The trip to the museum was uneventful and disappointing. What was more interesting was how few cars there were on the roads - in fact, there weren't any. Nor were there any people. Just a dark road, *like in the dream,* Willow thought. Even if people were sleeping, there should have been a few empty vehicles parked on the road somewhere. When they arrived at the museum, it wasn't much better. She dismissed her feelings that something was off as a result of the lack of clues as to where Mike was. The whole situation was throwing her for a loop.

The tour led them to the judge's quarters, the hanging poles, as well as where witches were put on trial and sentenced to death. It was interesting, but not helpful. The group, being smaller, moved faster. Soon, they were off to the church and graveyard, which Lilabeth promised would be sensational, seeming somewhat disappointed in the last stop herself.

Willow, Clairity, and Jade found the church fascinating. Their home world had provided no experience with religion, although each believed in a superior being or creator. They found themselves wanting to spend more time exploring the stained glass window pictures and the notion of worship, but Camile refused to enter. Instead, she insisted on sitting outside and waiting for them to look around. One person was forced to stand in the doorway to watch her, while the other two explored, occasionally switching places.

"You know we have to stick together," Jade said. "Remember what happened to Lester?"

Camile laughed loudly. "I am not going to disappear like that moron. Don't worry about me. You best watch each other's backs." There was something different about her voice that the others couldn't quite put their finger on.

When it came to walking around the cemetery she had no issues, laughing to herself about names and inscriptions on various tombstones. Even the other women on the tour noticed how strange she was behaving, whispering comments to one another just loud enough to be heard. Denny was staring at Camile constantly now, as if there was some strange attraction flowing between them - a circular river of infatuation.

"We will be heading through the forest now. It's a bit of a hike to a clearing in the centre. That's where rituals were performed and it is rumoured even some sacrifices were made." Lilabeth's voice carried an eerie tone, which was accentuated by a wicked smile.

Willow considered a possible connection between sacrifices and the blood wars. Perhaps that area had been used to harvest the blood of poor unsuspecting magical creatures. Before she could finish her thoughts, the tour group was moving again. There was still no sign of Gavin and the others.

This forest was an odd place. Usually being surrounded by nature, Willow felt at home. Here, the trees whispered dark warnings rather than playful thoughts. Placing her hand on one brought visions of blood and death. Backing away, she shook her head. Trees weren't supposed to show her horrors. Normally, they were a pillar of strength she could lean on. These trees were the opposite. They wanted someone to take away their pain. That was something she didn't know how to do.

Camile lagged behind, moving slower and slower as the tour went on. "Hurry up," Jade yelled back to her. "We need to stay together and the group is moving way too fast for your pace."

Hearing their friend's words, Willow and Clairity glanced back. By then, Camile was barely moving at all. Something was wrong. The girls backtracked to their friend's side. The only movement she was making now was a swaying motion from side to side, without falling over. Her shirt was open enough to see her new charm had left a scar burnt into her skin. It appeared as a picture, similar to the way guardians looked on Willow. That in itself was a wake-up call. How had she not noticed she hadn't heard from either Aslo or Kiera all evening? A simple glance at her shoulder confirmed they were still there. Something must have been blocking telepathic communications. How long had they been out of the loop?

"I can't contact anyone. Can either of you..."

Both Clairity and Jade shook their heads before she finished her sentence. Willow pulled the sleeve of Camile's shirt up and gasped. The portal guard symbol was gone. Something very bad was happening. What could be so terrible that she would lose her position as a portal guard? This was beyond their knowledge.

"We can't leave her here. We have to move her." Willow trembled, her mind saturated with negativity. "I can try to get the trees to carry her, but they aren't the friendliest in this forest. They have issues of their own. It sounds strange, but the trees have memories of terrible acts. It's like they are in shock. I am not sure how far we would get."

"Wait, let me." Clairity lifted her wand and closed her eyes, streaming all of her energy to lift Camile off the ground. "The clearing isn't too far. Hopefully we can catch the others and figure out what's going on."

The girls moved Camile's body carefully through the forest path until they came to the clearing. Clairity placed the girl back on the ground, in the same standing position as she was earlier. Lilabeth and the three other women ran over, each full of questions, wondering where the girls had been.

"Oh good, we were worried we lost more from the tour," the guide said.

"Good? Good?" Clairity yelled. "Does my friend look good?" She pointed to Camile swaying back and forth in some sort of a trance.

"What happened?" Denny asked, not taking her eyes off the bewitched girl. Her voice suggested she wasn't surprised at all, but rather happy to see the state Camile was in.

Intuition was a powerful tool. Willow's was demanding to be heard, refusing to allow her peace until it was. There was no shaking the feeling that Denny had a hand to play in what was happening to her friend. Ever since seeing them in the curiosity shop together, an odd vibe radiated from both of them. Whatever it was that controlled Camile, the same feeling radiated from the other woman as well.

"We were hoping one of you could tell us, since something hasn't been right this whole tour!" Clairity continued yelling.

The arguing voices faded in Willow's mind. Something else caught her attention: a stone table the centre of the clearing. It was similar to the one she had found in the keeper's library in her home world. She was drawn to it, finding herself standing over it. Her hands grazed over the etchings in the stone. The engraved words were written in an ancient language, the same one Nathan had shared with her the day she learned about his abilities back in their world - their secret language.

Astahkil Glaquool, she thought. *Beware Glaquool.* Glaquool wasn't a word she knew. She looked at the corners. It was definitely a portal. Her fingers traced across the top with her eyes closed. It was old. There were more words, but some were worn and faded. There was nothing legible. If only she could contact Aslo and Kiera to ask them about it. They were bound to have some insight. Without a telepathic link to her guardian counterparts, she had no voice that could reach them.

Then she realized, even if they couldn't hear her, they could still see. Her shirt fell to the ground, allowing her back to face the table. Under the cotton, button-up shirt was a tank top which left her shoulders exposed. When she turned her line of sight away from the stone portal base, the two cats were given a perfect view of it. Within seconds, Willow felt a tap from behind and turned around to see her two guardians sitting on the stone.

"Thank goodness," she said, exhaling the breath she was holding in.

"What is going on?" Kiera rubbed against Willow's arm with a purr. "All night we haven't been able to speak to you and we haven't heard anything since the hotel."

"Something or someone is affecting telepathic waves. I didn't realize anything could stop us from using our bond to communicate, but I guess the same principals apply as with any other form of telepathic speech." Willow went on to explain the night's experiences, from the hotel to where they stood now. "So do you know anything about this portal?"

"It's old," Aslo said. "From before the blood wars... before the time of the guardians. What was put in there is dangerous to every living thing. I suggest we leave it sealed. No need to mess with the danger that lies within."

"Problem is, I think whatever it is... is here."

The rest of the tour group took notice of Willow standing in the middle of the clearing with two black cats. Lilabeth crept closer, her feet landing softly on the ground as if she were weightless. She went up on her tiptoes with her neck outstretched trying to peek at whatever secrets were being hid.

"Private party?" the tour guide asked, knowing she had been spotted. "Mind if I ask what you are doing on the altar? It's considered a sacred place. I cannot allow anyone to defile it." She made a motion with the back of her hands towards the cats.

"Party? Without us?" Gavin asked.

Lilabeth's voice hit a high note. She almost jumped out of her skin at the sight of the four. Her reaction was contagious, sending a tidal wave effect through the other women, each letting out a little yelp or squeak of their own.

"Did you find Lester?" Jade asked, still catching her breath.

"Oh yes, Mildred and Lester are definitely... together," he answered. His friends smiled at his words in an unsettling manner. "So what do we have here? A witch's altar for sacrifices? Perhaps poor virgin maidens were stabbed through their hearts in this very place. Or maybe it was used for something else." His eyes fixed on the two cats sitting on the stone base.

"And what's up with Mesmer Girl?" Naomi asked, pointing to Camile.

"I don't think this is an altar," Willow said. "I think it's a sealed door keeping something very dangerous out."

"Or us in," Russ peered at her with contempt. He knew the comment held meaning for Willow and the two cats. It was a reference to when the portals were being created. Guardians meant to seal danger away from people. Some, however, believed they were sealing people in and taking away their right to freedom.

Clairity moved forward, looking at the stone base and then at Willow. "Do you think something escaped? Could there be something here?"

"I don't know. It's old, really old. It dates back before the blood wars. Whatever is in there was one of the first creations. Something sealed them in and put warnings on the door so no one would unseal it." Willow ran her hands over the four portal stones, a spark of energy jolted her hands as she touched each one.

"And how would a young thing like you know about the blood wars?" Gavin asked.

Willow hadn't thought about being overheard. *Guess the cat is out of the bag,* she mused, chuckling a little at her own sense of humour.

"It could be them," Jade said.

"We are honoured you think us that powerful, but we take no credit for that portal, nor did we touch your friend. We have done no wrong here." Gavin moved to position himself between Willow and the rest of his group. He crossed his arms over his chest, issuing a challenge for anyone to come closer.

"Of course not..." Clairity was about to go off on them when Willow cut in.

"They aren't the ones." She motioned for her friend to back down.

"Glad we established that," Naomi said, moving out from behind her living shield.

"Be careful, vamprite. We are not dealing with you today. There are more important issues for us to deal with," Aslo said, making the group of four jump backwards hissing. "If we are right, these beings are just as much a threat to you as anyone else. They have potential to wipe out all of existence. There are some creatures who cannot be allowed to roam freely in all worlds - no matter what you may think."

"Your cat spoke... it talks," Lilabeth said, taking a step backwards.

"What are they?" Gavin asked, ignoring the shocked tour guide. "The things locked behind the doors? Perhaps if you explained, we might understand better."

"I only know of legends told to me. The Glaquool were an advanced bodiless race made up of different gases. They craved experience and knowledge. It was like a drug for them. They found their form limited their ability to advance and sought out a way to change that. It wasn't long before they discovered that they could hide in everyday common objects that would allow them, on touch, to transfer to a host. Any living being was vulnerable. The Glaquool was believed to then devour the soul of the creature it infested, taking its place like a parasite. Their advanced metabolism, however, meant shorter life spans for the host body, requiring frequent changes."

"They were destroying far too many innocent beings to be left in the open. Their lack of concern for other life forms made them dangerous - too dangerous to be allowed to roam freely. They were sealed in a world of their own, by a power far greater than the guardians possess, doomed to live alone through eternity." Aslo perched himself on Willow's shoulder so he could see everyone directly, wanting a view that would allow him to size up the vamprite clan.

"Can they be destroyed?" Willow asked.

"I don't know. Their human bodies can definitely be destroyed, but presumably their essences will revert into whatever item they used to transfer to the body in the first place."

"Can the host be saved?" Jade asked, her eyes swelling with tears, fearing the answer she would receive.

"No. At least, not that has ever been recorded."

Silence followed. The clouds swirled above and rain fell in rhythm with Willow's tears. She reached for the umbrella, remembering how Camile gave it to her - excited that she might get to use one. Now she never would.

Looking up from her thoughts, she saw Denny staring at her friend again. *Denny,* she thought. The symbol on the chain around Camile's neck was the same as the mark on Denny's. The necklaces were the same. That's where she saw it before… in the hotel lobby. Denny, in the curiosity store, was talking to Camile. Denny was the enemy.

"It's Denny!" she yelled, pointing to the woman.

"What? Me?"

"Yes, you! You have the same mark on your neck. It's from the necklace you were wearing earlier. You were with Camile in the curiosity shop. You gave her the charm necklace and book. What did you promise her?" Willow asked.

"She simply promised your friend power. It was so easy. After being humiliated in the potions shop, Camile wanted to make it up to you - to look like she was ready to stand by your side. The poor girl was distraught worrying all of you would think her inferior. It's so sad." Although Camile was speaking, it wasn't her voice.

"Camile, can you hear me?" Jade yelled.

The girl laughed. "Camile isn't here anymore. Nor will she be returning. I have displaced her. This is my new vessel now and I plan to stay."

Willow couldn't contain her sadness. Rain poured down on them. "We have to send them back!" she yelled over the wind. "There is no other way."

"No, don't open the portal!" Aslo screamed.

A bolt of lightning came crashing down from above. Everyone ducked, covering their heads. When they looked up, the altar was intact, but Denny was gone. In her place was a smoking necklace with a charm like the one that was given to Camile. Gavin walked over and looked at it lying on the now-scorched black ground.

"Don't touch it. It isn't safe," Willow warned, her eyes not leaving Camile. "Can we destroy the charm?" she asked, directing her question to the two black cats.

"I don't know," Aslo said. "Most of the information I have are only stories. I don't know what is fact and what is fiction."

"You are quite the witchy, aren't you? Maybe you could hit it with another bolt of lightning?" Gavin said.

"I assure you, young man, she did not create lightning. You have read too many witch books. We do not control weather in such a drastic manner," Lilabeth said. "I don't know what's going on here, but we need to finish the tour and move on."

"Yes, take the others and go," Willow said. "I will stay with Camile and… chat a bit. We have a few things we need to work out."

"I am staying to help," Clairity said, Jade beside her nodding in agreement. There was no way they were going to allow anyone else end up with a similar fate.

"We are staying, just to make sure you three don't do anything stupid," Gavin said, motioning to his friends to get comfortable for a long haul.

"Okay then, and I assume the talking cats will stay too. Ladies," Lilabeth said to the remaining two women, "if you are ready."

"I am a seventh-generation witch. We will stay to help," Delilah said. "If there is something that threatens this world, we cannot stand by and watch."

Camile laughed. "Do you really think you can kill your friend? Do you have it in you to strike her down?" Her words faded as a bright light broke through her stomach. She exploded into dust, a smoking locket falling to the ground.

"No. But I can," Clarity said, shaking. "I knew we had to and I knew you couldn't. I had no choice." Tears streamed down her face - never having hurt anything before.

"So now, if we can't pick them up, what do we do with the lockets?" Gavin asked.

Clairity dried her tears and asked Lilabeth, "This forest is protected, right?"

"Yes, it is a historical site."

"And you said they transfer their essence to any living thing - right?" Clairity asked Aslo this time.

"That is what the legends say," he answered.

"I can use my wand to magically move the necklaces onto a branch where the charm can touch the trunk of a tree."

"No, not a tree that is here," Aslo said. "They cannot handle that amount of power. It would never work."

As if knowing what he was thinking, Willow said, "I can't use my telepathic connection to call anyone." Acacia most likely would have easily been able to deal with the problem. At least, she hoped the ancient tree would be able to - none of them knew for sure.

"True, but if we can package them in some way... make the charms so they don't pose a threat. Then when the tour is over, it may be a way to send them back, without having to open the portal," he answered.

"Maybe? We don't even know if that will work. So hope for the best and put them in a container? They can't transfer from inside one object to material other than a living being, right?" Willow's voice cracked when she spoke, letting on she wasn't confident with the plan.

"Theoretically, that is correct," Aslo replied. "Of course, there is no way to test it."

"No way to test it? So one of us may be in danger still? There are an awful lot of unknown factors in this endeavour. Are we sure we want to risk it?" Gavin asked.

"We can't very well leave them here, now can we?" Clairity argued. "And we can't send them back. So that leaves taking them with us for the moment. At least until we come up with another plan to dispose of them. Does anyone have a metal container, something small?"

"I do." Delphine handed a silver case to Clairity. "It's for cigarettes really, but it is big enough to hold two charms and chains."

"Thank you. It will do. I don't suppose anyone has any duct tape?" Willow asked.

"Actually, I do." Jessica spoke for the first time that evening. "As an assistant, I like to be prepared for anything," she said, handing the silver roll of tape to Willow. "You would be amazed at what duct tape can be used for."

"Perfect, thanks. I can imagine the uses are limitless."

Clairity sat the open silver cigarette case on the altar and used her wand to move the two necklaces without touching them. Once arranged inside, magic closed the case. Making it float in the air, Willow taped it all around several times in every direction possible, using almost the entire roll of duct tape to seal it tight. She asked for a plastic bag from anyone who could spare one. Luckily, Lilabeth had one. She held open the bag. Clairity moved the taped up cigarette case over top. It hovered for a moment before dropping in.

"Voila. All safe, for now," Clairity said. The girls found that since learning different languages from books Nathan shared with them, every now and then, they would mix a word from one in with their regular speech. It wasn't something that happened on purpose. It just slipped out. She emptied one of the backpacks contents into the other and then used the empty one to carry just the plastic bag holding the essences of the Glaquool.

"Safe?" Gavin laughed "A brutally evil being who could wipe us all out is in there and you think we are safe from it because of a little duct tape?"

"It has a lot of uses. Had it over my mouth once - not pleasant. I can't imagine they are happy right now," Willow said, causing a low chuckle.

"I have an idea," Lilabeth said. "Let's forget the rest of the tour and find ourselves a way out of this forest. We could all just head our separate ways. I think we all have had enough excitement for one evening."

"You really haven't figured it out, have you? We are stuck finishing this tour. We are in some spell or virtual reality. Until this moment, I actually thought you were behind it." Willow looked at the guide with a hint of disbelief. Aslo and Kiera took the opportunity to disappear into picture form while everyone was preoccupied with the tour guide.

"What do you mean, we can't?" Naomi asked.

"Exactly what I said. Have you not noticed that there are no other people, no vehicles on the road, no other tours? We are the only ones here."

"It's late. People sleep," Delilah offered.

"Not everyone. Then there is the issue of communication, no phone land lines or cells, no telepathic links. How easy was it for you to find us?" she asked Gavin.

"Easy, a path led right to you. It should have been harder."

"Go ahead, try backtracking to the graveyard." Willow sat on the altar.

Gavin's group agreed and turned to walk down the path, the way they came from earlier. After about fifteen minutes, they reappeared on the same path they left on. "That's impossible," he said. "We were walking a straight line and never turned around. How can we be back where we started? Are the Ghoul-whatever behind this?"

"It's some sort of an illusion. I think most everything on this tour is. I don't think the Glaquool were intended to be a part of the group. It was a coincidence Denny's body was taken over - a fluke. In the hotel, she mentioned only having bought the necklace earlier that morning. Which means it was still her when we started the tour. Sometime in the curiosity shop, she must have changed. Everyone was busy, so no one noticed. Then she used another charm to recruit Camile. It was probably in the store already and radiated to her - another strange coincidence." The redheaded girl turned her attention to the tour guide again. "My guess is there was some reason each of us are here. Something that drew us to taking this tour. Lilabeth, why are you here and who hired you?"

"I was looking for something... well, someone. My girlfriend was a tour guide before me. She was upset about something. She was very secretive and even called in her estranged brother to help her. He showed up and they argued about something. They lost all their family a few years back, as did I. They left together to take the tour. I think he hurt her. She disappeared that night. She is everything to me... the only family I have. I came to look for her. I don't know what I will do if I don't see her again."

"What was her name?" Jade asked.

"Annabelle, and her brother was Mike."

Clairity jumped forward, but Willow stopped her. They needed more information before playing all their cards.

"What about everyone else?" Willow asked. "Any other stories of why you are here?"

Delphine spoke first. "It was supposed to be an initiation into a very prestigious secret coven. I received an invitation for two, based on my birthright. Of course, I couldn't refuse. Jessica and I packed immediately. I am assuming no legitimate coven sent the invites."

"We were also invited, but to join a secret society that was supportive of our people and their right to be a part of this world. We figured it was either a joke or someone trying to trap us. Either way, we took it as a challenge," Naomi answered.

"Mildred and Lester won their tickets out of the blue. She mentioned she thought she used her powers to make that happen," Clairity added.

"Lilabeth, how did you get hired? Where did you find out about the job?" Willow's mind swirled, trying to piece together what they were all involved in.

"There is an underground witches' newspaper, called *The Empowered*. It lists everything from jobs to used items for sale, as well as supernatural news. It's a real community we live in and we like to support others from the same background. The job was posted the day after Annabelle went missing. I met with... I can't remember his name. It was only the once we met. He had amazing blue eyes and black hair with blue highlights, good looking," she answered. "There was a real charm about him."

"Lance," Willow said, staring at the tour guide.

"Yes. That was his name... Lance, and he talked about his three sisters running this tour for some time. He gave me instructions from them. Most of what I say is scripted. I memorized the lines. I figured it was for fear factor."

"You know him?" Gavin asked Willow.

"Yes," she responded, staring into space rather than acknowledging anyone. After a few moments, she shook her head and looked around, everyone locked their eyes on her. "He is King Cornelius' son. They are the ones trying to break the fabric of space between worlds. They are dangerous and recruiting. No is never an acceptable answer to them."

"What about you?" Gavin asked. "What brought you here? We all shared. I think it's only fair you tell us your story."

"We are looking for Mike," she answered.

Chapter Thirty-Seven

There were six stores left on the tour. The group made their way out of the forest, the path behind them disappearing a little more with each step they took. The tour members found themselves on a street, which led to a section of road with three doors on each side of the street. Just as in the dream, there were no windows and a sign above each door.

"This is the end of the tour. Please pick a door to finish your experience and someone will attend to your safe return to the hotel," Lilabeth said, her voice shaking as she recited the words.

Willow knew exactly which door they were going through. Without waiting, she walked straight to the sign which boasted a picture of a giant serpent on it and went in, with Clairity, Jade and Lilabeth following. Gavin shrugged his shoulders and followed them through the same door, with all the other tour members behind him.

"What now?" he asked.

Willow jumped. She hadn't realized the whole tour group was coming along. "Spread out and look for a big red button marked *help* or... stairs going down. We need to get to the lower level somehow. We will also need some light." Her words were cut off.

"Like this?" Lilabeth stood beside a large red help button attached to a silver wire hanging down in the middle of the room. Before Willow and Clairity could protest, she pressed the button and they were falling again.

"Talk about deja vu," Clairity said, trying to look around in the dark.

"Yeah, can you guys get off me?" Willow yelled from the bottom of the pile - Jade, Clairity and Lilabeth on top of her. It was an uncomfortable position, to say the least. She had never actually wanted to know how an orange felt being squished for juice.

"You okay down there?" Gavin asked. He couldn't see anything but darkness below. He waited for an answer before making a move.

The girls scrambled back to their feet and yelled up that they were fine. The search up top began. They needed a rope or something to climb down, but there was nothing.

Among all the ruckus, Delphine noticed something strange. "There is no door anymore. We can't go back the way we came," she yelled.

"Guess we go forward then, or downward, rather." Gavin jumped without hesitation, landing on his feet. Russ followed. "Ladies, we will catch you. Take a leap of faith," Gavin ordered once the two men were positioned.

"The walls are moving, closing in." Naomi dove, but needed no help, landing safely on her feet without so much as a wobble. Delphine followed in the same manner.

"Time is ticking, ladies. We will catch you. Please jump." The vamprite stood staring at the hole above him waiting for someone to leap down.

Delilah stood dazed, staring at the hole. Her body shook but wasn't budging.

"I think she is in shock. What do I do?!" Jessica exclaimed.

A chorus of "push her" rang out.

Jessica panicked. The walls were closing in, with crunching and breaking noises coming from items being destroyed. There were only seconds left, when Delilah's body came flying down. Russ caught her and moved out of the way. Jessica jumped into Gavin's arms just in time. The gap above closed over.

"That was close," she said. "Why can't I see anything?"

"There are no lights," Clairity said. "Don't suppose you have a flashlight in that bag of yours. It sure would help right now."

"Yeah, I do… or rather, I did. The bag didn't make it." The girls moaned at the news.

"How about a lighter or matches?" Clairity was already ripping a piece of her shirt. Willow, with her night vision, was easily able to find a stick to bring back to the others.

The girls lit the poor excuse for a torch, instantly realizing that idea worked better in the dream world. The cloth burnt quickly, leaving them with nothing more than a piece of wood in the dark. Without light, the sighs from the rest of the tour group seemed to echo. Willow took the lead, forming a single-file line behind her, having everyone put one hand on the shoulder of the person in front of them. Before moving, they each called out their names to make sure no one was left behind.

The hallway was longer than the girls remembered it being in the dream, or perhaps they were just moving at a slower pace. What seemed like an eternity in dark silence was interrupted only by the occasional scream as someone accidentally came in contact with a cobweb or something slimy on the walls. A horrible odour surrounded them - the mixture of earth and rot combined, with a touch of the usual damp musty smell one might expect from an underground dungeon added in. Occasionally a particularly strong whiff of something putrid grabbed a hold of one of their gag reflexes.

Finally, they came to the wall where the path split. Willow looked it over to make sure there wasn't something written somewhere, or directions, but ended up confirming to Clairity that it was the same as in their dream. Having no idea which way to go, she suggested, "Still left? We have to make the choice again."

"Yes," Clairity answered. She had chosen to leave the two kittens at the camp. They were still too young for battle, although probably quite able. That decision meant she was in the dark as much as the others and relying on Willow to guide her. "I still don't think anything in here could be right."

Following the left side, they came to a closed door with light shining through the crack at the bottom.

"Go in," Clairity said. "It would be nice to see again."

Willow opened the door to a familiar sight: the same room the girls had seen in the dream with cages in it. Cells lined the walls. A warning sprung from her lips, for the others not to get too close to the bars, born from the memories of the random hands that had grabbed at her before.

Entering the room, it was much bigger than expected. The main section was lit with torches, but the cages were dark and, at first, quiet. When the group were about halfway in the room they started to hear noises - moans and groans from behind the bars.

"What is that?!" Lilabeth screamed.

"Look! Something is in there," Jessica said. "What... what are they?"

As predicted, hands reached out from between the bars, as if trying to blindly latch on to anything they could. As the captives came closer to the light, their facial features came into view, distorted as if still forming. The skin in one place would stretch and a feature would appear, sometimes an eye, others a mouth or nose. Each time one appeared, another would disappear. The sight was unusual and something it would take a long time for any of them to get used to, if they did at all.

"Disgusting," Delilah said, speaking for the first time since freezing in the store. "What are these creatures?"

"Help me!" a woman cried out from a pathway between two of the cages.

"That's Annabelle! I know her voice," Lilabeth said, running down the space trying to avoid being grabbed by her hair or clothes. Clairity, Jade, Jessica and Delilah ran after her.

"We are going to head to the other path and look for a way out," Gavin said.

"How will you see?" Willow asked.

"You aren't the only one who can see in the dark. Our shape-shifting abilities give us certain... advantages over the terunji," he said, turning to leave. "If we find something, we will come back for you."

"Terunji?" she yelled at their backs.

"You need to get out more, Keeper... with others like you. There are many more than you know in this world. Perhaps we could show you around sometime." He showed off a sly smile and winked at her before walking away.

Willow was left wondering what they meant as she watched them disappear. Looking around, she realized she was alone, except for the creatures behind the bars. But that wasn't all. She was face-to-face with the door that might lead to Mike. In the background, wild dogs howled, keeping their location a secret.

Well, no sense waiting, she thought, opening the door and stepping through. She jumped when it slammed behind her.

Willow quickly realized that Mike wasn't in this room, but two large wild dogs were. They were wearing thick collars made from some sort of metal. Chains ran from them to the wall, one on either side of a closed door. There were no dishes for food or water.

The colour of their fur was impossible to make out, matted with blood and dirt. Both snarled fiercely, teeth bared and saliva dripping. With the lack of food, she couldn't rule out the possibility that she might be on the menu if the chains came loose.

"Nice doggie," she said, moving backwards. She grabbed at the handle, but the door she came through was locked. Unable to go back, the only other way out of the room was a door situated directly between the two hell hounds.

Perfect, she thought, trying to inch closer to the two beasts. They snarled and snapped at her making her jump backwards. *Two steps forward, one big jump back. Not exactly productive.* Normally, one of the guardians would answer her. That didn't happen. Silence was her only companion.

"Okay, listen. I mean you no harm. I am a friend," she said, figuring reasoning with them might help. Animals were, after all, intelligent creatures too, and these ones weren't straining to get any closer to her. In fact, they were staying in exactly the same spot.

"Who are you?" the larger beast asked, followed by a whine which made him sound like he was in pain.

"The collars," she said. "They hurt you in some way. That's why you don't move?" It was more a statement than a question, but she would have been happy to hear an answer.

"Why do you care?" it snarled back.

"She is the first to try to speak to us, Nero. Perhaps she is not one of them," the other dog said in a female voice before turning her attention to the red-haired girl. "Yes, there are sharp spikes on the inside of the collars. They keep us here. It hurts to speak, but more importantly, if we pull on the chains, the spikes dig in tighter, gauging the flesh on our necks. If we try to escape, the spikes would most likely decapitate us."

"Can they be removed?" Willow felt genuine concern for the two animals. No creature should be exposed to such horrific torture.

"There is a magic seal on them, which I do not believe can be broken easily. We are meant to stay here for eternity - never to see the daylight again."

"Well," Willow said, "since you can speak, I guess you are not ordinary dogs..."

She was cut off by Nero. "We are not dogs!" he yelled.

"Sorry," she said, watching blood trickle down his neck from the collar. "I didn't mean to upset you. Maybe I can help take them off or break the chains."

"You can try, terunji, but I doubt it will do you any good. You should run before they come for you," Nero snarled, lying down from the pain.

"Terunji, I have heard that twice today and have no clue what it means," she said, shaking her head. "Could you explain?"

"It means the people of this world, oblivious to what is happening around them or the possibilities of something more, outside their mundane lives. The non-magical that inhabit this world," the female animal replied. "I am Tika and he is Nero."

"I am Willow."

Both animals sat up. Their eyes widened at the sound of her name.

"My name, you have heard it before? From where?"

The two beasts exchanged looks before Tika answered. "It was long ago and brought back some memories. It is nothing to concern yourself about."

Willow began examining the chain connections to the wall while they were talking. "So if you aren't dogs, what are you?"

"Not that you would know what it means, but we are Olcsanka," Nero said.

She froze for a moment, before turning to the two with a look of disbelief on her face. "These chains will not break. I am not even sure magic could help, but there is another way."

"Another way? How?"

Willow moved forward and reached out to touch Tika's face gently. The animal responded, closing her eyes and rubbing back, as if she hadn't felt kindness in a very long time.

"You recognized my name. Did you know my mother and father?"

Tika let out a little gasp. "Is it possible? She would be the right age," she said to Nero.

"Where is your keeper?" Willow asked. It was a risk revealing so much to the two animals without knowing more about them.

The two exchanged glances again before Nero answered. "He was captured, taken prisoner. We were told he was injured and led here. He was in fact hurt, as they said, but once in this room they threatened to kill him if we didn't have these collars put on. After the restraints were on, they took him away as a prisoner of war and we were trapped, doomed to remain here forever. If we tug too hard we would decapitate ourselves and same would happen if we try to transform into our larger forms. We may be immortal, but living in two pieces isn't a pleasant thought."

"No. I suppose not," the girl answered. "You did know my parents though, right? I can tell from the way you reacted to my name."

"Yes," he answered. "I believe our keeper is your father."

Silence followed. Willow fell over on the ground and held her hands to her face, trying not to let her emotions take over. She expected them to know of her parents, but never imagined they were so close to her father. The urge to cry consumed her: thoughts of being an ordinary girl who still had her parents taking control. Tika broke the silence.

"He is alive somewhere, maybe," her voice faded off and she lay beside the girl, snuggling to her for comfort.

After a while, Willow spoke. "I don't remember them… my parents. I don't know what they looked like or even their names. No one would tell me anything." She paused for a moment. "But I miss them so much. When I am alone, it hurts. It's as if there is this big hole in my heart and nothing could ever fill that space again, except them." Tears fell steadily from her eyes. Somewhere, no doubt, rain was pouring down.

"We miss him, too. It feels the same for us," Tika said, nudging the girl with her nose. Neither guardian had considered how hard it must have been for the girl growing up without either her mother or father.

Willow sat up, wiping the remaining tears from her face. "Okay, well, we can't stay here, and we can't go back, so looks like we need to go through that door."

"We can't go anywhere. You must save yourself," Nero said.

"No, we will go together." Willow placed one hand on each of the animals and closed her eyes. Both Olcsanka changed to shimmering light particles, reforming on her skin as pictures of wolves. The collars that had bound them fell to the ground, blood still dripping off the spikes that had been embedded in their hides. She pulled up her sleeves and looked at them, smiling, then covered them up again before heading to the door.

Once again, she was faced with a closed door. Why stop tempting fate now? Turning the handle and opening the door was all it took. She was inside with it slamming behind her. This time, there was a chair with a high back in the middle of the room, facing away from her. Someone was in the chair, but she couldn't see who.

Slowly, Willow crept up to the back of the chair and peeked around; all the while, one hand remained on the wand in her back pocket. She was prepared to see something horrible, maybe even Mike hurt and bleeding or a dead body, but instead it was someone else.

"We meet again."

"Lance? What are you doing here?" she asked the young prince, relaxing a little.

"I should ask you the same thing. Not to mention how you got by the wolves outside that door. Not an easy task, even for the most accomplished of witches."

"I let them go," she answered.

"Let them go... again, not an easy task, breaking one of my sister's spells. Care to elaborate? Well, it doesn't matter. Although Ophelia will be upset her pets are gone. I would stay away from her if I were you." He stood up and moved to face her. "But I guess the real question is, what should I do with you?"

"You could tell me how to get out of here," she suggested.

Lance laughed. "That would be far too easy. No, you will have to figure that one out on your own. I am afraid I cannot intervene in my sisters' plans - not even for you. You do understand, my hands are tied."

"What is this place?" she asked. Instead of pulling out her wand, she found herself holding the bag containing the Glaquool charms from the backpack she carried.

"You know I can't answer that. My family would not approve. Perhaps we can talk about something else, like... what brings you here?"

"I... was looking for you," she said, smiling.

"Looking for me? Hmm. Well, I would think there to be easier ways..."

Willow cut him off. "I need your help. Your necrid flames, can you control them? I mean direct them to destroy something specific and just that thing?"

Lance looked at her with curiosity. "You have my attention. I am intrigued as to what I could possibly help you with. We are unlikely allies."

"Will you listen?" she asked.

He nodded, listening attentively as she explained the events that had transpired and the Glaquool being dangerous to everyone, including his family.

"You want me to destroy them? I had you pegged for pro-life somehow. Are you sure you don't want to give them another chance?" he joked.

"I am pro-life, but these creatures could destroy all other life. There has to be something to protect the innocent. My friend is dead because of them." She took out the wand and used it to remove the small package from the bag.

"Is that... duct tape?" Lance laughed. "I guess it is good for everything. I am impressed. Unwrap it then and let's see them."

Willow used her wand to remove the duct tape and open the cigarette case. Lance knelt down and held his hands over top of the charms, sensing the life force trapped within. His eyes lit up with sparks of gold as a stream of blue flames left his fingers and hit the two charms.

"You know you will owe me for this," he said without taking his attention away from the burning of the jewelry. The whole process took about five minutes before the charms burst open with a black smoke rising up from them. The prince stood up still watching the last of the blue flames going out. "It's done."

"The life forces are gone. You are sure?" she asked.

"Yes, they are no threat anymore. But tell me, if they were sealed away tight somewhere, how did they get into this world?"

"The same way you did. I am sure you realize the holes in the fabric of space you are creating are not just being used by your people. There are some things that are dangerous to us all out there that should not be set free."

"Agreed, but I cannot change the movement, I am afraid. I will report on the find, as best I can, without arousing suspicion and ask for limited activity in this area, but it is my sister's territory in the end, not mine."

Willow pointed her wand at the charms and silver case and let everything inside her flow into a magic stream which engulfed the items and left only dust when she was finished. Even she was stunned by the amount of power released.

"Emotions make magic stronger. We are not so different after all." He turned his head to the sound of a blood-curdling scream. "There is one of my sisters now and she is not happy her toys have been set free, from the sounds of it. Time for me to go." He walked around Willow and from behind brushed her hair from her face before gently kissing her cheek.

Willow's heart raced, her breath becoming heavy. She closed her eyes, enjoying the feeling of his lips on her cheek. His soft touch sent tingles through every part of her body. She wanted to move but couldn't. Her body froze in that moment enjoying every sensation. She replayed the events over again and again in her mind.

Opening her eyes, she saw Lance turn and head for a dark corner, vanishing into the shadows. Following him, however, led to nothing but stone walls. *He must have gone somewhere,* she thought, running her hands over the rough stone looking for a secret doorway or something. She was startled when she found her arm went right through one part. *An illusion,* she thought. *Of course there are ways out. We just can't see them.*

She put one foot through the wall, followed by the rest of her body. Magically, she was back where they first fell in. *How odd,* she thought, *the beginning was also the end.* Heading back, she decided to try the right side of the path this time, figuring everything down there connected in some way like a riddle needing to be solved. A fear of running into Ophelia might have aided in the decision as well. There was no desire to come face-to-face with an angry witch who had lost her toys. The priority now became finding the tour group and a way out as soon as possible.

After walking a fair distance, a similar room to the one with cages appeared. In these ones, however, beautiful women with stunning features were locked up. The group of vamprite stood in front of the cages just staring, their gazes locked on sheer radiance.

"Gavin? Gavin!" Willow yelled as she circled the vamprite, assessing what was holding his attention.

Her distraction was successful. He turned his face and shook his head. "Where am I?"

"How long have you been standing there?" she asked as she watched him shake each of his friends back to reality. There was no softness in the way he handled them. Any normal person would have been covered in bruises from the strength he used.

"I don't know," he admitted. "We were trying to figure out how to set these people free."

"I don't think that's a good idea." Willow remembered Clairity's words in the dream that nothing down this path could be right, and decided they best take that tip to heart. "We should try that path between the cages. It might lead to the others. I think I might know a way out."

"What makes you think that way leads to your friends?" Naomi asked.

Willow explained her theory that the entire basement was actually a series of tunnels, using illusions to hide secret passages in and out. Besides, there wasn't any other choice but to go that way or turn back. The group began their trek without making further eye contact with the hypnotic women in the room, leaving all but a hissing in a profane language behind as they made their way down the path. Apparently, the women were unhappy the vamprite were set free from the trance.

From that point forward, the whole passageway was filled with cages on both sides, but empty. The further they went, the more clear it became that the women were put there as a security system for anyone who managed to escape other cages. They would hold the beings in a hypnotic state until they could be locked up again. When she thought about it, it was really an ingenious plan.

They found the rest of the tour group standing in front of one of the doors to a cage, trying to figure out how to open it.

"Willow!" Clairity yelled. "We found Mike and Annabelle. We just can't open the lock. We tried everything."

"We don't have a lot of time. This place is run by Cornelius' daughters and one, Ophelia, knows we are here. I think the empty cages are for new beings - a holding cell of sorts until they can move captives back to their home world." She took out her wand and aimed it at the lock. "Stand back or to the side, everyone. Let me try." Willow focused all of the energy and power of the wand, but it didn't make even the slightest difference.

"Get out, Willow. Go before they find you." Mike's voice was weak, revealing he was injured, needing medical attention.

She thought back to when she first got into the jeep with him. She wanted to know how to control her thoughts, so none of the other guards could hear her. How ironic was it, now that she wanted nothing more than to tell him alone how she felt and she couldn't use the telepathic connection that normally flowed between them? Mike had mentioned he thought their mental connections were controlled by emotions. Lance said something similar about magic in the other room.

"Emotions," she said out loud. "Of course." She aimed her wand again.

"We tried this already, all of us have," Lilabeth said. "It's no use. The spell on it is too strong. It's hopeless."

Willow didn't hear her, or any other noises, for that matter. She was thinking about her parents, about Tika and Nero and how they were so close to her father for so long when she barely knew him at all. She was thinking about all the people back home, murdered or prisoners, and Camile, who gave her life so they could be there right now. Then she thought about her friends - about Clairity and Ashlyn, their times together alone in the forest - about the Shinning boys and the games they played together - about Aslo and Kiera and the kittens, whose names she still hadn't learnt - about William when they first met - about Mike, how he made her feel… and then about Lance: the way his gaze could hold hers, the way his lips felt when he kissed her cheek. Her desire to feel that way again sent her emotions over the top.

A beam of light exploded from the tip of her wand. It was everything she felt - everything she longed for. It was the good and the bad, all the things that made her who she was. A small explosion went off at the lock and Willow stepped backwards. Clairity reached forward and pulled on the bars. The gate swung open. Mike and Annabelle were free. The others searched Willow's face for an answer as to how.

"No time," she said to them. "We need to find a way out. I have an idea, but we will need your help, Jade."

"My help?" Jade was clearly surprised anyone would ever need her help. "What can I do?" she asked.

"Illusions," Willow answered while they walked. "I need you to try to detect them so we can locate where we can go through the walls."

"I am not sure I can do that." She held her gaze down, refusing to make eye contact with any of the others. "I have only ever used illusion on myself, to change my appearance."

"Give it a try," Clairity suggested. "You never know. It might be easy. We are all still learning what we can do."

Jade nodded. The group continued walking, checking all the cages for ways out, but coming up empty every time. Worry set in. Too much time was passing. Lance's sister couldn't be too far behind and Willow had no idea what to expect. One thing she did know, it wasn't going to go well if they all met up.

They came back to the first cage room. The prisoners were still reaching for them and making noises.

"Shh," Willow said, motioning for quiet so she could listen.

"Help," one of the prisoners said.

"Us," came from another.

"Please," from another.

The group continued alternating words, which Willow made out as "We." "Can." "Help." "You." "Escape."

"Why are we listening to a bunch of mumbled garbage? They don't even have a mouth formed long enough to speak," Delilah grumbled.

"They are speaking," Willow explained. "They can't make a sentence alone because their faces keep changing. They are working together, each saying a word, a part of a sentence. I think they know a way out."

"You have to be kidding." Gavin banged his head against part of the brick wall, indicating his lack of approval.

Willow raised her wand and channelled her emotions again making a stream of power strong enough to open the gate.

The strange prisoners filed out, each of the first five saying one word. There were at least fifteen, although there wasn't enough time to do a proper count.

"Thank."

"You."

"This."

"Way."

"Follow."

They formed a line, similar to what Willow and her friends had used to make their way through the darkest part, with one hand on the shoulder of the person in front.

"Amazing," Clairity said, following their new friends. "It's much easier to understand them when only one is speaking."

The group found themselves back at the place where they fell in. It was slightly bigger than the rest of the tunnel, having an alcove-like appearance.

"Why didn't I notice this before?" Willow asked, not expecting an answer.

"Great, the place we started at," Russ snorted. "We already knew we couldn't go back the way we came. This has been a big waste of time. The hole is closed over."

"No!" Jade pointed. "Wait! Over there in the far corner, it looks different."

None of the others could see what she was referring to. It all looked exactly the same. Willow glanced at her and back at the wall. Of course, the room she visited had also led back to that point. It must have been the way to leave. She moved forward and began feeling the wall, until her hand went through.

"There they are! Get them!" a screechy voice echoed from behind.

"Quickly, everyone just run through! Don't think about it! There is no wall!" Willow yelled to the others.

Jade went first, followed by the rest of the tour group. The strange ex-prisoners were next. Willow and Clairity realized there wasn't enough time, and looking at each other, they pointed their wands at the ceiling in front of the incoming witches, bringing it down.

"That should buy us some time. They will have to backtrack through the two rooms, but it won't take them long," Willow said, trying to inspire the people in front of her to move more quickly through the hidden passage.

Clairity went through next, still carrying a backpack. Willow followed. There was no sign of their pursuers yet.

As expected, the passage led outside. It was daytime and there were people hustling about their daily routines. The non-magical would never be able to understand the unusual faces of their new friends.

"Jade!" Willow yelled. "Illusion on them, please. We need to find a place to hide in public. The people here might not be able to find an explanation for them."

Jade glanced at them. Her eyes darkened to a shade of green that Willow hadn't seen before, with shiny specks.

Remarkably, their new friends' appearances all changed to hide their morphing faces. They looked as *normal* as anyone walking down the street and could pass for terunji. Pride was written on her face for using that word even if it was only in her own mind. Jade, however, looked exhausted.

Increasing our vocabulary, are we? Aslo asked.

"I can hear you again!" Willow yelled out loud, attracting the attention of all within ear shot. "We better move," she added. "Look for some landmark or something we can use to ask Faramund to come teleport us out of here. Oh, in case you didn't know, telepathic communications work again."

Chapter Thirty-Eight

It didn't take long for William and the others to reach the forest. By the time they did, the storm over top had dissipated. There was no other choice but to split into groups and search the woods unless someone came up with a better plan.

Faramund was least likely source, but the first to have an idea, suggesting they bring in one more recruit. Taking leave without explanation, he returned quickly with Ashlyn by his side. After filling her and Shelby in on the important details, Faramund laid out his plan. He asked the guardian bird to fly over top of the trees, providing a better view and hopefully a general direction for them to head in.

Shelby took flight, disappearing into the horizon. The sun would be coming up soon, but in the forest, it probably wouldn't make much difference. After several passes, the bird returned.

"There is a clearing to the east. Looks like there may have been a recent lightning strike. It is a fair way in, though," she said, landing on a branch.

"Okay, let's head in and stay together. This was a great idea!" William turned to Faramund, patting him on the back. "Shelby, stick close. If we get lost, we may need your help."

"I may be able to help as well." Iskander opened his fist and released his *little star* to go ahead, plotting a course through the trees.

"Brilliant!" Dezi exclaimed. "If they are in here, we should find them quickly." He didn't need to finish his thought. Everyone else was already thinking it: *as long as they weren't too late*.

The group headed into the forest, following the direction of the ball of light and Shelby. Every so often, the guardian flew up, making sure they were still on the right track. Everything was going well, until they came close to the clearing.

"It's just up ahead," Shelby said, returning from a flight. "We should be there in less than five minutes."

After ten minutes, William stopped. "Seems like you misjudged the distance."

Iskander sent out his sphere of light and waited for it to return. "It appears we somehow turned around. We need to go back the other way."

"We didn't change directions." William said, perplexed. "Shelby, take a look again, please. I would prefer not to get lost in these woods."

The bird took flight and returned a moment later. "He's right. I can't explain it, but we are heading the wrong way. I suggest we try walking ten minutes in the other direction, then check again."

The group agreed and began the walk. Ten minutes later, they stopped and followed the same procedures again. This time they went around the clearing - completely missing it.

"Any ideas?" William asked, sitting down for a rest.

"I believe there must be a magical explanation for this," Shelby said. "Some form of a barrier that makes people change course to avoid a certain piece of land. It is rare, but would explain the disruption of telepathic communication as well. The same idea was applied to the keeper's library back home. Only a keeper could find the building - no one else would ever know it was there."

"Is there any way to get inside the barrier?" Jessie asked.

"Since I can fly over it and the sphere can see it, I believe so. My guess is the storm disrupted part of the magical force field. It's similar to the barriers between worlds, just on a much smaller scale. Of course, it isn't anywhere near as powerful, either. Most likely this type of barrier is based on a strong illusion magic rather than the type of magic that was used to divide the realms," Shelby answered. "We have to remember that although it acts the same as a divide between space, it is still an illusion. Since it is set to make travellers avoid whatever is hidden within it, we still need to find a gap to enter. If we don't, the enchantment will continue to redirect us every time we come close."

William stood up again and brushed off his pants. "So how does that help us?"

"If I am right, the storm we saw basically made a hole in the illusion. Again, it would be similar to the holes in space between worlds we are experiencing. There should be openings that occur in different spots at certain times. We need to find one of those to enter. I believe Malarchy should be able to detect anomalies in the illusion."

"I can," Malarchy said with no emotion on his face. "If I am in the right place at the right time. We could stand here forever and not see a thing. We also don't know what the intervals are for the holes to open. It could be days, months or even years. Unfortunately, we haven't figured out how to measure or predict such events."

"That is true." Shelby flew to Ashlyn's shoulder. "There is another possibility. Just one, but it could be dangerous."

"Spill it," William said, anxiety creeping in. Every second they wasted was a moment that could make the difference between life and death.

"Faramund should be able to teleport us inside. The hole from above is stable and should allow access."

"But," William said, anticipating a problem, "we don't have the exact coordinates to use."

"I may be able to help with that." Iskander pulled out a small crude-looking machine made out of thrown-away electronics from the camp - a screen made from an old tablet with wires running to what looked like a computer board and a battery. He lifted up a small round piece which resembled part of a webcam. "Zsiga and I have been experimenting on this for some time. It's more of a hobby than anything else, but it has some useful applications we thought might come in handy. If Shelby can fly over top of the clearing from here, I think we can map coordinates."

Disbelief had stolen most of their voices, leaving Malarchy the sole speaker. "This is a hobby? It seems rather advanced. Especially considering there were no electrical items in our home world. How is it you built something like that?"

"Electronics seem to come naturally to us for some reason. We can see how things work and possibilities of how things can go together. It has only been tested once, but I think it will be fine." He placed the small camera part in the palm of his hand. "This part has to face like this. I could strap it on if it would be easier."

The bird tried to pick it up in its talons. It was light enough to carry in that fashion. She took flight. Seconds later she was soaring above the clearing. It took several passes for the guard to collect all the information he needed.

Iskander turned all of the power on. The tablet lit up green. After inputting some information, white grid lines appeared. Within moments, data began flowing from the remodelled camera. The screen showed trees and the clearing, picking up details as small as the spot where lightning had struck. Shelby returned and dropped the equipment into Iskander's hand.

"Thanks." He put away the small piece carefully in the bag before turning his attention back to his work. "There," he said, turning the screen to Faramund. "Those are the numbers to use. It will put us right in the middle, away from any objects."

After packing away the rest of the equipment, the group gathered together. Faramund recited the figures. A green gas escaped from his hands. It swirled around them before retreating back again.

"Did we make it?" Ashlyn asked, her hands still covering her eyes from the journey. She moved her pinky finger to peek out at where they were.

"Yeah." William chuckled. "We're good, champ."

He did a double take, glancing back at her. It was the first time he had seen Shelby as a picture on her skin. Somehow, it looked strange to him. The pictures suited Willow, with her almost bronze tone and red hair. Clairity was similar. Although she had a very white complexion, black was a good look for her, matching her midnight hair. It looked natural. Ashlyn, however, was different. Against her white hair with pink highlights and pale skin, the black bird really stood out.

He turned his attention back to looking around the clearing. He could sense the portal stones radiating from the altar in front of them. Walking over, it was obvious that this portal wasn't the same as the others.

"Can Shelby come over?" he asked without looking away from the design of the table. When the bird landed beside him, he added, "What do you make of this?"

"It's old, before my time. There are stories I have heard. We had best leave it alone for now and not disturb it. We can discuss it further when we have more time. I don't think it is relevant to finding Willow and the others... at least, I hope not."

"Okay," he said, turning to look where the smoking black spot was on the ground. "Why would she have made lightning strike this spot?"

Iskander squatted in front of it, examining the remains. "Looks like it hit hard. Whatever was there was completely obliterated."

"Let's check the perimeter. Look for any paths they could have taken. These girls couldn't have just vanished." William headed to the tree line, finding a path easily. "Let's try this."

The group began walking and five minutes later were back in the clearing again. They took turns glancing at each other before agreeing to try a different route. The results were the same.

"Seems all the trails bring us back here. An illusion must be used to keep people in as well as out." William sighed, another dead end. "I don't think we are going to get any further. We best head back to check in with Zsiga and the others."

The group left the clearing the same way they entered, having Faramund transport them to the abandoned hotel where Zsiga was stationed. After confirming that no one came or went, they walked back to the other motel, stumped. Iskander remained behind with is fellow guard, sharing the excitement of how their invention had been of use.

Back at the strip motel the weary group sat down and filled in Diana and the others about their night. Nathan was sleeping on one of the beds. The sun was up and outside the streets were becoming busy.

Where are you, Willow? William's thoughts were heard by all of the portal guards.

Here, echoed back to all of them.

It was Willow. They could hear her.

Chapter Thirty-Nine

Willow and the others waited patiently at a statue of a woman with a broom, presumably a witch. It was a place which was easy to find for everyone to meet. The streets were busy with people, some taking pictures of each other with the statue, others just stopping to look. For the first time, she realized Delilah and Jessica were gone. They must have bolted at the first opportunity that presented itself. No one could blame them. It would be safer in a group of two to hide from evil witches than it would be staying with the rest of the tour. For a moment, she wondered if they would ever run into them again. Somehow she thought they would.

The four vamprites were also getting nervous. Naomi came over and said they would meet again, shaking her hand. Deep down, Willow was glad they decided to go off on their own. It would have been hard to explain to Sarah. This gave her the opportunity to bring up the suggestion that perhaps there were some unlikely allies out there. They were still left with the large group of faceless creatures. That was going to be interesting to explain to William.

She wondered how they could transport all of them without the general public noticing. With their new friends, there were too many to go by car and Faramund's teleportation was far too noticeable.

Perhaps an illusion, she thought. Looking at Jade, she quickly changed her mind. She was draining every ounce of energy just hiding the odd faces of the ones who made the escape possible.

Willow was just as tired. Expending as much magic as she did the previous night meant she was physically drained - adding in the emotional factor and mentally she was tapped out as well.

She glanced over at Mike. Annabelle and Lilabeth stayed by his side, tending to his wounds like he was a baby. He didn't appear to mind. She wanted to talk to him - make sure he was okay, but decided to wait until they could have a minute alone. She snapped out of her daze when she heard William's voice calling out to her.

"You are a sight for sore eyes," he said. "Who are your friends?"

"Long story. Right now, I would feel better if we could go somewhere safe." Willow's voice faded as she noticed William wasn't paying attention to her and was instead heading for Mike.

"You alright?" he asked. "You gave us a good scare."

"It wasn't the greatest experience. I can think of better ways to vacation, that's for sure." Mike patted William on the back. "Thanks for coming for us. I knew you would figure it out."

Willow and Clairity exchanged eyerolls at the statement.

"We should get to somewhere safe," William said, motioning to Faramund.

"Why didn't I think of that?" Sarcasm dripped off Willow's words. "We will need someplace a little less public."

William looked at Jade, her illusion abilities clearly tapped out. "Between those buildings there is an alley. It's the best we can do in a hurry." He turned to Faramund, "Take them back to camp. Settle our new guests and make sure Mike visits the medical centre to get checked out. We will be ready when you return."

Willow saw William drive off in a car just before they teleported back to their base of operations. A certain level of relief accompanied their return. After watching Mike and his sister head off to see the doctor, she decided it was time to wash up and change. Once back in her sleeping quarters, Aslo and Kiera came out to stretch their feet and find their children. For the first time, she thought about the two wolves, slowly healing. Looking at their pictures, they were doing much better. Their fur was no longer matted with blood and the wounds on their necks were smaller than before. It would only be another day or so before they were ready to separate from her.

She reached in her back pocket to pull out her wand and found something else with it: an envelope. It, however, came with no recollections as to how it got there. She opened it out of curiosity. Inside was a white card with gold lettering on the front which read:

Prince Lance

requests the honour of your presence

at his annual

Witches' Halloween Masquerade Ball

October 31

Costume is required. Refreshments provided.

Underneath was a handwritten note which read, *Looking forward to our next meeting. Lance.* The back side of the card listed an address and time.

Willow sat staring at the invitation. It reminded her of the first ball she was invited to, but was never able to attend. Jade used a love potion to convince Dezi not to go with her. The townsfolk spent so much time making her clothes, jewelry and shoes. She laughed, remembering the shoes and her lessons on how to walk in them. If she was going to this ball, she would need to practice a lot.

She shook her head. What was she thinking? There was no way she could go to a masquerade party on Halloween with... the enemy. She returned the card to its envelope, placing it in the backpack beside the second copy of *The Portal Prophecies* she had found in the curiosity store.

She headed into the bathroom to wash and change. Looking in the mirror, she fixed her hair. Her clothing was carefully chosen. It was best to wear long sleeves until the opportunity arose to fill in the rest of the camp about the new guardians. She was the only one who knew about them still and wasn't even sure how much Aslo and Kiera knew. If the felines were aware of the Olcsanka, they weren't mentioning it.

It was time to check on Mike. Walking into the medical building, Willow scanned the room quickly. She wasn't fond of her memories of the room or what modern medicine offered, but for now it was the best thing available. One day, Victoria's healing abilities would be fully formed and she could take over the job most of these machines did in a fraction of the time.

Annabelle was on the far side of the room, sitting with Lilabeth. They hadn't noticed her enter and were embraced in a passionate kiss. Willow had never seen two women in a relationship before, but it wasn't that which caught her attention. The two were giving off such a strong aura of love. It was all around them - engulfing their beings - combining them together. The colours were powerful and mesmerizing, flowing between them. She couldn't remember having ever seen anything quite as beautiful. It would have been easy for her to stand and admire their devotion for hours.

Annabelle noticed her stare. "Is something wrong?"

"No," Willow answered. "Your connection is so beautiful. I can see your aura... true love. It's stunning. I am sorry for staring." She looked down and headed towards where Mike was sleeping.

"I... didn't mean it like that," Annabelle said apologetically. "We have a lot of people who don't understand or approve of our relationship because we are both women. Even worse, two women who both practice witchcraft. I can be a little defensive sometimes."

"I admit, I have never seen two women as a couple before, but I can't believe anyone could deny the feelings you have for each other."

"You're Willow," Annabelle said, smiling.

"Yes," she answered, sitting down in a chair beside the bed. "And you're Annabelle, Mike's sister." Smiling, she turned her attention to Mike. Someone had cleaned him up, leaving only a few bruises and bandages. She thought he could still use a few visits from Victoria. Bruises were the girl's specialty at the moment and she enjoyed being needed.

"Willow," Richard said, walking in. "I heard you had a long day. Shouldn't you be resting?" He looked at Mike and then back at her and sighed. "How about I move a bed closer so you can sleep and still be here when he wakes up? Okay?"

She agreed and the doctor prepared her a bed. Lying down, she realized exactly how tired she actually was. It took less than a few minutes for her to fall asleep holding his hand.

Willow woke to Mike watching her. "This is backwards," she said. "I was supposed to be waiting for you to wake up."

Mike smiled. "To what do I deserve the honour?"

"I feel responsible for what happened… and I never had the chance to thank you for taking me to town that night. It was more fun than I have ever had… so thank you." Inside, she was beating herself up for sounding silly. At least she finally understood what the expression tongue tied meant.

"No problem, and no need to feel responsible. You couldn't have known what was going on. I am just glad William sent you guys to find us. He's a great friend."

"Yeah," was all she could manage. It seemed as if William was getting the credit for everything. "I better go clean up to meet with the others." She stood up and reached the door. Opening it with one hand, she stopped to look back at him. "Mike, I am glad you are okay."

Willow went to wash, change, and grab the backpack before meeting the others to tell the tale of the past few days. When she arrived at the cabin, everyone else, including Mike and Annabelle, were already settled in.

"Sorry," she said. "I didn't realize everyone was waiting."

Willow moved forward to sit down, but was caught by a big hug from Sarah. Her red puffy eyes made it obvious there had recently been a steady flow of tears.

"I am so sorry. I should have realized. I let you walk into a trap."

Willow took her arms and moved her to a chair. "It's okay. Sit down. It's over now." She hoped no one would mention Camile. From the look on Sarah's face, it might push her over the edge. Of course, it hadn't been her fault. There is no way she could have stopped them from going on the tour, even if she wanted to.

"Right." William locked his gaze on Sarah. "Who wants to start? We have filled Mike and Annabelle in on the dream and how we pinpointed locations, and Sarah's side of what happened."

"Our hotel room was actually an old abandoned place, all dirty. It was all an illusion. There were bugs and everything." Clairity spit out. "Just like you figured out in the forest. It was a big lie from the beginning. I can't believe none of us noticed. Not even Jade."

"You knew that?" William asked.

"Not until after the first set of stores. At least, that's when I started to suspect. I was sure by the forest. There was no doubt we were separated from the rest of the normal world."

"So who wants to fill in some details?" William looked around the table to see who was willing to speak.

Clairity jumped at the chance. She went over the first stores and the wands, handing Ashlyn the one they bought for her. Her rendition included how the potions store reacted to them, and the story about Lester and Mildred. She paused for a moment after telling them about the necklace and Camile. Sarah excused herself and William took a break to speak to her. They returned a few minutes later, the girl's eyes swollen shut from crying. She dried her tears and took a seat again.

Willow's attention focused out the window on nothing particular, but rather simply staring into space. Her mind was on Camile and what happened. There had been no time to mourn her loss, until now. While she was lost in her own thoughts, she completely missed Jade and

Clairity fill in all the details regarding the forest and Aslo retelling the information about the portal and the Glaquool.

Tears flowed from almost everyone in the room, at the news of what happened to Camile, Willow still oblivious to everything around her. The girls continued to tell their story right up to finding Mike.

"Willow?" William said, sensing the girl's mind was somewhere else.

"Sorry," she answered again.

"What happened to the charms?" he asked.

"They are taken care of," she answered, still looking out the window.

"Where were you while the girls were looking for Mike and Annabelle?"

"I went through the door, the one in the dream."

"Alone?" Even Clairity was surprised by her comment. "That place was creepy. Anything could have been lurking in there."

"I was alone. I needed to know what was behind the door," she said. "It was the place in the dream where we saw Mike. With everyone else gone in different directions, it seemed like the only thing to do."

"And?" Ashlyn pried.

Willow didn't have a chance to say a word before Nero and Tika appeared beside her. "Don't be scared!" she exclaimed. "They are guardians." She wished they had let her explain how she found them before appearing like that. From the look on William's face, he was upset she hadn't mentioned it earlier too.

Nero and Tika took turns telling their part of the story, leaving out nothing. "Without her, we would still be doomed to a life of torture. We owe her a great debt."

"Seems to be a theme," Shelby said, happy to see them. "It's good to see you again, my friends."

"Shelby!" Tika exclaimed. "Is Lasel here as well?"

"No, he is captive with our keepers."

"Sorry to break up the reunion, but we have a lot of ground to cover. Willow..." Aslo looked to his keeper to continue her story.

Willow picked up the story about how the prince was in the room and how the charms were destroyed, leaving out most of the conversation and the way he kissed her on the cheek. Shivers went up her spine just thinking about it again.

"He helped you?" Ashlyn asked.

"Yeah, he said I owed him. I suppose one day he could show up and ask me for a favour. I would be obliged to help." She finished the story with the prince leaving and how she found the secret about the tunnels. Jade took over to complete the tale of how they escaped. She did a particularly interesting job of describing the people with mutating faces.

"Well, your dream was right about one thing. We were captured. The witches' brother just happened to be by to give them a message. I don't know what it was, but they were deep in discussion. He saw the portal guard mark on my arm and asked for some time to interrogate me. He wanted to know about you." Mike stared right into Willow's eyes, albeit she couldn't read what he was thinking.

Willow put the backpack on the table and pulled out the book she bought, hoping to change the topic, but the invitation flew out with the book. William picked up the envelope and opened it. Willow's face turned several shades of red.

"When were you going to tell us about this?" he asked, examining it.

"That's why I was bringing out everything, to... talk about it," she lied.

Clairity flashed her a glance that told her she was busted, at least by her best friend. She was thankful no one else knew.

William read the invitation out loud for everyone. "Seems our prince has a fixation on you. Is there anything else we should know?"

"No," Willow said.

"Willow." Clairity only needed the one word to tell everyone that the redhead was lying. So much for her friend keeping quiet.

"Okay, maybe. It's a little embarrassing." She filled in the missing information. How Lance said he couldn't do anything against his sisters, *not even for her.* She paused for a moment and after another glare from Clairity, mentioned the kiss on her cheek and how the prince basically showed her how to escape. She looked up and everyone was completely still, just staring at her. "What?" was all she managed to say.

"Okay," William broke the silence. "How about our new guests?"

"Kriller," Nathan said. "They are thought to be the most intelligent creatures to live. The speed at which their brain works causes the changes in their faces. It is really fascinating. They communicate to each other telepathically and then work together to speak or walk or do anything really. They are far more advanced than anything else we have come across and probably ever will."

"Do we know why they are here?"

"I have spent some time with them and it seems they became stuck here after stumbling through one of those holes between the realms. The princesses were on the other side and captured them as soon as they entered the main world. They would be happy to go home." Nathan was busy looking at the new book.

"Problem is, the portal stones to their home world are on the missing list," Sarah added. "There is absolutely no information on them anywhere."

"Perfect." William rubbed his eyes. "I guess they are going to be our guests for at least a little while longer. Anyone want to input anything else?"

"Yeah." Willow turned her attention to William. "We know there are beings from other worlds living here. I don't think we realize just how many are. I believe there is an underground society of potential allies we should look into."

"We can help with that." Annabelle spoke for the first time at the meeting. "Willow is definitely right. There is an underground movement, including parties and clubs. That ball you were invited to is probably one as well."

"She's not going," Mike blurted out. "It's too dangerous."

William threw his pencil in the air out of frustration and leaned back in his chair, balancing it on only two legs. "Go ahead, tell me how you plan to infiltrate?"

"I don't know," Mike admitted, still watching Willow. "But she isn't going to that ball. I can't be the only one to feel this way. The risk is way too high."

"Okay," William looked from Mike to Willow, then back again. "Until we figure this out, you two are going to stay away from each other. I need everybody's head in the game. Don't even try to argue or say anything. I don't want to hear it."

Mike calmly answered, "Okay."

Willow agreed in the same fashion, pretending she was clueless as to what the big fuss was about. Secretly inside, she wondered if there was anything between her and Mike. He had dismissed spending time with her so easily. Maybe it was all in her head. She glanced at Annabelle and Lilabeth. Their aura was still flowing between them in a perfect rhythm. One thing was for sure, she didn't see that from herself for anyone, at least not yet.

"Is it possible to see your own aura?" she blurted out, realizing that it had nothing to do with what the others were discussing.

"Is there a relevance?" William asked, brushing his hair out of his eyes. "Cause I don't see one." Tension strung his words together.

"No," Willow didn't want anyone to know she hadn't been listening to the past twenty some odd minutes, but daydreaming about… love. "I was just wondering. Since I joined with Nero and Tika, I can see some auras. I know it is a gift you receive when joined with the Olcsanka, but I think I have developed the skill even without them. They must have jump-started a latent ability and I thought it might be relevant if I could analyze my aura's interaction with different groups." She was pushing this story way too far. How could seeing energy patterns ever really help?

The look on William's face told the story. She could tell he wanted to wring her neck while asking what was wrong with her. Of course, he didn't. The silence was actually more painful. She felt like an alien, understanding for the first time how the Kriller must have always felt.

"Well," she said. "I could use some air, excuse me." Willow stood up, walking outside she headed for the forest. Stopping dead in her tracks, she screamed. She expected one of her friends to come after her, but to her surprise, it was William who put his hand on her shoulder.

"Are you okay?" he asked.

"No," she said, shaking. Why couldn't he see something terrible was happening? "Look." She pointed at the forest.

William looked where she was pointing and then back at her. He walked closer to see if there was something he was missing. She followed, staying behind him.

"I don't see anything, Willow."

"The trees, they must be sick. The leaves are changing colours and falling." A horrified look crossed her face. "We have to help them. Maybe it's bad magic. I have never seen this happen before."

William started to laugh, thoroughly amused by her. She, however, was less than impressed by his reaction.

"I don't see what's so funny."

He tried to speak, but he couldn't stop laughing. After a few minutes, he managed to blurt out, "They aren't hurt. It's just a season change. In fall, the trees prepare to hibernate for the winter. Their leaves turn colours and drop off their branches. During the winter, when it is cold and there is snow, the trees are dormant. In the spring, the trees wake up and grow new leaves. It's a completely normal thing in this world."

"Oh," she said, pouting. "You didn't have to laugh at me." She started to walk away.

William grabbed her. "Sorry," he said, hugging her. "Now what about inside? What was that about?"

"I don't know, things pop into my head sometimes. I just figure they have some relevance. Sometimes it does and other times people look at me like... I am from another world." She was amused at her little joke -

even managing to chuckle a little. "Sometimes, things make more sense when I say them out loud."

"So it has nothing to do with Mike?"

"No," she lied. "Why would it?"

"I don't know. You two seem to have something going on."

"Like what?" Willow decided acting ignorant was best, especially since she was questioning both of their feelings. Being a girl was hard work.

"Nothing, I just thought," he said. "Never mind. I guess I was wrong. I am going to make up the teams, if you don't mind, and hand out some assignments to prepare to follow up on the clues we have."

"Fine." She smiled. "I think I just need some alone time to catch up. Everything happens so fast around here. There isn't much time to breathe."

"Yeah, I know what you mean." William turned and headed back to the cabin.

Willow watched him until he disappeared inside and thought about how he must have felt. She only dealt with some of what happened around there. He was stuck dealing with everything and everyone. She felt guilty for putting her silly lovesick girl thoughts before saving the world. She had a lot of growing up to do.

Chapter Forty

The next couple weeks seemed to pass at a tediously slow rate for Willow. William asked her to take time off from the prophecies to rest her mind. That meant lots of extra time to do absolutely nothing. Even worse, everyone else was too busy for her.

Aslo and Kiera were teaching their little ones, who were growing fast and needed constant instruction now. They even started taking their young on nightly patrols. Not having at least one of them there when she needed someone to talk to was a new experience for her - one she wasn't exactly fond of. If the kittens weren't so busy, maybe she could have learnt the little one's names.

Things were also much quieter with the first group already gone to investigate the writer of the second copy of *The Portal Prophecies*. On the back cover was a picture of the woman from the amusement park. The same woman who also appeared in their dream. The article underneath the photo indicated the town she had grown up in. It was a place to start. They needed to find out who she was and why she wrote the second copy of the book. Mike took Ashlyn, Pete, Malarchy and Zsiga with him to find the gypsy witch and figure out if she was friendly or not. At last contact, they were still tracking down where she was last known to have lived with nothing to report.

Annabelle and Lilabeth took Clairity, Dezi, Jessie and Jade to infiltrate the underground network of the empyral. They had already learnt that *empyral* was the word most of the magical living in this world was using to describe beings who came from other realms. Willow envied them. Most of what they needed to investigate included nightclubs, dances, and other fun supernatural hotspots. While she was stuck twiddling her thumbs, they were probably having the best time of their lives. Inside, she longed to be with them.

Heading out of her sleeping quarters, she saw Iskander working hard on another one of his inventions in the training field. He was the only one out there. Even Acacia left after hearing of the thinning of protection around the Glaquool's world. Apparently there was more than one race that had been isolated as dangerous long before guardians or men existed. The ancient tree went to check on the magic barriers that kept the most dangerous beings away from the main world.

She walked towards the cabin that was their command centre. Inside Nathan, Diana, Sarah and Neil were hard at work, with Victoria pretending to help. She longed to walk in and delve right into the prophecies. To do something. But, orders were orders, so she stayed clear of the building.

Out front of the cabin, William was playing with Nero and Tika, running around and wrestling. Since arriving at the camp, the Olcsanka became particularly attached to him and vice versa. They slept in his quarters and rarely left his side. *He would make a good keeper,* she thought.

William sat on the ground, petting both of the large wolves. They rolled around, loving every minute. All of a sudden, the two animals turned to a flashy silver colour and disappeared. There was an expression of confusion on his face, as he searched everywhere for where the two had gone.

Willow walked up to him with curiosity. "Take off your shirt," she said.

"Pardon?" William asked, caught off-guard by the request.

344

It wasn't something she imagined she would have to say to the guard often. "Your shirt, take it off." She chuckled at how the request had probably sounded to him.

He did as she asked. Willow smiled and ran her hand over the picture on his shoulder of a silver and grey wolf. There was a large brown wolf on the opposite side. Looking at him like that, she couldn't deny he had an attractive physique. His muscles were a nice size, not overbearing but definitely noticeable. He would have made a good model for one of the magazines Sarah was always looking at, if it weren't for the scars on his back and chest. She wondered what caused them, but dismissed them as war scars from before her time. She shook her head, realizing where her thoughts were leading.

"You're a keeper now," she said. It crossed her mind that she had caused the change. She was the one who decided he would be a good keeper. She thought back to when the others became portal guards, and then too, she thought they would be of help. She was the one who was choosing their team, not Acacia. Perhaps that ability was passed on to her the night she was healed. Not knowing for sure, she felt it best not to discuss that with the others. Of course, there really wasn't anyone to discuss it with.

William was gone, heading to show Aslo and Kiera the good news. She was alone again. He left her there standing on the lawn, feeling like an idiot. She sighed, heading to the forest.

The leaves continued to fall steadily, although there was still a lot of red, orange, and yellow colours left to look at. It was a pretty sight. She placed a hand against the trunk of one of the trees. The communication was sluggish. She could tell the forest was almost ready to sleep until spring. The light whispers of fun that had been her constant companion over the years, listening to all of her life's experiences were absent. Even here, she felt alone.

Walking back, she ran into Faramund writing poetry. It became apparent over the last few days he was developing a crush on Sarah - writing mushy odes in her name ever since. Sarah, of course, was oblivious to what was going on. Love was an impossible thing to understand. Why couldn't it be easy?

"You busy?" she asked.

"Not extremely," he answered, putting down his pencil and paper to give her his full attention. "What can I do for the little lady today?"

"I thought with everyone being so busy that maybe we could take a trip somewhere. We could take a look at the Kriller portal... see if there is anything I can do. Maybe I could find a way to open it."

"Have you asked William?" He picked back up his pencil and paper, anticipating the answer.

"He is so busy. I thought it would be one thing off the list if I could figure it out." Pleading her case wasn't going well.

"Well, last I heard we still didn't have the missing portal stones and you should be resting. There is no need to look at a portal that has no stones. Even your talents can't open that."

"I am tired of resting. If I don't do something, I am going to die of boredom. Please?" She kicked the grass with her shoe, making a small hole of dirt.

He put his paper back down and looked at her. "If William asks me, I will take you. Otherwise, find something to do... a hobby, maybe."

A hobby, she thought, *great.* Her mind wandered to the prince. He wouldn't have sent her away. Of course, he wouldn't save her from his sisters either. She wondered if they knew about her, or any of his family, for that matter. It was doubtful. She could imagine what they would say if they did. No, she figured he was keeping their meetings his secret for now, in much the same way she wanted to leave out details of their time together at the meeting.

Memories returned of the way he touched her hair and kissed her cheek. It was warm and nice. His lips were soft. She couldn't remember anyone else ever having kissed her, not even her parents. Maybe that was why it affected her in such a powerful way.

If they want me to find something to do, she thought, *then I will.* She was going to find a costume for the witches' ball. No matter what was decided, she was going to go and nobody was going to stop her. She made a mental note to fill William in on her plan later - when the time was right.

Chapter Forty-One

Mike felt his body temperature rising. Sweat trickled down his back, soaking his shirt. He stretched the muscles of his neck and shoulders. Every time they tracked down a place where the woman from the amusement park lived, they found out she had only been there a short time and moved on, even as a child. It seemed this was the life of a gypsy, never staying in one place for long. Many locals were afraid of her name. There were local legends that formed about the band of gypsies she travelled with and their powers. That meant finding someone to talk to them about her was extremely difficult.

So far, they had learned she was an accomplished witch, practising in the area of clairvoyance. According to people in each of the small towns she took up residence in, she could see past, present, and future as if it were a movie playing before her. She used crystal balls, cards, runes, dice and fire to channel her visions. After asking enough questions in one particular area, a concerned citizen would come forth, usually without identifying themselves, and point a direction in which the caravan headed. It was more an act of desperation, wanting to make his group move on than to actually help them. The citizens didn't want someone or something to know they helped. It was a puzzle stacked on another puzzle. Unfortunately, Mike wasn't the most patient person; his blood was reaching its boiling point.

The latest town they came to was no different. After getting nowhere quickly with the locals, they headed to the only motel in town to rest for the night. There, they were greeted by a man, of medium height, with long, pure white hair. He wore plain loose clothing and open-toed sandals. "The legends of the gypsy curse have a deep meaning in these parts. There are those who would prefer things not to be disturbed," he said while processing Mike's credit card.

"Can you tell us about Estonia, the author of this book?" Mike asked, holding up a photocopy of the cover of *The Portal Prophecies* written by the gypsy.

"Patience, this town is rich in information, if you know where to look. Might I suggest our museum?" The old man pointed towards a section of the motel through two doors which was labelled *The Gypsy Connection: A Tour Through The Ages*. "You are in luck, there is a special presentation tonight. Shall I add tickets to your room for the low price of $29.99 each? It may answer exactly what you want to know."

"Yes, thanks, one for each of us." Mike grabbed the keys to the rooms so he and the others could unpack. "$29.99 each, I hope this isn't a waste of time," he mumbled while walking away, unsure if they were making a frugal investment.

They were the only people staying in the motel and most likely the only visitors to the area in a long time. The town definitely wasn't a hot vacation spot and Mike made his reservations known as to whether or not they would learn anything from the presentation, emphasizing the not. Ashlyn convinced him that it couldn't have been a coincidence that the show just happened to be playing when they came to visit. She didn't have the visionary powers Clairity did, but she was sure it was a sign. Besides that, it was the first time anyone offered information to them since they started their quest.

The doors to the exhibit were open when they returned to the lobby. There was no sign of the old man, so they proceeded to let themselves through. The first part was set up as a museum. There were items under glass and on walls, each with a plaque nearby with information on what they were looking at. At first glance, the room appeared to hold promise.

"See," Ashlyn said, taking the lead and heading straight to the first item. "There could be some good leads in here."

Mike followed her and looked at the first glass display. "A scarf from Blad, one of the first men to be named a gypsy," he read from the plaque, which was more a hand written piece of paper that was framed. "Yup, this is gonna be great." His lips pressed together tightly as he shook his head. The sound of air releasing from his flaring nostrils resembled wind flowing through an empty tunnel.

"Okay, well, it's just the first item. There must be other things in here." Ashlyn moved to a picture on the wall. Another handwritten note said:

Storm, caused by a sorcerer after Blad and his townsfolk turned down his offer of extended life and great power. The villagers cited the sorcerer's connection to the dead as the reason for their rejection of the generous offer. This was the turning point for the gypsies. They would now be forced to choose a nomadic life in order to avoid the wrath of the necromancer and his army.

"Yup, that storm is informative. Never seen one like that before. There is rain and stuff," Pete said sarcastically before walking over to the next item up for view.

Mike was spending a bit too much time reading over the write-up on the storm. Ashlyn thought back to the story of what happened with his brother. Taking his hand, she led him away from possible thoughts of his brother's reanimated corpse.

The next item they viewed was a poorly handwritten journal belonging to someone named Durikken. The note claimed it was from the time of the black plague and evidenced acts of necromancy, vampires, and werewolves.

On the wall across from them was a picture of a cloaked man standing alone on a foggy night. The note underneath titled *Fear of Strangers.* Gypsies believed that any stranger hanging around a place without reason could potentially be the necromancer, following them throughout eternity.

"Maybe that's why people are frightened to speak to us. They might think one of us is the sorcerer." Ashlyn flipped her white hair, revealing some hidden pink underneath.

"Yeah, sure, and the rest of us are undead." Pete wasn't going to give up the opportunity to use sarcasm. Usually, it would be his brother Dezi cracking all the jokes. A pretentious grin spanned his entire face.

As they moved further into the makeshift museum, the exhibits didn't improve much. They viewed a horse shoe, a statue of a dragon and various stories of different beasts. Apparently, gypsies were thought to have a strong connection with animals.

The next display was a series of tribal tattoos. The description underneath them revealed that each gypsy clan would use a different area of the body to mark and a different animal, depending on their beliefs. Those depicted were of a black bird, a black cat, and a wolf.

"That's interesting," Zsiga said, taking a photo with another device he was working on - one which allowed him to send pictures directly back to William in the camp. He was documenting everything carefully so as not to miss a clue. "Seems we are finding a lot that could tie in with guardian influences in this world. At least it's progress."

"I bet there are other animals too," Mike said, unimpressed with the poor excuse for a museum. "This doesn't look like anything to me. Not worth wasting William's time, that's for sure. It wouldn't surprise me if he was getting tired of all the things that are being brought to his attention when they all turn out to mean absolutely nothing."

They followed stories and items outlining a trail of immigration paths that the caravans followed - some settling in swamps and hiding among mossy trees. Certain groups tried to assimilate into society and blend away from the sorcerer's reach. Still other clans were continually moving from place to place.

The last glass-encased exhibit was a deck of tarot cards. They were old and possibly handcrafted, the pictures still vibrant with colours. The one showing face-up was a picture of a woman with red hair wearing a green and gold dress. There was magic flowing from her hands towards the sky.

Following that was another room with a few rows of folding chairs set up. In front of them was the old man. "Come, come take your seats," he said. "We'll just wait for everyone to finish their tour of the museum."

"I think we're it," Mike said, looking around.

"Young man, if you are going to cause a disturbance, I will have to have you removed. Please take your seat."

Mike grumbled as he sat in one of the plastic seats. They were small and uncomfortable for a large guy. He changed the positions of his legs constantly, letting out a huff with each movement. Ashlyn took the seat beside him, trying to keep him calm. After approximately fifteen minutes, the presentation began.

"Welcome, everyone, and thank you for your patience while people were finding their seats for tonight's presentation," the old man bellowed out.

Mike glanced around the room, then rolled his eyes. No one else had joined them.

"Tonight, we have a very special topic. We are going to look at the history of the gypsy witch. If you bothered to look at the displays on your way in, you should have a basic knowledge of the past and how these brave people became known as wanderers or nomads."

"Can we just ask a few questions?" Mike interrupted.

"Am I going to have a problem with you, young man? There are other people who have paid for the whole evening," the hotel attendant said.

"We are the only ones here." Mike's blood pressure rose, threatening to erupt. His face turned red, his teeth letting out a grinding noise which mixed in with his words.

"Really?"

Everyone turned to follow the old man's crooked finger, pointing at a short elderly woman. Using a walker, she wobbled slowly towards a chair.

"You've gotta be kidding," Mike whispered under his breath.

Ashlyn took his hand and leaned over to his ear. "It won't take long. Who knows, it might even be fun. Let's just sit and watch. Please?"

He took his seat again, waiting until the woman had found a suitable place to settle in before their host resumed his speech.

"My name is Vincent and I will be taking you on a powerful journey tonight. By the time we are done, you will all have a better understanding of who a gypsy witch is.

"A very, very, very long time ago, there was a small village of good, upstanding, hardworking individuals. One day, a great sorcerer visited them and, seeing their abilities and resolve, he extended them a cup of blood, drinking from which bestowed extended life and great strength. The townsfolk knew the sorcerer as one who practised a form of death magic which allowed him to reanimate corpses. They refused his offer and have had to move around to hide from him ever since, as well as having to avoid the dark magician's allies, vampires and shape-shifters.

"Here in this area of the world, we have been influenced by nomadic gypsies for several hundred years. They have been integrated into our culture. Many modern-day witches and psychics use the ways of the gypsy in their craft.

"So I hope you have enjoyed the presentation and have a wonderful night," Vincent said.

"That's it?" Mike's voice became two levels higher than before. "We paid $29.99 each for that pathetic show?"

"Did it not give you information you didn't have before?" Vincent's tone remained soft and steady.

Mike stomped out of the room, knocking over his chair on the way. Ashlyn ran after him. It was Malarchy who remained level-headed and approached the old man.

"My apologies for my associate. He is a little impulsive sometimes." He extended his hand in friendship. The two men shook. "I enjoyed your show very much. Perhaps you could tell me if there are any specific patterns that the gypsy caravans from this area followed?"

Zsiga moved closer. He set his machine to record for the presentation, not wanting to miss any of the conversation, especially since it sounded more promising than anything else they learned that evening.

"Well, yes, there are a few paths. There is a map in the lobby. Let me show you." Vincent motioned to a door which led directly back to the main room of the motel. "Here you can see a map of all the towns in this area. The red lines are main caravan routes. Blue and yellow represent smaller, less used ones."

Malarchy needed to keep the man talking. From all that he acquired to make the gypsy museum they just viewed, there must be some connection between him to this group of people… a passion of some sort. "I understand from your talk that gypsies are the victims. They have been given a bad rap, so to speak."

"Yes and no. As in all living creatures, there is always a choice to do good or bad. Gypsies are no different. Some chose a less than honourable existence and were given a *bad rap* as you say. Others have lived a noble life. Of course, living on the run did have some disadvantages, which added to the exaggeration of many of the stories."

"What of psychic powers? We have heard much about clairvoyance. Is this true? Have their abilities been exaggerated as well?"

"There are always those that are exaggerated, my friend. However, there are those who were extremely gifted as well. Quite a few gypsies were known for their future-reading talents and ability to communicate with the departed."

"We are looking for a specific woman, named Estonia. Have you heard of her?" Malarchy asked, fishing for the answers they were looking for.

"Yes, you are not the first to come through here looking for her. Her talents were unusual," Vincent said.

"How so?"

"Well, she wrote books, prophecy books that mirrored other prophecy books." The Inn keeper was amused with himself for the language.

"I am not sure I understand." Malarchy admitted, raising one eyebrow. "Mirrored how?"

"Well," Victor said, smiling. "You have a book of prophecies, written by someone you know. Then you find this other book, named the same thing, written by the gypsy woman. She did that on purpose, knowing you would cross one country, maybe two, to track down how to interpret her version. Following so far?"

"Yes." In reality, Malarchy couldn't shake the feeling he was being made fun of.

"She was a genius, really. Let's say your book says, *The moon was bright. In the distance, you can see a rat*," he said. "Estonia's book reads, *Only three stars had light, look again, it is being chased by a cat.*"

"Okay," Malarchy said, trying to follow where the old man was going.

"Each is a prophecy, which when the time comes you may be able to figure out. Obviously, there would be more to them. This is just an example," he said, scratching his head with one hand. "The beauty of her prophecies is this: put them together and you now have, *The moon was bright, only three stars had light. In the distance you can see a rat, look again, it is being chased by a cat.* See how they fit together and make the wording easier to understand?"

"Yes, I see. Do you know how I could contact her to discuss her work?"

"Only if you know a good medium. Estonia died several years ago. An accident near the swamps, they said. She was found covered in black leeches. They sucked her body dry of all its blood. Not sure that can happen by accident. If you know what I mean."

"Was that near here?"

"Follow the blue line on the map. It ends at the swamp where she was found and her body is buried there as well. Some folks say on a foggy night, you can see her ghost walking through the swamp waters."

"Thank you for your help," he said, shaking Vincent's hand.

Returning to the room, Malarchy found that the bags were all packed. Zsiga had kept everyone filled in on the conversation and took pictures of the map in the lobby.

"It's a full day's drive," Mike said. "Let's sleep tonight, but be ready to pull out early tomorrow. William wants us to check out the swamp."

Chapter Forty-Two

Willow could have jumped for joy and done a back flip when she heard William was calling a meeting of all remaining persons in the camp. Something must have happened and hopefully it meant the end of the rest and relaxation that was driving her crazy.

By the time she entered the cabin, everyone was already assembled. Apparently, she was an afterthought. She wasn't entirely sure how she slipped in the ranks from a leader to almost forgettable in such a short amount of time. Rather than complain, she decided her best line of action was to sit and find out what was going on. At least it was something to do.

"Well," William said. "Now we are all here, shall we begin?" He continued, relaying all the information that Mike's team had found out.

Willow slammed both her hands on the table. "Estonia is dead? How can that be if I saw her and she talked to me?"

"That's what we don't know," William said. "For now, I want to concentrate on researching ghosts and spirits."

"Do you think they are real? Ghosts, I mean," Faramund asked.

"I don't know. It's a new concept for us," he answered. "With everything else we have seen, I suppose anything is possible. There very well could be another realm for the essences of people who have moved on. There are definitely enough theories in this world. Heaven and Hell being two names that have been given to a *spirit realm*. Let's see what else we can come up with."

"The prophecy books," Nathan said, flipping through the pages of one of the volumes without bothering to look up. "Shouldn't we try to put the prophecies together? Finding the way the two books interact could be the key we need."

"It is something we will have to look at, but with Halloween approaching fast, we need to follow the clues we have." William stood up to make a cup of coffee and realized the pot was empty. He chuckled. "I am starting to miss Zsiga's brew. Who knew I'd ever say those words."

Diana stood and offered to make a new pot.

"No," he said, smiling at her. "I'm okay. I should cut back anyways." He sat back down, rotating each of his shoulders in a backwards circular motion to stretch his muscles.

"I have already done some light research on the topic of ghosts," Nathan said, still looking through the pages of the book in front of him. "There are a lot of different variations in lore throughout the history of this world, some of which can be explained as phenomena directly relating to an otherworldly experience."

"Illuminate us." William folded his arms together in front of him, leaning back in his chair, the two front legs lifting off the ground. He was ready to hear a few long stories.

"Funny you should say that," Nathan said, smiling. "The first thing we can look at are the orbs people associate with ghosts. They are most often described as floating balls of light." He paused, waiting for a reaction to his joke. No one did. The beginnings of a frown formed on his lips. Nathan believed the play on words he had used was amusing and the lack of laughter annoyed him.

"I have heard of that," Sarah interrupted the silent awkwardness. "Sometimes you can see them, sometimes they only show up in pictures."

She noticed everyone staring at her. "What? There are tons of ghost hunting shows on television. I watch them when I can't sleep. They use all kinds of tests to see if a spirit is present. It's educational."

Nathan sat up straight and directed all his attention to Sarah. "I'd like to see some of those... strictly for research purposes, of course."

"Okay, we are getting off-topic. Let's keep it to the subject for now." William's chair crashed back down on the ground. He tossed his pencil on the table in front of him. "We can view the programs later, if need be." Satisfied his authority was being adhered to, he pushed his chair back again.

"Wisps." Nathan's expression returned to indifference as he resumed flipping through the pages of the prophecy book. "They are a race of bodiless beings who generally appear in the shape of a sphere. Their natural form is a raw energy, or light."

"Of course," Willow said, jumping in the conversation. "They are friendly and trying to make contact. When they meet a new entity, they scan their mind for a form to take - an image of someone or something that is familiar. After taking that form, they are still made of energy so they appear as an illuminated see-through copy of a person."

"Oh!" Sarah exclaimed. "Because they are energy, they would be able to control a flashlight or equipment of the ghost hunters as well."

"They have no vocal chords so, in general, they can't speak. There is a report of a couple of them who learnt how to radiate their energy frequencies at a rate to create noises that sound like certain words, but usually only one or two at a time and it is difficult to hear," Nathan said.

"What do they want with people?" Diana asked.

"They are really friendly and usually only make contact to help others," the boy continued. "If you lost something, they might try to lead you to it, or if there was something dangerous, they may try to keep you away from it."

"So how do we round them up and send them all home?" William asked.

"Well," Nathan answered. "We don't. They were one of the few magical beings who posed no threat to… anyone. They were never given a world to be confined to, inhabiting any and most likely all worlds. They can appear as large or as small as they want - so small they could be undetectable. There was also some discussion that perhaps their unique form allows them to pass between worlds without the use of portals. We don't know."

"It does explain a vast majority of ghost stories." Sarah's eyes lit bright, her gaze never leaving the face of the boy who had been speaking. "At least the stories we hear a lot about."

William's chair came back down on all four legs. He sat for a moment in deep thought, bouncing the eraser end of a pencil on his notepad. "So we are debunking the notion of ghosts?"

"No, not at all," Nathan answered. "There are many other things to look at. That was an example of just one that we can explain." He paused for a moment, as if collecting his thoughts, almost like a computer accessing information. "The next interesting group would be what this world calls poltergeists."

"Poltergeists? You can explain them?" Sarah was clearly interested in this topic much more than anyone else. Her enthusiasm, however, had a contagious effect.

"What's a poltergeist?" Faramund asked.

"It's a supernatural force or ghost that creates physical disturbances," Sarah jumped to the answer before anyone else could. "Doors slamming and things moving around a room are common. The lights could flicker, static on television, oh… and they could physically come in contact with the living, like a pinch, or pulling hair." She obviously was much more informed than she had been letting on. Her knowledge exceeded that which one might expect to learn from a television program.

"Exactly!" Nathan exclaimed. "These occurrences could be Winks. They are the smallest of the fairy family. I mean really small. A scale for them would be from the size of a fruit fly to that of a house fly. They all have wings and, unfortunately, a mischievous nature. Although they mean no harm, their pranks and jokes often lead to destruction."

"I am assuming their size might hinder us finding and returning them to their home world." William was scribbling on his paper, what appeared to be three-dimensional boxes.

"Absolutely." Nathan stretched his neck to try to glimpse at the drawing from his position at the table. "Then there are the spectrim. They aren't so nice - a bodiless race, generally made of some gaseous substance. They can mutate their form to create pictures in things you find in this world, like water or clouds. Using an ability to read minds, they choose a person who is emotionally unstable over the death of a loved one. Then they create pictures of the deceased in, for instance, a lake. Luring their target into the water with the images, they would attempt to take over their victim's body. Unfortunately, they are not compatible with living tissue. The end result, the target dies and it looks like a suicide from emotional distress."

"Do they have a world they are confined to?" Willow asked.

"Yes," he answered. "We can send them back, if we come across any. They are rare, though."

"Are there any examples of ghosts we cannot explain? Anything that would suggest they are real? Maybe we should concentrate on those." William seemed distracted, as if his mind was somewhere else.

"Of course. We can't dispute many mediums of this world. They appear to be able to contact the deceased. According to some of the most renowned experts, at least that I have researched, the easiest way for the deceased to contact the living is through our dreams. The description is similar to what a dreamwalker does, except they have no control of the dream and often use symbols to express what they want to say. They can use noises the dreamer would understand or scents to show they are present. The dreams still have to be interpreted for them to make any sense."

Nathan looked proud of himself for the extra research he was doing. "One other thing. Since they can't break through into our world fully, it is believed they leave symbols in everyday life, like little messages. Often in number forms or sometimes noises and scents. Seeing a certain number or combination of the same number over and over again is said to be communication from the other side. As would smelling someone's favourite perfume or hearing their favourite song."

"So that would explain why the lady in Willow's dreams and the number thirteen keep popping up over and over again," Sarah said. The keys on her computer made a loud clicking noise from her fingernails. She could type faster than anyone else in the camp could.

"But not how she appeared in the amusement park," William was quick to add. "Where do these mediums suggest the spirits are?"

"In another dimension." Nathan turned his gaze to meet William's, feeling the weight of concentration being sent in his direction. He closed the book. "Basically, another world which is separated by a barrier from this world. Mediums can telepathically connect to that other realm. Now, on Halloween, or Samhain, which is basically the witches' new year, the divide between these particular two realms is thinnest, allowing activity." He paused. "I believe that on that evening, there is a recurring rip in the space between one world and another, allowing something to come through."

"So the question is where, then." William's lips turned downwards. "And is there a danger? If this has been happening for years, why are we worried?"

Willow looked around. The room was full of people she considered friends, but not the usual people she confided in when she thought she knew something. Even all the guardians were out on patrol and not there to run her ideas by, before blurting something out and looking silly.

She finally decided to speak. "I think we know where. I was invited there." That was enough she thought to at least to get the conversation going.

"What makes you think the witches' ball is where everything will happen?"

She considered a snarky answer for a moment, but decided it was in her best interest not to push her luck and end up sitting in her sleeping quarters alone again. "The person who sent the invite is a necromancer. I understand they practice death magic."

"Interesting," Faramund said. He had remained fairly quiet through most of the meeting, looking as if he was concentrating hard on a task of some sort. "I can see the connection. Ghosts are dead people." That statement sounded almost as awkward as his poetry.

William looked at the other guard with an expression of disbelief. "Yes," he answered. "They are." He shook his head.

Everyone in the room knew Faramund was trying to be helpful. His skills on a battle field were hard to match, but here, in the command centre, he was out of his element. It was rare he interacted at all. Perhaps he was trying to impress Sarah. From the look on her face, it wasn't working.

Willow decided to take attention off of the guard. "The prophecy, or curse, fits too," she said. Noticing most of the others were still staring at Faramund, she recited the old woman's words again:

Be forewarned on Hallows Eve

Those who are not of this world shall take to the streets,

Blood shall flow and death shall follow.

Your presence attracts what we cannot explain.

Your destiny is written. You best make sure you listen.

"All the more reason for you not to attend the ball," William said.

"If it is a curse, it will happen wherever I am, so it won't make a difference," she answered with a frown. "However, if it is a prophecy, I am meant to be there to stop it." Her logic was sound. She knew the others would have a hard time finding anything to argue about in her statement. Now was as good a time as any to let them know she was going to accept the invitation. She would leave out the part about wanting to see her prince again.

"True," William conceded. "But I don't have to have Clairity's abilities to have a bad feeling about this."

"I know," Willow answered. "I have a feeling it all ties in with what happened to Mike and Annabelle's family, too." She didn't know why she had said that out loud. There was sure to be a lot of questions, and she didn't have any answers. It was just another thing that popped into her head and she blurted out.

"How so?" he asked.

"I don't know yet. Whatever is going on, with the witches, the princes, the missing people, the tour, the old woman and the dead is all connected. It's like a puzzle we only have half the pieces for. We can guess the meaning or wait for more pieces to fill in."

William seemed impressed by her answer. Thinking about it, she was too. It was true. Everything that had happened since Estonia first appeared seemed to be linked in some way. It was like a word stuck on the tip of her tongue that she couldn't quite remember. Her thoughts were cut short by Sarah.

"So," she said, "what are our next steps?"

"We still have a bit of time before Halloween," William answered. "Mike and his team are continuing on to the swamp where Estonia died to check out her grave and the rumours of her ghost haunting the area. Annabelle's group has settled in and is still trying to find access to the underground. The rest of you will need to concentrate on anything helpful you can find on necromancers and ghosts. I will bring out books that will help."

He looked at Nathan, who was engrossed in the prophecy books again and added, "You should probably continue your research on the connection between the two books."

Nathan smiled. It was obvious he already had every intention of spending his time with his nose between the two books. It was a challenge for him. He could use his gifts to memorize the words and understand them for each book, but in the end, seeing how they could fit together was visual. It required him to actually look through the volumes. The task wasn't going to be easy, either - none of the prophecies appeared to be in any particular order.

"Willow and I will be heading to the town where the ball is being held. We will be gone for a few days. It will give us a chance to look around and settle in. I want to take some pictures of the layout of the house the ball is being held in. We need to be prepared if something does happen."

Willow was shocked by the statement, but thrilled at the same time, curious as to why it had been so easy to convince him she needed to be there. The thought passed quickly. There were more important things to concentrate on, like packing and her prince.

Chapter Forty-Three

Annabelle led the others down a street to a small store, its front old and unkempt. It was hard to imagine anyone would want to buy anything from the run down shop. The windows were dirty, as if they hadn't been washed in years. It would have been easier to see their reflections in a lake of mud than look inside. A sign that said *Unusual Circumstances* in black letters formed in an arch on the window. Under that was smaller writing, *Your gateway to an out-of-this-world experience.*

Once inside, they were met by the undeniable presence of burning incense lingering in the air. Shelves were filled with typical merchandise found in any occult store. Fragrant oils in tiny vials lined the wall behind a counter. Every scent possible filled the large space. Beside them, were jars holding thin sticks of incense, again in hundreds of different varieties.

A tall man, wearing a pin-striped suit without the jacket, stood alone behind the counter. What used to be a long-sleeved white shirt, now dulled from time, sat under a proper vest covering his thin frame. A chain leading to a pocket watch hidden within the vest dangled down in an odd position. His long white hair had a noticeable bald spot in the middle. His nose, having been broken one too many times, was a little flat.

"Good evening," he said. "Is there something you are looking for?" The man closed one eye and used the other to look up and down at his new patrons, taking his time to examine each one carefully.

"Yes," Annabelle replied. "A copy of *The Empowered,* please."

The man pointed to a stack of newspapers in the corner. His finger was as crooked and as long as his nose. A cracking sound emanated from his bones with every movement.

"Anything else?" The man raised one of his bushy white eyebrows. Wrinkles covered his visible skin with folds on top of folds.

"Actually," Lilabeth said, stepping forward. "We were looking for somewhere that we could relax with others who have similar interests as us. Perhaps you could recommend somewhere magical?"

"And those interests might be?" His voice lingered on the *be*.

Jade moved beside the two witches and said, "We enjoy the unusual." She flipped through several different illusions, changing her appearance from one to another effortlessly.

"Of course," he answered in an unimpressed voice. "Do you have transportation?"

"No," all three girls replied in unison, their voices each a different level as if they were singing in a choir.

"Then you will need these bus tickets. One for each of you?"

"Yes, thank you," Annabelle replied, somewhat skeptical at how easily he was offering them. "Where do we catch the bus from?"

The man smiled, showing metals of different colours in spots where teeth should have been. "That depends on you. Anyone can buy tickets, but catching the bus, that is a different story," he said. "Good evening." The man then sat down, put his feet up on the counter with a loud creak and covered his face with a newspaper as if having a nap.

The group exited the store. Clairity let out a sneeze. It was only the second time in her life that she had that experience. The first happened when she was younger and was lying to Willow about not being able to smell some wild flowers in the forest. Her friend kept moving the bunch of small yellow blossoms closer and closer to her nose until the tips tickled her. The sensation caused her to let out a strange noise. The whole thing scared both girls so badly they ran all the way back to her mother. The explanation of sneezing had been interesting enough that the two spent weeks trying to recreate the event, without success.

"Incense can be overwhelming, especially the more unusual scents." Lilabeth offered her a tissue.

"Thanks," Clairity said. Coming to an abrupt stop, she titled her head sideways towards an alley. Noticing she was not moving, the others turned around to walk back to her.

"What is it?" Jessie asked.

"I don't know, but I have a feeling we need to go down there." Clairity moved her head from side to side, trying to see. Even though it was daytime, the lane was hidden in shadows.

"Down there?" Jade made a face showing her disapproval. "It's dark and anything could be hiding in spots we can't see."

"We need to follow her instincts." Annabelle pushed through the others and headed down the lane way, her pace quickening with every step.

It was definitely dark. The area appeared to be nothing more than the backs of stores, used for dumping garbage. A stench rose from bins of decomposing food and waste. Jade covered her nose with her hand as they walked. At the end of the buildings, they came to a large chain fence.

"Well, that's a dead end." Dezi placed his fingers in the metal holes of the fence and shook it - echoing a rattling noise all around them.

The fence started to move, creating an opening similar to a doorway. The group exchanged glances with each other. Jessie took the lead heading through to the other side. Bright lights shone in his face before he could see anything.

"That must be our bus," he said, his eyes still squinting from the shock of a flash of light shining directly in them.

Stepping up the stairs to board the bus, each one handed their ticket to the driver and took a seat. The bus looked like an ordinary city bus. The blue interior seats were worn with a few rips that were taped back together. They were the only ones along for the ride.

Clairity couldn't help but notice the bus driver was so thin that she could see the bones of his face. As if feeling her stare locked on him, he turned around and glanced in the general direction of what she assumed was towards her, it was difficult to tell. His eyes pointed two different ways and neither one was straight. She wondered how he was going to be able to drive. Turning her head, she looked out the window, not wanting to appear rude.

The ride started out as any normal bus route. The driver followed all the rules of the road and made regular stops, although in unusual spots. People got on and off at various places. There was an old lady being walked by a small dog and a large hooded group wearing all black. No one was able to see any part of any of their faces, but a distinctive odour drifted from their direction of decomposing tissue. Next a woman got on with her three children covered in what looked like a large amount of bubble gum. The driver yelled, "No gum under the seats, or on them," at her when they boarded. Even people who looked normal seemed to be hiding something.

The bus stopped at the bottom of a mountain. All the other passengers exited and Annabelle's group found themselves as the sole group on the bus again. The driver turned the route sign to *end of the line* and started up the side of the mountain. The road twisted and turned. Jessie, looking out the window, commented several times that the road was barely big enough to hold the size of the vehicle they were travelling in.

After about twenty minutes, they all noticed that there was something up ahead in the road. As they came closer, Annabelle's eyes widened. She grasped the seat in front of her tightly. "Is that a road closed barrier?"

They all turned their attention in front of them. It was, in fact, an orange barrier which read R*oad Ends.* Past that was nothing. The road literally ended at a cliff.

"Why aren't we slowing down?" Lilabeth asked. "What's he doing? Is he going to drive over the edge?"

There was no time to react other than to close their eyes and hold on tight to anything they could reach as the bus went speeding through where the barrier was positioned.

Clairity opened one eye. "Are we still falling?"

"Phew." Dezi wiped the sweat from his brow. "We seem to be okay." He looked out the window. The bus appeared to be driving on nothing.

"It's an illusion," Jade said, looking out another window. "I think it's similar to the one we experienced on the tour, except on a much larger scale. There was no cliff. We are still on solid ground."

"Our telepathic connection is affected again," Clairity added.

Annabelle pulled out a cell phone. "It must be the illusion. Somehow the magic blocks signals from going through. My cell phone isn't working, either."

"Well, at least we know why now." Clairity placed one hand on the window as she watched the clouds disappear and the road form beneath them. They were inside the magic completely now. Out each side of the bus, the group could see fields of open land. Up ahead, there were tall gates leading into a city.

"I expected something shinier," Lilabeth whispered.

"You watch too many movies." The driver had remained silent the whole way, but listened to everything that was said. "Probably thought it would be made of gold or diamonds? Maybe glass or emeralds? Tell me, what other than to make a good story, would be the point? I think you will find that the folks around here would rather use precious metals and gem stones for more practical uses, like magic. Tales made for the terunji have to be dressed up, to keep their attention and grab their imagination. Their subconscious yearns for them to accept what they can't explain."

Annabelle laughed. "I suppose you are right. There really isn't a need to jazz it up. The illusion used to hide the city is impressive enough."

"We have to keep the terunji out, as well as the riff raff... if you know what I mean." The driver seemed to be more talkative now.

"I think I do. There are those who would destroy this world, including all of us," Annabelle said, trying to keep the man talking.

"Yes Ma'am, there are," he answered. "And the people round here want nothing to do with them."

"Out of curiosity, why did it take you so much time to speak to us?" she asked.

"It's my job," the driver answered. "I not only drive the bus, but use my discretion as to the people who I bring into the city. I make sure they are the right sort of folks. Unless you have been approved by a city official, that is."

"And we are?" Dezi asked.

"You are new to here, that's for sure. But I have a knack for weeding out folks who don't belong. You are good people. Not sure how many of you are empyral and how many native, but you belong. This is it folks, end of the line." He pointed to the bus' route sign. "Have a good stay and enjoy the festivities."

The city looked as any normal city did. There were cars and taxis, all with special licence plates. Tall buildings overshadowed small businesses. One building stood out, almost looking out of place. Its architecture suggested it was older by far than the other buildings in the area. Out front was a long sign which read *Your Destiny*. It appeared to be an old-fashioned hotel.

"Well," Dezi said. "It could take a long time to explore this place, maybe we should check into a room?"

Inside the building was much smaller, with only a front desk and an elevator, leaving the group to wonder how it seemed so much wider on the outside. Behind the main desk was a man who stood over eight feet tall. His long nose curled under at the end, as if it was once pointed and he ran face first into a wall. His stringy reddish-brown hair hung down below his shoulders. The plain brown coat he was wearing draped down low enough to cover his ankles with only two boots sticking out from under it.

"Can I help you?" he asked in a deep, whiny voice.

"Yes," Annabelle said, stepping forward to the desk. "We would like to enquire about a room. Do you have any available?"

"And what happened to all the space this hotel takes up outside?" Dezi threw in.

"You don't expect us to waste valuable space on a check-in area at this time of year?" The man pulled out a book, then looked over his potential new guests. "Two rooms, I would imagine?" he asked.

"Yes," Annabelle responded. "That would be perfect. Thank you."

The man gave her a look of curiosity. "And how will the madame being paying?"

"Oh," she answered. "We have cash or credit."

The man let out a laugh that sounded like a dying pig. "New to town, are we? You should have stopped at the foot of the mountain and changed over your cash to more usable currency."

"Guess that explains why everyone else got off the bus," Jessie said.

"Yes," the man said, closing his book.

"Wait," Annabelle pleaded. "What would be acceptable currency?"

"That would depend on where you are." The man said, tilting his head to look at Jade. "Some places accept precious metals or gems, some hard-to-find ingredients or potions. The politicians, of course, would prefer you add magic to their enchantments. Any city-run establishments require you to use magic to help advance or repair the surroundings in some way. The more unusual places have more, specific needs, like blood donations."

"I am guessing you prefer gems?" Jade said, stepping forward and removing one of her earrings - her favourite pair made by Mr. Shinning. The front piece against the ear was a large diamond attached to a dangling string of rubies that ended in a star of sapphires and emeralds, all embedded in a fine gold. The main world didn't have anything close to the quality or value. She placed the single earring on the desk. "What would this get us?"

The corner of one side of the man's mouth curled up as if trying to smile and hide it at the same time. Jade couldn't help but wonder if she placed both earrings on the desk if the other side would have curled up as well.

"I could give you two nights for that."

"We should look somewhere else," Clairity said, having a feeling the earring was much more valuable to the man than he was letting on. "There are other establishments who will give us a fair deal."

"Wait," the man said. He looked like he was having a silent argument with himself. "We can offer a week," he finally spit out with some difficulty.

"Um," Clairity said with a frown. "Two weeks, throw in breakfast and dinner daily and we have a deal."

Annabelle looked at her with concern, but said nothing. She witnessed Clairity's abilities at work before and decided questioning her while she was negotiating might be counterproductive.

The man seemed distressed with the negotiations. After spending some time with his back to the group, whispering to himself, he turned back and handed Jade two keys to a suite.

"We hope you enjoy your stay," he said, motioning towards the elevator to take them to their floor. Right after, he appeared to be having some sort of a seizure. The flesh on his face began shaking and stretching. Then his head popped off onto the floor.

Lilabeth let out a little scream. Jessie and Dezi moved forward, pushing the girls behind them. Clairity and Jade turned their gazes away, clenching their eyes tight.

"Is it over?" Jade asked.

"No," Jessie said. "It's changing again."

They couldn't help but to look; out of the headless body grew a new head and the head grew a new body. The original man was still over eight feet but the new man was only about three feet. Their clothes were identical except for size.

"Sorry about that," the smaller version said. "It's hard to find good help. I prefer to do things myself." He showed his new patrons into the elevator and up to the thirteenth floor. "You can call me Clyde."

"I thought hotels didn't ever have a thirteenth floor," Lilabeth said, watching their porter push the button inside the elevator.

"Not at this time of year," he answered. "Things tend to book up fast for Samhain. We utilize all spaces."

The elevator jerked to a stop and they stepped out onto the thirteenth floor. The man pushed by them to a door.

"Key," he said, waiting.

Jade handed him the key and he opened the black door to a beautiful sitting room. He motioned with one hand for the group to enter. The door was marked in the same pattern as had been in the dream. Apparently, the entire thirteenth floor used only Roman numerals to identify rooms. Theirs was marked in gold as number MCCCXIII.

"This is your sitting room, to the left is a room for the gentlemen and to the right two rooms for the ladies. There is a bathroom attached to each." He pulled out a small wand and motioned at the curtains. The beautiful peach coloured drapes opened, revealing a gorgeous view of the city. From there they could tell everything here was all much larger than any of them anticipated.

"Do excuse any noises you may hear beneath you," he said. Before anyone could ask what he meant, he was gone.

"Maybe we should have brought our things." Clairity said, thinking about how nice it would be to change her clothes.

"If we knew the underground was a hidden above-ground city, we would have." Annabelle's voice held a condescending tone. "Looking at how big this place is, I don't know how we will ever find anything."

"We already have," Clairity said, turning her attention to the window.

"What?" Mike's sister asked.

"Remember the dream we talked about? The one that led us to you and Mike." She didn't wait for an answer. "When we were looking for Mike in the dream," she paused, staring out at the lights of the city below them. "We had to find a door to go through to lead us to him. The door we picked was the door to this room." She walked to the sofa and sat down, her mind racing faster than a horse.

"You're kidding," Annabelle said. "Exactly?"

"Yes, except there were three numbers." She took the pen and paper on the table in front of her and drew XIII, MCCCXIII and XXVI.

"I wonder who is in the other two rooms," Jessie said. "Maybe we should go visit."

"And say what?" Annabelle asked with a snarky sound that reminded everyone that Mike was her brother. "Hi, I dreamt about your door. Mind if we take a look around to see if you are planning to invade the world? That should go over well."

"There is no need to act like that," Clairity snapped. "This is connected. Everything I saw in that dream, everything that happened on that tour and what we are doing here is all connected. The dream directed us to that door. It means something, whether you want to believe it or not. It's no coincidence we are in this hotel. I think we should check it out."

"Well, it's a good thing I am in charge then," Annabelle said, dismissing the other girl's opinion. "I say we have a good sleep. Let the freaks from other worlds do their creepy things out there in the dark and we take a look around in the morning. Lilabeth and I will take the first room."

"Whoa." Dezi rubbed the back of his neck. "Didn't see that coming."

Annabelle turned to him. "Problem?"

"Yeah," he answered. "I don't like being called a freak from another world." He crossed his arms and rested against the back of a couch.

"Agreed!" Clairity exclaimed. "No one put you in charge." She wished deep inside Willow was there to take control of what was happening.

"Look," Annabelle said, sitting down beside Clairity. "I promised I would take care of us. I don't want to take any unnecessary chances. In that place I was in, I saw a lot of strange and dangerous things. We could be in way above our heads here and we have no way to call for help. I am not trying to be… well, a witch, but we need to be sure we can handle what we are getting into." She tried to take Clairity's hand, but she pulled it away too fast.

"We came here for answers and whether we like it or not, those other rooms are a part of it. This is the job you signed up for." Clairity stood up and moved to a single chair. "We can look tomorrow, but that's where we are going to find out what we are here for. I can feel it. Your approval isn't needed."

Annabelle conceded. "Fine, but during daylight hours when things that go bump in the night are sleeping. Oh, and sorry about the freak remark. I guess I forget you guys are different, too. Pleasant dreams."

"Prejudice comes in all forms," Clairity said, not accepting the apology. She stood and headed to a bedroom without saying another word.

Chapter Forty-Four

The drive to the small town bordering the swamp land was uneventful. The smell of a busy gym filled the vehicle - sweat dripping off of each of them. Outside, the sun was still shining bright, although there were only a few hours of day left. A chance to step outside and move cramped muscles was foremost in their minds.

First, they needed a place to stay. The town was small and Mike was concerned that they may have to go somewhere else to find lodging.

"Ask and ye shall receive," he said, smiling. "Looks like they have a small motel right in town. Lady Luck is with us."

"Something is with us," Malarchy snapped. "But I don't know if it's luck. There are far too many coincidences for my liking."

"Ah relax, a lot of these towns have small places like this for people passing through. I saw a sign for swamp tours too, so might be for the business."

"Yes." Malarchy raised an eyebrow. "I am sure that is a big draw. Who would miss a chance to see swamp land?" Sarcasm dripped off his words faster than the sweat down his face.

Malarchy may have done a lot of things people didn't agree with, but no one could deny he was the most level-headed person one could meet. He was gifted a natural ability to think things through and assess possible outcomes.

"The sooner we check this place out, the sooner we head home." Mike parked the car and opened his door. Stepping out, he inhaled deeply and immediately wished he hadn't. The stench of earthy compost filled his senses and caused him to gag. "So much for fresh air," he said, still coughing. "We must be very close to bog lands."

After getting two rooms, side by side, and settling in, the group decided to take a look around the neighbourhood. Their trip didn't take long. The whole town consisted of basically one road named Main Street, with a total of about ten businesses. Other than that, there were a few scattered houses and one church. On the far side of the church was a very large graveyard, which was at least ten times the size of the rest of the town combined. The remainder of the surrounding area was swamp lands.

"Why would there be such a large graveyard in a place with so few people? How do they have enough bodies?" Ashlyn asked.

"Good question," Mike answered. "We have a bit more time before we lose sunlight. Let's check it out."

The cemetery gates were a classic storybook fashion, made of a black finished wrought iron. Driving in the first section of the grounds, everything appeared quite normal. The grass was well kept and flowers adorned the graves of loved ones. The road led to a parking lot attached to a building, which was closed. Mike assumed it was either the caretaker's storage or some sort of funeral parlour for services and perhaps body preparation.

The group continued on foot through a section of above ground columbaria, which held the cremated ashes of presumably deceased townsfolk.

A man wearing dirty overalls and carrying a shovel tapped on Ashlyn's shoulder from behind. She jumped, letting out a scream. She had stayed back a bit from the rest of the group. The thought of walking in an area with the remains of so many dead people was frightening. The idea of a dead body itself was new and she hadn't embraced it the way Pete, Zsiga and Malarchy had. Her male friends found the idea fascinating and were willing to explore it to the best of their abilities. They were reading out names and inscriptions, as well as dates, particularly commenting on how old the flowers were that had been left to honour the deceased.

"Sorry ma'am," he said, taking off a baseball cap to reveal a completely bald head. "Didn't mean to scare. Just thought I might be of some help to you folks. You don't look like you come from round here."

Mike filled the spot standing beside her and extended his hand. "Thanks," he said as they shook. "I'm Mike and this is Ashlyn. My other friends are Malarchy, Zsiga and Pete."

"Nice to meet you. I'm Samuel, the caretaker here. If you are looking for a loved one who lived in town, I may be able to help you."

"Brilliant. We do actually have a few questions." Mike motioned to the others to have a seat on a bench while he did the talking. "We were actually wondering why there is such a large cemetery in such a small town."

"This here cemetery is as old as the town. The first people to settle in this area are buried here and all their ancestors thereafter. Even folks who move away ask for their bodies to be brought back here as their final resting place. I guess once you have been a part of this town, it's hard to leave."

"Interesting, sounds like you could give a history lesson on this area." Mike smiled as if he were interested. "Anything unusual happen?"

Samuel's face turned pale and he replied with a scowl. "Interesting how?"

Malarchy sensed Mike's ability to interrogate heading south again and intervened "Are there any important historical figures buried here? Graves we should see before we leave the area?"

"Oh," the caretaker answered. "That I can help you with. Over here, we have a judge from the witch trials." He led the group to a large fancy cross marker, with angels clinging to both sides. "He was on vacation here. It's believed a swamp witch tracked him down and murdered him. His family was too frightened to have his body moved, so they chose to bury him here. Nobody ever visited, either. I keep the grave neat and tidy just in case."

"Worried about curses?" Malarchy enquired, wanting the man to continue talking about this topic.

"Most likely. Not too many people in these parts who aren't, even in this day and age. It's a part of the culture round here."

Ashlyn moved closer and noticed at the base were a series of Roman numerals. "Excuse me," she said. "Can you tell me what these markings are for?"

"Of course," Samuel answered. "That's how we locate a particular grave. The back area over there are all unmarked graves, without names. The numbers indicate where they are in our records. Every grave has one."

"Why would there be people buried without names?" Pete asked. He had been so quiet the others almost forgot he was there.

"Several reasons. The main one being the swamp. Lots of people head in and never come back every year. Their body or parts wash up all the time. Can't identify them, so eventually they end up here. Some are never claimed. Folks round here are very superstitious and if they think someone has been taken by evil, they won't have anything to do with the body after life. Either way, those poor folks get a town burial and a headstone with just numbers."

"Fascinating," Malarchy's voice sang with enthusiasm. "Would you mind if we take a look? It's the things they don't put on tour guides that makes this part of the country so rich historically."

The caretaker beamed with pride. "Of course, just don't get lost and I suggest you leave before night. It's been mighty hot today, but they say it'll cool right down this evening. That means the fog will be rolling in after dusk. I'll be round tomorrow if you have any other questions. Was a pleasure meeting you folks."

"Thank you." Malarchy's ability to captivate an audience was on full power. "You have made this trip more enjoyable than I ever imagined possible."

Samuel, satisfied with himself, turned and walked back to the building. The others headed to the unused section of the cemetery to look for clues.

A second iron fence split the two areas up. It stood approximately half the height of the gate leading into the cemetery and appeared as if it was in need of repair and possibly a new coat of paint, some sections completely missing.

The grave sites on the other side of the fence weren't much better. Broken markers lined the ground in positions that made it look like they were as close to each other as possible, each one marked with Roman numerals. Weeds and moss grew unkempt. The further in they walked, the worse condition the graves were in.

Mike read the Roman numerals as they walked by, occasionally having to stop and move something aside to see the stone hiding underneath. "Looks like a bit of a walk still." He stopped for a moment and looked down at his shoe sinking slightly into the ground. The earth beneath him felt more spongy than solid. Lifting his foot he could see an imprint left by standing there. "The ground is softer here too. Be careful of your footing. We must be near the swamps. Hopefully, it doesn't get much worse."

Looking back, Ashlyn could no longer see the front area they came from. She bumped right into Mike. "Sorry," she muttered. "Why did you stop?"

"These graves have been recently dug up and filled in again," he answered, pointing to mounds of fresh dirt.

"Why would someone do that?" Pete wandered around a couple of graves looking for anything he could find.

"Not sure, but I bet our gypsy witch's grave is one of them." Mike stood back, rubbing his chin for a moment before examining the ground. When they came to the resting place with the Roman numerals matching Ashlyn's dream, it too had recently been exhumed.

Zsiga moved forward to get a good picture of the stone monument for documentation. "Guess the question is, are people still buried here? If not, what happened to the bodies?"

"There is really only one way to know the answer to the first part." Mike swivelled around in a circle, his eyes searching for something.

"No!" Ashlyn cried out. "No way are we digging up any graves." Everyone knew what Mike was thinking, but she was the only one to disagree with his plan.

Mike ignored the girl's comments. "We need something to dig with. Spread out and look around."

"The woman in the dream said don't touch anything. I made that mistake once. Let's not do that again." Ashlyn took a few steps backwards and almost tripped over a root sticking out of the ground. She came to a complete stop, her bottom lip quivering.

The others, still ignoring her ranting, continued to look for something to use to move the dirt from at least one of the burial spots so they could see what was inside. She could tell it was going to take them a long time to find anything suitable.

"Fine, if we have to do this, I'd rather not be here all night." Ashlyn pulled out the wand Clairity bought her and concentrated on the dainty sceptre. A beam of pink and white light exploded from the crystal adorning its tip. Immediately after, dirt from the grave began flying through the air. "Sorry," Ashlyn said, shrugging her shoulders, whenever earth hit one of the others in the face.

When the soil appeared to be settled, Mike moved forward and peered into the grave. "Nothing," he said, moving safely away from the edge. "Can we look in one more?"

Ashlyn let out a frustrated huff. "Why? We know Estonia isn't in there; isn't that good enough? What more do you need to know?"

"We need to know if all of these graves are empty. If they are, then we have a lot of missing bodies. That might be relevant."

"If I do this, we leave and if you want to come back tomorrow you guys can, without me," she said. "And bring a shovel."

"Agreed." Mike stood out of the way.

Again, the soil began flying through the air. This time the dirt seemed to target Mike wherever he moved. In the end, the result was the same. There was no body. This time, however, there was something left in the grave. Zsiga jumped into the hole without waiting for discussion. He picked up a picture of a woman none of them recognized. He wiped off the dirt it was covered in. Whatever was in the grave had spent time studying it. The picture was just another piece to the growing puzzle they didn't yet have a place for.

Time passed the group by without them noticing. A putrid smell was flowing from the swamp as a low-lying fog rolled in over the cemetery grounds. The thick mist crept eerily around grave markers as if it were seeking out the living in a place where everything was dead. It would only be a few moments before it would surround them and stunt their senses.

"I think it's time to go," Pete said

"I think you're right." Mike took Ashlyn's arm and pulled her quickly back towards the exit. Light was fading fast - before long it would be completely dark. As fascinating as the guys found the excursion, none of them wanted to be stuck fumbling around there at night, especially in a creepy fog.

Once safely in the cemetery parking lot, Mike took Ashlyn's hand and pulled her to face him. "What was with the mud-slinging?"

Ashlyn laughed. "I haven't had any time to practice. Guess I am just not used to channelling magic yet. You didn't think it was intentional, did you?" The devious smile on her face suggested she was lying.

"No, of course not." Mike's voice implied he didn't believe her. He released her hand. "Well, we have one more place to check out tonight. Who's up for a swamp boat ride?"

"Gee," she answered. "Just what I always wanted to do."

"Great, cause that's where we are heading." Mike swung his body into the driver's seat and started the engine.

"Might I enquire as to why we need to do this at night?" Malarchy's shoulders squished together. He stretched to move his legs.

"Because," Mike chuckled, looking in the rear view mirror. "That's when the ghosts come out. They walk on the fog and hide among the moss-covered trees." His devious grin told Ashlyn how much he was enjoying teasing her.

****

The boat they rented for the evening was equipped with lanterns along the sides for light. The vessel itself was wooden with a covered area in the middle and a few benches. Propelling the boat through the water was going to take a lot of muscle. Ashlyn took a seat, watching the others battle it out for the strongest alpha male title, which came with the prize of being named best suited to handle sticks. Men seemed to always want to compete with each other, as if it were some tribal ritual. In the end, Malarchy was happy to have been counted out - content to sit and watch while someone else took care of the manual labour.

Shortly, they were on their way. The fog clung tight to the water, making it impossible to see anything that might be lurking underneath. A rotting odour lingered all around, which Ashlyn imagined she would never get out of her clothes and possibly her hair. Her stomach turned, but it wasn't clear if it was from the stench, general fear or because it was her first boat ride.

The river echoed with sounds of frogs croaking a song in the glowing moon, mixed with the occasional splashes of some creature or another heading into the water around them. The moss covered trees had low hanging branches that appeared to move in the shadows and provided places for the swamp's inhabitants to hide. At night, everything seemed to be a shade of grey. The water was still except for the ripples protruding from the movement of their boat gliding across its surface.

Ashlyn and Malarchy glanced in different directions, hoping to see if they could find anything that might help. She ended up noticing some writing on the side of the boat. "What does that say?" she asked, trying to see the words without getting too close to the edge. "I am not getting any closer. Falling in isn't an option."

"It's probably the name of the boat," Mike answered without leaving his post.

Malarchy came over with a lantern and lowered it to the words. "*Your Destiny*. Fascinating."

Mike looked at them. "Are you sure? That's the name?"

"Yes." Malarchy moved aside. "See for yourself." His hand outstretched, indicating the way to the side of the boat from where he read the words.

Mike put the large paddle down. Taking the lantern from Malarchy's hands, he looked at the side of the vessel. "Guess we are on the right trail."

"How so?" Pete asked.

"Part of what the woman said to Willow in the amusement park," he answered, then recited Estonia's words:

Be forewarned on Hallows Eve

Those who are not of this world shall take to the streets,

Blood shall flow and death shall follow.

Your presence attracts what we cannot explain.

Your destiny is written. You best make sure you listen.

"That's very literal," Malarchy said.

"A little too strange to be a coincidence, though. Don't you think?"

In the distance there was a chiming noise which drew their attention. At first, none of them could identify the sound, but as they came closer to its source, Mike recognized it as wind chimes. Not metallic but something more hollow, like ceramic or bone.

"Someone has to own them. There is no reason for wind chimes to be hanging in the middle of nowhere. If we find them, we could find some answers. Maybe that's what we are listening for." Mike remained at his station at the front of the boat, directing the others which way they needed to manoeuvre the vessel to head in the direction of the sound.

"Or we could end up dying," Malarchy commented, sitting down beside Ashlyn on one of the benches in the covered area. The other men either didn't hear him or chose to ignore his comment.

The clamouring noise became stronger the further down the river they travelled, but there still wasn't any sign of anything out of the ordinary. An hour went by and still nothing other than something in the water hitting the side of the boat a few times, making it rock and Ashlyn nervous. She shivered at the thought of what could be lurking under the water, biding its time until one unlikely soul accidentally fell in. Her imagination played havoc with her senses, each splash or knock becoming louder and more frightening.

Zsiga was the first to see a white silhouette in the distance. From where they were, it appeared as if a white dress was floating on the water, holding a lantern. "Do you think it's a ghost?" he asked, pointing to the figure.

"Guess we'll find out," Mike answered, turning the boat to head towards the woman. "If it is, let's hope she can talk."

The closer the small vessel came to where the ghostly figure was, the more evident it became that a living person was the source of what they were seeing and hearing. Everything stemmed from a small shack, anchored in the water with a series of pier type walkways attached on all sides.

After docking the boat and tying it tightly to a pole, the group rounded the house, stopping to admire the wind chimes carefully placed to provide the best sounds. Ashlyn was glad they were ceramic, although if you didn't look at them closely, one might mistake them for bone - each designed to give off that appearance from a distance. Animal skulls of all different shapes and sizes hung on the sides of the shack, some adorned with feathers and fur, their white surfaces illuminated by the moon. Mike knocked on a small door. A woman answered. Her skin was as dark as Zsiga's and she wore a pure white dress.

"What do you want?" she asked. "How did you find me?"

"It wasn't really that hard. You are anchored in the middle of the river," Malarchy said. He had a way of belittling almost anything anyone could say.

"Most people don't come this far down the river. The spirits keep them away."

"Your wind chimes and attire do help give off that illusion, without the use of any magic. Quite ingenious, really." His knowledge of illusion only spanned the use of enchantments. The idea of creating a false impression without mystic involvement was completely new.

"Magic is a precious gift that does not need to be wasted on things we can do for ourselves," she answered. "But you are not here to discuss the ethics of magic, now are you? Come in and tell me what has brought you here. Only those who are destined to meet me make it this far, in my experience."

"Thank you," Mike uttered, taking a seat inside. After introducing himself and the others, he continued, "We are looking for information about a woman named Estonia. She was believed to have passed away near here. We were told her spirit haunts this part of the swamp. Anything you can tell us would be most helpful."

"Estonia," she said, heading to a closet nearby. "I was wondering when you would come. She left something with me for you." She handed Mike a package, poorly wrapped in plain brown construction paper. Written on it were the words *For Willow*. "As for her spirit, I have not seen it for some time. I cannot help you there."

"You knew her?" Ashlyn moved closer to the woman. She couldn't help but wonder how Estonia knew who Willow was two years ago.

"Aye, she was my friend and a powerful witch. Her abilities were unmatched. But there are those who do not want the powerful to exist in this world. They do not want anyone to challenge them. They found her and destroyed her. The same as they do to many covens. I have seen it in the cards. I stay clear of anyone involved now. I have to protect myself - stay out of the conflict, if you understand what I mean."

"Her body is missing from her grave, as are many others. Do you know why?" The girl wasn't sure why she asked the woman. It popped into her mind and she blurted it out. Willow must have been rubbing off on her.

"Bodies missing?" The woman sat at a small table covered with a red and gold cloth and put her hand over her open mouth. After a few moments, she picked up a set of cards with beautiful pictures painted on them and put three in the centre of the table face up. "The omens are bad. Death magic lingers in the air. Come, child, sit." She motioned to the chair across from her.

Ashlyn sat in the chair. "What is it?"

"Shuffle the cards and ask your questions. Let me look into your past, present, and future. The cards will hold the answers you seek."

She shuffled the cards and handed them back. The woman placed a pattern down on the table in front of her. "This is strange, you have seen so much for such a young girl. You have the craft within you. Yes? It manifests itself in the dream world. Much talent I see. Now, your future." The woman gasped. "Your friend, she is in grave danger."

"Danger? How?" Ashlyn pleaded. She looked down at the cards on the table. On top in the middle was the same card she saw in the gypsy museum. A red-haired woman in a gold and green dress, with her arms outstretched as if they were holding something. Magic flew from her hands up to the sky. "Those cards, I have seen them before."

"Estonia made them for me as a gift. She gave them to me at the same time she gave me that parcel. You must go now. I cannot help you any further. There is nothing more the cards can tell you. You are left to your own devices, I am afraid."

The woman stood and opened the door for them to exit, slamming it behind them without saying another word. They heard a lock click and the shack went dark. Whatever the fortune teller saw, it obviously frightened her. Ashlyn felt a chill run down her spine.

Back on the boat, Mike opened the package. Inside he found a set of portal stones. Estonia kept them safe from whoever had murdered her. At least now they knew, the gypsy woman was a friend and her words a prophecy, but about what? He motioned to Zsiga to send all the information to William for review and ask Faramund to meet them at the hotel to head back to camp.

Chapter Forty-Five

Willow awoke to her name being called out loud. Opening her eyes, she saw Ashlyn standing over her. She jumped up, hugging her.

"You have no idea how much I missed you!" she exclaimed, squeezing tight.

"Ditto!" her friend answered. "We need to head over to the cabin. We have lots to go over. Have you heard from Clairity?"

"Nothing." Willow grabbed some clothes and quickly changed. She didn't want to miss a thing about what they found out.

Before long, the two girls were sitting in the command centre waiting for William and Mike to arrive. When William did walk in, he inhaled deeply, revelling in the smell of Zsiga's coffee brewing again. A smile crossed his face as he headed straight for the pot and a fresh cup. Taking their seats, Mike and his team went over everything they saw and heard.

"Have you heard from Annabelle?" Mike asked, slouching back in his seat.

"No, we lost contact sometime yesterday. Most likely some form of a force field again, perhaps around the underground they were looking for."

"Maybe Ashlyn and I could contact Clairity in a dream, just to make sure they are okay." Willow stood up, examining the new portal stones and the brown wrapper with her name on it. "Do we know which portal these stones belong to yet?"

"No," Sarah said, looking up from behind her computer. "I haven't had enough time to figure it out yet. It may take a few days."

"So what do we know?" Willow asked, not wanting an answer, but rather speaking out loud to herself. "The old woman died some time ago. Her body and others are missing. She knew of me, what we are doing here and was trying to help us. She was a gypsy witch with strong gifts in future telling and a powerful medium. Someone is eliminating anyone with strong powers from this world, maybe?"

"Well if I was wanting to take over a world, I would take out threats first too," Faramund said without shifting his view from his poem book.

"Brilliant!" Willow replied to him. "Why didn't I think of that? Of course, the princes and princesses are going to try to take out as much magic as possible from this world before their invasion. That's why witches are disappearing! That's what the tour was about!"

"And that's what the ball is probably about too," Ashlyn said. "The woman said you were in danger, Willow. The card on top of the pile was a red-haired woman."

"We have already decided that I need to attend the ball." Willow looked at William to back her up. "I have some connection to all this and we need to use that to our advantage."

"She's right. If we are going to stop whatever it is that is going to happen, we need her to be at that ball. Let's get some rooms in the area and head there tomorrow. Tonight, you girls see if you can contact any of the others and find out what's going on in the underground." William stood and indicated for Willow to follow him.

Together the two walked silently to a building she never noticed before. He unlocked the doors and opened them. The room was filled with clothes. Not like the ones she saw before with Sarah, these clothes were different.

"Having been around for so many ages in this world's time means we have a pretty good collection of clothes from all different eras. They aren't good for much anymore, since no one dresses in these styles, but they could make good costumes. They are all authentic and some quite lavish. Pick something you like and we will get you a mask to match." William took a seat to wait for her to go through the racks of dresses.

"Wow," was all she could answer right away, stunned by the selection in front of her. "I don't even know where to start." Willow headed to a rack of full-skirt dresses. Some boasted brilliant colours in satin, a small waist and a hoop-style skirt, while others had layers of clothing - all beautiful. "Can you turn around so I can try some on?" she asked.

"Sorry, of course." William's face flushed just a touch, but enough to notice. He pushed his hands into the pockets of his pants while rocking back and forth between the fronts and backs of his feet.

The first dress she tried on was blue. The weight of the petticoats was too much for her. She changed her mind before even finishing putting it on. The next dress was gold and green with a hoop style skirt, the type without under-carriage. Although she thought she would have far less mobility because of its size, it was much more comfortable. Looking in the mirror, she liked the look. The colours made her red hair and bronze skin tone stand out beautifully.

"This one," she said decisively while admiring the dress in the mirror.

William turned around and stood - awkwardly stunned by her radiance. "Um, wow," he finally said, pink returning to his face.

"It looks that bad? I rather liked it, but if you think..."

He cut her off. "No, it looks great. I mean, you look great," he said.

"Are you sure it's okay? I don't want to look silly walking into a witches' ball and have everyone single me out."

"You will be the belle of the ball," he answered.

She winced, remembering the last time she heard someone say that - Martha, Ashlyn's mother. She was making a dress for her to go to a dance at the castle in her home world. Those days seemed so far away now. Things had changed so much. She looked into his eyes and smiled, managing a "Thank you."

He turned around again so she could change back into her normal clothes. He would handle the packing of the dress so it wouldn't get damaged and attend to a mask to match.

She thanked him again before heading off to find Ashlyn so the two girls could spend some time together before the evening's adventures.

Chapter Forty-Six

Ashlyn opened her eyes to a familiar sight. She was in the staging area of her dreams again. Shelby looked up at her. "Nice of you to bring me along this time," the bird said.

"Glad to have you here." She was about to ask if they would join together, but the bird had already found a place as a picture on her shoulder. "Guess we should find Willow."

"Right here," Willow said, tapping on her other shoulder.

"How did you do that?" Ashlyn asked.

"The door was open. I walked through. Guess you are getting used to me being here."

It didn't make sense to either of them, but they weren't there to discuss Willow, so they began the search for Clairity.

After calling for their friend for some time, they finally found a door. It was the same door the three of them went through before - the last time they dreamt together. Ashlyn didn't look as high-strung about opening it this time. Willow couldn't help but feel her friend must have faced some real horrors when she was away. It made her stronger; less timid. Her new confidence was appealing.

The door opened and the two girls were pulled into the middle of the dream, walking down a street in a city neither of them knew. Everything was still and perfectly quiet. It was like walking through the middle of an abandoned city.

"Willow! Ashlyn!" The girls spun around to see Clairity running towards them. "Am I glad to see you two," she said.

"Likewise. Everyone is trying to reach you guys. Is everything okay?" Ashlyn asked as the two hugged.

"Yes and no." Clairity motioned for them to sit with her on a park bench. "Annabelle has gone super power-hungry witch on me. She believes we all have to follow her orders. She is acting like a completely different person. I don't know what is going on with her. I have a bad feeling though. Something is way off."

"Annabelle?" Ashlyn seemed surprised.

"Really? She didn't seem the type." Willow turned around in a circle taking in the scenery. "Where are we? I don't recognize anything."

"It's a city just for magical people. It's well hidden." Clairity went on to tell them about the way they arrived and everything else that happened. Then she told them about the hotel rooms, the doors and the argument.

"Hard to believe she said that. She is so self-conscious of people being prejudiced towards her relationship. I would have thought she would be more sympathetic." She paused for a second. Her thoughts we broken when she caught something moving out of the corner of her eye. "Did you see that?"

"See what?" both girls echoed.

"Nothing, I guess. I just thought for a moment I saw... Annabelle." She shook her head, dismissing the thought, then found herself concentrating on Estonia's prophecy again. "I don't get why there would be two places that fit the prophecy so exactly."

400

"What do you mean?" Clairity asked.

Ashlyn filled her in on what her group had found and the new prediction of danger. "Can you show us around?" she asked, changing the topic.

The three girls walked through the city. Clairity showed her friends what she knew, which really wasn't much. They only just checked in the night before. They passed a window with a picture of a woman in it.

Ashlyn paused to look at the portrait. "I have seen her somewhere before, but I don't know where."

Since the other two didn't recognize her, it couldn't have been anything important. One the way to the hotel, Clairity suggested they could take a look at the rooms in the dream world.

"I see no reason not to," Ashlyn said without hesitation.

Both Willow and Clairity were shocked by their friend's new confidence. Normally she would want to try something a little bit safer.

The small lobby was empty, so the three girls entered the elevator alone. Inside they found that there were no floor buttons for them to press. The doors closed and opened again on the thirteenth floor. Clairity showed the other two to the room they were assigned. As they neared the suite, they realized the door was wide open.

"I was wondering when you would get here. You were almost too late," Estonia said. "Your presence is required." The woman smiled then walked out of the room and disappeared in the hallway.

Looking around, there was no sign of the others in Clairity's group. The room held no clues as to where they went or if they had even been there.

"Back to the elevator?" Ashlyn asked, shrugging her shoulders.

The other two agreed - they were riding again. This time, the doors opened to the second floor. Willow led the others to the door marked twenty-six in Roman numerals. Again, the door was open.

Inside was a different scene. The floor was littered with bodies. The first four, Willow identified as Gavin, Russ, Naomi and Delphine, the vamprite from the tour group. The others were all small replicas of the man from the front desk. There must have been at least ten of him - each murdered.

"It's hard enough to kill one vamprite, but four? That must have taken some power," Willow said. "But why? I really don't understand. I wonder what they are doing here."

The girls looked around for a bit, but in the end saw no indication as to who could have committed the crime. They headed back to the elevator and found themselves on the first floor. The thirteenth door was closed. Willow turned the handle and opened it. She gasped. Inside were two princes, Joseph and Simon, and one very large snake. There was something odd about the serpent. It didn't quite look real.

"Well, well, who do we have here? Should have listened to the witch and left the other rooms alone," Joseph said, smiling.

"But then they wouldn't be here with us. Nosy witches." Simon took a step forward.

That was enough to make the three girls bolt, but the elevator was gone. The hallway changed as they ran. They were no longer in a hotel. Willow outstretched her arms to feel for an illusion in the walls - some form of an exit. She let out a yelp. The flesh on her fingertips ripped on the jagged rock that replaced the smooth wallpaper. They were in a maze of some sort. They continued to run, but more often than not every corner they turned was a dead end. Willow threw her hands to her head, spinning in circles. None of them knew which way to go. Behind them they could hear the princes' cackling laughs shadowing their every move, closing in on their position. They were in trouble.

You are late. Move it. Move it. Move it, rang out loudly in William's voice from down a path to their right making all three girls jump. Looking at each other, the girls knew they all heard the same thing. It was the alarm on the watch that William gave Camile. But how? Why would it be here in this dream? Remembering what Nathan said about spirits finding it easier to communicate in the dream world, Willow motioned to her friends to follow the sound.

They rounded the turn and followed the path. Again the alarm went off, this time to their left. The pattern continued as they wove right turns and left turns through the maze, finally ending at the door leading out of the dream.

Willow stopped at the door. There wasn't a lot of time before the two princes still pursuing them would catch up. "Thank you, Camile," she said, turning the handle.

Willow and Ashlyn sat up straight in their beds. They contacted their friend thinking they had almost all the answers, and now there were more questions than before. Willow turned her hand over slowly, revealing fresh wounds on the finger tips. She closed her hand before her friend noticed.

"William needs to know." Shelby ordered, separating from Ashlyn. "I suggest you speak with him alone about what you have learnt and let him share what he feels appropriate with Mike about Annabelle."

Annabelle, what was she up to? Was she working for the other side? Were the others safe? For the moment, Clairity seemed okay, but something in Willow's mind lingered over what Mike's sister's whole role in this mess really was.

The nights were getting cooler outside and Ashlyn decided to stay under the warm covers, letting her friend venture out to talk to William. Deep down, Willow felt Ashlyn just didn't want to have to tell anyone that Mike's sister could possibly be an enemy.

After throwing on a couple of sweaters, she headed out. It was late and the camp was silent. Aslo and Kiera were on patrol with the kittens again. It was the best solution for everyone. The men and women in the camp all ended up with proper rest and it gave the guardians a chance to do some one-on-one training with their offspring.

She headed straight to William's sleeping quarters and knocked on the door. It took a few knocks before he answered with a yell.

"Who is it?"

"It's me, Willow," she answered, jumping from one foot to the other, trying to stay warm. She wasn't used to the temperature being so low. William warned her not to interfere with the weather patterns. Apparently, it could disrupt the cycles for the whole world and create a disaster somewhere. She wasn't sure she understood, but agreed to allow their seasons to happen as they did before she arrived. "It's cold out here. Can I come in?"

The door opened. "People do like to sleep sometimes, you know."

"That is completely unfair," she said, pushing passed him to enter the warmth of his room. "I haven't been waking you up lately at all."

She hadn't seen his sleeping quarters before and was surprised to see the number of books lining the walls. It made sense though, thinking about it. Whenever they needed information for research, he always showed up with a stack of books from somewhere. She never considered where they came from.

In one corner of the room was a single bed with several warm blankets. It was messy, like he hadn't made it in weeks. On the other side, there was a small wooden desk with a chair that could swivel around in circles. On the desk was a light and paper work of some kind. He had already sat back down and picked up one of the papers, seeming to be reading it.

"What's that?" she asked.

"Did you come here in the middle of the night just to ask what papers are on my desk?"

"No," she answered, taking a seat on the corner of his bed. She was still cold and had an urge to take a blanket and wrap herself up, but decided against it.

"Perhaps you could share your motivation for this visit." His voice mocked her.

"Sorry," she said. "The dream... we found Clairity."

He dropped the paper and spun around in the chair. His attention changed to focus on what she was saying. "Is everything alright? None of them are hurt, are they?"

"No," she answered. "Not yet." His eyes locked on hers while she retold the entire story. "We thought someone should talk to you first and let you handle what you want to say to Mike. Ashlyn didn't want to get out from under the covers. That left me to come bother you."

"Didn't see that coming," he said, rubbing his temples. "They should be safe in the city until after Halloween. I don't want to spread us too thin. We can have Sarah track down possibilities for where this mountain access might be so we can find them right after the ball."

His voice faded away into the background. Her attention locked on his bare chest - drawn to the scars that he acquired over the years. Was there a story for each one? Willow's eyes scanned upwards to his shoulders and the pictures of Tika and Nero. They looked completely natural, as if they were always meant to be a part of him. She bit her bottom lip, noticing his muscular physique; possibly due to all the wood he cut. This year she had made things a bit harder for him, since he was only allowed to cut down trees that died naturally. She didn't understand why he spent so much time chopping it all. There were others who could help and he already had so much to do. She made a mental note to one day ask him.

He spun back around and continued talking about different plans. Willow was listening to the sound of his voice for some time, before she drifted off.

Opening her eyes slowly, Willow focused on the wall in front of her face. It wasn't her room. She had fallen asleep on William's bed. She stayed perfectly still, not wanting to disturb him. Closing her eyes again, she felt the warmth of his body against her. His arm cradled her waist, pulling her into him. His breath felt warm against her neck. Relaxation flowed through every inch of her.

A thought popped into her head about Mike, how she had felt the same way when he carried her - how silly she was thinking there was more between them than there actually was. She decided right then that wouldn't happen again. She turned around slowly, trying not to disturb him, but he was already awake.

"Good morning," he said.

"Hi," she answered with a half-smile. "Sorry."

"No problem." A sheepish grin matched his messy hair and stubble beginnings of a beard. "It's getting late. We best meet the others and update them."

She completely forgot about the dream. How could she? Boys! They consumed her thoughts. When did this happen to her? They had become more important than anything else. She made a mental note to work on changing that as she sat up. Sliding out of the bed, she stood, gathering her senses. "I'm going to wash up real quick and meet you over there." As she approached the door to leave, she thought of Mike again and the intense feelings that accompanied not thanking him right away. That was one mistake that wouldn't happen again. She quickly added, "Thanks for not kicking me out last night."

"No problem, small fry." He smiled at her. The warmth of his gaze made her want to run back to his arms. She opened the door quickly to escape her own thoughts and ran right into Mike.

"Willow," he said. "Where's William?" Questions were written all over his face - each one wasn't something she could answer.

"Hi," she said, keeping her face down. She didn't want to stick around, knowing William needed to talk with Mike about his sister before the meeting. "He's inside changing," she muttered, trying not to look him in the eyes and give away that she knew something. Pushing by him in the doorway, she added, "See you in a bit," and headed back to her sleeping quarters to change.

Ashlyn was wide awake, waiting for her to return. "Where were you all night?" she asked. "I was about to send out a search party." Sitting on her bed, she crossed her legs and pulled a pillow to her chest.

"I fell asleep listening to him talk about different plans."

"And he didn't kick you out?" her friend asked.

"I know, right? Weird." She grabbed some clothes and headed to wash up. "We have to rush. Everyone is meeting up in the cabin."

The two girls barely finished getting dressed when they heard a scuffle from outside. It was Mike and William yelling and fighting.

Standing in the doorway, the two girls could see every punch they threw at each other.

"That looks serious," Ashlyn said. "I guess Mike didn't take the news about his sister being on the wrong side well."

Aslo was rounding up everyone and sending them inside. "Best we let them get this out of their systems before the meeting. Everyone into the command centre and take a seat. No need for an audience."

"Come," Kiera ordered. "That means you two."

"Are they going to be okay?" Willow asked. "They might hurt each other." She let out a sigh. A part of her felt bad that William was the one stuck telling Mike the bad news. The rest of her was glad that no one was using her for a punching bag.

"They are big boys. They can take care of themselves," the guardian answered, nudging Willow towards the cabin.

They were the last two to enter the cabin and it went silent when they did. Willow felt the entire room staring at her, blaming her for what was happening. She couldn't help but feel that maybe they should have kept the news about Annabelle to themselves. They knew Mike probably wouldn't take it well, but neither of them imagined he would be this upset. The others couldn't have known that though. So why were they staring at her?

It seemed like an eternity that they were sitting there, waiting. Everyone was still watching them, occasionally whispering something to each other. Finally Mike and William walked in, both bruised and battered. Victoria stood up to try to heal them, but Jessie motioned for her to sit down again.

Guess they need to feel the consequences of their actions some before the pain goes away, Willow thought to herself

"Let's get right into the meeting," William said, wiping some blood from his lip - his right eye swelling. "The girls managed to contact Clairity in a dream last night. Their dream brought to light some new information." He motioned for the two girls to take over.

Willow nudged her friend to speak. She already did enough in her opinion. Ashlyn told the story up to the part about Annabelle, where she stopped. She looked at William and Mike. She didn't know what to tell everyone, especially after the fist fight outside. Willow shrugged her shoulders. The two sat there quietly trying to figure out what was safe to say.

Mike, sensing the awkwardness, intervened. "It appears my sister is working with the princes. We aren't sure what she is up to, but Clairity is aware of the deception now and hopefully will handle it."

Ashlyn picked up the story again about how they escaped with Camile's help.

"Are you suggesting you believe in ghosts?" Malarchy raised an eyebrow at the girls. "The mind is a clever thing. Perhaps your subconscious put her into your dream - a mere desire to see her again."

"I don't know." Willow wasn't sure what she believed. "It brings us back to the question of whether or not there is an afterlife. None of us can know a definitive answer to that. If you want my opinion, I would like to believe we are more than just physical beings. Regardless of whether or not I believe, the alarm showed us the way out."

"I think we need to stay focused on the ball. After that, we can deal with Annabelle," William said, trying to defuse the tension brewing between Willow and Malarchy. He ended up right back in a confrontation.

Mike took in a deep breath. "It's too dangerous. She could get hurt."

"She won't be alone. She is our only way into the event." The expression on William's face beneath all the bruises was frustration.

"I don't think we should use her like that." Mike's voice raised. "And I suppose you think you're the one who should be with her?"

William stood. "Yes, as a matter of fact."

The tone in his voice reminded Ashlyn of the men on the boat back in the swamp. It was the same argument, just with a different topic. Who was the stronger alpha male was the underlying question they seemed to be trying to answer.

Aslo cut the two off. "Outside now, both of you."

The two walked out the door, followed by all of the adult guardians. As soon as the door closed, there was a race for a spot at a window to watch. Willow imagined everyone was hoping to see fists thrown again. For a moment, she wondered if it came down to it, who would win between the two men.

*****

"What are you two doing?" Surprisingly, it was Kiera who started the conversation. "Acting like a couple of kids arguing over a toy."

"It's not like that." Mike looked at all the guardians in front of him and realized how severely they were taking this. "What's the big deal, anyways?"

"What's the big deal?" Tika answered. "She is fragile."

"Who?" William asked.

"Willow, of course." Kiera took over again. The male guardians seemed to be content hanging out behind the women, staying clear of their wrath. "You of all people should understand, William. I know you were only twelve when you lost your parents."

"What does that have to do with anything?" Mike asked, almost instantly wishing he hadn't. The three female guardians gave him a stare that sent chills down his spine.

"You two baboons don't see at all, do you? She doesn't even remember her parents. Willow has always been alone. It's all she knows. Having never felt anyone comfort her, take care of her or hold her, it's confusing. She has never felt real kindness from another person before and can't distinguish feelings of different kinds of love. We were there for her, but not physically."

"What exactly are you trying to say?" Mike asked.

"I'd like to know that too." A scowl crept over William's face.

Shelby moved forward and pecked him in the head. "She isn't ready yet. She needs time to figure out which feelings are which."

"And she doesn't need you two making it more complicated. Let her decide what she wants, in her own time. Until then, be her friend and stop trying to kill each other." Tika turned to William before he could speak and added, "Don't even try to deny it, guard! We have seen your thoughts." She walked away to do a perimeter run with Nero.

Seeing the other guardians heading back towards the cabin, everyone inside rushed back to their seats again. William and Mike returned a few minutes later and resumed the meeting as if nothing happened.

"Maybe we all should go," William said. "One team can locate possible mountain entrances to the underground city and the others can help Willow with the dance. The more people to keep her safe, the better." Whatever the guardians had said to him, it worked.

Ashlyn used her perfect timing and added, "What about Prince Lance? He really seems to have the hots for her." She was clueless as to the possible reactions to her statement.

Malarchy stood before anyone else could speak. "Seems we have a disease that is spreading. Perhaps we should all give up now and duke it out to see who the biggest neanderthal is?"

Half the room broke out in a chuckle and the other half looked as if they had missed the punch line. Willow and Ashlyn were definitely left in the dark. It was Diana who would comment, though.

"Can someone please tell me what's going on? Did I miss something?"

"I think a lot of us did," Nathan replied. "Might be best that way. I don't want to duke it out with anyone."

Willow laughed. "Me neither. Can we get back to the ball? We only have today and tomorrow, and today is passing quickly. Whatever everyone is fighting about needs to wait until we are all safe and back together."

Malarchy chuckled. "Yes, indeed." Both Mike and William flashed him a disapproving glance.

The meeting concluded. William and Mike were to make suitable lodging arrangements. Sarah lifted a piece of paper high above her head for William to take on his way out. It contained information for possible entrances to the underground. Everyone else prepared what they needed to travel.

Before long they left the camp once again and were settling into hotel rooms for the night. The girls in the group shared two rooms. Zsiga assigned himself to watching their doors. He could keep a low profile and still make sure the girls were secure. The rest of the group shared another three rooms.

The sun set quickly. Tomorrow brought with it Halloween.

Chapter Forty-Seven

Clairity's eyes opened wide. She sat up, the memory of the dream still fresh in her mind. Leaning over, she peeked to see if Jade was still sleeping. Her mind was working overtime, processing thoughts at a million miles a minute. What she should do? Annabelle was a danger to them. What wasn't clear was whether or not Lilabeth was involved as well.

Jade stirred on her own. Sitting up, she noticed the expression on Clairity's face. "Is everything alright? You look like something scared the life out of you."

"Something did. I need your help," she said. "I need you to get us over to the boys, without Annabelle noticing. Can you do that?"

"Of course, but why?" Jade asked, confused at the request.

"There is no time to explain now." She popped her head out the door to see if anyone was up or not. "When we wake Jessie and Dezi, I will fill you all in."

Darkness filled the main room of the suite. The silence left an uneasy feeling in the pit of Clairity's stomach. The sun would start to rise any time. Even with no one noticeably awake, Jade used her abilities to hide them as they crossed the sitting area and entered the boys' room. At first they debated knocking, but the noise might attract attention, so the girls both closed their eyes tight and walked in.

"Jessie? Dezi? Are you guys awake?" she asked. "Is it safe to open our eyes?"

Jessie rolled over in the bed and looked at the two girls. He snickered at the sight of them both trying hard not to look. "Yeah, it's all good. Why are you two here?"

Dezi glanced over at them through one eye. "Obviously trying to sneak a peek at a couple hot guys." Even half-asleep, he couldn't help but tease them.

Clairity filled them in on the dream and their new enemy. They needed a plan. The question was what could they do? "We have no choice but to take them by surprise this morning."

"Do we know if Lilabeth is involved?" Jade asked.

"No, but we can't take the chance," she answered. "Either way, they are in love and when you care that much about someone else, logic isn't always first in the mind. I am pretty sure she will protect Annabelle at all costs."

Moving to the sitting room, they each found a spot to wait for the two traitors to wake and come out. There were no noises, just silence. Time slowed to a crawl until finally a door opened.

"Good morning," Annabelle said, smiling.

"Sit down." Clairity pointed her wand directly at the girl. "Both of you. We know what you are doing."

"I don't know what you mean." Annabelle took a seat on the couch beside her lover. "We haven't done anything." A look of innocence was plastered over her face.

Clairity observed her movements. "You were there, last night. You were in the dream. Willow thought she saw you for a moment, because she did. Don't try to deny it. The princes told us."

Lilabeth became anxious about what was going on. "What is she talking about, Annie?"

A single tear cascaded down her face. "I did it for you, Lil! I couldn't let them hurt you."

"You did what for me?"

Annabelle's lip began to quiver. Her one leg shook up and down so hard it vibrated the floor. She couldn't hold back the tears. The story of what happened streamed from her lips. "It started about five years ago." Her words continued over a gasp from Lilabeth. "Our coven was young. We wanted more power, faster and with less effort. We were all inexperienced and naive, experimenting with the unknown. One day, we met what we thought was another coven. They were all cloaked and we never saw their faces, just heard their voices. We asked them if they knew of a way we could delve deeper into magic right away. We were looking for advice and willing to take shortcuts. We never considered there could be a negative effect."

A deep husky noise came from her throat, clearing some of the shakiness from her voice. "They offered us a potion of power. It came with a warning. If we used it, each of us would have to give up something close to us."

"We thought they meant an heirloom or prized possession, something financial maybe," Lilabeth blurted out.

Annabelle reached for her hand, clasping it tightly. "But the night we used the potion, each of us lost a family member. After we attended services at the funeral home, we all met again to look for the strangers. We found them easy enough and begged them to bring back our loved ones. Again, they warned us they could bring their bodies back to life, but there are consequences to everything. Again, we didn't listen."

Lilabeth broke in, an expression of pain masking her natural beauty. "We were distraught, grieving. We all agreed. We wanted our families back. None of us saw how wrong it was. We wanted to make right the wrong that was already done."

"What came back looked like our loved ones, but it wasn't them. They lacked the essence that makes us all us - a soul. The creatures went on to destroy all of our families. Mike was the only one to survive. Then William and his team showed up. They took my brother in, but not before they were noticed."

"Noticed? By who?" Clairity asked.

"The group of cloaked strangers." Annabelle answered. "I followed the strangers and watched them disappear through some hole to another world. It was there, then it wasn't. I have hated empyral ever since. That's why I am so narrow-minded. I don't regret the way I feel about them, either." Annabelle's eyes puffed out red and swollen from her tears. "Years later, coven members started to disappear. They were picking us off one by one. No one even noticed until it was too late. One night, they came for me. The man in charge recognized me from years earlier. He had been one of the hooded coven members. He made me a deal. He would let Lilabeth and myself live free, if I helped him get information on the guardian forces left in the main world. My choices were limited, so I agreed."

Lilabeth covered her mouth with her hand as she gasped in horror. "No! Why? You must have known they would never keep their promise? Look what happened before."

"I couldn't take the chance they would hurt you. I love you more than anything, my beautiful girl. I thought losing a few other-world freaks wasn't a bad thing to trade." Annabelle turned her attention back to the others. "The tour was operational already, run by three sisters. They used it to capture and eliminate risk to their future invasion. Their main goal is to destroy any chance of resistance, especially magical, before it could become a threat. I made the call to Mike. I figured he knew all the details that the prince wanted to know. They would rough him up some and he would talk. Then he would be useless to them and hopefully they would dump him somewhere injured."

"He's your brother." Dezi's eyebrows clenched close together, forming two lines between them, his face expressing a wish to vomit at the sight of her.

"Yes, many years ago he was." Annabelle paused for a moment, staring into space before continuing her story. "In the end, that red head friend of yours had to come and not only save us, but set that witch's pets free. The princes control my dreams and that night they came to me. They were upset I didn't keep my end of the bargain. I argued that I brought them my brother. They believed I set them up and there would be consequences. It was Lilabeth's life they threatened. Not just death, but unimaginable torture."

She cleared her throat again. "They offered me another deal. They would forgive my failure if I could bring all of the loose ends here. They weren't concerned about Mike. The only one I was missing was Willow. Then you girls offered me a solution to the problem last night. Your dreamwalker friend called my name without even realizing it and I entered your dream, but only long enough to let Prince Joseph in. Then I left. None of you were supposed to escape that dream. They had plans to deal with the three of you."

"But we did." Clairity sat on the coffee table with the wand pointed directly into the girl's face. "Who are in the other two rooms?"

"The rest of the loose ends. The two witches are in one and the four vampires in the other. They have no idea all of you are in the same place."

"What do the princes want with them?" Jade asked.

"Like I said, they are loose ends. They know too much and the princes are worried they may alert too many of the magical folk. Last thing they want is for people to be prepared for their attack. They are trying to stop resistance to an invasion from happening. If people know, they could ban together and fight."

"Okay," Clairity said. "Let's find some rope and tie them up. Then Jessie and I are going to go find the others. Maybe together we can figure out a plan of what to do with them."

"Lilabeth has nothing to do with this. It was all me." Tears streamed down Annabelle's face like a waterfall.

"We can't take that chance." Dezi found some rope in one of the drawers and used it to tie up the hands of both girls.

Heading to the first floor, Clairity and Jessie rapped loudly on the door marked thirteen. Jessica answered. Her eyes widened at the sight of Clairity from the tour. Opening her mouth, a high-pitched shriek escaped. "What are you doing here?"

"No time to explain. It seems someone wants us out of the way. We need you to come with us." Clairity motioned for them to hurry. Their next stop was on the second floor to pick up the group of vamprite. It took little to convince them something was going on. They figured something wasn't quite right as soon as they arrived.

Back in the suite on the thirteenth floor, Gavin circled the room, watching the two women tied up on the couch. "So what's up with the tour guides?"

Clairity took in a breath and let it out slowly. She corrected her posture and closed her eyes as if meditating. In her mind she selected the right words before filling the others in on what Annabelle did. They needed to understand the danger they were all in. Her concern lay with how the vamprite would react to the deception.

"Well," he said. "This is brilliant, isn't it? What are the ways to kill a witch?"

"We need a plan, not vengeance." Clairity gave him a little push away from the two captives. "Is there somewhere we could take them? Somewhere around here where we could notify people of the danger that is out there? The necromancers aren't just coming for us. They want to eliminate all magic before they invade."

"We could go to the mayor, Hilary. She is a personal friend of mine." Delilah was still the same, very much impressed with her social standing. "She would know what to do with them. Her office should be opening any minute now. It's only four blocks from here."

"Perfect!" Clairity clapped her hands together, making a loud slapping noise. "It's far too easy for them to find a way to escape if we leave them just tied with rope. I think it's better if we don't have them running around until after the ball when Mike and William get here. They can deal with these two."

Annabelle laughed loudly. "You don't really think you can get away with walking two women four blocks with their hands tied, do you? All we would have to do is scream and people would rush to our aid."

"You don't think that the four of us are without abilities, do you?" Clairity echoed the tone of voice the woman used. "We may not have the same gifts as Willow, but we do have talent."

"Oh yes!" Annabelle exclaimed with a smile. "You get feelings about things and Jade can do some glamours. You can work a wand not too badly, I will give you that." She laughed, stopping abruptly when she noticed the upset look on Lilabeth's face.

"Illusion is a strong ability. I can make people not even notice your existence." Confidence flowed from Jade's lips to the words she spoke, her demeanour reminiscent of her former self from before the invasion on her homeland.

The group made it all the way to the Mayor's office without incident. Occasionally, they would pass someone by who heard a muffled cry for help from Annabelle, but since they couldn't see anyone, they would go on about their business. Approaching the building, the vamprite decided to wait outside. Politics weren't their specialty.

Inside the office, things were bustling. Clairity recognized the smell of fresh coffee as they walked through the front door. She scanned the room quickly. In front of her there was a woman standing at a counter with a wand directing papers and files on where to fly to. Old-fashioned telephones sat on every desk - the type with stretchable cords. When the phone rang, the receiver would pick up and head to the nearest employee who wasn't otherwise engaged to answer the call.

Pictures of the mayor lined the walls. Clairity immediately recognized her as the woman Ashlyn thought she knew from the dream. Coincidences were starting to add up, but answers were still lacking.

In one corner they watched a woman meet her colleague at the water cooler. Instead of having a regular conversation, the woman opened a notepad, tore off a page and handed it to the man. It contained everything she was going to say, if they actually talked, written down to save time.

There was already a line formed for complaints and questions for the mayor. Even with Delilah's influence there was no avoiding having to take a number and wait.

The woman behind the main desk had blue hair, which was styled in a beehive. Her mouth opened and closed in a chewing motion, revealing a wad of pink bubble gum. Every so often, she would twirl a loose curl from her do and blow a massive bubble. Clairity imagined that if it popped, it would be stuck in the woman's hair forever, but she seemed to always make it go back in her mouth without incident. On her pink sweater was a name tag that read *Esmerelda* in bright blue letters that matched the colour of her coiffure. Occasionally throughout the day, her pencil or pen would go missing and she would reach into her stiff ringlets to pull out another one. Clairity couldn't help but giggle at the thought of what else could be stored somewhere in the woman's hair.

The first person in line was a cab driver - fined for having slime covering his passenger seats. Esmerelda's eyes rolled upwards throughout his whole spiel about how he hadn't realized he had taken a slime-producing client on board and it was his first offence. She let him finish, then cited a bylaw which said slime must be removed from all seats within an hour of the ride and stamped his appeal *DENIED* in bright red before yelling, "Next." The more loudly she spoke, the more noticeable her irritating nasal voice was.

Over the next several hours, they listened to complaints about lack of bylaws for walking alligators after two in the afternoon - the need for people with wheels instead of feet to follow road rules not sidewalk rules - too many potholes - not enough potholes - and store hour requests for amendment to name a few. They were particularly amused by a woman with brown hair woven into a basket shape on her head. There was a tiny hat sitting on top, which at first looked silly. Every so often a small dog would pop up and look around. After people realized it was the dog wearing the hat and not the woman, they would comment about how cute it was. She was complaining about men with removable eyeballs peeping under skirts.

Finally, it was their turn. Stepping up to the counter, they requested to see the mayor. Esmeralda let out a laugh that sounded more like she was having an asthma attack than finding something amusing. When she calmed down, she said, "The mayor is a busy lady. She can't drop everything to see everyone, now can she? That's why she has me. Now you tell me what the problem is and we will see what we can do." She blew a bubble in Clairity's face.

"Excuse me, darling, I am Delilah. The mayor is a personal friend. I know she will make time to see me."

The clerk rolled her eyes. "Of course she will. Wait here, Your Highness." She disappeared to a back room and came back moments later. Pressing a large blue button, part of the desk moved, creating a pathway. "You can go through. Follow the blue lines and only the blue lines. Next."

On the floor and ceiling were a series of different colour lines. The blue one started out with black and red beside it all heading in the same direction on the floor. The red one broke off and headed to a separate room marked *Caution Red Tape Area*. Every so often, a scream could be heard from behind the closed door. The black one split and ended up at a wall filled with pictures and reports of missing people. Clairity couldn't help but notice how many there were. Every possible spot on the wall was covered. It seemed covens weren't the only ones being targeted. Almost every type of magical being was on the hit list.

The group continued following the blue lines. On the ceiling there were yellow, green and purple lines, all heading towards a staircase leading upstairs. Finally the blue stopped at an office. Clairity went to knock, but the door flew open and a woman said, "Come in then."

The mayor looked much older than her pictures. She obviously touched up the portraits to make her appear her best. Jade wondered if magic or technology was used. Her yellow hair was tied into a large bun on her head and she wore a light beige blouse tucked into a tan skirt with a matching jacket over top. She was very bland looking. No one could complain she was too loud, or that they didn't like her taste.

Delilah and Hilary greeted with air kisses and loud *muah* noises. Taking a seat, the seventh-generation witch introduced everyone else.

Exhaustion leaked through Jade's illusions. She flopped on a chair, her body slouching backwards, resting against its back. The two women materialized before the mayor's eyes.

"Why are there two women tied up in rope in my office?" she asked.

"Madam Mayor, I assure you, we have been victimized and should be immediately released." Annabelle struggled with the ropes that bound her.

"She has committed a crime," Delilah blurted out.

"A crime?" The mayor almost choked on the words. She motioned for the telephone. "Call the constable, please." The receiver moved itself to the mayor's ear. "We may have a situation here that warrants your presence."

Before the receiver returned to its resting place, a rectangular box descended from the ceiling. It was made out of a dull silver colour and resembled an oversized birdcage. The lift was suspended by a black metal cable from the floor above. Looking at the ceiling, however, none of the group could actually see where the apparatus came from. In the front was a door, which opened and a small chubby man stepped out.

"Has something transpired?" he asked, twirling the end of his moustache. The officer was unusual looking. His black hair was tied back in a ponytail. It was obvious from the way his hair sat that he usually wore some sort of a hat. His facial hair was all blonde, including his eyebrows, sideburns and moustache. Constant revolving of the ends of the hair resting just above his lip caused strands to stick out at the ends. He paired the mustard yellow suit he was wearing with a bright orange tie.

"Apparently, we have a crime being reported." Hilary kept her eyes directed at paperwork on her desk avoiding contact with the man's colour choices.

"A crime? Please do bestow on us the information." The man took a seat on the corner of the mayor's desk. Hilary glanced up with a look of disgust then promptly returned her attention to her work.

Clairity offered to explain to the officer, retelling the dream. She made sure to include how Annabelle expected the three girls not to return.

The officer listened occasionally raising one eyebrow or the other and nodding at the most interesting parts. When he was sure the girl was done speaking, he replied, "Well, that is a fascinating tale. However, there are no laws against anything that happens in a dream." He turned to the mayor. "Although maybe there should be. Can we put that on the list for an enquiry?" After Hilary smiled and agreed, he continued, "So unless there is something else..." His deep voice trailed on the *else* for what seemed like minutes.

Clairity interrupted the continuing flow of the word. "It is connected to all the missing persons cases you have."

Both the officer and the mayor's eyes shifted to the girl's face. Hilary stood and rounded her desk, resting on the front edge beside her constable.

"How?" was all she said with a stern look in her eyes.

"The men in the dream, they are the ones behind the abductions and murders. We are just loose ends they are cleaning up. We know too much. They plan to one day invade the main world. First, they are thinning out those who could form a resistance, the most dangerous... the magical. They either recruit you or they destroy you."

Annabelle sighed. "You can't hold us. No crime has happened. Clearly, Clairity is fine. A dreamwalker called my name, pulling me into that dream. I didn't stay, nor did I plan it."

"She has a point, madam." The man tucked his notebook away in the inside pocket of his suit jacket.

"It's all true!" Lilabeth bellowed, still in tears. "Bad things are going to happen."

"Lilabeth!' Annabelle exclaimed, disbelief written in her expression.

"I won't be a part of this, Annie. I can't. People are dying. It's not right. You need to tell them everything. Make this right."

Annabelle looked deep into the eyes of her mate. She saw sadness, disappointment, and confusion. Everything she did was to keep Lilabeth happy and safe and now the opposite happened. Suddenly the witch realized she failed the princes again. They would be coming for her and there would be no more chances. Perhaps others didn't have to suffer her fate as well. Perhaps if she explained, the city could keep Lilabeth safe.

"I'm sorry," she said, breaking down. From the beginning she explained the entire story again, emphasizing her mate was not involved at all and required protection.

"Be that as it may, you still haven't broken any laws," the officer said at the end. "We will need to take some precautions here in the city, though. Pity you don't know any exact plans."

Dezi moved forward. "Madam Mayor," he said. "I notice it is an election year. With tonight being the biggest celebration of the year, wouldn't it be better to hold these two, just overnight? We will come tomorrow when our friends arrive and take them off your hands. There is no sense taking chances on ruining the evening's festivities."

"Now, young man," the constable started, but was cut off by the mayor.

"Don't be so hasty, Safron. The boy has a point. We can hold them for one night on suspicion of accessory to a crime." She motioned to the man to take the girls away for processing. "The group of you best be here in the morning to collect them and escort them out of the city."

They were almost at the front door when they heard the officer calling from behind them. His words mixed with heavy breathing. He handed Clairity his card, which read *Constable Safron Black*. "Ask for me at the desk in the morning. No need to disturb the mayor." He turned and disappeared behind the counter.

The vamprite were waiting when they stepped back into the street. The hustle and bustle of city life commenced while they were in the office. The streets were lined with people running from place to place finishing their last minute errands for the night's celebrations. To stay out of the way of the commotion, the group took seats at an outdoor patio of a small cafe.

"Do you think they have change for an earring?" Jade said with a half-smile. Her stomach let out a loud growling noise. The hotel agreed to give them meals, but there had been no time to take advantage of the offer. Now, there was little chance they would be returning there. It was far too dangerous.

"You forgot to change over currency, I am guessing." Jessica's smile looked sympathetic.

"First time here... we didn't know we needed to," Jade replied. Another gurgling sound came from her stomach.

"Well, we can't have that." Delilah motioned for a server and ordered something for everyone to eat and drink. "That should do for now." A look of satisfaction covered her face like she saved a starving kitten found on her doorstep.

The next hour was spent enjoying the food and uttering thanks to the seventh-generation witch for picking up the tab. After everyone was completely satisfied the conversation turned to the issues at hand.

"Do you think they will still come for us? Try to tie up the loose ends?" Naomi asked the question everyone else was thinking.

"I don't know," Clairity answered. Somehow all the questions were being addressed to her. For a moment, she thought that must be how Willow felt. A deep longing for her friend to be with her developed in the core of her being. "We should stay away from the hotel and try to blend in."

Jade's attention veered from the conversation as she watched a lady walk by wearing an elaborate Egyptian costume. It was stunning, even the mask. The woman had black straight hair, shoulder length with a golden net that draped over top of the back. The outfit split into two parts an upper and lower, joined only at the midsection by a few threads. It was made of a crisp white linen, trimmed in a sparkling golden weave. A gold chain adorned her neck which the top attached to. The bottom part was a long skirt which began just below the belly button and continued to the floor. There were several full-length slits in the material allowing people to see both her legs and her golden flat sandals. The mask adorning her face glistened with gold metal strands intricately woven into different circular patterns. After the woman disappeared from sight, Jade used her illusion abilities to create the same look for herself.

Jessie smiled at the costume, his eyes fixated on Jade's legs. "Too bad we all can't dress up. Then it would be harder to find us. We would look like everyone else."

"That's a good idea, mate," Gavin said, slapping Jessie on the back. "There must be a costume shop around here someplace. Everyone will be dressed up tonight. Wearing a disguise would make it much harder for anyone to track us down."

"I know a place. It's right around the corner. Shall we?" Delilah offered.

The costume shop was different to the other shops they were in lately. It was well lit and sparkling clean. Several sales ladies scurried about the floor, occasionally bumping into each other while attempting to match masks to costumes for their patrons - each one was dressed in a vibrant costume and smiling as wide as a smile could be.

One approached the group from behind. "Do you have something ordered?" She was tall and thin, wearing a pink ballerina costume that looked more like a piece of sexy lingerie with a fancy pink and white mesh skirt added to it. Her hair was tied back in a spiral bun adorned with a flashy tiara. Around her neck was a necklace that attached to a plastic name tag which read Cecile. The look on her face told them she knew they didn't have anything on order.

"No, it's terrible, Cecile," Delilah responded, appearing distraught. "We had a luggage mishap... lost everything. I do hope you can find us something." No one in the city would leave something as important as their costume to this late a time.

The perturbed look on the sales clerk's face changed to a pout. "That is so horrible, and on such an important day. Come along. We will figure something out."

Cecile led them to a room with couches and chairs to wait in while she attended to finding whatever stock was left. She returned towing a rack on wheels behind her. Hanging neatly on it were different odds and ends - some were full costumes, others they would have to put together and be creative with.

She held a pirate costume up to Jessie's neck. It appeared to be his size. He wasn't sure what exactly a pirate was, but the fancy fake sword and funny hat sold him on the idea. His shirt was white with a black and gold canvas doublet to wear over top. The store was out of the usual pirate leggings, so she gave him a pair of tight black pants to substitute.

Clairity managed to piece together a cat costume, which was basically a black skin-tight outfit with ears and a black mask. Dezi stood in a mirror examining how he looked in *mighty fine* cowboy gear. His outfit included two toy guns, which he claimed could decimate Jessie's sword any day.

The four vamprite were more enthusiastic than anyone anticipated. Clairity realized the group had a pretty good sense of humour when they all chose outrageous vampire outfits. The clerk was thrilled with their choice. Apparently vampire and witch costumes were the hardest to get rid of. The terunji depiction of the two races was considered distasteful to most.

Delilah looked radiant in a stunning white angel costume with beautiful feathered wings and silver mask. Jessica chose a red devil costume to complement her mentor.

Adorned with their new outfits, the group decided there was no better way to twiddle away the time than to join in the festivities. They stepped out of the shop and into the street party that was already underway.

It was late afternoon. For safety, large orange barricades blocked off all roads in the area, closing them for the rest of the celebration. A parade was flowing by to kick off the official start to the new year. Several establishments in the city donated an attraction to the ritual to advertise their businesses. A marching band playing a song about monsters over and over kicked off the beginning of the train of displays winding through the streets. Band members were dressed in red outfits complimented with big golden feathers. What looked like roller skates covered their feet. Clairity's thoughts returned to the memory of the complaint made earlier in the mayor's office. She bobbed her head up and down attempting to find a good vantage point to see if the wheels were in fact a part of the band's actual feet.

Jade's mouth dropped open when she saw the next participant in the parade. The mayor chose an Egyptian theme. She was wearing an outfit almost identical to Jade's and standing on a chariot. Instead of animals, two scantily dressed, muscular men pulled her as she waved to the crowds. A large sign flew behind the chariot which read *Re-elect Hilary for Mayor*. Jade swallowed with a gulp. She repositioned herself in the middle of her friends. Looking from side to side to ensure no one was watching, she switched her Egyptian illusion to one of a ninja. The guys couldn't help but snicker.

The next few parade floats weren't much to look at. They were the other candidates for the mayor's race, not wanting to appear too flashy or too dull. Following them was a float by *The Empowered* newspaper. The parade announcers' voices seemed to become several levels louder proclaiming the display to be made entirely of magic. It was supposed to reflect life of the good witch as depicted by terunji media. Several more bands and floats passed by. Every so often one would toss streamers and paper stars onto the masses lining the sidewalks. Dezi was most impressed by the ones that levitated candy into the crowds. Clairity was touched by the animal adoption float. It was in the shape of a giant black cat and covered by pets of all types, each one currently available to be adopted in the city.

Everyone was so completely enthralled by the parade they hadn't realized how long they were watching. The entire afternoon flew by without a second thought and the final float of the day was announced. A pristine-looking lady dressed in a full-length black dress was standing by a desk in the front of the display. The base resembled a book opened at the middle, the entire scene illuminated with a vibrant orange glow. The whole display hovered over the ground. Clairity couldn't see where anything was supporting it, or pulling it for that matter. She wondered how much magic it would take to create such a float.

"Who is that?" Clairity asked.

"The Director of Knowledge, Cassandrhea Tibbins," Jessica yelled back, directly in her ear. The noise level around them intensified as the sun started going down. "She runs all of the schools. There are over a hundred of them. She is probably one of the most important and respected witches alive."

"There are empyral schools?"

"Yes," she yelled back. "It's very sophisticated, really. Students write an entrance exam and the results determine which school is best suited to their needs. To apply, you have to be magical or from other worlds. I've been trying to get into one for years. Competition for spots is fierce. I am apprenticing with Delilah hoping to improve enough to get a spot next year. You should write the exam too. The best students… the ones with the top results, attend Sleeping-Sands School and study under the direction of Ms. Tibbins herself."

As the final float made its way through the streets, the sun went down. Crowds overflowed into the roads behind it. Fireworks of every colour erupted in the sky and the celebration was officially underway.

Chapter Forty-Eight

The afternoon passed fairly quietly for Willow. Her personal role in the events that were to unfold would take place later in the evening. Everyone else busied themselves with the details of any last-minute plans. Maps covered beds and clues were tacked neatly to a corkboard. Pete, Iskander and Sarah had already left for the first possible location for an entrance to the underground city. They hoped to find the way in before the evening was over. With time running out, William called a final meeting to go over the night's plans leaving nothing to chance.

"I took a drive by the location of the ball earlier and took these pictures." He threw a handful of photos on the empty bed.

The ball was being held at an elderly house. It was hard to imagine using the word *house* to refer to the property they were discussing, it was so incredibly grand. From the sidewalk, there was a path that led to about ten steep steps heading to a double front door. The mansion took up most of the block, including its fenced-off lawns and gardens. Standing three stories tall, it overshadowed the other houses of the area. Iron bars were placed outside every window making everyone wonder if they were for the protection of those inside or out. A four-foot hedge bordered the outside perimeter of the property. Across the street was a city park approximately the same size.

"Unfortunately, we can't go inside. We will be taking up spots in the park and hopefully near the hedges. There will be people out for Halloween festivities, especially children. We need to first and foremost make sure none of them get caught up in the evening's events."

"And if Willow needs help?" Malarchy asked.

"I take it we are assuming our telepathic link will be broken by some form of magic? I'll have to yell really loud, if that's the case." She turned her head, distracted by a picture pinned to the corkboard standing in the corner of the room.

Mike followed her line of sight. He walked over to the board and pointed to the photo. "We found this picture of a woman in the graveyard. We need everyone to study it and if they see her let us know."

"I have seen her before," Willow said.

"In the dream." Ashlyn walked over to get a better look. "She is the mayor of the underground city. Her picture was in the window we walked by."

"What could she have to do with this? It doesn't make any sense," Mike said.

"We aren't sure about anything yet, but let's keep an eye open for our good mayor tonight," William said. "Just in case."

"And the other thing we are watching for is a massive hoard of zombies." Mike had a look on his face like there was little chance any of this was going to actually happen. "That shouldn't be hard to miss."

"Do we really think that all those missing bodies are going to be walking around attacking people later?" Ashlyn asked. She leaned back in the chair she was sitting on and pulled her knees to her chest.

"Again, we don't know. But we need to be prepared for the worst."

"So what do we do if they do show up?" Ashlyn made a valid point. None of them were trained in the finer art of zombie slaying.

"Go for the head," Mike answered. "It works in the movies. Take off the head and the body can't continue to function." He made a motion that looked more like he was swinging a bat at a baseball than using a sword to decapitate a dead body. His tongue and cheek made a clicking noise at the end of his pretend swing.

"I am glad we have such a tactical plan," Malarchy used his normal sarcastic tone to answer while rolling his eyes.

"Okay, Willow needs to get into costume. Everyone else, prepare for a long night. We all need to be alert to any possibility. Truth is, we don't know what we are going to be facing tonight, so stay vigilant." William handed out some backpacks for the group to start preparing anything they might need, including weapons.

Willow returned to her room eager to unpack the dress she was to wear to the Halloween ball that evening. It was as beautiful as she remembered. William added golden gloves, shimmering green shoes and a beautiful mask adorned with peacock feathers.

The dress fit her like it was made especially for the shape of her figure. For the first time, she looked at the reflection in a mirror of herself and saw a feminine body with curves in all the right places. Daydreaming for a moment, she thought about how wonderful it would have been if she lived through the dress' era in the main world. It suited her. The green and gold colours perfectly complimented her bronze skin tone and red hair.

Adding the finishing touches, she put on the gloves and mask. Her wand slid easily up the sleeve of the dress, giving her easy access if she needed it. Returning her attention to the reflection in the mirror, she noticed Ashlyn was standing in the doorway behind her.

"So," she said, "what do you think?" Willow twirled around, completing a circle so her friend could see the entire dress, front and back.

"Amazing! You look so… different. It reminds me of a tarot card I saw…"

"Is it okay? I don't want to look silly tonight." Willow turned from side to side in the mirror still looking at every view she could.

"You won't look silly. It's just, that's the same dress the red-haired woman on the tarot card was wearing. I think you should be worried about more than how you look. This could be a trap for you." Ashlyn sat on the bed, watching.

Willow thought about it for a moment, her mind drifting to her guardians. Aslo and Kiera were still in the other room going over details for the evening with William. She flashed back to what happened to Shelby, Tika, and Nero. The guardians needed to stay with the others she decided. It was too dangerous to expose their existence to the prince at the moment. It would make them a target.

With a strong resolve, she headed over to William's room. For a moment she forgot she was still wearing the costume. The look on the faces of the others quickly reminded her. She sighed as her face flushed red. Compliments made her uneasy. She was used to being the punchline of a joke, not the girl everyone adored. Honestly she didn't know which was worse, deciding she would rather be lost somewhere between the two.

"You look fantastic," Kiera said as proudly as a cat could.

The others agreed, some in words, some just nodding. She mumbled a *thank you*, happy that the mask she was wearing covered her blushing. She was nervous enough about what she was about to say. The attention she was receiving made speaking harder.

"I," she stuttered a little. "I have a suggestion. I think it might be wise if Aslo and Kiera remained here."

"Not a chance." Aslo stood up from sitting on the bed. "This is far too dangerous for you to be in there alone."

"I know how dangerous it is!" she exclaimed. "But they don't know you exist and it is best we keep it that way for now. If they knew, they would come for you... for us."

"You may need us. What if it comes down to a final battle?" Kiera was twitching her tail nervously. Her ears curled forward slightly, anticipating an answer.

"I think we all know tonight isn't the endgame. Whatever is going to happen is only a part of the final plan for them, but not a takeover invasion. More like a test of what they could do and what won't work... experimentation at its finest." Willow moved to sit beside the two guardians. "I won't take any unnecessary chances. I promise."

"The girl has a point," Malarchy said calmly. "Our advantage at the moment is that no one knows you exist. We should make sure we keep that edge. We can't afford to lose any guardians at this time."

"We can't afford to lose Willow, either," Ashlyn cut in. "Look at her, wearing that dress, she looks identical to the image on the tarot card. The card the swamp witch used to predict danger for my friend." She was angry no one was listening to her about Willow's likeness being displayed on the fortune teller's hand painted picture.

Aslo made a noise similar to a roar. "We will be with her this evening. We will stay hidden. If you are not concerned with her safety, then there is no reason to be worried about ours. The discussion is closed."

The two cats took their place as pictures on the girl's skin, well hidden by her costume. Willow removed her gloves and looked down at her hands. She rubbed them together, her palms clammy. Everyone had become silent since Aslo's temper erupted. The sun was going down and it was time to head to the witches' ball.

*****

Willow looked out the window of the van William was driving. It was a challenge just packing her large dress into the vehicle, forcing her to sit at an unusual angle. Her elevated position provided her a good view of the outside. The houses they passed were all decorated for the night's festivities, orange and black being the predominant colours she noticed along the way. Decorations of ghosts made out of white sheets were scattered in gardens and skeletons of paper dangled in windows. Front lawns were made to look like graveyards, littered with tombstones. Every so often, there would be one house with decorations so realistic it made her shiver.

Parents were walking their small children down the street made up in various costumes. She saw some clowns, witches, ghosts, cloaked figures, cartoon characters and some she knew were costumes, but wasn't sure of what. Each child was running door to door, collecting candy in big bags.

She thought for a moment about what a strange tradition it was, going to neighbours' houses to collect sweet treats. She could definitely see the appeal to the children.

All that sugar can't be good for a child, Kiera's voice echoed in Willow's head.

It's fun. I wish I had done something like that when I was younger. Anything like that. You two need to be quiet tonight. No comments. Okay? she said.

We will be non-existent, unless a problem arises, Aslo promised.

They parked about a block away and walked through the park. Silence hung in the air, the unknown frightening everyone. William nodded to Zsiga to continue walking with Willow. His stealth abilities would allow him to escort her further without being detected. She turned around just in time to see the others split up into different locations in the park. She was happy to see Ashlyn stayed within proximity of both William and Mike, where she would be as safe as possible.

Willow focused her attention on the people up ahead climbing the steep stairs, all dressed in beautiful costumes. Women were dressed in stunning dresses from every era. Men were dressed in elaborate black suits with crisp white shirts and black masks. She was especially happy with the costume she chose to wear after seeing the others entering the building. She could at least relax a little now, knowing she wasn't going to stand out like a sore thumb. Zsiga motioned to her; it was time to continue on alone.

She only managed a few steps when she almost ran into a group of zombies. Their costumes made her jump back, her heart racing. The makeup they were wearing was so realistic, it actually made their skin look as if it was rotting. Willow caught her breath and composed herself before continuing on. She almost blew everything over a group of party-goers heading for a local bar to celebrate. She didn't even know if that was what a zombie would look like. The only real information she had was from a few movies. Scanning her surroundings, she suddenly realized how hard their job really was tonight. With people dressed in costumes, figuring out which were their enemies and which were terunji wasn't going to be an easy task. It was the perfect plan for an invasion. No one would notice until it was too late.

The grand house's lawn was decorated to attract attention. People walking down the street with their children would stop and admire the decor. Mechanical monsters were scattered inside the fences. Some stirring cauldrons with lights and fog rising up from underneath. Others leapt out of bushes or jumped up out of nowhere, scaring anyone that came too close.

A man-made graveyard was strategically placed to be noticed. The headstones contained within looked like they were made from real stone. In front of some were hands or bodies appearing to break out of the ground. Others were engraved with names. She read a few out loud and realized they were made to be amusing. *Fester N. Rott, Yule B. Next, Bea A. Fraid, I.M. Knotwell.* She giggled a little until a fake spider behind one jumped out at her, making her squeal and stumble backwards.

The pathway leading to the steps was lined on either side with pumpkins boasting elaborate carvings of spooky scenes, each one lit with a candle inside. There was so much to take in, she wasn't sure she would ever make it into the ball. She stood and admired the work of the carver, not being able to decide if her favourite was the one that looked like a hand reaching up out of grass, or the one that resembled a black cat. Every one of the intricate patterns contained incredible detail and could be considered a fine work of art.

She slowly walked up the path, stopping at the bottom of the steep steps to look up at the door. She took in a deep breath. There was no hiding she was nervous, frightened even. When the door opened, she staggered a few steps backwards, almost falling.

"Careful," Lance said, smiling. "You aren't frightened by the decor, I hope." He dressed as most of the other men did, in a black suit with tails, a crisp white shirt and bow tie. There was no denying his crystal blue eyes, even behind the black mask. His midnight black-blue hair was tied back neatly for the occasion.

He ran down the stairs to her side and escorted her inside the house. The indoor decor was just as effective as the outside. The house was lit entirely by candles with a few red and green lights highlighting corners for effect. The front entrance opened to a sitting room on the left and two closed doors on the right.

Webs lined the walls and giant spiders appeared to follow her everywhere. Green lights directed to one wall made it appear as if bats were swooping down through a hallway. Black cats with hunched backs looked as if they had been scared and jumped to the ceiling, clinging upside down by their claws. There were more pumpkins, filled with flower arrangements made from black roses and bare sticks. Each arrangement was adorned with orange and black ribbons made into big bows. The time and care someone put into the decorations was unfathomable to Willow for one night's celebration.

Straight ahead was a fancy hall with an elaborate staircase to the upper levels in the middle. A giant crystal chandelier lit with candles hung over the centre of the room. Two large doors opened, leading to an elegant ballroom. Inside music played while couples swirled around as if they were floating.

Willow suddenly realized she didn't know how to dance. That was a big oversight on her part. Who showed up to a dance without having any idea of what dancing even was? Panic set in, her face flushed red. It was too late. Lance grabbed her waist.

To her surprise, her body glided easily in time with his. She felt as if she knew the steps and had practised them her whole life. Other dancers cleared the floor for the prince and his date, watching them move perfectly to the music from the sides of the room. It was as if they were meant to dance with each other. Their motions were as one. When the music halted, the other guests broke out into a round of applause.

He directed her to the far side of the room, where a section of the wall opened to an outside courtyard. Waiters walked through the crowd with trays of drinks. Lance picked up two glasses from a server and offered one to Willow.

"Thank you," she said, sipping the drink. "What is it?" The taste was a little dry, but sweet at the same time. The bubbles ticked her noses and her senses.

"Champagne," he answered. "Normally, I would suggest my date have a few." He looked in her eyes. "You, however, I would prefer not to overindulge. It has alcohol in it, which can numb the mind in larger amounts."

Willow admired the surroundings. The entire affair felt beautiful. On one side of the courtyard a man was carving the images of couples into pumpkins with extreme detail. All around her, everyone was smiling and enjoying the festivities. She suddenly began wondering when the bad part would come. "So," she said, "what now?"

"What do you mean?" The prince finished his champagne and put the glass on a tray of a waiter walking by. "We enjoy the evening." He put one arm around her waist and with the other, took the glass she was holding. He disposed of it the same way he had his own, then pulled her closer to him. Her back was to him and he whispered in her ear, "What would you like to happen? I am here to please you." Lance moved her hair to one side with his free hand and kissed her neck gently.

A shiver ran down her spine. It felt so natural, melting in his arms, his lips soft on the exposed skin of her neck. Then it occurred to her, she felt safe. There was no sense of danger like she felt with him before. This time he radiated warmth, kindness, protection.

She spun round and looked at him. "You didn't bring me here to hurt me. You brought me here to keep me safe!" she exclaimed. "Nothing is going to happen here, is it? This was never a trap. I was never in danger."

Lance rubbed his neck, pressing his lips together tightly. From the look on his face, she could tell he wasn't going to answer. Willow bolted back through the house, straight to the front door. As she reached the bottom of the outside steps, she heard him call to her. She stopped in her tracks.

The others seeing her running from the house moved in closer to make sure she was okay. The prince ignored them and called to her again. "Willow!" he yelled, running down the steps to face her. "I can't protect you if you leave here. It will be out of my control."

"I know." Willow didn't know what came over her, but she threw her arms around his neck and kissed him softly on the cheek. "Thank you for trying. If it were your friends and family, you would want to help them too."

He nodded at her. Shoving his hands in his pockets, he slowly climbed back up the steps, stopping briefly to give a little salute to Mike and William on the way. She watched him disappear back inside the house before joining her friends.

"It isn't me," she said, heading back to the park. She lifted the sides of her dress up with her hands so her feet could move faster.

"What do you mean?" Mike asked, trying to match her pace.

"I mean, he was trying to protect me... keep me from whatever is going to happen, so I wouldn't get hurt." She looked at Ashlyn. "The card reader, she must have been talking about Clairity, not me. We have to find them before it's too late."

Chapter Forty-Nine

They caught up to Sarah, Pete, and Iskander in a small log cabin store at the foot of one of the bigger mountains in the area, with purchased tickets for the last bus entering the underground city. Boarding, they took seats for the ride up the mountain. They were the lone riders; presumably, anyone else attending the festivities arrived in the underground city hours ago. Fixed on the task ahead of them, they didn't even notice the bus driver watching them through mirrors and listening to their conversation.

"How do we plan to find them?" Sarah asked.

"Not sure." Willow sat watching out the window of the bus for the road ends sign her friend told her about in the dream. "Clairity wouldn't have gone back to the hotel, although we may want to check out the area around it. Someone should probably look for the mayor. She could be a target."

"You don't think she is involved?" Malarchy asked, looking at the photo he brought with them. "She could be in on the whole thing. It would explain how the princes and their zombie hoard are getting into the city.

Someone must be on the inside working with them. I think we are just starting to understand the extent of connections our enemy has in this world. I would suggest an open mind for the time being."

"No, it makes more sense they were using the picture to show someone or something what the mayor looked like before it ended up dropped in a grave. If she was their ally, why would they need to know exactly what she looks like? If there is an attack, we probably won't have much time once we get there."

The driver hit the brakes. The bus came to a screeching halt. "I don't know what you people are up to, but not tonight," he said.

"What are you doing? We need to get to the city!" Willow cried out.

"Not with all that talk about finding the mayor and attacks, you don't. My job is to make sure possible threats don't get into the city. The lot of you fit the description of a possible threat."

"We aren't the threat, you numbskull!" Malarchy blurted out. "We are your precious city's only hope." His voice seemed unusually angry. No doubt his emotions hinged on the fact his daughter was also in the city - the only family he had left.

The driver exited the bus. Everyone else followed him. They were only about halfway up the mountain from what Willow could tell. This disaster wasn't going to be easy to resolve. The bus was their sole hope to find Clairity.

Nero appeared. "Shall we send you back to your own world?" The wolf took his full form, appearing with the body of an oversized bear and the face of a giant wolf. Willow had never seen an Olcsanka in its natural shape before. Their size alone was impressive. She finally understood the descriptions she read about them. He was a most formidable guardian.

"There are no guardians left in these parts. What are you folks trying to pull?"

Tika took Nero's side. "Are you willing to bet on that?"

"Perhaps we shouldn't bother waiting for an answer." Aslo appeared on the other side of the driver. He spun around to see the feline in his glorious guardian form. Kiera stood still by his side.

"Shall we continue?" Shelby landed beside the cats also in her true from. Sensing the man was scared she added, "We mean you no harm. We aren't here for you or any other peaceful empyral."

"Then why?" he asked.

"Your city is in great danger. We have been tracking a foreign kingdom's activities. They are convinced they should rule all of this world and every other realm as well. The trail leads here, tonight. We believe your mayor may be a target as well." Shelby slowly backed away from the man, giving him no reason to be startled and stood beside Ashlyn.

Willow moved forward holding her hands up in front of her. "We have friends inside, but they will not be strong enough to stop a necromancer's army of undead."

"Necromancers?" The man paused. "There have been reports... let me call ahead and speak with my superiors."

Mike was growing impatient as usual. "Can you do that along the way? We are wasting valuable time sitting here. How can you argue with guardians?"

The man glanced at each of their faces, then at the guardians. He paused for a moment tapping his forehead with two fingers. "Alright, get in. But I am going in with you. We head straight to the mayor's office. They can decide whether or not to let you walk around. Folks won't take kindly to thinking we are letting guardians in to send them all home. They haven't done anything. You have to understand the panic it could cause."

"We will work out something about that with your mayor, after the evening's threat has been eradicated. We have no problems with those who wish to peacefully coexist, as the inhabitants of this city are doing. It is with those who would threaten war and wish to conquer that we take issue," Shelby said, disappearing into picture form on Ashlyn's leg.

Chapter Fifty

"Looks like we are right on schedule, brother," Simon said, looking down from the top of a building.

"We have some loose ends to tie up first. Shall we take care of our sister's mess for them?" Joseph opened the door leading into the hotel from the rooftop. The girls may have gotten away in the dream, but they had no intention of letting them get away tonight.

The brothers visited all three suites. Finding each completely empty, rage consumed them. They destroyed the final room in a fit of anger, breaking furniture, mirrors, and windows.

"Perhaps we should have a talk with the slimy owner. He hasn't kept up to his end of the bargain," Simon suggested, running out of things to smash. His anger needed another outlet. "I was never fond of their kind."

"Yes, and find that witch, Annabelle. She appears to have failed us again. I am not in a forgiving mood."

In the lobby, they found Clyde in his usual place behind the desk. He paid little attention to the two men at first. "We are all full. Try somewhere else," he said without looking away from the book he was writing in.

"Oh, we don't want a room," Joseph said, knocking on the desk.

"We were wondering where your guests are? The ones you were to keep here for us? That was the deal we made, wasn't it?" Simon moved around to the other side of the desk and pulled the man out into the middle of the small lobby.

"Yes, but I couldn't. Let me explain," Clyde cried. "They teamed up, all together and they left. They used some form of illusion to take two witches with them bound in ropes. They had no idea I can see through illusions. I followed them. I know where they went." The man knew he was pleading for his life.

"Where?" Joseph's eyes rolled up. Examining his fingernails, he let out a breath of air suggesting his impatience with the man and his excuses.

"The mayor's office. The two witches never came back out. The constable must have taken them upstairs. Most likely, they are being kept in the holding cells. The office will open again tomorrow morning."

"And the others?" Simon pointed a knife at the man's chest, cutting a button off of the coat he was wearing. It flew across the room, smashing the light it hit.

Clyde swallowed with a gulp. "They bought some costumes to blend into the crowd. I lost them during the parade. The crowds were too thick."

Simon plunged the knife into the man's chest and pulled it out again, wiping the liquid off the blade on the carpet. Clyde fell to the ground. His body separated into ten smaller bodies, each one stabbed in the same place and lifeless. The brothers stepped over the smaller Clydes and exited the hotel as if nothing happened.

"Let's take care of the coven witches first. If worse comes to worse, my minions can deal with the others in the street. I highly doubt they will be able to refrain from sticking their noses in where they don't belong as usual." Joseph stepped onto the sidewalk. The thick crowd parted making room just for them as they strolled through the street.

The mayor's office was basically empty. Most everyone in the city was at the evening's festivities. One unlucky janitor found himself assigned to working on cleaning up the offices for the busy day to come. Waste paper baskets flew through the air to a larger container where they emptied their contents before returning to their normal places. The worker was listening to some form of music through small earphones making him oblivious to the pending danger. Joseph took advantage, throwing a spiked weapon similar in appearance to the blade of a circular saw. It spun round and struck the unsuspecting worker in his head, exploding into a black dust on contact. The man instantly fell over motionless, leaving only a black bruise on his forehead as a clue to what killed him. The trash baskets fell to the ground wherever they were, scattering their paper contents everywhere.

"Nice shot, brother. It's a shame Lance isn't here to join us."

Joseph chuckled. "Yes, well, his talents aren't what we need tonight. He deserves to have a little fun with the ladies. I think we can handle this."

The brothers added a skip to their steps as they climbed the stairs to the city's police department. One deputy was alone in the office, left on duty to handle any complaints that might come in. The celebration outside warranted that all available officers be outside to maintain control of the crowds. Constable Black ordered everyone to be on the lookout for anything unusual after listening to Clairity and her friends' stories earlier in the day. No one anticipated an attack on a closed building.

Joseph made quick work of killing the young officer before he even uttered a single word. Simon took the keys from the body. They continued to the holding cells. Although they found the key that fit, the door didn't open.

"It's enchanted," Joseph said, pulling out a long black wand with a silver tip. He motioned for his brother to move aside. A blast of black energy streamed from the wand. The door didn't just open, it melted to nothing. All that was left was a gaping hole with red embers on the edges where the door once stood. "Guess the keys are useless. You can toss them." He chuckled.

The holding cells were all empty, except for two. Annabelle was in the first and Lilabeth in the other.

"Ladies," Joseph said.

Annabelle jumped to her feet. "Prince Joseph!" she exclaimed. "How did you find us?" Her body trembled at the sight of the brothers.

"Do you not think we are capable of keeping track of our... investments? Perhaps you felt we would be too busy and overlook your failure?" Simon pointed his wand at the lock on her cell. After a small explosion, the door opened wide. He continued to do the same for the other door. Both women backed up in fear.

"I led you to them in the dream. After they escaped from you, the girls knew everything. I was outnumbered. There was nothing I could do. Please? I can make it up to you and help you find them tonight," Annabelle pleaded, biting her bottom lip.

Joseph laughed. "For a moment, it sounded as if you were saying this was our failure. Surely you wouldn't suggest such a thing."

"No," she replied, her voice shaking from fear. "Of course not, it was my fault. I should have been prepared for them to figure out everything."

"Good. Then you understand why I won't accept another disappointment from you. We had a deal and since you did not live up to your side of it, we will not be honouring ours..." Joseph motioned to his brother to bring Lilabeth to him.

"Wait!" Annabelle said in desperation. "It was my fault, not hers. Punish me. I will accept any torture you chose." She knelt in front of the prince with her hands together as if she were praying.

Joseph sighed. "If I had the opportunity, I would let you live knowing the pain your lover felt before she died was because of you. However, since we can't have people knowing our plans, I unfortunately have to kill you as well. You will, however, watch her die first."

They were defenceless. The constable had stripped their wands from them before putting them in the cells. Lilabeth tried to yell out an incantation, words flew from her mouth without the opportunity to finish. A blast of power hit her directly in the chest. Her body slammed to the ground. Annabelle screamed, grabbing the bars that separated her from the woman she loved. There was nothing she could do. Simon used magic to slam the witch's body against walls until the final breath left her lips and she lay motionless.

Annabelle fell to her knees crying. She looked up at Joseph and knew it was her turn. Without her soulmate, there was nothing left for her to live for. She summoned every ounce of her power in an incantation to take her own life and deprive the prince of the satisfaction.

"Time to conquer this city, brother," Joseph said as they exited the building content that the evening's plan was going exactly the way they wanted it to.

Chapter Fifty-One

The bus parked outside the city gates and the driver led the group through the crowds to the mayor's office. They opened the door and instantly knew something was wrong. Waste paper baskets and their contents lay strewn all over the floor.

Mike called out, "Over here." He motioned to the body of the janitor, lying on the floor with music still blaring from his headphones. Whatever weapon had been used was gone. There was no visible damage to his body except for a strange bruise on his forehead. Ashlyn took out her wand and the others prepared themselves for confrontation. The bus driver moved to the back of the group, placing his hands on Sarah's shoulders, occasionally peeking around her to see what might be up ahead. Moving slowly from one end of the building to the other, they determined the rest of the lower level was empty, checking every room and under every desk. There were no clues as to what may have happened before they arrived.

"The police are on the second floor," the man said, still hiding behind everyone else. Curiously he didn't consider the possibility of someone attacking them from behind.

When they reached the top of the stairs, the office was deserted. The lights flickered on and off creating shadows that sent shivers radiating down the line they formed.

Ashlyn called out, "Hello," without answer. The others sent her a glare of disapproval. The looks on their faces asking *who in their right mind would say hello to a hiding killer?*

Slowly, they crept around the counter making as little noise as possible, hoping not to alert any intruders, who hadn't already heard Ashlyn, as to their exact location. William stumbled over something, sending the rest of the tightly packed group tumbling to the ground. It was the body of the officer. He was young, probably new to the force. William felt remorse they hadn't reached him in time to save him. His thoughts were interrupted.

"Over there," Ashlyn said, pointing to the hole in the wall.

"Stay here," William ordered, motioning for only Mike to follow him to check out the other side of the hole. Coming across the bodies of Annabelle and Lilabeth, he mumbled, "Sorry." William placed his hand on his friend's shoulder for support, then headed back out to join the others, leaving Mike alone for a moment.

Mike emerged from the hole in the wall a minute later. No one knew what to say. She may have been working with their enemies, but regardless, Annabelle was and always would be Mike's sister. "Let's find the others," he said, emotion drained from his face.

"You sure you are okay?" Malarchy asked.

"Yeah. There will be time to think things through after everyone else is safe. Let's make sure no one else ends up having the same fate." Mike said, descending the stairs without making eye contact with anyone.

"Where do we start to look?" Iskander asked.

"I doubt they will be in the hotel, but it's the best start we have," Ashlyn replied.

The bus driver led them to the hotel; having a personal tour guide was working out much better than any of them could have anticipated. None of them were prepared for the size of the city. Without help, they could have been wandering around lost for most of the evening. Outside the hotel, the group found themselves staring at the sign *Your Destiny*. William narrowed his eyes, his face close to the glass doorway leading into the lobby. It was difficult to see, but he made out Clyde's ten bodies scattered around the small room. Even with reduced vision, it was obvious they were too late to help them.

"Look!" Faramund exclaimed, pointing down the street.

Strangers walking by turned, snickering at them. The lot of them stood in a line, mouths parted, fixated on what was taking place in front of them. Not far ahead, at a crossroads, there was a gigantic snake balloon filling the space of at least three city blocks. Crowds were cheering and running to get a closer look at the enormous serpent.

"Guess we know where we will find the others," Willow said. Without waiting for a response, she started following the crowd.

Trying to find a spot with a good view was as difficult a task as any she faced since arriving in this world. The scene attracted everyone in the city, each one pushing and shoving for space, believing it was something the city thought up to end the evening's festivities. Partygoers hoped for some lavish gifts to be bestowed on them or a spectacular show that couldn't be missed. Willow managed to push her way forward to the edge of the sidewalk. Shifting her eyes to her left, she realized she was standing right beside the mayor. *That was sheer luck,* she thought to herself, not taking her eyes off of the woman.

Hilary was complaining to one of her aides about her competition putting on this big production to show her up. A tone of disgust stemmed from her words over the display that was chosen. She mumbled something about the creatures being better served on a dinner table than used as a brilliant display on a sacred holiday. Snakes apparently weren't her favourite creature. Willow turned to William and motioned towards the lady, who was still trying to figure out which one of the candidates had masterminded the extravagant event. Malarchy used his illusion magic as he and the bus driver each took one of her arms, escorting the mayor to safety. Iskander and Zsiga went with them.

"Over there," Ashlyn yelled, pointing to a group across the street.

Willow spun around to look so fast she almost lost her footing. A smile crossed her face, Clairity was standing on the other side of the street dressed in cat costume. Her friend was motioning towards the top of the snake. Following her line of sight Willow saw the two princes standing on the head. Neither one was making even the slightest effort to conceal themselves.

The face of the giant serpent bobbed up and down as it slithered through the streets attracting as many people as possible. It came to a complete stop, its chin touching the ground. The crowd cheered, excited about what was about to happen, still believing this to be a city sanctioned part of the celebration. They didn't have to wait long. The serpent's mouth fell open, revealing a gaping hole and the undead army began to emerge.

"I expected them to look more zombie-like," Sarah said, glued to the spot she was standing in, watching the events unfold. "There must be something in death magic that restores their flesh. Are we sure they are the missing dead bodies?" The corpses were all improved from the state of decay than they should have been in. Some of them looked almost normal.

"Whether dead or alive, they are attacking people. We need to stop them!" Mike yelled, running towards the mouth of the snake - a sword appearing in his hand.

He was right. Whatever they were, they were hitting people and biting them. Some used weapons. The crowd started screaming. No one was prepared for what was happening. Had even a few individuals taken a moment to think, their magic could have saved many lives. Panic set in and no rational thought prevailed - survival was all that mattered. The crowds stampeded, trampling anything in their path, trying to get away. Magic flew through the air without direction, more often missing targets than not. Danger no longer attached itself only to those attacking. Everyone around was a possible threat.

Willow was still fixated on the two princes, ignoring the pushing and shoving that surrounded her. There was some sort of an aura coming from Joseph's hands, unlike anything she had seen before. It was as if a black light was dusting down over the dead forces he unleashed. She wondered if anyone else could see it. A thought crossed her mind... perhaps the aura might be what he was using to control the army of corpses. It might be a trail of his magic. If she could disrupt it...

Willow bolted across the road. Ashlyn was the only one to notice the swiftness of her movements. Following, she grabbed Clairity's arm and pulled her along to find their friend, resulting in an outright battle against the flow of empyral traffic desperately trying to escape.

The serpent's head rested between a store on one side and a park on the other. A tree bent down forming a bridge leading to the top of the head. Willow followed the trunk of the tree climbing quickly to the top.

"Up there!" Ashlyn yelled.

Clairity looked up to where her friend was pointing. "What is she doing?"

"I don't know, but she needs help. She can't take them both on alone."

The two girls followed the tree bridge, catching up to their friend at the top. Willow's plan was still in the process of forming. She figured out how to get up there, just not what to do after that. Whatever she was going to do, it needed to be fast. People were being slaughtered below her. For some reason, the magic the living were using didn't seem to be having any effect on the zombie army, barely slowing them down.

"There is a power I think that is controlling the corpses radiating from Prince Joseph. I need to distract him long enough to stop whatever spell he is using. If you two could keep the other one busy..."

Her words cut off. It was too late. They had already been spotted.

Simon headed towards them. All three pulled out their wands and directed them at the prince. A stream of bright light exploded from the tip of each, suspending the prince in the air high above. He couldn't move. The commotion caught Joseph's attention. He turned to face the girls with a look of disdain forcefully aimed at them. A burning sensation radiated through to their bones.

"We got this one!" Clairity yelled. "Stop Joseph!"

Willow changed the direction of her wand and moved closer to the other prince. The aura she saw before was gone. Briefly glancing down, she could see the bodies of the zombie invaders falling to the ground, decomposing where they fell. They were reverting to the state they were in when they were found in the grave.

Joseph smiled at her. "You are the ones who have been giving my sisters so much trouble. But who, exactly, are you?" He looked at the two girls imprisoning his brother as if sizing up the situation.

"Up there!" Mike yelled, pointing at the girls on top of the head of the snake. He couldn't help but notice Willow looked exactly like the picture on the tarot card they saw, lacking only a flow of magic from her hands.

Joseph looked down at the ground and then back at Willow. A smile crossed his face. "Until we meet again." He pointed his wand at the balloon head. A loud bang exploded through the air, causing all three girls to cover their ears. Clairity and Ashlyn dropped Simon from where he was suspended. He landed on the deflating balloon head. The prince had pierced the snake's head and they were all falling. That was the last the girls saw of either one of them.

Willow lost her footing and ended up tangled in the material that once formed the giant snake. Jessie and Dezi pulled her out by her arms, fabric still woven around her legs, dragging the knotted remains of the serpent's tongue along with her. Clairity and Ashlyn had already found a way out of the mess and were safely on solid ground. The search of the deflated balloon continued for some time, but there was no sign of the two princes. They somehow managed to slip away.

"We should regroup, find Malarchy and the mayor. We need to make sure everyone is okay," William said.

They found the mayor standing outside her office. Constable Black was inside with a team of officers and medical attendants cleaning up the bodies. The crowds were dispersing now. Officers were directing everyone to head home. A missing persons line was set up for people to report loved ones who didn't make it back. It was going to take a while to sort through the bodies scattered on the street. Some were the missing corpses stolen from graves and others, people who were unfortunate enough to have been killed before the princes were stopped.

"Perhaps there is somewhere else we can go to speak?" William asked the mayor.

They found themselves sitting inside a small cafe, hidden away in a back room. A woman wearing a purple apron brought in a pot of coffee with cups, leaving them on the table for anyone in the group to ask for. When the pot lifted into the air, Ashlyn pushed her chair back away from the table in shock. The carafe proceeded to pour a hot drink for the mayor, adding milk and sugar. A stir stick mixed the drink well before the cup slid over the table stopping in front of Hilary.

"Will someone please tell me what is going on?" the mayor demanded. "Does this have to do with those two women we are holding?"

William explained the story to her as the others sat around listening. Every so often Clairity would fill in details that were missing from his view.

"We will need to move the location of the city immediately." She looked around the room. "I hope you understand those two girls will have to be punished for their involvement. I can't release them to you now."

"Annabelle and Lilabeth are dead." Mike looked down at the table. The reality of what happened was now setting in. "The princes took them out quickly. Probably why they went to your office first."

"Why?"

"To tie up loose ends," Clairity responded, taking the attention away from Mike. "They needed to make sure no one knew who they were or what their plans were. They were silently eliminating anyone capable of resisting a takeover of this world, starting with your city."

"There is a lot we will need to discuss now." Aslo appeared on the table. "We can see that the people who reside here can live peacefully in this realm and we have no desire to change that. However, there are those who are a danger. Those are the ones who need to be returned to their home worlds."

"What do you propose?" Hillary asked.

"An alliance of sorts. The details would need to be worked out. There would be laws against interfering with the terunji," Aslo responded. "We would agree not to deport any of your residents living peacefully."

The mayor took in a deep breath and let it out slowly. "I can only speak for our city, but we will agree to work with you."

"How many cities are there?" Ashlyn asked.

Hilary laughed. "Hundreds. Each one would have to be approached and agree on their own. I have no say in their affairs."

"Is there no connection between them?" Malarchy asked, surprised as to the system of government being suggested. None of them expected the underground to be so large. It was amazing they were able to stay hidden. There must be something that protected their secrecy.

"The mayors set their own laws to abide by for each city. We get together a few times a year. But normally, there is little to discuss. Things may be about to change."

"You have directors who run things for all the cities, though. We saw one in the parade earlier," Clairity said.

"Yes a few: the Director of Knowledge, Director of Ancient Artifacts, Director of Dangerous Substances, Director of New Residents and Director of Secrecy. There are several low-level governmental positions as well. They work to ensure the safety of our kind, but their involvement in city affairs is usually minimal. Given the circumstances, they may take a bigger role in the alliance you are suggesting."

"Can you set up some meetings? We need to establish common ground with everyone," William said.

"After clean-up and the city is safely moved to a new location, I can try. Not too many will jump at the chance to meet with guardians and possibly be exiled. This is a delicate situation."

"You do understand that guardians created portals between the realms to ensure the safety of magical beings," Willow said. "Safety of all beings is their main concern and always has been. There is no reason to interfere in this situation."

"Yes," she answered. "But the blood wars were long ago. Only those who have studied history know anything about them. There aren't many of us around. Education has only become a priority in the past few decades and history, unfortunately, is not the most important subject on the curriculum. With the random openings into this world becoming more and more frequent, there are more and more empyral migrating here. The schools need to teach people how to fit in, live in this world and control their magic. We try to help newcomers from the time they arrive until they either pass on or go home. Even with as many different schools as we have now, there is still a need for even more."

"What about threats? There are some races who cannot be rehabilitated to live in peace with other races." Willow kept her eyes on the woman. There was something odd about the mayor, almost like a blank aura. She couldn't quite figure out what it was she was sensing.

"There is a special task force that assesses and handles threats," Hilary answered. "They have averted many disasters before they happened. Such events are few and far between."

"Seems they dropped the ball tonight." Mike chose to stand and was pacing around the table.

His energy was reading nervous. Willow felt for him. The pain he was experiencing was one she was familiar with. Her mind wandered to her parents. At least there was hope she could find them again. Mike's family was gone forever.

"This is the first I have heard of this king and his family. They will be on the radar now. Hopefully our people will help find them and end whatever plans they have. If they are planning an invasion, they will be in for a fight."

William agreed they would help with the clean-up of the city, which lasted most the night. A Special Forces team came in and returned the stolen bodies to their proper graves. They left a report with the mayor that all bodies were recovered except one, noting the Roman numerals on the grave stone. It was Estonia's. The bodies of victims were taken to the city's funeral parlour. After identification, loved ones were contacted and grieving began.

The Empowered printed a headline of *Guardians and Keepers Save City*. Apparently, there was a leak from the coffee shop as to what really happened the evening before. Perhaps it was the woman who served the coffee. The story included a lot of information about King Cornelius and his sons as well. The picture on the front page was of William and Mike swinging swords at the heads of two of the attackers to protect a group of young children.

After that, the mayor found she didn't have to make any calls; everyone was calling her to set up meetings. They all wanted an appointment with someone from the guardian camp. The mayor took it upon herself to inform them official invitations to a conference would be sent after her city was moved and safe from any further attacks.

William decided it would be best to leave some people to help with the relocation and security of the city. They could also work with the mayor on awareness seminars for scared people, which there were a lot of. Malarchy, Iskander, and Jade would remain behind. Diana would also be sent in a few weeks to help with the efforts, if they could spare her.

Delilah created her own position, which she named Director of Enemy Awareness, with Jessica by her side. Gavin and his three friends agreed to act as liaisons to the vamprite. He warned that not all of his kind were interested in peaceful relations, but he would spread the word. A common foe could change some minds.

Everyone else headed back to camp with the help of Faramund. They were all tired and ready for a long sleep before dealing with anything else.

King Cornelius

Lance was awoken by a summons from his father to breakfast. It was an unusual request, since the princes all liked to sleep in. After dressing, he headed down to the dining room. He found all of his siblings already seated at the table.

"Good morning," he said, slipping into the chair reserved for him. The large wooden table was filled with pastries and breads. Pots of coffee and tea were placed strategically so that they were easily accessible by everyone.

"Is it?" his father asked. "What exactly is good about it?"

Lance glanced at his brothers, having absolutely no idea what was going on. "Sorry, did I miss something?"

"Perhaps if you were with your brothers last night, they might not have failed, or at least not as miserably as they did." His father's face turned red with anger. "All I have seen from the lot of you is failure this past while. With no victories, the men are starting to talk. They are beginning to perceive us as weak. They doubt our resolve, our cause, our abilities. The kingdom whispers behind my back. I will not appear as a fool."

"You are exaggerating, Father," Joseph said, sipping his coffee.

"Am I? Perhaps you would like to inform Apopp of your endeavours last night." The king took his seat at the head of the table. "I thought not. What happened? I shall have to report your mess myself."

"The same witches who thwarted my sisters interfered. We don't know who they are, or where they came from, but we will find out," Joseph replied.

"So in summary, my wonderful children have lost three guardians, put the entire empyral society on notice of our plans, and lost the Kriller," the king bellowed.

"Why do we care about those freaks, anyways? I am glad the Kriller are gone. Watching their faces made me ill," Ophelia said, dropping her biscuit on the table with a look of disgust.

King Cornelius let out a growling noise. "They are possibly the only race smart enough to figure out how to bring down the barriers between the worlds completely. You have risked our entire operation. Do I not have anyone who will bring me a victory to show our kingdom we are still effective? Are my children that weak and pathetic?"

Zoe stood. "We will, Father, the next opening we find. We won't disappoint you."

"Make sure that you don't." The king went back to eating a cream-filled cake. He waved his hand in a shooing motion, dismissing his children from the table.

Zoe motioned to her sisters to prepare for another invasion. They headed off to pick out troops and weapons to take to a new world.

It was afternoon before an opening was stable enough to travel through. The plan was simple. There were about two hours to enter, conquer, and return. Stepping through, they faced something they never expected. The world was entirely snow and ice. The girls were not prepared for the extreme weather change and found themselves shivering from the temperature drop.

"Let's just quickly see if there is any sign of life in this forsaken place and meet back at the entrance. I don't want to be in this cold long," Zoe said, her teeth chattering.

Ophelia took her men to the left of the hole they entered through, while Sissy went right. Zoe headed straight forward. All they found as far they could see was snow and ice, nothing more. It was Sissy's group who would find life. Even with the distance between them, the other two heard blood curdling screams coming from their younger sister's direction.

Hurrying over to see what happened, they found the bodies of men from their army lying in the snow, frozen to death. Zoe and Ophelia exchanged glances. There was no sign of Sissy.

"Spread out, look for footprints. Find my sister!" Zoe yelled.

A small creature came into sight. It was a couple feet tall with a face that looked like a goat, but in a silver and blue colour. From the scant clothing covering its body, it was obvious that cold was not an issue for the beast. Two men approached it with weapons drawn. It hardly looked like it would be of any consequence to their forces.

"Do you know where my sister is?" Zoe asked it. She received only a strange look back. She tried again. "Do you know what happened to these men?"

The creature smiled, revealing sharp claw-like teeth. "Yesssssssss."

It jumped up and bit one of the men near the elbow of his arm. The man screamed in pain. His arm turned blue and black with frostbite. His blood was freezing. They watched the frost travel through the man's veins. Once the cold hit his heart, there was silence and the man fell over dead. Zoe pulled out her wand and aimed it at the creature, sending light flying at it. She missed and the beast laughed. The laughter multiplied as more and more creatures popped out of the snow.

Zoe ordered the men to attack as she and her sister retreated. Once inside their home world again, she commanded whoever was nearby to watch the gateway while she tried using any magic she could to close the gap. Nothing worked. Ophelia ran for more troops to watch the gateway until it closed in case any of the creatures tried to slip through. After they were sure the hole was safely shut, Zoe and her sister called for all of the family to meet immediately. They gathered in front of a fireplace, where their mother was sipping tea.

"Where is Sissy?" the queen asked.

"She is lost." Tears swelled in Ophelia's eyes.

Zoe described what they encountered in detail, her head hung in sadness. There was a real concern for Sissy in her voice.

"And you left her there?" Lance asked. "She could be hurt. How long before the hole closes? Why are we wasting time?"

"It's closed," his sister answered. "We don't know what world it was. Nor do we know if or when a hole will form again."

"We need to do something. We can mount an attack and find her somehow. We can figure out how to open the door again." Lance was ready to put together a rescue mission. "We have people studying these things. Someone must have an idea how to duplicate the entrance way. We have to at least try."

"No!" his father exclaimed. "You have disappointed me again. How many men did we lose?"

"Father?" Zoe was surprised by his reaction.

"How many?" The king yelled.

"Three hundred, maybe more," she answered, looking down.

"I ask for victory and all I get is failure. You disappoint me, all of you. I will waste no more men on a foolish girl who couldn't find her way back home. This will cause more disruption in our forces as it is." The king turned his back to them. "How can men believe they can follow me to victory, if my own children can't? Three hundred men is no small number."

"Mother," Lance started.

"She is no longer your sister, forget her. I suggest you work harder to please your father or you will all be in the same position," the queen answered without emotion. "Don't worry, your father and I can have another child to replace your sister. It will be as if none of this ever happened. You will be just as happy again."

Lance started to walk out.

"Where are you going?" his mother asked.

"To call in some favours. I am going to get my sister back, with or without your help." He left and headed to wait for an entrance to the main world to open. He half-expected someone to come after him, maybe even offer to help. No one did.

Chapter Fifty-Three

Willow found she was one of the last to wake up. She stretched her stiff back, no doubt a result of wearing the dress for such a long period of time the day before. She joined the others at the table in the command centre. Sitting in plain view were the portal stones Mike brought back from the swamp.

"We figured out where they belong." Sarah's face beamed with excitement. "They are the portal stones to the Kriller's home world. We can send them home now."

"Great!" Willow exclaimed. The Kriller didn't fit in this world, or perhaps it was this world that wasn't ready to accept them. She knew they were uncomfortable here and longing for their home. Who could blame them? Most of the time they were here they spent locked up like animals to avoid being seen. "When are we sending them?"

"Nathan is saying his goodbyes now," Diana said. Her grandson took a real interest in the Kriller. He was highly intelligent and found he understood their race. They had a connection. It wasn't hard to tell he was going to miss them dearly. Diana promised her grandson that he could visit sometime. The beings liked Nathan as well. He took good care of them in the camp. Where some would see an odd-looking person, the boy saw an amazing race. He was one of the few in the world who could look past their appearance and see their persons. He gave them hope that one day this world would be ready for them to visit and share their knowledge.

Faramund transported everyone to the portal site. This time, Aslo opened the portal. There was no need for Willow to create a storm to open it. Instead, the stones simply flew up into the correct positions and the gateway opened. She sighed to herself in the background. Using that amount of power was exciting - something she looked forward to.

After goodbyes were said, the group of Kriller headed back to their homeland. Willow moved beside Nathan and put her arm around his shoulders. They had been good friends for as long as they both could remember. She could see his pain - how he was struggling to keep back tears. She felt for the boy. There hadn't been a lot of time for any of them to spend one on one with him, especially since he was always working on the prophecies. Willow made a mental note to speak to William about doing some kid stuff with him. At his age, he shouldn't be stuck with his nose in a book deciphering prophecies every day.

Faramund transported the group back. Walking over to the cabin to check in, Willow realized that Acacia was sitting in the training field again. The rest of the camp was gathered round.

"What's going on?" she asked.

Shelby appeared and answered. "There are some questions you still would like answered?" The avian guardian agreed to take patrol again while everyone else was busy with the Kriller. "Is there something that still bothers you about what happened?"

"Yes," she answered. "There is something." Willow moved closer to the tree and placed her hand on its trunk. She felt a warm sensation. The tree was glowing. It illuminated her face.

"What troubles you?" Acacia asked.

"Estonia, her body was never found."

"Yes, in life she was a strong medium, able to cross barriers others couldn't. Her essence was displaced from her body before it died. Effectively, her spirit was trapped in this world but had no physical body to live in. When her body was reanimated by the princes, they basically replenished the living tissues. She took control of it again. The other corpses held no being within them. Their essences had long since moved on. She contacted you because she saw the future. She knew what was going to happen."

"Why did she run?" Willow asked.

"She was afraid. She didn't know who she could trust. She is well and you may one day cross paths again."

"So there is another world after we die?"

"I can't answer that," Acacia said. "There are some journeys you must take for yourself. One day, all living things find out that answer. You must wait until it is your time."

"You said her essence was displaced?" Willow asked.

"Yes, like another you know," the tree answered. as if reading the girl's mind. "Your friend's essence is with us right now, but she has no body to return to."

Clairity gasped and covered her mouth. She destroyed Camile's body and now the girl was stuck between worlds.

Acacia's branches began to sway and glow gold, silver, pink, green, and blue. Beneath them formed a figure. The whole camp watched as features began to form. It was Camile. When the colours retreated, she took a breath and fell to the ground. Willow rushed to her side.

"Camile?"

"Hi," she said in a quiet, squeaky voice.

"I trust you have learnt your lesson?" Acacia asked the girl. "There are no shortcuts to life, child. Learn things as they come."

"Definitely," Camile answered.

Willow helped her to her feet and gave her a big hug. She turned to the tree. "How?"

"A body is just organic matter. It is our essences that make us who we are. I can duplicate matter, but not a soul. Camile's soul was not destroyed. It has been with you since she lost her body. She has helped you more than you know, leaving you clues and coming to your aid in dreams. All I did was give her essence a place to go." Acacia addressed Camile, "Make use of your second chance. A third is unlikely. Learn from your mistakes and help others avoid what you endured."

Camile agreed and the two stepped back. Again, the branches swayed and glowed. A second figure appeared. It was Denny, the woman from the tour. She fell to the ground and both girls rushed over to help her up.

Before she even regained her senses, the ancient tree disappeared again. The rest of the camp ran to them. Everyone wanted to touch them, make sure they were real. They heard the words Acacia said, but it was still a miracle in their eyes.

Once Camile and Denny were fed and everyone settled down in the cabin the questions came.

"What was it like?" Ashlyn asked.

"Strange. I mean, I was there, right beside people and no one could see me or hear me. There are others who are stuck in that state as well. It's sad, really. A lot of them don't even know they aren't inside a body. Denny was the only one I recognized. I tried to keep her with me after I found her." Camile smiled. "I am so glad to be back. You have no idea. It was scary being alone and not knowing what sort of a future I would have."

"Were there any who were actually dead? Ghosts?" Ashlyn asked.

"I only saw those who had been displaced in some way. I don't think any of them actually died. But I never really asked. If you are asking if there is an afterlife, I don't know."

Denny was still quiet, sipping on a tea while listening to the others talk. "I don't understand any of this. How did I get like that? I don't remember anything after leaving on the walking tour." Her face was pale white, showing signs of shock. Her pulse was elevated and her skin turned clammy.

The girls took turns explaining to the woman what happened with the necklace she bought and the Glaquool. Since it was clear the story was frightening her, they left out the part about destroying her body, simply ended it with the camp helping to reunite her essence with her physical body. She was still going to need some time to process everything. Zsiga offered to take her to a place to lie down. There would be time to worry about taking her home when she felt better. After she agreed, he escorted her over to the medical facility where Richard and Mary could monitor her situation.

Faramund excused himself to go check in with the guardians who were outside on patrol again. They were doing more than their fair share of security sweeps and thought he should offer to help.

Most of the others, knowing there would be lots of time in the future to speak with Camile, decided to let the girl have some peace. Diana and Nathan headed off to find something to eat. That left the girls to catch up and spend time together. It was exactly what Camile needed.

"I am so sorry for sending your other body into oblivion," Clairity blurted out with the most sincere look on her face.

For a moment, there was silence. The girls all looked at each other, then broke out into laughter. It was such an odd comment to ever have to make.

"It wasn't your fault. You couldn't let that thing go loose. I understand." Camile stood up and walked around the room. "Can we go outside? I really want to move around and feel things again."

"Of course," Willow answered.

Walking outside, Willow was reminded of how different the seasons were in this world. A cold wind blew, leaving them all with a chill. Only Camile was happy to feel it.

"Jack Frost is nipping at our noses already," Sarah said.

The other girls all came to a dead stop and looked at her strangely. Sarah, far too often, forgot that the girls didn't know all of her world's sayings or traditions.

"Why is someone going to bite our noses?" Ashlyn asked, covering hers with her hand.

Sarah laughed. "No, it's just a saying, I don't even know where it comes from. When the weather gets colder, we talk about Jack Frost."

"Who is he?"

"No, he isn't real. I mean, I don't think he is real." Sarah stopped and thought for a moment. She wasn't sure anymore what was real and what wasn't. There was a possibility that the stories about Jack Frost came from some blurred form of reality. "Maybe we should check those stories out sometime."

Willow turned around to comment to Sarah, but something else caught her eye. Walking across the lawn, Faramund was escorting someone. She watched William and Mike rush out to meet them. As they came close, she could see it was Lance.

She headed over in time to hear Mike say, "What are you doing here?"

"I need to talk to Willow," he answered.

"How did you know where to find us?" William had a tone of concern in his voice.

"We have known about your little base for some time. You were too small to be a threat to us. We left you alone. My family hasn't put together the connection between you and the girls," the prince answered.

"And you aren't going to share?" Mike enquired

"If I was going to, I would have already. I have known for some time." Lance seemed unimpressed by the guard's line of questioning. "I will, however, suggest that it won't be long before they figure it out. You might want to consider relocating in the near future. I suggest far away."

"Why, exactly, haven't you told them? And why are you helping us? Why would we trust you?" William seemed truly interested in a possible answer.

Lance sighed. "I have my reasons. You can choose to trust me or not, but they will eventually come here looking for her."

"What's going on?" Willow broke into the conversation.

"Apparently, he knew we were here the whole time." Mike moved to stand between the prince and Willow.

"I need to speak to you," Lance said, looking into her eyes.

"Anything you have to say to her, you can say in front of us," William said.

The prince's face showed signs of desperation. "I need a favour."

Willow gasped. What could she possibly help the prince with? She looked down at the ground, kicking a few leaves aside with her shoe. He helped her when she asked him to. He risked everything to come to her. She looked up and nodded her head in agreement, resolve exploding from her eyes. She would help him now, no matter what anyone else said, even if she had no idea what she was getting into.

Chapter Fifty-Four

Over the past few months, a pattern had formed with each day that passed being equally as bizarre as, if not more than, the one before it. A week ago, if anyone had whispered sneaking suspicions that she would be sitting in the command centre having a conversation with William, Mike and Prince Lance at the same time, she never would have believed them - a certain level of hysterics most likely accompanying her disbelief. Yet here she was, wondering if the three of them were going to kill each other before a chance emerged to find out exactly why they were there.

Lance expected a favour in exchange for his help. She knew that day would come, but never expected him to walk into their camp and ask her for it - a dream, perhaps.

The prince's necrid flames were instrumental in the destruction of a couple of pendants - charms possessed by beings from an obscure race known as the Glaquool. They were dangerous bodiless creatures made of gases, who could displace a person's essence or spirit from their physical body. Once a body became an empty shell, the Glaquool were free to take control of it. The worst part was this race hid in everyday items like charms. All an innocent person needed to do was touch a possessed item for the process to begin. It could be anything and anywhere, although she figured the item would be marked with a symbol on it - something similar to a warped sideways number eight.

Camile and Denny both experienced the whole process. Luckily, they weren't killed, although their bodies were destroyed. Their essences lingered, unnoticed, walking between life and whatever came after that. Acacia, the tree of justice, re-created duplicates of their bodies. In the end, their physical and spiritual selves were reunited.

"We aren't getting anywhere," Mike argued, pushing his chair back from the table, its legs making a loud scraping noise on the wooden floor. "How did you get here?"

"Do we really need to go over this again? Your camp has been here for a very long time and we have known about it for a very long time. I came here to speak with Willow."

"To ask for a favour," William added, cutting off the prince's words. "Why would she help you?"

The prince laughed. "Because I helped her when she asked."

"Helped her? You're holding her friends and family prisoners. How about releasing some on good faith?" William asked.

"I can't do that," Lance replied. "I am not in control of the prisoners. My family would not permit it. They do not know I am here, nor are they interested in what I need to do."

"Which is what?" Willow asked.

Willow extended her hand, a message to her friends to hold back on their urges to interfere, at least for the moment. She sighed, leaning back in her chair. The muscles of both Mike and William held a certain level of tension - primed and ready to jump in front of her to protest any chance of her agreeing to help the prince.

William stood. The table shook, the chair he previously sat in slamming hard against it, making a thud. He turned away from them, his fingers rubbing the strained muscles at the back of his neck. Closing his eyes, he recited the numbers one through ten in a whisper.

A loud crack shifted Willow's attention to Mike. Only slivers of pencil remained in his grip. The rest lay broken on the table, jagged edges facing outwards. Anxiety steamed from the two like a kettle boiling on a stove. The situation unfolding in front of her required diffusing, but how?

"I figured there was going to be far too much testosterone in this room for you three men to handle," Malarchy complained. Amongst the commotion, slipping into the cabin without detection was the easiest task put before him in a very long time.

Spinning around to face the newcomer, William redirected his emotions. "You are supposed to be helping the good mayor. Why have you returned?" he demanded, slanting his eyes slightly in a search for anything that could be construed as defiance.

"Yes indeed. Things are fine in the city and I have every intention of returning," Malarchy replied, his voice calm and unemotional, unaffected by alpha-male rituals. "Faramund contacted me to tell me of our visitor. He thought you boys might need some mediation. I have to admit, I agreed. So I have returned for a few hours to help. How about I take control of this meeting and you three lovesick puppies calm down?"

Mike flashed him a disgruntled look. Folding his arms over his chest, a gruff sounding *huff* escaped his lungs. His eyes remained glued on Malarchy. As if joining in a primal ceremony, William added his own crass grunt before taking a seat at the table again. The prince shifted his eyes between the two, sizing them up, a quirky smile never faltering from his lips.

"What?" Willow yelled.

"Our innocent naive girl," Malarchy teased. "Please don't pretend you haven't noticed these three playing for your affections. Not even you could have missed the fist fight in the yard the other day."

Willow's face glowed, turning fifty-one shades of red. Every corner of the room bore witness to the irregular beating of her heart. Looking up, three sets of eyes met hers, each watching her carefully for signs of an unspoken choice.

"I thought that was because of the news about Annabelle," she mumbled. "I think I need some air." Anxiety demanded an exit be found, to escape not only her own emotions, but those of would-be suitors as well. She side-eyed the door. It was close. She could make a break for it.

"Sit down," Malarchy demanded, his voice superimposed an undeniable stern authority over every word. "We are going to figure out what is going on and to do that, we need you."

She planted her bottom firmly in the chair, but turned her head away, avoiding all eye contact. There wasn't enough time to process the new information hurtling at her from what felt like every direction. How could all three of them have feelings for her? All this time she thought she was being a silly, lovesick girl, fantasizing about the men in her life wanting to be with her. The truth didn't set her free - it made everything a million times more complicated.

"Lance was about to tell us about the favour he is asking," she explained, figuring someone should break the silence before Malarchy became really upset.

"Do we care what he wants? We can't actually be thinking about helping him. He's the enemy." Mike's voice deepened, teetering on the fine line between yelling and screaming. "Don't think for a second I am going to agree with this farce. It's probably a trap."

"We need to hear him out," Willow argued. "He helped me when I asked and I am going to give him the same courtesy. If you two don't want to be involved, that is your choice."

"Well then," Malarchy said, glancing between the three men. "If no one is leaving, let's hear what is so urgent. I personally am very interested. It took a lot of courage to come here. You must know you aren't thought of fondly in the camp."

The prince smiled. "Yes, I do in fact realize that." Looking down at his thumbs, he began twiddling them, almost as if thumb wrestling with himself. "My sister is missing. I need help finding her."

"Not the one who wants to eat me for breakfast, I hope," Willow blurted out, forgetting her own advice to hold her tongue at the first thing that came to mind. She slipped down in her chair clenching her eye lids tight, not wanting an answer or reaction to her previous words.

"No, not Ophelia. She hasn't forgotten about the wolves, though. It's Sissy, the youngest of my brothers and sisters. After the events of the past few weeks, my father is quite upset. I don't even know what happened in the city, but you must have really put a wrench in my brothers' plans. Combine that with my sisters' problems from their previously successful tour, the one you destroyed and his anger raged at all six of us. None of us are used to anything less than victory, at least until you and your friends showed up."

"And what does that have to do with us? You want us to apologize to him for you?" William asked.

"No, not at all. I would prefer Willow never go near my parents, or my brothers. It wouldn't be safe for her."

"Right, and Willow's safety is your number one priority?" Mike scoffed.

"Back to the story. We aren't here to discuss Willow." Malarchy's teeth ground together. He straightened his back, folding his hands together on the table in front of him.

Lance nodded and continued. "He insisted his children prove their allegiance and bring him a victory of some sort immediately. Joseph and Zoe often compete for his favouritism. It was the girls who accepted this particular challenge. They waited for the first stable way into another world and without even knowing what realm it was, they entered, taking three hundred soldiers with them. Only Zoe and Ophelia returned. Sissy was lost and the soldiers were dead."

"So why doesn't your family go find her?" Mike asked. For the first time, his words held no contempt, replacing it with an odd level of civility - something he hadn't offered since the prince's arrival.

"My father was angry at the loss. He disowned her. He refused to lose any more men. The entrance way to the world closed. I don't know what world it is or when an opening will happen again. My sister is out there alone. I can't leave her there. Please help me find her." His eyes glossed over.

William rubbed his hands over his face, then in one swift motion, moved them in front of him, popping the joints in his fingers until satisfied with the loud cracking sounds. "I can't believe we are even discussing this, but… what can you tell us about the world?"

"You have to be kidding!" Mike yelled. "You aren't really thinking about helping him? This is nuts. The guy tortured me."

"That wasn't torture. I merely smacked you around a little. Sorry about that." There wasn't an ounce of remorse hidden in Lance's words. In fact, if anything, he sounded pleased with himself.

"I want to assess the risk to this world," William explained, his answer directed at Mike. "If there is something that can kill three hundred men that easily, I think we need to look into it and make sure the realm in question is secured. If we end up having to go into this world, there is no reason not to find the girl at the same time."

"I agree," Willow said. "Leaving someone to perish isn't our style." Not that she knew what their style was, "But how do we figure out what world we are looking for?"

"Are there any details can you tell us about the realm? Details of what it looked like or what its inhabitants looked like?" William asked.

"Zoe mentioned it was a frozen land, all ice and snow. The girls were shivering from the cold. There was a storm the whole time they were there. It made it hard for them to see. Neither Zoe nor Ophelia saw any buildings or roads - no signs of civilization. The creatures they came across were small, maybe a couple feet tall. Their faces resembled goats, but more silvery-blue in colour. They understood our language." He stopped for a moment, trying to remember the details from the story Zoe told. "They weren't affected by the cold... didn't seem to have to dress to keep warm."

"How did the men die?" William asked. The pencil he held furiously scratched on a pad of paper. The scribbles held no meaning, at least to anyone other than William himself.

"The first man they saw die, a creature jumped up and bit his arm. It turned a black blue as if frostbitten. The colour seemed to travel through his body. They described it like a venom made of ice had been injected into his arm. When it reached his heart, he fell over dead. We have never encountered anything like them before."

William let out a breath of air. The look on his face told the story of a man who had come across these creatures before and the experience wasn't a good one.

"Do you know something?" Lance asked.

William sighed, concentrating on his doodling. "Yes, I know of them. We lost a few good men and women to them a long time ago. They are known as the Frostica, another cousin to the faeries. We are going to need more people in on this," he said. The pencil fell from his hand, rolling away on landing, its path aided by a slight vibration - a result of his chair pushing away from the table.

"I need a moment with Lance." Willow's expression held every emotion and none at the same time, making it impossible for anyone to read. Ignoring the strange looks Mike and William flashed her, she continued, "Maybe you could send Nathan and his grandmother in too."

"My work here is done. William, Mike, maybe you could see me off?" Malarchy motioned for the two to leave the room. He nodded at Willow, giving his approval of her plans. Closing the door tightly behind them, the three walked across the field to where Faramund waited to return to the underground city.

With the others gone, an uneasy silence grew - faster and stronger than a weed out of control. Finally the door opened again, breaking the awkwardness that threatened to suffocate them.

"You wanted to see us?" Nathan asked, finding it difficult to conceal his excitement at the premise of being summoned.

There was little for a boy to do in the camp. Being twelve meant he was too young to join the adults and there weren't really any other kids his age. When the chance there might be a need for a prophecy to be deciphered or his opinion on something appeared, his face lit up, beaming with the joy most children only experienced on Christmas morning.

"Yes," Willow replied. "I want you two to meet Prince Lance. Lance, I want you to meet Diana, your aunt and her grandson, Nathan." If she thought the room uncomfortable before, it was a hundred times worse now. Diana and Nathan both took seats at the table, after which, no one moved or uttered a word - the ticking of a clock indicating precious time passing.

Out of the blue, Nathan spoke. "Why do you want to kill us?"

"Nathan!" Diana yelled. She covered her mouth with her hand, staring at the boy. Leave it to a kid to ask the uncomfortable questions without any problem.

Lance glanced at the boy, emotion running rampant in his eyes. "I don't. We don't want to hurt family." He paused. "We have been searching for your grandmother to bring her home."

"And my mom, my dad, my grandad? Where are they?" Nathan asked, the sadness in his expression demanding an answer.

Lance glanced at each of them. Silent questions flowed from his perfect blue eyes. No one mentioned his aunt had a family.

"They are missing, like my parents," Willow explained, biting one side of her bottom lip. Even if he couldn't release them, maybe he would at least be able to tell them news of their loved ones.

"I don't understand," he said, revealing nothing. "We were told you were a prisoner. That you were being held captive against your will. No one ever mentioned a family."

"I am not," Diana replied. "I never was. It was a long time ago that the guardians asked my help to protect the realms. I accepted. Your father wanted to go as well, but he had tasted the blood of the magical creatures. It tainted him... chilled his heart. Not being included in the offer made him angry. I didn't realize just how angry until Willow met you." She reached across the table and took Willow's hand, silent affection exchanging between them. "I married a wonderful man a year after that. My son is Nathan's father."

"My father would never hurt family," Lance said.

"Except your sister," Willow stated.

The prince darted a look in her direction. The blue in his eyes now held an image of fire - burning bright. She could see his world turning upside down in the flames, shattering self-imposed defences. Willow shivered, thinking back to when she found out the world she was living in was a lie. Everything changed so fast after that, leading her to the seat she was sitting in right now.

"What happened to his sister?" Diana asked.

It didn't take long for Lance to fill them in on the world Sissy was lost in and the Frostica. Willow sat quietly, the image of the burning flames in Lance's eyes etched into her mind. She had seen them before, but at the time, dismissed it as lighting. The flames were somehow attached to his anger. There was something about emotions and how they affected magic that she was just starting to understand. Feelings - love, hate, happiness, sadness, anger, kindness, jealousy, pride, hope, fear - all seemed to enhance magic, or maybe even create it. That's why magic had an aura.

"There isn't anything I have read on them," Nathan stated, breaking her train of thought with his confusion. "William knows them? Weird." He tilted his head slightly to one side, his pupils shifting back and forth, accessing information from the deepest parts of his brain. "There is a prophecy or two about ice and snow. We should probably take a closer look at them before you go anywhere."

"You have no problem helping me?" Lance asked. He leaned back in his chair, observing the three. The blue flames dimmed back to a glow, no more than a shadow of what they had been only a moment ago.

"I have no problem helping you." Diana reached across the table, taking his hand in her own. "I am glad I had the opportunity to meet at least one of my nephews."

"I have no problem… if Willow has no problem." Nathan stood and grabbed the two prophecy books from a shelf behind him. "Ashlyn says you have the hots for Willow. Is that true?"

Shades of red made a return appearance on her face, heat rushing to her cheeks. "Nathan!"

"It's okay," Lance answered, smiling. "I guess I do."

"Neat," Nathan said, opening the books. Pages flipped, searching for the passages he mentioned earlier.

"We need to wait for the others first," Willow said. "Mike and William won't be happy if they aren't here for this. You want to call them?"

"They going to duke it out again?" Nathan normally liked using his telepathic powers to call the others. He wasn't allowed to use them nearly as much as he would have liked to.

"I hope not," Willow answered, rolling her eyes.

Lance seemed more amused by Nathan's comment than concerned. "Do they fight over you often?"

"Oh," Diana exclaimed, her eyes lighting up in revelation. "That's what everyone was talking about yesterday." She glanced at Willow, smiling. "You are a popular one, aren't you?"

Willow's face hit the table. Circumstances warranted banging her forehead a few times. The prince's laughter only egged her on. The situation was far from funny to her. Most of her life she had spent alone, the guardians her only family. This newfound popularity was frightening and enticing at the same time. She had no idea what to do.

Then do nothing, until you do. The voice in her head belonged to Kiera. She often forgot the feline guardian was joined with her. It didn't help they had remained so quiet through everything else.

Can I do that? Won't they get mad? she asked. Having someone she could talk to, without having everyone in the room hear the conversation too, was a relief.

If they really care for you, they will wait till you are ready. If they don't, it is best you find out before you lose your heart. There are different types of love. Take your time and be sure of what you, and the man in question, feel. If it's meant to be, you will know.

Kiera's words always made sense. Willow was still a small child when her parents went missing and were declared dead. Without Aslo and Kiera, she would have grown up completely alone. Without them, she wouldn't be the same person she now was.

No sense wondering. There are more important issues at hand, Aslo reminded her. He was her voice of reason and the more stern of the two guardians.

Willow mused at how she sometimes forgot they could hear everything she thought. In fact, the only places they couldn't hear her were in dreams, unless invited, and within any magical barrier that disrupted communications.

She snapped back to reality at the sound of the door opening. The rest of the camp filed in, seemingly unimpressed at the thought of another meeting. All eyes concentrated on the new guest. Whispers of speculation circulated the room. Willow glanced at the faces of those arriving, trying to find the lips from which she heard her name amongst the rumblings.

Zsiga began brewing coffee as usual. Meetings wouldn't be the same without his freshly-made pots of liquid energy. Even though William hadn't come in yet, he poured a cup for him, sitting it on the table in front of his usual seat. Gasps broke out when Zsiga offered Lance a cup as well. The prince accepted the offer of hospitality, glancing into the swirling liquid as if searching for an explanation.

"Just because we aren't all on the same page, doesn't mean we can't all agree coffee is a fine drink." Zsiga smiled, filling a few more cups before starting a new pot.

William entered last, smiling at the sight of the steaming mug waiting for him. He nodded a *thank you*. "We have another possible breach from outside this world to investigate. I am going to give you a bit of background on the subject before we discuss anything else." He leaned back, pushing the chair into a position balancing on two legs, waiting for the whispers and rumbles to settle down. Everyone in the room knew he meant *before they discussed the prince being in the camp*.

Satisfied eager gossipers were finished with their discussions, his chair slammed back onto all four legs. "A while back, we came into contact with an unusual group of beings called Frostica... direct cousins to the faeries. From what we have all seen in the past, I am sure you can imagine that they have a side that can be helpful, light and fun and a side that is more destructive and dangerous. Of course, we all have those two sides in us, but these beings have extremes. In particular they have a hostile side, which could be described as children having temper tantrums."

"Jack Frost," Sarah blurted out.

William laughed. "He very well could be based on one of them. I hadn't really considered that. We will have to do some research into those stories. I doubt there will be anything helpful that we don't already know, though. Having said that, we should understand the number of myths and legends in this world are tremendous in number. I doubt we have enough time to look at them all."

He returned to the story. "The Frostica are ice faeries. They live in extreme cold and enjoy ice and snow. Standing about two feet tall, you might find them unusual looking to say the least. Their bodies appear humanoid, but their faces are more animal-like. If they want to communicate, the Frostica will use our language fluently. Their bite is deadly. After the initial penetration of the skin, fangs extend from their jaw, depositing a venom directly into the bloodstream of their victim. The bite effectively sends frostbite throughout the body, resulting in death."

A few grumbles made their way around the room. Willow understood the apprehension around her. She didn't particularly enjoy the sound of that description herself.

"A female named Lanzia proclaimed herself Queen of the Frostica. She was a powerful sorceress, trained in cold magic. Her wand could turn anything into snow and ice. She recruited forces from among her kind and broke the treaty we had with their people. They managed to cover most of the known world in frigid temperatures before we were able to capture them all and send them home."

"Are we talking about the ice age?" Sarah peeked up from her laptop screen, waiting for an answer.

"Yes, we are still under its influence in some regions of the world. Its effects were devastating... complete races wiped out. That wasn't the only problem we had to deal with, though. There were those among the Frostica who didn't want to destroy anything. Like any creature, they had the chance to choose between good and bad. We couldn't punish the whole race for the mistakes of a few. We decided to split their world into two sections. Lanzia and her followers were confined to one and the rest lived in the other."

"So you created a barrier inside a barrier?" Mike asked.

"Effectively, yes. We lost a number of good people through the whole process and guardians too. Some were never accounted for." He paused for a moment, staring into his coffee cup. "Frostica are very energetic. They need to be kept busy. They like to work with their hands. The guards who were stationed outside their portal decided to take it upon themselves to live with those remaining... to teach them to use their energies productively. They used raw materials from their world and began making things. Workshops were built. Soon their creations became too vast. There was nowhere to store them anymore."

Sarah gasped. "Are we talking about what I think we are talking about?" Her eyes widened, revealing a twinkle of excitement in them.

"The guards, Nick and Meredith, decided to put the items to use. So much was lost in the ice age. They went through the portal and delivered the items that were made to the needy. It was their way of giving back."

"You have to be kidding," Mike blurted out. A smile crept over his face. He shook his head. "Is there anything that you people aren't involved in?"

William smiled. "Once a year thereafter, Nick would make a trip to the main world, loaded with gifts. Only Nick uses the portal because the treaty between the Frostica and the guardians states they cannot enter this world. Meredith always stays behind to look after them."

"You are talking about Santa Claus. It's brilliant!" Sarah exclaimed, beaming with joy.

"Yes."

William handed Nathan a book about the history of Mr. and Mrs. Claus as depicted by the main world. His ability to read books and share the information with the others was about to prove valuable once again. Lance sat, watching in awe, leery when it was his turn to learn from the boy. His arm extended with caution. The resulting expression on his face mimicked pure amazement.

"So first area of business is to make a journey to visit Nick and Meredith, to see if anything has changed lately and bring them up to speed. I would like to send a few people first to let them know we are coming. There are no hotels there, so we will be relying on hospitality.

Any volunteers?" William turned his attention to Sarah, already knowing she was definitely interested.

"You know it!" she squealed with delight. "How could anyone give up the chance to actually meet Santa Claus?"

"I'm in, too," Mike blurted out. Seeing everyone looking at him with curiosity, he added, "I can't pass it up... this is too good."

"Great! The two of you will leave as soon as you are ready. Pack warmly. No one is exaggerating the cold. Keep in mind, in another realm you won't be able to contact us. If there are any problems, you will need to come back to the main world to let us know."

"Can we look at the prophecies now?" Nathan asked.

"Did you find something?" William replied, surprised to hear there was news. There had been problems identifying anything from either book as of late.

"Yes, one from each book. They appear to go together, but it's our first attempt. Do you want to hear them separate first?" Nathan's excitement bubbled. He hadn't often had anything solid to offer to meetings lately.

"Let's hear them both, just in case," Willow said, knowing the boy was enjoying the spotlight.

Nathan read from the book written in his homeland first.

When a blast of cold from the north does blow,

A hero's heart will go missing,

To save us it must be the chosen,

Time past by, while doors were locked,

Finally free, they seek to return the favour,

Hidden in ice and snow and sleet,

Locked away in time, it happened before.

"I don't suppose we have any idea what we are talking about yet?" William asked.

"Not really. I imagine parts are referring to the Frostica. It gets better, though, in Estonia's book." Nathan recited the second prophecy.

A single touch stops a river's flow.

Enter lonely sprites, their queen reminiscing.

Her will is cold and heart is frozen.

Now the childcare's joy has been blocked.

While you fight over who is braver,

Careful not to miss exactly what you seek.

Heed this warning or it will happen once more.

"A river? I wonder what river it is talking about," Sarah said, frowning.

"I don't know, but the real fun stuff happens when you put them together." Nathan's smile grew tenfold, as if he had just won an award for being the smartest kid in history.

When a blast of cold from the north does blow,

A single touch stops a river's flow.

A hero's heart will go missing.

Enter lonely sprites, their queen reminiscing.

To save us it must be the chosen,

Her will is cold and heart is frozen.

Time past by, while doors were locked,

Now the children's joy has been blocked.

Finally free, they seek to return the favour,

While you fight over who is braver.

Hidden in ice and snow and sleet,

Careful not to miss exactly what you seek.

Locked away in time, it happened before.

Head this warning or it will happen once more.

"Wow, that really does fit," Willow said, impressed with his success in combining the two books. "I still have no idea what it means, though. We should keep in mind the last few prophecies have had different meanings for different people. I think it will come up again. Keep your eyes open for anything the words could apply to."

"Okay, I have to attend a meeting with Malarchy tomorrow. Willow will be attending as well. When I return, we can go over whatever information Mike sends us. Until then, pack what you will need to be ready for the cold and get some rest." William turned his attention to Lance. "I am sorry, Your Highness, but you will have to be confined to your quarters until the next meeting. Food and drink will be provided for you. Two guards will be posted outside at all times. You do understand, for safety reasons."

"Of course. I would expect no less," the prince answered. "I would appreciate haste, if possible. The longer Sissy is left in the cold, the worse her chances for survival are."

William nodded.

Lance stood, holding his hands out in front of him as if waiting to be handcuffed, a cheeky smile plastered on his face.

"Very funny, Your Highness," Mike scoffed. "Your suite is ready. Let's go." He bowed, mocking the prince, then motioned towards the door.

Chapter Fifty-Five

Faramund's teleportation abilities transported William and Willow to meet Malarchy. When the green gas dissipated, it revealed a very small island.

After the attack on the underground at Halloween, it was necessary to move the entire city somewhere new - the original location having been compromised. People were too scared to remain. Even in a magical world, an army of undead marching through the streets was considered unsettling. Malarchy spent his time helping with new security protocols and speaking to some of the officials from non-represented realms in the city.

She ignored directions to walk straight out into the water. The idea of going anywhere near the shoreline made Willow uneasy. The lack of bodies of water in her home world meant she never learnt how to swim or float. Arguing did little more than waste time.

A muffled squeak was all she could manage from where her head hung down on William's back. Being carried was one thing, having her bottom sticking in the air over someone's shoulder was another. Complaining, however, proved useless - her curly hair swung back and forth with every step he took.

When they finally stepped off the rocky surroundings and touched the water, it was as if they were still walking on solid ground. "Being able to walk on water." William snickered to himself. "Just another everyday kind of miracle."

"It's an illusion," Malarchy explained. "There is no water where you are standing. The whole area is known for having extreme depths, alternated with very shallow sections containing sharp rocks. It naturally keeps away boaters and swimmers. Ingenious really - it takes less magic to hide everything this way."

"Doesn't anyone wonder about things moving on top of the water?" Willow asked, still upside down. She spit out a few strands of hair that invaded her mouth while her lips parted to speak.

"That's why we have to walk. Nothing big is allowed on the pathway. The whole area fogs over on the outside when in use. From the other side, all you can see is mist," Malarchy boasted, seemingly impressed with the whole system. It was obvious he must have had his hand in the design in some way. "No magic is allowed on the pathway either. It would draw an immediate response from the city's police."

It took about ten minutes before the illusion gave way - ground forming beneath them again. Willow felt queasy, her head still hanging upside down. "Think I could get down now?" she begged.

William stopped, setting the redhead down. Everything around Willow turned fuzzy, her world spinning in circles. Stumbling backwards, she almost fell. William's arm grabbed her by the waist, waiting until she was stable on her feet before letting go.

"If you two are done with your moment," Malarchy snapped. "People are waiting." For some reason, he hadn't been keen on anyone experiencing love lately. She shrugged it off as understandable, most likely stemming from the death of the man's wife in the invasion on their home world. There was no time to linger on thoughts. Their guide was already a fair distance ahead of them.

"Right behind you," William yelled out, taking Willow's hand and moving quickly to catch up. "Is this the only way in or out?" he asked.

"For the moment. They are working on a system to teleport between empyral cities. It just hasn't been perfected yet. Hopefully in the near future." Malarchy's words remained faint, showing he had no intention of slowing his pace to wait for anyone.

The city looked different. The last time they visited was in the middle of the biggest celebration of the year and during a zombie attack brought on by a couple of crazy necromancer princes. Now, with everything cleaned up, it looked no different than any other city a person might visit. A sign posted on the way in read, *Welcome to Pewterclaw.* Underneath the population number updated automatically when anyone entered or exited.

The mayor, Hilary, ran out to greet them. "So good to see you two again. It's such a pleasure to welcome you to our new location. Everyone is waiting to meet you." She shook their hands, hurrying them along the road towards a convention centre.

Jade waited outside for them, fidgeting. Willow gasped for breath under the pressure of the girl's embrace.

"I missed you so much," Jade exclaimed. "You are going to have so much fun here. There is so much to see and do. Not to mention, you two are famous - everyone knows about you and what you did. You are the biggest news ever." She pulled out a stack of *The Empowered* newspapers, each one prominently displaying articles that were in some way about them. The first one included a picture of Willow in the gold and green dress she wore for Halloween with her wand outstretched. Even she couldn't deny it was a good picture.

Turning her attention back to Jade, she realized she too looked good. She was wearing a skirt with matching jacket, almost like a uniform. Her blonde hair was tied neatly back in a bun which was a new style for the girl and one Willow didn't recall ever seeing before. The glimmer in Jade's eyes, however, she did remember from their homeland. Of course, it also might have been all the new shiny jewelry that brought back memories.

A sense of worry pulsed through Willow's veins, her mind flashing through scenes of how Jade used to be. The green-eyed girl helped bring about the destruction of their world - a result of a temper tantrum. Looking at her now raised doubts in Willow's mind. Perhaps Jade was reverting back to her old self again after coming in contact with the comforts of Pewterclaw.

William grabbed the paper, clenching the edges firmly. "How did they know all this? The information in these articles isn't common knowledge and not all completely accurate. Surely a paper can't publish whatever it wants without proof to back it up."

"We don't know. The newspaper has a history of knowing things no one else does. It's a big mystery. We tried to ask someone who works at the paper, but no one is ever there," Jade answered in a nonchalant manner. "I did manage to find a business card for the young intern at the paper." She handed Willow a card which read *Keith Quidnunk, Intern Journalist. Call for appointment. All tips confidential*. "He seems to write most of the articles on us and takes the pictures as well."

"There is no number to call," Willow said, frowning.

"Great." William slammed the newspaper into a trash container as they walked by. "This much attention isn't something we needed or wanted. Now everyone will know who we are, anywhere we go."

"Don't be silly," Hilary said. The mayor dressed in a plain fashion again, except for her blazer. It was a bright yellow colour and prominently displayed her name, city and her position of mayor on it. Her hair was tied back neatly in a bun in the same fashion as Jade's. "You are heroes. It's a good thing - something we desperately needed. You have inspired us to connect our cities and governments for the common good. Shall we go inside? I can't wait to hear what the others have to say."

Inside the building, a large hall led to different sections. The mayor showed her guests into a room with a large oval table in the centre. Willow bumped into William, her attention fixed on the ceiling, or rather the lack thereof - the sun shining brightly and clouds floating by like fluffy cotton balls. Hilary, seeing the girl's lack of attention to the important people who gathered for the meeting, quickly identified those sitting round the table. Neither of them caught any of the names, but both William and Willow had a general idea of who was present for the afternoon's discussions.

Each of the directors were there in-person, representing their branch of a possible new government. The remainder of the seats available were for the mayors of the largest cities. Standing around the outside of the room were representatives of all the other cities as well as delegates from realms who maintained their own towns in this world. Each had a pencil and notepad to record important information.

Malarchy took his seat at the table beside Hilary, with Jade standing behind him. William and Willow were positioned at the other end of the table. Iskander and Faramund stood behind them. There was something strange about the way they sat opposite each other, almost as if someone wanted them separated.

On the table in front of each person was a neatly organized pile of papers. The first page holding a diagram of the table with the names and positions of everyone seated filled in. Around the edges was the information for those standing. A couple times, Willow thought she saw names change place, reminding her of the ledger from the hotel she visited before Halloween. Names that were written in it magically disappeared, in front of people - perhaps a similar form of magic was used to create both.

"I am very pleased to host this meeting, here in Pewterclaw. I know we are going to accomplish a lot here today," the mayor said, standing. Her voice was sickly sweet, dripping with the aspirations of a woman looking for new opportunities to advance her position.

"Sit down, Hilary," the Director of Secrecy, Kasper, demanded, his tone impatient.

The mayor immediately took her seat, forcing a smile on her face. She exchanged glances with Malarchy. Doubt crawled under Willow's skin, nagging at her faith in the loyalty of the man and his daughter. Had he returned to his former self? He held a position here, similar to what he had with the council in their home world. Perhaps his desire for power took over - the memory of losing his wife and son becoming irrelevant. She shook off the feeling. It was after all mere speculation. Nothing transpired to warrant such an accusation. Still there was something she was sensing from that direction that bothered her.

"If you don't mind, I will be taking over this meeting," Kasper announced. A strand of his grey hair fell loose from where the rest gathered, tied back with a blue ribbon - the style reminiscent of some of the pictures Willow saw in the museums on the witchcraft walking tour. His thin frame was masked by a jacket similar to Hilary's, but in a deeper golden colour. It was hard not to notice that each time he swallowed, his eyes glazed over yellow like a reptile. "If we are to consider letting you run loose, there will have to be some changes. We are pleased you realize your own shortcomings and have attended this meeting voluntarily to set some parameters."

Willow was confused. Who was he talking to? She looked at the others she knew at the table, each seeming just as surprised. She was about to ask what was going on when William handled it for her.

"I'm sorry," he said. "Who are you referring to?" A scowl forming on his face indicated displeasure rather than anger.

Whispers filled the air as the officials and representatives mumbled to each other. The director called for silence. "I am speaking to you, of course, and your so-called guardians. The way you handle yourselves is a danger to our very existence."

Willow took a deep breath in and let it out, shock preventing her from doing much else. Her eyes focused on Malarchy. Had he set them up? Had he brought them there to further his position in this magical world? Could Jade have forgotten the second chance she had been given by Acacia? Her thoughts broke at the sound of William's agitated voice.

"I think you have this backwards. We are here to offer help to you. Our people spent a good part of the beginning of time protecting the realms, including this one, from danger. If it weren't for the guardians, none of you would be sitting here right now. Your magical ancestors would have been destroyed in the blood wars." Upset couldn't begin to describe the message that rested in his words. His gaze rested on Malarchy. His concern about the loyalty of the father and daughter clearly written in his expression as well.

"There is no proof of guardians here. A talking cat in front of Hilary is all we have to go on and, of course, your word. So much time has passed since the era of the guardians. We simply don't believe you are who you say." The Director of Ancient Artifacts, Tereza Scarab, took the floor.

Willow tried to focus on the woman's words, but couldn't help but notice her glasses. They were silver, with teal-coloured lenses that became brighter in the sun. She was also the only woman in the room, other than Willow, who didn't have her hair tied back in a bun, although she was wearing a hat. Curiously, it looked like some form of a safari hat. From the bits of hair that stuck out underneath, it was obvious it was frizzy - probably dried out and damaged from the sun.

"Perhaps if you demonstrated? Call forth one of these mighty beasts. I don't mean an ordinary house cat made to look like it could talk... an actual guardian, the stuff legends are made of. If we could see them for ourselves, maybe we could accept the incredible stories we are being asked to believe."

Every bone in Willow's body screamed *no - it's a trap*. All eyes were on the two of them - waiting for an answer. William pulled his jacket back over his shoulders. Before he signalled for one of his guardians to join them, Willow grabbed his hand and smiled. Even though their telepathic communication should have been broken inside the city, he heard her, darting a look of confusion only she recognized.

I don't know how, she thought. *I just needed you to hear me and you did. This feels like a trap. Something is very wrong here.*

I can't contact anyone else. It looks like it's just us two, he replied in the same manner.

We are here also, Aslo said. *We knew, as time progressed, Willow would develop more abilities. This is just part of what is to come.* His familiar voiced calmed her down. She felt better knowing that her guardians could hear her and offer advice.

We can also hear you. The voice was Nero, one of the Olcsanka, joined with William. *From the thoughts going on in your mind right now, we have a good idea of what is happening. Let's let this play out some. It would appear someone or something is trying to push us into the open. To come out now could leave us vulnerable.*

"The bus driver saw them in full form... all three types." Malarchy stood to input his observations.

Willow couldn't decide what side he was on. He seemed to effortlessly move his positioning right before her eyes, without looking any different from one moment to the next.

"The driver is missing," Kasper proclaimed loudly, followed by a rumbling in the background again. "Rather conveniently, if you ask me."

"Missing?" Hilary hissed, surprised by the news. "Why didn't I know about this?"

"Why indeed? As mayor, you should know if a city employee goes missing." This time, the Director of New Residents, Fuscia Magnetal, spoke. Oddly enough, she was wearing all different shades of pink, which, although it matched the sound of her name, clashed horribly with the yellow jacket.

The whole afternoon had the beginnings of an inquisition or witch hunt. The meeting to work out an alliance disappeared as if it never existed. Something had happened between Halloween night and now, but what?

Kasper motioned to the woman to sit. "We are not here to discuss Hilary's shortcomings." He paused for a moment, looking as if he was sucking his teeth and puckering up for a kiss at the same time. "Yet."

"You can't deny this girl saved the city from an army of undead led by a pair of ruthless princes. They could have succeeded in wiping out Pewterclaw if our people had not intervened." Malarchy seemed to be running defence for them now. Willow frowned, wondering if it was all a show or an attempt to save grace.

"Actually, we can. We don't believe there was that much of a threat. A couple boys got a little rowdy and decided to try out what they could do. No more than a big prank. That is why a girl this young, with her obviously limited abilities, was able to stop them so easily." Kasper smiled at her, goading her emotions and begging for the release of anger.

She took the bait. "A prank? People died. I don't consider that a prank. We went through a lot to track them to this city and stop them." The tone in her voice revealed emotions were still under control.

Vern Hemlock, the Director of Dangerous Substances, looked at her with sympathetic eyes. "No one denies you did a service to Pewterclaw. Of course, we are in debt to you child, for stopping them much sooner than the city's inadequate police force would have been able to. These boys need to be taught a lesson for what they did, but they are just children the same as you are. Therein lies the problem."

He wiped sweat from his brow with a handkerchief embroidered with his initials. The heat from the sun, combined with his chubby physique made him uncomfortable. The added weight of the jacket he wore to match the other officials didn't help the situation. "Children are not able to control what they do at all times. It's a danger to us all. One tantrum or hormone imbalance could ruin our way of life forever. We need to make sure they stay within certain boundaries. Your camp is made up of mainly underage youths. We simply cannot allow you to run wild. You do understand. It isn't personal."

"Bottom line, we don't believe there is a mad king planning any invasion. We don't believe there are guardians in existence anymore. For that matter, history has little proof they were in fact real. What we do know is the younger members of your group cannot yet control their abilities. They have not been properly taught or mentored. Being at a very emotional stage in their lives, makes them a threat." The Director of Secrecy dripped with pride, patting himself on the back for his dominance over the meeting.

"I may have a possible solution." Cassandrhea Tibbins, the Director of Knowledge, stood and began walking around the table. The black dress she wore instantly grabbed the attention of everyone in the room. The top part appeared frugal and boring. The bottom skirt, however, flared out, spinning when she walked, creating a mesmerizing effect. With the group engrossed by her attire, almost to the point of entering a hypnotic state, she continued, "They could write the exam and be placed in schools for this coming year. It's not far away, just after the terunji holiday season. They would be in a safe environment and would learn how to control their craft."

Kasper contorted as if he had just been hit by a bus. "You think they will agree to this?" he said, recovering.

"Why wouldn't they?" Cassandrhea turned her attention to Willow. "Knowledge is the key to what is hidden inside. Sometimes we all have to listen. If one is not careful, one might miss exactly what one seeks."

The wording seemed odd. It was a strange thing to say, yet there was something familiar. It took Willow a moment to figure it out. Of course, it was similar to a line from the prophecy. Could she have known about *The Portal Prophecies*? It seemed unlikely. But maybe this was a clue. Everything that happened, happened for a reason. "I think it would be a good idea," she blurted out without thought.

William raised both eyebrows then shook his head in disbelief, stopping himself from engaging in argument. It was impossible to keep up to wherever Willow's mind was heading. He slouched back in his chair, deciding to wait for an explanation.

"You don't mind attending a school? You would have to abide by the same rules as everyone else. There would be no talk of guardians or invasions. That would scare the other children and we can't have that." Fuscia searched for a reaction.

"Fine," Willow agreed.

"You would have no connection to the older members of your camp while in school." Kasper said, making a last attempt to change her mind.

"Okay," she said. "I will talk to the others in camp about writing the test. I am sure Jade will be happy to join us as well." She wasn't sure why she singled the girl out like that - yet another case of speaking her mind without forethought.

"I was hoping to stay in the city. Hilary can watch me and make sure I am behaving."

"I think it would be good for you," Malarchy intervened. "You were just saying how much you miss the girls. Yes, she will write the test as well."

His reaction confused Willow even further. She decided it would be a good plan to see if there was a way to get both father and daughter back to camp for a while, although she doubted it would happen, at least not right now.

"All settled, then!" Cassandrhea exclaimed.

"Yes, yes. Except..." Kasper put on a pair of square frame, reading glasses for the first time since the meeting began. His fingers shuffled through some papers in front of him before settling on one in particular sheet. "The issue of murder." Whispers erupted through the room again.

"Murder?" William bolted into a straight sitting position, wondering what the man was going to try to pull now. The whole meeting was nothing more than a trap - one they willingly walked into.

"Yes, murder. It is a crime in this world as well. Since we have evidence two people were killed during the tour, we must examine that evidence and deal with any potential killers. Justice needs to be served in this world as in any other. Jade, would you step forward, please? We will need to hear your testimony about the day." The director slid back into his seat, arranging his papers neatly in front of him, then turned his attention solely towards Jade.

Willow shot a glance at her and then at her father. Jade walked to the director's side, keeping her head tilted downwards so as to never once make eye contact with anyone from the camp. Malarchy's expression revealed a similar level of shock as her own, that his daughter was aiding this farce of an investigation.

"Thank you. Would you please tell us in your own words what happened in the forest clearing on the walking tour you took with your friends?" Kasper asked.

"Camile was acting strangely. It was as if she was in a trance or something. She simply stopped walking. None of us knew what was wrong with her. We were all frightened. In the clearing there was an altar. Willow went and looked at it. She told us it was a portal to another world that had been used to seal in the Glaquool."

"The Glaquool? Could you elaborate?" the Director of Secrecy asked.

"Apparently, they are a race of bodiless beings, who have the power to hide within objects and then take over a physical body when the object is touched."

"Did you ever actually see one?"

"No," Jade answered. "But the lockets Denny and Camile were wearing were thought to be the objects they hid in."

"We don't need speculation, just the facts. What happened to the two ladies?"

"A bolt of lightning hit Denny and she turned to dust, except for the locket. Clairity used her wand to eliminate Camile in the same fashion. But they were doing it to protect us. The Glaquool had to be confined."

"So you know the Glaquool exist?" he asked

"No, not exactly. I believed Willow. Everything she said fit. It made sense. I had no reason to doubt her."

"So you believe due diligence was made before the execution of the two women? There was no doubt that something else couldn't have caused their conditions? Another spell, perhaps? All avenues were explored."

"I don't know." Her voice shook, revealing exactly how nervous she was.

"Could another spell have caused the same reaction? Is it possible Willow was wrong?"

"I suppose..." Her words were cut off.

"Did anyone suggest that the two could be under the influence of anything other than the Glaquool?"

"No, but..." Her words were cut off again.

"So who decided their fate?"

"Willow," Jade said, almost stuttering.

William jumped up, as if he was going to intervene in the questioning. Willow grabbed his arm, pulling him back down to his seat. She wanted to hear what Jade had to say. It could help her piece together whether or not the girl was reverting to her former self.

"Did she consult anyone before carrying out a lethal sentence?" Kasper's voice became louder with every question.

"No. When she figured it out, she sent a bolt of lightning through Denny immediately. We didn't know what she was doing till it was over.

She was distraught. Our friend was gone and we couldn't save her. Some weird thing had possessed her body."

"But she had no problem dealing with her friend Camile, as well?" Kasper looked down at his papers, making notes.

"No, Clairity used her wand to disintegrate Camile. She knew Willow wouldn't be able to." Jade looked at Willow and mouthed *sorry*.

"So these two young witches took it upon themselves to sentence two living beings to death, without any trial or investigation. It was simply because they were upset and believed possession had taken place. There was no contemplation that perhaps there was another reason for the condition of the two young ladies. There was no thought put into alternate avenues that could have saved the girls' lives. Thank you, Jade, you can step away now." The man waited for her to take her spot again before continuing. "Emotions took over and two young women paid the price. There was no proof that they were possessed and would harm anyone..."

"Excuse me," Willow said, her interruption creating a loud uproar among the observers. "If we had known this was a trial, we could have been more prepared. Of course, I am not suggesting this proceeding to be similar to the witch trials so many unjustly endured a century or two ago." She looked up, meeting Kasper's gaze with confidence. Learning wasn't all bad. Paying attention at the museum and the history of the witch trials came in handy. It made an impact on the crowd, grumbling to one another around her. "I would think we are missing a few people. Clairity, for instance, perhaps should be here."

"Of course. By all means, send for the girl." It was Kasper's turn to interrupt. "It would be easier to take care of everything here and now."

"Brilliant. I should think it might save some time for all these busy people if we have Camile and Denny come as well." Willow locked eyes with the director, issuing a challenge.

The whole room exploded into conversation about those last few words. Kasper stood, the palms of his hands flat on the table, staring at her in disbelief. Jade's jaw came close to hitting the floor.

"Are you suggesting the two women in question are alive and well?" Cassandrhea asked.

"Yes. Denny was still in a bit of shock last time I saw her. Being displaced from one's body apparently isn't the nicest feeling. Both were glad when we helped them reunite their essences with living tissue. Faramund could fetch them, if you like. I do hate taking up any more of your valuable time over this issue."

"I must insist we see them." From his voice, it was clear Kasper was unsure of his position on the subject. This was not something he anticipated. Being outstaged by a young girl fuelled his dislike for her. Those congregated in the room bore witness to the birth of a personal grudge.

William's smile spanned from ear to ear. He was completely impressed with the way Willow handled herself. It was, however, his turn to take over the conversation. "Of course." He turned to Faramund and nodded. The guard exited to bring back the three in question. "While we are waiting, I would like to go over our position in this alliance. You have to admit things have been very one-sided so far."

While listening to William cover laws that would need to be made and enforced about interaction of the empyral with the terunji, Willow drifted off into a daydream. This was his strong point, not hers. He would tend to all the details necessary. She began thinking about Ashlyn, wondering what she was doing.

"Why are you asleep?"

Willow looked around. She was sitting at the same table, but it was just her and Ashlyn in the room. "I'm not," she answered. "I was just daydreaming about us being back home, sitting under a big tree. Are you asleep?"

"I was tired and decided to take a nap. But if you are only daydreaming, how are we talking? Is that even possible?"

"It must be or we wouldn't be here." Willow said, stating the obvious. Of course, she had a point. There was no sense wasting the opportunity. It was the perfect chance fill her friend in on what was going on at the meeting, leaving out some of the details, including her suspicions about

Jade and Malarchy. It was best to leave those accusations until they met in person, if she discussed them at all.

"So you are on trial? That's insane," Ashlyn said.

Willow heard her name being called. "I have to go. Talk soon." Zooming back into reality, she faced an entire room staring at her. "Sorry," she mumbled.

"Is there anything you would like to add?" William asked.

There were questions hidden in his expression. His concern for the way she reacted filled the lines of every wrinkle on his face. It was strange that after such a short time she could read him so well, always seeming to know what he was thinking or feeling. The way his eyes moved, the lines around his mouth, even the way he moved his hair out of his eyes, all told a story of what was going on inside him.

"No. I am sure you have been quite thorough," she answered.

"Well, then," William said. "There is nothing left to do but wait for Faramund to return with the girls."

Just as he finished speaking, the door opened and the group walked in. The three girls took their places behind William and Willow before introducing themselves. There was an eruption of whispers after Denny and Camile said hello.

Chapter Fifty-Six

Willow was glad to be back in the camp. She originally hoped to bring Jade and Malarchy back as well, but after being accused of murder, she just wanted to leave without further argument. Hilary was apologetic about the situation, claiming she had no idea that was going to happen and assuring them that they were still heroes in her eyes. The mayor always seemed to don a blank canvass on her face that turned Willow's stomach into knots, giving her a queasy feeling similar to food poisoning. There was something wrong with the woman - something deeper than could be seen at a glance.

Jade spewed out a few lines about how bad she felt, emphasizing her lack of choice in answering the questions. It was possible what she said could have been true. Her answers hadn't actually proved either way which side of the fence she stood on. There was one thing for sure, there was something going on in Pewterclaw. Someone was working against them... Willow just didn't know who it was yet or what they were trying to accomplish. All of her own people were on the suspect list, that included Iskander as well. She couldn't trust any of them. Then there was the mysterious journalist, Keith Quidnunk. Who was he? How was he involved in all this? Where was he? There were probably a few people working for the city who were involved as well. There were too many pieces to the puzzle missing, pieces that could only be found in Pewterclaw - enough to warrant a late night visit with William to discuss.

Denny decided to remain in the city. Since things were more familiar there for her, it lessened the stress of adjusting to life again after having been a displaced spirit. There was little for the camp to worry about. She couldn't remember anything that happened between starting on the walking tour and waking in the medical centre in the camp. If anyone had decided to question her, the answers would be less than helpful for any growing investigation.

Arriving home, the camp was already buzzing with the information Willow gave Ashlyn in their meeting. The biggest news wasn't about the directors' investigation, but rather about Willow's ability to dreamwalk while not asleep. That, combined with her other new ability to telepathically communicate *while under a silence spell*, caused a buzz in the command centre. This was new territory for everyone, even the guardians.

"Can you contact Mike and Sarah in the ice world?" Faramund asked. "Just to see how they are." His eyes lit up with anticipation.

"No, I am sorry. I cannot," she explained. "I had to physically touch William's arm to make the telepathic connection. I was able to connect to Aslo and Kiera, though. I don't even know if I could duplicate it."

"But in time, you may develop that skill even further. These abilities have never been documented before. They are unique to you. You are exceeding even our expectations." There was a touch of concern rather than happiness in Aslo's voice. "One good thing, there appears to be more ways to communicate in areas where we have been silenced up until now. I believe that will work to our advantage."

"Have we heard from Mike or Sarah yet?" William asked.

"Not yet." Diana said.

"Maybe the girls should take a stroll into the dreamworld tonight and see if they can find out what is happening up north." William settled into his chair, focusing his attention on a set of perfectly-formed three-dimensional boxes sketched on the paper in front of him. He darkened the lines around each square as he set the plans in motion inside his head, following possible outcomes before speaking.

Willow watched him for a moment, thinking how completely different they were. Where she would have blurted out everything she was thinking, he was calculated, only letting people in on the part of the plan they needed to know.

"What about our young prince? How is he holding up?" he asked, looking up from the paper he was doodling on.

"He is fine, although a bit eager to be set free," Jessie said.

"Perhaps he could try dreamwalking tonight as well. See if he can contact his sister. The more we know about the situation we are walking into, the better." Willow avoided making eye contact with William after the comment. The last thing she needed right now was for him to start throwing punches at Lance like he had with Mike. His reaction took her by surprise.

"That's a good plan. If we are going to help him, we need something to go on. At least confirmation she is alive would be nice." He looked around the table. "That brings us to the school tests. Maybe Willow should explain this part to you all." He raised his eyebrows and let them fall quickly into place, a quirky smile appearing on his lips.

"I agreed we would take the placement tests for entry into the empyral schools." A grumbling of disapproval travelled through the room. "It's not that bad. Anyone under eighteen cycles has to take the test from the camp and go to a school if placed. It made the directors happy... and I think it might be beneficial to us as well. I know I would like to be able to control my abilities better. It would be nice to not have to worry about it starting to rain when I am sad."

"I agree. It would be good for most of you. The training we can provide here at the camp is limited. We don't understand enough about your unique abilities to mentor each of you properly. In their system, they will teach you how to better control and focus your talents," William said. "You may even learn some new skills."

"I think it's great," Camile added. There was no doubt she wanted to delve further into her craft. There was no way to accommodate her in the camp. The items she needed to make different potions simply weren't available.

"I have a feeling," Clairity started. When she said those four words, the rest of the camp had learnt to listen to her. Her feelings were always right. "There is another reason we will need eyes and ears in the school system. We have more enemies than just the royal family. It's there we will find out more."

"Is it safe?" Diana blurted out. "Perhaps the younger children shouldn't be involved in this for another year or two." Her words laced with concern for her grandson.

"I am not sure anything is safe anymore. We have been exposed to a lot of people and it seems everyone knows where we are," William said. His pencil pressed hard against the paper, breaking the sharp point of lead with a crunching noise. "Regardless, we are obligated to send everyone for the test." He sighed. "I hate to spread us too thin, but we need to move camp as well. Over the years, I have acquired quite a few other properties. We can transfer everything from here to one of them. So when some of us visit the North Pole, the rest will be discreetly packing and moving. Diana and Jessie, you two will be heading up the camp transfer project. Richard and Mary will see to the medical centre transfer and set up. Faramund will transfer some people to start patrols this evening, as well as Aslo and Kiera's children. Ashlyn should go as well, that way Shelby can watch over security at the new location to make sure the site is safe. Is there anything else we should discuss?"

"One thing," Willow said, looking around the room. "We have someone who is spying on us in the city and doing a good job too. I suggest we keep our plans secret from the others who are staying there for now. We don't know if there might be a mind reader or something causing the information leak." The urge to blurt out her suspicions rushed through her body like a wave. She pushed her words back down her throat with a gulp, wanting to talk to William about her theories before airing them in front of everyone. Accusations could be devastating for those in the city if she was wrong.

"Sounds good. Make sure your things are packed tonight and ready to move. I'll let the people know later who is heading north in the morning."

The grass was crisp and made a crinkling noise under Willow's feet as she strolled across the training field to the building Lance was staying in. When she arrived she found him lying on a bed staring at the ceiling, the boredom of being confined to the one room written in his expression.

The prince jumped up at the sight of her. "Any news?" he asked.

She was rather disappointed his excitement hadn't been about seeing her. "No, not yet. Actually, that is what I was coming to talk to you about. Tonight, I am going into a dream with friends to try to contact Mike and Sarah. We were thinking you could do the same with your sister. See if you can find anything that would help us before we head there tomorrow."

A perplexed look crossed his face. "I have never tried to explore dreams before. I am not sure I would know what I was looking for." He sighed, returning to his seat.

"But you have such control in dreams."

"Yeah, I can enter a dream and change it to whatever I want, but I have never tried looking at what is there already." Lance's lips curved down slightly. His eye lids closed, he turned his head from Willow to avoid her gaze.

She watched him for a moment. The expression of failure on his face was so intense, a feeling of pity rushed through her. "Well then, I guess we will all have to go together. Leave it to me. I'll see you tonight," she said.

It wasn't until later that afternoon that Willow was able to find William alone in his sleeping quarters, busy packing all of his books from the shelves that lined the room. She tried sitting then standing - neither making her comfortable enough to speak. Her fidgeting, picking up books and trinkets that hadn't been packed yet, drew William's attention. There wasn't an easy way to tell him that the prince was going to join her in dream land that evening, so she just blurted it out and hoped for the best.

William's face had absolutely no expression on it. "Do you really think that is a good idea? It could be a trap."

"If he wanted to wipe us out, all he had to do was bring his whole family along. I doubt he is planning anything for tonight. I believe he genuinely wants our help."

"You have a point," William admitted. "Okay." He went back to packing books.

"Okay? That's it?" Surprised showed in her tone at how easy the conversation with him was going. She expected at least a little resistance. She looked down at the book she was still holding, her body slumping from standing to sitting on the bed.

"Yup," he answered. "I'll see you back here when it is time to go to sleep. I am going with you too. There is no way I am leaving you girls alone with him in a dream."

She smiled. That was the William she expected. Tonight was going to prove interesting. The three girls now had two guys to drag around who had no clue what they were doing. *The blind leading the blind,* she thought as she headed off to finish her own packing.

Chapter Fifty-Seven

Mike and Sarah were travelling for what seemed like hours in the freezing cold. Faramund's abilities were putting in overtime with the rest of the camp's needs. That translated into leaving them to their own devices at the portal gate. The doorway itself was hidden in an unusual way. The pair found themselves staring at a giant wall of ice and snow with a spherical hole cut into it. Mike swung one leg inside and ducked his head down to enter, mumbling something about the gap being made for short people.

Stepping through revealed a cavern-type room carved deep into the cold, which housed the portal itself. If they hadn't known they were out in the middle of nowhere, they might have thought they had stepped into an elaborate hallway. Above the stone portal base, a series of giant icicles hung down from the high ceiling. The light from the open gateway illuminated the formation giving the illusion of a magical glittering chandelier reflecting hues of different shades of blue all around them.

Getting that far had been easy. It was what was on the other side of the portal that was the real problem. Since no one knew they were coming, it meant navigating the rough terrain without any form of transportation. Similar to the main world, the realm they entered was experiencing a period of almost total darkness, both day and night. There were no maps to follow and no roads, leaving them no choice but to trudge on, cold white layers crunching beneath their feet, hoping to find something... anything, to show them they were at least heading in the right direction.

Sarah began to wonder if the trip was worth it, even if it was to meet Santa Claus. Although she was in fairly good shape, her legs were tired. A burning sensation forming a dull ache. Walking in deep snow for a long distance was taking its toll on her. She stopped for a moment to catch her breath. Her legs buckled beneath her. Stumbling slightly, she let out a scream, muffled by her scarf, before falling face-first into the snow.

Hearing her cry, Mike moved as quickly as he could to her, his legs trudging through the deep snow felt more like navigating sticky tar. There was little choice but to carry Sarah now, but he wouldn't get far. Even with his strength, the extreme elements were having an effect on his body as well.

A strange noise came from beside them. It sounded like... a train. Mike turned towards the commotion. Some smoke hovered over a small mound of snow close by. There was definitely something there. It was their only hope. Picking Sarah up over his shoulder, he carried her, his legs burning with pain from each step.

Neither of them knew whether to be in shock or delight at what they found. Sitting in front of them was, in fact, a train. It wasn't a regular train, though. This locomotive was small, standing only about half Mike's height. The bright red and greens were a welcome contrast to the fluffy white snow surrounding them. Surprisingly, there was no conductor. It was being controlled from another location.

The majority of the train's cars were open at the top, resembling carts that might be used in a diamond mine. It was obvious from their design, they were used to transport some sort of physical items. The last attachment had the appearance of an old-fashioned horse-drawn sleigh, without the horses, of course. There was enough room for two people to sit.

A whistle blew from the engine. A sign they had taken enough time to look things over. Not wanting the train to leave without her, she stepped into the sleigh and sat down, letting out a sigh of relief after finding the seats were heated. Wiggling herself around so the warmth would reach every cold part of her backside, her face displayed pure satisfaction that her *fanny* would soon be warm. As soon as Mike joined her, the pint-sized train began moving.

With the stress of the hike, neither of them had taken the time to notice how truly unique and beautiful the scenery around them was. Being able to sit back and relax meant the two could now enjoy the landscapes this world had to offer. The train zig-zagged them through carved passages in gigantic mountains and over top frozen lakes. Everything around them formed stunning gigantic ice sculptures. The designs and formations in each passage the train twisted through were unique, capturing the imagination of the passengers, each of them pointing to show the other the different patterns they found. Sarah thought she saw a duck followed by a bunny, while Mike picked out what he thought formed a skull and cross bones.

"It's like watching clouds form patterns, except in the snow," Sarah said. Looking up at the sky, she noticed light from the moon reflecting off the ice caverns. She let out a gasp, nudging Mike to make sure he shared the same sight she was experiencing. The reflections created an array of colours, appearing to dance in the skies like a rainbow being indecisive about where to put its pot of gold.

The train whistled twice as they rounded a bend to what appeared to be a town. When it came to a full stop, both Mike and Sarah hopped out and retrieved their belongings from one of the carts near where they had been sitting. No sooner than they finished, the tiny train was off again, making its next stop up ahead between two buildings.

There was no sign of anyone in the town. The lights, if they were any, appeared to all be off, except for in one house. Obviously, that was where they needed to go.

The house was a small bungalow, decorated with bows and garland outside. Inside the front bay window stood a beautifully decorated Christmas tree lit with small bright white lights that twinkled - its branches adorned with beads, ornaments, ribbons and bows. On top stood a single star shining ten times brighter than the other lights.

Mike rang the doorbell, letting out a chuckle when the noise of sleigh bells rang out after pressing the small button. After a moment, a pudgy little woman with short curly grey hair answered the door. She was dressed in a bright red dress with a frilly white kitchen apron over top.

"How did you know we needed help?" she asked, wiping tears from her eyes, which were puffy and red as if she had been crying for an extended period of time.

"We didn't. There were some reports of activity in this area. A woman is missing as well. William sent us to check in with you," Mike said. "From the looks of things, it's a good thing he did. Are you okay?"

"Please come in where it is warmer and I will tell you everything," the woman offered. "I am Meredith and my shy friends are the Frostica. They help us run everything around here. You two are very lucky they noticed you in the snow and sent the sleigh to pick you up." She led them to a sitting room, offering hot drinks to warm up with by a fire. The hospitality was welcomed by both of the weary travellers. Although their bottoms had been warm on the train ride, the cold air made the rest of their bodies quite chilled.

"What happened? You said you needed help." Sarah didn't wait for Meredith to tell them her story. She was nervous she hadn't heard anything about Santa yet.

"It's Nick. He's missing." Tears swelled in her eyes at the sound of her own words. She turned her head away from Sarah's view attempting to hide her pain. Tiny drops streaked down the sides of her face leaving traces of their line of descent and red blotches on her otherwise perfect white skin. An aura of helplessness surrounded the woman.

"Missing? When did you last see him?" Sarah asked, placing her cup of hot chocolate on the table in front of her. Standing, she put her hand on the woman's shoulder to offer support. Meredith greeted Sarah's hand with her own, welcoming the comfort.

"Two days ago. As you can imagine, all of us are at a loss. He never goes off on his own for longer than a couple of hours. I don't know what we are going to do. It's going to take a lot more than luck to make it through this."

"Do you know where he last was?" Mike decided it would be better if he took over the questions, seeing his partner in this expedition was becoming a little too emotional over the news of Santa being missing. Touching Sarah's hand, it was as if he could feel her thoughts and for an instant he imagined what might happen if they didn't find the jolly old man. His eyes looked at the floor - visions of all the children who might be disappointed this year filling his thoughts. Christmas was too close for comfort. Mike snapped back to reality at the sound of the woman's voice.

"Yes," Meredith answered. "Warm up some and then I will take you there. Maybe one of you can find some clue as to what has happened. Fresh eyes are always helpful."

Mrs. Claus, as she was known in the main world, insisted they stay by the fire for at least an hour before heading back outside. Although Meredith introduced the Frostica, Mike and Sarah had yet to actually see one of the creatures who lived in the town. They remained hidden while inside the house. Once outside, however, they made their presence known. Taken off guard at the sight of them, Sarah jumped backwards a few feet. Using Mike as a human shield, she peeked her head out slowly to take another look. They were the most unusual creatures she had ever seen, which was saying a lot after the Kriller.

Mike turned his head to look behind him. He wasn't sure why she was so surprised. The Frostica were exactly as William described. Standing about two feet tall, they were unusual to look at, but hardly the scariest looking creatures the pair had encountered. Their bodies appeared humanoid, but with faces which were more animal-like, some features similar to a goat. Their extremely shiny and white teeth were the most surprising, having sharp jagged edges that jutted out - the kind that one would expect to see fill the mouth of a predator... a predator who had regular dentist appointments. The creatures were naked exposing the skin of their bare chests. The rest of their bodies were covered in a thick blueish coloured animal fur, including the tops of their hands and feet.

"Their body temperatures are so very hot, they require the cold to even them out to a comfortable level. We don't have many visitors here. Nick and I don't mind; they go without clothing to keep the temperature of their bodies down. The Frostica would find it very hard to survive for any length of time in any climate warmer than it is here in the open. We even have to keep air conditioning in the workshops to make sure they don't overheat. They spend limited time in the house as well." Meredith, sensing uncertainty in her two visitors, broke the silence. "These ones are quite harmless. They enjoy the lives they live here and are just as curious about you as you are about them."

The train stopped beside the bungalow-style home. This time the sleigh attached had four seats instead of two. Meredith and Sarah took the front spots. Mike climbed in back, stretching his limbs out across the whole seat.

They headed in the opposite direction from where Mike and Sarah entered the frozen land. The journey took about twenty minutes from start to finish. Along the way, Meredith pointed out areas of interest, including a naturally-occurring hot spring where she and Nick went swimming. The heat the water gave off caused the Frostica to stay clear of that area, so it was very private for them. As the train passed by a forest of pine trees and a few polar bears, Meredith told stories of how Nick rescued the bears from the main world. Her eyes lit up as she spoke of his love of animals, explaining that with the climate changes that were happening on the other side of the portal lately, Nick feared the beautiful white bears might not survive much longer. This was his way of saving them from possible extinction.

The train came to a stop at what looked like a series of ice bridges woven between caverns. As the group walked closer, it became obvious that the whole structure was suspended over a body of water which was not frozen over.

"This entire realm is actually made completely of frozen water," Meredith said, seeing the looks on her guests' faces. "It's basically a gigantic ocean. There are fish and sea creatures that live underneath the top layer of ice that we are walking on. The Frostica's basic diet is made up of various types of small fish. We have a greenhouse out back to grow fruits and vegetables for Nick and myself. If we have time, I can show you it later."

She motioned for them to follow her on to one of the bridges. "While I love spending my time gardening in the greenhouse to relax, this is Nick's favourite place to come to. As you can imagine, things have gotten progressively busier for us every year. The population increase in the main world is beyond belief. Sometimes, I think it's out of control. With that comes the additional stress and pressure of increasing our production levels every year, not to mention delivering everything. It can get to all of us, but not as much as it affects Nick. He bears the load, so to speak. When he needs alone time, this is where he comes and we try not to bother him when he is here. That's why we didn't know he was missing right away. It wasn't until he didn't return for several hours more than usual any of us worried."

They walked across several bridges to one with a small platform in the middle. Looking down, they had a good view of the ocean below. Several whales were swimming playfully at the surface, each one with a spiral horn on its head.

"Are they..." Sarah never had a chance to finish her sentence.

"Unicorn whales," Meredith answered. "A somewhat unusual thing for your world, but here, where there is no pollution or hunting, they flourish. We aren't sure why, but they are not on the Frostica menu."

Sarah and Mike couldn't believe what they were seeing, the whales were playing right below them. Their horns touched together, lighting up in all different shades of blue, which in turn reflected off the ice all around them, illuminating all of the caverns and bridges.

"Imagine what a lineup they would have if a marina had these for an attraction," Mike said as he and Sarah stood in awe of the sight. Then something spectacular happened. The whales began giving off a musical sound.

"Are they singing Christmas songs?" Sarah asked, her face lighting up with a big smile.

Meredith laughed. "Yes," she answered. "As I said, Nick tends to get stressed. Hearing the songs written about him from the main world always seems to cheer him up. At first, he would bring a machine to play them while he sat and talked with the whales. Eventually, they learnt the noises and imitated them. He doesn't even bother to bring the machine now. He just sits here and talks to them. They sing back. Sometimes they get so loud, we can hear them from the house."

"That's incredible!" Sarah's eyes gleamed with excitement. She never imagined there could be anything this wonderful packed away in snow and ice. She moved closer to the frozen railing that edged the platform they stood on and reached her hand down to one of the whales.

"These bridges and caverns, what do they lead to?" Mike asked. As much as he enjoyed the whales, they were becoming far too preoccupied with the creatures. All of them needed to get back on track.

Meredith's face turned pale and her expression went blank. "The portal to the other Frostica land. It's still sealed. I checked. I didn't think it could be opened without the stones and a guardian. We dismantled everything and gave the pieces to Kristophe... the guard for the portal that led to Yeti lands. Presumably, he hid them somewhere deep inside, where no man or beast would find them. Of course, we have no way to verify that, since it is believed his life was lost in a battle many years ago. William would know all of the information. We all lost so many friends, some we know were killed, others captured and still others are just missing."

"Are the portal stones for the Yeti lands intact?" Mike asked.

The woman turned and walked across the bridge. They followed her to one of the ice caverns. She placed her hand on a table made of ice and the wall beside it began to shift. "We hid them here. It was Nick's idea so that no one would know there was anything behind the ice. No sense taking any chances."

"A secret room?" Sarah asked, surprised to see such a thing could be built out of ice.

"The Frostica are not without their abilities. They built all of this. This room was designed especially to hold the portal stones after Kristophe couldn't protect the gateway anymore. Letting a group of Yeti into the main world could be just as dangerous as any other beast. Nick and I know little about them. Kristophe preferred to keep to himself. He even requested his post alone." She removed the stones and handed them to Mike. "You think Nick is behind the sealed portal to Frostica lands don't you?"

"It's one explanation," Mike answered, looking at the stones.

"If he is there, it's a trap. You do know that, right?"

"Yeah, that's what I figured," he answered. "Everything we do now seems to be a trap set by someone." Without looking at either woman, he headed back towards the train.

The total darkness that spanned day and night of this world made it hard to judge what time it was. The hours passed by quickly. Exhaustion caught up to the two explorers. They agreed it was best for them to spend rest of the night at Meredith's house. A storm was brewing outside that neither of them wanted to get caught in.

"Tomorrow I will send message to William about what we have found out. If there is any way possible, we will save Nick," Mike said, hugging Meredith.

She set up beds for them by the fireplace made from air mattresses, pillows and blankets. Once Mike and Sarah were tucked away in woolly covers by the warmth of a raging fire, they both drifted off to sleep without any trouble at all.

Chapter Fifty-Eight

The last thing she remembered was landing on her backside. Then there was a long slide down what looked like a tube made of ice, and an extremely slippery one at that. She grasped and grabbed at the ground beneath her, but everything was too slick to catch a hold of. There was no way for her to stop herself. At the bottom, she must have hit her head. Everything went black.

Now awake, she realized she was inside some sort of a cage. The bars surrounding her looked like they were made from… ice. *How hard can it be to break ice?* she thought to herself, standing up and jogging on the spot in an effort to warm up. Feeling her pockets, she moaned. Her wand was missing. That was going to make things a little harder. Lifting one leg and using the force of her body, she directed the heel of her boot in the form of a kick at one of the bars of ice.

"Not a good plan."

She spun around, looking for where the voice came from. The area was fairly dark. A torch burnt green flames outside her cell, but only illuminated the middle of the space she was confined to.

"If you don't have any night vision abilities, you won't be able to see me. I am in a cage further down. My name is Jawfree and beside me is Decon."

"I am Sissy. How long have you been here?"

"For a very long time. We lost track. Something is coming. Stay back from the bars. Don't aggravate them."

She did as the others suggested, moving to the very back of the cell. Sitting down on the ground again, she pretended she was still passed out. She heard footsteps followed by some hissing. A plate of some sort of food was tossed into her cell. Whatever made the noises left as quickly as it appeared.

"We could break the ice," she said, moving to the front of the cell again.

"The noise would attract them. Even if you could escape, where would you go? Outside is a barren land of ice and snow. The temperatures alone would take their toll on your body. The Frostica would catch up to you and their bite is deadly. Even if you beat all the odds and managed to get away, there are no active exits from this world. I am afraid we are prisoners here. I am not sure how you found your way into this land, but it was a terrible mistake coming here."

"My family will come for me," she said, sitting down leaning her back against the bars, pouting at her situation.

"They are counting on it. It is the only hope they have to escape this world. If they do get out, they will freeze whatever realm they enter. Dead creatures are their diet. They like raw meat and bodies stay well preserved in the cold for them."

Sissy looked at the food that was left for her. "This could be one of the men from my father's army?"

"No, that they would save for themselves. What they give you is a mixture of fish parts," Jawfree answered.

"Did no one come for you?" Sissy asked.

"We do not believe anyone knows we are here. If they did, I would hope they wouldn't waste lives in a rescue attempt. The danger to other worlds is far too great a chance to take. Two lives are not worth the possible death of thousands, if not more."

Days and nights passed slowly and no one came. The only source of interaction Sissy had was with Jawfree and Decon. She was grateful they were there to keep her company.

Unusually early one morning, the clamour of the creatures entering the dungeon told the captives to move from sight. This time it was different. It wasn't time for feeding and locks were already checked for the day... or night. She realized she couldn't remember which it was, or how many days she had been held captive. There was no way to tell from inside her small cell. A tear ran down her face as she contemplated spending the rest of her life in this manner. How could her family have forgotten her so easily?

She heard a voice amongst the footsteps. Creeping just close enough to see, she watched them walk a man dressed in a red suit by her cell to the cage next to her. He was tall with a big belly. His white hair matched his bushy beard and moustache.

"This is a mistake, even for Lanzia. Please reconsider," he said. "If you want to renegotiate terms, this won't help any. Let me go and I will see what I can do for you."

The Frostica ignored him, locking him in an ice cell like the other prisoners. *They must believe he is very important,* Sissy thought. She doubted he wandered into their world on his own and he seemed to know them.

"Nick?" Decon asked.

The man squinted his eyes trying to see who was speaking to him, before pulling out a small pair of glasses. "Decon! Is that you? I thought you were gone... lost with the others."

"Don't strain to look. The darkness won't let you see us," Decon said. "Iris and Helena didn't make it. Jawfree and I were stuck here when the door was sealed."

"My dear friends. I had no idea you had survived and all this time. If I had known..."

"You could not have done anything," Jawfree responded. "We knew the chances when we came here. We were prepared for the worst to happen. But enough about us. Why are you here?"

"They found a way to enter and bring me back without using the portal. I don't understand it. It was like there was a hole in the barrier between our worlds for a short time. If this is a sign of what is to come, I can't even fathom the outcome." Nick paced in his cell. "I think they expect someone to come for me and provide a way out of this world for them. What I don't understand is that they know only a guardian can open the portal. I don't know if there are any keepers or guardians left anymore. Last I heard, William was the only guard left in the main world."

Sissy listened intently to the conversation, torn over the decision of whether or not to speak to them about what she knew? Her family wouldn't approve. She didn't know who any of them were. In the end, she chose to speak of William and his new friends to them. What her family didn't know wouldn't hurt them. Maybe she might even learn something useful about the witches who had been so bothersome.

"I have seen this William you speak of. He seems to have some new friends. Witches of incredible power. Their leader has long curly red hair. I believe I heard someone call her Willow," Sissy said, hoping for a reaction.

"Willow?" Jawfree's voice didn't hide his surprise at hearing that name.

"You know her?" Sissy asked.

"Yes, we know that name," Decon answered. "Before Iris passed on, she gave one last prophecy: that Willow would be the last hope for all the worlds. She is the only one who can stop the barriers from coming down and total destruction of all life."

"Why would there be total destruction?" Her interest piquing in what she wasn't being told at home by her father. These people seemed knowledgeable, for some reason.

"There are creatures far worse than the Frostica out there. They have been sealed within barriers for longer than the guardians have existed. They alone could destroy all life. Then you have all the different realms being thrown together again. The blood wars are sure to restart again. The force field that separates the worlds is all that protects them at the moment." A candy cane dangled out of one corner of Nick's mouth.

He threw an extra one through the ice bars at the girl. The rustle of the wrapper told him she opened it. "Thank you," she said, smiling at the taste of peppermint. "This is wonderful." She took it out of her mouth, examining the swirling colours. "Do you think someone will come?"

"I don't know. There isn't enough luck in all the worlds for Meredith to be able to help us alone. I don't think she would try to contact anyone. So unless William and his new friends figure out something is wrong, we may be stuck here. Even if William does try to help, without a guardian..." Nick's words faded. As broken as his sentences were, their meaning was understood.

"But they have guardians!" Sissy exclaimed. "A bird named Shelby and two dogs, Tika and Nero."

"We are not dogs!" Jawfree snarled. "How does a child like you know so much about the ancients? Who are you?"

"You," she stuttered. "You are guardians." She turned her back to the bars of ice, sliding down to the ground. Once in a sitting position, she pulled her legs to her chest, wrapping her arms around them.

"Does it matter what we are? We are all stuck here together with the same problem," Decon suggested. "We should try to get along."

"I think Jawfree is correct. We need to know how this girl knows so much about us." Nick moved as close as he could to the ice bars that separated them.

She figured she had no choice now but to tell them. "I am Cornelius's daughter. My name is Sissy."

Jawfree let out a deep roaring laugh. "You are the reason the barriers are breaking down. Well, I wouldn't count on your father coming here for you."

"Why? My father loves me. He is only doing what he is, to right the wrong that was done to our people," Sissy cried.

"Silly girl. He is a man bent on having war. That is his only purpose. Do you think you conquer and kill off worlds so their inhabitants can enjoy freedom? Not even a young girl like you could be so naive. Open your eyes and look around."

"You sealed us in a world and took my Aunt Diana prisoner." Sissy refused to turn from her position. She flopped her head down on her knees.

"Diana." Nick smiled. "I haven't heard that name in a long time. The finest storyteller I ever met - a wonderful woman. If, in fact, you are her niece, you should be proud. But a prisoner she was not. We all chose to join the guardians, my child. They asked us and we agreed. They took no one against their will."

"I am afraid your father, after participating in the blood wars, was bent on war. Surely you do not believe that when the barriers come down, he will let everyone live happily ever after. You have seen firsthand how he treats the creatures he comes across. We had no choice but to give his kingdom its own world to protect the other realms." Jawfree knew what he said would affect the girl deeply. "I am sorry, but it is all true."

Sissy said nothing. Deep down, she knew what she was told was true. For some time, she felt the urge to question her father's practices. There was no one to speak to about her feelings. If she had said anything to her siblings, she ran the chance of being accused of treason. She also knew it wouldn't be her father who would come for her. There was hope for her sisters, though. She refused to believe they would just leave her there.

She sat and cried. It was time for her to accept this small cage could be her home for a very long time, if not for eternity. "It's what we grew up believing. We had no idea that it wasn't all the truth. The stories and legends were told to us as bedtime stories. If what you say is true, I am sorry for what I have done."

Chapter Fifty-Nine

It was time to head over to William's quarters to prepare for the evening's dream adventures. The sun would be going down soon. Richard provided everyone with a sleeping pill - the whole group would fall asleep at exactly the same time.

Once inside the dream realm, Willow found Ashlyn in the staging area of her dream. The girls added Lance next. His advanced skills in dreamwalking not only made finding the others easier, but gave Ashlyn a few new tips as well. Once Clairity and William joined them, the group set out together to find Mike and Sarah.

Doors appeared before them in the room - as was usual in their previous dreamwalking experiences. The choice was obvious, the one made out of ice had to be it. Cold radiated towards them from it. Willow silently wished for something warmer to wear. She rubbed her shoulders, while moving her legs in a walking motion on the same spot.

The prince, seeing her discomfort, took no time to make her wish come true. They were immediately all bundled up for a day of fun in the snow. He opened the door and the group was pulled through before anyone even had a chance to say thank you.

"Thanks for the clothes. Next time, can we agree to do something as a group before rushing in?" William's tone made it obvious he wasn't impressed at being drawn into the dream without knowing what was going on first.

"Sorry," Lance answered. "I hate wasting time. I forgot you haven't spent any time in the dream world before." A familiar smirk graced his face, suggesting he wasn't all that sorry. "Besides, we all want to get back quickly." He winked at Willow. The simple gesture was enough to make her face turn bright red.

Diffusing the situation before it became any more volatile became priority number one. "We should move on," Willow proposed. "There is probably a long way to go before we find out anything. Even if it is a dream, none of us want to be exposed to the cold any longer than we have to be."

She was wrong. They stepped over a hill of snow and were in the middle of a small town. There was no sign of movement anywhere, other than blowing snow whipping against any exposed skin it could find.

"Let's check the buildings," Ashlyn suggested.

The distinct scents of chocolate and peppermint floated towards them, luring them towards the first building. A single whiff was enough to warm the girls on the inside, their bodies drifting mindlessly towards the source. Seeing the door open increased the urgency of their movements. Without warning, it slammed shut in their faces, leaving them disgruntled and disappointed. A sign on appeared which read *Not This Way*. The next two buildings were equally as frustrating.

"Well!" Willow yelled, glancing up. "If we aren't supposed to go that way, which way are we supposed to go?!" She held open her arms as if asking anyone who could hear her.

A large arrow lit up in the snow on the ground, made entirely out of red and green flashing lights and pointing to the west.

"You're kidding, right?" Lance asked.

"I was going to ask the same thing," William added. "I don't remember your dreams ever telling you where to go before... at least not this bluntly."

"We never asked before," Ashlyn said, staring at the arrow. "I guess we follow it. Someone must be pointing us that way. It's better than having another door slammed on us."

"Your powers of deduction are second only to your beauty," Lance said sarcastically. He bowed majestically before her as if she was royalty.

Ashlyn took it as a compliment, completely missing the tone in his voice. She smiled, allowing a sigh to escape her lips. Her eyes focused dreamily on the prince as he straightened back up and gave her a wink.

William, as always, found himself forced into being reality's advocate. He pinched Ashlyn hard, making her scream "Ow!" and breaking her daydream.

A smile crept over Willow's face. For the first time she realized how funny the lovesick girl stuck between two men was... as long as it didn't involve her.

The arrow became their guide. The group headed in the direction they were being steered towards. A few minutes later, they stumbled upon an idling train with enough open sleighs to fit them all. As soon as they were seated, the train took off, leading them on a non-stop route to the bridges and caverns. A mere minute later, they arrived.

Simply walking over the bridges was enough to make the girls queasy, finding the water below unnerving. Those emotions might have been tenfold had it crossed their minds that not knowing how to swim wouldn't matter. Falling in would have resulted in an almost instantaneous death from the freezing temperatures.

Only certain bridges allowed them to walk across, others crumbling as they neared. They were being directed to somewhere. Before long, it became obvious their destination was an open portal.

"Took you guys long enough to get here," Sarah said. "This whole dream thing is weird. How can we feel the cold? Can't someone warm it up a little? I know, why not add some sun and sand, or maybe a nice beach?"

"Did you have to bring Prince Creepy?" Mike asked.

Lance chuckled quietly at the comment. The look on his face told Willow he had made a mental note of it and would one day bring it back up. "We are all heading the same way. Why not enjoy each other's company at the same time?"

"Yes, I suppose we are," Mike answered. He filled them in on Nick's disappearance and the stones to the Yeti land.

William frowned. "Yeti territory is very dangerous. We are going to have our hands full just trying to locate the stones to enter Lanzia's domain."

"The door here is open," Ashlyn said, causing everyone to turn and smile at her. Stating the obvious was her strong suit.

"Well," Willow said, "let's go see what awaits us."

"Is that a good idea?" Sarah asked. "I mean, we don't know what's through there. It could be dangerous."

"That's the point... we don't know. That's what we came to find out. We need to know what exactly is out there. Anyone who wants to stay can, but if we are to mount any type of a rescue, we need more information about what we are up against." Willow held her breath and took a step through the portal.

The others all followed. The terrain in the new location was almost identical to the world they had just come out of. There was no sign of roads or pathways and Willow highly doubted a train was coming to usher them on a tour. They were stuck walking.

Lance positioned himself in front of the others, suggesting they head in the same general direction his sister had. It wasn't long before they came to a hill. Although it was dark, the moonlight reflecting off the crisp white snow and ice illuminated the area enough to see the outline of large castle sitting on a lone cliff. It too was coated in sparkling ice. A single shimmering bridge was the only thing that connected the castle to the rest of the world.

Far below them, that single mountain, was surrounded by ocean on all sides. The tips of waves, far beneath the castle peaks, were frozen in place, never having the opportunity to finish crashing against the sides of the cliffs.

Ashlyn, looking for a better vantage point, inched forward. The ground beneath them gave way, sending them spiralling down an ice slide. They twisted, turning sideways, upside down and right side up again before crashed into a pile at the bottom.

"Maybe we could not fall through the ground in a dream sometime," Clairity said to Ashlyn from the bottom of the pile. Her face formed a frown, which quickly changed to an expression of pain.

Ashlyn tried to move, almost making it to a standing position. Slipping on the ice, she came crashing back down on top of her friend.

"Well, you can't tell me you knew that would happen," she answered. "There wasn't any big warning button this time."

"No, but I wasn't going to try to get any closer to the edge," Clairity replied, finally managing to stand up. A cramp formed in her lower leg. She balanced on one foot while trying to shake it off.

Willow smiled. Her friends always made her see the humour in things. From the corner of her eye, Willow noticed Lance bending down to pick something up. Moving closer to him, she could see it was a wand.

"It was my sister's," he said, putting it in his pocket for safekeeping. "When we find her, she will need it."

"Looks like we are way down here and need to get way up there." Mike glanced at the top of the cliff the castle was perched on. "We better start looking for another way back to the top."

"Watch your step," William advised. "The ground is sheer ice and there are sharp points in these waves that you could easily fall on. We don't want anyone impaled by accident." He moved by Willow's side, taking her arm to ensure her safety before anyone else could.

They walked along the shoreline hugging the walls of the cliff as best they could, but found no way to climb the smooth sides. Mike let out a big breath of air, which mixed with the cold outside, forming a smokey appearance. He chuckled at the sight. Making a fish face, he blew rings into the air.

"Looks like we may have a problem. We could be stuck down here. Should we start the dream over?" he asked.

"Maybe there is a way in from down here," Clairity suggested. "We could try the base of the structure under the castle."

The walk over to the separate cliff, which housed the ice tower, proved to be a difficult obstacle course. They found themselves ducking under some frozen waves while carefully avoiding the sharp edges of others.

"Look! There is a cave!" Sarah exclaimed.

The alcove appeared to be naturally formed. Most likely created back when waves were still able to smash against its walls. Coming closer, it was still hard to tell if there was any rock underneath the layer of ice that coated everything.

William ran his hand against the smooth surface of the wall, testing its strength. Inside, large icicles hung down from the cavern ceiling. If any one of the icicles fell it would, no doubt, cut straight through any flesh it happened to land on. Crystallized ice made displays in patches, appearing as white flowers lining the floor.

Torches lit with green flames were positioned in equal intervals from each other about five feet from the bottom of the walls on either side of them. The flames, however, provided no heat.

Willow moved her hand close to one, fascinated by the appearance. Lance grabbed her from behind. The two tumbled to the ground, with her body ending up lying directly on top of his. Their eyes locked. A warmth flushed to her cheeks as he playfully winked. William and Mike rushed over to help her up.

"Flames that burn green can instantly freeze organic matter," Lance stated, dusting himself off. He took her hand in his. "Just touching it with the tip of one finger could have cost you your hand." Slowly, he lifted her hand to his mouth, delicately kissing it, his eyes never leaving her gaze. The sides of his lips curled up at her undivided attention to his actions.

When the prince released her hand, Willow's expression turned to horror, his words sinking in. She glanced at her hand, realizing what he had just saved her from. "Thank you," she said, giving him a hug.

William nodded his head in approval at the prince for looking out for Willow's health, but took her hand in his, separating the two.

The cavern split into four different paths, resembling tunnels etched out over time by a series of rivers. A cold wind snapped at them, sending chills down her spine.

"Which tunnel did that gust come from?" she asked.

"Why? What are you thinking?" William asked her back.

"The prophecy that Nathan recited, its first line was about a cold wind blowing. That could be the sign we need to tell us which way to go. I think we should follow it." Willow stood in front of one pathway and motioned for the others to pick a tunnel. They waited for a gust of wind to return. When it did, it came from the far left direction.

"Looks like nothing in here could ever be right, either," Clairity mused, referring to a similar choice she made in a previous dream they entered together. The choice there had only been between going left or right. Still, they stayed to the left.

The further in they travelled, the more difficult the route became to navigate, their feet slipping and sliding in every direction.

"I think the ground is actually on a slight incline. We are heading upwards, making it harder to walk on the ice. If we aren't careful, we could slip all the way back to the entrance," Lance said, not helping the mood.

A set of stairs leading to a door offered them momentary relief. The whole structure was entirely crafted out of ice, with a gigantic padlock securing the door.

"The prophecy does mention locks. This could be another sign." Ashlyn carefully inspected the door and lock, clearly not interested in going back down the steps. The top part of the path had been particularly hard for her to navigate. "We could use magic to open it." She pulled out her wand and before anyone could say a word a loud bang sounded. The lock crumbled, falling to the ground.

"We were hoping not to attract attention," Clairity said. "Remember, we talk before we do?"

"Right. Sorry," Ashlyn mumbled, rolling her eyes.

"Might as well push on now it's open," Lance said, squeezing by Ashlyn. Opening the door, he walked through without hesitation, seeming to have a good sense of direction for not having ever been to this world before.

Thinking back to the visions Shelby had showed her of the prince's castle, Willow understood. His home was also built into a mountain with lower levels that extended all the way down the heart of the summit. This dungeon was probably very similar to what he was used to.

The inside of the castle was cloaked in as much ice as outside. The group followed Lance around passages and upstairs. He seemed very confident in his directions, until they came to another shut door.

"This should be the main part of the dungeon. I don't know what we will find behind the door for sure, but the design of this castle suggests prisoners are on this level somewhere." Lance moved aside, suggesting he wanted one of the girls to use magic to open the door.

To everyone's surprise, it was Mike who moved forward. He grasped the handle, turning it with ease. "No lock," he said, smirking at Lance. "Not so big on attention to the details that aren't on a female body, are you?"

"I figured there would be more security. My mistake," he said, a challenge lingering on his lips. "As for the beauty of the female body, perhaps if you paid a little more attention to that, you might stand a better chance." Lance locked his eyes on Willow.

Behind the door was a table and a few chairs. On the wall above, hung thousands of keys. *Did they really have that many prisoners? Why would they need that many keys?* Willow moved closer, her hands clasped together behind her back. After the episode with the green flame, she wasn't taking any chances. There were a total of zero plans that involved touching anything in that world again. A single brave finger broke free from its confines. Shaking, it pointed towards one of the keys - the only one that wasn't made from ice. It was black and a bit smaller than the rest.

Lance leaned over her, his arm brushing her shoulder as he snatched the key off the wall. Smiling, he handed it to Willow. "The keys won't hurt you."

"Thanks," she replied, returning the grin.

A noise caught their attention from behind an adjoining door. Like its predecessor, it too was unlocked. Behind it they found themselves staring at empty cages, hundreds of them.

"Looks like the Frostica have big plans," Willow said, keeping her distance from either side. The middle was close enough. "They must intend to fill all these."

"Probably with us," Lance said, walking past her again. Following the cages, every so often finding a staircase leading up. "We need to go up."

"Lance!" a female voice exclaimed, from inside one of the dark cages. "I knew you would come." She stepped forward out of the shadows, to the front of the cell.

"Sissy," he answered, moving up to the bars that imprisoned her.

"Why are they here?" she questioned, carefully watching Willow. "Where are the others?"

"They are helping me find you." Lance replied, taking her hand through the ice bars. He handed her the wand.

"They were going to leave me here, weren't they? Father probably doesn't even know you are here. He didn't send you, did he?" she asked, already knowing the answer. A look of despair flashed in her eyes, sadness quivering on her lips.

"It doesn't matter, Sissy. I am going to get you out of this world. I promise," Lance announced.

Willow moved forward, her eyes resting on Nick. Shock returned her gaze. From the cage across from him came a scream, "Willow! It's a trap. Run!"

She turned to the side, finding herself face-to-face with two unknown guardians. The fear reflected in their stares chilled her to the bone. They weren't looking at her, but rather past. She licked her lips, biting the bottom one before peeking over her shoulder at a female Frostica with a large white staff, adorned at the top with a crystal ball.

The creature opened her mouth and, in a hissing loud-pitched voice, yelled, "GET OUT!" Her staff banged down on the ground, sending a shock wave hurtling towards them.

Willow sat up in bed, sweat dripping down her face. The Frostica Queen's words echoed in her mind, competing with the sounds of her own laboured breath. There was nothing that could stop her uncontrolled shaking.

"Sh," William whispered in her ear, sitting up beside her. His arm stretched around her, alleviating some of the fears. He gladly shared them, making her stronger.

The bits of nails not destroyed from her constant biting dug into her palms. Looking down at her hand she realized something was clenched in one fist. Fingers slowly pried open, stiffer than a rusty bolt. She gasped. There lying in her possession was the key from the dream. Somehow, she managed to bring it back. How was that possible? The look on William's face told her he was just as confused as she was.

Chapter Sixty

Jade glanced in the mirror at her reflection. Donning a pair of shiny earrings, she looked exactly like the girl she used to be. She tied her hair up into a neat bun on the top of her head. Hilary suggested she try to look more presentable when helping in the mayor's office. What choice did she have but to comply? That was, after all, what she had been left in the city to do. Her new job involved helping sort out issues from the attack, the city's move and work on a future alliance with the guardians.

Her first day in the city had been difficult. Feelings of loneliness consumed her. After the atrocious things she had done in her homeland, it had taken her a long time to even attempt speaking to the others. Then, just as she was starting to feel as if she was accepted, perhaps even forgiven on some level, she was shipped off to the city - dumped like trash on garbage day.

Her memories faded back to that fateful day when she singlehandedly caused the invasion of her home world. The face of her toddler brother Jordan being carted off as a prisoner haunted her. That was the first and only time when he didn't appear to be dripping in cuteness. The next image was worse: her mother's body lying lifeless on the ground. Her death had replayed in her mind a thousand or more times. It was a neverending loop, reminding her of her crimes. In a way, it was a self-inflicted punishment. Tears streamed down her face as she stood motionless, staring in the mirror yet not seeing her own reflection.

She hadn't been able to speak to anyone about what happened - not even her father. How could she? No one would have understood. No one, that is, until Hilary.

The mayor caught her in one of her more vulnerable moments. Illusion usually hid all of her emotions in public, but Hilary saw through it, bearing witness to an emotional breakdown. After which she insisted on lending an ear. Once Jade started, there was no stopping. Her emotions streamed out - a flowing river rushing to a waterfall. Nothing could have stopped the force. She revealed everything in her soul… every feeling… every regret. The mayor hadn't judged her nor had she tried to correct her. She simply listened to Jade as she poured her heart out. That was exactly what was needed and something no one else could have given her. She felt a bond to the woman now - a gratefulness.

"Miss Jade?" A knocking at her door snapped her out of the trance. Constable Safron Black had arrived. He picked her up every day, delivering her in a timely fashion to the mayor's office and her new job.

None of them expected to be split up. Being there to help meant accepting what they were each asked to do. She was assigned to help the mayor with Pewterclaw's relocation, defences and negotiations with the camp. Her father, Malarchy, on the other hand, was assigned to helping delegates from other cities and the directors. His job was more difficult than her own, now that the directors had basically denounced the existence of guardians. That translated into a lack of time. They hadn't seen much of each other since before Halloween.

She opened the door, applying her happy face illusion as makeup. "All ready. Sorry if I kept you waiting."

The constable was, as always, dressed in an orange suit with a yellow shirt, leaving her to question if the man owned anything else. She pressed a finger over her lips, stifling a giggle. Someone important in his past must have told him those colours suited him.

Today, his black hair was tied back into a neat ponytail. The rest of his facial hair was blonde, and for the first time since she'd met him, looked as if he had brushed it all straight. It was a contrast from the pronounced curls he usually wove by hand into his beard and moustache.

"Not at all, my dear. Lots of time... lots of time. Shall we?" he asked.

It was a short drive to the office. Inside line-ups were already formed for various complaints and problems. Since Halloween, the number of reports filed had tripled. Esmerelda stood behind the main desk, filling her tall, beehive-styled, blue hair with the office supplies that would be needed for a busy day. She offered a quick good morning in her usual nasal voice as she opened the counter for them to pass through.

The two followed the coloured lines on the floor towards the mayor's office. Jade slowed her pace, nearing the missing persons wall. Right in the middle, on top of all the other reports, was the bus driver that first brought her to the city. After disappearing mysteriously, he had become nothing more than one more face in a growing pile of missing persons. His case was especially odd since he was the only witness who actually saw any of the guardians in their full form. The circumstances were suspicious, to say the least. Thinking about it now, she understood why the guardians didn't appear at the meeting. It was far too dangerous. Somewhere in the city, there was a spy. At this point it was impossible to figure out who, but she was going to spend her free time trying.

A new office had been added for Jade to work in. Space for the addition had suddenly appeared right next to the mayor's office. The hotel owner had done something similar, easily moving space around to maximize its use. There was so much she didn't yet understand about how some magics worked.

After entering through the main door, she took a seat on the comfortable high-back, leather chair that rested behind a wooden desk with her name displayed on it in large gold letters. Behind her was a second door which led directly to Hilary's office. When the mayor wanted to see her, there would be a knocking noise, followed by the door flying open.

Since she began working with the city, Jade found herself constantly in the company of the mayor. She attended all meetings and events, basically shadowing Hilary's every move. She didn't mind. Having someone to talk to and confide in was a comfort. In exchange, all she needed to do was to keep her appearance professional, which translated into looking like the mayor. All the clothes and accessories she needed were provided to her as gifts. Deep down, a part of her didn't mind having new things. Having the finer things in life and every comfort was addictive. Wanting to live well, in itself, wasn't a crime.

A knock broke her train of thought. Her office door opened, allowing a fat wrinkly dog in. Leaping onto her desk, it dropped a newspaper and daily memos, then wagged its tail before jumping down and exiting.

A smile crossed her face at what she witnessed. She picked up the first memo, announcing the city decided to adopt many of the homeless pets and was providing them with various jobs. They would now be handling delivery of memos, mail, newspapers and other inter office communications. *That explains the dog,* Jade thought to herself, chuckling.

She picked up the newspaper and opened it to the first page. The headline read *Rumours of Guardians Debunked* written by Keith Quidnunk. There was no desire to read the article, knowing it was information she had already heard firsthand - information no one from the newspaper should have ever known. She turned to the next page. The articles there weren't much better, covering the teenage heroes and their next transition into empyral schools.

Jade glanced up for a moment and let out a huff. School was a complete waste of time for her. She had carved out a position for herself in the city that gave her access to valuable information. It seemed counterproductive to leave now. Hilary had also voiced her disapproval for any of them to attend the schools. The mayor was deadset against it and planned to have a discussion with the Director of Knowledge in-person.

The question lingered in her mind as to who was behind the information leaks to *The Empowered* and who was this Keith Quidnunk? Someone on the inside was feeding this guy information. But who? And why? Whoever it was, must have also been the one providing intelligence to the directors. How would anyone benefit from making it appear guardians did not exist? She desperately wanted to figure out the endgame, but there just wasn't enough information.

Jade flopped the paper down on her desk. There was other work to do. At the moment, she was looking into the way in which the princes and their zombie hoard had managed to enter the city. It was a real puzzle. The only way in or out had been by the bus. The driver was very careful as to who he let into Pewterclaw. She saw that firsthand. He had, however, mentioned that he provided rides for those cleared by high-ranking city officials without asking questions.

She picked up another file from the pile to see if she could find anything that might incriminate the culprit among city officials. If she went through enough files, her luck was bound to change and she would end up stumbling upon some clue. Paperwork must have been filled in allowing a group that size into the city. She was sure of it.

Opening the file in her hands, she recognized the picture on the inside flap. It was Clyde, the man who ran the hotel. Apparently, he was on the city books as a paid consultant. It didn't say what he was consulting about. Since he was deceased, his file should have never been sent to her. She slumped back in her chair, her mind jumping between how the file found its way into her pile and what Clyde could have possibly done for the city.

Jade jumped, startled by a knock. The door behind her flew open. She quickly hid the file in the bottom drawer of her desk, using an illusion spell on it to make it look like a blank notebook in case anyone tried to snoop in her office.

"You wanted to see me?" she asked, smiling as she entered the mayor's office and sat down.

"Yes," Hilary answered. "I thought we could go for lunch. We can try another new restaurant you haven't been to before. *The Blinking Barman* is opening today and I need to be there for the grand ceremony. It might be a fun experience for you."

"Sounds great!" she exclaimed. She froze. A shriek escaped trembling lips. "Kill it, please!"

Crawling across the mayor's desk was a small blonde spider. It terrified her. Jade had been born with a silver spoon in her mouth and a father who handled any creepy-crawly problems.

Hilary glanced at the spider, then at Jade. "Don't be silly, child. This little creature is our friend. It isn't like a snake. Those we could do without in this world. That's why I was sure someone had chosen the giant snake on Halloween. I figured they knew how I felt about them and were trying to scare me out of office." She stood up, escorting the spider safely out of the room.

Jade wasn't about to follow. She wasn't sure where the mayor went, but presumed she took the critter outside to release it. A few minutes later, Hilary returned. "I am surprised you reacted so to a spider. They are, of course, the first and strongest illusionists to exist. You share their power. That should mean something to you. If you do a little research on them, you might see they really aren't bad at all."

Jade gasped. Spiders used illusion magic. Who knew? And why did the mayor know? The abilities of ancients wasn't common knowledge. "Have you considered the possibility that the princes are working with the Xiuhcoatle?"

The mayor's eyes widened with curiosity. "You don't believe that, do you? I mean have you seen them, the serpents?"

"No, not directly. But why would the princes lie?" Jade asked.

"It would make them seem much worse than they actually are. No dear, I expect they made the story up to strike fear in their opposition. If there are any serpents out there, they are locked away somewhere else. If they do come here, we will handle them."

"They were in Willow's dream as well," Jade said. "Doesn't that mean something?"

"Dreams are interesting things. Some things we see are merely images from our mind or symbols meaning something else. From what I know of that dream, it was probably just a foreshadowing of the Halloween parade and that terrible blown-up serpent float."

"You do believe us though, right? You believe the guardians are here?" Jade asked.

"Why, of course, dear. I think after the reaction today, we should stay hush-hush on the subject though... for safety's sake. It is an election year and I won't be of any use to anyone if I don't get re-elected. Unfortunately, popular opinion isn't in favour of the existence of guardians. I told you before, only some people have been educated on our history."

"I understand." It was best she agreed with the mayor for now. She had Hilary's favour at the moment. There was no reason to change that.

"I have a few errands to run. I will be back to meet you for lunch," the mayor said, preparing to leave.

After saying goodbye, Jade returned to her office. It was the first time since Jade took the position as aid to the mayor that she hadn't gone along on errands. Why was today different? Where was Hilary going that she wanted to be alone?

Another knock sounded at her door. A frown crossed her face. She wondered why they had given her a door at all. It was much easier before when people simply approached her.

"I was looking for the mayor," Esmerelda said. "Do you happen to know where she went to? She isn't in her office."

"She said she had some errands to run," Jade answered. "Can I help with something?"

"Errands? There isn't anything in her appointment book." The girl blew a big pink bubble from her gum. It popped. "I wonder if she has a new date?" She snorted a laugh.

"She dates?" Jade asked, confused by what was so funny.

"Oh my, yes. She has been engaged more times than I have pencils in my hair. She never gets to the aisle though. They break up right before the wedding and the guy never comes around again. I think she may be a runaway bride and tells them to hit the road when she gets nervous. No way to tell, though. Folks round here joke if she married them all, she would be nicknamed *The Black Widow...* the way them guys just disappear. But you didn't hear it from me. If you hear from her, be a doll and let her know I am looking for her."

Esmerelda left. Jade sat back in her chair twirling a pencil through her fingers as she wondered what that was all about. She hadn't thought of the mayor as the type of woman to date many men. Perhaps at lunch she would have the opportunity to discuss it. There were other topics that were more important, though - staying in the city and not taking the school placement tests topping the list.

She went back to looking through the stack of files on her desk until it was time to meet Hilary for lunch.

Chapter Sixty-One

Here she was, back again. The command centre had become a second sleeping quarter for Willow and her friends. This morning they were gathering to go over the dream from the night before.

Outside, the wind howled as if it were screaming a caution of a storm that would surely follow. Flames raged to new heights in the fireplace. The smell of wood burning, mixed with brewing hot coffee, was a delight to the senses of anyone coming in from the rapidly dropping temperatures outside. For the first time, she felt a chill in the cabin. The fireplace usually kept things balmy... not today. A mumbling of the word *snow* from somewhere across the room caught her attention, although she wasn't sure from who.

The door opened. Lance immediately headed to the fireplace. He walked on the spot for a few minutes, rubbing his hands together in the glowing heat. "It's hard to believe anyone would choose to live in this part of the world. Give me a warm climate any time."

William laughed as if they were good friends. "You are going to be a whole lot colder for a while if we are to have any hope of rescuing your sister."

"I have to be careful of time now. I have a few days left before there is an opening between our worlds. To avoid explanations of where I was, I will need to return. The less I divulge about you, the better for all of us." The prince took a seat at the table beside William.

"Well, then the sooner we get going, the sooner we can come back. The camp should be fully moved by the time we are done. I hope you don't mind if we don't tell you where that will be, assuming you don't already know that too." There was almost a tease in his words. "Last night's dream adventure has left us with a few questions. We know where to look for the portal stones so we can enter the land of the Frostica."

Willow was uncomfortable with the way the two men were becoming so friendly. She wasn't sure exactly why it bothered her, but it did. Avoiding looking at either one, she locked her gaze, focusing her eyes on the key she brought back with her from the dream.

"And," William said, watching the key flip around in her fingers, "it seems Willow has developed yet another talent. She brought that key back from the dungeon."

She felt the gaze of every eye in the room focused on her as if there were something hideously wrong with her face. For a brief moment, she realized how the Kriller felt. Her eyes remained on the old-fashioned key. Looking up wasn't an option - at least, not one she was willing to take.

"How is that possible? Even with my family's advanced skills in dreamwalking, I have never heard of such a thing." There was a sense of uneasiness in Lance's voice - one that Willow never heard before. Just hearing it somehow made him less attractive.

"No one has. I don't know how and I don't know what the key is for. I imagine its use will present itself to me somewhere. Can we concentrate on the portal stones? Mike said they are hidden in the Yeti world. Do we know anything about that realm?" Drawing attention away from herself was the plan. Her stomach churned, turning upside down and making her glad there hadn't been time for breakfast.

William opened his notebook and bounced the pencil up and down a few times before speaking. "We actually don't have that much information about the Yeti, or abominable snowmen, as they are known in this world. The stories say they are large savage beasts, usually with white fur, who live in snow-covered areas... normally mountain tops. They are hard to track and even harder to prove they exist. I was hoping Nathan might enlighten us a bit more." He pointed the end of his pencil at the boy. "You might know them as *Transmutton*."

Nathan's lips curled up at the edges just slightly, his eyes narrowing. "I do know them. They are snow shifters. When hunted by anything, they can become a mound of snow, basically disappearing in plain sight. That would be why they are considered so elusive."

"Are they dangerous?" Lance asked.

Willow lifted her eyes from the key to the prince's face, wondering if it was fear she heard in the tone of his question. Now, without an army behind him, was this the real Lance? She dismissed the thought. He did, after all, come there on his own accord, against the will of his family, to try to save his sister. That was not the act of a cowardly man. Her mind shifted to Malarchy and Jade. Why had she been questioning everyone around her the past few days? Maybe it was her. Maybe, with all she had been through, she was trying to see the negative in people even if it wasn't really there.

"That's a good question," William said.

Willow's eyes bolted to the guard before resting back on the key in her hand. A half-smile formed on her face, thinking about how silly she had just been. Of course, it was completely normal to wonder what the risks were. Why was she being so critical of Lance?

"Oh, most definitely. They are beasts. There are no records of them communicating with each other or anyone else." Nathan's eyes widened, gleaming with excitement. His face gave off an aura of pride. Knowledge was his forte. "I should also mention that they do use their snow-shifting abilities to hide and wait for prey."

"Great," Clairity said. "So a mound of snow could eat me now." A frown crossed her face as she considered how being devoured by a hairy beast would feel.

"There is no evidence of people going missing in areas where these snow beasts exist. I expect they choose smaller prey than humans... perhaps elk. Of course, they would have the ability to attack if provoked, I am sure." William looked around the room at every person as if sizing them up for duty.

"That could be said about almost any creature," Lance replied. The prince's face was emotionless and cold.

"Alright, Willow, Lance, Dezi, and Clairity. Go find some warm clothes. Everyone else help pack and move. We have two days to find the stones in Yeti land, use them to enter the Frostica world and retrieve Nick and Sissy, before Lance needs to head home and someone I know has a test to write." A smirk crossed his face.

Chapter Sixty-Two

After a brief stop to pick up Mike and Sarah with the portal stones, Faramund teleported them all to the portal base for the Yeti world. Snow whipped against their faces, making their noses numb and visibility poor.

Mike made quick work of setting up a tent in front of the portal. Sarah, Faramund, and Dezi would remain there, to make sure no Yetis escaped, while the rest of the team were inside the other realm searching for the hidden portal stones to open the doorway to the Frostica world. Faramund had already decided Sarah was to stay inside the tent to keep warm. For a moment, Willow found herself pondering over why the three guys who were supposed to be crazy about her weren't insisting she stay warm.

They know you too well. You would argue you were going no matter what, Kiera's voice echoed in her head.

Willow giggled. Of course, Kiera was right. Where Sarah was happy to stay warm and safe, Willow craved the knowledge of what was happening. She was standing there chuckling to herself when she realized everyone else was watching her.

"What?" she yelled out, moving closer to them. It didn't take long for her to see they were in front of the stone base, waiting. "Oh." How could she be so stupid? She hadn't even thought with Lance there the guardians were staying hidden unless absolutely necessary. They were waiting for her to open the portal.

She stepped in front of them and looked to the skies. There was already a storm right over top of them, making her task easier. She lifted her arms upwards. Lightning bolted down from above, hitting the stone base. The stones flew up, spinning from the force of the blast for a moment before settling into their respective corners. The portal opened.

"So that's how you managed to escape. Another talent that has never been heard of before. I am starting to see you are much more special than even I had thought." Lance said, watching her walk away. He tilted his head, keeping the best possible view of her.

The tone of his voice sent an extra shiver down her spine, one that wasn't caused by the temperature. Was he implying this was useful information to take back to his family? Guilt overwhelmed her for her thoughts. Lately, she was seeing something terrible in a lot of people. Maybe it was a phase. It was wrong to second-guess someone. Why was doubt creeping in now? There had to be a reason. Was she sensing the future?

"Well, no time like the present," William said, motioning for the group to head through the portal and suggesting Lance take the first position.

The Yeti realm wasn't much different from where they came from, except there was no storm this side of the doorway. The landscape was a crisp white, untouched by man. The sun glared off the ice around them, causing Willow to squint.

Lance pulled out a pair of sunglasses. Their dark lenses trimmed by thin black frames were elegant to look at. The prince hadn't actually been prepared for the adventure. He simply always carried a pair with him for appearance reasons. Still, Willow wished she had done the same.

"I am not close enough to the stones to know which way to go," William stated, looking in every direction.

"I think we should head for that mountain," Clairity said, pointing towards a peak to the north of them. "I have a feeling that's where we need to go." Her feelings were starting to become more regular now - a muscle she was stretching daily. Her ability was growing.

The hike through the snow wasn't a pleasant one. Even with no storm, the wind ripped at their skin, leaving welts from the cold in any spots not covered by cloth. They were crossing flat plains. Their feet sunk into previously untouched snow as they walked, making each step painfully slow and heavy. Even with all the extra clothing Willow had worn, she still felt a chill deep in her bones that rattled her teeth. Surprisingly, sweat also trickled down her face from the sheer exercise of the trek.

Things didn't get any better when they reached the mountain. There were no paths in sight and no caves to use. They were going to have to climb to the top. The sides of the mountain were sheets of ice formed as frozen waterfalls.

"You can't expect us to climb up a popsicle!" Clairity exclaimed. "We would never make it."

William removed his backpack, taking out boot covers with spikes on the bottom. He handed a pair to each of the group, suggesting they get moving before dark.

Willow brushed him off, having little interest in mountain climbing lessons. She surveyed the side of the mountain, losing herself to deep thought. Pacing back and forth, she examined every angle until she found the lowest landing.

As usual, the men paid little attention to her request for them to wait for a moment. William and Mike had already begun scaling the side, searching for a safe place to help the others up to.

Clairity moved close to her friend and looked up. "What is it?"

"A ledge, a ways up. Do you see it?" Willow asked. "It's just barely visible."

"Yeah, could be a cave or something. You think that is where the portal stones are?"

"Not even thinking about them yet." Willow smiled. "I was only hoping for an easier route. Shall we race the boys to the top?"

"Mind if I join you?" Lance asked. "I have a feeling your way up is going to be a little more appealing than theirs. I can see how tired the two of them are already."

Willow looked at the ground. The snow parted, making way for a fir tree sprouting out from under the layers of untouched white. As it grew, so did a staircase of branches, leading all the way to the ledge above. The three began walking up with little effort.

In the distance, they heard Mike's voice echoing, "You have to be kidding."

Willow winced at the tone of his voice.

They waited for William and Mike to join them. Once at the top, William flashed Willow an angry glance. Without saying a word, he pushed past her, sitting down to rest for a moment.

"What?" Willow said. "I told you to wait. I was trying to figure out if I could find an easier way up."

He still didn't answer her.

"So what's next?" Lance said, looking around.

"Ask Willow," Mike answered. "She's in charge now." Evidently he wasn't in a forgiving mood either.

"Fine," Willow said, turning her back to the pair. "If you two want to be like that, I will take over. So, we can either follow the ledge in either direction or enter the cave. I personally think the cave is the better idea. Clairity, any feelings?"

"I agree. Let's hit the cave." Clairity answered, flashing the two men a look of disapproval for their behaviour.

Lance glanced at the two men not budging from their spots and shook his head. "Guess I will go first, you two stay behind me." He motioned to the girls to stay close and moved in.

The cave was dark and damp. The temperature was warmer than outside, causing a thaw which became more evident the further in they travelled. The walls of the cave were smooth rock, almost as if they had been handcrafted. Glancing back, there was still no sign of Mike or William.

They pushed on, coming to a three-way branch in the tunnel. Willow walked to one side. Using the advanced eyesight provided by her feline guardian companions, she surveyed the area. She ran her fingers over a series of crude pictures carved into one of the walls.

"What is it?" Lance asked.

"Three pictures," she answered. "Looks like the first pathway has an 'X' through it. The second seems to lead to death and the third has a picture of a man... probably the guard who hid the stones. I suggest we take the right side." Willow moved back to the openings. She removed a scarf and was looking for somewhere to attach it to.

"What are you doing?" Clairity asked.

"Leaving a trail for William and Mike to follow, in case they decide come after us."

"No need," William said. "We are here." He looked around at the options and let out a sigh when he realized the three were doing fine without them. "Lead on, boss."

Willow grabbed Lance's hand, pulling him down the path they had chosen behind her. "We are going this way," she yelled back.

To her surprise, Lance snatched his hand back. "Not that I don't like holding your hand, but leave me out of trying to make William mad." He took the lead down the dark path.

A rush of regret flowed through Willow. She hadn't even noticed what she was doing until it was too late. William and Mike pushing by with smirks on their faces intensified her guilt.

"Boys: can't live with 'em, can't live without 'em." Clairity grabbed her arm and the two girls walked together behind the others.

The path led to a cavern. Stalagmites and stalactites formed in some areas reminiscent of sharp teeth biting down. Water dripped from the ceiling. This new area was warm. The layers of clothing adorning them became heavy, each member of the party shedding them at one point or another. Resting a minute the extra clothing was packed tightly into backpacks. Lance stood to one side alone.

Willow approached him, unable to hold his gaze. "Sorry," she mumbled, her lips quivering slightly. "I..." she started, but her words were cut off.

Her prince pulled her in tightly and kissed her. Not on the neck or the cheek, but full on the lips. Her eyes closed. She gave into the passion of his kiss. It was warm and soft. Tingles flowed through her body rushing to reach every tip: fingers, toes, even her nose.

When the kiss was over, he whispered in her ear. "I will always make you feel like that. Neither of them can." He brushed the hair from her face, before walking away with a smile.

There were no words strong enough to express how she felt. She wasn't even sure how long she had been standing there. Her fingers touching her lips, retracing where Lance kissed her.

"Willow, you okay?" Clairity asked, waving a hand in front of her face.

She snapped back to reality. "Yeah, great." A smiled formed on her face, which seemed to glow a little brighter than usual.

"How was it?" Clairity asked.

"Amazing," Willow said, the smile on her facing having no plans on disappearing any time soon. Neither of them had experienced a real kiss before. It was exciting news for the girls that would require further discussion when they returned.

"If we are done with the performance, perhaps we could get back to what we came here for!" Mike yelled, anger lingering in his eyes, more so when he glared in Lance's direction.

It was the opposite for William, there was a lost look on his face. His eyes filled with sadness and disappointment.

A sharp pain stung Willow in the chest. She looked away, unable to handle the hurt she'd inflicted. Something in the pit of her stomach ached, gnawing at her insides as if she had just made the biggest mistake of her life. All these feelings confused her. She wanted to cry - to run away. It felt like the ground beneath her was shaking.

Suddenly, she realized the ground beneath her was shaking. It gave way. The two girls found themselves hanging on to the edge of a cliff on the opposite side of a hole from the others. All three men bolted forward. There was nothing they could do from where they stood. The gap between them was simply too big.

Looking down, Willow couldn't see the bottom. Aslo and Kiera were about to intervene when a doorway opened. A pair of Yeti stepped through. They were tall, clearing at least ten feet and three times as wide as any man. Their bodies were covered completely in white fur or hair - Willow couldn't tell which. Huge sharp yellow teeth protruded from their mouths, resembling the rock formations they had passed earlier.

Both girls let out screams. The noise caused the beasts to glance at them. The Yeti reached down, grabbing an arm of each of the two girls and pulling them up to safety. The doorway in the wall opened again. Willow only had enough time to glance back at William for a moment, hoping he would notice the remorse in her eyes.

Chapter Sixty-Three

The pathway the beasts led the girls through seemed more extensive than either one of them believed possible. It wound in S-like patterns, leading to a room where other beasts were gathered. The two girls huddled together as the Yeti made growling noises at each other around them.

"Guess they do communicate with one another. Our information on them must be wrong. Let's hope they are friendly too," Willow whispered.

"Those teeth don't look friendly to me," Clairity answered, her body shaking.

The beasts stopped. The two girls found themselves in the middle of a circle of Yeti. Willow glanced around trying to find where growling noises were coming from, unable to decipher any message the beasts might be trying to communicate. "Nathan must not have had time to read any books on the Yeti language. At least, he never shared any with me."

One of the beasts moved forward and grunted at her while pointing to the ground. Unsure what to do, Willow sat. The ground was soft like sand. She ran her fingers through it and looked up at the creature staring back at her. What was it trying to tell her?

Taking a chance, she drew a picture of a girl and her depiction of one of the beasts holding hands in a friendly manner. It wasn't her best artistic work, but in her opinion, it could pass for a not too bad sand drawing. The beast bent down and grunted. He drew a picture of a man.

"That must be the guard who used to visit here. They probably wonder what happened to him. I think they were close," Clarity said.

"Great. So how do I tell them he died?" Willow rubbed her neck, thinking about it for a moment, then ended up drawing a picture of the same man lying down. She poured sand over top of the drawing.

Shrieks of pain rang out, intensified by echoing. The beasts were crying for the man that had been their friend. How could the information on the Yeti have been so wrong? They weren't savage at all, once one figured out how to communicate.

Willow found her fingers were already moving in the sand without her even realizing what she was doing. The pattern formed a copy of the portal stones that were missing, asking the Yeti where they could be found.

The beast in front of her lashed out, swiping at the sand the picture was drawn on, while letting out a fierce growl. Both girls scooted backwards. The creature moved back to his spot with the others, forming a circle around the two girls. They joined hands and began moving in a counterclockwise motion while making a low humming noise. Clarity spun around, looking in every direction. There was no way for them to escape.

"What are they doing?"

"I don't know," Willow answered. "Looks like some sort of ritual."

"Shouldn't we do something?"

"Like what?" Willow scanned the room for something that could help them. "We can't go through them. Most of my abilities are useless in this environment. Have you tried a telepathic link with them? Maybe you can explain why we are here and that we are not planning anything harmful."

"I can try, but that isn't an ability I have been able to use before." Clairity closed her eyes and filled her mind with thoughts of the Frostica and the prisoners. She thought of what had happened in the dream, of the guardians and what their people stood for.

Nothing happened.

Clairity shrugged her shoulders. "Guess that didn't work. Now what? Wands?"

"That could be construed as an act of aggression. I don't think that will help us find the portal stones." Willow answered.

"But we could escape."

"To where? We don't know where we are or which way to go. Somehow we need to communicate with them. There must be a way." Willow took a seat on the ground again, resting her head in her hands. She needed to figure out how to handle this before the others found them. She imagined the three men running in weapons ready. That would be a disaster. She lifted her head examining their surroundings again. There was one chance, but it was risky.

Aslo? Kiera? she thought. *Maybe you two could communicate with them? I know you have been monitoring everything. Lance isn't here so if we hurry, he would never know.*

The two guardians appeared. Aslo moved forward to try to communicate with the creatures, while Kiera remained back to protect the girls if the negotiations ended up taking a turn for the worse.

A low husky growl escaped from Aslo's throat. The same beast that was attempting to communicate with Willow moved out of the circle again, making a similar noise. The two continued exchanging grumbles, groans and growls for some time.

Aslo twitched his tail. "The guard, Kristophe, apparently took the time to learn how to communicate with them. It's amazing, really. He was teaching them to draw, among other things. He was their friend. Others who they tried to communicate with before were always afraid of them. They are hunted as elusive wild beasts. The people they encounter shoot first and ask questions later, especially when the fame of being the one to capture a Yeti is involved. Kristophe was trying to keep people away from the snow beasts, rather than the other way around. Seems they are misunderstood creatures who just need a hug." Aslo went back to growling noses again.

"Do they know anything about the hidden portal stones?" Willow asked.

"Kristophe brought the stones into their world one day. He asked them to guard them and never let anyone touch them. He warned the Yeti of the great danger that losing the stones could pose to all living things in every realm," Aslo answered.

"Can't you explain to them why we need them? You two are, after all, guardians. They seem intelligent enough to reason with." Clairity clung to Willow's arm, half-hiding behind her friend.

The growling came to a stop. Aslo returned to the group. "They are considering whether or not to disclose the location to us. Although they understand our situation, it seems their bond to Kristophe was extremely strong. He was their mentor... like a father figure."

"So where does that leave us?" Clairity asked.

"We wait," Aslo answered. "They will tell us their answer soon enough."

"You might want to explain the others to them. I bet the first reaction those three will have will be to attack rather than figure we are safe." Willow said.

"Good idea," Clairity agreed. "With the way Lance kissed you, I bet William and Mike are both dying to hit something." The edges of her lips went from full grin to grimace in seconds, realizing the pain the words held for her friend.

It appeared a decision was reached. Aslo returned to meet with the beast again. After a lengthy discussion, they heard a noise that sounded more like laughter than the usual growling noises.

"They have agreed to help us. It seems Kristophe mentioned his good friends Nick and Meredith. They feel they owe it to their friend to look out for those two. I have explained the situation about the young men and they were thoroughly amused with the problem, but understand."

"Am I the only one who isn't amused?" Willow asked.

"Seems like," Clairity snickered.

"Great," Willow said. "Let's find the stones and then the guys." Aslo and Kiera rejoined with her, appearing as stunning pictures on her skin again.

The girls followed the snow creatures through another series of paths, which after winding in many different directions came to an opening into the cold again.

"Are we on the other side of the mountain?" Clairity asked.

"Looks like." Willow peeked outside the doorway.

They had lost their extra clothes back in the room when they were separated from the group. Simply glancing outside made them both shiver.

The snow beasts seemed to understand their dilemma. One large, extra-furry Yeti moved forward and picked Willow up. The heat radiating from its body was intense. "Don't worry, Clairity, let them carry you. Trust me, they are warm."

The group continued following the ledge on the outside of the mountain. Willow tried to refrain from looking down, knowing they were much higher up the mountain than a tree could reach. Falling wasn't something she wanted to experience. She hid her face deep in the fur of the snow creature that was carrying her, pretending to be shielding herself from the cold. The sweet smell of jasmine surprised her nose.

Previously, when she thought of an abominable snowman, she pictured a smelly, dirty beast. These creatures were different. Their fur was clean and soft. In fact, the only thing that was unappealing about them was their sharp yellow teeth. There was little they could do about that considering where they lived and what they had access to. A type of plant that could produce a chewing stick that would provide them with natural tooth brushes popped into her thoughts. That was something she could leave for them. A gift of sorts for agreeing to help.

The ledge veered to the right, taking on a slight uphill grade. The path itself narrowed, becoming quite small and icy. The creatures showed off their extreme agility in manipulating the environment with ease and grace. When they came to a stop, Willow peered up from the fur that had been covering her face. Up ahead, several creatures were pushing a large ice boulder blocking the entrance to another cave.

Entering, the girls immediately felt a blast of warm air circulating around them. This area was even warmer than before.

Pools of water collected drips of moisture, each surrounded by green moss-covered stones. Parts of the ground were covered in a layer of soil. Willow bent down, her fingers feeling a lacked nutrients. To one side, she noticed some crude tools. The Yeti had been learning the basics of farming, probably just before Kristophe passed away.

She blew a handful of dirt back onto the ground, replenishing it with everything it needed to sustain plant life. She turned her hands upwards, allowing sparkling magic to flow to the soil. A series of trees sprouted, maturing before their eyes.

Breaking off a branch, she showed the creatures how to peel back some bark and chew on the end, making a brush for their teeth. Willow continued planting, choosing a variety of vegetables beneficial to teeth. When she was finished, the girls ate a few of each as an explanation of what vegetables were. Then break was over and they were continued their journey further in the mountain.

"I think we are following this stream," Willow announced.

The small trickle of flowing water turned into a full river. Both girls were surprised they were boarding a small boat. This area was a totally different ecosystem from the exterior of the mountain. It was warm with green moss and grass growing along the shore lines. The boat came to stop at a small town made up of crude huts.

"This must be their home," Clairity whispered.

The two girls were led through the huts to the other side of the small town, where another boat awaited. Willow slid into a seat with Clairity by her side. They sat quietly through most of the ride, taking in the scenery. Occasionally, a small bird would fly down and tease them playfully, or a colourful butterfly at least five times the size of any they had seen before would flutter by.

The small vessel came to a stop at some jagged rocks. Taking turns, the Yeti lifted the two girls off, securing the boat safely before they proceeded on foot. Their direction led them into a maze of sharp edged rock walls that reminded Willow of the dream in which she had been chased by Lance's two brothers and barely escaped. She shivered at the thought.

After winding in many directions, they came to a room containing a single stone pedestal in the centre, on top of which sat the portal stones. The snow creature, which Willow decided was the leader, handed them to her. Bowing before her new friend, she accepted them.

Stopping in the town on the way back, the girls were offered fresh cool water from an inside spring. At first, they were leery of the drink, wondering where the flowing water was coming from. They watched as the creatures placed cups under the flowing water and drank. Handing both girls a cup, they followed the same procedure, coming close to the spring and holding out their mugs to collect a small amount of the liquid. Willow opened her mouth and poured in a few drops. It was crisp, clean and refreshing. The best water she had ever tasted. She finished the entire cup, filling it a second time afterwards. Her mouth revelled in the feeling as her tongue soaked up wetness like a dried out sponge. Neither of them realized how dehydrated they were until the precious life fluid was being replenished in their bodies.

Willow's mind wandered to the William, Mike, and Lance. She wondered how they were, where they were and if they were thirsty. It didn't matter that they had supplies. A guilt overcame her for enjoying the water without them.

As if sensing what she was thinking, the Yeti motioned for them to move on. After travelling back, they arrived at the room where the floor had caved in. It was only moments later when the three men returned to the same spot, still searching for a way across the gaping hole. Seeing the girls surrounded by Yeti, all three prepared to attack. Willow bolted forward, throwing herself between man and beast. Holding her hands up in front of her face and closing her eyes, she acted as a human shield.

"Wait!" she yelled. "They are friendly." Willow opened one eye slowly and peeked out, hoping the attack had stopped. "Thank goodness," she said, letting out a puff of the air she had been holding. The next few minutes were full of explanations of the events that the past hours held, leaving out only the part about the best water anyone ever tasted and the involvement of the guardians. After her story was finished, she handed the portal stones to William.

They had what they came for. It was time to head back to the main world. The Yeti escorted them all the way to the open portal. Willow hugged each of her new friends as if they were gigantic teddy bears. She heard William chuckle in a low voice from behind her and turned to see a smile on his face.

Looking back one last time before leaving, she nodded. She would be back again. Kristophe started something with these creatures and they needed to continue on his legacy.

Chapter Sixty-Four

The door flew open. Safron Black raced into the room, huffing and puffing harder than usual. Placing his hand over his chest, he stopped moving until his heavy breathing subsided. "No time to waste. The mayor is waiting for us at the restaurant for lunch."

Jade slipped out from behind her desk and followed him. She knew from firsthand experience, keeping Hilary waiting wasn't something a person should do.

When they arrived, there was already a line-up on the street, waiting to enter the new restaurant. A giant red ribbon floated in front of the door, blocking the entrance. As soon as the mayor caught sight of Jade and her constable, she squeezed down on an enormous pair of scissors. The ribbon floated down on either side of her, falling to the ground. Flashes from a number of cameras went off, adding a momentary strobe light effect.

Jade spun around, hoping to catch a word with any reporter who might have been covering the event. Even on her tiptoes, peering over the heads of people in the crowd, there was no sign of any. The owner of the establishment thanked the mayor, shacking her hand for good measure. They held the pose, cameras taking advantage. Jade's head moved twice as fast this time. She thought she saw something at first, but it proved to be only a shadow.

Leaning over to Safron, she whispered in his ear, "Are the press covering this? I don't see anyone from the paper."

"Of course. It's even bigger news now that there is talk of forming one government to manage all of the empyral society. Hilary's name is on the list of potential candidates." The constable never took his eyes off of the mayor, all the while twirling his moustache at the ends.

"Where are they?" Jade asked.

"Where are who?"

"The reporters."

Safron glanced sideways at her for a moment before returning his attention to the mayor. "Don't be silly, girl. What sort of reporter would they be if everyone could see them in the open? It's their job to stay well hidden. That's how they get the best stories. Not the sort of life I would want, but to each their own, I say."

That was going to make things problematic. How was Jade supposed to find a link between the reporters and what was going on if she couldn't even find the journalists? Jade's attention turned back to the event at hand. The doors were open now and the crowd was filing in with hopes of trying all the new delicacies the restaurant had to offer.

As they reached the entrance, they were immediately escorted to the mayor's table where Hilary was already seated. Several extra place settings made it difficult to distinguish her spot. The mayor indicated for Jade to sit beside her, sending the constable to the bar to order drinks.

"Are we expecting more guests for lunch?" she asked.

"Yes," the mayor answered. "It's a special lunch today. Isn't that your father?" She motioned across the room.

Malarchy was sitting at a table with several dignitaries from other cities. There hadn't been much time for her to spend with him in the city. They both were overloaded with work. Looking at him now, his face glowing with the illusion magic he handled so well, she realized how much she missed him. "Yes," she answered, smiling.

"He is still single, isn't he?" Hilary asked in a higher pitched tone than usual.

Jade's attention zoomed to the woman she was sitting beside. "He is still mourning my mother," she snapped. "I don't think he is ready to date." Jade's mind replayed Esmerelda's words from earlier about the mayor and the nickname *the Black Widow*. She bit her top lip. Could Hilary have her sights set on her father? "Do you date?" Jade asked, feeling this was at least her opportunity to bring up the conversation.

"Hm?" Hilary turned her attention back to Jade. "We all like a little romance in our lives, dear. I am afraid my position in life scares off most potential mates. Seems when I reveal my true self to them, they... well, disappear."

"That's horrible," Jade said. "How do you handle it?"

Hilary laughed loudly. "Men are like flies. There are thousands of them. Surely you have seen how replaceable they are."

Remorse filled her thoughts. She had done some things she wasn't proud of. The Shinning boys almost died from her love potion cake and poor Neil believed she was going to run away with him. She sighed. That was what caused the end of her world. Prince Joseph had tricked her in much the same way she tricked boys. "Love is vicious," she said.

"Yes," Hilary agreed, smiling. "Yet we still want it, don't we? It's a primal urge all creatures have... to find a mate and reproduce."

"Reproduce?" Jade said, a little too loud. Having a child was the furthest thing from her mind.

"Yes, dear," Hilary answered. "That's why we have all those feelings. The desire that drives us to make love to one another is merely a means to ensure the continuation of our species. Once you accept that, it makes things much easier."

Safron returned with three glasses of a yellow liquid. "House specialty," he said. "They insisted we try it."

"Are we late?" Kasper Deogole asked.

"Not at all. Not at all." Hilary stood, greeting the Director of Secrecy and the Director of Knowledge.

"Fetch a couple more drinks will you, Safron, good man?" Kasper asked, smiling.

"I am so glad we could meet like this," Hilary said. "There are a few things I would like to discuss. You both know my assistant, Jade."

"Yes," Cassandrhea replied. "We are well aware of Jade and her situation."

"Of course. That is actually one of the things I wanted to discuss with you. I was hoping you two would reconsider the need for her to attend the testing." The mayor opened the menu in front of her and scanned it quickly.

"You want me to place her without being tested?" Cassandrhea flipped open a crisp white napkin and placed it neatly on her lap.

"No. Of course not." The mayor motioned for a waiter to attend to their needs. "A basket of bread for the table, please." Turning her attention back to the Director of Knowledge, she said, "I don't want her to attend school at all. She has become invaluable to me and I do think her time with me will give her a better education than she could receive anywhere else. There are so many applicants to the education system. I am sure there is someone who needs the spot more."

"With everything that has transpired, we cannot simply let these children run loose," Kasper said. He took a piece of the fresh bread that had just arrived and buttered it generously before taking a bite.

"Of course not, and those who were directly involved in the whole mess should go. Jade's part was coerced. She isn't aligned with them anymore. That part of her life is over. I will take responsibility for her."

Jade's mouth fell open. She wanted to scream out that it was all a lie. She wanted to stand up for her friends. Words refused to form. It was as if her voice disappeared - replaced with compliance.

"Coerced?" Cassandrhea's gaze shifted to Jade. "How?"

"For crying out loud, Cassie, the girl's home world was destroyed. She was forced here without any other option. The only people she knew were those children. If that wasn't bad enough, they never liked the poor girl. They treated her poorly. She had to try to fit in. I don't blame her one bit for following their lead. If we look at who performed the magic, it was never her."

"She still had her own free will," Kasper said. "Is she denouncing the existence of the elusive guardians as well?"

"She only went with what she had been told. The poor girl was brainwashed," Hilary stated.

Jade's mind raced a hundred miles a minute. Why was Hilary talking about her friends like that? The mayor was supposed to believe them - to be on their side. How could she betray them like this? Her voice remained absent.

"While I appreciate your position, you are not her parent. Malarchy has agreed she would be best served attending one of our fine institutions and I agree," Cassandrhea said.

"She wants no interaction with the others." Hilary said, offended.

"I can arrange for her to write the test ahead of time at Sleeping Sands. You could bring her yourself, Hilary. Perhaps tomorrow?"

"A lovely invitation. Jade will attend. I, unfortunately, must decline. Things are very busy at the moment. You do understand."

"Yes, I do," the Director of Knowledge replied.

"We have heard your name has been thrown into the fire for the new Governing Authority position that is being created. That wouldn't have anything to do with your change of heart about the guardians, would it? I would imagine it would be hard to find votes if people thought, well you were siding with these people." Kasper took his third piece of bread and began slathering it with butter.

"I appreciate what they did for our city, of course. Whether on purpose or by fluke is no concern. They saved lives. The rest of the mess I have no involvement in. That is your department, Kasper. I know you will figure it all out."

"I will. There are quite a few things that still don't add up. It's time to look at everything very carefully." Kasper motioned for a waiter. "I think we should order now."

Hilary looked at her watch. "My goodness, is that the time already? You will have to excuse us. We have another appointment to attend to. Enjoy whatever you like. My office is picking up the tab. Always a pleasure. We should get together more often."

Safron returned with the drinks and placed them on the table for the two directors. "So have we decided on lunch?"

"We are leaving, Safron. Come along," the mayor said, heading to the door.

Jade's stomach growled in the car, matching a similar noise coming from the constable. She had experienced this feeling on more than one occasion before. Out of all the times she went to lunch with Hilary, she never actually saw the woman eat anything.

Once back in the office, the good constable went to find them something to eat. Jade took the opportunity to find out exactly what happened at the restaurant. Luckily, her voice had resurfaced. "I was curious about earlier," she started.

"Yes, I am sorry, dear. I should have filled you in. Things are moving so very fast right now - there just wasn't time. I was hoping that the directors would let you stay here under my care. Unfortunately, it looks like I will be without you for much of the campaign." Hilary leaned back in the comfy chair behind her desk.

"Campaign?"

"Yes, much of it is your father's doing. I must thank that man properly. Somehow, he convinced the directors and other city officials that we need a central government. I was blown away when I found out that my name was in the race for running it. Fabulous news, isn't it?"

"Yes, brilliant," Jade said, taking a seat in front of her desk.

"Oh, cheer up. School is only a few months and then you will be back here with me, where you belong. Who knows what could happen in that time? I have to say, I would adore to have you as my own daughter."

Jade's eyes darted forward at her. Illusion was the only way to form a smile on her face. She needed a way to talk to her father and warn him.

"What's wrong, dear? You don't look happy," Hilary said.

Jade forced a real smile. "Nothing," she replied. How had Hilary seen through her illusion? "Just my friends, I worry about them."

"That is a problem. My office needs to stay away from controversy. If you want to return to your position after school, I need you to stay clear of your friends. Just until I am in power, of course. Then we can work with them again."

Jade sighed. "Can I tell them what is going on, at least?"

"No!" Hilary yelled. "The election itself hasn't been announced. There are spies everywhere. Eyes and ears are following you and not just here. When you go to school, there will be people who want to bring down this office. You must be very careful. Don't speak to anyone about anything. We cannot trust anyone. Another person in power, say Kasper, would not be as sympathetic to your friends' cause."

"I understand," Jade answered, nodding. Being as alone as she was, she needed to be able to trust someone. Her friends would understand when she explained after the election. This was, after all, the job she was assigned to do. That didn't mean she would be as lenient when it came to her father. She still had every intention of warning him not to date the mayor. "Would you mind if I stepped out to grab a salad? We left before lunch."

"No need. I am back. Here you go... your favourite." Safron Black always had impeccable timing.

"Perfect," Hilary said, going back to her paperwork.

Jade thanked the constable for her lunch and spent the rest of the afternoon in her office trying to find a way to sneak off to visit her father.

Chapter Sixty-Five

Faramund and Dezi were standing guard outside the portal when the others returned - relieved to see it was their friends and not something trying to escape they would have to battle.

With the portal stones to the Frostica land in-hand, it was time to save Christmas. The thought of the story of Santa Claus made Willow as happy as the children he delivered gifts to. She recited a line from the prophecy in her mind, *Now the children's joy has been blocked*. That had to refer to Nick being missing. Unless they found him, there wouldn't be any gifts this year.

The walk through the Christmas realm was longer than in the dream. Luckily, Mike and Sarah knew exactly where the train made its stops. There were enough sleighs attached for the entire group to be transported to the holiday town. Everything was exactly as Willow remembered from the dream, with the exception of Frostica walking around. Her first sight of the creatures caused her to jump backwards, grabbing a hold of William for protection. He gave a sideways glance to Lance, acknowledging the victory.

"Welcome," Meredith said. "Come on inside, where the fire is on to keep warm."

"Thank you," William answered, moving forward to take her hand. The two embraced in a friendly hug. Anyone watching them could tell they had been through a lot together.

Willow's mind wandered back to the scars on William's chest and back. She wondered if Meredith had been there when he got any of them. Her imagination soared, filled with visions of a glorious battle in which William rushed to the aid of his friends, being wounded saving them. The visualization of the scene brought about the sigh of a teenage fangirl.

"Ahem." Sarah nudged her, recognizing the dazed look of a daydream in Willow's eyes.

Everyone heard the sigh, turning to see what caused it. Willow managed to whisper a *thanks* to Sarah before turning her attention back to discussions of what was about to transpire.

"We appreciate the offer, Meredith, but no time. We need to get in and out of the Frostica realm as soon as possible for everyone's sake. We visited with Nick in a dream. He is okay for now, but time is of the essence. We know where we are going and with a little luck, the rescue will go without incident. Faramund and Sarah will remain on this side of the portal while it is open." William paused for the moment, looking at the faces of the others. The twinkle that usually shone in his deep chocolate brown eyes was noticeably absent.

"And if the Frostica try to enter?" Meredith asked.

"They will disassemble the portal again." William said, his tone colder than the ice around them. "If it comes to that and we survive, we will make contact through the dream realm and arrange a way out. If not, no one is to open the portal again. The sooner we leave, the better."

Clairity let out a gasp. This was by far the most dangerous adventure they had attempted to undertake. No one had anticipated there was a chance they would not be returning.

Sensing the uneasiness in the team, William turned to them. "If anyone here wants to change their minds about going on this mission, now is the time. I cannot guarantee your safe return. Once through that portal, anything could happen."

There was no time for sightseeing on this trip. The train was set to high speed and moved so quickly the scenery was a complete blur. After hopping out, they followed the ice bridges to the cavern. Even the unicorn whales were silent, appearing to know the urgency of the situation and trying to avoid being a distraction.

Reaching the ice cavern which encased the portal, they came to a situation no one had considered. The base was inside the cavern. There were no open skies for Willow to call a storm. That meant there was no choice other than to use a guardian to open the portal. The question was, which guardian? If Aslo or Kiera appeared, Lance would know she was a keeper and that there were guardians his family didn't already know about still in existence. If Tika or Nero appeared, the prince would know where his sister's toys had gone and that William was a keeper.

Willow glanced at William and was about to suggest that Faramund escort Lance away from the area when Nero appeared.

Lance took two steps backwards. "How is this possible?"

"I told you, I set them free," Willow answered. "Where did you think they went?"

"I didn't realize there were any keepers left in this world," Lance said, a sly smile crossing his lips. "You and your friends are full of surprises."

"You have no idea," Mike replied, bumping his shoulder against the prince's in a macho display of power.

"Can we just get on with this? Time is of the essence, remember?" Willow's eyes followed Nero - the stones flew into place and the portal opened.

"Faramund, you and Sarah are this world's protection. I think Willow should remain as well. Anyone else who wants to stay is welcome to." William moved forward to stand in front of the portal without looking back.

"No way!" Willow exclaimed. "I am in all the way." She walked to his side, gripping his arm.

"I'm in, too," Mike said, patting William on the back. "Always got your back." The two shook hands.

Lance let out a sigh. "I am the one who wanted to go, so I am in."

Clairity moved behind Willow, tossing her arms around her friend's neck. "I couldn't let you go with these three alone," she said, a tease in her voice. Her joke was a welcome change to the dismal atmosphere that surrounded them.

"I don't know what's in there, but I will join you if you need me." Dezi was the only one who hadn't been in the dream world to see what they were up against.

"Perhaps you should stay here, Dezi," William suggested. "Your fire power could make a big difference if the portal was rushed. The Frostica cannot handle high temperatures."

"Just keep in mind, you are standing on an iceberg. If you melt it, all that is beneath you is water. Might wanna go easy on the flames." Mike pointed at Dezi, smiling before backing up and being the first one to cross over through the portal.

*****

The temperature on the other side of the glowing doorway was comparable to the world they just left. The terrain matched as well, making it easy to see how the two worlds had once been connected as one. Willow paused, wondering how easy it was to divide worlds or connect two together. There was no time for standing around contemplating things. There was a job to do. Her slight hesitation meant Mike already had a rather large lead crossing the icy plain.

Clairity remained close to Willow. The two girls struggled with the walk; not only was it longer than in the dream, it was much more difficult. Every so often, one of their feet would crunch through the icy surface of the snow, causing them both to stop to free it before continuing on again. The men all arrived at the ledge first and were searching for strategies when they caught up. Not one of them looked back at the two girls to see if they needed help. This mission was well past that. Clairity and Willow both needed to carry their own weight for the rest of the journey.

Moving closer, they could see the guys were looking at a slick part to the hill presumably to slide down to the bottom as they had in the dream.

"What are we waiting for?" Lance asked. Sitting, he pushed himself down the side. The others took turns doing the same, with Mike insisting on going last.

Even leaving a small amount of time between each person, they still ended up in a pile at the bottom, except for Lance.

"Seems the ice gets slicker and faster with each person that goes down. Who knew?" A wicked smile crossed his face. He stopped at the same place where his sister's wand had been in the dream and looked around, but it was nowhere to be found.

"There is no sense trying the walls. We should head straight over to the caves," Clairity suggested. Her eyes fixated on the frozen waves with their sharp points. Each one held the potential to be deadly from even the simplest misstep, causing a slip on the sheet ice they were walking on.

William reached into his bag and pulled out the shoe covers with spikes again. "We will need these. This walk is going to be nowhere near as easy as it was in the dream. You'll be glad to grip the ice better. Trust me."

No one was going to argue with that. They each put on the unusual looking overshoes. William was right. Even with the grippers latching onto the ice, they found manoeuvring the walk difficult. The men positioned themselves so the girls were each sandwiched between two of them. That way, if one slipped someone was there to catch them in any direction. They found their hands full a few times, dealing with close calls accompanied by shrill shrieks.

The cave was exactly where the group found it before. Inside the same torches burnt. Willow, remembering the warning about the flames, stayed clear of them.

Again, the walk was longer than anyone had thought and with more twists and turns. They came to a tunnel choice they hadn't made before.

The group stood, staring at the two different paths. Willow exhaled, watching her breath turn to smoke, waiting for someone else to decide the proper course to follow. Clairity suggested they stay to the right.

A faint clicking noise could be heard coming from the left. The men discussed amongst themselves what the cause was. In the end, they chose to ignore Clarity and head towards the unusual sounds.

"I really think the other way is the best choice, guys," Clairity yelled to their backs. "Curiosity is dangerous. Remember what happened to the cat?" She let out a huff, taking Willow's arm to follow. "At least slow down. We can't move that fast." All three moved out of the girls' line of sight after rounding a corner.

"William? Mike? Lance?" Willow called. There was no answer. The two girls exchanged glances, removing their wands for added protection. "If this is a joke, it isn't funny!" she yelled. Again, there was no answer.

The two slowed their pace, taking each step carefully so as not to fall flat on the ice or rush into something horrible. The chattering noise intensified the closer they came to the bend in the path. Stopping at the corner, they carefully peeked around the side. The room awaiting them was stunning.

A light source was shining in from somewhere, although neither could figure out where. It reflected off both the walls and the thin blue strands of what appeared to be glass attached to them. The lines were reminiscent of wire, but glistening like crystal, forming shapes and patterns all over the room. It was a work of art - each strand perfectly formed, yet different from the others in one way or another. All of them were woven together in intense patterns similar to the doilies Clairity's mother put all over their house to make furniture last longer.

There was no sign of the men. They had simply vanished.

"Let's not touch them," Willow said. "We don't know if they could freeze us. I think I see a path that we can follow if we take our time."

Clairity agreed with a nod, her body shaking. Willow moved forward, making sure to dig the spikes of her shoe covers in for every step. Falling into the designs wasn't a desirable outcome, especially since neither of them knew what would happen if they did. At best, they would be sharp enough slash through skin. Clairity followed in her exact footprints, neither one noticing the noises had completely stopped.

They followed the path, ducking under some ice strands and stepping over others, until they came to a large circular room. The girls stood at the entrance looking in. Glass statues were scattered all over the room, some with intricate designs including detailed features of people and animals. The top of the walls glistened with sculptures of gigantic crystal spiders. Willow took the initiative, stepping in. She moved forward to look at the first statues - a man and a woman, each with a similar look of fright etched onto their face.

"That's creepy," Clarity said. "It's like they posed in terror for it. I wonder who the artist was."

Willow had already moved on to the next group - a couple of Frostica. Both looked as if they were about to bite down on something. "Everything here seems so wrong." Her heart pounded faster by the second. She inched towards two birds that reminded her of Shelby. Could they be depictions of guardians who had been there? Clairity touched her shoulder. Willow jumped, almost losing her footing.

"Sorry," Clairity said. "Any clue what is going on here?"

"None," Willow answered, continuing on. They passed several more animals - polar bears and fish, mainly. "Do you hear that? It sounds like water running."

"It's coming from over there." Clairity pointed to a dark spot on the rounded wall. A pathway led to a warmer spot with a river. "It's like the Yeti world. There are hidden warm springs."

The ground was soft where they were walking and the spikes from the shoe covers left marks. She looked down at the ground and sighed. "They didn't come this way. There are no foot marks up there." Willow turned around, heading back to the strange room. She squinted her eyes while glancing around the room. "Does something look different to you?"

"The spiders look creepier, if you ask me. Let's find the guys and get out of here. I knew we should have gone the other way."

Willow came to a dead stop, placing her hand over her open mouth, muffling a scream.

Clairity bumped into her. "What?" she asked. There was no need for an answer. Following her friend's stare, she saw crystal statues of the William, Mike, and Lance. "You don't think?" Her words cut off as the clicking nose returned.

Willow glanced up in time to see the crystal spiders on the ceiling moving - preparing to descend on top of them. She froze to the spot.

Clairity clung to Willow's arm, letting out a shriek. "Any ideas?" Her breath was heavy and her body shook even harder than before.

"Just one... the river. I think if we can get them into it, the heat of the water could destroy them. But I'm not sure how to get them there. How many do you see?"

"Too many," Clairity answered.

"Look up there, the big one. I bet she is the queen. If we move her, the rest might follow."

"How do you figure?" Clairity asked.

"It kinda fits with the prophecy. We need to melt her heart," Willow said. "And we are out of time." She pointed her wand at the largest spider. It came crashing down to the ground, landing on the statues of the two Frostica. "Use your wand! We need to move her to the stream!"

The two girls focused their magic on moving the spider queen down the path in front of them. Additional spiders came down in full force, racing to her aid - increasing their speed in a deadly chase. Willow and Clairity bolted to the river, dropping the spider in the middle after reaching the opposite side. The queen shrieked in pain, twisting and turning in the warm water as it melted to nothing. The first spiders to follow melted from the heat as well, trying to reach their beloved queen. Smarter ones scattered, retreating, realizing their defeat.

After the movement all of the creatures in the water ceased, they disappeared, leaving nothing behind. The two girls returned to the circular room.

"What do we do now? They can't just be gone. We need them. We can't do this on our own." Tears streaked down Clairity's face as she paced back and forth, holding her head as if it were in pain.

"Calm down. I have an idea. Help me move the birds." Willow used her wand to move one of the crystallized birds into the river. Clairity followed her friend's lead, bringing the other.

"What are we doing?" she asked.

"A test," Willow answered. "I think these two are trapped guardians. If I am right, the water will melt the shell around them. Hopefully, we can do the same for the guys."

The glass-like casing cracked, leaving the bodies of two blackbirds lying in the water. Willow rushed over to them and reached down. Their immortality had preserved life, but left them in poor condition. Willow allowed the pair to join with her in order to heal.

"They were in there for a while. The best we can hope for is that the guys are still okay. It hasn't been very long for them. We have no choice but to melt them free if they are to have a chance." Willow's eyes never met her friend's. She could hear the tears falling down Clairity's face. Each of them knew coming to this world could be dangerous - the reality of that was setting in.

The two girls combined their powers, lifting the three glass sculptures to the water. They waited for the casings to melt and crack. Willow rushed to William's side. Gently pushing his hair out of his face, she listened for breath from his lips. Putting her head against his chest, she felt a faint heartbeat. She glanced at Clairity and smiled, letting her know William was okay. Her friend checked the other two. All three remained unconscious.

Willow leaned over and whispered in William's ear. "Come back to me. I need you." Running her hand against his face, she bent down close and kissed him gently on the lips before sitting up again.

The corners of his mouth curled up slowly. He opened his eyes. "What took you so long? I thought we were done for." He sat up slowly, the spider's freezing venom still affecting him. "They took us by surprise.

Once we were stung, we couldn't move. We had to stand there and watch them encase us in that crystal."

"Told you we needed to go the other way." Clairity said from behind them. The other two were waking up as well.

William was first to his feet. "I won't ever doubt you again - promise," he said. Focusing his attention on Willow again, he offered his hand to help her up from kneeling. As soon as she was on her feet again, he pulled her into a tight hug, whispering gently in her ear, "We will talk about that kiss later." He winked at her and went to check on the condition of the other two men.

"Guess you are glad Willow didn't listen to you and came along, huh?" Clairity teased as he walked by where she was helping Lance to his feet.

William smiled at her briefly, paying more attention to Mike, who was only just regaining consciousness. "You okay?" he asked, offering his friend a hand getting up.

"Yeah," Mike answered. "Thought that was the end. Let's hope the worst is over."

"I doubt that," Lance said, joining the two men. "But this river could be our way out after we rescue the prisoners. The Frostica don't like heat."

"Um," Willow interrupted them. "Bad idea. The prophecy could be a warning. If they have the ability to freeze things on contact then freezing this river would be easy for them. If we were wading in the river when it froze, we would be stuck."

"How else are we going to get out of here, then?" Lance asked, his voice taking an argumentative tone.

"The front door. We walked under an ice bridge earlier. It connected the castle to the top area we slid down from." Willow shook her head as a flash of dizziness came over her. She stumbled backwards a couple steps before Clairity caught her.

"Are you okay?" William asked.

"I," Willow started and stopped abruptly, looking at Lance. She paused for a moment. "I hurt myself while we were trying to deal with the spiders. No big deal. I'll be okay."

William took her arm and walked her out of sight of the others. In the background, she could hear Lance complaining about her plan to take the main door out. It appeared that the good prince had come close enough to death for one day and wanted a safer exit strategy.

Willow turned her attention back to the man in front of her. Concern flowed from his eyes. "It's okay," she said, moving back a piece of the sweater she was wearing to reveal the two birds she found and perhaps a bit too much cleavage.

He traced the outline of the birds with his fingers gently before covering the spot back up with her sweater. "You sure you will be okay?"

"Isn't much we can do about it, anyway. We can't turn back. Forward is the only choice," Willow replied. She took his hand and steadied a telepathic connection between them. *Don't let him talk you into returning here. It would be a mistake. I think it's a trap. The spiders are probably some sort of pet. Anyone escaping from the castle who made it by them are forced into the river area. I think the line in the prophecy was a warning about it.*

William nodded. The two returned to the rest of their group. They took a moment to try to thaw the other frozen statues, however, what was left inside the crystallized casings had long since expired. They backtracked to where the original path split. After heading in the opposite direction, everything was familiar. It was the same as in the dream right up to the stairs leading to a door. This door, however, was not locked.

"Think they are expecting us?" Clairity asked.

"Either that or they ran out of locks." Mike answered, pushing past her to open the door. He let out a sigh. "It's empty. They must have moved all the keys that were here too."

Willow reached in her pocket, making sure she still had the key she found in the dream. No one knew when or if it would become useful. She watched Mike carefully open the next door, leading to the holding cells. With no sign of opposition, he stepped inside.

Lance took the lead, heading straight for the cell in which his sister was being held. "Sissy," he said, smiling. "Are you okay?"

She took his hand through the bars that kept her prisoner and rubbed it against her face. "I knew you would come."

He looked at her other hand tightly holding her wand. "How?"

"I don't know. After the other night, I woke up and had it again." She answered his question as if she could read his thoughts. A flame burnt deep in her eyes when Willow walked by. "You!" She lifted her wand. "You are the reason for all of this."

Lance moved in front of her wand to block her, but it proved unnecessary. Her attention dropped almost instantly from Willow. The flames of hatred dimmed as her gaze locked on Mike. To everyone's surprise, he appeared just as infatuated with the witch.

"Are we good here? Because I would prefer not to let you out if you are going to try to kill us," William said.

"Yeah, fine," Sissy answered.

William alternated his glance between his friend and the witch. "Great! Mike, how about you watch Sissy?" he said, shaking his head. He patted Lance on the back of his shoulder, acknowledging the shock on his face at what was transpiring.

"William," Nick said. "You are a sight for sore eyes. I don't know how you made it this far. I hope there is a good plan to leave." The two men engaged in a talk about the exit strategy, while Clairity used her wand to open the cell doors.

Willow moved in front of the cage across from where Nick was being held. She took out her wand and aimed it at the lock.

"Wait," a voice said in the dark. The two Olcsanka moved to the front of the cage. "The lock on our door is a trigger for an alarm. If you open it, everyone here will die. You must leave us and hurry. They will check on us in exactly twenty-two minutes. Once they see the cages empty, you will have little time to escape. Make every moment count."

Willow put away her wand. She glanced at William. "Do what you must," he said, reaching out to touch her face.

The two wolves were backing away. "Wait!" Willow exclaimed. "Come here, please." The guardians returned. She reached in and touched both of them, one with each hand. She heard a gasp from behind her as the two beasts turned to glittering light before taking their place as pictures on her arms.

"You're a keeper?!" Lance asked, although it sounded more like a statement than a question.

"I don't think we have time for revelations now. I suggest we save the explanations for when we are safely out of this world," Nick suggested, pushing by everyone and looking round the corner of a wall leading to a staircase heading up. "Let's go."

"Hang on," Lance demanded. "If we are going to try to make it out this way, let's at least do it right. The next set of stairs up should lead into the courtyard. The top exits closest to the bridge out." Before anyone could question how he knew, he added, "It's the same layout as another castle I know well." The prince took the lead, followed closely by his sister and Mike. The staircase wound in circles, passing several sublevels, without the sign of any Frostica.

Clairity tugged on Willow's sweater and whispered, "Doesn't anyone else think this is way too easy?"

"I was hoping they simply didn't know we were here yet," Willow answered. The ease at which they were moving wasn't going to continue much longer. The line came to an abrupt stop at the top level.

The men moved forward to survey the situation. The courtyard and exit were made completely of a sheet ice that looked as if it had been polished to maximize how slippery it was and rendering the spikes on their shoe covers useless. The surface of the ground was simply too hard to penetrate. There were four Frostica guards positioned in front of the exit. The rest of the courtyard was empty.

"There are probably four more on the outside." William said. "They are too fast to handle if they are alerted to us. Not to mention, there is probably an alarm somewhere one of them could sound. We need to lure them over here and deal with the first four quietly... then take out the ones outside."

"I have an idea." Nick reached into his pocket, retrieving a handful of small chocolate balls wrapped in shiny coloured tinfoil. "The Frostica have an addiction to sweets." He rolled a couple of the balls just outside the door. The flashy foil caught the eye of one of the Frostica guards, who came over to investigate.

Picking up the small candy, the creature opened it and placed it in his mouth, making a low humming noise, indicating his satisfaction and drawing the attention of another guard. The second creature headed over to see what had been found, arriving just in time to see the candy devoured. The two argued for a moment, trying not to attract more attention and have to share any further chocolate they might find. They headed to the doorway and began down the stairs.

A blast of energy escaped from Willow and Clairity's wands, stunning the creatures. Sissy created a golden magical rope that bound the two together so they were unable to move, just in time to hear Nick say, "The other two are coming over." The three girls followed the same procedure again.

Nick motioned for them to stay put while he carefully moved to the middle of the room and made a small pile of candy. He then headed for the wall beside the doors. One by one, the others followed him. Cold radiated through Willow's back. Her body stiffened, afraid to shiver. Several more tinfoil covered balls rolled outside the door. The Frostica guards devoured them, making loud chewing noises. When the sounds ceased, all four guards entered the room. Without looking around, they headed straight for the pile of goods.

That was their opportunity. They rounded the corner, running straight for the bridge at full speed. The ground beneath them was slick. Willow's feet came out from under her. She landed on her back, sliding into Clairity and making her fall as well. After that it was a domino effect as the speeding pile of bodies grew in size, knocking each of them down, one by one. The bridge slanted downwards. There was no way to stop the force at which they were moving. Although the effect was they were actually travelling much faster than they could have by foot, the commotion attracted attention. Lanzia was already at the door, screaming for her forces to follow them.

They were moving too fast, spinning in all directions - out of control. Willow couldn't reach her wand. Neither could either of the other two witches. She opened her eyes wide, looking up at the sky, summoning the clouds above to swirl. As their body pile left the bridge, a blast of lightning struck it, crushing the ice into dust and sending the Frostica pursuers plunging to the ground far below.

It took a moment for everyone to regain their senses and footing. Looking back at the castle, they saw the Frostica Queen already making another bridge of ice to allow chase. Lance stepped forward and opened his arms wide, letting out a fierce roar. Blue flame escaped from his chest aimed directly at the castle. It hit and engulfed the building. Screams of pain echoed from the structure as every living thing began to burn. The spectacle was frightening yet beautiful at the same time. Clairity hid her head in her hands. Willow looked on, a single tear falling down her cheek.

Lance's expression held no remorse. "They would have killed us. There was no choice. I suggest we move quickly; the flames will seek out all life and destroy it." He took his sister's arm. The two moved swiftly towards the doorway out of the dying world. The others followed in silence.

Once safely through the portal, Willow, ignoring the welcome back comments from Faramund, Dezi, and Sarah, headed straight for Lance, slapping his face hard enough to leave a red mark.

The prince rubbed his jaw, a smile creeping over his face. He grabbed her arm tight. "Would you have preferred to die?" he asked, rage burning in his eyes. "Those things were a menace to everyone and now they won't ever hurt anything again. Is that not a choice for the greater good?" His hold on her wrist grew tighter. "Is that not what you do? Make choices for the greater good?"

"There were other things alive in that world who didn't deserve to perish." She struggled to pull her arm away. It was aching now. His grip was hard enough the blood supply was being cut off to her hand. She let out a whine.

"Let go of her!" William yelled, pushing Lance's shoulder.

He did as requested and let Willow go. She had been tugging so hard to get away, the sudden release sent her flying back into a wall of ice. Everything went black.

Chapter Sixty-Six

Willow opened her eyes slowly. Pain radiated through her body. She lay still, imagining the number of bruises it would take to make her hurt so much. Trying to move her arm, she cried out in pain. The spot where Lance had grabbed her was black and blue and puffed out twice the size of her other arm.

William and Lance, she thought, sitting up quickly. She looked around the room. Everything was unfamiliar. She was on a couch covered with a knitted blanket that reminded her of her home world. Flames raged in a stone fireplace. On the floor in front of it, two sets of eyes watched her - the Olcsanka from the Frostica realm.

"They aren't here," Jawfree said. "There was no time to waste."

"Not here?" Willow said, perplexed. "They left me here?"

The door behind her opened. "Our guest is awake," Meredith said. She sat down on the edge of the couch. "Are you feeling any better?"

Willow looked at her and Nick, then Aslo and Kiera who entered with the them. "Why did they leave me behind?"

"You were in no condition to travel, my dear. That was a nice bump you got on your head. Combine that with the stress of all the guardians you were carrying and healing..." Meredith handed her a cup of hot chocolate. "It's lucky you weren't hurt worse."

Willow took the cup from her. She watched a small marshmallow swirl in circles in the middle of it before melting away into a foamy white froth. She thought back to waking up in the hospital after healing Shelby. "How long was I out for?" she blurted out.

"About twelve hours," Nick said, smiling. "You needed the rest." He handed her a piece of paper. "This is from Lance."

Willow sat staring at the paper for a moment, then turned her head away. She didn't think there was anything he could say that would change how she felt about him after what happened.

"You should read it. Whether we like it or not, he was right. Had the Frostica built that bridge, we would not have outrun them." Nick walked over to Jawfree and sat on the ground beside him. The man had a bond to the two that radiated as an aura, one she had seen before between William, Nero and Tika. "One other thing you should know," he said. "The prince can't control his emotions after using that much negative energy. It takes him a while to subdue the extreme rage it takes to manifest necrid flames that strong. Anyone who challenged him in that state would have been in trouble. The fact that he didn't hurt you further is a credit to the boy." He stood. "Well, Meredith, we best leave her alone to her thoughts. I will head to the portal and step out to let William know she is awake."

"Wait!" Willow exclaimed. "What happened? After I hit my head, I mean."

"William knocked him out in one punch. He was out about ten or fifteen minutes and was much calmer when he came to. He had a nice shiner, though." Nick closed the door behind them.

She looked at the paper he left on her lap. With her good hand, she opened it.

Dearest Willow,

I cannot express how sorry I am for how I hurt you. I can only hope to explain to you that it was not done consciously. If you can find it in your heart to hear me out, I will set out my explanation for you.

When you channelled enough force to destroy the charms the Glaquool had used to conceal their essences, you were directing the negative feelings you had into your magic. I know it wasn't a pleasant feeling for you.

For me, all of my magic is based solely on negativity. Death magic is dark. The very worst part of me has to come forward to use it. To summon a power such as I did in the Frostica world requires me to allow my being to be consumed by hatred, greed, jealousy and rage. Once it comes out, it is hard to suppress it again.

I know it isn't an excuse for what I did. I put you in danger, something I promised myself I would never do. I deeply regret everything that transpired. I will not contact you further unless necessary so as not to subject you to any further risk. I can rest easy knowing you are in good hands.

Perhaps one day I shall find the ability within myself to control the rage. Until then, know you brought me inspiration and showed me new direction. You will always have a place reserved in my heart.

Love, Lance

Tears flowed from her eyes. She held the paper against her chest as if she were hugging it - hugging him. Her prince was gone and it was her fault. All those times she sensed anger from him, now she knew why. It was something he couldn't control - forced on him by the nature of the ability he was cursed with by his parents. If he had told her before... if she had known, she never would have slapped him. She understood him better now... the things he said... the way he acted.

The sour taste of guilt filled her mouth. She felt sick - a churning deep within the pit of her stomach threatened to send its contents back up. The burn of bile in her throat sent her running to an open door leading to a bathroom. Holding her long curly red hair back, she heaved over the toilet. Nothing came out. She couldn't remember that last time she had eaten anything, but the dry heaves still contracted through her stomach.

When the feelings subsided, she cupped some water in her hands from the sink and drank it to wet her mouth and throat.

Returning to the couch, she rested her face in her hands, her elbows planted firmly on her thighs. She wasn't sure how much time passed when the door opened again and Kiera sat by her side. Willow braced herself for a pep talk, but none came. Her guardian was just there for her, not judging or trying to make it better. It was what she needed. The two sat silently, cuddling together for a while before Kiera joined with her keeper.

William will be here soon to pick you up. It's time to pull yourself together. I have a feeling that isn't the last you will see of your prince, if that is truly what you want.

The door opened and the others entered. Willow watched as Jawfree and Decon moved in perfect timing with Nick. She hadn't even noticed William was with them.

"They were meant to be," she said out loud.

The two Olcsanka mutated into a gold dust and reappeared as pictures on Nick's skin. She could hear gasps in awe of the beautiful transformation from the others.

"You did that!" William exclaimed.

Willow's head spun round to see him standing with Faramund in the doorway. She swallowed with a gulp and forced a smile. "Yeah," was all she answered.

William sat down beside her. "How long have you known you could make people keepers?" His eyes locked on hers waiting for an answer.

She let out a sigh. "I sort of figured it out that day with Tika and Nero," she said. "I saw the three of you together and how much you bonded. The interaction between the three of you was beautiful. It gave off an aura... one I am sure you just saw around Nick." He nodded and she continued. "I thought back then you were meant to be with them, that you would make a good keeper for them, and then they joined with you. Thinking back to the night with Acacia, I realized something. I had decided who should be a portal guard. I chose Clairity and Ashlyn to be keepers as well. I thought it in my mind and it happened. I think it was part of the gift Acacia granted me that night. I wanted to make sure before I told anyone my suspicions.”

“You should have told me,” William said. His scowl turned to a smile. “Thanks for choosing me. It's an honour to be thought of as worthy.” He put his arm around her, squeezing affection.

“It's amazing,” Nick said. “Are you sure you want to leave these two with me? I don't know if they will be any help to the cause here.”

“For now, they have a good home. We are pressed for time. Willow has a test to write. When everything is settled again, we will return. Maybe we can give you a hand this Christmas seeing as you are behind schedule now. I know Sarah has quite a few questions she wants to ask you. She keeps mumbling about how you manage to do so much in one night. She would like to know how you stop time.” He shook hands with Nick and gave Meredith a hug before helping Willow to her feet. The letter still held tightly in her hand. She put it in her back pocket without meeting William's gaze.

“You okay, little one?” Faramund asked. “You gave us a real scare.”

Willow smiled and hugged him. He had looked out for her since the first time they met in the market back home and she imagined he always would. She whispered “thank you” in his ear. He nodded, understanding what she meant.

After proper goodbyes and hugs, the three of them headed back. Willow had completely forgotten that the camp changed locations. They were now in an area surrounded by trees. It was perfect for her. She glanced sideways at William.

He moved in behind her and whispered, “You love it, admit it.” He placed his arm over her good hand. “We need to have that fixed up before you get to explore.”

She smiled. It was as if he read her mind. Did he really know her that well? She was surprised when he led her to visit Victoria rather than the doctor.

"Victoria has done a great job lately. She healed everyone's bumps and bruises when we returned," William said.

The girl was beaming. Her smile couldn't have gotten any bigger. For so long she had yearned for purpose and now there was some. Victoria's hands ran gently across the surface of Willow's wrist, leaving a glittering pink trail of magic which absorbed into the skin. The swelling and discolouration began to disappear almost instantly.

"Don't go rushing off yet. You need to stay with someone until it has a chance to fully heal," Victoria said, waving her finger in Willow's face. "It's going to take a few hours. That was a nasty hurt."

Willow let out a breath of air in a huff. That meant no exploring. There wouldn't be enough time before she left to write the test for school placement.

"I can show you around. I have some free time," William said.

Her eyebrows lifted. Free time and William in the same sentence was hard to believe. The tour began with several of the buildings. Not everything had been built yet. There were more people who had joined the camp in the past couple of days. Willow clasped onto William's hand as they passed a group of girls who she hadn't seen before. The looks they shot at her were as cold as the ice world she just left.

"I hope you don't mind," William said. "Not all the sleeping quarters have been built yet so I had your things sent to mine for now." He held the door open for her.

His new living quarters were bigger than before. His desk and chair were familiar - as were the books that lined the shelves on the wall. The bed, however, was double the size of the one he had at the last camp. Willow couldn't help but wonder if that was because of her. The few times she spent the night sleeping in his old bed, they were cramped for space.

"It's big," she said, sitting down and bouncing a little. "And comfy." He showed her dressers and closets that were just for her things. Everything was arranged as if she was meant to stay. "Is this permanent?" she blurted out, her face turning bright red as soon as she did.

"Maybe." He rested against the desk, looking at her. "I think we need to talk sometime about things. Right now, I thought you might like to wash up and change. After that, you need something to eat. You must be starving by now."

He was right. She was hungry. Her stomach hadn't stopped growling since they arrived in the camp. Grabbing some clean clothes, she headed to the washroom to shower and change. The hot water pouring on her sore bones felt wonderful. She hadn't realized how much of a chill was left in her body until she felt the beads of water hit her skin and trickle in streams down to her toes. Although she wanted to see everything before heading to write the school test, the hot water felt too good to cut her shower time short. When she was changed, she returned to see William lying on the bed reading a book while he waited for her. She smiled watching him. Even with Nathan's ability to read books and transfer them to another person, William still preferred to read the old-fashioned way, one page at a time. She jumped on the bed beside him and nudged her way under his arm to take a peek at what he was reading.

"You could just ask," he said, putting the book on the side table after carefully marking his spot with a bookmark.

She looked up at him and smiled. "What fun would that be?"

"Okay, let's go get you something to eat," he said, getting off the bed.

"What should I do with this?" Willow held the key from the dream up, in her other hand she had the letter from Lance. The two items were the only contents of her other clothes. "Should I leave the key with you?"

"No," he answered. "I think you will need it." William took off the gold chain he was wearing and put the key on it. Moving behind her, he placed the chain around her neck. Gently moving her hair to the side, he fastened it.

She move her hand to the key around her neck and felt it. The sides of her lips curled up slightly. She turned around and hugged him. "Thank you," she whispered in his ear then kissed him on the cheek.

"You wouldn't want to tell me what the good prince put in that letter, would you?" William said, their faces almost touching.

She put the letter in his hand. "Read it if you want. I don't mind."

He shoved it into his back pocket. "Maybe while you are writing the test. It'll be one more thing we can talk about later."

"Later?" She tilted her head to see his eyes under the hair that had fallen in his face. "Why not now? Just get it over with."

The smile that crept across his face turned into a laugh. "We don't have enough time to give all the topics we need to cover justice. How's your arm feeling?"

"Way to change the subject." Willow stopped at the door. In front of them, she saw Mike and Sissy walking together holding hands. The aura emanating from the pair was beautiful. She had seen a similar display only once before between Annabelle and Lilabeth.

William's gaze followed her line of sight. "You okay?"

"Yeah." She smiled at him then looked back. "The aura between them is beautiful. It's hard to look away. I am glad they found each other." She took his hand.

He let out a satisfied sigh. "That's one thing off the list we needed to talk about."

Her head zipped to the side to look at him. "What do you mean? You can see the aura too, can't you?" Willow knew exactly what he meant, but decided to play dumb. She really didn't want to bring up the whole crush thing from the past tonight.

"Yeah," He answered. "I can see it because of Tika and Nero. I don't see all auras, though, just some."

"I think it's magic auras we see. I see trails, in different colours. Love is a form of magic - it is flowing between them." She looked at him, but as always saw nothing radiating from him towards her. The smile on her face faded. She looked away.

As if sensing her emotions, he pulled her close to him and whispered in her ear, "It's on the list for later. Trust me."

"Hey!" Ashlyn yelled from across the field. "It's time to go. I don't think we should be late."

She nodded at him, not quite sure what she had agreed to. It was time to meet the others and head to the location they were given to write the entrance test for the empyral school system. She quickly grew an apple tree to grab a snack before they headed off.

King Cornelius

Lance stepped through the portal and was immediately greeted by his brothers. "I figured you would return the next available opening." Joseph's lips curled upwards in a sly smile. He slapped his brother on the back. "I hope you burnt off some steam." He glanced at Lance's black eye. "From the looks of it, you did." He laughed.

Lance touched the area around his eye and made a whining noise. "Yeah, it was a great fight, wish you had been there. The other guy didn't fare so well."

"You mean there was only one? Perhaps you are losing your touch, brother." Zoe rounded the corner and eyed him up and down.

"I had a few too many drinks and stole a few too many kisses. It was worth every moment, I assure you." Lance donned a crooked smile. His brothers erupted in laughter.

"Father is waiting for you." Zoe returned round the corner from where she appeared. The laughter ceased.

"Come on, then," Joseph said. "Best not keep him waiting." He took the lead as they followed their sister to where the king waited.

Lance let out a little chuckle under his breath. The room was exactly as it had been when he walked out days ago. Even his mother was sitting in the same chair, sipping on tea.

"So the wandering son has returned," Cornelius said without looking away from the window he was standing at. "Feeling better, I hope." He turned around and smiled.

"That's it?" Zoe shrieked.

"What did you expect, dear?" her mother asked, putting her tea cup and saucer down on a side table.

"Punishment!" she yelled. "He walked out on us. He defied you, Father."

"Enough!" Cornelius bellowed. "Lance is different. His necrid flames are a gift we have to nourish and feed. Perhaps you haven't figured it out yet." He raised an eyebrow, looking at each of his children separately.

"Figured what out?" Zoe asked.

"The flames aren't something a necromancer or witch can learn," the king answered, the edge of his lips quivering as they turned slightly upwards. He walked over and put a hand on Lance's shoulder. "They are a part of him. His soul burns in anguish every day, the likes of which none of you will ever experience." He walked back to the window again. "It is his rage and anger that keeps them lit."

Ophelia gasped. "You can feel it?" she asked her brother.

A blank look came over Lance's face. His eyes glazed as if they were seeing something no one else could. "Yes," he answered. Until that moment, he hadn't realized what it was he was feeling. He was born with it and never questioned the pain and sadness inside him, at least until he met Willow. She awakened something different in him. The two forces had been battling within his soul ever since. Now he understood. Love can't exist in a soul burning with rage and hatred, and yet he did love her.

"It is a part of him. Should the flames go out, if it didn't kill him, he would be very ordinary and quite useless. So you see, we must encourage his emotions. Temper tantrums feed the power we need to win our war. But enough about that for now. You all have a mission to attend to."

"A mission?" Lance asked.

"Yes," Zoe answered. "We have linked that red-haired troublemaker to the portal guard camp. It's time to finish off the last of them once and for all."

"Brilliant. When do we leave?"

"As soon as the hole opens. You may want to clean up a bit," Simon said.

"Before you go, dear," the queen said. "There is the question of Sissy."

Lance turned to face his mother. "I won't look for her again, I assure you."

"Oh, good." The queen let out a sigh of relief. "You know even if you found her, she would never be welcome back here again. We banished her and that won't change."

"She is left to her own devices now." Lance headed to his room to wash and change - glad to leave the scrutiny of the room.

Turning on the tap, he splashed cool water on his face and looked at himself in the mirror. His heart raced, sweat trickled down his face. What if they found her? He couldn't think of things his brothers would do to her. His fist smashed the mirror. He felt the pain of the flame burn stronger from his anger.

He placed both hands on his head and closed his eyes. There was no answer to his dilemma. His soul was charred beyond recognition from the blazing fire of destruction. He could not take the chance it would consume Willow as well. He loved her, but love had no place in his existence. He knew now more than ever he could never see her again. It was too dangerous - he was too dangerous.

He took a towel and dried off. After changing into some fresh clothes, he put on a pair of sunglasses to hide his bruised eye and returned to his siblings. There would be no stopping them. All he could do was hope the camp had already moved to a new location.

The hole opened on schedule and the remaining five of Cornelius's children walked through with an army behind them. They entered the main world in the forest that bordered William's camp.

"We should have done this a long time ago," Joseph said.

"They held no threat. It was a waste of our time," Zoe answered. "If she wasn't there, they still wouldn't be. Do we know who she is yet?"

"No," Simon answered. "People seem to know very little about her. The reports are conflicting from our sources. Seems she knows a lot about us, though... too much for comfort."

The walk was short and after entering the camp, Zoe let out a high-pitched scream. It was empty. "How did they know we were coming? They stayed in this location for years and now all of a sudden they pack up and move right before we attack? Someone tipped them off."

"Spread out," Joseph said. "Check every building."

Lance found himself walking in the direction of the sleeping quarters. He singled out the building he wanted to search - William's. Opening the door, he walked in and tried to imagine what it had been like when the guard lived there. The walls were covered in shelves that were empty. From traces of dust, he could tell books once filled them. The only other thing in the room was a single bed. He imagined it would have been tight for two people to share. His mind wandered to Willow. William most certainly would win her heart now. The rage built and engulfed him. Moments later, he was standing outside, looking at what was left of the building he had destroyed in blind rage.

"Don't worry, brother," Joseph said, looking at the pile. "We will find them eventually and when we do, you can have first turn with the girl." He smiled and motioned for their forces to return home.

Lance took in a deep breath. That day was bound to come. He had no idea how he would handle it. One thing he did know, while he was alive, neither of his brothers would ever touch the woman he loved.

*****

King Cornelius awaited the return of his children in his throne room. Sitting upon a perch high above those that would dare to come before him, he sipped on a gold and gem-encrusted goblet of wine. His eyes locked on the closed double doors at the end of a long tapestry runner before him. His wife by his side made no noise to dare interrupt whatever was running through his mind. The edges of his lips curled up slightly when his children walked through the threshold to approach him.

"Ah, at last. Have we destroyed the camp and its pathetic inhabitants?" the king asked.

In an unusual turn of events, it was Lance who stepped forward and not Joseph. "No, Father, the camp was deserted when we arrived."

A fire exploded in his eyes as they turned bright red, his face quickly matching the same colour. "Why, after all these years, would they decide to move? Someone told them of our plans." Cornelius threw his goblet at his five children. "Only those in this room knew of the plan to attack. So it seems we have a traitor amongst us."

"You can't mean that," Zoe said. "Why would one of us do such a thing?"

"Why indeed." The king sized each of them up with his eyes. "You, Zoe, have always been jealous of your brothers."

"Never!" Zoe exclaimed, taking a step backwards and bowing her head to her father.

"Ophelia, your feelings about what happened to Sissy have not gone unnoticed. Has revenge taken over your soul?"

"Me?" she shrieked. "Lance was the one who left to find her. I stayed. If anyone, it was him. He was upset and had opportunity being stuck in the main world."

The king's laugh exploded like a roar. "Lance knew nothing of the plan to attack, my dear. How could he warn someone of something he didn't know was going to happen?"

Ophelia bowed her head, shuffling in a backwards motion to join her sister. Neither of the girls dared to look up to their father's face in case it was seen as a sign of defiance.

"Simon, your activities of late have not gone unseen. Extra trips to the dungeon to visit with the guardian's people. Illuminate us as to what motivated your visits?"

Simon looked up and immediately turned his gaze away from his father's face. It was the first time any of them saw the king for what he actually was - a man driven by rage and hate, willing to stop at nothing to achieve his goal. "I burn off some extra steam sometimes. I hadn't realized the prisoners were off-limits."

"It's one girl in particular you visit, isn't it?"

"There is one I prefer to take for nightly escorts. She appeals to my taste." Simon hid his hands behind his back to avoid notice of their shakiness.

Lance felt for his brother. In one brief moment, he saw a glimmer in Simon's eyes that reminded him of how he felt about Willow.

"Perhaps I should try this girl if she is as tasty as you say. The guards may also like to share in her talents." The king's face held a devious smile.

"Father," Lance interrupted, holding the king's gaze. "I should like to spend some time with her. Most days, we do need an outlet for our frustration. Might I suggest we make this girl a chamber maid for my brothers and myself?" It was the best he could do to save the girl, whoever she was.

Cornelius ignored Lance. "Joseph, always quick to reap the rewards of victory and take credit. I haven't seen you so eager to take responsibility for the failures of late. Does it bother you so much that your brother is favoured in my eyes, that you would turn your back on all I have done for you?"

Joseph looked at Lance, then at his father briefly before turning his gaze back to the floor. His lips pressed together tightly. At first, no answer came. An awkward silence filled the room before the prince spoke. "Think what you will, Father. I have always been your most loyal son. I would give my life and soul for you."

"And so you shall if you are guilty." The king pulled on a golden cord hanging beside him - six guards entered the room. The final two escorted the girl from the dungeons. "Take Joseph and imprison him until further notice," the king said, making a shooing motion with his hand.

All five of his offspring gasped at the words. One guard took each of Joseph's arms and began to walk him out.

"Wait!" the king bellowed. "Bring him back." Cornelius turned his attention to his son. "I am going to give you one more chance. If you fail me again, I will kill you." The guards released him. The king motioned for the six men to leave. "Lance, take the girl. Make her whatever you want. She has no appeal to me. The rest of you understand this... I am watching you. Make no mistake about your fate should I find out any of you have deceived me. Your mother is already pregnant with a child to replace Sissy. It would be just as easy to wipe the slate clean and start again with all of you. Do you understand?"

"Yes, Father," Zoe said, her voice shaking slightly. Her siblings answering the same except Lance.

The king turned his face to the prince. "And you, Lance? Do you understand?"

Lance laughed. "We both know you can't replace me, Father. The odds of having another child who not only has the gift I do, but can live with the pain I endure are not in your favour. If you wish to kill me and end the torment of life, I offer myself to you now." He outstretched his arms and knelt before his father.

For the first time, all four of Lance's siblings looked up, each one wondering how the king would react to their brother's offer.

Cornelius stood. He stepped down the stairs which led to his throne, stopping in front of his kneeling son. Placing a hand on Lance's shoulder, he broke out into laughter. "To offer your life to me as you have is a true sign of your loyalty. The five of you make yourselves useful. Put a bounty on the girl's head, dead or alive, and bring me that portal guard we allowed to live for far too long. I want him alive." The queen joined his side and the two left the room.

The five royal children stood perfectly still at first. After several moments, Lance let out a sigh and walked over to the girl who was left in his charge. He took her arm and pushed her to his brother Simon. "You should be more careful with something so important to you."

Simon grabbed the girl and hugged her tightly. "Thank you," he mumbled.

"You aren't in the clear yet," Joseph said. "I suggest the next way to the main world might be in order. The girl will have to wait a few days until we can find a way to smuggle her out."

Lance smiled and shook his head. He hadn't expected his brother to want to be involved in something that could be construed as treason.

"We will do as Father asks and place the bounty on the two." Joseph sighed, looking at Simon. "After we get this girl to the main world you can leave her there, but know this, you may never see her again. Lance can convince Father he killed her in a fit of rage. That is as far as my deception goes. All of our lives are on the line now. I doubt even you, Lance, will escape Father's rage if things do not change in his favour soon." He turned to face his siblings. "If I find out one of us is a traitor, I will kill them myself. Prepare to enter the main world. The girl will stay in Lance's quarters for now to avoid suspicion."

Chapter Sixty-Eight

Willow found herself outside a building. It was the only thing around other than the paved walkway they were standing on. A thick fog behind them made it impossible to see if there was anything in that direction.

"Think there is anything out there?" she asked the others.

"I don't think I want to find out," Ashlyn said, shivering.

"It radiates only cold and empty," Clairity said, looping her arm with Ashlyn's.

Willow held William's hand tightly. Victoria came over. Breaking them apart, she took a spot in between the two, holding both of their hands. "I don't like cold and empty," she said, her small lips forming a pout that puffed out her cheeks, resembling an adorable chipmunk. Dezi moved forward to take his sister away, but William stopped him, saying it was okay for Vicki to stay where she was.

The interior wasn't much more inviting. It was a single hallway with a number of different doors attached to it. Each door was exactly the same. They were all made from a blonde wood with a silver door handle. One small rectangular window was placed in a position that most people could look through without the need to bend down or find something to stand on.

A woman standing by a desk at the front of each room was holding tests to hand out as possible future students entered. The woman appeared to be the same person in each room, wearing exactly the same clothes. Some applicants were writing tests already. They watched people enter the rooms, change rooms, leave the building and disappear altogether.

"So now what?" Jessie asked.

"I think we are supposed to choose a room. It might be part of the test itself." Willow wasn't sure why she thought that, but as usual couldn't keep her ideas to herself.

"Should we all just go in one room together?" Ashlyn asked.

"I don't think so," Clairity answered. "We each have to decide for ourselves. I am pretty certain that's how it works."

Willow glanced at her friend. She was usually completely sure about her feelings. Something must have been attempting to block her abilities, most likely to force them all to individually choose where they wanted to go.

"I am going in there," Victoria said. Before anyone could answer, she opened a door and walked in. Willow watched through the window. The young girl took a test from the lady and sat down to begin writing her answers. Nathan decided to follow her into the same room.

Willow looked down the hall. She had already decided which room she was going to enter. She hugged William, whispering, "See you when I am done," before opening the door and disappearing.

When she entered the classroom, there was a low rumble of noises. Everyone stopped writing their test to look at her. "Are you sure you want this room, dear?" the woman holding the tests asked. She was of medium height with short grey hair that looked as if a salon had recently styled it. Her teeth were as white as her blouse, which was made more noticeable by the black full-length skirt and knitted shawl she was wearing. She stood with perfect posture beside a desk. Behind her was a blackboard which had *Ms. Petal* written on it in extra large letters.

"I am sure," Willow answered, holding out her hand to take a test. Ms. Petal gave her a half-smile, reluctantly placing the paper in her hand.

All the other applicants continued watching her. It was obvious most of them were from one of the races of the elf realm. There were beautiful blonde forest elves. She had read their appearance was stunning, but wasn't prepared for exactly how true that was. Each one had long, almost pure golden coloured hair, complimented by a pale flawless complexion. Their features were chiselled to perfection and crisp white linens covered their thin frames. As gorgeous as they were, they could have used a few more muscles. The other group she recognized from a book Nathan had shared with her as dark elves. Their hair was cut short and pitch black, with clothing matching the darkness. It was their crystal baby blue coloured eyes that stood out - like nothing she had seen before. There were a few other people in the room, who came and left, usually quickly after sitting down.

Taking a seat, she looked at the paper she was given and let out a muffled laugh. The pages flipped back and forth in her hands. There was nothing written anywhere. She heard a few mumbles from the blonde elves of, "Wrong room."

She wasn't about to ask Ms. Petal what to do and be ridiculed, so she pretended she knew what she was doing and started doodling on the paper.

What do I need to do? she wrote.

Leave and choose another door if you don't know, appeared underneath her question.

No. I chose this room.

This room is for people who know what to do, formed beneath her writing again.

She took an eraser and deleted all of the writing. *What do people do when they write a test?* she thought to herself.

I would start by putting your name on the paper, Kiera replied.

I forgot you guys were there. I don't think you are supposed to be helping me, though, she answered back.

Last I heard, we don't exist, so how could we be helping you? Aslo offered.

Willow let out a little chuckle that caught the room's attention again. She mumbled a *sorry* and went back to her test. At the top of the page she wrote her name and waited for an answer.

Hello, Willow. If writing could pause like normal speech it did. *Please summarize what it is you would like to learn this year.*

Okay. Who are you? she wrote back.

Who I am is irrelevant.

I don't think so. Everyone is relevant in some way. Obviously, you are intelligent or we couldn't be having a conversation. I would find it hard to believe you are just a test or piece of paper. So who are you? What type of magic is being used? she wrote on the blank paper.

You are supposed to write what you would like to learn.

Fine. I would like to learn who you are, she replied again. The eraser was in her hand ready to clear the page again, but, before she had the chance, the words faded on their own.

Why?

She sat back, chewing on the end of her pencil for a moment while she stared at the one word on the page. *I told you already. You must be a sentient being of some sort. It's only proper I know your name, since you know mine,* she wrote.

How do you know I am not just this piece of paper?

How do I laugh in writing? Seriously, you have an essence. An inanimate item doesn't have that. No, more likely a spell was used to displace your essence and transfer it to this paper for this test. After I am done writing it, you will rejoin your organic body form. There must be a lot of you seeing how many people are writing tests, so I would think you to be an older student, one who has been around a few years. Perhaps hoping to become a teacher or work in the government. At least that is my guess of what is happening here.

Willow looked up. Most of the others were leaving the room still holding their papers. She wasn't getting anywhere. Playing with the key on her necklace, she focused her attention back on the words forming before her eyes.

If I don't know what you expect to learn, how can I hope to place you?

She sighed, taking her time to answer. *I don't think it matters what I answer. You don't know what my abilities are and don't seemed concerned about that, either. I think placement is based solely on expectations. You expect the elves to do well and have advanced abilities, so they will be placed in the higher learning schools, probably at Sleeping Sands. I can deduce from the reaction to me entering this room, I am not expected to be quite as bright. It was already decided that I don't belong in this room before I even entered.*

So why are you still here?

Because I knew in my heart when I saw the door that this was the room I wanted to be in. I know I am as talented as, if not more than, the others who wrote this test. Bottom line, I am trying to convince you to give me a chance. Willow hadn't even noticed she was resting her head on her hand - her elbow on the table. Her other hand was still pulling the key back and forth on her necklace. She watched the pencil write what she was thinking on the paper, but she wasn't touching it.

She was the only applicant in the room at the moment. Ms. Petal set the tests down on the desk and moved to the seat in front of her. The teacher stared at the pencil for several minutes before Willow looked up startled to see her there. The pencil fell to the paper. "Sorry," she said.

"No," Ms. Petal said. "It's fine, just rare." She stood again and walked back to her place picking up the tests from the desk.

Willow wasn't sure what to make of what the woman said. What was rare? Not moving a pencil on paper. Clarity was always making writing utensils move on the table in front of her. She looked back down at the paper.

The only thing written on it was, *Take this paper to Cassandrhea Tibbins in Room C.* Willow took in a big breath of air and let it out slowly, making a huffing noise. She stood and gathered her things before exiting the room.

William was sitting on the floor in the hallway waiting. He jumped to his feet at the sight of her. Willow put her hand in front of him. "Don't ask," she said. "I have no clue. I don't suppose you know where Room C is?"

"Yeah, it's at the end of the hallway. A few of the others have already headed there." He took her hand and led her to the room, taking a seat on the floor again when they reached it. "See you soon, I hope." Before she entered the room, Willow noticed he was holding Lance's letter in his hand.

Room C was a gigantic meeting room of some sort. People were standing in sections that were roped off and individually marked with different school names. As she figured, the elves from the test room were all inside Sleeping Sands Academy's area. They snickered as she walked by to enter the line-up of applicants trying to find out if they were placed in a school and if so which one.

At the front of the line, Camile was handing her test paper to the Director of Knowledge. "Black Beakers Collegiate!" Cassandrhea yelled out. A cheer came from one of the areas in the middle. She watched the girl walk across the room and join her new schoolmates. There was no announcement for the next four applicants in the line up. A group of students dressed in uniforms escorted the rejects to a door, each one crying. Willow took a deep breath. The thought crossed her mind that she too would be leaving by that door. Perhaps she shouldn't have argued with the test paper quite so much.

Nathan was in front of her in the line. She wondered how the test went for him. If he could absorb whatever a book had in it, perhaps it was possible for him to absorb everything the tester knew from that blank paper. She watched him hand in his paper. "Sleeping Sands Academy!" Cassandrhea yelled out. There were no cheers but rather mumbles of surprise from the prestigious school's section.

The closer to the front of the line Willow came, the longer it seemed to take for it to move again. Her heart raced at full speed, perspiration lightly wetting the curls that framed her face. How could she face anyone again if she wasn't placed well? She hadn't thought about that while arguing with her test paper. She watched the person in front of her being escorted out of the building, begging for another chance.

It was her turn. She took a deep breath and held it. Holding out the paper, she did her best to steady her hand. The white pages still bobbed up and down in a shaky manner. The director looked her over before taking the test from her. She glanced at the paper, then at Willow, repeating the same procedure several times. Cassandrhea's hand carrying the paper fell abruptly to her side. The woman's eyes narrowed and her lips pressed together for a moment. "Sleeping Sands Academy!" she yelled out. Her face changed to a smile as she whispered, "Welcome, we will be seeing quite a bit of each other. I have high hopes for you based on your test results."

Willow smiled and moved to her new school's designated area. Several of the elves locked eyes with her out of sheer curiosity. She stood beside Nathan, who was the only one ecstatic to see her. This was going to be a long school year for them if the elves were their only classmates.

The rest of the afternoon was long and boring. They stood in their area and watched potential class mates go through the line. All of their friends were given spots in schools, although no more than two in any one institution. She was separated from those closest to her and couldn't help but wonder if that was on purpose.

Willow watched the line and the crowds, but never saw the one person she was looking for. The idea that Jade somehow got out of writing the test made her want to scream. It wasn't fair - reminiscent of a life she thought she had left behind. Why would Jade end up privileged again? She clenched her fists, her teeth grinding. Before they returned to the camp, she wanted an answer.

The sound of a horn blasted through the room and silence fell among all those who had been accepted as students to the various schools. Cassandrhea Tibbins took a position to address the new students.

"Good afternoon and congratulations on your acceptance to one of our schools. As I am sure you are aware, you here today are only a fraction of the students who will be attending this year. The test was administered to many groups over several days to make things easier."

Willow scanned the room to see if there was a microphone or something making her voice carry so well across the room. There was no visible evidence of any.

"There are a few details that are important to your success in the upcoming year that I would like to go over. First, all of the schools are protected by an anti-magical enchantment spell designed by myself. That means no illusions or enchantments will work after you walk through the gates. I suggest our avid illusionists who don't normally wear clothing take that warning to heart."

A rumble of laughter exploded from most of the room. Willow looked around and noticed that neither of the types of elves she was with were showing any emotion.

"It also means only sanctioned magic will work on school grounds. There will be no duelling to establish rank. To make things easier, you will be sorted by race in groups to work and live with during your first year. Competition between races is often quite intense. Expect to work hard if you want to place well in grades."

Nathan whispered to Willow, "Think we will be on our own? We can take these guys no problem." Several elves turned around and glared at them. A flush of heat ran to Willow's cheeks, turning her bright red.

"Most importantly, bring what you need. Once all students are accounted for, the gates to the schools will seal. There will be no leaving the grounds after that. No one in and no one out. There will be no communication with the outside world. That includes dreamwalking and telepathic connections. You will be isolated from the rest of the world until the end of the term. There will be no dropping out. No failures are allowed. Punishment for unacceptable behaviour will be administered by school staff. If you do not agree to these terms, leave now. If you need support, you will have to find it with your fellow schoolmates. I suggest you don't rock the boat, so to speak, or you will find the year difficult."

A few applicants had stood up and were escorted out. Her speech was harsh. The idea of being cut off from everyone for so long was eating away at Willow. She wondered if her extended abilities would also be affected by Cassandrhea's spell.

"On your way out, each of you will pick up a backpack. Inside you will find an information package with the place and time you will be escorted to your school. Make sure you are on time. If there are no questions, we will see you on January first."

She stepped down and left the room. The future students were let go one school section at a time. At the door, a backpack appeared for every student.

William stood outside the door, his hands shoved in his pockets. Together they headed out of the building to where the other portal guards were waiting.

"I didn't see Jade," Willow said.

"The director did say there were different days for testing. Jade probably already took it," Ashlyn said in an over bubbly tone. "Clairity and I were placed in the same school. I was so worried I wouldn't have a girlfriend for the whole school year." She looked at Willow and her smile disappeared. "Would have been better if you were with us. Sorry." She walked over to join Clairity and the Shinning brothers to discuss their test results.

Willow watched her friends chattering with enthusiasm about their placements. Jessie and Dezi were at the same school, as were Neil and Pete and Camile had Victoria. Although she was placed with Nathan, she couldn't help but feel left out somehow.

William put his arm around her. "It's only for a few months," he whispered in her ear. "You'll be fine. If anyone can make new friends, it's you. Let's head back to camp."

Chapter Sixty-Nine

Jade returned to her office after writing the entrance exam at Sleeping Sands Academy. Placing her purse on her desk, she peeled off her matching gloves and unbuttoned her suit jacket. She had chosen a teal colour for everything she wore today. Somehow she felt naked when there wasn't bit of green in her outfit.

She let out a breath of air as she plopped down in the leather chair behind her desk. She was accepted to one of the schools, but not the most prominent. She sighed, feeling a burst of failure radiate through her bones. She had never even heard of *Green-Eyed Recluse Collegiate.*

Taping her fingers on her desk, she noticed there were new files she hadn't seen before. The first was a record of suspected assassins living in the city. Opening the file, she was surprised to see Gavin and his friends at the top of the list. Her eyebrows moved closer together, forming lines between them. She bit her lower lip and continued reading the classified information.

There wasn't a lot of time for her to review everything. At any moment, someone could walk in wanting her to do some strange task they considered important for the mayor's future. She stuffed the file in her purse and continued on to the next one, containing written notes on results of various people from the exact test Jade had just taken herself. The first name was Jessica, having written the test three times and failed miserably. The notes indicated she possessed next to no magical talents.

So how is it she found an apprentice spot with such a prominent witch? she thought to herself.

Turning the page, the next name was Keith Quidnunk, the intern journalist she had been trying to contact. Seems he wrote the test multiple times but never attended any school. The page after was a Krissy Quidnunk. Comparing the reports, it appeared they were born on the same day. *Twins, perhaps,* she thought. Their test results were identical in every way, except the tests themselves were written on separate days. Krissy also never attended a class, even after being accepted several times.

Jade's lips quivered and her eyes burnt from the swelling of tears as she flipped through another file. It was filled with missing children, mainly orphaned, abandoned, or poor.

The final file was an internal affairs investigation of Hilary. She took in a big breath of air and let it out again. Inside were pictures of various men and reports of when they disappeared, each only days before a scheduled wedding. At the back of the file were photos of Constable Black handing envelopes to different people, including Gavin, Clyde the hotel owner, the bus driver, and the Director of New Residents, Fuscia Magnetal.

She closed the file and rubbed her eyes. What did all this mean? How was it all connected? She opened her purse and put the files in it, making sure she closed it tightly before she placed it in the bottom drawer of her desk. She glanced around, looking for any notes or anything to show who had left them for her, but found nothing. Whoever it was had to have access to all of the various official records.

Slouching back in her chair, she closed her eyes. When she opened them a few moments later, Hilary was standing in front of her. "So how did the test go?" the mayor asked.

Jade swallowed with a gulp. "I was placed but not in the school I expected," she said. "I will be attending *Green-Eyed Recluse Collegiate.* I haven't heard about it before."

"I have. It's the second-best school, in my opinion. It specializes in illusion magic. That would be why you were placed there." Hilary sat in a chair and crossed her legs. "Most of the schools specialize in one area of magic or another. That is how they place you. *Sleeping Sands* places those who practice several types of magic - jacks of all trades, so to speak. Occasionally they do accept someone who has such a strong unique talent that it cannot be ignored. Usually something very unusual that the director hasn't seen before."

"I suppose I do only practice only one form of magic."

"You should be proud. Illusion magic is one of the strongest of all magics. I believe you will excel." The mayor smiled.

"What type of magic do you practice?" Jade asked, realizing she had never seen the woman actually perform anything extra-ordinary in her presence.

A shadow passed by the door to Jade's office. "My next appointment is here. Can we pick this up again later?" Hilary asked. Without waiting for an answer, she exited through the door which joined the two offices.

Jade sat for a moment, contemplating everything that happened during the day. It was time for her to visit her father. Without telling anyone where she was going, she grabbed her purse and gloves and headed out the front door using an illusion to change her appearance.

Her father lived in an apartment on the other side of the city. It would take her a long while to walk there, but she didn't fancy anyone tracking her movements. Every couple of blocks, she ducked into an alley or closed doorway to change the illusion she was using to conceal her identity, hoping to throw any would-be spies off her tail. When she arrived at the building, she made herself appear as a delivery person taking a package to Malarchy.

Her father saw through his daughter's illusion immediately and invited her into his suite. "So what's with the disguise?" he asked, pouring a drink.

"Something strange is going on. I need to talk to you." She took the glass Malarchy offered her and sat on the couch. Opening her purse, she pulled out the files and handed them to her father.

"What are these?" he asked, taking the seat beside her.

"Files that appeared on my desk. I don't know who put them there, but the information in each is disturbing." Jade took a sip of the drink and coughed, almost choking on it.

Malarchy patted her on the back. "Are you alright?"

"Yes," she answered. "Fine... just went down the wrong way."

Her father opened the files and read each, while she sat waiting for his reaction. After Malarchy finished studying them, he placed the files on the coffee table. Letting out a breath of air noisily, he said, "We are in a big mess. Like a gigantic web of lies everywhere."

"Yes." Jade slouched back on the couch. "I've missed you," she said. "Things are going to get worse, aren't they?"

Malarchy wiped the tear from his daughter's face. "Yes," he answered. "Although the information we are finding out here is important, I am afraid we are too disconnected from the others for it to be of any use. If what's in those files confirms my suspicions, it's only the beginning of the truth. We have another enemy somewhere and one that might be more dangerous than Cornelius."

"Who?"

"I don't know yet. Better we don't trust anyone other than ourselves."

"I am just getting to the point now where I am trusted enough to learn information and I am being sent off to school. Why did you agree to have me write the test?"

"That meeting was a farce, child. We were set up from the beginning. Every day that passes, Pewterclaw becomes more dangerous for us. The schools are the only place you and the others will truly be safe. The Director of Knowledge is the only one at that meeting who had nothing to hide. It will also give you the chance to advance your abilities."

A buzzer rang and Malarchy said hello while pressing a button on a remote control box. "Malarchy? It's Hilary. I thought we might have a drink and chat."

"Can you give me ten minutes and I will come down?" Malarchy asked.

"Perfect!" the mayor exclaimed. "I will be in the car and have Safron leave it running."

A look of horror crossed Jade's face. "You did read about her dating habits, right? I would rather you not become involved with her."

Malarchy let out a laugh from deep inside his throat. "I don't plan on dating her, Jade. No one could replace your mother, especially not her. That reminds me, we should have a talk about the Pledge sometime. You are at the age where you may consider taking a husband."

"Sure, how about you stay here and we talk about it?" Jade suggested. She would have said anything to stop her father from going out with the mayor. The idea of it made her want to throw up. She liked Hilary and was grateful for all the help and support she gave, but no one should be dating her father, no matter who they were.

Malarchy let out a sigh. "Not tonight, but before you go off to school. Perhaps we can go back to camp and Diana can explain it better. I never was good at the more delicate subjects."

Jade smiled. She knew it would be some time before she saw the camp again. Her father was being a little optimistic. Hilary hadn't wanted Jade to leave for school. She most certainly wasn't going to allow her back to the camp, especially after ordering her to not be seen with or speak to anyone from there. She kissed her father on the cheek and waited five minutes after he left before heading down herself. Perhaps a good night's sleep would make things clearer in the morning.

Chapter Seventy

Willow's first sight back in the camp was Diana sitting with her niece, laughing and smiling as if they had been close to one another for all their lives. Nathan ran over and joined them. A warmth grew deep inside her as she watched the three, a beautiful aura of love encircling them.

"Can you see it?" William asked, moving beside her.

"Mm-hmm," she answered, still watching them. "Stunning." Her hand reached for the key around her neck. Fiddling with it calmed her. In the short time it hung around her neck, she had become accustomed to having it there to play with.

"It's on the list." he smiled.

Willow watched him walk away. This was a very long list they had to discuss. She wondered for a moment how they would find time to cover everything. Looking around, she realized she was standing alone in a field again. Apparently, the new theme in her life was isolation. Even her guardians wouldn't be with her at school.

With William off to check on the progress of construction in the camp, Willow headed to the food building to see what they had for dinner. With more and more terunji joining the camp every day, the menu often contained foods she found less than desirable. Today was no different. The main meal being offered was hamburgers and french fries.

Willow thought back to the first time she heard of a hamburger - it mortified her. Poor Mike had no idea she was a vegetarian. She had no idea this world ate animals. She smiled. In the end, the evening turned out to be the most fun she ever had.

The smell of searing meat dragged her back to reality, sending her running for the door, gagging for fresh air. The field was probably the best place for her. She sat down on the ground and an apple tree sprouted behind her supporting her as she leaned back. After the wave of nausea passed, a branch bent down, allowing her to easily pick its fresh fruit to eat. Taking a bite, she savoured the crisp flavour.

She wasn't the only one who had experienced a similar reaction to the dinner menu. Before long, most of her friends discovered her small oasis in the middle of the field and joined her. She added several other types of fruit trees.

"Gotta love a pick-your-own-fruit-salad night," Dezi joked, standing under a peach tree.

"Better than what this place has been offering lately," Clairity made a snarling noise as she spoke.

"We can't force our way of life on those who don't agree with it," William said.

Willow hadn't even realized that William joined them. He took an apple from the tree and sat beside her.

"Maybe we could do two separate eating times. The smell is really hard to handle." Ashlyn said. She made a face and stopped eating again, sickened by the memory.

"That's not a bad idea. I think we can work on some sort of a rotation. Thanks for the food," he said to Willow before walking away to meet with Mike, who had chosen to eat the camp's food.

A noise rang in each of their heads, stopping everyone in their tracks. It was as if a message was being distorted by something. A screeching noise caused several of them to whine and hold their ears. The only words anyone could make out was *meet*, *now* and *city*. The same message played several times in a row before suddenly stopping.

Every portal guard headed for the trees to see who else heard the sounds. Apparently, it was relayed to each of them.

"It must have come from either Malarchy or Jade. Given the obvious choice, Malarchy would be the more likely of the two," Faramund said.

"Agreed," William said. "But why was it sent in such a distorted manner?"

"Regardless, there is only one way we will find out," Willow said with a sigh. It appeared her talk with William was going to have to wait a little longer. "We have to go to Pewterclaw. I suppose we could pick up all the school supplies at the same time. We each have a list of stores in the city where we can find the things we need. That gives us a reason to show up there without raising suspicion anyways."

"Okay," William said. "I want everyone to bring their list to the meeting room. We can make one master list and take less people to pick up everything. Sarah can quickly catalogue the stores and items before we go."

*****

It was Willow's first time in the new meeting room. The table itself was twice as large as the old one. William was already sitting at one end, furiously doodling on a pad of paper in front of him. She didn't even have to look to know there was nothing important on the notebook. He was deep in thought and probably didn't even realize his hands were moving. She took the seat next to him quietly so as not to disturb his concentration. She sat and watched him until Sarah walked in.

"Hey guys. Sounds like a fun night."

William looked up from his trance. "Yeah, loads," he said. He turned his attention to Willow. "How long have you been here?" he asked.

"Not long," she answered. "I didn't want to disturb you. Want to share your thoughts?"

The edges of his lips curled up a little. He let out a chuckle. "Not yet."

"Just don't tell me it's on the list. Seriously, we are going to need a full week to get through that list soon."

William laughed.

"What's so funny?" Mike asked, taking a seat.

"Nothing," William answered. "It's a long story."

Everyone was filing in now, handing their papers to Sarah, who after tying her hair back with an elastic, started typing at an incredible rate. For a moment, Willow was mesmerized by the speed at which Sarah's fingers were gliding across the keyboard. It was much faster than she remembered. Shaking her head, Willow added her school list to the pile.

Returning her attention to the rest of the table, Willow realized she wasn't the only one who had been hypnotized by Sarah's new ability.

"They're finished," Sarah said, smiling with satisfaction.

"Sarah," William said, starring at the girl. "When did your typing speed become faster than the speed of light?"

"What do you mean?" she asked, a blank look on her face.

"It took you maybe three minutes to enter all the information on all of those pages." William pointed to the stack of lists.

Sarah's gaze alternated between the pile and her screen a few times. "Oh, I see what you mean. I don't know. At least it saved us some time tonight." She handed a copy of the printed list to William for him to look over.

"Okay," he said. "This is quite the list. Let's split it into two. Faramund and Sarah can fill the first part. Jessie and Clairity can take the second half. I am going to visit with Malarchy. Willow and Ashlyn, you two can visit Jade. Hopefully, we can figure out what the message was all about quickly."

"You don't want me to come along?" Mike asked.

William shot a look at Sissy. "I was hoping you could take care of things here. We need this place functioning fully. Everyone else can lend a hand where you need them." He stood. "We will be heading off first thing in the morning, so try to get a good night's sleep."

Willow couldn't help but wonder what it was that was bothering William. She followed him back to the sleeping quarters they shared.

"Is everything okay?" she asked.

He turned quickly. "Yeah," he answered. "If you keep sneaking up on me, you might give me a complex."

"If you weren't so deep in thought, you wouldn't think I was sneaking up on you. Is it Sissy? It crossed my mind that maybe we are giving her a bit too much trust. She was our enemy, after all. I can't imagine being thrown into this lifestyle is easy for her. Turning us in would put her in good favour with her family again."

"Thanks for that," William said, rubbing his neck. "That wasn't what I was worried about, but now you mention it, I suppose I better have a talk with Mike and Diana." He fell backwards onto the bed. "The message is what is bothering me. It was made to sound like distortion on purpose. Something bad must be happening in Pewterclaw. There is the possibility that we are walking into a trap."

"We could try to contact them through a dream tonight. That way, we wouldn't be walking in blind," Willow said, lying beside him.

"No, if Malarchy believes his messages are being intercepted enough to try to code them, I would imagine even dreams aren't safe. I have a bad feeling about all of this. I know we were supposed to have our talk, but I am afraid it will have to wait."

"I know, until we get back from the city. I figured. We need to concentrate on the issues," Willow pouted.

"Thanks," William said. "I am going to find Mike and discuss Sissy with him. Get some sleep. I think tomorrow is going to be a long day."

Chapter Seventy-One

Willow had no problem walking across the water that led to Pewterclaw this time. They entered the city in pairs. Once inside, they each went their separate ways. Willow and Ashlyn took a direct route to the mayor's office to find Jade.

There was no escaping waiting in a line-up to ask to speak to their friend. Esmerelda seemed to be taking her time helping those in front of them. After what seemed to be an extraordinarily long wait, they approached the desk.

"Oh!" Esmerelda exclaimed. "I know you! You're that girl who thinks she talks to guardians." The blue-haired lady let out a loud nasal laugh. "So what can we do for you today?"

"We came to see Jade," Ashlyn said.

Esmerelda's smile faded from her face. She blew a big bubble from the gum she was chewing. "I'll see if she is available." She turned and disappeared in the back offices. When she returned, it wasn't Jade who was with her.

"What a surprise!" Hilary exclaimed. "What are you girls doing in the city?"

"We needed to pick up the supplies for school. The information packet said we could find everything we needed here in Pewterclaw. We thought we would stop by and visit with Jade while we are here," Willow said. Her eyes never left the mayor's face. That strange feeling shot through her body again. It wasn't so much an uneasy feeling as it was an empty one. Her hand reached for the key around her neck as if it was the answer to all of their problems. She moved it gently back and forth on the chain William had given her.

"Oh, what a shame," the mayor sighed. "Jade is so swamped right now. She asked me to tell you she just can't take any time today. I suppose you know all about how busy one gets with your camp moving and all."

Willow's eyes narrowed. "Where did you hear that?"

"From Jade or maybe Malarchy. We have no secrets, you know," the mayor said.

"Are you sure Jade can't see us? Not even a minute to say hello?" Ashlyn asked.

"I am trying to be delicate with you girls," Hilary explained. "She has graduated past your childhood adventures. Jade has a new life here and you are not a part of it. I suggest you forget her and move on yourselves." The mayor turned and walked away.

"Next!" Esmerelda yelled.

"Wow," Ashlyn said, as they exited the building. "What was that about? Do you think Jade actually said that?"

Willow shrugged her shoulders. "I don't know," she said. "Ow!" A woman hit her square on the shoulder. She turned around to look at the stranger, but her eyes wandered towards a shadow.

"What happened?"

"I don't know. This woman bumped into me. I turned around to see who it was and I thought I saw something. It's like someone has been following us since we got here," Willow said. Looking down at her hand, she realized she was holding something. "And now I have a strange piece of paper in my hand. I have no idea where it came from."

"Well!" Ashlyn exclaimed. "What does it say?"

A shiver ran down Willow's spine - another familiar feeling she didn't like. She looked around, hoping to catch sight of whoever was watching them this time. Her vision failed her, finding no one. Resting her back against the wall of a building, she positioned Ashlyn in front of her. Once she was sure no one else could see the contents of the note, she opened it.

The cafe down the street. Take a seat outside with your back to the one you know. Pretend you and your friend are talking.

"Feel like a coffee?" Willow asked.

The cafe was packed with patrons. Willow, following the note's instructions, requested a seat on the patio. There was only one available, right behind a familiar face - Gavin. She sat down with her back to him without showing any inclination that the two knew each other.

"I think someone may be following me," Willow blurted out.

A waitress came over and took the girls' order for drinks. She left a complimentary copy of *The Empowered* newspaper on the table. Willow opened it without reading any of the news and pretended to be absorbed in an article.

"I am not surprised," Gavin said. "You are being followed by quite a few people. The Director of Secrecy's office, reporters, and as of this morning, you have made a most-wanted hit list."

"What?!" Willow yelled, immediately pretending she was surprised by an article in the paper.

"Two different people have offered large rewards for you dead. I am afraid the city is not safe for you. By this afternoon, every type of assassin possible will be after the reward," Gavin whispered.

"Is it just me? Are my friends on the list as well?"

"Just one for now... William, but they want him alive. I wouldn't suggest it is safe to be close to you, either. An assassin won't care about collateral damage, if you know what I mean. Leave the city and stay hidden is my advice... trust no one. Not everyone is what they seem."

A large crash sounded inside the cafe. "They are gone," Ashlyn said. "I only looked away for a moment."

The waitress returned. She placed a receipt on the table and smiled. "Your bill has been paid. Thank you." There was something about the woman that Willow recognized but she couldn't quite place it.

She picked up the bill to see if there was any indication as to who paid for their drinks. Letters formed before her eyes at the top of the receipt: *RUN*. Willow stood and grabbed Ashlyn's hand, dragging her outside the patio just as a truck rammed into the area right over top of where they had been seated.

"Are you alright?"

Willow jumped back two feet, startled to see Jessica standing beside them, looking at the disaster that had just occurred.

"I was about to come over and say hello," Jessica said. "It's a good thing you moved when you did. I hope no one else was hurt."

"We have to go," Willow said, starting to walk at a fast pace.

Jessica followed. "What's going on?" she asked.

"It isn't safe for you to be seen talking with me. I have a couple of bounties on my head. You should go."

"Bounties? You mean someone is trying to kill you?!" Jessica shrieked.

"Yes, that is exactly what I mean," Willow answered.

"Who?"

Willow stopped for a moment. "I have no idea. Two rewards have been offered to kill me and one reward to take William alive. Obviously, I have more enemies than I thought."

"We should go to the directors. They could help with this sort of thing." Jessica wrinkled her forehead upwards, anticipating a response.

Willow laughed. "No, they would hardly believe me considering my track record. The only proof I have is an anonymous tip and the accident you just saw. You better go." Willow grabbed Ashlyn's arm again. The two continued towards Malarchy's apartment.

The buzzer made a horrible sound, which reminded Willow a little of the garbled telepathic message that was the reason they were in the city in the first place.

"Hello?" Malarchy's voice came loud and clear through a box in the apartment building lobby.

"It's Willow. We need to see William right away."

"Take the elevator up three floors - second door on the left," Malarchy said.

The door was open when the girls arrived. The apartment was very modern and quite comfortable - a lifestyle that suited Malarchy. She thought back to the director meeting and wondered how much she could trust him or his daughter.

William was sitting down on a couch looking through some files. "What's the problem now?" he asked. He tossed the papers he held down on the table and sent her a glare that made her feel insignificant.

"Sorry, didn't mean to intrude," she answered. "Just thought you'd like to know we have assassins after us is all."

"Assassins?" Malarchy motioned for them to take a seat, anticipating a long story was coming.

William rubbed his eyes. "You did say assassins, right?"

"Yeah," she answered, sitting beside him on the couch. "I have two different bounties on me payable on proof of my death."

"Of course," William said. "Why is it always you?"

"I wouldn't get too high and mighty. There is a bounty on you as well. Just... they want you alive." Willow sat back and hugged her purse. She realized she was still holding the newspaper from the cafe.

"Actually, we were almost killed just now at the cafe. If the receipt hadn't told us to run, a truck would have smashed right into us."

"I suppose it's Cornelius who wants you to out of the way," Malarchy said.

"That might work, except there are two different bounties on me placed by two different individuals. I think we have another enemy, perhaps even worse than Cornelius," Willow said.

"Well, we are stuck here until the others return with the school things. You two might as well take a look through these files," William said, picking up another file.

Willow looked at the newspaper in her hand. She read the headline: *Blast Of Cold Air From The North Chills City*. Underneath another article read: *Cold Spell Causes River To Freeze Over.* "There wouldn't happen to be a file on children in there, would there?"

Malarchy arched an eyebrow. "How did you know?"

She handed him the newspaper. "It fits."

He handed the paper to William. "I am not sure I see what you mean."

William shrugged his shoulders while shaking his head.

Did they both forget about the prophecies? Willow sighed. "The prophecy," she said. Looking at their faces was like staring at a blank chalk board. She recited the prophecy out loud to refresh their memories.

When a blast of cold from the north does blow,

A single touch stops a river's flow.

A hero's heart will go missing,

Enter lonely sprites, their queen reminiscing.

To save us it must be the chosen,

Her will is cold and heart is frozen.

Time past by, while doors were locked,

Now the children's joy has been blocked.

Finally free, they seek to return the favour,

While you fight over who is braver.

Hidden in ice and snow and sleet,

Careful not to miss exactly what you seek.

Locked away in time, it happened before.

Heed this warning or it will happen once more.

"I thought the prophecy was referring to what happened before in the Frostica land." William used the eraser end of a pencil to scratch behind one ear.

"I think we have seen the past prophecies have held several meanings for several different people. This is too coincidental to ignore." She stood up and walked around the couch in a full circle, stopping directly in front of William. "If I am right, the line *A hero's heart will go missing* refers to you. It very well could be that you end up captured from this bounty."

"I think you are over-thinking it." William took her hands and directed her gently to sit down again. "The ice, snow, sleet, frozen are all words that refer to Frostica land. The hero and children reference was about Nick being captured. He wouldn't have been able to deliver gifts this year if we didn't free him. The queen was Lanzia and the *it happened before* I have no doubt was about the Ice Age. It all fits."

"It's snowing," Ashlyn said, starring out the window.

Willow stood up and went to look outside. It wasn't a little bit of snow. It was coming down like a blizzard.

"When it's winter, there is snow, sleet, ice and things are frozen." Willow's voice was emotionless. "I can't help but feel there is something we are missing. Promise me you will be careful."

The others came through the door just in time to hear Willow's last sentence. "Everyone needs to be careful in this snow. It's slippery out there and cold," Jessie said. He came to a complete stop, feeling the mood of the room.

"Why do I have a feeling we missed something important?" Clairity asked.

"Is everyone alright?" Sarah asked.

"Yes," Malarchy said. "Yes... quite fine for the moment. We seem to have an assassin problem and need everyone out of the city as soon as possible, so no waiting." He grabbed a coat. "Is Jade going to join us?"

"I almost forgot," Willow said. "The mayor told us Jade never wanted to see any of us again. She also seemed to know we moved camps somehow."

"I don't know which part of that statement to question first," Malarchy said. "Did you see her? I suppose the other question is, did we move camp?"

"No, Hilary wouldn't let us near Jade. The mayor said she heard about our location change from either Jade or Malarchy. Obviously, that was a lie since no one ever told them we were moving." Willow looked at the group crowded in the doorway dripping from the melting snow, utter confusion plastered on each of their faces. It was almost humorous to watch.

"We best not wait any longer. You need to leave here now. It won't be safe for anyone you are seen with. I can hide you with illusion to the city limits. After that, you will have to cross the bridge on your own. It's a bad place to be in the open, but no magic is allowed there. Once across, teleport immediately. I don't want to know where the new location for camp is. I will find a way to pry Jade from the mayor's grips for a family trip. I will contact you to pick us up once we are clear of Pewterclaw. It may take a few days." Malarchy motioned for them to take the stairs.

Outside, the wind was blowing fiercely, cutting at exposed flesh like a knife. The weather was definitely similar to that of the Frostica land. It would be a long walk to leave the city. They were almost at the furthest possible place from the bridge. Malarchy cast an illusion on them to disguise them as snow dwellers. They were perhaps the only beings who would be out in the current weather, except for maybe a few ice imps. The only real problem was they were slipping and sliding on the fresh snow like they had never seen it before.

"Over there!" cried out from behind them, sending panic through Willow's veins.

"We need to split up," William yelled. "Malarchy, get them out of here. I will keep these guys busy."

"Not alone, you won't!" Willow yelled back. The wind caught her face and made her whine from the blast of cold. "I am staying with you."

"There isn't time to argue over this. Just go."

Faramund took Willow's hand. "We stand together. We leave together."

Ashlyn and Clairity pulled out their wands. If the assassins were attacking, they would fight them as a group.

Willow's heart skipped a beat as they were approached. A man stopped in front of William and reached in his pocket. She took in a breath of air ready for the worst.

"Hey, mate. This is the way to the all-night bar, isn't it?" the man said, lighting a cigarette.

Malarchy pointed towards a bright pink neon sign.

"Over there, guys!" the man yelled out. "Thanks, mate."

As he walked away, almost everyone let out the breath of air they were holding. Willow watched him put his lighter back in his coat pocket. There was still something not quite right about the man. She looked in the other direction for his friends but she couldn't see any. William took her arm. They began walking quickly again. Willow's eyes watched the man disappear into the bar.

"Malarchy," she said. "Are there people who can see completely through illusions?"

"I am not sure now is the time for lessons," he snapped. His breath creating a long trail of mist from the cold. He glanced at her and sighed. "Yes, illusion masters can. Why? I assume it is pertinent to our survival tonight."

"The man," she said, looking back quickly. "His friends never followed him."

William glanced at Malarchy. The two quickened the pace, almost pushing the others forward.

"I have a feeling," Clairity started. Her forehead wrinkled and a look of anguish crossed her face, "we are being followed. We won't make it to the bridge."

"Which way?" Willow yelled at her best friend.

"Behind us to the right," Clairity answered.

Specks of gold in Willow's eyes began to shine brightly, until all that was left visible was shimmering gold. Storm clouds swirled above as the wind behind them picked up the snow, which had already accumulated on the ground, and threw it backwards at anyone who might be following. The use of magic slowed her pace. William picked her up and carried her while she maintained a wall of snow to block any possible attackers.

Making it to the bridge was only the first step to leaving the city safely. Malarchy nodded at William and disappeared into the storm. Covering just himself with an illusion spell would be far harder to track than a large group in the open.

Willow had no choice but to drop her snow wall before they entered the bridge. No magic was allowed there; breaking that rule would be detrimental to their future relations with anyone in the empyral society and would cause a rush of police to arrest them. Remembering how Annabelle and Lilabeth were executed while imprisoned in the city, Willow realized they wouldn't last an hour incarcerated by the constable.

All they could do was run. Jessie used his strength and speed to pick up Clairity and Ashlyn over his shoulders. He raced them to the other side of the bridge and returned to take Sarah and Willow. Once he had her over his shoulder, all the protesting in the world wasn't going to make a difference.

It was just as cold at the end of the bridge. The storm which raged inside the city also wreaked havoc on the outside of it. Willow grew a few trees to block the wind from blowing them over and as a line of defence should someone or something attack. After that, there was nothing to do but wait for William, Iskander, and Faramund to finish crossing. Minutes passed and nothing.

"We have to go back! They could be in trouble!" Willow yelled.

In the distance, they heard some muffled yells. Jessie raced back onto the bridge. Willow attempted to bolt forward to help. Ashlyn grabbed her arm. "You can't leave us!" she cried. "We would be sitting ducks."

She was right, of course. If Willow left, the three girls would probably not be strong enough to outlast an attack on their own.

Indecision filled her. Either way, if someone got hurt it would be her fault. She had no answers this time. Letting out a couple heavy breaths, Willow alternated her view between the scared faces of her best friends and the empty bridge ahead.

"We go together then," Willow said. "We can't just leave them."

The other three agreed. They inched closer slowly, and were just about to step on the bridge to leave the main world again when Jessie appeared in front of them carrying William. He was hurt. Faramund and Iskander came running after them. As soon as the two cleared the final step of the bridge, a green gas surrounded them and they were travelling. Moments later, they were back in camp.

The smile on Mike's face at the return of the group faded as he realized something was wrong. He rushed over, yelling to some men to find Richard. He dropped to his knees where Jessie placed William's body down on the ground. Tears flowed from Willow's eyes. Faramund held her back from rushing to his side.

"Is he okay?!" she screamed through her sobs.

Mike looked up at her. "I don't know. It's bad. What happened?"

Iskander relayed the story of how they escaped the city. "Once it was the three of us, something attacked. We don't know who or what it was. We never saw it coming. If it weren't for Nero and Tika, we would all be gone."

The two Olcsanka appeared beside the injured portal guard. They both let a howling whine for him. "They were assassins," Tika explained. "The most deadly killers for hire we have seen."

"I don't understand," Willow said, sniffling from the tears. "Whoever wanted him, wanted him alive."

"He is alive, barely." Nero lay down beside William. "It is much easier to transport someone incapacitated. They didn't anticipate our intervention. Perhaps we should consider Aslo and Kiera always joining you in future."

The two Leander arrived from patrol. "She will not leave our sight now. The camp will be protected by the avian guardians. We have put too much emphasis on protection of the camp and not enough on Willow. That will change," Also said.

"Move aside." Richard slid on the ground, stopping at William's side. He opened a black case he brought with him and took out some instruments. His face turned white as he began working on the motionless body.

"Victoria!" Willow yelled to Jessie. He darted to find his sister without another word.

"There may not be anything the girl can do for him," Faramund said, tightening his grip on Willow in a hug.

"I hope there is," Richard said, standing up. "I can't help him. He is dying."

Willow screamed. Her heart snapped in two. This was her fault. They should have stayed together. Tears streamed down not just her own face, but everyone else's as well.

Victoria and Jessie arrived just in time to hear what the doctor said. The girl knelt beside the injured man and placed her hands over the main cut. A light pink dust escaped from her hands. It was working. She could see the bits of magic trying their hardest to put William back together again.

"It's no use - she isn't strong enough," Mike said.

"Wait, no!" Willow cried. "It's working. Can't you see her magic? The pink shimmer!"

"There is nothing shimmering, Willow," Clairity said.

For the first time, Willow realized she could see magic trails. All this time, she had thought she was seeing auras of some type, but it wasn't. It was magic. Every type had its own signature colour.

"Please, one more time," Willow begged. This time, she took one hand of the young girl. She watched a blast of rainbow colours flow from her body to Victoria. The pink stream intensified from a light pastel colour to a strong hot fuchsia. She watched as the magic began to repair damaged tissue and smiled. It was working.

She felt her shoulders slouch and her eyelids started to grow heavy - her energy draining. He wasn't healed yet and she was faltering. The flow of colours was between her and Victoria faded in and out. She put every ounce of magic power she could muster into the healer already.

Willow looked up and saw Mike standing with his arms around Sissy, the aura of their love for each other flowing solid even in this time of sadness. *Love,* she thought. It was a form of magic. That was why she could see it between people. She took in a big breath and looked at William. She did love him in some way. After admitting it, she let her feelings flow. Every ounce of power and feeling flowed from her body and into Victoria.

She watched the beautiful colours she had once hoped she would one day see coming from her for another person. In the background, she heard someone call her name. She fell over, landing on the ground. Everything went black.

Chapter Seventy-Two

Willow opened her eyes slowly. She didn't recognize the room she was in, but she definitely knew the machines that were around her. She focused, slowly realizing she must not have been out too long since there were no wires attached to her.

"You gave us a scare," Mary said. "We weren't sure if you were going to pull through for a moment."

Willow shook her head. She was still fuzzy, but alert enough to know that this was too backwards to be true. "Worried about me?" She found the strength to mumble. "William?" She closed her eyes again, exhaustion returning.

"I'll fetch your friends. They can explain what happened to you better than I can. Give me good old-fashioned strep throat to diagnose any day over what you lot go through." Mary left the room.

Willow lay in the silence for what seemed like an eternity. Nobody came. A white curtain was drawn around her bed separating her from other beds in the same room. She wondered if William was on one of them. Mustering her strength, she sat up. She rested her head on her fingertips for a few moments, trying to find the energy to move. Taking a deep breath, she supported her head on its own again. For the first time, she realized her skin had turned from a golden bronze to pure white.

"You should be resting," Kiera said.

Willow fell back on the pillow again. "I need clothes," she said.

"I brought you some," Clairity said. Her friend looked odd somehow, like she was forcing a smile.

"What happened?"

Clairity placed the clothes on the bed and moved aside, allowing Aslo to jump up on the bed. "You did a very foolish thing," he said.

"Foolish? I don't remember. What did I do?" Willow asked.

"You tried to transfer your life force. You almost did it, too. Another minute and you would have been gone. I understand you had feelings for William, but..."

"Had?" Willow cut him off. "You said had!" she screamed, sitting up her eyes swelling with tears and the storm of the century trying to brew outside.

"Stop!" Kiera yelled. "You don't have enough power back yet."

"William," she said, trying to calm herself. "Is he..." She couldn't say the words.

"Not exactly," Richard said, joining the conversation. "He is in a bad state. We don't know if, with regular medicine, he will wake up again. Victoria did more than we expected with your help. That's the only reason he has even a slight chance. We have to accept the fact that he could remain in a vegetative state forever."

Willow gasped for air. It was as if a hot stick had just been pushed right through her and was burning her from the inside out. The pain she felt at that moment was more intense than anything she could have ever imagined.

Her mind raced. "The guardians must be able to do something for him," she blurted out.

"This is beyond our power," Nero said. All of the guardians in the camp had arrived to see how she was fairing.

"What power?" Willow yelled. In each fist she clenched the white sheet on the bed tightly. "When have any of you shown even an ounce of power, other than to hide behind us? You use our mortal bodies like a shield posing as pictures on our skin while we take all the chances. We have risked everything for you. We fight for your cause. Why? None of you do. You leave it all to us. You are supposed to be powerful beings. Where is the power?"

"You are angry right now," Kiera answered. "We understand that. This isn't something we have the ability to do."

"You don't have the simple power of healing? What can you do? If not you, I will call Acacia to help." Willow attempted to get out of bed.

"She will not come," Aslo answered. "She knows what has happened. You must understand, we cannot interfere in life and death."

"You still haven't answered what you can do," Willow snapped. "Is there anyone who could help him?"

"I heard some yelling. Is everything okay?" Mike said, looking around the curtain.

"Answer me," Willow barked.

"Perhaps a full healer, maybe. The longer he remains in this state, the worse the chances he will ever recover. We will be around should you decide to want to speak to us." Aslo turned and walked out, the other guardians following him.

Willow noticed Sissy standing beside Mike for the first time. Her eyes locked on the girl. "Clairity, I need Ashlyn. Can you get her for me please?"

"I don't know if I like the sound of that," Mike said, sitting on the edge of her bed. "What's going on inside that head of yours?"

"I need to contact Lance," Willow answered.

Sissy's mouth dropped open. "Why?" she screamed. "It's too dangerous. All of my family is probably on high alert right now. My father could have some way to monitor dreams. You have to listen to me..."

Willow cut the girl off. "No, you listen to me. Somewhere in that nasty dungeon of yours is a man named Micca. He is William's only hope to come back to us. If I have to break in there and find him myself I will, but if your brother can help find an easier way it would be a lot quicker."

"Mike," Sissy started.

Mike held up his hand to tell her to stop. "William saved my life too many times for me not to try to save his. I'm in. I'll call a meeting."

"I'll find Ashlyn, I guess," Clairity said.

"No, I got that," Mike said. "Help her get dressed and over to the meeting room. We need to prepare to invade if Lance won't help us."

"You can't be serious!" Sissy shrieked. "It's suicide. Sheer numbers alone are against you. Willow is only at half-strength. She will be useless."

"Don't worry about me. I heal quick." Willow sat up and took the clothes from the bed. The white curtain fell closed - everyone now gone except Clairity.

After changing into regular clothes, she stood and took a few steps. At first, Willow was as wobbly as a newborn giraffe trying out its legs for the first time. That didn't last long. By the time she reached the bathroom, she was back in control and walking almost normally.

The mirror in front of her reflected the girl she used to loathe to see every day in her home world. She examined her face. It was more slender than it was the day before. She looked sickly. All the curves she had noticed as of late seemed to have disappeared. She was that stupid girl who grew vegetables and was good for nothing else. Feelings of inadequacy lumped in her throat, making it hard to swallow.

She splashed water on her face and dried off with a towel. She could feel the concern from her friend burning into her back. "Stop!" she cried out. "I don't need you to pity me. I will be fine. I am going to fix this."

Clairity broke down in tears. "If Ashlyn, Sarah, and I had let you go help them..." she sniffled. "If we hadn't stopped you, things would be different."

"It isn't your fault. I made the choice. It could have just as easily been you three they attacked if I left." Willow splashed a bit of cool water on the back of her neck and sighed. "Let's go meet the others."

*****

Mike stood outside the doorway to the meeting room. All the guardians lined up in a row watching him. Willow made Clairity go far around the line to avoid contact with them. She wasn't ready to make up with the guardians - there was probably a lot of work to be done on both sides before they would see eye-to-eye again. The fact of the matter was, the guardians really hadn't done anything to aid in their war. Everything that happened was left to keepers and portal guards. That would have to change.

"Glad to see you walking so well," Mike said as they approached the door. "I made sure no guardians were joining us tonight. If you want to change that, let me know."

Willow looked back at them. "After we know where we stand. If we have to invade, we will tell them. They can choose their own fate at that time."

Inside, the whole camp was in deep discussion over what was going on. The moment Willow walked into the room all fell silent, eyes locked on her. She moved to the table and almost sat in her normal seat. Looking at the empty seat where William normally sat, she moved to it. She was running the show now. Mike sat down beside her. It took a second glance for her to confirm Malarchy and Jade were both there as well.

Mike leaned over and whispered in her ear, "They don't know any details about him yet. I sent for Malarchy and Jade. I figured we would need everyone."

Willow took a deep breath. "As most of you know, we went to Pewterclaw yesterday. What you don't know is that assassins have been hired to kill me and William."

A rumble filled the room. Mike requested silence until she was finished.

"Malarchy escorted us to the city bridge to leave. We were followed. Jessie managed to bring the girls in our group, including me, to the other side safely using his speed." Willow paused for a moment. He shouldn't have been able to use his speed. The city would have been alerted to magic being used on the bridge. The police should have come and arrested them.

"Willow?" Mike said, breaking her thoughts.

"Sorry," she said. "A fight broke out and William was injured."

Mike again had to call for quiet so Willow could speak.

"I know a lot of you watched from a distance last night as Victoria bravely tried to heal him. I lent her every ounce of power I had to boost her own ability. She did a fantastic job." Willow smiled at the girl. "He would be dead at this moment without her."

Sighs of relief rang out through the camp members.

"However," she continued and silence fell again, "he isn't well still." She rubbed her fingers on her forehead. "Diana, could you take Victoria and Nathan in the next room and let them pick out something to watch please?"

Willow waited for the woman to return. "There is a chance William will never wake up again. He could remain in his current state forever. The longer he is unresponsive, the worse his chances are for recovery."

"The guardians must be able to help," Zsiga said.

"I begged them." Tears fell from Willow's eyes and the sky at the same time. She swallowed the saliva filling her mouth. "Neither the guardians nor Acacia will aide in his recovery." She paused, looking at the window. "There is one chance to help him. A full healer might be able to bring him back if we hurry." As if on instinct, Willow reached for the key around her neck. It slid from side to side with ease, but the calming feeling it usually provided was gone.

"We don't have a healer in the camp," Malarchy said.

"I know, but we know where one is," Willow answered. "Micca was taken prisoner by King Cornelius' sons. He is somewhere in the dungeon of the king's castle."

"Are you suggesting we invade?" Malarchy raised an eyebrow at Willow.

Willow took a deep breath and let it out again. "Tonight, Ashlyn is going to help me find Lance in the dream realm. Before anyone says anything, I already know it is dangerous. We are taking the chance of running into anyone from the royal family by entering their domain. If we can find Lance through dreams, there is a chance he might be able to help us free Micca."

"If not?" Faramund asked.

"You each have to make up your own decision. There is no pressure on anyone, but if I cannot find a way to rescue Micca from here, I am going there."

"And the guardians?" Malarchy asked.

"They will be given the choice as well should that time come," Willow said. The door creaked opened. The guardians sat at the threshold listening.

"I'm in. William saved my life enough times. I owe him," Mike said.

"I cannot leave the little lady unprotected. I gave my vow as a portal guard and I will fight as one again," Faramund said.

"I too will fight if need be," Zsiga said. "William likes my coffee more than anyone else." His attempt to lighten the mood wasn't as well received as he had hoped.

One by one, each of them agreed to try to free Micca and save William if necessary. Aslo moved forward. "The guardians will join you in battle if this is what you choose. Although we cannot save William ourselves, we are not without ability, even if some of you believe that." The guardians turned and exited the room.

"Ashlyn and I will need sedatives for tonight," Willow said directly to Richard.

"I'm coming, too," Clairity demanded. "Safety in numbers, remember?"

"I'm tagging along, too," Mike added.

Sissy gasped. "The dream world is where they are the strongest. You won't be able to fight them there. I could go with you. It might throw them off to see me."

"I could go as well. If you encounter Cornelius, you may need me," Diana said.

"No," Willow said. "Sissy. Diana. The fewer people who go, the better. We are hoping to contact Lance and get out. Either he agrees to help us or he doesn't. All we are doing tonight is deciding which course of action to take tomorrow."

Chapter Seventy-Three

Opening her eyes, Willow found herself in the middle of a white room. She recognized it as the place Ashlyn called her staging area. The only problem was, Ashlyn wasn't there. She looked at the doors leading to people in dreams. Normally, she came from another room - from behind one of those doors.

"Hey," Ashlyn called from behind her. "How did you get here before me?"

"I was trying to figure that out too. Let's not waste time on it now, though." Willow moved forward in the room, checking the different doors for signs of their friends. Ashlyn found Clairity from behind a mirror again. Mike's door had a big hamburger on it. Normally that would have made the three girls laugh.

Taking a big breath, Willow called Lance's name. The four of them stood looking around. Nothing happened. No door appeared that could link to the prince and there was no sign of Lance himself.

"Maybe he isn't asleep yet?" Ashlyn asked.

"Lance, I know you can hear me. Please. I need your help," Willow pleaded to the ceiling. She wasn't sure exactly why she was looking up.

The room shook and a familiar scene appeared before their eyes. Lance was sitting in a comfortable chair in front of a fireplace. He sighed. "You are taking a big chance coming here like this. It's a risk to all of our lives." He stood and laughed. "I see you brought the pack. Only missing good old William. Where is he?"

"He's dying," Willow said. "An assassin attacked him."

"Dying? Are you quite sure?" the prince asked.

"Yes," Mike said. "Quite." He shot Lance a look of anger.

"I need to ask for your help," Willow said.

Lance pressed his lips together and tilted his head sideways at her friends. "Then you alone should ask," he said, waving to the others, who flew backwards and disappeared.

Willow was alone with him in a dream again. He seemed different somehow. His eyes displayed the blue flame burning in his soul.

"So," he said, "what is it now?"

"There is a man in your dungeon, Micca. He is a healer from our world. There is a chance he can save William. It would have to be soon." Willow looked down at her shoes. "I know it's a lot to ask."

"A lot?" The prince laughed loudly. "You have no idea what you are asking of me. My life and all of my brothers' and sisters' lives are at stake. If my father were to find out, or my brother, for that matter." He laughed again. "If they even suspected I was speaking to you." He stopped and rubbed his hands vigorously through his hair, messing it up. "And to save the life of the man who will probably end up with the woman I love." He let out a sigh and sat down in the chair again.

Willow knelt before him and took his hands in hers. She rested her head on his lap. "Please," she begged. "I would do anything to save him."

Lance took his hands back and put them over his face. "I would not ask of you anything you were not willing to offer me." He put his hand on her head and played with her long red curls. "You are going to be my downfall."

"I don't want to be. I wish there was a happy way for everything to end," Willow said.

"Happy endings are for stories the terunji tell their children at night. In the world I live in, happy doesn't even exist." Lance paused for a moment. "Do you remember the witch statue where you met William after escaping from my sister's tour?"

"Yes, but how do you know about the statue?" Willow asked, raising her head from his lap to look at him.

"Don't pretend you don't know that back then I was keeping an eye on you." Their eyes connected. The raging flames had dimmed to a beautiful glow. He caressed her face gently. "Tomorrow after one o'clock. Send only Faramund. He is to wait to approach the statue until my siblings are all out of sight."

"Of course," she replied.

"This is important, Willow. You are not to be there. Promise me."

"I promise," she said, getting to her feet.

Lance stood and pulled her close to him. His lips pressed against hers. She closed her eyes and kissed him back. A tingling sensation flowed through her body. He was her prince. A part of her hated him for the atrocities he committed and a part of her wanted to love him for the man she knew he could be.

A wave of guilt engulfed her. How could she be so hopelessly in love with two different people at the same time? She opened her eyes and searched for the aura she had seen with William, but there was none. She gave up the trying and gave into the enjoyment of the kisses the two were sharing.

Chapter Seventy-Four

Lance sat up in his bed. He was so preoccupied with the thought of how to release a prisoner without anyone knowing that he almost didn't notice two eyes watching his every move. When he did see her, he froze for a moment.

"What's your name?" Lance asked.

"Sabrina," the girl answered in a shaky voice.

"Well, Sabrina, you don't have to worry. I am not interested in you in that way. I do, however, need your help if I am to find a way to get you out of this world safely. Do you understand?" He watched the girl nod. "Good. So we need to make it look like I hurt you. Okay?" He didn't wait for an answer this time. "Lie down on floor and don't move a muscle. I am going to make some noise and break some things, but you are not to move. I am not going to hurt you." He looked at what she was wearing and sighed. "I need you to change too." Lance went to a drawer and threw the girl a sexy satin nightgown.

Sabrina froze when she saw it.

"I told you I am not interested in you. If you want out of here, this has to look good. Now change."

When she was done dressing, Lance positioned her on the floor at the foot of his bed. He tossed blankets and pillows around, then changed into a black robe. A smile formed on his face. It was time for his favourite part - smashing things. He started with bottles of wine and escalated to mirrors and furniture. The noises coming from his bedroom were loud enough to attract the attention of all of his family.

"Lance!" Cornelius yelled, knocking on his door. "What is going on in there?"

Lance opened his door. "I broke the girl," he said.

"So get a new one and let us get some sleep," his father said.

"I wasn't finished with this one." He looked past his father to Simon. "I see what you liked about her now." He licked his lips and donned a half-smile.

Joseph restrained Simon from bolting forward in anger. Lance laughed.

"If she is broken, I am not sure what you want me to do," Cornelius said, yawning.

"There might be a medical person from her home world in the dungeon. I'd like to try to save her. At least enough to finish what I started," Lance said.

"Fine," the king said. "Fine. See if there is someone to revive the girl, but keep it quiet." He returned to bed.

Simon broke free from his brother and lunged forward, fists flaring. Lance rubbed his jaw where his brother's closed hand connected. Joseph walked in and shut the door.

"Thanks for that," Lance said, still rubbing his face. "You can get up now."

Sabrina sat up. Simon rushed to her side.

"Mind filling us in on what you are doing?" Joseph asked.

"The girl can't walk around alone in the main world. She'd be dead in a day or two. I am going down to find someone to go with her and at least give her a fighting chance to survive."

"Yes, well there is still the issue of getting them off this world or did you forget about that, brother?" Joseph said.

"That would be why you two are going to find me two army uniforms." Lance said, smiling.

"You are deliciously devious, brother," Joseph said. "But what reason do we have for taking men to the main world?"

"Oh that's the best part. Seems one of your assassins got a little too playful yesterday and attempted to murder the portal guard. My sources say he has a fifty percent chance of survival. Now we did ask for him to be brought in alive, did we not? What was the assassin's name who took the job? *Falkone-A* or something like that?"

"Something like that," Joseph answered. "How do you know this?"

"I was called into a dream. I think it's worth checking out. If these assassins can't do the job right, perhaps they should be added to our hit list." Lance dressed and headed for the door. "I will be back in a few minutes. Try to remember, the girl is supposed to be hurt."

*****

Lance motioned to the prison guards to open the rooms where prisoners from Willow's home world were being kept. "I need medicine men," he said to the guards. They returned with only one man. "I expected there to be more of a choice," Lance said in a disappointed tone. He shrugged his shoulders. "What's your name?"

"Micca," the man answered.

"Well, Micca, I have a job for you. Follow me." The prince led the man up to his sleeping chamber. Joseph and Simon were still inside.

"I am very interested in what the next steps of this plan are as I can't seem to connect the dots. Although it is very creative up to this point." Joseph rested against the backside of a chair.

"It's quite simple really," Lance said. "Micca is here to fix the girl. When he fails, I break out in another bout of rage over not getting my way and destroy them both."

"I'm sorry? What am I fixing?" Micca asked.

"I tell Father of my frustration of losing the girl as well as of our issues with the assassins and ask to take a couple good men to take care of the problem and to work off some steam. I ask to take my brothers along as well, of course. Sabrina and Micca dress in the uniforms my brothers acquired. Once in the main world, they change. We go find us an assassin to play with. They go the other way. We grab a couple recruits or just pretend the assassin knocked off the men." Lance smiled.

Joseph laughed. "It might work. What about the assassin, though?"

"I thought we would pay the one responsible a visit. I know how you like to make an example of those who fail us. I will leave his punishment to you. The correct entrance to the main world will happen in four hours."

"I appreciate that," Joseph said. "Come, Simon, we have uniforms to find."

*****

Lance took a seat at the breakfast table with his parents and sisters. The aroma of fresh baked cinnamon rolls and dark roast coffee filled the room. "Good morning," he said.

"Yes," his father said. "It might have been better if we had a little more sleep last night. I trust you have sorted everything out?"

Lance filled his cheeks with air making them puff out. "Well, the medicine man was a bit useless. It was frustrating, to say the least." He buttered a roll on his plate. "I lost my temper and killed them both."

Ophelia gasped. "You killed them? Dead?"

"You sound surprised, sister. They aren't the first I have killed."

"But Simon!" she exclaimed.

"Yes," Lance answered, sipping some coffee. "He may be a bit put out. I suggest we don't mention it to him."

"Is the mess dealt with?" Cornelius asked.

"Yes, I was enraged. The flames took care of the rest," Lance said.

"You have learnt how to control the flames to burn specific targets?" Zoe asked.

Lance looked up. That was the part of the plan he hadn't considered. He hadn't told them he could destroy individual targets with his abilities and not just entire worlds. "It's a work in progress," he answered his sister.

"A work in progress. You could have destroyed us all," Zoe complained.

"Are you afraid of me, sister?" Lance asked.

"Perhaps we should all be afraid of you, brother," she answered.

"Enough squabbling between my children!" the king bellowed. "Now, what are the plans for the day?"

Lance took the napkin from his lap and wiped his mouth with it before tossing it on the table and pushing his chair back slightly. "It seems my brothers and I need to pay a visit to an Albino assassin today."

The king looked up from his pastry. He took a moment to use his tongue to remove food from his teeth making a sucking noise. "Do we have news of our bounties, then?"

"The portal guard we asked for alive is apparently fighting for his life. If these people are to be our allies, they must learn to respect our requests. We will take a couple of men with us and make a statement," Lance said.

The king slammed his hand down on the table. "Outrageous! I needed him."

"He isn't dead yet. I hear he has a fifty percent chance of survival. It shouldn't take us long today. The portal will be opening soon," Lance said.

"Well done, son," Cornelius said. "Stay on top of things. We can't afford any more mistakes. I want to be back to entering worlds as quickly as possible."

"Where are Joseph and Simon?" Zoe asked.

Lance laughed. "Sleeping, I expect, after I disturbed them last night. I think I will go wake them up, come to think of it."

Chapter Seventy-Five

Lance stepped through to the main world and put on a pair of sunglasses. "What time is it here?" he asked.

"Early afternoon," Joseph answered. "Let's get on with this. I could use a drink. Simon, those two need to lose the uniforms."

The hole through which they entered the main world was on top of a tall building. Using the stairs, Sabrina and Micca removed the uniforms. Entering the street below, Lance directed them to move to a popular tourist spot. They were to walk to the statue and remain there, appearing interested in it until the brothers left the area.

"You have already had your chance to say goodbye, brother," Lance said to Simon. "Now is time to walk away and not look back. It is the safest thing you can do for both of you. Hold on to what you are feeling. You can have first crack at the assassin."

The brothers headed to their standard suite at a posh hotel nearby. Word was sent that they were waiting for *Falkone-A* to update them on the portal guard's condition.

Joseph walked to the bar and filled a glass with ice and bourbon. Waiting aggravated him, which in turn made him that much more deadly. Simon paced by the full-length windows, his mind clearly on the fate of the girl he helped to release. Lance lounged in a chair with a leg hanging over one of the arm rests and the other leg on the ground.

"What do we know about these beings?" Lance asked. They put out the bounties with their usual contacts. The assassins in question, however, were freelancers who jumped at a chance to take the offered contract.

"Not much, really. Albino assassins are good at what they do. They rarely miss a mark and leave no evidence behind. They come well recommended for more difficult targets. I am curious as to why they messed up our contract so badly." Joseph took a seat in another chair.

"Should we be concerned?" Simon asked

"With what, brother? An assassin? Need I remind you, we are also in the same line of work? Our methods may be slightly different. But overall, I am sure we have killed more people than their entire clan. I can settle your nerves a little. Your sisters should be here any time now to join us."

As if on cue, Zoe and Ophelia walked into the suite and plopped down on the couch. Neither one looked thrilled to be there. "Have we heard from the loser yet?" Zoe asked.

"Patience is a virtue, sister," Lance said.

"We aren't exactly the virtuous types, brother," Zoe replied.

Joseph's laughter from his sister's comment was interrupted by a knock on the door. He stood and answered it, showing three hooded figures into the suite.

The largest one in the middle removed his hood, unveiling his white complexion. When he took off his sunglasses, he revealed pure white eyes, lacking pupils and slanted at the sides. His two companions followed his lead removing the hood that covered their pure as snow, white faces. They were both women, boasting similar features.

"I take it one of you is *Falkone-A*?" Joseph asked, circling them - sizing up his competition.

The woman to his right spoke. "We have been called here, I assume to collect the payment for the contract on the portal guard."

Joseph laughed. "Do you hear that? They want payment," he said. Turning his attention back to the three Albino assassins, he asked, "Why would we pay you, when you didn't do the job we asked to be done?"

"The portal guard was severely injured. He will not live. A poison flows in his veins that only the leaves from a passion flower plant that lives in the remotest area of our homeland can cure," the woman answered with no emotion.

"Be that as it may," Joseph said. "The contract was to take the man alive. He is useless to us dead."

"There were circumstances that required force. There was no mention in your contract of ancient interference."

"That," Joseph said, as he touched a strand of the woman's white hair, "is not our problem. Your failure is unacceptable."

One of the woman's legs flew up and kicked the prince in the stomach, sending him flying onto the ground. Zoe pulled out her wand behind them and sent a flash of magic at the woman, throwing her against a window. A cracking sound came from either the pane of glass or the woman's bones. She fell to the ground, humped over. Simon walked over and grabbed the woman's white hair, forcing her head backwards. Satisfied the assassin was of no further threat, he shoved it back down.

"That was a bad move," Joseph said, looking at the remaining two. He pulled out his wand and placed it under the chin of each, teasing them with their impending doom.

The remaining two assassins threw off their robes, revealing massive black wings on their backs. The contrast between the colour of the wings and their entirely white bodies was mesmerizing. The assassins used that window of opportunity, flapping their wings once and disappearing. Joseph spun around to see them reappear in opposite corners on the room only long enough to send a star shaped weapon hurtling through the air at each of the members of the royal family.

Lance jumped to his feet and dodged the star. It impacted on the chair behind him, erupting into a ball of red smoke. He turned, in time to see another star just barely miss Joseph - his sisters used their wands to destroy the ones directed at them. Simon was not so lucky, a star hit him in the shoulder, the red vapour released, seeping directly into his veins.

Lance watched his brother fall to the ground in slow motion. Magic was flying around him in the background as his remaining siblings tried to battle the two assassins teleporting from spot to spot. Anger turned to a rage. Lance's eyes became engulfed with the blue flames that dwelt deep within him. He turned but the assassins were in mid-transport. A violent scream erupted from deep within him. He opened his arms and his chest arched forward, a stream of blue flame protruding from it. The necrid flame at first appeared to have no direction but connected with the second woman knocking her body from the path it was travelling in. She screamed in pain as the fire consumed her - leaving nothing, not even a single ash.

A blast of dark magic flew past Lance and struck *Falkone-A* who was sneaking up behind the prince. The assassin stumbled backwards and fell to his knees. Zoe grabbed his head from behind and punched him in the back. Taking her wand, she used magic to remove the black wings and destroy them. A black liquid poured from the scars left where the wings had been. A single black tear formed in the man's eye.

"I die knowing at least one of you will be joining me shortly. In the afterlife, we shall meet again," *Falcone-A* said

Zoe moved aside and watched as her brother sent a black dagger twirling through the air, connecting with the assassin's heart and killing him instantly. Joseph straightened the jacket of the suit he was wearing and joined Lance to see how their brother was.

"He is unconscious," Lance said. The prince thought back to the description Willow had given him of William's condition. "He is dying."

"What can we do?" Ophelia asked.

Joseph knelt by his brother's body. "I don't care how. Find him a cure." the prince stood up and faced Lance. "I know you can."

Lanced sighed. "I may know someone." He rubbed his neck. "It will be a few hours before I can contact them. They are his only hope." He paused. "We will have to leave him here and return home. Let's clean up this mess and make him comfortable until then."

"The woman!" Ophelia yelled. "She is still alive."

Joseph ran over to the assassin who had hit him earlier. She was waking. The prince grabbed her shirt at the throat with one hand and raised his other arm. A dagger appeared in his free hand.

"Wait!" Lance yelled. "We may need her to save Simon."

Joseph lowered his arm and let go of the woman's clothing. "She is dangerous as she is. I will let her live, but we removed the wings that give her power."

Chapter Seventy-Six

A green mist appeared in the middle of the field. Willow ran over, almost slipping on the newly fallen snow. Faramund appeared just in time to catch her before she fell. Willow couldn't believe her eyes. Not only did he bring back Micca, but Sabrina was with them as well. For a moment there was an awkward silence.

"We can save the reunion for later," Faramund said. "Let's get to the medical centre."

Micca moved straight to William's side, only stopping for a moment at the sight of Nero and Tika watching over the man.

"What happened to him?" Micca asked.

"He was attacked by assassins. Their weapons appeared magical. He was unconscious within a moment of being struck." Faramund took a seat on a neighbouring bed.

Willow watched Micca's hands hover slightly above William's body. A warm glow in a mixture of orange and yellow radiated down from them as they moved from head to toe. The process was slow and the silence frightening. Not even a pin dropping would have dared to make a sound as they sat eagerly waiting the potion maker's words.

The glow subsided and Micca pulled his hands back. He used one hand to cup his own chin and frowned while still looking over his patient. Letting out a breath of air, he said, "Do we know if a poison was used?"

"A poison?" Willow echoed the man's words.

Micca sighed again. "Rather I should say do we know what poison was used? From the tone of your voice, I imagine that is a no." He backed away from the bed and took a seat next to Faramund. "I can tell you he has been poisoned."

"Can you make an antidote?" Mike asked from where he stood in the background, watching everything.

"I can make an antidote to anything," Micca said. "Provided you can tell me what I am making an antidote for. I need to know what the poison is."

Willow's eyes moved to Nero and Tika. As if sensing her question, Nero answered. "We do not know who they were. The storm was fierce and we did not see our attackers well. They moved fast and used stealth."

Willow stood, frustration surging through her body. Needing to regain control, she moved to a bed on the other side of the room. Crossing her legs in a sitting position, she closed her eyes and tried to focus. Her hand reached for the key around her neck as she concentrated, looking inwards for a solution. Now she had someone who could cure William and they didn't know what they needed to cure. There must be a way to find out. Who were these assassins? *Lance,* she thought. If there was anyone who could find out, it would be him.

"I'm here," sounded in her head. She opened her eyes to a familiar sitting room with a fireplace. She was daydreaming Lance's dream world. Her prince was in a squatting position facing the fire. "It's my turn to ask you for help."

Willow took a seat in the room for the first time and listened to Lance's story. She let out a big sigh. "Where are they now?"

"Still in the hotel room. The creature is bound, its wings removed. Zoe used a sleeping spell to make sure it didn't escape." Lance stood and faced her. "We have returned home. You are my only hope." He walked over to her and knelt before her. "Please," he said, taking her hands. He placed the key to the hotel room in her hands. He rested his head on her lap and she stroked his hair gently, attempting to offer some comfort. This was more emotion than he had ever allowed her to witness - except for rage.

"Do you know who they are or what world they are from?" she asked.

"Just that they are known as Albino assassins," he answered.

"We will do our best. All we know at the moment was that William was poisoned. Without knowing by what, we cannot make an antidote."

"The woman assassin," he said, looking up. "She told us the antidote could only come from the leaf of a rare passion fruit plant that grew in a remote area of her home world."

Willow's face lit up at the news. "I will send Faramund to bring them back immediately. If there is any news, I will try to contact you."

Her eyes opened and she was back in reality, a hotel key clenched in her hand. Etched in the key were coordinates to travel to. That was only the second time she was able to dreamwalk while daydreaming. The odd thing was it wasn't her ability that allowed her to access that world, she needed a dreamwalker. She pushed the questions out of her mind. There were more important things to attend to at the moment.

Willow heard her name in the background. It was Mike. "Willow, are you coming?"

"Sorry?" she answered. "Coming where?"

"To the meeting room. I called everyone together to discuss the news," he answered.

She walked with him silently. Her mind was racing without direction. At least the meeting would help her let the others know what she planned.

Willow took William's seat at the table again. This time all the guardians were present in the room, each one eyeing her carefully. Mike began the meeting with William's condition. He asked everyone to try to research any possible poisons that could have been used. That was Willow's cue.

"Actually," she said, "there is some more information that I have just found out. Someone else was affected by the same poison and one of the assassins has been captured."

Gasps and whispers darted around the room. Mike's eyes fixated on her. "Go on," he said.

"They are known as Albino assassins and the cure for the poison comes from a rare plant in their home world. Unfortunately, we don't know which plant or which world. The assassin does, though." She paused and took a deep breath. "I would like to send Faramund and Zsiga to bring back both people."

"Seems like a good course of action. Do we know who the injured person is?" Mike asked.

"Prince Simon," Willow answered.

Gasps and whispers erupted again, this time slightly louder than before. "Are you crazy?" Ashlyn said. "He wants to kill us."

"He won't!" Sabrina yelled. "He isn't like that."

"Lance asked for my help," Willow said, ignoring Sabrina altogether. "He helped us free Micca and Sabrina. He is also handing us an assassin to find out how to make the cure."

Aslo jumped on the table and faced her. "Albino assassins are deadly creatures. Their knowledge of combat exceeds that of all other known races. Combine that with deadly black wings which power their shadow and teleportation magics and the odds are against survival if you meet one. Bringing one to the camp is far too dangerous."

"The creature's wings have been removed. She is bound and currently under a spell to induce sleep. We could contain her to one room. This is the only hope for both William and Simon. We were ready to invade a kingdom to try to save William. This plan has slightly better odds."

Aslo looked around the room. "If this is your choice, we will help contain the assassin. You should all understand, before making a final decision, you risk the lives of many others to save these two. The guardian way is to always save the most possible in any scenario."

"We know what the guardian way is," Willow blurted out. "It doesn't mean that it is always the right choice to make."

Aslo backed up, bowing his head. Jumping to the ground, he joined the others, his tail between his legs. He turned his head once to meet the gaze of his keeper.

"Aslo," Willow said. "Guardians are old and wise. Your ways are noble. My personal feelings aside, we need William." She knelt beside him. "I know people look at me and see the girl who was meant to be - meant to save the world." She paused for a moment and gazed into the fire. "But it isn't all about me. It's about all of us together. I am not meant to be the one to lead us. I never was. We need him as much as we need you."

The feline's eyes widened at her statement. He raised his head. "I am proud of you. You have learnt so much in such a short time."

Willow stretched out her arm and touched Aslo's face. The guardian disappeared from where he sat, reappearing as a picture on Willow's arm. Kiera moved forward and did the same. They were at least understanding each other now. It would take some time for them to work through all of what happened. There would be time for that later.

Willow looked around the room. Nathan and Victoria had been left out of the meetings so as not to alarm the children about William. "Diana," she said. "I need to speak to Nathan." The woman stood and left the room.

"About time," Nathan said, returning with his grandmother. "I figured someone had to need me eventually."

Willow smiled. "Albino assassins," she said. "Not sure if that is their actual names or a made-up one. White appearance except for black wings."

Flashes of light flew by in Nathan's eyes as he accessed all the information he stored in his mind from books. "That narrows it down to about twenty different species," he said. "None go by Albino assassin, though. Pretty sure that was made up for this world."

"William left these in my apartment," Malarchy said, placing a stack of files on the table. "He meant to bring them back that night and review them here. There might be some useful information in them." He pushed the files in front of Nathan.

It took only a moment for the boy to scan each file and scour the contents for the information they needed. "There is research on Albino assassins. Seems they are as deadly as vamprite assassins."

Willow had been focusing on a blank pad of paper in front of her. On top of it was a pen slightly chewed at the end which belonged to William. Nathan's words shocked her into looking up. "Vamprite assassins?" she asked.

"What did you expect?" Sarah asked.

"The vamprite are the ones who warned me," Willow picked up the pen and traced a cube on the page the same as she had seen William do a hundred times. Surprisingly, she found it calming. "Why would an assassin warn me?"

"Good question," Malarchy said.

"The ones we are looking for seem to have a base they work out of on an island. The coordinates are in the file. It's near the North Pole," Nathan said. "They prefer the cold and cannot survive in direct sunlight. They have a unique ability to survive underwater for extended periods of time. There are some names listed."

"Can't you just grow the plant we need to make the antidote?" Sabrina said, filing her nails.

Willow focused her eyes on the girl. She wondered for a moment what Sabrina had been through at Cornelius's castle. "I could, if I knew what plant it was," she said. "Perhaps you could make yourself useful and write down everything you remember about the dungeon you were kept in." Willow shoved the paper and pen across the table and it landed in front of the girl.

"They have returned," Shelby said, sitting by a window.

Mike and Willow headed to the field to meet the returning guards. "I'll take this one straight to the medical centre," Zsiga said, carrying Simon's motionless body.

Looking at the bundled-up pile that Faramund was carrying, Willow could hardly tell there was a person in there. "We have a holding room for her," she said. "Mike, can you find Richard to come have a look at her wounds?"

Willow chose one of the newer buildings that was still not in use to confine the creature to. The woman was apparently still under the effects of the sleeping spell, showing no signs of movement, even once resting on a bed. On another bed were the two black wings that had been removed from her back. Willow touched the ends of them. They were soft in her fingers. The woman made a noise as if she felt her touch.

"Perhaps the wings should be confined in another place," Aslo said, appearing with Kiera at Willow's feet.

"I agree," Faramund said, picking them up and exiting the building.

The assassin woke still bound. She scooted backwards on the bed as far away from the guardians as possible.

"Who are you?" Willow asked. There was no answer. "Where do you come from?" The woman's reaction remained the same.

Aslo turned to his full form and let out a roar.

"My name is Asil. I was born on an island to the north. It isn't shown on any maps or charts and there is no name for it in your language," the assassin said.

"We want to know about the poison you use. You must carry some with you to put on your weapons." Willow looked in a box sitting on a bed containing every form of small blade possible. She carefully picked up a dagger with two fingers by a handle and dropped it right away.

"The blades are all soaked in the poison before we leave. The metal used in our weapons has the ability to soak in liquids."

Richard, Mike, and Micca entered just in time to hear what the woman said. Richard immediately attended to the wounds of the woman. Micca looked in the box of blades. Choosing one with a long handle, he examined it carefully.

"Can you extract enough to make an antidote?" Willow asked.

"Yes, but..." Micca paused. "It will take an enormous amount of time. Time I am afraid we do not have for either of the men."

Willow looked down then back at Asil. "The cure. You told the princes the only cure was from a plant in your home world. Where is that? What plant? What is the poison made from?"

"I have never seen the plant. My world was destroyed by men led by guardians years before my birth. All we have are legends. A blue flame erupted and destroyed everything living. A small group of my kind were saved by the Aquanor who dwelt in the depths of the sea where the flames could not reach. Underwater there is a rogue portal that we used to escape the world. It is a poison from the tentacles of the Aquanor that seeps through your friends bodies."

"Aslo?" Willow asked.

"Unless you can freeze time, there is nothing we can do," the Leander replied.

Freeze time, she thought. A memory popped into her mind. William said Sarah had questions for Nick as to how he could make time stop. "Mike!" she yelled. "Send Faramund to get Nick for me, please. It's urgent." She turned her attention back to the woman. "You say guardians were involved in the destruction of your world. Which ones?"

"The Xiuhcoatle. After the split of ancients, none of the ancient races remained together legends say."

"You are wrong," Willow answered. "Three still work together and attempt to protect the innocent."

The door opened and Nick was ushered in quickly. "You," Asil said. "I know you. Every year, when the terunji celebrate their religious holiday, you come and give us gifts. Things we never ask for. We have been grateful for your service over these years." She bowed her head to the man.

"Yes," Nick said. "You are welcome. The holiday may have been born from a religion of this world, but no matter what you believe, the magic that lives in this tradition transforms us all for the better."

Willow took Nick's arm and walked him to the medical facility. "You have an ability that deals with time?" she asked. "William has been hurt. We are working on antidote to a poison that is killing him and the man beside him, but it will take time. They don't have enough of that left."

"I can help," Nick said. "Normally, I don't use my ability for something like this." He stepped back and rubbed his white beard. "We will have to clear the room. No one will be able to enter except me while William and Simon are in the time rift."

Willow asked everyone to leave. Richard and Mary took what they needed from the room quickly. Once everyone else was out, Willow nodded at Nick and stepped outside herself. A flash of light exploded and an aura of red magic surrounded the building.

Nick stepped outside. "I have made time slow as much as I can. Anyone walking inside without me will become stuck in the time rift. When you have your cure, I will remove it."

"Thank you," Willow said. "Any suggestions on what to do with the assassin?"

Nick laughed and his belly jiggled. Willow couldn't help but join in. "Happiness is contagious," he said. "Perhaps you should show her some compassion. From what I have heard, her people have been misled. Show her who the guardians really are."

"She is the reason William is in there. He could be dying. How do I forgive that?" Willow asked.

"Tell me," Nick answered, putting his arm around her shoulder. "The other man in there. Is he an ally of ours?"

"No," Willow said, her lips pressed together in a puffy pout.

"Yet you are willing to save his life. Extend the same privilege to the woman. Remember, Willow, happiness is not the only thing that is contagious. We can all do our part to spread goodness at any time of the year." Nick looked down at her over the top of a small pair of round reading glasses. "Why don't we go talk to her?"

Asil was still bound on the bed, surprised to see them walk in again. "Are you back to finish me off?" she asked.

"Goodness no," Nick answered. "Why would we do that?"

"I would prefer it to the fate you have left me with. You have stripped me of my wings and they cannot be reattached. I will not be allowed to return home. I welcome death."

"We didn't do that to your wings," Willow said.

"Then who?" she barked.

"An evil king who went mad. He follows the Xiuhcoatle. From your description, it is possible his kingdom was responsible for the fate of your world as well." Willow sat beside her on the bed.

"And whose will bends your mind?" Asil asked.

Jawfree appeared. "We do not bend the will of our keepers," he said, taking a place beside Aslo.

The door opened. Shelby flew in and joined the other guardians. "Ashlyn said you needed me. Sorry it took so long. I have been working with the avian guardians from the Frostica world. They are starting to adjust to the changes that happened while they were frozen. Who do we have here?"

"This is Asil," Kiera said. "We were explaining to her that Leander, Olcsanka, and Allaren work together as guardians still. Only the Xiuhcoatle, Achaear, and Aquanor split and went their own way in search of power."

"Can we remove her bindings? They look like a magic spell of some sort," Willow said, examining the glowing rope tied around her arms and waist.

"Is that such a good idea?" Mike stood from the bed he was sitting on in a corner.

"Have you been here the whole time?" Willow asked. Lately, Mike seemed to go unnoticed a lot - then all of a sudden he would pop up.

"Yeah." He shrugged his shoulders and tossed a ball he was playing with at Willow.

"Her wings give her power." Willow caught the ball and threw it right back again, aiming for his face.

He caught it and smiled. "I am sure she is still trained in hand-to-hand combat."

"Scared of a woman?" Willow asked, laughing a little.

"No," Mike chuckled. "I was worried about your safety."

Asil eyed the two through the whole conversation. "Who are you people? This has to be the strangest military unit I have ever seen."

"Well," Willow said. "We aren't military, exactly. We are just a bunch of people trying to keep the world in one piece."

"If you are this world's hope for a future, we are all doomed," she said.

"Hey," Willow said. "At least we are trying. You must be hungry. Is there something you would like to eat?"

"You want to feed me now?" The woman shook her head. "Um yeah, anything is great."

"Vegetarian or meat eater?" Mike asked.

"I eat meat," Asil answered. Mike stuck his tongue out at Willow and headed off to find a hamburger for the woman.

Aslo moved forward. Asil leaned away from the guardian. "Don't worry, assassin, I have no desire to hurt you." He used a claw to cut through the magic binding. The glowing rope fell to her sides and disappeared.

After she finished eating, she settled back on the bed, her back resting against a wall - knees pulled up to her chest.

"Could I be so bold as to ask for a favour from you all?" Nick asked. "Perhaps we could gather everyone together so I could speak to them?"

"Of course," Willow answered. "I can show you to the meeting room."

"Wonderful," he said. "Asil, do join us."

Willow looked at the assassin. She was shocked by Nick's invitation to include the woman, but at the same time felt confident the man knew what he was doing.

Everyone gathered in the meeting room. Asil found herself seated at a table beside Willow. All of the rest of the camp filed in the room and took their places. Zsiga offered the woman a cup of coffee. Her eyebrows clenched together, forming two lines between them. Scrunching her nose slightly, she looked at Zsiga and then at the others in the room. For the first time, she actually wondered what the story was behind the girl she was hired to kill. She shook her head - the thought was gone.

The camp members broke out in a Christmas song at the sight of Nick. He stood and smiled, enjoying every moment. It wasn't often that he could take credit for the good deeds he did. After a few choruses he said, "Thank you," to settle everyone down. Keeping an ear-to-ear grin, he sat back in his chair. "I would like to start by asking everyone to stay away from the medical building until further notice. Everything is fine, but it is quarantined."

A rumble of whispers flowed through the room as if riding on a wave of questions. "Is William okay?" Sarah asked.

Willow just stared at the girl, unable to answer. A glossy haze appeared in her eyes.

"Yes," Mike said, seeing her discomfort. "We just need to give Micca a bit more time to make the antidote."

"With everything that has happened, I am afraid my work is behind at the North Pole. I need your help," Nick said. "It's hard work, but fun and I think you all could use a little distraction for a few days."

Willow slouched back in her chair. "What can we do?"

"You'll be my guests. We will put together the gifts and deliver them. Afterwards, we can have our own little party to celebrate the spirit of Christmas," Nick explained.

"We will help," Willow said. "I am not sure about celebrations. That will be up to everyone individually." She looked down at the table.

"My child," Nick said. "The spirit of Christmas isn't something you decide upon. It lives inside each of us. If there has been one thing I have learnt over all these years, it's that the magic it creates is stronger than anything any of us can wield. It can change things in wondrous ways... if we let it."

Chapter Seventy-Seven

The little Christmas town in Frostica world buzzed with activity - every building being used to capacity to fill the tall order of gifts that needed to be provided.

"How do you make things for everyone? The number of gifts you bring each year..." Sarah was in awe of the production of goodies. The spirit of Christmas danced in her eyes like the sugar plums of a poem her father used to read to her.

"It has become more difficult over the years. Of course, most adults don't believe I exist," Nick said, smiling as he showed his new campers where everything was.

"I'm sorry," Sarah started.

"On no, don't be. It's a blessing, really. Parents go out and buy their children items thinking I won't come. I simply supplement what they buy. On Christmas, when a child receives something that the parents don't recognize, each assumes the other bought it. It works for them, the children, and me."

"That explains a lot, actually. I always wondered why some people say you weren't real and why rich kids always seem to get more," Sarah said.

"Yes," Nick said, rubbing his beard. "That is a problem. I give a little more to those who have nothing, but with the amount we have to give, we can't match what some parents can buy. We also try to be understanding of families who are of another religion. There are some children we cannot provide things to - no matter how much it would improve their lives."

"Do you actually have a naughty-or-nice list?" Sarah asked.

"William warned me that you would have quite a few questions." Nick let out a deep laugh. "Not exactly a list," he said. "Inside you lives both naughty and nice. We all make choices every day which are either one or the other. None of us are perfect. We all make a choice to be naughty sometimes. Some more than others. That doesn't mean that we give up hope that next time the nice choice will be made. I like to think everyone I have gifts for has shown the potential to still choose to be nice in some way."

"So what can we do?" Willow asked.

"I was hoping Asil and you would help in the candy section." He opened the door, showing them into the most delicious smelling room. The scents of peppermints, chocolate, marshmallows, and caramels filled their noses.

"That smells like heaven," Clairity said.

"Why don't you join them too, and Sissy as well." Nick moved inside. "That will free up the Frostica to help in other areas. Running this room is fairly simple. Make sure the machines keep moving. You can mix as many or as little of the flavours as you like. Create new tastes. All you have to do is turn the valve on the side of each of the containers and they mix together coming out here." He pointed to where a stream of candy was filling trays of shapes. "The trays then go through a cooling chamber on this conveyor belt and come out on the other side over here." The girls followed him to where the candy came out completely hard and cool. "Next it goes into that machine." He pointed in front of him. "There they get wrappers and it spits them out into one of the bins of the train outside."

"Where does it go from there?" Willow asked.

"The main warehouse, where everything gets sorted so it's easy to package by person."

"Anything else we need to know?" Asil asked.

"It can get a bit messy. With a little luck, Meredith has some outfits for you to wear, just in case." Nick's lips curled upwards, forming a devious smile.

Nick continued assigning his volunteers to different rooms. The Shinning brothers joined the wooden toy department. Neil, Mike, and Camile were asked to help in metal works. Faramund, Iskander, and Zsiga jumped at the chance to work with electronics. Everyone else worked in the main warehouse, putting together items for people all over the world.

Meredith handed the members of the candy team white jumpsuits to wear and asked that they tie back their hair covering it with a net over top.

"Don't even bother laughing," Asil said, walking out of the room she had been changing in. She took one look at Willow and came to a stop, turning her back to the other girls to conceal a smile from them.

Sissy had been attempting not to laugh for several minutes. Seeing Asil's reaction was too much for her to handle. She burst out in a full cackle.

"Great," Willow said, realizing everyone was laughing at her. "Let's get to work."

At first, everything was going smoothly until a yell came from outside to pick up the pace. The girls split up the machines so that each of them had two different flavours to handle. They hadn't, however, been able to figure out a way to make the system go faster.

"Maybe if we add more?" Clairity started turning valves. The machines she was in charge of began twisting and tilting until a big gob of marshmallow flew through the air and hit Willow in the face.

Willow wiped the candy from her eyes. Her mouth open, she licked her lips. Clairity and Sissy bent over, grasping their sides, tears of laughter rolling down their faces. A half-smile formed on Asil's face. Willow nodded at them and opened the valves on her machines as far as they could go. The device let out steam and began rocking. A blast of caramel flew across the room and landed on Sissy's head.

"Oh no, you didn't!" Sissy exclaimed, liquid caramel dripping down her face. She used her wand to open her valves full tilt. A grinding noise began, followed by a high-pitched whistle. A candy coating spewed all over Asil. She was covered head to toe in rich creamy milk chocolate.

"Nothing like an assassin coated in milk chocolate, yummy," Willow said.

Asil stood still for a moment, shaking the rich candy off her hands. Suddenly, she burst out into laughter and the others followed suit. When they settled down, Asil looked at Clairity, the only clean girl left. She opened her valves on full. Candy started spraying everywhere. Flavours mixed together and coated the walls and floors. The girls slipped and slid, falling over and occasionally throwing handfuls of candy at each other. They laughed and squealed so loud, it attracted attention from outside. None of them noticed the machines stop.

Nick opened the door and pressed a button. Everyone in the Christmas town stood at the door. They scrambled to their feet, covered from head to toe in every type of candy one could imagine. Laughter erupted from outside the workshop as everyone took turns glancing in at their appearance.

"Good job, girls," Nick said, laughing. "We have enough candy now." He pressed a button and closed the door. Water rushed down washing the walls, floor and the girls. The candy washed away and down a large drain that opened in the floor. After the water ceased, fans appeared, blowing everything completely dry. All four girls' hair was blown in awkward positions. Willow's was frizzed out and fluffy, making her head look ten times its original size. Clairity's was blown to the side. Both Asil and Sissy's hair stuck straight up.

Nick opened the door. His eyes widened at the state of the girls, giggling uncontrollably at each other. "Oh dear," he said. "It's a good thing

I sent everyone else back to work or we would never finish. You four best visit Meredith in the house. She can help you sort out your new hairstyles."

The laughter didn't stop when the girls entered the house. They took turns looking at themselves in a mirror, finding their own appearances even more humorous.

"Oh my," Meredith said, rushing to see what the commotion was about. "Showers for each of you. There is no other way to fix that."

By the time the girls were cleaned up and dressed again, everyone else was in the house enjoying a hot chocolate.

"So," Sarah said. "What's next?"

"Ah, this is where the magic starts. I use my abilities to slow down time and start making deliveries. I have a hovercraft the Frostica built that makes good time. I fill it up, deliver, come back and do it again. I will take Willow, Asil, and Sarah to help - everyone else can relax between loads. Fill us up when we come back."

Sarah jumped up and down, clapping her hands. "This is the best day of my life," she said. "Are there reindeer?"

"No," Nick replied.

After finishing the best hot chocolate any of them ever tasted, they moved outside to see the red hovercraft Santa used to travel the world. It was shiny, resembling a boat more than a sleigh. Nick opened a door and let the girls take seats inside, while the others filled the vehicle with goodies to deliver.

"It looks small, but it holds enough gifts for a small country. We do one country at a time. We have to work with the time zones as well, so we will be starting as soon as we are loaded." Nick jumped in the driver's seat. He watched in his mirrors for one of his Frostica helpers to give him the thumbs up. The engine started and they were off.

"How do we get the gifts into each home?" Sarah asked.

"That's Meredith's department. With a little magic and a lot of luck, she can enchant anything to find its way to where it belongs. Each parcel is separately enchanted. Normally, I have to hover in a spot, release some and move over a little to repeat. With you girls here, though, I can continue driving while you three release gifts as we go. It will be the fastest Christmas Eve I have ever had."

The hovercraft moved at speeds none of them knew possible. Before long, they were over a vastly populated area. Nick motioned for them to begin dropping the parcels. All three girls reached into the back grabbing whatever they could, tossing it over the edge of the vehicle. When the final items began their descent to the town below, Nick turned around and returned to Frostica land to reload for another trip.

The girls lost count of how many trips they made. It was a long night, but they had fun ringing bells and singing songs as they dropped presents all over the world. The warehouse emptied. Jessie yelled out, "Last load!" from behind them.

When the trip was finished, Nick stopped the sleigh outside the portal and stepped out. The girls followed him.

"Why are we stopping?" Sarah asked.

"I have a few gifts left to give," he said.

"The back is empty," Asil said, watching him reach into the vehicle.

"Sarah," he said. "This snow globe is for you. It shows you our little town and everyone who is in it."

Sarah shook the snow up and looked into the globe. In the window of the house she could see Jade and Malarchy looking out. "Does it work like a video playing?"

"Yes," Nick answered. "You will be able to watch our progress every year."

"This is amazing," she said, hugging the plump man. "Thank you."

"Willow," Nick said. "This is for you."

She opened the package and found a pink crystal heart on a golden chain. "It's beautiful," she said.

"May it remind you that there are certain types of magic that dwell inside all of us. No one can control them or take them away from you. They are more powerful than anything a witch can do." Nick smiled at her. "I can't take the credit for the crystal; that was Meredith. She wanted to make sure you had a little luck with you, wherever you went."

"Thank you," she said, putting the small box in her pocket.

"Asil," Nick said. "I was hoping you would deliver gifts to your island for me."

"I cannot. I am not allowed to return to my home now that I have lost my wings. There is nothing in that trunk that can help me," she answered.

"Are you sure?" Nick asked. "Willow, would you reach in there, please?"

She pulled out the black wings that had been cut from Asil's back. The assassin knelt down to them and stroked them gently. Tears fell down her face. "There is no way to reattach them to me."

"Who told you that?" Nick asked.

"The Aquanor have told us many times. Failure is not rewarded," Asil said.

"The Aquanor have misled you," Aslo said, appearing in full guardian form with Kiera by his side.

Jawfree and Decon joined them. They took positions around the girl and let out a growl that shook the ground. Willow watched a white magic flow between them, intersecting at Asil. The wings floated up in the air and opened, taking their place on her back. A bright white line formed where the wings met body and then silence.

Asil stood and stretched her large black wings out. She flapped them and took flight, zipping from one place to another. A smile covered her face.

Nick placed a large bag of gifts for her people on the ground. Asil picked up the bag and without a word disappeared.

"Hopefully, she doesn't try to kill you again," Sarah said, patting Willow on the back.

Willow glanced at Sarah out of the corner of her eyes. That had been the furthest thought from her mind, until now. "Yeah, that would be good," she replied.

Asil appeared in front of them again, carrying a wooden box. She handed it to Willow. "There is a legend among my people. Long ago a cure for the venom of the deadliest of the ancients, the Achaear, Aquanor and Xiuhcoatle, was placed in this chest, which was then locked with a magic key. The key was hidden and its location forgotten over time. One day a great warrior would need the contents and only then would the key surface again. It would change the odds in the battle for freedom." She flew up and twirled in a circle. "If you can open it, you can save your friends. I don't know if you will save the world, but I think you could if you wanted to. Either way, only time will tell."

Willow looked down at the box then up in the sky. Asil was gone again.

"I need to get back to camp," Willow said. "Can you take me?"

"Let's tell the others where you are going. I think a few of them may want to return with you." Nick slipped back into the driver's seat beside the girls and headed back to the small town he called home.

Willow took the opportunity to discuss one more gift that needed to be given on the way back. "Nick," she said. "The Yeti. I would like to figure out some way to connect their world to yours. They have come so far. Kristophe taught them so much, perhaps you and Meredith could continue on where he left off? I believe Jawfree and Decon could help set up what would be needed to make the changes."

Nick smiled. "That's our girl. What a wonderful idea. There is good to be found in this world if you open your eyes to it. Remember that."

Chapter Seventy-Eight

The camp was dark and quiet when they first arrived. Willow headed straight to the meeting room and placed her Christmas gift on the table. She tried to open the lid, but it was stuck tight. She picked it up and turned it every way possible to see if there was another way to open it. There wasn't. A frown crept onto her face as she tried in vain to find ways to get into the box.

"Maybe we could break in?" Sarah said.

"We would chance breaking one of the bottles inside," Willow replied.

Mike took out a knife and tried to pry the box open at its hinges. A flash of light blinded them. When they could see again, Mike was climbing to his feet from the ground where he had been thrown. "That's not the way," he said, dusting himself off.

"She didn't have any idea where the key was?" Clairity asked.

"No," Willow replied. "It was hidden long before she was born and the location forgotten. I have a feeling it was before the blood wars, when all the worlds were connected." She plopped down in the chair and sunk back, staring at the small wooden chest that might contain a cure for

William. Her hand reached for her necklace. She fumbled with it for a moment while thinking. "It can't be!" she yelled.

"What?" Mike asked.

Willow undid the clasp of the chain William gave her, dropping it on the table. She removed the key that had hung around her neck every day since she brought it back from the Frostica dream.

"Nothing would surprise me," Sarah said. "Give it a try."

Willow positioned herself in a way in which she could get hurt the least, half expecting to be thrown clear across the room. Picking up the key, she inserted it into the lock. So far so good - it fit. She looked up briefly at the others, then took a deep breath and held it. With one hand she turned the key. The lid popped open. Inside were three flasks of liquid; red, blue, and green. "I think we need Micca."

Mike was already on his way to find the healer before she opened her mouth. Her gaze admired each of the concoctions while keeping a good distance away. Her fingers didn't dare touch any of the bottles.

"We have an antidote?" Micca asked.

"One is for each of the ancients who opted out of being guardians," Willow explained. "But I don't know which is which."

"Green would be for the Xiuhcoatle," Sissy offered. "Their venom is green... among other things." Everyone in the room knew she was referring to the green tinge of her own skin colour.

"If that is the case," Micca said. "Red would be for spider venom and blue for sea creatures." He lifted a bottle, shaking it around a little. "Do we know for sure what is in here?"

"No," Willow said. "Just a legend."

"I have a feeling, it is what we think it is," Clairity added.

"Let me release the medical centre," Nick offered. "We need to give it a try... while the magic of Christmas is still with us."

Walking into the medical centre, Willow immediately felt uneasy. It was as if something sucked every bit of happiness and light from the room. She crossed her arms, rubbing her shoulders to escape the chills running up and down her spine.

Micca went right to work, with Richard and Mary assisting where they could. Willow watched as they filled two needles with the blue liquid and moved towards William with one. Richard prepared a sedative in another - in case anything went horribly wrong.

Micca bent over William's body, glancing up one last time at Willow and Mike for approval before administering the liquid into his bloodstream. He moved to the second bed, following the same procedure for Simon. Minutes passed.

Simon's eyes opened. He jumped to his feet. "Where am I?" The prince looked around the room, focusing on Willow. "You!" he yelled, fumbling for his wand.

"Relax," Sissy said.

Simon moved his focus to his sister, taking a few steps back from her. "You're dead," he said. He looked at Nick. "You're a terunji legend." He smiled. "None of this is real."

Richard plunged the sedative into the prince's arm; seconds later he fell back onto the bed. "That wasn't going well," the doctor huffed, disposing of the needle. "He will be out for twelve hours. I suggest we figure out what to do with him before then."

"Faramund can take him back to the hotel room," Willow said. "When he returns, I can contact Lance to pick up his brother. It won't be hard to convince him what he saw here was a dream brought on by the poison." She moved to a chair beside William. "Why hasn't he woken up yet?"

Micca stood behind her and put his hand on her shoulder. "Be patient," he said. "The poison was in his system for much longer."

Willow sat perfectly still in the chair watching William for hours, only looking away from his face briefly when Faramund returned from dropping off Simon. Her eyes stung as if someone had dried all the liquid inside them. Finally, she closed them to escape the pain.

Her mind went through every scenario possible, from what she would say and do if he woke up to the utter devastation she would feel if he didn't. Depression had a hold of her. She needed something to take her mind off of the world around her.

Lance, she thought. Her eyes opened. She watched everything around her change into the comfortable sitting area her prince used as his staging room for dreams. This time, she was the only one there. Taking a seat by the fireplace, she waited.

"How did you get in here?" Lance asked.

"I don't know," Willow answered, standing to face him. She wanted to run into his arms - for him to hug her and tell her everything would be okay. "I thought of you and I was here."

"How long have you been here?" he asked.

"I don't know that either," Willow said. "Your brother is back in the room. We had to sedate him. He should sleep for several more hours. He may be confused when he wakes. Just convince him everything he saw was a dream caused by the poison."

"He is alright, then?"

"Yes," Willow said. "I wouldn't leave him too long, though. The assassins know that location." She turned, staring at the fire.

"And William?" Lance asked.

Her body trembled at his name, tears begged for release. "He hasn't responded. The poison was in his system much longer than in your brother's. I should go."

He caught her arm, pulling her close to him. She broke down in tears. Her prince gave her exactly what she needed. He held her silently while she released all the emotions built up inside her. She cried until she couldn't cry anymore and then she stayed in his arms until she felt like she could continue again.

"Better?" Lance asked.

"Yeah," Willow answered. "Thanks."

"After Simon returns, there will be questions," he said. "It isn't safe for us to meet like this for a while."

"I know," Willow answered. "I am going to be locked away in a fancy empyral school with no contact anyways."

"A school?" Lance smiled. "With your friends?"

"Afraid not," she answered. "I am going to be very much on my own for months."

"Perhaps that is for the best," Lance sat in his chair and pulled her onto his lap. "Take some time to find yourself. Figure out what Willow wants. A lot could change in the time you are away. It's time to go." He moved her hand to his face and kissed it gently. She closed her eyes, enjoying the warmth of his touch.

Willow opened her eyes. She was sitting beside William's bed. A wave of guilt rushed through her. How could she be so fickle as to turn to Lance's arms when William lay possibly dying in a medical centre? She pulled her hair, wanting to scream.

"Slow down there, little lady," Faramund said. "Don't beat yourself up. This isn't your fault."

She did her best to mask her true emotions, donning a fake smile. Faramund meant well. He didn't understand what she was feeling through. How could he?

"You need to remember we all need someone to lean on sometimes. It isn't a crime to need someone to tell you everything is going to be okay," Faramund offered.

Willow looked at him, grateful for the words he expressed. It was exactly what she needed to hear. She took his hand in hers, clasping it tight. Faramund nodded, remaining with her for several hours.

The days and nights passed as she sat by his bedside watching carefully for any sign he might be recovering from his injuries. Clairity and Ashlyn tried everything to help ease her mind. In the end, Clarity had no feelings either way as to the outcome. Numerous attempts to contact William through dreamwalking failed. Sarah and Sissy brought Willow food, which mostly sat untouched.

The visits of friends became shorter and less frequent over the next couple of days. Aslo and Kiera brought their children in to visit. Willow smiled at the sight of each of them. The thought of not knowing what might happen at any time made her cringe. She decided learning their names wouldn't wait another minute.

"Tibo, Jenx, Cameo, Sugar, Hans, Theo, Cleo, Dusty, Pazely, Gretta and Toby," she said, quite proud of herself for getting each name right for the first time. Each one passed by and kissed her on the nose. "I'm sorry," Willow said, facing Aslo and Kiera. "For what I said before."

"It's okay." Kiera nudged her. "Tragedy never brings out the best in anyone. If we could save him right now, we would. This battle is for him to fight and he is. The fact that he is still here with us means there is something he feels is important enough to come back for. Not everyone can defy the odds like he has. That night on the bridge, with the amount of poison his body was subjected to, he never should have survived at all. It is a miracle that he is hanging on. Do you understand?"

"Sorry to interrupt," Mike said, walking around the bed and squatting in front of Willow. "There are only a couple days left before you leave for Sleeping Sands. You need to prepare."

"Prepare?" Willow asked, her eyes stinging with tears again. "I can't go. I can't leave him. If something happens, I need to be here."

Mike took her hands in his. "Listen to me, sweetie," he said. "You sitting here won't help him. This is something he has to do on his own. He knows you care and he wouldn't want you to stop doing things for you. The best thing you can do right now for both of you is go to the school."

"But maybe I could do something..."

Mike cut off her words. "You already have. You gave him a chance when no one else could have. Now you have to let him do the rest. Believe in him."

"If something happens while I am gone, I won't know," Willow cried.

"If he passes, we will find a way to let you know. I promise," Mike said. "If you do not hear from us, know he is no worse than he is now."

Mike helped Willow stand and walked her back to the sleeping quarters. Luggage was open on the beds waiting to be filled. Uniforms, books, and other school needs were already neatly packed. Beside the luggage on the bed lay an assortment of clothes Sarah had picked out for her to take to school. On William's desk was a list of things not to forget. Willow fumbled around the room checking each item off as she put it neatly in one bag or another. As each suitcase filled, she zipped it up and placed it outside the door for Mike to move to a more suitable location for teleportation.

Willow sat down at the desk and picked up William's chain that he gave her to wear with the key. Micca now had possession of the box and key to keep the liquids inside safe - in case they were ever needed again. She put it back down on the desk and picked up a long box beside it. She opened it and took out the pink crystal heart Nick gave her. Undoing the clasp, she put it around her neck and fastened it again.

Willow picked up a pen and a blank piece of paper and began to write.

William,

If you are reading this, I couldn't be happier. I wish I had been there to see your eyes open again for the first time. School is about to start and I am most likely at Sleeping Sands. You know they said no contact in or out for the whole school year.

Problem is I am having a hard time leaving. There was so much on that list we were going to talk about. So much I wanted to say and never made the time to say it. I keep thinking there must be something else I can do.

I guess what I want to say is I need you. Nothing feels right without out you here. I look around and I think of you. I miss you more than I can express in words.

I love you.

Willow

She folded the paper, placed it inside the book William had been reading, returning it to its place on the shelf. She looked around the room. There was no way she could stay there without him. She decided to stay with Clairity and Ashlyn until it was time for them to leave for school.

Closing the door behind her, she knew she would be leaving this life behind her - at least for a while.

GLOSSARY

These terms may be found throughout *The Portal Prophecies*. Not all terms may appear in every volume. Additional terms may be added to future volumes as needed.

Acacia - An ancient tree with consciousness. Acacia is thought to be one of the first creatures in existence. Its physical appearance is depicted as a type of willow tree.

Achaear - An ancient spider race. Once guardians, the Achaear preferred a life dedicated to their own race rather than the protection of others.

Albino Assassin - A race of beings white in appearance with deadly black wings which power their shadow and teleportation magics. Their knowledge of combat exceeds that of all other known races.

Allaren - Avian Guardian who takes the form of a black bird to bond with another being.

Ancients - Those in existence before the mass population of the worlds. They are thought to be some of the oldest living beings. There are different aged Ancients, ranging from supreme beings to guardians.

Apopp - One of the most prominent Xiuhcoatle (Serpent Race). He controls all contact from his race with other worlds.

Aquanor - An ancient sea creature race. Once guardians, the Aquanor preferred a life dedicated to their own race rather than the protection of others.

Blood Wars - Wars created by men in order to expand their kingdoms. The blood wars were started by certain ancient races to gain advantage over guardians. Men became obsessed with obtaining and drinking the blood of magical creatures to gain temporary abilities that aided them in battle. The wars ended in the creation of the portals.

Council - A group of mentors, originally appointed to train new abilities in those who were aiding the guardians. After a prophecy was made about the end of the guardian home world, the power of the Council was taken over by men and quickly corrupted.

Coven - A group of witches who practice magic together. There are usually thirteen members.

Cycle - 1 cycle is 10,000 years in main world time.

Displaced - The essence of a living being which was removed from its body before physical death occurred.

Dreamwalker - An individual with the power to enter and control dreams. They can also call people into their own dreams.

Empowered, The - The underground newspaper for empyral and the magical.

Empyral - Beings living in the main world, but having come from other worlds. They are generally happy to take residence in the main world and do not pose a threat to society.

Faeries - A magical race. Their eyes are a shimmering white and silver. The females have wings. Not much is known about actual faeries. They rarely interact with other races and it is much more common to find one of their many cousin races.

Frostica - Ice faeries. Their bodies appear humanoid, but their faces are more animal like. They are about two feet tall. Their bite is deadly.

Glaquool - An advanced bodiless race, made up of different gases, who crave experience and knowledge. They discovered they could hide in objects, which on touch, allowed them to displace the essence of the being and take its place.

Green-Eyed Recluse Collegiate - A school specializing in illusion magic.

Guardians - Combination of ancient races who protect the rights of all beings to exist and grow in which ever direction they choose. If faced with a choice, they will always choose to protect the greater good.

Gypsy - Term used to describe a group of witches who travel around constantly, hiding from a powerful necromancer.

Hannulate - Peaceful and fun-loving creatures who live in magical realms. A direct cousin to faeries. They were once one of the most beautiful races to exist. During the blood wars, they were forced to adapt to survive, by developing sharp teeth and razor claws that could extend at will.

Keeper - Individuals who can host guardians to allow them to pass through portals. It was believed a keeper could only carry two guardians of the same race at a time.

Kriller - A race of the most intelligent creatures to live. The speed at which their brain works causes changes in the formation of their facial features. They communicate with each other telepathically and then work together to complete necessary tasks.

Leander - Feline Guardians who take the form of a black cat to bond with another being.

Light - A person able to read energies and can lend energy to another person to enhance their natural abilities.

Main World - The modern day world. It is the largest realm and connects all of the worlds by portals.

Medium - A witch who specializes in contacting the deceased.

Necrid Flames - A blue flame that engulfs and destroys all living material.

Necromancer - A witch who specializes in death magic.

Olcsanka - A wolf/bear guardian who takes the form of a wolf to bond with another being.

Portal - A doorway to another world that can only be opened by guardians. Once open any creature can use it if it remains active. Guardians can only pass through a portal when bonded to a keeper.

Portal Guard - Those chosen to protect, who travel through portals and ensure the safety of all realms.

Portal Prophecies, The - A book of prophecies made by Iris and Raven prior to the wars and recorded by Diana. There is also a book written by a gypsy named Estonia by the same name.

Portal Stones - The four corner stones required to open any portal.

Samhain - The witches' new year, when the divide between the realms is thinnest, allowing supernatural activity or contact.

Sleeping Sands - The most prestigious of the schools for the Empyral.

Terra former - A person with a rare ability to manipulate weather and soil to sustain life. They can also grow plant life on command. There are few documented people with this ability. The extent of their abilities is not known.

Terunji - People living in the main world who are completely oblivious to the magic around them.

Transmutton - Yeti.

Underground, The - A hidden city. Its inhabitants are all magical, whether from the main world or other realms.

Vamprite - A race of shape shifters led by a young prince, Drake. During the blood wars they learnt that drinking human blood could keep their people young, strong, and beautiful. The main world knows them as vampires.

Wand - A wooden rod used to channel any form of magic and turn it into any form of physical magic the user needs.

Wisps - Bodiless beings who keep their form generally in the shape of a sphere composed of raw energy, or light. Considered a possible explanation for ghosts.

Winks - The smallest of the Faery family. A scale for them would be from the size of a fruit fly to that of a house fly. They all have wings and, unfortunately, a mischievous nature. Although they mean no harm, their pranks and jokes often lead to destruction. Considered a possible explanation for poltergeists.

Witches - A name given to any humanoid with unusual amounts of magical powers. There is some difference between main world witches and those from other worlds. There are different types of witches, practising different types of magic.

Wizard - A witch who practices alchemy and potions. They have a more scientific approach to magic. Wizards can still channel magic through a wand.

Xiuhcoatle - An ancient serpent race, once guardians.

Yeti - Abominable Snowmen.

Author's Message

I hope you enjoyed reading *The first Volume of the Portal Prophecies* as much as I did writing it. The story doesn't end here. *The second Volume* contains the final three books in the series.

ABOUT THE AUTHOR

C.A. King is the recipient of several awards, including: The Hamilton Spectator Readers' Choice Award for 2017 Best Author; The Brant News Readers' Choice Award for 2017 Best Author; Readers' Favourite award in the short story/novella category; the 2017 SIBA Award for Best New Adult; the 2017 SIBA Award for Best Novella; 2018 Readers' Favourite International Book Awards: Gold Medal in the Fiction - Supernatural genre; and 2018 Readers' Favourite International Book Awards: Bronze Medal in the Fiction - New Adult genre

Currently residing in Brantford, Ontario Canada, she lives with her two sons. She began her writing career after the tragic loss of her parents and husband. Redirecting her emotions through writing became therapeutic in her battle with depression and in 2014 she decided to publish some of her works.

The Portal Prophecies

Volume I

By

C. A. King

Cover Design by Eyes of a Crow

Editor: J.D. Cunegan

This book is dedicated to the memory of James Huntington Turner, who taught me anything is possible if you try.

Look for other books by C.A. King, including:

The Portal Prophecies:
Book I - A Keeper's Destiny
Book II - A Halloween's Curse
Book III - Frost Bitten
Book IV - Sleeping Sands
Book V - Deadly Perceptions
Book VI - Finding Balance

Tomoiya's Story:

Book I: Escape to Darkness
Book II: Collecting Tears

Surviving the Sins:

Book I: Answering the Call
Book II: Pride
Book III: Lust

When Leaves Fall: A Different Point of View Story

Peach Coloured Daisies: A Cursed by the Gods Story

Flower Shields: A Four Horsemen Novel

Drawing Strength From Words: A Four Horsemen Novel

Miracles Not Included

Twisted Tales of A Dead End Street
Shot Through The Heart: A Faerie Tale